The *objects* who people the pages of THE TOMORROW FILE:

ANGELA BERRI: Sophisticated in the ways of primitive sex, Angela kills as casually as she loves.

PAUL BUMFORD: Behind his rosy-cheeked innocence and innocuous manners lies a Machiavellian mind. He advocates tattooed identification numbers and rule by a scientific elite—led by himself, of course.

GRACE WINGATE: A beautiful romantic in a world of realists, Grace pursues two dreams with passion—total devotion and total surrender.

HYMAN R. LEWISOHN: Within his decaying body lives the mind of a genius, the mind that must be kept alive—at any cost.

and

NICHOLAS BENNINGTON FLAIR: Brilliant, damned, determined to make sense out of a senseless world he never made, Nick has one fatal flaw: he wants life to have charm—an archaic concept in the mechanized world of THE TOMORROW FILE

The Tomorrow File

Lawrence Sanders

BERKLEY BOOKS, NEW YORK

The clock on the cover is through the courtesy of
Computime Limited, Department 3A
P. O. Box 3392
Poughkeepsie, New York 12603

This Berkley book contains the complete
text of the original hardcover edition.
It has been completely reset in a typeface
designed for easy reading, and was printed
from new film.

THE TOMORROW FILE

A Berkley Book / published by arrangement with
G. P. Putnam's Sons

PRINTING HISTORY
G. P. Putnam's Sons edition published 1975
G. P. Putnam's / Berkley edition / September 1976
Sixteenth printing / November 1982

ISBN: 0-425-05770-4

A BERKLEY BOOK ® TM 757,375
Berkley Books are published by Berkley Publishing Corporation,
200 Madison Avenue, New York, New York 10016.
The name "BERKLEY" and the stylized "B" with design
are trademarks belonging to Berkley Publishing Corporation.
PRINTED IN THE UNITED STATES OF AMERICA

"We can no longer afford an obsolete society of obsolete people."

—PRESIDENT HAROLD K. MORSE
Second Inaugural Address
January 20, 1988

ORGANIZATION OF THE DEPARTMENT OF BLISS (1998)

Department of Bliss (DOB)
Director (DIROB)
Headquarters Staff

Prosperity Section (PROSEC)
Deputy Director (DEPDIRPRO)

Wisdom Section (WISSEC)
Deputy Director (DEPDIRWIS)

Vigor Section (VIGSEC)
Deputy Director (DEPDIRVIG)

Culture Section (CULSEC)
Deputy Director (DEPDIRCUL)

Satisfaction Section (SATSEC)
Deputy Director (DEPDIRSAT)

ORGANIZATION OF SATISFACTION SECTION, DOB

Satisfaction Section (SATSEC)
Deputy Director (DEPDIRSAT)
Headquarters Staff

Division of Research & Development (DIVRAD)
Assistant Deputy Director (AssDepDirRad)

Division of Security & Intelligence (DIVSEC)
Assistant Deputy Director (AssDepDirSec)

Division of Data & Statistics (DIVDAT)
Assistant Deputy Director (AssDepDirDat)

Division of Law & Enforcement (DIVLAW)
Assistant Deputy Director (AssDepDirLaw)

BOOK X

X-1

She was naked, riding without saddle. In the cold moonlight her green hair was black, her slender corpus as pliant as a rod of white plastisteel.

The thunder of hooves on hard-packed sand faded. I looked about slowly. The great earthquake of 1979 had taken up this section of coast south of San Francisco and shuffled it like a pack of stone cards. Much had been destroyed, many had perished. But the quake had created new cliffs and coves, sand beaches and clever openings through which the sea came murmuring.

Her house was above, built on stone. I sat in a kind of beach gazebo, infrared heated, and waited patiently.

I heard the sound of hooves again, thundering, thundering. . . . She reined up, the sea behind her, and slid smoothly from the stallion's back.

She held up an arm. The em in an earth-colored zipsuit, standing behind my sling, left the gazebo and went down to her. He took the reins and led the whuffing horse away. I watched them go. That horse was partly my triumph.

In 1985, an extremely virulent form of multivectoral equine encephalitis had swept the globe. Almost 60 percent of the world's horses had stopped. The East claimed the outbreak had started in a Maryland laboratory operated by the US Army's Research & Engineering Section. They were working on mutant viruses. I knew that to be operative. The East said the outbreak of encephalitis was deliberately planned. I think that was inoperative.

Fifty years previously, breeders would have despaired of replacing this epizootic loss of horse flesh in anything less than a hundred years. We did it in five. We used artificial insemination, artificial enovulation, genetic manipulation, and a new category of hormonal and enzymatic growth drugs that reduced the natural equine gestation period to three months. The program was a dramatic success.

But that wasn't the entire reason I admired the stallion as it was led away. Because, as I saw from the first day I was assigned to the Planning Section of the SOH (Save Our Horses) Project, the same techniques we employed—a crash program to restore a grievously endangered species—could be used for the human race in the event of nukewar.

My paper outlining such a program caused considerable comment, much of it favorable. It certainly led to my present service. My name was Nicholas Bennington Flair. I was an NM (Natural Male). My official title was AssDepDirRad. That is, Assistant Deputy Director of the Division of Research & Development, of SATSEC, the Satisfaction Section, of DOB, the Department of Bliss, formerly the Department of Public Happiness, formerly the Department of Health, Education and Welfare.

The ef waving her white arm at me from the beach was Angela Teresa Berri. She was DEPDIRSAT, Deputy Director of the Satisfaction Section of the Department of Bliss. She ruled me. I took up a magenta alumisilk cloak and went down to her.

When I proferred the cloak, she thrust it away with a short, angry gesture. We paced slowly down the deserted beach. Her corpus was not trembling in the chill sea wind. I guessed she had taken a mild Calorific tablet to raise her body temperature.

"Nick," she said. Abrupt, almost rude. "Do you remember that night in Hilo, two years ago, the last night of the International Genetic Control Association meeting?"

I turned my head to look at her in astonishment. Remember? It was a silly question, and she was not a silly ef. Of course I remembered. Not because it had been a particularly memorable evening, but because it was practically impossible for me to forget anything.

Fortunate in having a superior natural memory to begin with, I also took monthly injections of Supermem, a restricted drug administered to everyone in my Division, and annually I underwent surgery for hormonal irrigation of my hippocampus and electronic stimulation of my amygdala. In addition to all this, I was an honor graduate of the GAB, the US Government's Academy of Biofeedback, where I had majored in theta.

We strolled along the beach, her long, thin fingers on my arm. Her nipples were painted black, a tooty fashion I found profitless.

"What did we do after we left the meeting in Hilo?" she asked. Demanded.

"We stopped at the Hi-Profit Bar for a vodka-and-Smack."

"And then?"

"We went down to the beach, took off our plastisandals, and waded in the wet sand back to our hotel."

"And then?"

I couldn't understand the reason for this examination. She was on Supermem too; she remembered that evening as well as I.

"And then?" she insisted.

"We went up to our suite. We used each other. We both took a Somnorific and I left in the morning to fly back to the mainland."

She smiled briefly, tightly, and turned me around. We went back to the gazebo. She put on her cloak then. We climbed to the house, passing a lower level of Thermaglas. Inside I saw a young em bending intently over a workbench, doing something with a portable Instaweld tank.

"Beautiful home," I said. Our silence was beginning to disturb me as much as her questioning.

"It's not mine," she said. Too fast. "It belongs to a friend Who's away. I borrowed it for my threeday. Nick, thank you for coming. You were right on time."

We turned to smile at each other. Because, of course, I had arrived before she summoned me.

X-2

I had been in bed with Paul Thomas Bumford, my Executive Assistant. He was an AINM-A, an artificially inseminated male with a Grade A genetic rating. We had been users for five years, almost from the day he joined my Division.

Paul was shortish, fair, plump, roseate. He wore heavy makeup.

All ems used makeup, of course, but he favored cerise eyeshadow. Megatooty, for my taste.

Strangers might think him a microweight, effete, interested only in the next televised execution. In fact, he was one of the Section's most creative neurobiologists. I was lucky to have him in DIVRAD.

It had been a dyssynaptic evening. It started with a long, angry meeting with my Chimerism Team. I had ordered them to produce a fifteen-minute cassette film on our progress to date. I had approved the preliminary script. It ended with a two-minute closeup sequence of a cloned grizzly bear cub (*Ursus horribilis*) that had been fitted with human hands (to provide the apposable thumb) easily performing a variety of simple mechanical tasks: picking up small screws, handling a sheet of paper, turning a valve, etc.

But the rough-cut of the film we viewed was all wrong. It was too cute. The bear cub in the experiment was a natural-born comedian. It didn't help when the voice-over narrator kept referring to him as "Charlie." It was an amusing film. But the intent was not to amuse. Far from it.

When the lights came on, Horvath, the team leader, an NF, and her film producer looked at me expectantly. I stared at them in silence. Paul Bumford said nothing, made no movement. He knew my moods.

Then I made the following points:

1. The experimental animal was to be referred to only by its breeding code: UH-4832-A6.

2. All shots of the bear cub cavorting were to be cut.

3. More footage would be devoted to the actual transplant, and more voice-over to the use of immunosuppressive and learning drugs developed by DIVRAD.

Then the arguments began. I let them shout. I would have my way, but they wouldn't understand why I was so intransigent. They had no need to know. Finally, grumbling, they took their foolish film back to their lab.

"What was that all about?" Paul asked, when we were on our way to *La Bonne Vie*, one of the less execrable restaurants within the government compound.

"Obsolete history," I said. "You weren't in Public Service during the Presidency of Morse. He was our first scientist-President, the first Chief Executive to understand the consequences of the Biological Revolution. He had a doctorate in microbiology, you know."

"From where?" Paul asked sharply.

"London. At the time, they were doing some marvelous things over there. Now they're just coasting. No love. If you want input on the quality of Morse's mind, scan a paper he delivered on July 16, 1978, at a meeting of the American Chemical Society. We have a spindle in the film library. He completely demolished the icebox theory."

"Now you've lost me completely," Paul said. "What was the icebox theory?"

"In the 1970's, neuroscientists were becoming increasingly concerned about the political, social, ethical, and economic consequences of their service, as well they should have been. The icebox theory was suggested. Biological research wouldn't be halted or curtailed, but discoveries would be stored away, put on ice, until the public had a chance to debate fully their possible consequences."

"The public!" Paul burst out laughing. "What the hell do they know about it?"

"Precisely. That's what Morse said. He also pointed out that by putting biological discoveries in an icebox, we were condemning a lot of objects, particularly children, to pain, subnorm lives, or early stopping. But most important, he said that by keeping research completely free and unfettered, we were increasing the possibility that means might be discovered—chemical or electronic—to increase learning to the point where we *could* understand all the potential problems of the Biological Revolution and cope with them."

"Beautiful logic."

"Yes. And he had luck. A week after his address, von Helmstadt in South Africa published his definitive study on the results of oxygenation of the fetus. Those kids could learn at an astonishing rate. It proved exactly what Morse had said. A remarkable em."

"You met him a few times, didn't you?"

"Once. I met him once."

It had been an early spring. We strolled along slowly. The compound was a bleak place at night—and not much more inviting during the day. The wide cement walks had been intersected with squares of green plastigrass. There were a few plastirub trees, some bearing wax fruit. The floodlights went on automatically at dusk, freezing everything in a white glare. And the fence, of course: chainlink with triple strands of barbed wire at top. A total of six double gates, with guardhouses.

"How did Morse stop?" Paul asked. "Assassinated?"

"Never been definitely determined," I lied. "A lot of rumors. Anyway, on the day he took office, Morse started working on the Fertility Control Act. We *had* to have it. First of all, it insured zero population growth by federal licensing of procreation. But in addition to Z-Pop, it gave us the beginnings of genetic control by law. Morse finally got the FCA passed a few months before he stopped in 1990. And ever since, obsos have tried to chip away at it. The latest is an amendment that would allow unlicensed breeding between natural ems and natural efs."

"You're against it?"

"I'm against anything that weakens the FCA. So is DEPDIR-SAT. So is DIROB. But this time the obsos have some clout. It comes from two directions: the Department of Peace and the Department of Creative Services. The generals want more bodies because it increases their options in the event of a popwar. The labor pols want it because they're getting a lot of kaka from union leaders whose objects are steadily dwindling as consumption declines under Z-Pop."

A two-em security patrol passed us, sauntering slowly. They had flechette guns slung over their shoulders. Each had an attack beast on a chain leash. The beasts were a new mutant our San Diego Field Office had developed: DNA from hyena, jackal, and wolf. Prototypes had no tails, but more recent models were bred for tails, to improve their balance when attacking.

"So that's why the film is being made?" Paul asked. "To defend the FCA?"

"Right. It's intended for Public Service distribution only, with a restricted PS-3 rating. You won't even be able to view it, legally. But it's political clout. It holds out hope to the generals that the possibility of sending chimeras into battle isn't as remote as they may have thought. And it scares the Department of Creative Services, because if we can put animals to work on assembly lines, what's going to happen to their precious unions?"

"I'm computing," Paul said. "A promise and a threat, all in one."

"Correct," I said. "Maybe now we'll get an answer to the great CR debate. In Conditioned Response, which has the higher efficiency—the promise of reward or the threat of punishment? How do you opt?"

"Threat of punishment," he said. Promptly.

"I'm not so sure. And there's another factor involved that makes me want to defeat that amendment to the FCA. If natural ems and natural efs are permitted to breed without licensing, it's only a matter of time—little time—before naturals will consider themselves as elite. Then our society will become structured strictly by genetic classes."

"Now you're talking like an obso. There's elitism right now. The scientific elite. And it exists because we *are* elite."

"*That's* a lot of kaka."

We turned into the restaurant. We had to wait almost ten minutes, but finally got a table in the Executive Dining Room. We didn't need menus. Few in the restaurant did. Most of the customers were from my Division, all on Supermem.

If I was asked to name the greatest technological discovery of the past fifty years, I would have to say it was the synthesizing of protein from petroleum, first in the lab and then in a commercially viable process. If I was asked to name the most disastrous technological discovery, it would be that same development.

When my square of prosteak, rare, was put before me, surrounded by propots and probeans, I knew I was in for a mild attack of RSC. Sighing, I fumbled in the side pocket of my bronze-colored zipsuit for my pill dispenser.

About a year previously I had become aware of a curious and bothersome mental irregularity. It first occurred after my annual hippocampus and amygdala treatment. In effect, my memory, triggered by a sight, sound, smell, or almost any other input, ran wild. I could not control a flood of associative memories that engulfed my brain and temporarily extirpated my ability to respond normally to subsequent stimuli, or to learn, deduce, or fantasize.

After the second attack, I went to my Memory Team leader, a molecular neurologist, and described the symptoms. He was not at all surprised. I was suffering from RSC, Random Synaptic Control. It was fairly common in both ems and efs who had been memory-conditioned in the 1975-1985 period. It was due to an inaccurate stereochemical configuration of the hormone administered. Therapy was by ingestion of a corrective hormone isomer.

If Proust could write a novel of that length inspired by a piece of madeleine soaked in tea, you can appreciate why a plate of food derived from petrochemicals and artificial flavorings might drive my synapses out of control. The memories came flooding in. . . .

. . . my father's shrewdness. He was a successful toy manufac-

7

turer with a BS in chemistry. When the production of protein from petroleum was announced as commercially feasible, he had immediately put a lot of love into companies producing spices, flavorings, and seasonings. He made a bundle, and then, as he followed the chemical journals carefully and noted the inevitability of synthetic salt, pepper, thyme, tarragon, garlic, curry, mustard, dill, etc., he withdrew with a tremendous orgasm that made him a decamillionaire in new dollars.

. . . my mother's adamant refusal to consume *any* synthetic food or drink, and especially artificially flavored whiskies made from petrochemicals. She existed in an alcoholic stupor maintained with a rare Eastern vodka produced from natural potatoes.

. . . Millie's service. The young ef was a CF-E, an embryo-cloned female with a Grade E genetic rating. She was a packer in the Qik-Freez Hot-Qizine factory in Detroit. It was possible she had packaged the prosteak I was about to eat. Millie and I were users.

. . . almost atavistic memories of the taste of farm-fresh eggs, vine-ripened melons, cucumbers, fresh beef, gravel-scratching chickens, wine made from grapes. . . .

I popped my RSC pill. Paul watched me sympathetically.

"Bad?"

"Not too," I said. "There are some memories I can do without."

"Tememblo?"

"Too gross," I said. "It erases everything."

Tememblo (Temporary Memory Block) was a restricted drug we had developed. Given by injection, it produced complete forgetfulness, either immediately before or after the events, for periods of one to forty-eight hours, depending on its strength. But the duration of the effect was limited.

Paul was instantly alert and interested.

"You're suggesting a specialized memory inhibitor?" he said. "To block, say, a color memory without inhibiting a scent memory?"

"Something like that." I nodded. "But we can't take it on now. Better put it in the Tomorrow File."

We no longer smiled at that, though it had started as a joke.

Soon after Paul Bumford joined DIVRAD, he sent me a memo tape suggesting that every individual in the US have his BIN (Birth Identification Number) tattooed on his forearm. The idea was preposterous, but I admired the organization of his argument.

8

I called him in and explained why his suggestion was impractical for social and political reasons.

"If it's the cosmetic effect of the tattooing that might offend," he offered, "we could use a skin dye visible only under ultraviolet light."

"Paul, you're not computing. We still have some objects in this country who have harsh memories of Germany's Third Reich, the concentration camps, the arm tattoos. If I suggested such a program, all hell would break loose."

"Obsoletes," he said. "They can be manipulated."

"Obsos," I agreed. "And they probably could be manipulated if I felt the project was important enough. But I don't. Do you know how long it took us to get the National Data Bank accepted? Five years! By a massive-all-media effort to convince objects it was not a computer but just a highly sophisticated filing system. *Files*, not dossiers. And it was only after the Fertility Control Act was passed that we were able to assign Birth Identification Numbers. You must learn that what is practical and useful scientifically is not necessarily practical and useful socially, ethically, or economically. And especially politically."

"I still think it's a good idea," he said stubbornly.

"As a means of personal identification? Well . . . maybe. About as good, and bad, as fingerprints, I'd guess. But we're working on something much better.

He came alive. "Genetic codes?"

"No good. Not in the case of identical twins or clone groups. Ever hear of forensic microbiology?"

"No."

"Suggested about 1970. But nobody did anything about it at the time because most of the biomedical research then was therapy-oriented. But this could be big. Right now I have only one object serving on it. Mary Bergstrom, a neurophysiologist. She's good, but she needs help on the microbiology. I want you to serve with her."

"Will she rule me?"

"No. You'll be equals, reporting only to me. I'm very interested in this. I'll code you and Mary the IMP Team, for Individual Microbiological Profile."

He reached for his memo tape.

"Then I guess I can erase this."

"Don't do that." I smiled, putting my hand on his. "Have it transcribed and filmed. "It's not a *bad* idea. But for the future. Put it in the Tomorrow File."

"The Tomorrow File?" He liked that. He smiled.

We became users that night.

Since then, whenever we—together or separately—came up with an idea that could not be developed because of the current social, economic, or political climate, we put it in the Tomorrow File. Paul kept the film spindles in his office safe.

We finished our dinner.

"How do you feel?" Paul asked. "The spansule work?"

"Fine," I said. "So far. Knock on wood." I rapped the table top.

"That's plastic," Paul said.

"Old habits stop hard," I said.

"Yes." He nodded. "That's the problem."

We went back to my apartment. Paul wanted to watch the AGC Network—Avant-Garde Cable. They were presenting Walter Bronkowsky on the Leopold Synthesizer, playing his own symphony, *Variations on the Rock of Ages Mambo*. We watched and listened to about five minutes of Bronkowsky twiddling his dials and flipping his switches. Then Paul and I exchanged grimaces. He tried other channels.

It was a new laser-holograph three-dimensional set, with a one-meter box. But all we could get were sit-coms, talk shows, and the tenth rerun of *Deep Throat*. So we went to bed.

Paul's mucus membranes were gainfully tender. Our investment had endured long enough for each to be attuned to the physical and mental rhythms of the other. We were, for instance, able to go into alpha together.

Recently, almost as a hobby, Paul had been researching ESP. He had evolved a theory that during sexual arousal, as during moments of other emotional stress—fear, anger, etc.—the ESP faculty was intensified.

We had been conducting a series of experiments to test this out. Before sexual relations, Paul or I would write a single word or simple phrase on a piece of paper, keeping it hidden from the other. During using, the sender attempted to transmit mentally the word or phrase he had written, and the other to receive mentally the identical word or phrase.

Results had been inconclusive but encouraging enough to continue. That night Paul was sending.

After we summited, and our respiration and cardiac rates had returned to normal, Paul asked, "What was it?"

I hesitated a moment, then said, "Ultimate pleasure."

Paul switched on the lamp, reached to the bedside table. He picked up his note and unfolded it so I could read what he had written: "Ultimate pleasure."

I shook my head. "Not conclusive. Too subjective. It may have been an emotional or purely physical reaction on my part."

"Not so," Paul said. "You've never used that phrase before. And besides, it *is* objective. It's a subject I've been thinking about a long time. I put a memo on it in the Tomorrow File. It proposes the development of an Ultimate Pleasure compound. In pill form. Cheap. Addictive. No toxic effects. No serious side effects. Working directly on the hypothalamus or affecting the norepinephrine-mediated tracts."

"That's interesting," I said.

I turned off the bedlamp and we went to sleep.

I was in the middle of an REM dream when I was awakened by the chiming of the bedroom flasher extension.

"Flasher" was not the correct name for this device, of course. Technically, it was a Video Phone. Why flasher? Because the new devices had spawned a new breed of obscene phone callers. The conventional table or desk set consisted of a 3 dm viewing screen with a 5 cm camera lens mounted above and centered between the video and sound control dials and the push-button station selector.

The obscene caller, ef or em, stood before the flasher so the face could not be viewed by the camera lens, and exhibited naked genitalia after calling a selected or random number. Such callers, and there were many, were termed "flashers." The device took its popular name from them.

I pulled on a patterned plastilin robe and sat before the flasher on my bedroom desk. Paul climbed out of bed and stood behind the set where he could not be photographed. I flicked the On switch. The color image bloomed blurry and shaky, then steadied and focused. It was a pleasant-faced black ef, wearing the blue zipsuit of a PS-7. We stared at each other.

"Mr. Nicholas Bennington Flair?"

"Speaking."

"Mr. Flair, are you AssDepDirRad?"

"I am."

"Would you insert your BIN card, please."

I motioned to Paul. He rushed to get my card from my discarded bronze zipsuit.

Meanwhile the ef was looking at my image and then down at her desk, obviously comparing my features to a photo. Paul handed me the BIN card over the set. I inserted it in a slot under the screen. The ef read her output, sent by the magnetic-inked numbers on my card. She seemed satisfied.

"Mr. Flair, this is DIVDAT in San Francisco. We have a message to you from Angela Teresa Berri, DEPDIRSAT. May I show it?"

"Go ahead."

The printed message came on.

It was a memo, dated that day.

From: DEPDIRSAT.
To: AssDepDirRad.
Subject: IMP progress report.
    You personally rush urgent latest. Emergency. /s/ Berri.

The operator came on again.

"Did you get that, sir?"

"I did," I told her. "No reply, and thank you."

The screen went dead, a little white moon fading, fading. . . . I flicked the Off switch. Paul and I looked at each other.

"She's on a threeday," he said finally. "Someplace south of San Francisco."

"I know."

"That report she wants—I wrote it. Strictly NSP—No Significant Progress."

"I know."

"Listen," he said, "are you sure that was from her?"

"I'm sure."

"You are?" He looked at me narrowly. "Oh-ho! Section code. I get it. 'Rush urgent latest. Emergency.' R-U-L-E. Verification code—right?"

No idiot he.

"Right." I nodded.

I looked at the bedside digital clock.

"If we hurry I can make the 2330 courier flight from Ellis. Let me shower, shave, and dress. First, you lay on a cart and copter, and book me on the flight. Then put on some clothes and get me an

12

Instox copy of that report from your office. Meet me outside in twenty minutes.''

He nodded and we started rushing.

Twenty minutes later he handed over the sealed report and drove the electric cart to the copter pad at the other end of the compound.

"Nick," he said. "Be careful."

"Careful?"

"Something's up. If she really needed that report, which I doubt, it could have been scanned to her. But she started with 'You—You personally. . . .' ''

"That's right."

"What is it?"

"I have no idea."

"You have no idea—or I have no need to know?"

"I have no idea."

"Will you flash me after you see her?"

"No. If possible I'll take the return flight. I'll be back before dawn."

"Nick, I grabbed a couple of things in my office—amitriptyline and the new iproniazid. Want one?"

"I'd like the fast upper but I'm not going to take it. I better play this straight."

He parked in the shadow of the hangar, cast by the floodlights on the pad. The copter was waiting there, rotor slowly turning. Paul and I kissed.

"Take care," he said lightly.

I made the 2330 hypersonic from the airfield that had formerly been Ellis Island. We landed in San Francisco two hours later, and most of the time was spent circling over the Atlantic and Pacific Oceans, going and coming through the sonic wall.

Arrival was approximately 0130, New York time. I was coptered and then driven to Angela Berri's seaside home in less than 30 minutes. According to my digiwatch, I walked down to the beach just before 0200, New York time. But just before 2300, local time.

Ergo, I had arrived before I had been summoned. Amusing.

X-3

We came up from the beach into the main house. Angela Berri led the way into a living room-office-den, then closed and locked the door behind me. She motioned me to a white plasticade armchair, then switched on a cassette of a gamelan quartet. I remembered she fancied Eastern music. She turned up the volume of her hemispherical sound system. Too loud. The windows fluttered. She went to a small office refrigerator and, without asking my preference, poured us each a glass of chilled Smack.

She sat down behind the red plastisteel desk.

"You brought the report I wanted, Nick?"

"Yes. Here."

I leaned forward to scale the sealed envelope onto the desktop. She tore it open, scanned the report swiftly, tossed it aside.

"What is the status now?"

Curious. She received weekly progress reports, and I knew she listened to them. She had a double doctorate—in molecular biology and biochemical genetics. She would understand exactly what we were doing on the Individual Microbiology Profile Project.

But dutifully I replied, "Everyone in the Department of Bliss has been tested and coded."

"New employees?" she asked sharply.

"Not those coming aboard in the last six weeks. But we have everyone else. The computer has been programmed. We're tuning up now. We should be able to start blind tests in a day or two."

She nodded. "I'm beginning to work on my budget recommendations," she said tonelessly. "I must adjust the allocation for IMP."

Curiouser. She knew as well as I that no specific allocation had ever been made for the IMP Project. The new dollars came from my discretionary fund, as did the love for all pure research projects. Congress and the public were interested only in hardware. We hid the rest.

She came over to me and stood directly behind my chair.

"I'm glad you could bring the new report personally, Nick."

But it was not a new report. She had scanned it two weeks ago. What was—

Then, standing behind me, she began lightly stroking my temples, jawline, beneath the chin, with her fingertips. My initial reaction was ego-oriented. I knew she took profit from me, and thought she might want to use me. But then, as those cool fingers continued to search the outlines of my face, I knew what was happening.

That interrogation on the beach had been to assure her that I was who I claimed to be, Nicholas Bennington Flair. That I remembered events that only she and I had shared. But it was inconclusive. An object's memories could be drained, to be learned by another object. I had helped develop the drugs to do it.

This probing of my face with her fingertips was to confirm that I was the em I appeared to be, Nick Flair, and not the product of clever surgeons using the new Juskin. It was a synthetic product, bonded to natural skin by a technique not unlike welding. It left no scars or seams, but it did leave an invisible welt at the line of juncture that could be felt.

She feared me an impostor—a not unreasonable fear. Two months previously the Statistics Projection Chief of the Department of Agribusiness, formerly the Department of Agriculture, had proved to be an impostor, in the employ of a cartel of grain dealers. The original Chief had been assassinated.

She went back behind the red desk and sat there, staring at me. We both sipped our plastiglasses of Smack while she tried to make up her mind. I thought idly that the reason for her senseless questions about the IMP Project had been inspired by her suspicion that this room was being shared. That was also the reason for the high volume of the gamelan tape. The sound was sufficient to set up random vibrations of walls and windows, in case anyone was sharing with a long-distance laser beam.

I turned the glass of Smack in my palms. The Jellicubes of "ice" didn't melt. Unfortunately. They looked like little blocks of squid.

Smack was interesting. It was the best-selling soft drink in the world, by far. It had a sweetish citric flavor. Other soft drinks tasted better, but Smack had an advantage they didn't have: it was addictive.

The original formula was a serendipitous discovery. In 1978, Pace Pharmaceuticals, in St. Louis, was doing research on a drug that might be effective against the so-called "fatty liver" caused by alcohol addiction. Eventually, they found themselves working on the physiological effects of alcohol, caffeine, and nicotine.

Two years later, Pace had produced a powder that was, in solution, admittedly physically addictive. But it did not require increased dosage to provide mild euphoria over a long period of time. More important, Pace claimed, it produced absolutely no harmful physical or psychological effects.

It was a nice legal point. Pace decided to meet the issue head-on. They fought it through the courts for seven years. By the time the Supreme Court decided, in 1987, that addictive substances were not, per se, illegal, providing they had no toxic effects, Pace was ready with "Smack! The Flavor You Can't Forget!" It was widely rumored that two Associate Justices and five law clerks became millionaires overnight by prior knowledge of the decision and purchase of Pace stock. This may or may not be operative.

What was operative was that Pace's addictive formula was now licensed for chewing gum, toothpaste, ice cream, mouthwash, and candy bars. As the obsos were fond of saying, "Better living through chemistry."

So there I was, sipping my Smack like millions of others throughout the world, and watching Angela Berri struggle to make up her mind. It really didn't take her long. She rose, pulled heavy drapes across all the Thermapanes. She returned to her swivel chair, unlocked a desk drawer, drew out a tape cassette, placed it squarely in the middle of the desk blotter. She stared at it. I stared at it. Then she raised her eyes to give me that hard, tight half-smile of hers. I looked at her, computing.

When, at the age of twelve, I announced to my father that I had been accepted at the government's new National Science Academy, under the Accelerated Conditioning Program, and that I intended to make a career of Public Service, he gave me a sardonic look and said merely, "Save yourself."

It was five years before I understood what he had meant. As I moved up in PS, I became increasingly aware of the plots of Byzantine complexity and Oriental ferocity that swirled through government, and especially Public Service. Unless you were utterly devoid of ambition, it was impossible to remain aloof. You had to ally yourself with the strong, shun the weak. More important, you had to join the winners, reject the losers. It called for inching along a

16

political tightrope. You hoped that you would master the skill before falling.

Now Angela Berri was presenting me with what I guessed to be essentially a political choice. I hesitated only a moment. In politics, as in war, it is better to make a bad decision than no decision at all.

Without speaking, I raised my eyebrows and jerked my head upward to point my chin at the tape cassette.

Without speaking, she motioned me over to stand next to her.

Without speaking, I picked up the cassette and examined it. It appeared to be a standard commercial cartridge, providing about thirty minutes of tape on each side. The clear plastic container was unlabeled.

Without speaking, she took a pad of scratch paper and a gold liquid graphite pencil from a side drawer. I watched her movements carefully.

She tore the top sheet of paper from the pad and placed it off the blotter, on the bare plastisteel desktop. She didn't want to risk the second sheet of the pad or the desk blotter picking up even a faint imprint of what she would write. She scribbled a few words, then looked up at me. I bent over her. I smelled a pleasing scent of her sweat, the stallion's, and the exciting estrogen-based perfume she was wearing.

I read what she had written: "For you only." I pondered a few seconds, then took the gold pencil from her fingers. Directly beneath her note, I jotted, "Paul Bumford?" She read it, raised her eyes to stare at me a moment, then nodded. Yes.

She took a ceramic crucible from a side drawer, crumpled our shared note, dropped it in the crucible. From another drawer she took a small bottle of a commercial solvent, Deztroyzit. The cap was actually a dropper with a bulb of plastirub. She dripped two drops onto the crumpled note. It dissolved. We watched the white smoke curl up. Acrid odor. In a few seconds the paper was gone. Not even ashes left.

I slipped the tape cassette into the side pocket of my zipsuit. We walked to the door without speaking.

In the hallway, the young em was just coming up from the lower level workshop. He was carrying a beautifully crafted model of an antique rocket. I think it was a Saturn.

"Nick," she said, "this is Bruce. Bruce, meet my friend, Nick."

We smiled at each other and stroked palms. I judged him to be about twelve. No more than fourteen. Handsome. Big.

"Bruce's clone group is being conditioned for Project Jupiter," she said proudly.

"Lucky Bruce." I sighed. "I wish I was going."

But of course I was much too old. I was twenty-eight.

Bruce, not having spoken, left us and carried his rocket to an upstairs room.

At the outside door she put those long, slender fingers on my arm.

"Nick, thank you again for bringing me that IMP report."

"Sure."

"Perhaps when I get back we can use each other again."

"A profit!" I said. I meant it. She was an efficient user.

"For me, too," she said.

I made the return flight with minutes to spare. There were fewer than twenty passengers scattered around the cabin of the 102-seat hypersonic. It was a waste of the taxpayers' love. But if you worried about wasting taxpayers' love, you shouldn't be in Public Service in the first place.

Takeoff was right on the decisecond. After we were airborne, the Security Officer came down the aisle returning our BIN cards, surrendered for identification check at the boarding gate. As we circled out over the Pacific, I stared at my card. I had, as required by law, provided a new color Instaroid photo the previous year. But I felt many years older than that long-faced, rather saturnine em who stared back at me.

The BIN card noted I was 182 cm tall and weighed 77 kg. (The US had completed switchover to the Metric System in 1985.) Hair: black. Eyes: Blue. Race was not noted since by assimilation (especially interbreeding), classification by race, color, or ethnical stock was no longer meaningful (or even possible). Creed was not noted since religious persuasion was of no consequence.

My BIN was NM-A-31570-GPA-1-K14324. That is, I was a Natural Male with a Grade A genetic rating, born March 15, 1970, who lived in Geo-Political Area 1, and whose birth registration number was K14324. The invisible magnetic coding made it almost impossible to forge a BIN card. Almost, but not quite.

I put it away when the stewardess came down the aisle, pushing her cart of nicotine, caffeine, alcohol, Smack, Somnorifics, tranquilizers, decongestants, antidepressants, antibiotics, diuretics, steroid hormones, and nonnarcotic sedatives. In her white zipsuit and white cap, she looked exactly like a pharmaceutical nurse making the rounds in a terminal ward.

I asked for a two-hour Somnorific, but all she had was one-hour or three. I took the one. I settled back in my seat, the alumistretch strap holding me securely, and turned the inhaler over in my fingers before removing the seal.

About five years previously, the Space Exploration Section (formerly NASA, now a division of the Department of the Air Force) had let a contract to Walker & Clarke Chemicals to develop a controlled hypnotic. SES had found that on extended flights and tours of duty in the space laboratories, the crews frequently suffered from boredom and/or insomnia. SES wanted a precisely timed sleeping pill, inhalant, or injection with no side or toxic effects.

After some clever molecular manipulation of glutethimide, a nonbarbiturate hypnotic, Walker & Clarke came up with a powder that oxidized when exposed to air, releasing a gas that had the required somniferous effect when inhaled. After tests, the Space Exploration Section accepted the new product and felt it safe enough to license for unrestricted use. They claimed it was nonaddictive.

"It is nonaddictive," Paul Bumford agreed, "unless you want to sleep."

Anyway, Walker & Clarke, after a massive preproduction advertising campaign ("Don't wait for sleep; make it come to you!") brought out Somnorific—plastic inhalers of precisely controlled strengths, from one to twenty-four hours. You peeled off the foil seal, waited about ten seconds for oxidation to take place, plugged the Somnorific into each nostril for a deep inhalation, and away you went.

Initially, Somnorific was a colossal failure. Customer complaints mounted, unopened cartons were returned to jobbers by drugstores, to wholesalers by jobbers, and to Walker & Clarke by wholesalers.

Investigation soon proved where the problem lay: customers were simply not waiting the required ten-second oxidation period despite clearly printed instructions for use. They were yanking off the foil seal, plugging the bullet-shaped containers up their noses, and taking deep breaths. Nothing.

I knew all this because Tom Sanchez, Director of Research at Walker & Clarke, had brought his troubles to me. We sometimes did favors for lovers in the drug cartels. They, in turn, helped us on sweetheart legislation. In this case, I assigned the problem to my Human Engineering Team.

They came up with the solution in one day. It was a classic. They recommended that the foil seal on each Somnorific inhaler be attached with a more tenacious adhesive. It was now difficult to pick off with your fingernails. When you finally got the damn thing off, it stuck to your fingertips and you had to ball it up between thumb and forefinger before you could flick it away. By that time, oxidation was completed and the Somnorific ready for use. We were all manipulated, in small matters and large.

I finally flicked the foil seal off my fingers, took two inhalations of my one-hour Somnorific, and was gone: black, deep, dreamless.

I must have drifted into natural sleep after the hypnotic wore off because we were letting down when I awoke. The hypersonic had no windows or ports. But there was a cabin telescreen, and I saw we were over New York harbor, coming into Ellis. I could see the Statue of Liberty. For safety, they had outlined it in red neon tubing when the airfield went operational. It didn't spoil the lady's appearance as much as you might expect.

A SATSEC copter was waiting for me. That was Paul's doing, and I appreciated it. A few minutes later we landed on the pad in the compound. Paul was seated in an electric cart near the hangar. He leaned out to wave to me. I walked toward him, brushing the side pocket of my zipsuit with the back of my hand to make certain I still had DEPDIRSAT's tape cassette.

Paul waited until I climbed onto the plastivas seat next to him.

"What was it?" he asked eagerly.

I fished out the cassette and showed it to him.

"What's on it?"

"I don't know. For our ears only. We better go to your lab."

He nodded and started the cart with a jerk. He was a miserable driver.

Geo-Political Area 1 was a megapolis that ran along the Eastern Seaboard from Boston on the north to Washington, D.C., on the south. During the decentralization of government offices during the Presidency of Harold Morse, the DOB had assigned SATSEC to a complex of office and residential buildings on the lower tip of Manhattan Island.

The development had originally been called Manhattan Landing. It was excellent for our purposes, including offices, apartments, shops, restaurants, and small parks. The three level underground area had been converted to laboratories and computer banks at a cost of 200 million new dollars. Like all government compounds, ours was surrounded by a high chainlink fence, with constant security patrols, closed-circuit TV, infrared, ultrasonic, and radar monitors.

My apartment was on the penultimate floor of the highest residential building, since I was a Division Leader, PS-3, the third highest rank in Public Service. Paul Bumford, a PS-4, lived one floor below me. Angela Berri, a PS-2, had the penthouse. DIROB, the Director of the Department of Bliss, a PS-1, had his home and office in Washington, D.C.

Paul and I drove directly to A Lab, fed our BIN cards into the Auto-Ident, and took the executive elevator down, down, down. Another Auto-Ident check to get into the general lab area. To enter Paul's personal lab, he had to speak his name into a live microphone. It automatically checked his voiceprint with the one on file in the Security Computer. Then the door could be opened with his magnetic key. It was all a game. Everyone knew the whole system could be fiddled, but we all followed regulations.

Over in a corner of the lab, the fluorescents were on high intensity. Mary Margaret Bergstrom, an AENOF-B (an artificially enovulated female with a Grade B genetic rating), was serving with a polarizing microscope. She looked up in surprise when we entered. Paul waved to her. She nodded briefly and went back to the scope.

"What's she doing here at this hour?" I asked. It was not yet dawn.

"She serves all hours." Paul shrugged. "She's got no social life, no hobbies, no bad habits."

"Unless you call playing a flute naked in front of a mirror a bad habit."

Paul laughed. "Oh, you heard that story, too."

We went into his private office. He turned on the lights, locked the door behind us, pulled the plastopaque shade down over the glass window that looked out into the general lab area.

I checked the Sharegard monitor on the wall. It was supposed to register the presence of any unauthorized electronic sharing devices. Sometimes it worked. At the moment it showed a normal reading.

"When did you have your last sweep?" I asked.

"About a week ago. We were clean then. They found an unauthorized transistor radio over in B Lab. Some clone had been listening to the dog race results.''

"Beautiful. Let's get on with it."

Paul took out a portable cassette deck. The cracked plastic case was held together with plastitape.

"Earphones," I ordered.

I used an earplug set. Paul did, too, but in addition he clamped on a theta helmet: small steel plates, held about three inches from his temples. They sent a weak electric current, about 7 cps, through his hippocampus. Paul was studying biofeedback but had not yet mastered the skill of going into theta at will.

He inserted Angela Berri's tape cartridge and pushed the On button. He looked at me. I nodded. He pushed Start.

"This morning, at approximately 1045 EST, the corpus of an em was discovered lying in a bed in an apartment on West Seventy-fourth Street in Manhattan. The em was identified as Frederick Halber. That's H-a-l-b-e-r. The corpus was discovered by the guardian of the building in company with a uniformed officer of the New York Peace Department. The guardian had been alerted by flasher from Halber's employer. Halber had failed to show up for service that morning and wasn't answering his flasher. The employer is Pub-Op, Inc. You know that outfit, Nick.

"The New York Medical Examiner made a preliminary diagnosis of coronary thrombosis. The corpus was taken to the New York City Resting Home. His 'next of kin' listed in Halber's service file at Pub-Op, Inc. was a cover name for his control. That was how I was notified.

"The real name of the stopped em was Frank Lawson Harris. He was in PS, on my Section's Headquarters Staff, assigned to undercover service, reporting only to me, through his control. The Director of Bliss and the Assistant Deputy Director of the Security Division are not aware of this activity. They are not, repeat, *not* to be informed.

"Nick, I want you to find out what you can about how Harris stopped. I do not believe it was a coronary thrombosis. I believe he was assassinated. Claim the corpus from the NYC Resting Home and perform a complete autopsy, including tissue and organ analysis. Preferably, do it personally. If not, concoct a believable cover story for whoever does it. Lieutenant Oliver of the New York Peace Department will cooperate on releasing the corpus and allowing you access to Harris' apartment.

"I will be back tomorrow. I hope you will have answers by then. I know I can rely on your loyalty and discretion. Destroy this."

The voice stopped. Paul turned off the machine. We removed our earphones. We looked at each other.

"What do you make of that?" I asked finally.

He ticked points off on his fingertips:

"One: Angela Berri is involved in a covert and possibly illegal activity of X kind for Y reasons.

"Two: Her immediate ruler, DIROB, is unaware of this activity, as is the Department's Security Chief. Why? Either her activity *is* illegal or *they* are personally involved in an illegal activity which she has uncovered or suspects.

"Three: Her covert activity is organized and of some duration, since she has a system of controls for her agents and has enlisted the assistance of at least one officer of the New York Peace Department. And since she suspects Harris was assassinated, her activity is serious and not just ordinary politicking.

"Four: Halber's—or rather, Harris' employment at Pub-Op, Inc., is probably of some significance since we depend on them a great deal in our estimation of the Satisfaction Rate.

"Five: If Harris was in service with the Department of Bliss, his file is available to us, and we have an IMP on him."

He paused a moment, then: "How was that, Nick?"

I held up a finger. "Six: You and I are now involved, whether we like it or not."

"We can refuse to do anything."

"And risk Angela's vengeance? I know the ef. Good-bye careers."

"What do you suggest, Nick?"

"Do what she orders," I decided. "I interpret this tape as an order from our ruler, not a request. And you so interpret it. Agree?"

"Agree."

"Do not destroy the tape. It is our only hope in case this whole thing blows up. I'll keep a file on all this in my apartment safe. When you're finished with the tape, return it to me. From then on, we'll discuss this only in the open or in a closed area where the possibility of sharing is minimal."

"Understood."

"Tomorrow morning, or rather this morning, I'll get Lieutenant Oliver on the flasher and make arrangements to get into Harris' apartment. We'll take IMP samples. And I'll claim the corpus. Can you do the PM?''

His face went suddenly white. "I can, but don't ask me, Nick. Please don't ask me!''

I was shocked by his vehemence.

"All right," I said gently. "You don't have to. But I haven't done an autopsy in more than ten years. I'm not up.''

"Mary!" he burst out. "Mary Bergstrom can do it! She does them all the time. She *likes* to do them.''

"What will you tell her?''

He thought a moment.

"That the New York Peace Department requested our cooperation because the case demands a transmission electron microscope, an energy-dispersion analyzer, and a lot of other hardware they don't have.''

"You lie very well." I nodded approvingly. He grinned. "Will she ask questions?''

"Not Mary. She'll do what I tell her.''

"Fine. Tell her to get everything on color tape. She'll have the corpus later today. I'm going to sleep. You keep the cassette until you run the voiceprint. I'll call you after I've spoken to Lieutenant Oliver in the morning.''

He locked the tape cartridge in his office safe. Then he opened the door. I put a hand on his arm.

"Paul, that beachhouse of Angela's out on the coast. . . .''

"Yes?''

"She told me she doesn't own it, that she borrowed it from a friend. But she moved around in it like she's lived there all her life.''

"Oh?''

"There's a glassed-in gazebo down on the sand. And a small stable. I saw a stallion and at least one em server. The whole thing has got to cost at least a hundred thousand new dollars, plus upkeep. On Angela's rank-rate?" I pondered a moment. "Paul, does the Section have a contact in that area who could make quiet inquiries and find out who actually owns the house?''

"Sure," he said promptly. "I know just the em. An attorney in Oakland. DIVLAW let one of his clients plead *nolo contendere* in a case of mislabeling chlordiazepoxide. It might have been an honest packaging error, but I doubt it. Anyway, they ran a good recall, and no one got hurt. But if we had fought it, the client could have drawn a five-year reconditioning sentence instead of a ten-thousand-dollar fine. That lawyer will do anything we ask.''

''Take care of it. 'I know I can rely on your loyalty and discretion,' '' I quoted solemnly. He laughed.

Paul went over to talk to Mary Bergstrom. I went back to my apartment, to sleep. I didn't need a Somnorific. I had an REM dream of an ef galloping a black stallion. She had a death's-head.

X-4

I awoke irritably at 0700 when my radio alarm clicked on to the strains of ''Esperanti Street Songs.'' We were enduring one of the periodic Esperanto revivals, although linguists had proved—to my satisfaction at least—that the world had more to lose from a universal language than from a profusion of national tongues. The only valid universal languages were music, scientific symbology, and gold.

I did twenty minutes of slow hatha asanas, followed by twenty minutes of meditation. I showered, shaved, used my ultrasonic tooth strigil. I applied light pancake makeup, a rosy shade; my skin was rather sallow. Just a touch of lip rouge. An eyebrow darkener. My hair was still black, but my eyebrows were beginning to go gray. Probably an enzyme deficiency. I dressed while drinking the day's first glass of chilled Smack, laced with a packet of high-potency vitamin concentrate. I also ate two probisks. They tasted as you might expect: anise-flavored sawdust.

As usual, I arrived at my office before any of my three secretaries. Each was assigned one of the three general areas into which I had divided my responsibilities: (1). Day-to-day activities of DIVRAD; (2). Relations with Satisfaction Section and the other three divisions it ruled; (3). Relations with food and drug manufacturers, makers of prosthetic devices and organs, commercial laboratories, biomedical academies, neuroscientific associations, etc.

I found three neat stacks on my desk awaiting me, each left by one of my secretaries. All included memos, letters, and papers to be scanned; tapes to hear; films to see.

I glanced first at two bright-red teletyped messages. One was the weekly Satrat (Satisfaction Rating) Report from DIVDAT (Division of Data & Statistics). It showed the national Satrat was up .4 percent. That was encouraging.

The second red teletype was less encouraging. It was a medical report from SATSEC's Rehabilitation & Reconditioning Hospice No. 4, near Alexandria, Virginia. It stated that Hyman R. Lewisohn, the government's foremost theorist, showed no improvement under continued treatment. Lewisohn was suffering from leukemia. We had been trying a new manipulated form of methotrexate, with apparently no improvement. We might have to add vincristine and cytosine arabinoside. I jotted a note on the teletype to flash the Chief Resident at R&R No. 4 and discuss it. Lewisohn's survival was the responsibility of my Division. I did not take the duty lightly.

I then went through everything else rapidly, making three new stacks of my own: (1). Requiring immediate attention; (2). Leave till tomorrow or for a week at most; (3). When I had time. Or never.

I was still at this organizing procedure when Ellen Dawes, one of my secretaries, came in. She was an AINF-B, a female bred by artificial insemination. I had long ago decided that the Examiner who had assigned her a Grade B rating had been more impressed by her personality than her genetic code. I didn't blame him a bit.

At the moment, as she stood in the doorway and held a plastic cup out to me, her eyes were as wide as those of an addict preparing a fix.

Without speaking, I went to my office safe, inserted my magnetic key, swung open the heavy door. I withdrew the five-pound can that had cost me fifty new dollars on the black market. She watched me measure out five tablespoons into her plastic cup. She licked her lips. Her eyes were still glistening.

"Thank you, Dr. Flair."

"Thank *you*, Ellen."

We both laughed. She left with the precious grind. I put the can back in the safe and locked the door. Fifteen minutes later Ellen was back with a steaming mug, put it carefully on my desk on a little plastimat. I didn't touch it until she had left to enjoy hers with the other two secretaries, both ems.

Then I sat back in my swivel chair, took a sip, closed my eyes. It was so hot it burned my lips. But I didn't care. It was the genuine thing. The last can I had bought, from an unfamiliar pusher, had turned out to be mostly chicory, oregano, and ground-up peanut shells. But this was real coffee. Possibly from Columbia State.

It was 0942 before I could get through to Lieutenant Oliver of the New York Peace Department. My office digiclock showed 1020 before I had things organized. Then we left the compound.

Paul and I led in an internal-combustion-engined sedan. I drove; Paul never could learn how to shift gears. His IMP equipment was in the back seat. Behind us came a fuel-cell-powered ambulance driven by Mary Bergstrom. With her were two laboratory attendants. They were both young gene-variant ems, bred by electrical parthenogenesis before we had satisfactorily solved the problems of chromosomal injection of the egg. Their appearance was normal, but both suffered from Parkinsonism. It was controlled with an improved form of L-dopa.

We stopped at the New York City Resting Home, after driving around the block three times before we found a parking space. I went inside with Mary Bergstrom.

There was no problem; Lieutenant Oliver had already alerted them. I signed the release form. Before Mary and the attendants took the cadaver away on a wheeled stretcher, I zipped the body bag down far enough to take a look.

Face contorted in agony. Bulging eyes. Rictus. Deep lateral scratches across the thoracic area. It was difficult to imagine, but he might have been handsome. I wondered if he and Angela had been users.

The guardian let us into the apartment. I locked the door; we looked around. All the furniture, the rugs, the prints on the walls, the linens, the plates and cutlery, even the clothing in the dressers and closets appeared to be leased. That was not unusual. Few people owned more than trinkets and minor personal effects. Styles and fashions changed rapidly; you could trade in all your belongings annually and lease new, tooty "possessions."

Paul began unpacking his equipment. I wandered about. The guardian and the officers who had removed the corpus had already polluted the air, the rugs, possibly the furniture. It was not an ideal situation for gathering IMP samples.

I went into the nest. Neat and clean. A row of six-hour Somnorifics in the medicine cabinet, along with the usual array of unrestricted drugs. Nothing unexpected. Paul started taking adhe-

sive patches from the sink. I went into the living room. Cold, cold.
. . . Who had lived there? No one had lived there. A ghost maybe. It
was empty of human track. The bedroom wasn't much better. But
the bed was rumpled, the thermal blanket thrown back, the plas-
tisheet still showing an indentation where Frank Lawson Harris had
rushed to an excruciating stop.

Near one leg of the bed a glint caught my eye. I bent over to stare
at it. It appeared to be the foil seal of a Somnorific inhaler, balled up
and flicked away. I went to Paul's case for a little self-closing plastic
envelope. I slid the balled-up Somnorific seal into the bag and
pressed the lips tightly together. I slipped the envelope into the
pocket of my zipsuit. I went back into the nest. Paul was on his
knees, sleeves rolled up, probing down into the toilet drain with a
long, flexible instrument we called an "eel." It had a rounded,
adhesive knob on the end.

"I'm going now," I said to Paul.

"Right."

"There are Somnorifics in the medicine cabinet. Bring them
along."

He didn't answer. He was intent on what he was doing. He could
probe a toilet drain, but he wouldn't do a postmortem or even look at
a stopped em.

I went back to the compound. I had a lot of service to get through,
heavy because in two days I was due for a threeday and wanted to
train to Detroit, GPA-3, to visit my parents. And Millie.

First I took the little plastic envelope from my pocket and sent it
down to A Lab for analysis of the Somnorific seal. Then I went back
to scanning the daily team reports. My Division was organized
into teams: Nutrition Team, Transplant Team, Genetic Team,
Biochemistry Team, etc. We did a tremendous amount of original
biomedical research. In addition, we performed the functions of
what was formerly the Food and Drug Administration. We tested all
commercial drugs and foods for purity. Well . . . maybe not for
purity, but for nontoxicity. And our field forces inspected production facilities regularly.

I was proud of the fact that DIVRAD was self-supporting. That
is, we developed new foods, drugs, artificial and cloned organs,
new laboratory equipment and techniques, etc. These, when not
restricted, were licensed for commercial production. The fees
received more than paid for the expenses of DIVRAD

Only two other governmental departments were self-supporting.

One was the Atomic Energy Commission of the Department of National Resources (formerly the Department of the Interior). The other, of course, was the National Contribution Commission (formerly the Internal Revenue Service), a division of the Department of Profitability (formerly the Department of the Treasury).

(Incidentally, all these name changes of government departments were not made by whim. They were decreed by the Office of Linguistic Truth, OLT, formerly the Office of Governmental Euphemisms, OGE.)

The following morning, Angela Teresa Berri returned from her threeday in California. I met her by chance in the corridor outside her office. We chatted casually, all-colored zipsuits moving by us on both sides.

Finally, the corridor reasonably clear, she murmured, "Anything?"

"No," I whispered in return. "Not yet. It's very complex. I'll contact you when I have something. Or nothing."

"Who else knows?"

"Paul Bumford."

She looked at me steadily. Greenish, flecked eyes.

"You trust him, Nick?"

"Of course."

She nodded, and was gone.

Late that afternoon, A Lab returned my little plastic envelope with their report. They had identified the inclosed object as a standard Somnorific seal. Hardly earth-shaking news. But on the underside of the seal they had discovered minute quantities of a substance they "believed to be" (typical scientific hedging, there) 5-HT.

Now, 5-HT—5-Hydroxytryptamine—is known to biochemists as serotonin. Nanogram amounts of platelet-bound iso-serotonin were found. And platelets are particles suspended in human blood, formed by bone marrow, and necessary in the clotting of blood and the sealing of injured blood vessels.

It was interesting.

The following morning, at 1030, Paul Bumford, Mary Bergstrom, and I were in my apartment, seated in plastivas slings drawn up around my new 3-D TV set (leased). The shades were down, the door locked, the flasher disconnected. The set was switched to Tape.

I leaned forward so I could see her, past Paul.

"Mary, what lens did you use?"

"Infinite focus," she said in that cold, toneless voice of hers. "Wide angle. Electronic zoom by voice-actuated switch. But no sound. There was no need for sound."

"Of course not," I said. I leaned back, pressed the Start button of my control unit.

The guard glass flickered. Wild images. Then, as the lasers took hold, the holograph image steadied in the box. We were looking at the pain-racked features of the stopped Frank Lawson Harris. Focus was sharp, colors were lifelike—or rather, unlifelike.

The naked corpus was stretched out on a stainless steel table, slightly tilted, with a run-off channel at the bottom. Mary stood behind the table, masked, gowned, gloved, scalpel in hand.

She gave us a running commentary, in person, her voice flat, without inflection.

"Closeup of features. Contorted. Agonized. Notice lips drawn back from teeth. Rictus. Long view of total anatomy. Limbs twisted. More than normal rigor. Notice hands half-clenched. Now this—close-up of lateral scratches in thoracic area. Analysis of tissue under object's fingernails proved scratches self-inflicted. Clawed at chest. Long shot again. Here—close-up of genitalia. Penis and testicles flaccid. Now . . . autopsy begins. I'm going in. Butterfly incision. Firm skin. Good muscle tone."

I was fascinated. I was aware that Paul Bumford was not watching.

"Everything normal," Mary continued tonelessly. The camera zoomed in to show her knife at work. "Now I'm going into the chest cavity. Heart normal but aorta unusually small to the touch. My first clue. Liver somewhat fatty but not pathologic. Here's a close-up. Healthy."

I watched the tape hum along. I admired her technique. She was sure, deft, unhurried. She removed the organs swiftly, put them gently aside.

"Now I'm into the stomach cavity. Normal. Except for that abdominal aorta. Unusually tortuous. You'll see a close-up in a second. There it is. Rigid, nodular. Now I'm at the pancreas. Everything out. Everything normal. Intestinal tract normal. Within four hours prior to stopping object had consumed proveal, propep, natural starch—possibly spaghetti—red petrowine, and a few other things. I have it all on my taped report. Now I'm in the lower abdominal area. This took more time than is shown, of course. I cut and spliced the Instaroid tape so you wouldn't get bored. Genitalia normal. There they are. Testicles large but soft. I'm going into them now. Ejaculation two hours before stopping. Penis small. Here, close-up, discoloration on glans. Analysis showed it to be Amour Now, a popular brand of lip rouge. Color: Passion Flower.''

A sound came out of Paul Bumford next to me. Whether it was a groan, a sigh, or a giggle, I could not tell.

"Into the legs now," Mary Bergstrom continued, staring intently at the TV screen. "Nothing unusual. Good musculature. Strong. Good skin tone. But here again, close-up, tortuous and sclerotic femoral arteries. That completes the tape of the PM. Now we go to the tissue slides.''

Paul straightened in the sling, took his hand from his eyes, looked at the TV glass.

"Cross sections," Mary narrated. "Gross slices, gold-palladium coated. For the SEM. Arterial. One: Internal carotid. Two: External carotid. Three: Thoracic aorta. Four: Abdominal. Five: Common iliac. Six: Femoral. Now we go to venous. One: Jugular. Two: Iliac. Three: Subclavian. Four: Vena cava. Finally, sections of those 'healthy' organs. One: Heart. Two: Liver. Three: Kidney. That's it.''

The tape wound to whiteness. I pushed the Off button. We sat there in semidarkness, in silence. I couldn't believe what I had seen.

Paul Bumford spoke first.

"J-J-Jesus Christ!" he burst out. "Are those cross sections for real?''

"I have the shavings," Mary Margaret Bergstrom intoned. "I have the slides. It's all in my report.''

After my initial shock, I began to realize what had happened to Frank Lawson Harris. Those arteries and veins looked like obso iron pipes, the inside surfaces so encrusted with rust that flow was slowed and finally choked completely. It would take years, maybe a century, for iron pipes to become that obstructed. I suspected the stopped em's circulatory system had been plugged in minutes, and the intensive venous involvement suggested a nonphysiologic process.

I stood and raised the shades. We blinked in the strong south light.

"Anyone want anything?" I asked.

"Something stronger than Smack," Paul said. His voice was shaky.

I had been saving a bottle of natural apple brandy for a special occasion. This seemed like a "special occasion." I poured three small glasses—real glass—and served their drinks, then brought mine. I stood before them, leaning on the TV set.

"Paul?" I said. "you all right?"

"Fine," he said defiantly. "I'm fine."

"You saw the tissue slides. Diagnosis?"

"Extensive, widespread infractions involving multiple organ systems."

"Mary?"

"I concur."

"Any idea what caused it, Paul?" I asked.

"Ingestion. Injection."

"Not ingestion." Mary Bergstrom shook her head. "I'd have found traces in the stomach lining or intestinal tract. Not injection. I went over the object carefully with a high-powered magnifier prior to PM. He was clean."

"Inhalant?" I suggested.

They looked at me.

"Possible," Paul said.

"Probable," Mary said.

"All right." I nodded. "Now what did he inhale?"

"Something," Paul said. "Something that caused wild, uncontrolled platelet agglutination and limpid deposition."

"Serotonin," Mary said. I looked at her, surprised and pleased. She had learned a lot, outside her discipline. "It's got to be the serotonin. Probably a manipulated form of 5-HT. The East uses it as an interrogative technique. By injection. Very painful. Very. But this must have been by inhalation. Stopping him almost instantaneously."

"I concur." I nodded. "The military played with it in the obso days of hypothesized chemwar. But they rejected it. Too lethal."

"Too lethal?" Paul cried. "For a nerve gas?"

"Use your brain. It killed instantly. So we wipe out all of France. Seventy-five million humans stopped, plus all other warm-blooded animals, including those marvelous geese with their synthetic-hormone-injected livers. What do we do for foie gras then? Seriously, what would the military do? All those corpora to flame. Vegetation gone too, if we wanted. What's the point? War is geography. That's why the military put lethal gas in the icebox and switched to temporary incapacitators. Knock 'em out, walk in wearing masks, take away their weapons, wait for them to wake up. Then they go back to work, the horses pull, the dogs bark, the birds sing, and those geese feel their livers expand. Beautiful. Simple and humane. But at one time, back in the 1970's and '80's, a 5-HT gas existed. Probably still does. In a deep cave somewhere in Colorado.''

I paused.

"The New York Peace Department will be very interested in this," I continued smoothly. "Mary, you did a fine service."

If I had told her she was gorgeous, she couldn't have blushed a deeper hue.

"Thank you," she said faintly.

"Run a lung slice to confirm. I think you'll find it. Then put the object back together again. Paul will give you the final disposition."

She nodded to us and was gone.

"A very bright ef," I said, after the door closed behind her.

"Sometimes she scares me," Paul said gloomily.

"Pure intelligence is always scary. You've never met Lewisohn, have you? There's a creative intellect that's terrifying."

" 'Final disposition'?" he said. "You told Mary I'd give her orders for the final disposition of the object. What?"

"That's Angela's problem. I'm going on a threeday in exactly"—I looked at my digiwatch—"three hours and fourteen minutes. Angela knows you're in on this. Catch her alone and ask her what to do with it. She'll probably want it flamed."

"Probably."

"All right. Now let's get to you, what you found. Did you bring back those Somnorifics in the medicine cabinet?"

"You told me to."

"What were they?"

"Analyzed? Six-hour Somnorifics."

"Uh-huh. What else?"

He finally shook off his depression, came alive, started talking rapidly.

"Habitual and recent presence in the apartment of an ef, approximately twenty years old, one sixty-five centimeters. Long, blond hair, trimmed recently. She uses Quik-Eeze Creme Shampoo. She wears tooty shoes. Spike heels. One pair is oxblood red. No Reason perfume, a complete synthetic. Amour Now lip rouge. Color: Passion Flower.''

"Ah-ha," I said.

"Let's see . . . what else? Slight nasal drip. Low-grade bronchial infection. Fuchsia eye shadow. Ugh! Oh: here's an oddity; I don't think she's on the pill or any other fertility control. Blood type is O-Rh negative. That's not Harris'. She was recently on a threeday or vacation in a hot, southern climate." He paused. "Want to know how I know all this?"

I looked at him.

"I know exactly how you know all that. You used chromatography, electrophoresis, spectrophotometry, polarizing microscopes, X-ray refraction, the scanning electron microscope, and our very best energy-dispersion analyzer. All this high-priced equipment on hairs you found on the backs of chairs and the sofa. Ditto on stains from hair shampoo. Position of stains gave you height. Then we have rug indentations for the spike heels and rug stains for shoe color. Pillowcase stains and scents for lip rouge and perfume. You might have used the Olfactory Analysis Indicator there. Eye shadow from pillowcase or bathroom towel, which would also give you perspiration specimen, which would give you a partial immunoglobulin profile. Nasal drip and bronchial infection from discarded tissues in the bathroom wastebasket."

"And the vacation in a hot, southern climate?"

"Skin flakes all over the place."

"Gee, boss, you're real smart."

"That's why I'm an Assistant Deputy Director, and you're my Executive Assistant."

It was a mistake. I knew it the moment I said it.

"All right, all right," I said hurriedly. "Did you find an exhausted Somnorific inhaler? Near the bed? Anywhere in the bedroom? In the apartment?"

"No. No sign."

"I checked with Lieutenant Oliver. His ems didn't find it either. They took Instaroids of the scene in the bedroom. No empty Somnorific inhaler."

"Is it important?"

"Yes. But let's get on with it. I've got to catch a train. What about the IMP samples?"

Now, I shall be as brief as possible. Microbiologists interested in pursuing the subject further are advised that more than a hundred references exist on film spindles. The journals of the American Society of Microbiology might be a good place to start.

As I had told Paul Bumford, the idea of microbiological identification of the individual began as a forensic concept, the purpose being to establish the presence of a suspect at the scene of a crime. I felt this was of peripheral importance. Microbiology, I was convinced, could be used as exact means of personal identification of the general populace, far superior to appearance, physical measurements, fingerprints, voiceprints, hair, teeth, blood type, etc.

All humans are hosts to an incredible number and variety of microorganisms. Some exist within the skin, some without. Some are pathogenic. Most, fortunately, are inert or beneficial. Indeed without the ''good'' protozoa, bacteria, fungi, and viruses, we simply could not exist.

IMP, Individual Microbiological Profile, was a project concerned only with the external microbial populations that humans support on skin, eyes, nasal passages, genitalia, throat, anus, mouth—whatever organs of the body are exposed to the atmosphere.

After two years of research, the IMP Project (a temporary horizontal organization drawing specialists from all my teams) selected the fifty most common permanent and semi-permanent microorganisms to be found on the human body. Each was given a quantitative rating of 1 to 10, depending on the profusion in which it was found on a particular object's surfaces.

We then took IMP samples from every member of the Department of Bliss—quite an undertaking when you consider there were more than half a million in DOB service. And ''taking an IMP sample'' involved analysis of saliva, sputum, perspiration, semen, vaginal scrapings, skin scrapings, nasal and throat discharges, urine, and feces. Fortunately, most of these analyses were automated.

Having coded IMP's for the 500,000-plus DOB personnel, we fed the information to our largest DIVRAD computer and asked for duplicates. There were none. That was encouraging, but hardly surprising.

We were about to start testing computer retrieval of IMP information. If the blind tests were successful, I intended to suggest a campaign, low-key at first, to make microbiological analysis obligatory nationwide. We would then include every American's IMP in his file in the NDB (National Data Bank).

''I was able to get a good IMP of Harris from his apartment,'' Paul Bumford said. ''His dirty laundry, sink, bed, atmosphere, rugs, toilet seat, and so forth. What I couldn't get, Mary furnished from the corpus. But we already have Harris' IMP on file. I presume you want a blind identification test. Right?''

"Right."

"But why an IMP on anyone else I could find?"

I didn't answer his question. "Did you get an IMP on the unknown blond ef?"

"A partial. Fairly accurate, I would say. Thirty-two definite factors out of the fifty. Nine possibles. That leaves nine unknowns. And where does that leave us? Nick, do you think the blond ef is in service in DOB? Is her IMP on file?"

"Could be. Harris was in DOB. It's possible his user was, too."

"Possible, but chancy. There's something else on your mind. I can tell."

I paced around, looking down at the floor, hands jammed into my zipsuit pockets.

"A crazy idea," I muttered. "You'll laugh at me."

"I've never laughed at one of your ideas in my life and never shall," he vowed.

"I thank you," I said. Everything was all right between us again. "The crazy idea is this: Of those fifty microorganisms included in the IMP, I think about half could be inherited."

He sucked in his breath. "My God," he said, "you are incredible."

"If I'm right," I went on, "if twenty-five or thirty factors out of the fifty—particularly those in the respiratory tract—are inherited, then maybe if that mysterious blond ef who sucked Harris' cock the night he was stopped isn't actually in service in DOB, with an IMP on file, then maybe she's related to someone who is. What do you think?"

He looked at me, shaking his head.

"Mary scares me, and you scare me," he said. "What do I think? Definitely possible."

"Yes. Now here's what I want you to do while I'm gone. Take your construction of Harris' IMP to the Computer Team. Tell them you're running a preliminary blind test and see if they validate it. Then try input of the unknown blonde's IMP. I know it's incomplete, but *try* it. If the computer comes up with zilch, ask Jim Phelps if he can reprogram to give you a list of DOB people with identical quanta on the IMP factors you *do* have on the blonde. Follow?''

"Of course. I'll have it all for you when you return. You better get moving. Say hello to your parents for me."

"Thank you, I will. I'll be back in time for the Section meeting on Thursday. Meanwhile, keep the mill grinding."

"Bastard!" He laughed. He took Mary Bergstrom's cassette from my TV set and started out. The tape cartridge reminded me of something.

"Paul."

He turned back.

"This is for the Tomorrow File."

He brightened. The TF was his baby.

"I know you weren't watching the PM. That's all right. But you heard Mary's narration. Did you hear her say that the stomach was normal, the heart was normal, the pancreas was normal? And that the liver was slightly fatty but not pathologic?"

"So?"

"Paul, those organs were grossly normal. Microscopically, of course, they were totally infarcted. But if they *had* been totally normal, they would still be shoved back into the object and flamed. The waste! You know the figures on donated organs, in spite of that last telethon. And production of artificial and cloned organs just isn't enough. We don't have the love we need to increase production. Patients are waiting, hopefully. And we're going to flame a healthy heart, liver, pancreas, stomach. And every time anyone stops naturally and is flamed, we lose retinas, kidneys, hands, arms, legs, gonads, and ovaries we can use, that we need."

"Nick," he said soberly, "you were the one who taught me the difference between what we *should* do and what we *can* do."

"I know, I know," I said impatiently. "That's why this is for the Tomorrow File. The first sanitation laws this country passed, more than two hundred years ago, established the government's interest in and concern for public health. Then laws, laws, and more laws. Sanitation, hygiene, drinking water, sewer systems, inspection of meat plants, then Medicare, then hospitalization insurance, government payment for kidney dialysis, genetic counseling, then national health insurance, then the Fertility Control Act, the licensing of procreation. It's all been gradually, gradually evolving, coming to a time when we must realize the citizen's corpus is the government's responsibility."

"And property?" Paul said.

"Well . . . its concern, certainly. We should not flame healthy organs; that's all I know. They're too valuable. They could be used for research, transplant, or frozen for the nukewar bank. They're a national resource and should not be wasted."

Paul computed a moment.

"It would mean a federal license for stopping," he said. "Government inheritability of the corpus."

"I know." I nodded. "That's what troubles me."

He looked at me steadily.

"The future belongs to the untroubled," he said.

X-5

They had restored direct New York-Detroit train service in 1983. It was the southern route, via Philadelphia, Canton, and Toledo, Ohio. I took the Bullet Train. It was gas-turbine-powered, with a linear motor. We moved at 480 kph, riding on a cushion of air about 1.5 cm above the track. Beautifully smooth, quiet, comfortable. The service in the dining car was excellent, the food detestable. But no one complained. They had no basis for comparison.

I had taken a compartment. This was a threeday, but I had brought along a case of papers, film spindles, tapes. Fortunately, I didn't need to carry clothing or toilet accessories. I kept a civilian wardrobe and complete kit in my suite in my parents' home.

The morning I returned to GPA-1, three days hence, I would be expected to attend the monthly executive conference of Satisfaction Section. This was, of course, ruled by Angela Berri, DEPDIRSAT. Present would be the Assistant Deputy Directors of her four divisions. The five of us (DIVLEG had two Assistant Deputy Directors) would sit facing Angela across the white plastiglass table in the conference room. Behind each of us would be seated our Executive Assistant. In my case, that would be Paul Bumford.

Angela Teresa Berri was a rigorously efficient manager. Each Division was allowed ten minutes, no more, no less, to present and discuss a single topic.

The topic I had selected for discussion in this particular meeting was Project Supersense.

Almost fifty years ago, neurosurgeons believed they had isolated "pleasure centers" in the human brain that could be excited by implanted electrodes. It became obvious, years later, that the term "pleasure center" was something of a misnomer; there was no single center of pleasure in human brains, or even in a single brain. Pleasure was generated in a series of "islands of concentration" in the pathway leading from the forepart of the hypothalamus to the cortex. Tickle one, and the object was no longer thirsty. Excite another, and hunger was satisfied. Titillate a third, electrically or chemically, and sexual pleasure was produced.

After lengthy experimentation on animals, a technique was evolved by which needle-thin electrodes could be implanted in the human brain. Energizing the titanium-alloy electrodes with a mild electric current gave the object a feeling of well-being. One neuro-scientist termed it "reward" rather than "pleasure." Exact placement of the electrodes was crucial, but not as difficult as you might expect. During neurosurgery, the object might be administered an anesthetic sufficient only to allow cutting through the scalp and drilling a hole in the skull.

Once the surgeon was through the meninges, the patient could be conscious and responsive during surgery. Fortunately, the stuff of the brain itself cannot register pain. So a surgeon implanting elec-trodes could probe and test, probe and test, asking the wide-eyed object, "There? There? What do you feel? What's happening? Are you happy?"

Originally, after correct emplacement, these electrodes were fixed with glue to the object's skull, with a bit protruding beyond the scalp. Wires were attached to carry the required electric current. Later, using hardware developed in the space program, a mic-rominiaturized radio receiver, battery-powered, was taped to the object's skull. Upon receipt of a radio signal, it stimulated the object's "pleasure centers." Thus he was ambulatory, free from entangling wires.

Still later, a microminiaturized radio transmitter, battery-powered, was attached to his belt. The receiver was implanted beneath his scalp for cosmetic reasons. An object could now stimu-late his own brain, giving himself a jolt of pleasure, or reward, by pressing a button on his belt kit.

The purpose of all this research and development was therapeu-tic, to relieve the symptoms of epilepsy, depression, schizophrenia, etc.

But as frequently happens, what began as a biomedical blessing became a medical craze. It was estimated that more than two million Americans had had electrodes implanted in their brains for the sole purpose of self-stimulation. The operation was not inexpensive, and even with the development of plastitanium, the presence of electrodes (or any foreign matter) in the brain presented certain risks, especially during violent acceleration or deceleration of the object. In a car crash, for instance. But the risks did not lessen the human hunger for new pleasures. They never do.

Now enters Project Supersense. It was my idea. I realized that the brains of these two million electrode-implanted Americans were being stimulated by a radio signal, self-produced. I saw no reason, considering the state of our technology, why a film—either in a movie theatre or on a TV set at home—could not be coded along its edge, just as sound is synchronized to the visual image, to send a signal to all receivers under the scalps or within the skulls of the "Mind-Jerkers," as the people who had opted for the electrode implant operation were popularly called.

Then these two million, watching a film on any subject, would be automatically stimulated to pleasure, thirst, pain, hunger, or eventually any other appetite or emotion, if neurobiological research continued at its present rate. Their titillations would be synchronized with the scene being shown on the film. Mind-Jerkers would feel greatly increased sexual arousal during a love scene, increased pain during a torture scene, increased fear during a horror scene, increased glee during a comedy scene.

I discussed this concept with Paul Bumford. He enthusiastically concurred that it was feasible. It was assigned to my Psychobiology Team. After investigation and research, they reported the plan practical, valuable, and eagerly awaited a go signal to develop the necessary hardware and film synchronization techniques in conjunction with the Electronics Team.

It was the file on Project Supersense that I was reviewing and attempting to evaluate on my train trip to Detroit. I was trying to decide whether to recommend going ahead with it or stopping it.

The railroad station in Detroit occupied a concourse on the two lowest floors of a new high-rise crematorium. Carrying my case, I took the express elevator to the copter pad on the roof. My father's copter was waiting. In his inimitable style, the four-seater was painted a startling Chinese red. On the cabin, in block lettering of vibrating purple, it read: FLAIR TOYS: THE TOYS WITH A FLAIR! Subtle.

The pilot was a young ef with flaming blue hair. She wore a Chinese-red zipsuit. Across one breast the expected legend was embroidered in that jarring purple. But she was so pneumatic it read: "flAIRToys." She told me she would drop me at the house, have something to eat, then go out to the airport to pick up my father, who was coming in on a commercial flight from Denver. He had a factory out there.

We tilted out over the Detroit River and almost immediately began our descent over Belle Isle to Grosse Pointe. She hovered a moment over my father's beautifully tended estate, then let down on the front lawn. My mother wasn't too far away, near the water. She was seated in a garden chair of white-painted iron. She was wearing one of her gowns of flowing silk, all pleats and ruffles. Her thin arm poked out, resting on the table alongside. Her fleshless fingers grasped the glass.

I looked around for Mrs. McPherson. She was nearby, a wooden statue with folded arms, standing under a small copse of young elms. She never let my mother out of her sight. Never.

I walked slowly down to the garden chair.

"Mother," I said softly.

"Who?" she said vaguely. She looked up at me, dazed and faraway.

"Nick."

"Who?"

"Nicholas, your loving and devoted son."

Her face cracked into a million pleased wrinkles.

"Nicholas, my loving and devoted son," she repeated, reaching out her arms. "Come kiss me, chappie."

And so I did.

"How are you, Mother?"

" 'I never saw a purple cow,' " she said.

"What?"

" 'I never saw a purple cow, I never hope to see one; But I can tell you, anyhow, I'd rather see than be one.' "

"What on earth is *that*?"

"Long before your time."

"Mother, it's nonsense."

"Isn't it?" she said delightedly. "Isn't it just! You're so handsome."

41

"Mother's beauty, father's brains."

"You're lucky," she said, and we let it go at that.

"This world . . ." she said.

"Yes, yes," I said. "Let's go up to the house. It's getting chill, and we have so much to talk about."

I got her onto her feet and gave her my arm. We walked slowly, slowly up the slope.

"Nicholas, my loving and devoted son," she mused.

"I am that."

Behind us, trailing but catching up, Mrs. McPherson trundled along, somber in the dusk.

"Are you in love, chappie?" She used the word in the obso sense.

"Not at the moment, Mother."

She laughed again. She had been a great beauty. But she had resigned from the world; she no longer belonged.

When I got mother inside, Mrs. McPherson took over and helped her upstairs to her bedroom. Charles smiled a welcome and took my case. I didn't know what Charles was. Obviously an obso em, he had to be an NM—but I knew nothing about his genesis. I suspected he might be from GPA-2, from the Tidewater section of what was formerly Virginia.

I went into the library. I mixed a vodka-and-Smack, mostly vodka. Coming home always did that to me. I could analyze my reactions, but it didn't help. I wandered about the library. Almost two thousand books my father had never read.

I was finishing my second drink when I heard the copter overhead. I went outside and stood on the floodlighted porch. I admired the youthful way he leaped from the copter and came bounding across the lawn toward me.

"Nick-ol'-as!" he shouted as he came. "Nick-ol'-as!"

It was his joke. He never tired of it.

He caught me up in a great bear hug. What a ruffian he was! He pulled me close. He smelled of a lot of things: petroscot, a testosterone-based cologne, a scent of something softer—probably from a quick embrace with that blue-haired ef copter pilot.

In the library, under overhead light, his face, beneath his makeup, seemed old and tired. But his manner hadn't changed: loud voice; jaunty walk; hard, decisive gestures; barked laugh; the need for physical contact—fingers on arm, arm around shoulders, shoves, pats, strokes, thumps. It was his way.

He poured us drinks, a petroscot for himself, one of my mother's potato vodkas for me. We hoisted glasses to each other and sipped.

"You seem perky," I said. "Who's the new tootie?"

He barked his laugh.

"You wouldn't believe."

"I'd believe."

"Ever catch *Circus au Natural*? It's on Thursday nights at 2300."

"The contortionist?" I said.

"You bastard!" He barked again. "You know everything. Hungry?"

"Starved."

We went into the cavernous dining room. We sat next to each other at an oak table large enough to seat twenty. It was genuine oak, all right. When they destroyed an obso building and found reusable oak planks they fashioned them into tables for the wealthy. But first they dipped the planks in caustic, beat them with chains, drilled in fake wormholes, and then used a stencil to make false rings where wet glasses might have rested. *Then* they coated the whole thing with Plastiseal.

My father didn't give a damn about food. Put anything in front of him—he'd eat it. But he had a special fondness for new foods, synthetics, laboratory spices, and refinery flavorings.

After dinner, dominated by his long, loud discourse on the success of his new sex dolls, we moved back to the library for a natural brandy. He continued his monologue there.

The sex dolls were not obscene. They were the result of a government contract he had won to produce small Juskin dolls, efs and ems, to teach sex education to four-year-olds. The dolls were naked and complete with genitalia. They had proved so popular that my father had started commercial production. They were now available in three sizes: 28, 60, and 90 cm tall. Many adults bought them.

Chester K. Flair had long experience in the industry. Originally, he had been employed as a research chemist by a toy and doll manufacturer. He came up with a suggestion for a doll that vomited when you bent it forward sharply. The vomit was a viscous compound containing bits of sharp plastic. You fed it into the doll through a stoppered opening at the nape of its neck. Refills of vomit were to be available in half-liter bottles.

Also, my father cleverly suggested adding a stain to the fake

43

vomit so that after regurgitation, the doll's dress was stained ineradicably. The doll's owner (her parents, actually) would then be forced to purchase a new costume. This doll, my father was convinced, would be an immediate commercial success. He called it Whoopsy-Daisy.

His employer rejected the idea. My father then married the woman who became my mother. Her name was Beatrice Susan Bennington. With her money—she had an inheritance of 50,000 old dollars—my father resigned his service, formed his own company and, with additional financing, started production of Whoopsy Daisy. His confidence was vindicated. It was an almost instant success. He expanded his corporation to include the production of conventional toys, dolls, and novelties. He was a very knowledgeable and shrewd businessman.

When I was nine years old, one of my father's designers came up with the extraordinary idea of a baby doll that defecated. The "feces" were plastic turds, fed into an opening in the doll above the coccyx.

The production of the Poo-Poo Doll, as it was called, meant an enormous investment in new dies, formulae, patents, machinery, etc. I remember an incident that occurred during this period. I was then ten years old, and my father still had fantasies of my "following in his footsteps" and becoming a doll manufacturer and director of his enterprises after he retired. He insisted I accompany him to a bank meeting for the purpose of securing a large loan to finance tooling-up for production of the Poo-Poo Doll.

I listened to my father make his presentation to a tableful of hard-faced bankers. He demonstrated a handmade prototype. He explained, with charts, color slides, and samples, that he was basing his estimate of potential income not only on the initial retail purchase price of Poo-Poo but on continued consumption of packages of fresh plastic turds and miniature paper diapers.

They listened to his sales pitch expressionlessly. When he finished, they turned to look at each other. He was asking for a great deal of love. Finally, one banker with a skin of parchment made a tent of his hands, stared thoughtfully at the ceiling, and said, "I know we have dolls that piss. But dolls that shit? Isn't that in rather poor taste?"

I rarely forget anything. But *that* I particularly remember

My father got his loan. The Poo-Poo Doll proved to be the sensation of the industry. It made millions of new dollars.

My father ended his Panegyric to Sex Dolls abruptly. He poured us each another brandy, then flopped onto the leather couch facing me. "So what's new?" he asked.

I recognized that apparently casual "What's new?" My father was fearful of aging, especially of the loss of physical strength that aging imposes, particularly of the diminution of his sexual vigor. I knew he would never lose the hunger. His terror was of being deprived of the ability to satisfy it.

"Nothing much," I said. "We're fooling around with several things at the moment: a manipulated form of vitamin E that's had some interesting results on rats; a new steroid we're constructing; and the pituitary transplant program is continuing. I really think we'll find the answer there, in the antèrior lobe."

"How about injection of testosterone? I think that's the most obvious answer. After all, I have a BS in chemistry."

I refrained from sighing. This was the Bachelor of Science who had flashed me from Hong Kong to ask if there was really any aphrodisiacal benefit in swallowing a ground-up tiger's tooth, as he had been assured by a Chinese apothecary.

"Androgen would be the most obvious answer," I agreed. "If it worked. It's been tried for years, for half a century, and it doesn't. But there are so many psychological factors involved, it's difficult to make an objective evaluation of the results. We can clone ovaries easily, but we're having trouble with testes. So that leaves direct transplant. Would you like to leave your nuts to science?"

"Fat chance," he scoffed. "When they flame me, my nuts are going to be where they've always been—between my legs. Who knows, I may go to heaven and need them."

"Fat chance," I repeated, and he laughed.

We sat a few moments in silence, staring into the cold fireplace.

"Something bothering you?" he said finally.

"Not bothering me, exactly, but perplexing me."

"What is it?"

"I have a Section conference when I get back. I have to make a recommendation to go ahead on a project or to stop it."

"What is it?"

Ordinarily, I don't like to discuss DIVRAD's business with outsiders. The indepsec stuff I never do, of course. But it suddenly occurred to me that I might benefit from his practical judgment and shrewdness. I briefly explained Project Supersense to him, how film scenes could be synchronized to give Mind-Jerkers increased stimulation. He listened closely, fascinated. He was always fascinated by anything that affected sexual pleasure, however indirectly.

"What do you think?" I asked him when I had finished.

"How many Mind-Jerkers are there in the country?"

"About two million. Maybe seventy-five percent adults."

"How would they pay for this?"

"I don't know. We'd license the process, I imagine. The people who make TV tape cassettes might be interested."

"I doubt it. Two million isn't much of a potential market these days. Is there any other way of producing the same results? Say by a pill?"

"Not at the moment there isn't."

I didn't tell him about Paul Bumford's memo in the Tomorrow File on the UP—the Ultimate Pleasure pill.

"Then forget about Project Supersense. Stop it." He rose and began to pace about the library. "Try for a pill that increases pleasure. Why a pill? The two big C's of modern merchandising: Convenience and Consumption. You've got to have a product that's convenient to use, and that is consumed by use, and has to be repurchased periodically. The safety razor was the greatest product ever invented. The makers could give it away, because then you had to buy their blades. That's where the love was. Ditto the camera. What goddamn good is it without film? No, forget about Project Supersense. Strictly a one-time sale. Put your people to work on a pleasure pill."

"It's not as simple as you think," I objected. "First of all, what *is* pleasure? No one can define it. Too subjective. To an obso ef suffering from arthritis, pleasure might simply be absence of pain. To a young em, pleasure might be parachuting from one hundred fifty meters. To me, pleasure is this glass of natural brandy. To you—well, I know what pleasure is to you."

"Don't say it!" He barked his loud laugh.

"What I'm getting at is that there are no objective criteria. How can we possibly start synthesizing a pill? We don't even know what we're looking for."

I finished my brandy and stood up. I pleaded tiredness and work to do. He didn't object. He had work to do, too.

The copter was still on the front lawn, and I supposed the ef pilot was in the guesthouse, waiting.

My parents' home had been built in 1904 by a wealthy Detroit brewer. I was born a little after midnight in my mother's bedroom on the second floor.

The house was a charming horror, a dizziness of gables, turrets, minarets. My father had compounded the insanity by adding a glass-enclosed terrace, a futuristic plastisteel guesthouse, and a boathouse on the river done in Tudor style with beams brought from England. There was an antique coat of arms over the doorway with the motto: *Aut Vincere Aut Mori*. I told my father it meant "I shall conquer death," and no one ever enlightened him. He was pleased with it, and had *Aut Vincere Aut Mori* engraved on his personal stationery.

My suite was on the third floor. A huge bedroom had a four-poster bed, two enormous armoires that held most of my civilian clothing, chests of drawers, an ornate, gilt-edged pier glass, a few faded prints of sailing ships on the walls. An open doorway (no door) led to a modernized nest. Then there was a small study that was all business: desk, swivel chair, film spindle racks, reading machine, a tape recorder that took cassettes, cartridges, and open-end reels, a TV set, a small refrigerator, and file cabinets.

The final room was my "secret place." It was always kept locked. I had, as far as I knew, the only key. Each time I left to go back to GPA-1, I glued a fine thread from jamb to door, about 20 cm above the floor. The thread had never been disturbed.

Two walls of this hideaway were the lower slopes of the mansard roof, interrupted by two gabled windows facing south and east. The inside walls and ceiling were plaster, painted white a long time ago. Now they were almost ocher. There was a frazzled rag rug on the planked floor, a sprung Morris chair with the leather seat and back cushion dried and cracking. There was a metal smoking stand, a bottle of my father's natural brandy and a single glass, a small bookshelf that held four books.

That's all there was. Nothing very significant. Except for the four books.

In 1998, most "books" were published on film spindles, designed for lap and desk reading machines. The few actual books printed were paperbound. To buy a hardcover book, you had to patronize a rare book store, an antique shop, or a merchant who sold secondhand junk. Practically everything ever published had been reproduced on microfilm. It took up so much less space, people simply sold or gave away their actual books, or threw them out. As my father would say, the film spindles were convenient.

In 1992, to escape a sudden and unexpected summer shower, I had ducked into a tiny decrepit antique bookstore on Morse Avenue (formerly Second Avenue in Manhattan). I had passed it a few times previously, and was vaguely aware it specialized in obso art books. How it survived I do not know, since you could buy film spindles of most of the world's great art, and the color reproduction in a viewing machine was incomparably more vivid than on a printed page.

Waiting for the summer squall to pass, I idly picked up and leafed through a heavily illustrated catalogue of an art exhibit that had been held in New York in 1968. The artist was an em I had never heard of. His name was Egon Schiele.

It would be melodramatic to declare that coming upon that old art exhibition catalogue by accident on a rainy summer afternoon changed my life. It did not change my life, of course. I continued my service in DOB as before (I was then Executive Assistant to AssDepDirRad). I visited my parents, ate, slept, used around; nothing in my life changed.

But something in me was altered. I knew it now. How I was altered by seeing the work of Egon Schiele, in what manner and to what extent, I did not compute then and did not now.

Egon Schiele was an Austrian painter, born in 1890, stopped in 1918. He was twenty-eight. He was the son of a railroad server. He lived in poverty most of his life. He was imprisoned, briefly, for "immorality," for having shown some of his drawings to curious children. He died of influenza, on the day of his wife's funeral. She also died of influenza.

Those were the bare bones of the em's life. They tell you little, and what they do tell is without significance. The meaning lies in the man's work.

If you stared for hours, as I had, at the self-portraits, you would see the depth of demonic possession in that face, and you would·be disturbed, as I was disturbed. Did I like the work of Egon Schiele? I did not. But it obsessed me. There had not been a single day since 1992 when, at some time, awake or asleep, I had not suddenly remembered one of his drawings or paintings. With pain, and the sense of loss.

I had purchased the exhibition catalogue, and the obso shop-keeper promised to try to find more of Schiele's work. About a month later he mailed me a note—handwritten!—saying he had located another catalogue of a different Schiele exhibition. I bought that one, too. During the following years I was able to buy another book, in poor condition, of sketches Schiele had made while in prison.

Then one day the owner of the shop where I had purchased the catalogue flashed me, in great excitement. He had heard of an obso ef, a widow, a recluse, who owned a biography of Schiele. It was, reportedly, in mint condition, an enormous volume of 687 pages with 228 full-page reproductions (84 in color), plus 612 text illustrations. She would accept no less than 1,000 new dollars for this prize. I bought it immediately, sight unseen. It *was* a prize.

Those were the four books in my secret place: the life and work of Egon Schiele. I had never seen any of his originals (most were in museums in Pan-Europe). I had never been able to locate prints or large reproductions. Schiele's name was not included on the list of artists whose work was available on film spindles.

On the cover flap of the largest book, an unknown editor had written: "The anguish of the lonely, the . . . despair of the suffering, the desolation of the desperate, are the moods Schiele expressed. . . . The themes are genesis and decay, longing and lust, ecstasy and despair, suffering and sorrow. . . ." This was all true, but it was not the entire truth.

I sat in my creaking chair, alone in the world, turning pages to feed on those wonders. Yes, there was gloom there, pain and desperation. But I was once again shocked by the colors, the forms, the beauty he had seen and I had not. There was something indomitable there, something triumphant.

It was after midnight before I closed the book, switched off the light, locked the door, went into my bedroom. Even in bed, my lids resolutely shut, I saw an explosion of color, pinwheels, great rockets and fireworks, all created by that long-stopped em whose eyes stared at me so intently from the self-portraits.

I awoke at 0900 to the roar of the copter ascending: Chester K. Flair commuting to his office and factory near Mt. Clemens. The copter thrummed away, the noise faded. Then I heard gasping caws of delight: water birds over Lake St. Clair. I went to the south window but could not see them in the fog. But I heard their cries.

The break in my daily routine was welcome. I pulled on old slacks, a heavy turtleneck sweater, worn moccasins. In the kitchen, with Miss Catherine bustling about, trying to force a "good, hot, solid breakfast" on me, I had only a glass of orange concentrate in cold Smack and a cup of something called coftea. It tasted like neither. To please Miss Catherine, I ate one slice of toast. Most of it anyway. Every year our bread became fouler and more nutritious.

Then I wandered out onto the grounds. The fog was lifting from the lake. I could still hear the birds. I went down to the shore. I found a flat stone and tried to skip it over the surface of the water, but it sank instantly. I picked up another stone, almost perfectly round. I bounced it on my palm. How could a stone seem so alive?

I strolled about, no plan or destination in mind, just meandering. I passed the garage, the boathouse, the guesthouse, the empty stable. Once we had a horse, a gentle mare named Eve, with a back as broad as a desk, so fat you couldn't possibly fall off. Eve had died during the equine encephalitis epizootic in 1985. My mother had wept.

I sat on the cold, wet grass under an oak tree. I rubbed my cheek against the rough bark. I chewed a blade of grass, bitter and pulpy, and spit it out. I poked a finger down into the moist soil.

My mother came down for lunch, sweeping into the glass-inclosed terrace like an obso queen.

"Good morning, chappie! It's going to be a beautiful day. I just feel it!"

She held up her face to be kissed, then insisted I sit next to her at the table. It was glass-topped, on an ornate wrought-iron base. It was set with linen placemats, Georgian silver, a crystal vase of mums. Everything had been leased. The mums were plastic.

The lunch was delightful, except for the food. My mother was in a manic mood, laughing, shrieking, clutching my arm, telling me outrageous stories of the two young ems who had purchased the estate next to ours. Apparently, both wore false eyelashes, and one had a small gold ring suspended from his nasal septum. Mother was delighted with them; they had brought her natural crocuses they had found on their grounds, in early spring.

"What are their names?" I asked.

"Who, Nick?"

We went on to something else. She was like that now, and deteriorating. Her attention span grew shorter and shorter each time I came home. She would not seek help, and my father would not force her. Nor would I.

Later we strolled about the grounds, trailed by Mrs. McPherson.

The afternoon passed. It was a glory, the air washed, earth scented. We went back to the terrace, and Charles threw open all the windows. Another glass and pitcher were put on a small table next to the soft chair where mother lolled. I lay on the couch. Once we sang a song together, a children's song I hadn't heard in years: "If you needed a man to encourage the van. . . ."

Then, the pitcher almost empty, she fell silent. Her eyes became dazed: that faraway look I had noticed on greeting her the previous day. I looked around for Mrs. McPherson. She came out of the house and led my mother away.

I went upstairs to bathe, shave, clean my teeth with an old-fashioned brush, and apply makeup. I dressed in a manner I thought would please Millie: a collarless jacket of purple velvet with a lavender shirt and mauve jabot. My knickers were fastened below the knee with gold buckles. My hose were black lace. My shoes were shiny plastisat, with heels higher than I was accustomed to. But I wouldn't be doing much walking.

A few years previously my father had a brief enthusiasm for antique and classic cars. He had purchased twelve before his interest waned. He sold them all off (by then he was collecting Japanese armor), and I bought one of them, a 1974 Ford Capri. I kept it in our Grosse Pointe garage. It would have been useless in GPA-1.

I drove the Ford into Detroit, the gift I had brought for Millie on the seat beside me. It was a combination powder and music box, made of plastic, with a tiny ef and em on top who held each other and twirled in time to the music. It was dreadful. Millie would think it a profit.

I had arranged to meet her at a restaurant-cabaret in a crumbling section of the city, down near the river. I had no fear of appearing there in the costume I was wearing. Most of the young factory ems who frequented the place would be dressed in similar fashion, many more elaborately. Last year it had been plastipat tights and Wellington boots.

I had met Millie Jean Grunwald at a basement cockfight. We had both bet a winner, and stood next to each other in the collect line. I won much more than she, and invited her and her girlfriend to join me at the bar for a drink. They accepted happily. I ordered a magnum of "champagne." They adored it, so I said nothing, but drank as little as I could. I thought it might contain methanol.

They went off to the ef nest together. When they returned, the girlfriend departed suddenly, giggling. I suspected they had flipped a coin for me. Whether Millie had won or lost, I did not know.

She had a large one-room apartment over a porn shop. It was almost a loft, reasonably clean, decently enough furnished with leased possessions that were obviously in their third or fourth setting. But there were a few personal touches: a calendar showing a young ef hugging a kitten, a plastic imitation of an old-fashioned round-faced clock, a crimson sofa pillow stamped "Use Me."

She answered all my questions readily and with great good humor. She was fourteen then, a CF-E, and she served as a packer at the Qik-Freez Hot-Qizine factory. She traveled to and from work in an electric bus. She was paid 125 new dollars for a four-day week (twenty-two were take-home pay), plus two two-week vacations every year, plus free lunches every working day of the factory's products which, she assured me, were the best foods ever, sold in all the tootiest restaurants in the world.

She was jolly, companionable, undemanding. I could relax with her. When she came in from the nest (it was outside in the hallway), I stood up as she entered. She blushed, smiled shyly, and murmured, "Thank you." When she asked if I would like to use her, I said it would be a profit.

Afterwards, I offered her ten new dollars "to buy a gift." She would not take it. I urged her then to accept a plastigold brooch I had on, the kind of cheap trinket I wore on my excursions into the "lower depths." She was delighted with it.

That had been two years ago. I saw her every time I came to Detroit to visit my parents. I brought her presents and took her wherever she wanted to go. I think she liked me. But it was hard to tell; she liked *everything*.

Apparently something had gone wrong in the chromosomal manipulation of the embryo from which her group had been cloned. She was not quite a variant, but her Grade E genetic rating was warranted. Once I saw her trying to shove a grossly oversized plastic stopper into the narrow neck of a bottle. Her brow was furrowed, her eyes puzzled. Her spatial cognizance was especially deficient, her vocabulary limited, her speech rapid to the point of spluttering. But she was a sweet ef, not incapable of treachery but unaware of it. I liked her. I may have felt a sense of responsibility.

She was standing outside the restaurant-cabaret when I arrived, although I had told her many times to wait inside if I was delayed. Her face lighted up when she saw me. She came running to throw her arms about my neck, and smeared my lip rouge.

The restaurant was crowded, noisy, and smelled of phenol. Too many small tables had been jammed in under a low ceiling; the atmosphere was milky with smoke. But Millie loved it, waving to acquaintances as we threaded our way to our table.

We had an enjoyable dinner: wretched food, but served with great verve by a flatfooted obso waiter who obviously recognized a good thing when he saw one. He would get his pat.

Millie chattered unceasingly, sometimes with a mouthful of food. She told me about her mean supervisor at the factory, about her girlfriend Sarah who had consumed a liter of petrorye "straight off" on a dare, and had to be taken to a hospital to have her stomach vacuumed, about a kitten she had found abandoned, named Nick, for me, who had stayed two days and then departed for parts unknown.

I listened to all this, smiling and nodding. DIVRAD was far away. I ate my prochick, drank my petrowine, and asked myself no questions.

Millie was wearing a tooty transparent blouse. Her breasts had been painted in red circles, like archery targets. There was what appeared to be a wide aluminum "gut-clutcher" about her waist, fastened in front with a brass tongue, shackle, and iron padlock. The key hung from a wire loop about her neck. She wore a minikilt, her legs bare from calf to buttock. Her boots were synthetic fur. From the zipper tabs hung the "flying penis" ornament that was the current rage, advertised on TV with a remarkable animated film and the endlessly repeated demand: "How tooty can you get? How tooty can you get? How tooty can you get?"

After dinner I asked our solicitous waiter if any natural brandy was available. Regrettably no. But he promised something just as good. It turned out to be a fruit liqueur. I think it was natural. Much too sweet for my taste, but Millie loved it.

The lights dimmed, a siren sounded, the diners screeched in anticipation, and a Master of Ceremonies darted through the curtain onto the minuscule stage. He was wearing an enormous codpiece, the batting popping out through a rip. The audience roared with laughter. He told several jokes ("I'm in mourning tonight. I lost my wife. But she found her way back home").

Then the nude chorus line came kicking on. One had a scar from a recent Caesarian section clearly visible. Another one astounded me; I thought I might have discovered the first case of steatopygia in the Detroit area.

After the dance routine, the next act was introduced by a professional type as being a "serious sex lecture." It was two marionettes, nude ef and em, cleverly manipulated, demonstrating various copulative positions. Father would have loved it.

This was followed by an em transvestite who sang a song about his continual "hard luck," with the rhyming lines you might expect.

Then came two nude ef acrobatic dancers who were quite good.

The chorus line came on again for a tired number in which they wore animal masks. The ef with the *gluteus* that was the most *maximus* I had ever seen was the gorilla.

The final act, the "star attraction," lasted less than five seconds. The room was darkened completely. A single blue spotlight centered on the stage. The curtains parted briefly. There stood a naked em, obviously a genetic variant, with a circumcised *membrum virilis* at least 60 cm long. The audience gasped. The curtains closed. The house lights came on. There was a great snapping of fingers.

"Shall we go?" I asked Millie.

She profited from driving at high speed. I enjoyed it, too, though I rarely had the opportunity. We drove out to an automobile testing track we had discovered in the River Rouge area. For a ten new-dollar pat, the bearded obso night watchman would unlock the gate and allow us onto the track. It was oval-shaped, the end curves so steeply banked that it was impossible to climb them until I had the car up to top speed.

Around and around we went, Millie screaming with delight as we moved higher and higher, lying on our side as we neared the tops of the almost vertical end curves. It was a cloudy, moonless night. Only the fan of white from the headlights, rushing ahead of us, showed me the edge I was shaving.

On the final go-round, I switched off the lights. Then just the faint light from the sky provided dim illumination. Wind-howl, engine roar, and the pleased whimpering of Millie next to me. . . . I plunged through the darkness.

"Y'gonna stop yesself one of these nights," the bearded watchman said when we left.

"That's right," I said.

He shook his head. "This world. . . ."

I remembered my mother had spoken the same words in the same tone. "This world. . . ."

Back in Millie's apartment, I handed over her gift. She tore off the wrappings as a child might, almost frantically, ripping. She was delighted with the musical powder box and set the miniature couple to dancing, around and around, watching them with a pleased smile, head cocked.

Her body was young, young, the skin nylon, the flesh natural rubber. There was a patch of golden lanugo over the lumbar vertebrae. Her painted breasts stared at me like shocked eyes. I rolled atop her and penetrated. Her lips drew back in a lupine grin.

She had told me, "I like using the most," and that was operative. But she had a habit that amused me at first, then distracted me, then angered me, but that I eventually conditioned myself to ignore. During using she would continue her conversation, telling me of a prank they had played at the factory (they had put the supervisor's purse on the assembly line, and it had emerged at the other end wrapped tightly in plastic and frozen as hard as a plastibrick). Or of a tooty pair of black plastisilk panties she had seen, imprinted with crimson mouths. Or of her desire to learn to drive, to drive endlessly, at high speed, anywhere.

While she recounted these things, during using, her cardiac rate increased, her breathing became shallow and rapid, her eyes glittered, a sweat covered her plump thighs. She continued chattering, linking her heels behind my knees, grasping my buttocks to pull me deeper, talking, talking, until she summited, interrupting her recital for a small shriek, then gabbling again while her body continued to pump in diminishing rhythm and her fingers probed gently into my rectum.

I arrived back at my parents' home in Grosse Pointe about 0400 the following morning. I went immediately to bed and slept until almost 1300. Without a Somnorific.

X-6

The return to GPA-1, thirty-six hours later, was a series of small accidents that almost added up to disaster.

1. The Bullet Train left the Detroit terminal right on schedule. It moved about ten meters and ground to a halt. A small em had tumbled off the platform, onto the tracks, and broken his right tibia.

It was almost an hour before he was attended to and taken away.

2. East of Canton, Ohio, streaking for Pittsburgh, we hit the last section of a four-unit articulated truck-train, driverless, on the new AUS-1 automated highway. No one was injured or stopped, but it took almost three hours to clear away the wreckage and the hundreds of plastilap bags of probeans scattered all over the right-of-way.

3. In New York, getting close to conference time, it took me twenty minutes to get an electric cab. At Fourteenth Street we ran into a traffic jam and sat without moving for another twenty minutes. I was beginning to sweat under my zipsuit.

I signed in at the compound with ten minutes to spare. I swung aboard one of the open-sided, slow-moving cart trains that made continual circuits of the compound, driverless, following a wire laid under the pavement. I was in my office in five minutes. Paul Bumford was waiting with his big green accordion file.

"You like to live dangerously, don't you?" he said.

"Thank God for accidents," I said, "or we'd start thinking we can predict *everything*. What's hot?"

"Lewisohn's condition has stabilized. Everything else can wait."

"Good. I have the Supersense file. Let's go."

We waited for the executive elevator to take us up to the conference room.

"Were you faithful?" he whispered.

I looked about casually. No one in sight. I patted his cheek softly.

"Not to worry," I said.

We were the last division heads to arrive, but it was another minute before Angela Teresa Berri made her entrance. We all stood up.

The Satisfaction Section of the Department of Bliss was rigidly organized into four divisions:

—Division of Research & Development (DIVRAD). I was Assistant Deputy Director in charge (AssDepDirRad).

—Division of Security & Intelligence (DIVSEC). Burton P. Klein was AssDepDirSec.

—Division of Data & Statistics (DIVDAT). The AssDepDirDat was Phoebe Huntzinger.

—Division of Law & Enforcement (DIVLAW). The two Assistant Deputy Directors were identical (and, according to rumor, incestuous) twins, Frank and Frances von Liszt. Both, naturally, were called "Franz," to their delight.

In addition, Angela Berri, Deputy Director of Satisfaction (DEPDIRSAT) had her own headquarters staff. She ran a tight ship, especially on matters that affected policy rather than mere planning and operations.

"Nick, you lead off," she commanded.

"Project Supersense," I said, glanced at the digiclock on the wall, and began. . . .

Without consulting my notes, I delivered a concise recitation of the history and current status of the project, costs to date, estimated costs to completion, estimated potential income. I ended in a little more than five minutes by stating, "I recommend Project Supersense be stopped."

"Comments?" Angela asked, looking at the others.

Burton Klein was the first to respond. He felt Project Supersense should be continued. I knew he would; he had plastitanium electrodes implanted in his brain. He was a Mind-Jerker. He said he did not feel a potential market of two million was negligible. It could be exploited for a lot of love.

I replied with a condensed form of my father's lecture on Convenience and Consumption, pointing out that if synchronized movie films were made available, nothing would be consumed; it would be a one-time sale.

"Not necessarily," he said. He claimed that Mind-Jerkers would purchase large libraries of the high-stimulant movie films. And, he pointed out, the same technique could also be used on film reels of books for reading machines. "Even on tapes of music," he added.

It was an idea that hadn't occurred to me, and I was silent.

"Anyone else?" Angela Berri inquired.

Brother and sister Liszt passed. Phoebe Huntzinger agreed with Klein.

Angela asked me if we had anything in present status that could be leased.

"No," I said, "nothing patentable. At this stage, it's just a concept."

She nodded. "Stop it," she said crisply. "Too limited. Phoebe, you're next."

One of the responsibilities of Data & Statistics that we were all interested in, that the entire government was interested in, was the

Satisfaction Rate (Satrat). Data was gathered daily; Satrat Reports were issued weekly.

Briefly, the Satrat measured the quality of life in America, what percentage of Americans were satisfied with their lives and the way things were going and, conversely, what percentage were dissatisfied.

The testing was done by a dozen commercial and academic organizations, under government contract, that specialized in public opinion polling. One of the companies was Pub-Op, Inc., in which Frank Harris Lawson was serving when he was stopped.

The polling involved in calculating the Satrat included everything from yes-no questions to essay-type questionnaires seeking in-depth reactions, emotions, hates, fears, prejudices, etc. The technique had evolved from social attitude and motivational testing of the late 1970's when it was recognized that the public's well-being could no longer be judged solely by economic indicators: income, growth of the Gross National Product, employment, etc.

The Satrat was extremely important to policymakers, from the President and Chief Director to Congress and the courts. By closely monitoring the public's social attitudes, laws could be passed or repealed, funds spent in one direction rather than in another, potential dissension smothered before it escalated into an intractable crisis, etc.

Phoebe Huntzinger, with her army of demographers, multivariant analysts, and linear regression statisticians, was the ef who provided the precise weekly social barometer, with the aid of an extremely sophisticated computer, of course. Her ten-minute contribution to our monthly conferences was invariably not a problem seeking a solution but merely a review of where the Satrat had been, where it was now, and her predictions of where it would be in a week, a month, a year, five years from now.

She was a black ef with a Grade A genetic rating that was fully deserved. She spoke languidly, almost lazily, but question any of her conclusions and you'd find yourself sinking slowly in a quagmire of sine waves, hyperbolic functions, and angular velocities that would do you in. Right now, her report was optimistic: The Satrat was up and rising. The near future looked fair, the far future glorious.

No questions were asked.

The third offering was from the von Liszts, heads of the Division of Law & Enforcement. Usually their monthly reports involved their continual struggles with lawyers and the courts. The main problem was inheritance. The development and increasing use of artificial insemination, artificial enovulation, parthenogenesis, self-fertilization, cloning, etc., had created a legal jungle through which lawyers and judges moved cautiously, no paths (precedents) to guide them.

As one eminent jurist remarked, "The Biological Revolution has raised law into the realms of poetry."

But on this day, the von Liszts' report did not concern inheritance; it dealt with a proposed legal change in the IC (Informed Consent) Statement.

By law, we were forbidden to experiment on human objects without first obtaining their signed IC Statement. Prior to signing, we had to explain to them, whenever possible, the potential results of their cooperation. That "whenever possible" was our legal out, of course. When testing a new drug on a human object, for instance, who could possibly predict the potential results, even after lengthy testing on animals?

Most of our testing on human objects was done on prisoners in federal penitentiaries. The IC Statements were easy to obtain. The prisoner was paid one new dollar a day for submitting to the test, or he hoped his cooperation would be a factor when his parole or reduced sentence was up for consideration, or he feared refusal to sign an IC Statement might count against him in such a legal proceeding.

Patients in government hospitals represented a different problem. If they were obviously incompetent to scan and/or understand what they were signing, the IC Statement had to be signed by next of kin. It was invariably signed, relatives fearing that not signing might jeopardize the patient's treatment in the hospital, and hoping too, of course, that the proposed experimentation might result in a cure.

The third class of human objects of experimentation were formerly in government service but were now confined to Rehabilitation & Reconditioning Hospices "for psychiatric observation for reasons of public security." A little trick we had picked up from the Russians.

The "psychiatric observation" part was valid enough. If their acts had been antisocial, it was *prima facie* evidence of a disturbed mind. The second part, "for reasons of public security," was validated by the first; obviously, a disturbed mind represented a potential threat to public security.

A lot of kaka had recently been published in facsimile newspapers and publicized on TV news programs that when these patients signed Informed Consent Statements, it was under physical torture or threat of torture. This, I could testify, was absolutely inoperative. No patient in a government R&R Hospice signed an IC Statement under duress.

It *was* true, of course, that those patients were frequently under hypnosis, under the influence of drugs or electric and electronic behavior conditioning. But that was part of their therapy. The fact that they signed IC Statements while undergoing treatment in no way nullified the validity of those statements.

That was our policy.

The increasingly vociferous objections to that policy came mostly from the Society of Obsoletes (SOO), a loosely organized association of obsos (generally people born prior to 1970) whose activities were usually laughable, concerning such things as antivivisection campaigns, letters to newspapers denouncing televised bullfights and executions, parades to protest the federal licensing of prostitutes, meetings to object to the legality of Smack and other addictive drinks and foods, and similarly hopeless causes. Most of these were simply a nuisance.

But their current program against the existing Informed Consent Statement was a little more serious. It appeared to be well organized, cogently reasoned, and presented to the public with thoughtful moderation.

To counter the efforts of SOO, Frances and Frank von Liszt suggested the IC Statement be reworded to include phrases stating that the undersigned fully understood the significance of what he was signing, that he had been offered no reward—financial or otherwise—for signing, nor was he signing under any physical, mental, or psychic duress.

Having concluded their presentation, the von Liszts were silent. Angela Berri asked for comments. Burton P. Klein and Phoebe Huntzinger gave approval to the revised form. I had an objection. I asked if making even this minor affirmative response to the Society of Obsos' desires might not encourage them to increase their demands.

"Once we give in," I pointed out, "they'll up the ante. Then where do we end? Sooner or later we'll have to answer them with a loud firm 'No!' It might be better to fight them on this. We could

easily win with a well-planned media campaign stressing the anticipated therapeutic benefits to be derived from human experimentation. If we surrender on this small issue, they undoubtedly will be
inspired to escalate their demands.''

"What do you think of that, Burton?" Angela asked Klein
directly.

She surprised me. After the way he had savaged my report on
Project Supersense, she seemed to be deliberately pitting the two of
us, for what reason I could not fathom.

"Mountains out of molehills," Klein growled. He was an
enormous NM; heavy through the shoulders and torso, with ridiculously spindly legs. His face was all eyebrows. He had a Grade B
genetic rating, but I suspected most of his talents were in his
muscles. Of course, in his service that was of some importance.

"Look," he went on, "it's just the wording of the IC Statement
we're concerned with here. It won't restrict us at all. Give those old
idiots what they want and shut them up. They're no threat. No one
takes them seriously."

There was silence for a moment. We all looked at Angela. She
looked at Burton Klein.

"I'll think about it," she said finally. "I may discuss it with
DIROB."

That seemed to satisfy Klein. He smiled. He thought he had won.

"All right, Burton," Angela continued. "Let's hear from you
now and wind this thing up."

The report of AssDepDirSec was a compendium of statistics and
percentages. It concerned the numbers, categories, and frequencies
of acts of assassination, kidnapping, sabotage, terrorism, and
threats against PS, academic, and commercial research
laboratories. Klein rattled off the figures so rapidly that he was
finished in three minutes flat. I don't think the others had caught the
significance of what he had said. I was conscious of Paul Bumford
shifting his position and moving uneasily behind me. I knew *he* had,
and was trying to alert me.

"Wait a minute," I said, even before Angela had asked for
comments. "Burton, if I understand you correctly, acts of assassination, sabotage, and terrorism against scientific research facilities
are up almost five percent from last month and more than fifty
percent from what they were a year ago?"

"That's right," he said stolidly.

"Well, you seem very calm about it. Aren't you concerned?"

"Sure, I'm concerned. I'm taking steps. I've organized a working committee of government, commercial, and academic security directors. We're exchanging intelligence. We're beefing-up security precautions. And we're working closely with the BPS on this."

The BPS, Bureau of Public Security (formerly the Federal Bureau of Investigation), maintained the data bank on domestic criminals and dissidents.

"Well, what's the pattern?" I demanded.

"Pattern?"

"Yes. What *kind* of installations are being bombed and burned and sabotaged?"

"All kinds. There's no pattern. Listen, I realize this is serious, but our violence rate isn't so bad when you compare it to the big picture."

"The big picture? What big picture?"

"The national incidence of violence, against banks, corporation offices, universities, insurance companies, government compounds, railroads, oil fields, laser-fusion power stations, airlines, and so forth. In some categories—bombings, for instance—our growth rate is actually *lower* than the national average."

I stared around the room. I don't think any of them caught it.

"It doesn't compute," I said. "Burton tells us the incidence of terrorist attacks against research facilities is fifty percent larger than it was last year and growing at a rate of five percent a month. He adds that the growth rate of national terrorist activity is even higher. But Phoebe tells us the Satisfaction Rate has never been higher and is rising every month. Just what the hell is going on?"

Angela stared at me a moment. No expression.

"Yes, yes," she said quietly, "it's something to think about. Well . . . I believe we've accomplished a great deal. Good meeting. I thank you all. Adjourned. Nick, could I see you for a moment?"

There was a gabble of relieved voices, pushing back of chairs, gathering of papers and files. The room emptied. Paul waited for me near the door, I went up to Angela.

"Yes?"

"I want to see you and Paul tonight. Come up to my place. At 2100."

"Fine. We'll be there."

She nodded and was gone. I sank down into her chair, began

rubbing my chin. Paul came over to stand close to me. I looked up at him.

"What Klein said about using the Project Supersense synchronization technique on filmed book reels and sound tracks—we should have thought of that."

"I know." He nodded miserably. "I'm sorry."

"Not your fault. Mine. Put it in the Tomorrow File."

"Too late," he said. "I'll explain to you later tonight."

"We've got to see Angela at 2100. At her place."

"I'll be back by then."

"Back?"

"I have to leave the compound tonight."

I nodded.

"Aren't you curious as to where I'm going?"

"Should I be?"

"I may have a user on the outside."

"So?"

"Couldn't you be just a wee bit jealous?"

"All right, Paul." I sighed. "Where are you going?"

"Tell you when I get back."

Sometimes he acted like a flirtatious ef. I let it pass.

"What's gotten into Klein?" I asked. "He seemed out for my balls."

"I noticed that. I was hoping you'd pick up on his report. I should have known you would. An Instox copy was circulated yesterday. I scanned it and got curious. I borrowed their rough data. They wouldn't let me take it out of their office, but I scanned it. There *is* a pattern to the terrorist attacks against scientific facilities."

"Had to be," I nodded. "What is it?"

"About seventy percent are against laboratories doing procreation and genetic research."

"That's interesting," I said.

The problem with the four-day week, for executives, was that we were compelled to serve twice as hard during the first six hours we returned from a threeday.

I went down to my office from the SATSEC conference and dug into the three stacks of documents on my desk. As usual, I organized my own three stacks: Immediate, Soon, Later. Included in the Immediate pile were the daily progress reports from team leaders that had accumulated during my absence. Most were routine; I scribbled my initials to indicate they had been scanned. They would then be microfilmed and filed. But one report was of particular interest to me.

It was from my Gerontology Team. With some diffidence, the leader was bucking along a suggestion made by one of his young servers—a bright ef. I scanned her name again to make certain I'd remember it.

She had run a computerized actuarial study of what it cost the government to maintain an indigent and nonproductive obso until the object stopped. She had included costs of food, clothing, shelter, and medical care. The dollar total was shocking. And when I saw the grand total for all such objects, I was astonished. What I could do for the young, vigorous, and productive with all that love!

The bright ef on the Gerontology Team had suggested an unusual approach to the problem. It was called GAS (Government-Assisted Suicide) and proposed the government offer 500 new dollars to any indigent and nonproductive obso who signed up. Stopping would be painless, by ingestion of pills provided free of charge by the government. The benefit would be awarded thirty days prior to stopping, to be used for any purpose the object desired, or it could be bequeathed.

Assuming a minimum of 10 percent voluntary acceptance of GAS, it was estimated that, even after payment of the benefits, the savings to the government would be almost two *billion* new dollars annually. I could scarcely believe it. But the report stated: "Computer printout available if desired."

I made two Instox copies on my office machine. The original report, initialed, would be microfilmed and filed. On one copy I wrote "Original thinking. F&F," initialed it, and marked it for return to the Gerontology Team leader. The "F&F" was Division shorthand for "File and Forget."

The second Instox copy I put in my pocket, then drew it out to red-pencil every reference to "Government-Assisted Suicide." I was writing in "Government-Assisted Peace" when Paul Bumford came in. The other offices were dark; everyone else had left.

"You've got to eat," he said.

"I suppose so," I said. I rubbed my eyes. "What time is it?"

"After 1900."

"I've got to come back. Pick me up here and we'll go to Angela's together. Will that give you enough time?"

"Plenty."

"Here's something for the Tomorrow File."

I handed him the corrected report on Government-Assisted Peace. He scanned it rapidly.

"Nick, it's good."

"I know."

"Not for action now?"

"No way. Talk to that ef who worked it up. Creative thinking there. She could be your second secretary."

He grinned. "For that I'll buy you dinner. *La Bonne Vie*?"

"I suppose so."

"You eat and I'll talk. I've got a lot to tell you."

He ate, too, of course, but he did have a lot to tell me. We sat at a 'orner table, Paul spoke in a low voice, his lips close to my ear. He finished his recital.

"You don't seem very surprised," he said, disappointed.

"I'm not. Angela's original tape was the input. She said not to inform DIROB."

"Oh. I had forgotten that."

"I hadn't."

"Do you trust her?"

"Yes, I trust her. In this."

"She's *such* a bitch."

"I know. But I think she's onto something here. It could benefit us. Let me do the talking tonight. Pick up your cues from me."

"Nick, I always do."

"Play it very tight. Don't volunteer *anything.*"

"Where thou goeth, there goeth I," he said.

We left and separated. He headed for the gate. I went back to my office. I had completed the Immediate stack. Logically, I should have started on the Soon. But there was a file in Later I wanted to scan.

When a server in PS was sent to a Rehabilitation & Reconditioning Hospice "for psychiatric observation for reasons of public security," and had signed an Informed Consent Statement, the first task given him was to write a report or dictate a tape detailing his activities during the past year, two years, five—for as long a time as his interrogators believed would be of value.

In this account, the object sometimes revealed names, places, dates that were frequently useful to AssDepDirSec, or BPS or UIA, in uncovering others who harbored antisocial tendencies. The object was usually assisted with memory-intensifying drugs, hypnosis, electric stimulation of the hippocampus, etc. The journal the object produced invariably made fascinating scanning.

It was particularly fascinating in this case, since the object had been a genetic biologist attached to the Denver Field Office of my Division. He and his wife had been principals in a criminal trial that had created headlines in the nation's facsimile newspapers and was the subject of endless TV gabble shows. It was popularly known as "The Horse Triangle Murder Case."

The couple wanted to breed, desperately. Since both were Naturals, with good genetic ratings (hers was an A; his a B), they had no trouble obtaining a license. But the em's sperm proved sterile. No amount of hormonal or enzymatic therapy was successful. It may have been a genetic variance. In any event, the ef opted for artificial insemination, wanting to experience—according to the subsequent testimony of her friends — the "glory of birth," whatever that may be. The em opted for artificial enovulation, but his wife refused to carry another woman's fertilized egg.

Their arguments on this decision became rancorous. Neighbors testified that on at least two occasions peace officers had to be called to calm the squabbling couple. Finally, apparently, the husband surrendered and agreed to artificial insemination. Since he ruled the local sperm bank, and was entitled to the discount allowed all government servers, he provided the sperm injection, and even immunosuppressive drugs which, he assured his wife, "were necessary to prevent rejection of the sperm." Ridiculous. In any event, the ef became pregnant.

In the fifth month of pregnancy, it became obvious to the ef's obstetrician that he was not dealing with a normal fetus. X-ray and internal telescopic TV examination proved the ef had been impregnated with equine sperm. The immunosuppressive drugs had served well, as they usually do. The wife underwent surgery for removal of the equine fetus, but suffered a massive hemorrhage on the operating table. She stopped. The husband was charged with premeditated murder, but local authorities surrendered him to us. Not without a lot of arm-twisting.

The journal of the object dictated in the R&R Hospice had no political significance. It implicated no one else. It was merely the confession of an em, of good intelligence, who wanted to breed but was unable. In simple language, the object recounted his emotions, his motives, what compelled him to do what he had done. The object was obviously jerked, but his account had a curious human logic all its own. It was almost convincing.

I was sitting there, still staring at the file, though I had long since finished scanning it, when Paul Bumford returned.

"You said you had some new iproniazid in your office?" I said.

"When did I say that?"

"The night I flew out to the West Coast."

"My God, Nick, don't you ever forget *anything*?"

"I wish I could."

We stopped at his office, and I popped two, dry. Then we walked over to the apartment complex. I asked Paul for the computer printout and he handed it over. A short list. Twenty-nine names with their service title and BIN's. All members of the Department of Bliss. I folded the printout and slid it into the inside breast pocket of my zipsuit.

"I just flashed the Section's contact in Oakland," Paul said. "That's what I've been doing. It was my third call. I thought it best to flash from outside the compound, from a commercial pay station."

"That's wise."

"Angela's beachhouse south of San Francisco is owned by the Samatin Foundation. It's a small outfit. About ten million new dollars' endowment."

"What do they do?"

"Give grants for the study of exotic disorders—frambesia, beri-beri, tsutsugamushi fever, icthyosis. Things of that sort."

"Where does their love come from?"

"I thought you'd never ask. Mostly from Walker & Clarke Chemicals and from Pace Pharmaceuticals and from Twenty-first Century Electronics."

"Oh-ho," I said.

"Oh-ho, indeed." He nodded. "Dear Angela is on the suck. That's why she gave you that quick stop on Project Supersense at the conference. She's going to peddle the concept."

"She wouldn't dare."

"Want to bet?"

"No." I looked at him curiously. "You're enjoying this, aren't you?"

"A profit." He laughed. "I think I have a talent for it. Devious motives, complex plotting, smart guesses, and shrewd digging.

When you get to be DEPDIRSAT, I want to be your AssDep-DirSec.''

"You have it,'' I said, the iproniazid beginning to serve. "Let's go get it started.''

Angela met us at the door and led us into the huge living room. She offered a box of cigarettes. Bold, a good brand of *Cannabis indica* with crimson filters. They were legal. I declined, but she and Paul Bumford lighted up.

"Well, Nick?'' she said. The cigarette bobbed. "What have you got?''

I narrated our retrieval of the corpus, the autopsy, and what was revealed by the tissue slides. I described the apartment. Frank Lawson Harris had probably been stopped, I told her, by inhaling a platelet-associated 5-HT nerve gas contained in a six-hour Somnorific. She was a molecular biologist; I didn't have to spell it out for her.

"There were other Somnorifics in the medicine cabinet?'' she asked.

"Yes. All six-hour. All checked out normal.''

"How did the assassin get him to take the one that stopped him?''

"Offered it to him in person, pretending it came from the medicine cabinet. Or, if the killer wasn't there, by simple manipulation. Five Somnorifics in the medicine cabinet. Four of them against the back, neatly lined up. The fifth one, the lethal one, out in front, at the edge of the shelf, by itself. If you wanted to sleep, which one would you take? But I think the killer was there and handed the fiddled Somnorific to Harris personally.''

"Why do you think that?''

"Otherwise the killer would have had to return to the apartment to retrieve the used inhaler. We didn't find it. Neither did the Peace Department. But the killer forgot the crumpled seal.''

"All right. Go on.''

I described Paul's efforts in gathering IMP samples at the murder scene. The stopped em's sample had been coded and run through the computer in a blind test. It checked out: it was the IMP of HARRIS, Frank Lawson, PS-5, Hdqtrs Stf SECSAT, AINM-B-70973-GPA-1-M76774.

I then explained our inferential postulation of a blond ef at the scene, how her IMP sample was completed as far as possible and compared with the computerized records to determine duplication of inheritable IMP factors.

"Clever," Angela said. "Whose idea was that?"

"Mine," I said. "Paul did the workup. We've bred a list of twenty-nine possibles."

"Let me see," she said, holding out her hand.

"No," I said.

She looked at me a moment, then leaned forward to stub out her ciagarette slowly.

"No?" Angela Berri repeated, looking at me suddenly.

"Not until you tell us what this is all about. Paul and I are risking R&R on this. We need to know more."

She leaned back on the sofa, turned slightly sideways, slumped. Her long green hair fell across her face.

"Oh, Nick," she said. "Don't you trust me?"

I turned to Paul Bumford.

"Are you catching this?" I asked him. "Great performance. A lesser talent would have pulled the zipper lower and wiped away an imaginary tear."

Paul grinned. Angela straightened up on the sofa, took a sip of wine, lighted another Bold.

"How many doctorates do you have now, Nick?" she asked casually.

"What difference does it make? It's like collecting medals. The best soldiers have none."

"What if I tell you nothing?" she said.

"We'll have to take what we have to DIROB and hope for the best. We have evidence that we acted under orders."

"Nick, you must learn not to give people ultimatums."

"I never do. I'm not giving you an ultimatum; I'm giving you a choice."

"A fine distinction."

"A distinction nevertheless. Well?"

"Come out on the terrace. It's not too chilly. Bring the wine."

I heard a small sound from Paul, an exhaled sigh. We followed her out onto the wide terrace. It extended around three sides of the penthouse and overlooked the brightly lit compound. But the terrace was not lighted. We sat on pillowed garden furniture in a dark corner.

"You heard the reports of Phoebe Huntzinger and Burton Klein at the conference today," she started. "Nick, you said it doesn't compute. It doesn't. I became aware of the conflict about six months ago. Phoebe's computer said the Satrat was going up,

slowly but steadily. Klein reported increased terrorism again
scientific installations. Actually, the national terrorism rate is muc
worse than he stated this afternoon. I see departmental reports; yo
don't because you have no need to know.''

She didn't either, but I made no comment.

"So either Huntzinger or Klein was giving me inoperativ
input," Angela went on. "I knew it wasn't Klein because of thos
departmental reports on assassinations, bombings, sabotage, and s
forth. Most of it is pillowed; the public isn't even aware of it. But
does exist, and it *is* serious. That left the Satrat.''

"Phoebe Huntzinger?" Paul burst out, disbelieving.

Angela shook her head.

"Not Phoebe. I'll swear she's clean. It's her computer. It's bein
fiddled. And very cleverly. Not electronically.''

"GIGO," I said. "Garbage in, garbage out.''

"Exactly." Angela nodded. "All the Satrat input comes fror
about a dozen public polling organizations, commercial an
academic. They've been infiltrated. The tapes they supply t
Phoebe's computer are inoperative.''

We were silent. I pondered the enormity of what was being done
if Angela was correct. The Satisfaction Rate was the temperature
pulse, cardiac rate, and EEG of the nation, all the life signs com
puterized into one important index. We were in trouble—if Angel
was correct.

"How did you decide Phoebe's computer was being fiddled?"
asked her. I knew, but wanted to lead into another question.

"If Phoebe's Division was clean, and I was certain it was, ther
was no other possibility.''

"All right. Assuming it was exterior sabotage, why didn't you
call in Burton Klein and dump the problem in his lap? He's Securit
Chief.''

"He had his hands full with the bombings. And I had to conside
the possibility that, somehow, he was involved.''

She spoke a little more rapidly when she was lying. Many peopl
do, thinking fluency proves probity.

"Besides," she went on, "I had no evidence. Just suspicions. S
I handled it myself. I placed undercover agents in four of the publi
opinion testing organizations we have under contract. Each agen
reported to a control I trusted who reported only to me. Results wer
nil until about three weeks ago. Then Harris, assigned to Pub-Op
told his control that he was onto something. Someone, rather. An e

who lived in GPA-1 and worked at Pub-Op as an analyst of essay-type questionnaires. But she had access to the coding and taping room, and had a Master's in computer technology. She had the capability to fiddle their Satrat tapes."

"What's her name?" I asked.

Angela took a deep breath.

"That's why I've been playing this cloak-and-dagger game. Her name is Lydia Ann Ferguson. She's the daughter of Franklin L. Ferguson, Director of the Department of Bliss. Is his name on your list of possibles?"

"Yes," I said. "Have you ever met her?"

"About a year ago, at a party in DIROB's home in Washington. She's blond, about the age and height you mentioned."

"Were she and Harris users?"

"Yes, for the past three weeks."

"It can't be only her."

"Of course not. This is nationwide. Well organized. Dedicated people, very intelligent, very dangerous."

"What do they want?"

"I have no idea. At the moment, apparently, all they want is to destabilize the country."

"Maybe," I said. "What were your plans?"

"For Harris? I was hoping he'd get some hard evidence on Lydia Ann Ferguson. Then I'd have her committed and decant her. Her father would raise hell, but he couldn't stop me."

"He'd have to resign," Paul put in.

"Would he?" Angela asked, as if the idea had only at that moment occurred to her. This ef was toxic. "I suppose he would. Well, I was certain that under interrogation Lydia Ann would implicate others and tell us what is going on. But Harris was stopped. I suppose she did it."

"I suppose so," I said.

We were all silent then, running through the permutations and combinations. Finally Paul spoke: "Nick, are we in?"

"Yes."

"Then you could do it."

"Take Harris' place? No way. They know me at Pub-Op."

"Not take his place, but do his service. With Lydia Ann Ferguson."

"Yes," Angela Berri said. "Yes. You could do it, Nick. With your body and that smile, what ef could resist you?"

"Thanks a lot," I said. "But no, thanks."

"My annual Section Party is scheduled a little more than two weeks from now," she went on, ignoring my protest. "Ferguson will fly up for it, I know. I condition two clone efs for him every year. He wouldn't miss it for the world. I'll ask him to invite his daughter. She's in the city; it's logical. You'll meet her then, at a party of a hundred people."

"Is she profitable?" Paul asked.

"Yes. Very."

Paul was silent.

"Well, Nick?" Angela said.

"I'll meet her," I said, deciding suddenly. "I guarantee nothing."

"Don't be so modest," Angela said. "I *know*."

We moved back inside. The three of us stood there awkwardly, not speaking.

"Paul," Angela said finally, "I wonder if you'd mind leaving us? I have some things to discuss with Nick. Not concerning this matter. Section activities."

"Of course," Paul said genially. I knew he was furious.

Later, we lay naked in her bed, resting.

"Nick," she said, "do you trust Paul Bumford?"

"That's the second time you've asked me that. The answer is still the same: Yes."

"He's *such* a bitch. . . ."

X-7

One of my duties as Assistant Deputy Director of Research & Development was to conduct distinguished visitors on tours of the Division's facilities. The sight-seeing groups were generally of two types: politicians and scientists.

On the morning of Angela Berri's annual party, at which I was to meet Lydia Ann Ferguson, my first scheduled service was to conduct a group of visiting Japanese pols on my portion of a Section tour.

The tour progressed as expected—and ended as expected: They asked to see our most famous project—Fred. Or rather, Fred III, since Fred I had stopped after forty-eight hours, and Fred II after seven months. Fred III was the severed head of a Labrador retriever we had succeeded in keeping alive for more than three years.

As they clustered about the oversized, sterile bell jar in which Fred existed, I explained the project briefly in their language. A liquid nutrient was constantly circulated through Fred's natural blood vessels. A computer and automatic pump controlled temperature and pressure. A continual EEG signal registered on a cathode ray oscilloscope, and all other life signs, including hormonal and enzymatic levels, were monitored.

The Japanese watched, fascinated, while I shined a bright light in Fred's eyes. The pupils contracted. I spoke his name softly into a microphone: "Fred!" He heard it from the little speaker inside the bell jar and his muzzle lifted. I pumped in a synthetic odor akin to fresh beef. His mouth opened and he began to salivate.

I finally drew the visitors away from the bell jar and accompanied them down an underground corridor to the computer room where Phoebe Huntzinger would take over. I found myself walking alongside an em I recognized as a prince of the Imperial Household.

"Tell me, please," he said in a low voice, "what do you hope to learn from this experiment?"

"We have already learned a great deal, Excellency. The construction of the equipment necessary, the formulation of the liquid nutrient, the nature of consciousness, the rate of brain cell stoppage, and so forth."

He finally asked the question invariably asked by visitors. "Is it possible that such a technique could be applied to humans?"

"It is possible." I nodded. "Anything is possible. There is no problem that cannot be solved."

We bowed to each other when we separated. I went back to A Lab, to Paul Bumford's office. He was inside, but the door was locked. He was intently scanning a long roll of computer printout. It had folded up around him, in a loose pile almost as high as the desk. He looked up, rose to unlock the door. He locked it again behind me.

"Well?" I asked.

I had persuaded Angela to requisition the raw data of the previous week from the public opinion polling organizations that provided input for the computation of Satrat. Then, without Phoebe Huntzinger's knowledge, Paul had run a comparison of the raw data with the tapes supplied Phoebe.

"Angela's right." He sighed. He sounded almost disappointed. "Nine of the twelve tapes are inoperative."

"Strange," I said.

"What's strange?"

"Angela said she began to suspect the Satrat was being fiddled six months ago. The logical thing for her to have done then would be to run the kind of test you just did. That would have confirmed her suspicions and she could have stopped the faking. But instead she let it continue while she set up her little spy network."

"I suppose she thought it was more important to discover who was doing it."

I nodded and stood up, knee-deep in computer paper.

"Make a tight roll of this," I told Paul. "I'll add it to the file in my safe. I have to go to the bank. I need some love. Then I'll be in my office until 1700. Stop by the apartment about 1900. We'll go up to Angela's together."

"What are you going to say to Lydia Ferguson when you meet her?"

" 'Happy to meet you, Lydia.' "

"Be serious. I mean after, when you talk to her. Are you going to ask if you can see her home?"

"First I'm going to ask if she likes Italian food."

"Italian food? What's that got to do with anything?"

"You've forgotten. Mary's autopsy report. Harris had consumed proveal, propep, spaghetti, and red petrowine four hours before he was stopped."

I went over to the branch of the American National Bank located within the compound. The ANB was one of Lewisohn's ideas. It had been sold to the Congress as a "standard by which civilian banking could be judged." A lot of kaka, of course. Lewisohn realized that, with more than five million adult servers, the government was missing a good bet in not establishing a bank to cater to their financial needs. The ANB offered a full range of services. How would you like to be a banker with five million depositors?

I handed over my BIN and told the server how much love I wanted. Checks were obsolete, it was paperless banking. A computer checked my account, okayed the transaction, made the debit, and I was handed my 200 new dollars. Fast and painless. I didn't like to think of what would happen if the people fiddling the Satrat computer decided to fiddle bank computers. Instant chaos.

I walked back to my office slowly, wondering if there was any possible way to obtain a printout of Angela Berri's bank account. I was still pondering her use of a beachhouse owned by a foundation financed by corporations to whom we sold licenses and, on occasion, gave invaluable free assistance. It might be interesting to compare the dates of her deposits, for instance, with the dates of contract grants to Walker & Clarke Chemicals.

But even if I could obtain her bank record, I couldn't believe that intelligent, ambitious ef would be stupid enough to deposit any more than a reasonable percentage of her rank-rate in the American National Bank. If she was on the suck, she was hiding the love somewhere else. There were many ways to do it. I could compute a few original methods myself.

I omitted lunch and devoted the afternoon to catching up on my "correspondence." It went swiftly, since practically all communication was done by minicassettes. The dictation machine could make an original tape and up to five copies simultaneously, in case of multiple mailings. I usually made only an original and one copy for filing.

I rejected, as politely as possible, practically all the invitations I received to address conventions of professional associations, contribute to scientific journals, take part in symposia, engage in televised debates, etc. I accepted a few speaking engagements, offered by prestigious commercial and academic groups. Not solely for the personal prestige but because of the esteem my Division enjoyed. It was important, politically, to hyperactivate our image.

I got back to my apartment about 1730, stripped down, went into the kitchen, and mixed a tall vodka-and-Smack. It was petrovod—but with Smack you couldn't taste the difference.

Of course, the day wasn't over yet.

I took a bath. Something I rarely do, preferring to shower. But as a PS-3, I rated a tub. It seemed silly not to take advantage of it occasionally.

I dressed with more care than usual. A two-piece suit of the light blue metallic (the jacket collarless), and a turtleneck sweater of white plastisilk, woven with black bugle beads. I wore formal hoshoes of black nylon and black plastikid. My makeup, as usual, was minimal. I did wear a silver brooch studded with lapis lazuli. It had been given to me by Mother. She said it had belonged to *her* mother. It was pleasantly obso.

I was on my second vodka-and-Smack when Paul arrived.

Unfortunately, he was not very prepossessing, physically, but he did very well with what he had. I noticed first the sequined eyeshadow and lip rouge, and a small, star-shaped beauty mark at one side of his chin. He was wearing a plum-colored velvet suit with a ruffled blouse of puce lace.

"What would you like?" I asked.

"You," he said.

"To drink."

"Vodka, please. By itself. Chilled."

We slumped at opposite ends of the couch, sipping our drinks.

"I have something good for the Tomorrow File," I said lazily, "but I don't want to discuss it now. Let's just relax."

"Nervous?" he said.

I laughed. "You're hyper."

"It *is* important."

"I suppose so. Have you ever met DIROB?"

"No. Never."

"Meet him tonight. Introduce yourself. You've got to start meeting the movers and shakers."

"What's he like?"

"Pleasant enough. Dry palm-stroke. He smiles too much. And a gloss to him. Like all upper-rank pols. Hair, suit, eyes, skin—he *shines*. Not science-conditioned. He came up through social engineering. But don't take him lightly. He's survived. He smells the wind."

Paul nodded. "I'll be ever so worshipful. By the way, Mary Bergstrom hit the national lottery for a thousand."

"Good for Mary," I said. "Finished? Let's go."

Last year her apartment had been transformed into a *fin de siècle* Parisian bordello, all red velvet, black lace, and frolicking plaster cupids. This year her decorator had opted for a jungle village, with natural plants in tubs.

Angela Teresa Berri moved through the undergrowth smiling, white teeth gleaming against a skin dyed a tawny brown. She wore a sleeveless gown that appeared to be aluminum foil with a bonded surface of stretch plastic. It came high on her thorax, cleaved to her body, ended in a hemline of points halfway down her hard thighs.

If anyone doubted she wore nothing beneath, it was only necessary to view her from the back. She was almost completely exposed, low enough to display the Y-division of her buttocks. She wore no shoes, but leather thongs ringed her toes and wound tightly

76

to her knees. She had a golden serpent thrice encircling her left bicep. The snake's eyes were rubies.

Only she could have worn such a costume and made it believable. She was more than an ef, more than human. She was a primitive power. A force. It radiated from her. It went beyond sexuality.

Everyone in the Section with a rank of PS-4 and higher had been invited and was there. In addition, three other Deputy Directors were present, and a party of five had flown up from Washington, D.C.: DIROB Ferguson and his staff. All five were ems; none was accompanied by his wife. The Chief Director, it was rumored, had been invited but had sent his regrets. Something about another famine in Bangladesh.

No attempt was made at formal introductions. I slipped sideways through the crowd, carrying my sweetish petrorum punch in a plastic coconut shell, greeting familiar friends and acquaintants, sliding palms with two of Ferguson's assistants I had not met before. Both had the gloss I had mentioned to Paul: the polish that increases in brilliance as you move up in Public Service, like a waxed surface drying to a hard shine.

Finally I came face to face with the Great Man himself, Franklin L. Ferguson, Director of Bliss.

"Good evening, sir," I said. "Nice to see you again."

We stroked palms automatically while his glazed eyes sought to focus.

"Flair!" he finally burst out, with a politician's memory for names. "Nicholas Flair!"

"Right, sir."

He smiled proudly. "Never forget a name. Let's see—you're a scientist, huh?"

"Yes, sir."

"I met Einstein once. When I was a youngster."

"Did you, sir?"

"Sure did. As nice a guy as you'd want to meet."

We went through this routine every time we met. It no longer annoyed me.

"See m'daughter?" he said.

"No, sir."

"Around here somewhere," he said vaguely.

A chubby ef from the Division of Law & Enforcement was thrust tightly up against him by the press of the throng. She giggled.

"Well there!" he said, and slid an arm about her waist. I left them to their rapture.

It was better out on the terrace. Too chilly for most of the guests. The air quality for the day had been deemed "Unsatisfactory," but at least it smelled all right. You could see stars. In an hour, if I waited, I'd see Skylab No. 14 flash high overhead, southwest to northeast. There were efs and ems up there, serving, snoring in a Somnorific sleep, or watching *Circus au Natural* on TV. I wondered how my father's contortionist was doing.

I was staring down in the brightly lit compound, watching a two-em security patrol saunter along the chainlink fence, flechette guns slung over their shoulders, when I became aware of someone standing at my side. Blond ef. Approximately twenty. About 165 cm. I supposed the object was Lydia Ann Ferguson, and Angela had suggested she slip out onto the terrace. "Say hello to that very handsome em over there by himself."

She, too, was staring down at the chainlink barrier around the compound.

"Outside, the animals," she said.

I turned to her. "What an odd thing to say."

"The fence is to keep the animals out, isn't it?"

"No. I serve here. The fence is to keep the animals in."

She laughed at that.

"Nicholas Bennington Flair," I said.

"Lydia Ann Ferguson," she said.

We stroked palms.

"Your father is Director of Bliss, isn't he?"

"Yes," she said. "He is."

"He rules me," I said. "If you get a chance to talk to him—a deep, close, personal daughter-to-father communication—would you mind mentioning that the new PS-3 zipsuit doesn't have any inside breast pocket, and I, for one, object?"

She laughed again. She laughed very easily.

My first response was negative. I was not usually attracted to very feminine efs with a soft serenity and an air of self-assurance. I could not endure sympathy and suffocating charm. I always thought they must smell of lavender and suffer from primary dyspareunia.

"Hungry?" I asked. "I can get a big dish of food and bring it out here. Save you from fighting the animals."

"I'd like that."

"I think it's pseudo-native slop," I said. "Shredded coconut, rice balls, papaya, poi, roast pork, raw fish—things like that."

"Sounds good."

"It does? What kind of food do you really like?"

"I like all kinds. I enjoy eating."

Good-bye, Sherlock Holmes.

"Grab a table for us," I said. "I'll be right back."

I was returning through the mob with a heaped platter, moving cautiously to avoid sliding a chunk of pickled octopus down an ef's bodice, when Angela Berri caught my eye. She raised her brows in question. I nodded.

Lydia and I chatted casually while we sampled Angela's "native delicacies." Some had a surprisingly pungent flavor, to epithelial end organs atrophied by a constant diet of petroleum-based synthetics. The raw fish was especially good.

I asked Lydia where she served. She said she analyzed and coded essay-type questionnaires for Pub-Op, Inc. She asked me what my duties were. I was as brief as possible.

"Sounds fascinating," she said.

"Not really. Just routine. Most of the Division's responsibilities concern testing and approving or rejecting new commercial products: drugs, prosthetic devices, foods, toys, paints—things of that sort."

"But don't you do original research and development?"

"Oh, yes. A limited amount."

"You have Fred, don't you?"

"Yes, we have Fred."

"What are you interested in mostly, Nick? I mean you, personally?"

"Me? Oh . . . I don't know. I guess my main interest is in procreation research and genetic engineering."

She nodded, without speaking, and we resumed our nibbling. We talked of several inconsequential things, a pleasant enough conversation but hardly significant. She was patting her lips with a plastinap when, quite unexpectedly, she asked; "How is Hyman Lewisohn?"

Lewisohn's illness was not a secret. It had been announced on all the TV news programs and published in fascimile newspapers. Anyone who viewed or scanned knew he was suffering from leukemia and was under treatment at a government hospital. What *was* unusual was that she should ask me about his condition, as if my responsibility was common knowledge. It was not. Perhaps Daddy had been talking too much.

"His condition has stabilized," I said.

She said she thought she'd thank Angela and leave; she wanted to get home early. I told her that her chances of getting a cab after midnight were minimal and, if she'd allow me, I'd call the motor pool and see if I could requisition a car. If I could, I'd be happy to drive her. She hesitated a moment.

"All right," she said finally. "Thank you."

I went inside and made the call on the compound intercom in Angela's bedroom. I noted with some amusement that all her closets and dresser drawers were fitted with locks. A secret ef. I finally got through to the schedule server. He promised me a sedan in half an hour.

I went back into the noisy living room. I found Lydia Ann Ferguson standing just inside the terrace door, looking with some distaste at the clamorous bacchanal swirling about her. I told her it would be a thirty-minute wait. It obviously distressed her.

"We could wait in my place," I offered. "I live one floor down. It's quiet there."

She had no fear. Daddy's rank would protect her.

"Oh, yes," she said. "Thank you. Let's go."

In my apartment, she wandered about examining my library of TV cassettes. I handed her a drink and we sat at opposite ends of the couch, exactly where Paul and I had sat a few hours previously.

"Ballet and Greta Garbo." She smiled. "You're quite a contradiction."

"I am? I don't understand."

"I thought all that interested you was science."

"No. Other things interest me. Occasionally."

"You're a Renaissance man," she said.

"Now you're jerking me." I smiled.

"No, really. I know your reputation."

I could have made a smart answer to that, but let it pass.

After a moment she said, "Angela Berri is a beautiful ef. Don't you think so?"

"Oh, yes. Very beautiful. She rules me, you know."

"I wish you wouldn't say that."

"Would it be better if I said she was my boss? The Office of

Linguistic Truth tells us that words like boss, work, job, and labor have a pejorative meaning.''

"Like 'love'?'

"Oh, that's not pejorative. Just meaningless in the obso sense. 'Profit' is much better.''

"And 'use'?''

"That's economical,'' I said solemnly. "Instead of a four-letter word, we now have a three-letter word.''

She didn't change expression. I had the feeling I was being given a test and wondered if I was passing or failing.

She looked at her digiwatch.

"Another fifteen minutes,'' I said. "Then we'll leave.''

I'd be as relieved as she. I wasn't enjoying this.

"That's a profitable brooch you're wearing.''

"Thank you.'' I unpinned it and handed it to her. "Hammered silver and lapis lazuli. It belonged—''

"Damn!'' she said.

"What's wrong?''

"Stuck myself on the pin.'' She sucked her thumb.

"Here,'' I said, rising, "let me take a look.''

Good-bye, Sherlock Holmes. Hello, Lady Luck.

I squeezed her thumb. A small drop of dark red blood rose to the surface. I dabbed it away with my handkerchief.

"I'm a medical doctor, among other things,'' I said. "Shall I treat you?''

She looked at me, puzzled.

I kissed the ball of her thumb.

"All better?'' I asked.

She laughed. "You're a very good doctor. Profitable bedside manner. I'll recommend you to all my friends.''

"Thank you. I need the practice.''

It went over her head.

"Are you really a medical doctor?'' she asked.

"Of sorts. I am many things, of sorts.''

She smiled mechanically.

"Let me get a fresh handkerchief,'' I said. "Then we'll leave.''

In my bedroom, I folded the soiled handkerchief carefully and placed it in the top dresser drawer. Paul Bumford had analyzed perspiration on a towel in Frank Lawson Harris' nest and found the type of IgA associated with blood type O-Rh negative. Not Harris' type. We'd see, we'd see. . . .

She lived up on West End Avenue, near Ninetieth Street. It took
us almost a half-hour to drive, and I don't believe we exchanged a
dozen words. I was certain I had failed.

We pulled up before an obso town house that must have been a
hundred years old, converted into apartments. It had remarkable
carved stone trim in a classical Greek pattern. I got out of the car and
went around to her side. We stood a moment on the sidewalk. I
looked up at the building. It needed cleaning, badly, but the lines
and proportions were there.

"It was designed by Stanford White," she said. "Do you know
who he was?"

"Yes. American architect. Stopped by Harry K. Thaw at the
original Madison Square Garden in 1906."

She shook her head. "Do you know *everything*?"

"Everything." I nodded. Something flickered across her face so
quickly I couldn't catch it.

We walked up the stone steps together. I waited while she found
her key and unlocked the door. She stood a brief moment, her back
to me, then turned suddenly.

"Come in," she said.

It was as fast and unexpected as that.

X-8

Angela Berri, Paul Bumford, and I began meeting one or two
times a week in my apartment, at about 1730. Angela welcomed
this arrangement; she had an almost paranoiac fear that her apartment was being shared.

The first few meetings were devoted to planning and operations.
We all contributed opinions and recommendations. Angela listened
intently to Paul and me, but the final decision was hers. There was
never any doubt about that.

The most immediate problem, we all agreed, was the rigged
Satisfaction Rate.

In any bureaucracy, one soon learns that an error is *never* admitted. It is corrected, as discreetly as possible. Only when it is of
enormous magnitude, impossible to gloss over without a conspiracy
of impracticable size, is one's superior advised. The ruler, then,

82

being ultimately responsible, may be capable of arranging the gloss.

So our initial discussion was of ways and means to accuratize the Satrat, make it absolutely operative. Paul's analysis of the fiddled tapes had shown it was presently too high by at least 10 percentile points, perhaps as much as 15. Suddenly to reduce the Satrat by that amount in one week would be disastrous. There would be an incredulous outcry, perhaps a formal investigation. Down go we all.

After a lengthy discussion of our options, we decided on this plan: Angela would send a routine memo to Phoebe Huntzinger, suggesting that, in the interest of accuracy, it would be wise of Phoebe to work from the polling organization's raw data, rather than from the coded computer tapes they supplied. The first organization selected for the new system would be one of the three whose tapes, Paul's analysis had determined, were *not* fiddled. The second and third companies asked to supply raw data would also be, apparently, uncompromised organizations. The purpose of this was to avoid alerting those who were fiddling the inoperative tapes to the fact that their activities were suspect.

It was decided that the restoration of the Satrat's accuracy should take place over a period of six months. The loss of 10 to 15 percentile points in such a period would alarm government rulers certainly, but not, we hoped, to such an extent as to cause them to question the Satrat's exactitude.

I go into such detail in this matter to illustrate the complexity of our discussions and the depth of our concern.

The Satrat was Angela Berri's responsibility. Paul Bumford's assignment was to analyze in much greater detail the incidence, types, and locations of terrorist activities against government, commercial, and academic scientific research facilities. Angela said it would be no problem for her to requisition the raw data from Burton Klein's Division of Security & Intelligence. But it was an enormous service Paul would have to provide, in addition to his regular duties. He asked if he might enlist the aid of Mary Bergstrom, without telling Mary the reason for their activity.

"What is your reaction to the Bergstrom ef, Nick?" Angela asked.

"She has a Grade B genetic rating, but I suspect the Examiner had a subjective reaction. She is very closed-off. I can't get a control on her. I have no doubts at all about her intelligence. Grade

A plus, I'd judge. Paul tells me she is discreet, and he can control her. Her service on Harris' autopsy was profitable.''

"I vouch for her," Paul said. "Absolutely."

Angela thought a moment.

"All right," she said finally. "But tell her as little as possible."

At the fourth meeting we discussed my service. I had already informed them that Lydia Ann Ferguson and I had become users.

"Her blood type checked out," I said. "Two nights ago I learned she is not on the pill or any other fertility control. I believe that verifies her presence in Harris' apartment beyond a reasonable doubt."

"And she stopped him," Angela said.

"Probably." I nodded. "We know she had the capability and opportunity of fiddling the Pub-Op tapes. Harris' reports to his control show that he knew it, too. Then he blew his cover, by accident or deliberately. Perhaps she meant more to him than just a user, and he told her who he was and tried to get her out, tried to convince her to tell who her rulers were and save herself. So she stopped him. Either on her own or on orders.''

"It computes." Paul nodded.

"Yes. Now there are three possible roles I can play to uncover her degree of involvement in this intrigue, plot, conspiracy—whatever you want to call it. And to identify who is ruling her. One: I can play the clown, a microweight snagged on alcohol, cannabis, sex, anything. She or her rulers might find me useful. Two: I can pretend a heavy profit. For her. Beneath that pleasant, charming self-assured manner is a strong ego drive, an operative passion. I told you what a furious, violent user she is. She might respond to a similarly undisciplined passion in me. Third: I can act the Public Service malcontent, dissatisfied with the orders he is given, disgusted with official government policy. Reactions?''

I had expected Angela to opt for the third possibility. She approved of the second. But the real surprise was Paul. I had expected him to select the first role. He argued for the third, vehemently. My own choice was the third. After almost an hour of sometimes rancorous debate, we convinced Angela; she agreed I was to play the rebel looking for a cause.

"Good," I said. "I'll go ahead with it. There is something else. Lydia's apartment should be shared. Angela, I know you don't want to bring Klein in on this—at this point in time—but is there anyone else in DIVSEC you can trust?''

"No," she said decisively. "I don't want them alerted. But I know an em who can handle it. A private investigator. He's served me before."

I looked at her with wonder, trying to guess how many strings dangled from those long cool fingers, how many marionettes jerked when she gestured.

"Leon Mansfield," she said, looking directly at me. "Peace of Mind, Incorporated. At 983 West Forty-second Street. Got that?"

"Yes."

"Don't flash him, go see him. Mention my name, but tell him nothing except that you want Lydia's apartment shared. He'll ask no questions. Just reward him."

"How much?"

"Start with a hundred. Cover it in petty love."

I nodded. We separated then. I think we all had the sense of events set in motion, a quickening tempo.

Late that night, wearing a robe, I lay on the couch to watch a televised debate that involved one of Hyman R. Lewisohn's innovative ideas. He was much on my mind. After stabilizing, his blast count had fallen dramatically. We went to a manipulated methotrexate. His survival was important, of course. Even more important was that his therapy did not cloud the functioning of that marvelously clear, seminal brain.

Late in 1982, Lewisohn had proposed the United States of America open its federation of sovereign states to other nations. Upon application and approval, countries beyond our mainland, beyond the seas—just as Alaska and Hawaii—would be accepted for statehood with all the rights and privileges inherent thereto.

A foreign nation becoming one of our states could retain its native language, if it wished, but English would also be taught in the schools. Each nation joining, like a mainland state, would be entitled to two Senators, and Representatives commensurate with its population. The United States of America would become simply the United States. The abbreviation would be changed from U.S. to US, for semantic reasons.

The suggestion for a worldwide US was proposed in a special message delivered to the Congress on January 15, 1983, by the then President, Irving Kupferman. Enabling legislation was passed by Congress on October 21, 1983 (by a 2-vote margin in the Senate, incidentally).

The Dominican Republic was the first nation to make application, and won immediate approval. At once, teams of social engineers swarmed in. Enormous amounts of love were spent. It was vital that the first foreign state should become a showcase of the Lewisohn Plan. So it did. The birthrate dropped, public health improved, average annual income rose, and roads, factories, new towns, and an American life-style appeared almost overnight.

Realizing what was happening, Puerto Rico applied almost immediately for statehood. They were soon followed by Mali, Chad, Ecuador, Taiwan, Colombia, Upper Volta, and others. In 1998, the United States, US, consisted of ninety-seven states and was growing at an average rate of three new states per year.

The most recent development was a tentative inquiry from Great Britain. There was a great deal of domestic British opposition, of course. Crowds gathered before Buckingham Palace and sang an obso song, ''Rule Britannia!'' But the great majority of Britons, and their rulers, were weary of their endless economic crises. Pan-Europe (formerly the European Economic Community) had been referred to by President Kupferman as ''ten Switzerlands,'' and he was right. The main problem was whether Great Britain should be admitted as one state, which we preferred, or as three states—England, Scotland, Wales—as they preferred. That was the subject of the TV debate I was viewing.

My doorbell rang. Paul's distinctive ring: three shorts, one long. He wasn't aware he was ringing Beethoven, and I never told him. I switched off the TV and went to the door.

''Interrupting you?'' he said.

''No, no. Come in. Drink?''

''No, thanks. Mind if I have a Bold?''

''Of course not. May I have one?''

''I thought you were off.''

''One won't hurt me.''

I had sworn off cannabis cigarettes almost a year ago. After we lighted up, and I took the first deep draught, I wondered why.

''What were you doing, Nick? When I knocked?''

''Watching a debate on TV. Should Great Britain come in as one state or three?''

''Which do you prefer?''

''I couldn't care less—as long as we get them.''

''Why so important?''

''Seventy million underconsumers there. Through necessity, not choice. But I want them for different reasons. England has some of the most originative neurobiologists in the world. Scotland's surgeons and biomedical doctors are the best.''

"And Wales?" Paul asked.

"Well . . . we could use some good poets, too."

He laughed.

"Nick, can we talk business for a minute?"

"Sure. As long as you like."

"Remember the night of Angela's party? You and I had a drink down here before we went up, and you said you had something for the Tomorrow File. What was it?"

I looked at him. "Paul, your memory is improving."

He blushed with delight.

"You really think so?"

"No doubt about it. How's the theta coming?"

"Progressing."

He was beginning to imitate my speech patterns. Short phrases. Laconic. I was amused—and touched.

"Stick with it," I advised him. "Big advantage. Yes, I have something for the Tomorrow File. Inspired by a letter I received that afternoon from an obso. An old, old obso. He was a Nobel Prize winner a long time ago. An environmentalist. It had been a good brain then. Senile now. Atheromata, I suppose. We've made some great advances there, but too late to help him."

"You're suggesting a new antiatherosclerosis drug?"

"No. A drug to *reverse* the effects of atheromata, to flush out those clogged arteries, particularly in the brain."

"Brain cells can't regenerate."

"Thank you, doctor," I said with heavy sarcasm. "God damn it, Paul, don't lecture *me* on physiology. It seems to me that in a case like this—an old, old obso with what was originally a fine brain—a drug that could reverse atherosclerosis would be invaluable."

"You mean, keep objects alive for one hundred twenty-five, one hundred fifty, or two hundred years?"

"Well . . . if that was necessary. But not for everyone, of course. Can you imagine the social and economic chaos that would result if we shoved the average lifespan up by fifty years? No, it would only be for selected individuals. Or perhaps just their brains."

"What's the point?" he asked. "Why not a *new* brain?"

"We could start with an infant's brain," I acknowledged. "One with a Grade A genetic rating potentiality. But even that would not guarantee its creativity. A brain that over a period of years had demonstrated inventive genius—like that old obso's brain I mentioned—that would be best. But in addition to regenerating it in a biomedical sense, we would also have to erase its memory, totally. Get rid of old habits, conditioning, prejudices, conceived opinions, and so forth.''

"Didn't you suggest that for the Tomorrow File once before?''

"No, I suggested a selective memory block, less gross than Tememblo. What I am now suggesting is *total* memory erasure. Perhaps a manipulated isomer of eight-azoguanine might do it. Something like that. Well . . . it's for the future. Add it to the File.''

Paul nodded. "Now I've got one. Remember that ef on the Gerontology Team? The one who suggested a program of Government-Assisted Suicide?''

"Of course I remember. Maya Leighton. Only I changed her suggestion to Government-Assisted Peace. I told you she might be your second secretary. Did you speak to her?''

"Yes. We've had two lunches.''

"And?''

"Tall. Imposing. Wide shoulders and hips. Narrow waist. Red-haired. Wears her zipper down. A good brain, Nick. Really good.''

"Rating?''

"Well . . . Grade B, but some very original thinking. She's been working on another idea. She's running a computer study on what it costs the government to maintain nonproductive objects of any age who have a Grade F-Minus genetic rating.''

Genetic ratings were assigned by a government GE (Genetic Examiner) to every infant at the age of two, and updated every five years after that. The Grade F-Minus was assigned to all those in the retarded, feebleminded, moronic, imbecilic, and idiotic classifications, the single rating used for all of them since differentiating criteria did not exist.

"She says her preliminary findings indicate a program of euthanasia,'' Paul said.

"And what did you say?''

"I told her that ideas and programs that were logically and scientifically sound were not necessarily politically, socially, or economically feasible.''

I laughed. "You're learning. She seems to be terminally oriented, if her first two suggestions are any indication of the way she thinks.''

"Not necessarily," Paul said. "You marked the memo about her first idea as 'Original thinking.' I believe that inspired her to try something along similar lines. Besides, is her suggestion any more impractical than the required abortion of embryos with untreatable genetic defects?"

"You may be right. Well, if you want her for a second secretary, go ahead. Angela won't object after all we've been doing for her."

He stared at me a moment.

"What's bothering you, Nick?" he asked.

"Remember your telling me Angela's beachhouse was owned by the Samatin Foundation, and the corporations that financed it?"

"Of course I remember. We decided she's on the suck."

"Yes. Well, we suspected it. That's what's been bothering me. This afternoon I went over to Data & Statistics and asked to scan the films on sales of licenses to Walker & Clarke Chemicals, Pace Pharmaceuticals, and Twenty-first Century Electronics. You know the mechanics of a license sale?"

"A product or process we developed is put up for license and advertised. Sealed bids are submitted."

"Right. To Angela. At the cutoff time and date, the bids are opened. High bidder wins exclusive license. During the past four or five years, those three companies have been winning their licenses with late bids, some of them submitted just hours before closing. And they've been winning with bids just a few hundred thousand and, in some cases, just a few thousand new dollars higher than the second-highest bid."

He looked at me, his eyes growing larger as he realized the significance of what I was telling him.

"Nick," he said, not believing, "has she been scanning previously submitted bids and tipping them off?"

"Something like that. I don't know her technique. Perhaps it's as primitive as steaming open the envelopes and resealing them. Maybe it's a fluoroscopic or ultrasonic scanning process. However she's doing it, I'm convinced it's being done."

"But I thought all the big drug companies work together?"

"They do—on cutting up world markets for aspirin, birth-control pills, tranquilizers, antibiotics, sulfas, steroids, and things like that. But on new, untried products and processes, it's every em for himself."

"Then Angela *is* on the suck?"

"I think so."

"But *why?*"

"A very ambitious ef. With expensive tastes. And the talent for applying a knee to a groin that politics demands. Plus a complete lack of conscience. There may be psycopathology there."

"My God."

"That's not all. Now compute this: When I returned the filmed record to the file clerk at Data & Statistics she remarked—quite casually—that those were certainly popular records, that Security Chief Burton Klein had been in just a week ago scanning the same films."

Paul's eyes grew even wider. "Nick," he said, "what the *hell* is going on?"

"Let's go to bed," I said.

I sat up, my back against the headboard, and let him do what profited him most.

Then we snuggled down beneath the thermasheet and held each other. He was soft and warm, his pheromones sweetish.

"Pleasure?" he said.

"Oh, yes! And for you?"

"Pleasure."

"The last time I was home, my father talked about a pill that would give pleasure. I didn't tell him about your suggestion in the Tomorrow File for the Ultimate Pleasure pill."

"The UP pill."

"Right. But I explained to him how difficult it would be to synthesize, since pleasure is so subjective. What does pleasure mean to you?"

"Physical orgasm, for starters."

"And?"

"I'm not sure, Nick. A kind of surrender?"

I propped myself on one elbow and looked down at him.

"Surrender? That's interesting."

"Is it?"

"Yes. I think the first problem is to differentiate between pleasure and happiness. How about this: Pleasure is momentary; happiness, or content, is lasting. Well . . . at least longer than pleasure. Agree?"

"Agree."

"Then, for you, the orgasm is momentary pleasure, but the surrender is happiness?"

He was silent.

"Surrender implies mastery," I said. "Therefore you find happiness in submitting?"

Still he was silent.

"Surrender, or submission, means the recognition of a power greater than your own. Since I am obviously not coercing you by physical force or threat, you submit voluntarily, to obtain happiness. That's why you accept me as your master."

"Oh?" Paul said. "Is that what you think?"

I spent a few hours the next morning scanning and initialing monthly reports from Field Offices of the Division of Research & Development. These FO's, now scattered all over the country and soon to be established beyond the mainland US, had their origins as the National Institutes of Health which, as recently as 1980, were centered in Bethesda, Maryland. At one time, the eleven Institutes, plus several other divisions and units, constituted the world's finest biomedical research organization. They had perished.

They had simply been phased out of existence, budgets strangulated, because of their directors' intransigence in dealing with Washington. The scientists refused to face political realities.

Their epitaph was delivered in 1979 during a Senate committee hearing on a proposed NIH budget. The committee listened to the stubborn demands of the scientists. Then Senator R. Vachel Krumbaugh (R-Oklahoma) gave his reaction to the press.

"A bunch of goddamn Joan of Arcs," he snorted. "We can't burn 'em, but we can sure as hell fire 'em."

Sometimes idealism can be a terminal virtue.

At 1030 I left the office, left the compound, and rode up to Forty-second Street on the Seventh Avenue IRT. I hadn't been in the subway for years. The air-conditioned cars were on rubber-tired wheels; the ride was quiet, fast, endurable. But the graffiti hadn't improved.

It wasn't difficult to find 983 West Forty-second Street; it would have been difficult to miss it. The six-story obso studio building stood alone on one side of a block-square area that had been leveled, then excavated for the foundation of an enormous office-apartment-theater complex. Why 983 still stood, I did not know; perhaps the owner was holding out for more love, or fighting eminent domain through the courts.

In any event, the exterior sidewalls of 983 were ancient brick, showing scars and ruptures where supporting buildings had been ripped away. In front, some of the wide windows had been covered

91

with tin. The stone stoop was littered with garbage, I looked up at what had once been a graceful façade, curlicued and embellished with carvings. On the third floor, on a dusty glass window, was painted a gigantic gilt eye and the legend: LEON MANSFIELD—PEACE OF MIND.

I picked my way up the steps, into the dark interior. It smelled of urine, boiled cabbage, damp wood. The office directory, hanging crazily from a single nail, showed a violin repair shop; a wedding photographer; a wigmaker; an association to liberate Latvia; a personality development school; a union of kosher butchers; and Leon Mansfield, Peace of Mind, Inc. I climbed the creaking stairs and followed a scuttling cockroach to Mansfield's door.

I listened a moment, my ear close to the wood. I heard feet shuffling rapidly, harsh breathing, a muffled cry. I knocked firmly.

The man who flung open the door had eyes the color and consistency of phlegm, and a nose that went on and on. He held a rusty fencing mask under one arm; a bent foil dangled from his fingers. The cuffs of his soiled trousers were snugged with bicycle clips. He stared at me.

"Mr. Mansfield?"

"Yes."

"My name is Nicholas Flair."

"Yes?"

"I'd like to speak to you."

"On a professional matter?"

I nodded.

"Come in, come in."

He closed and locked the door behind me. He came close to me. I amy hypersensitive to personal odors. His was musty. It wasn't the building; it was him.

"Nicholas," he said. "From the Greek. Meaning 'victorious army.'"

I must have shown my surprise.

"Names are a hobby with me," he explained. "My own name, for instance. Leon means lion. I'm like a lion. Know what a good name for a Chinese gangster would be? Tony Kimona. Sit down."

He removed two wooden dumbbells from a cracked leather chair, dusted the seat with a blood-stained handkerchief. I sat down and looked around.

A fencing foil fixed to the wall, pointing out into the room. A

92

kitchenette in a small alcove with a sinkful of dishes rimmed with the golden halos of synthetic egg mix. A chess game laid out on a table. Obso books and magazines and newspapers everywhere. A brittle theatrical poster for a performance of *Ah, Wilderness!* tacked to the wall. A clipped ad from a defunct magazine pinned to the lampshade: a plump beauty pouting a crimson sheath, her eyes dark with unrequited love. Beneath, the legend: "My constipation worries are over."

And dust clinging to everything like a wet sheet.

He dropped his fencing mask and foil onto the floor, removed the bicycle clips from his ankles. He folded into a swivel chair behind the desk, began biting furiously at the hard skin around his thumbnail. His eyes never left mine. I guessed him to be forty to forty-five, in that range.

"Doesn't look much like a detective's office, does it?" he said, speaking rapidly, spitting out bits of skin.

"I've never been in a detective's office before," I said. "I can't judge."

"I'm not a detective," he said, almost angrily. "I'm a social investigator."

I was almost ready to rise and walk out.

"Who sent you to me?" he demanded.

"Angela Berri," I said.

I was staring into his eyes. When I spoke Angela's name, the pupils of his eyes contracted. I was certain he had done it consciously. Whether he was a student of biofeedback or whether it was a natural gift, I did not know. But it changed his appearance. Before, his face had been thin, bony, hard: whacked from a block of walnut by a hasty sculptor. But in those slanted planes, deep and stubbled hollows, crisscrossed ridges and lines, had been a kind of obso charm. Then his pupils contracted, and the stricken face became. . . .

"Angela Berri," he said in a toneless voice.

He unfolded abruptly, strode over to the chessboard, moved a pawn.

"You play chess?" he asked, studying the board. "I have a theory about it. Sex is sublimation for chess. Everyone wants to be a great chess player, but most lack the ability, the drive, the passion. So they substitute for it by using. Defend, attack, checkmate. Sex imitates chess."

"You're joking?" I asked.

93

"Joking?" he cried. "Mr. Nicholas Flair, I never joke. Life is a tragic thing. Know what a good name for an English farmer would be? Lester Square. What did Angela Berri tell you about me?"

"Nothing. Only that you might be able to help me."

"What's your problem."

"My user."

"Ef or em?"

"Ef."

"Cheating?"

"I think so."

"Evidence?"

"You mean like letters?" I asked him. "Or suspicious behavior? No, nothing like that. Just a feeling I have."

"A feeling." He nodded. "And you want me to find out if this feeling is right or wrong?"

"Yes," I said. "I want to know the truth."

"Oh-ho," he said. "The truth. Oh-ho. Believe me, Mr. Nicholas Flair, you wouldn't like it—the truth. But find out about your user I can. You want her followed?"

"No." I said. "I want her apartment shared."

He went back behind the desk again, sat down heavily in the wooden swivel chair.

"Would you wish for a drink?" he asked formally. "I have something special."

"All right. Thank you."

He took two mismatched empty petrojelly jars from a desk drawer, blew into them. Something flew out. Then he removed a bottle from a bottom drawer, placed it gently on the desk. I leaned forward to examine the faded label. Slivovitz. Obviously quite old. He poured us each a small drink, recorked the bottle carefully. We raised glasses to each other, then sipped. He looked at me.

"Well!" he said.

"I must tell you, Mr. Mansfield, it tastes exactly like petronac." A small sound came out of him. It may have been a laugh.

"Well . . . it *is* petronac." He sighed. "But the *bottle*—that's something special. No?"

I nodded and finished my drink.

"Angela Berri" he said dreamily. "How is the dear lady?"

"Fine."

"This ef of yours—you want her apartment shared?"

"Yes."

"She live alone?"

"Yes."

"What kind of a building?"

"Old townhouse on West End Avenue, near Ninetieth Street. Nine other apartments. I think all or most of the tenants serve during the day."

"And this user of yours—she serves during the day?"

"Yes, from 0900 to 1500."

"You have keys?"

"No."

He shook his head. "Doesn't matter. When do you want me to start?"

"As soon as possible."

"Give me the address, name, and apartment number. I'll go up today. How will I contact you?"

"I'll flash you."

"No, no," he said quickly. "I have no flasher. I'll call you from outside, from a phone, not a flasher."

I thought a moment. I wasn't pleased with the idea.

"I'll give you my apartment number," I said finally. "Call me there if you have to. Identify yourself as 'Chess Player.' Just tell me where I can meet you. Don't say anything more. Don't repeat anything. I have a good memory."

He nodded, as if such clandestine arrangements were the most natural thing in the world. As perhaps they were.

I opened my purse. I gave him the slip of paper I had prepared with Lydia Ann Ferguson's name, address, and apartment number. I added my flasher number. I was still holding my wallet. I looked at him, about to speak. . . .

"Angela Berri told you a hundred new dollars?" he said.

"Yes."

He nodded. "The dear lady. All right—a hundred. To start."

I handed over the love, stood up, started for the door.

"Mr. Nicholas Flair," he said, voice dead.

I turned. He was staring at me.

"I don't carry a gun," he said. "Never touch them."

I looked at him in astonishment.

"Why should I be interested in that?"

"Just thought you should know."

I was halfway out the door when he stopped me again.

"Know what a good name for a brawny Scotsman would be?" he said. "Jock Strap."

I went back to my office and popped an Elavil. I don't know why that meeting with Leon Mansfield had depressed me so much. The physical surroundings, of course: decay, destruction, must. But also the em himself, with his quick alterations of antic wit and . . .

I called the commissary for a bottle of Smack and a package of probisks. That would hold me until my dinner with Lydia Ann Ferguson. I went back to scanning the monthly Field Office reports.

I had some excellent objects serving me. Young, talented, innovative. I was proud of them and, as far as possible, kept my hands off and let them run. Many of them could have made much more love on the outside. But they wouldn't have the freedom. What corporation, for instance, would finance a team of ten genetic biologists to investigate color blindness? Everyone knew it was caused by a defective gene in the X chromosome. Where was the love in that?

But the corporations would be intensely interested if they knew the results of that team's work: Manipulation of the defective gene that could quite possibly lead to manipulation of a similarly defective gene that caused baldness. Genetic engineering sometimes led to chemotherapy for symptoms of the genetic variance. "Bald? Take Shaggy!" We could license *that* drug for zillions.

I went back to my apartment and took a one-hour Somnorific. I arose at 1830, showered, dressed carefully. I decided to wear a new wig I had purchased recently, a "King Arthur," down to my shoulders, silver-blond. As I tootied up, I rehearsed how best to play my role as a Public Servant malcontent, looking for a cause to which I might totally dedicate my energy, talent, and sacred honor.

I had my hand on the doorknob when the flasher chimed. I went over and flicked the switch, but no image came on. Flashers could receive voice calls from conventional phones.

"Hello?" I said.

"Hello?" a voice said. "Who's this?"

"Whom are you calling?"

"This is Chess Player."

"Oh. This is Nicholas Flair."

"There's a Mess Hall on Seventh Avenue between Eighteenth and Nineteenth. In half an hour."

He clicked off. I looked at my digiwatch. If the meeting didn't take too long, I could still be on time. And even if I was a few minutes late. . . . Lydia was a patient, sweet-tempered ef.

The chain of popular Mess Hall restaurants had been started in 1989 as one answer to the rising prices of restaurant meals. An ingenious entrepreneur—an ex-nightclub publicist—had bought up a supply of Army surplus compartmented steel trays. They were the key to the low-cost fast-service Mess Hall operation. Meals were served cafeteria style, only one selection a day; no menu, no substitutions, no seconds. The day's choice was posted in the window: Monday, beef stew; Tuesday, hamburger; Wednesday, fried chicken; and so forth. If you didn't like the main course offered that day, you didn't eat there; nothing else was available.

I saw Leon Mansfield from the sidewalk. He was seated at a table near the plate glass window. His steel tray was empty. He had pushed it away and was playing a chess game on a small pocket set. I went inside. I took the chair opposite him. He didn't look up.

"Nice perfume," he said.

"Thank you. Please make this fast."

"I put in two," he said. "One in the flasher in her living room, one behind the dresser in her bedroom. Transceivers. I'll pick up in a white van marked 'Kleen-Eeez Laundry.' Sound-activated recorders, so I don't have to be there."

"You have any problems?"

He finally raised his eyes from the chessboard and looked at me.

"Problems? No, I have no problems. But you—you got a problem."

"Oh? What is that?"

"Her place was already shared when I got in."

I thought about that for a moment.

"How many?" I asked.

"One. Under the slipcover on the side of the armchair in the living room. Butcher's work. A straight mike. The wire goes down through the floor."

"Into the apartment below?"

"It goes through the floor. That's as far as I could trace it. I left it there."

"Thank you," I said.

"Give my best to Angela Berri," he said. "The dear lady."

I met Lydia, on time, at an eastside Italian restaurant. The place was half-empty. With the love they charged, that was understandable. But they knew me. I *think* the wine they served me was made from grapes.

"You must be very wealthy." Lydia smiled, studying the menu.

"Not on my rank-rate," I said. "But occasionally I have to get out and unwind."

"Let off pressure?"

"Exactly. How about the veal? *And* peppers. *And* spaghetti. *And* a bottle of red wine."

Frank Lawson Harris' last meal. Her expression didn't change.

"Sounds marvelous," she said.

She looked quite profitable. Not tooty—but then she didn't have the body for it. Wide shoulders, heavy bosom, thick hips. She was smart enough to wear a loose, flowing shift. It tightened across her nipples, then draped straight to her knees. Seductive without being obvious.

Her face was broad, too. High, clear brow. Wide cheekbones. Rather Slavic. Her neck was soft, almost puffy. Her eyes were large, slightly protuberant. I wondered if she might not be suffering from occult hyperthyroidism. Probably not. Her mind was certainly not dulled, and I could detect no signs of irritability. She seemed as serene and self-possessed as ever. A very pleasant ef.

I asked her questions about her service as we dined. She was quite open about it. She was currently analyzing and coding essay answers to the question: "Do you approve of, disapprove of, or have no opinion on televised transvestite beauty pageants?"

"Did objects know what a transvestite is?" I asked.

"Interviewers were instructed to explain only when asked. Most of them knew. Even children. Some of the replies we received were hilarious."

She quoted some of the essays. I didn't think they were particularly hilarious. But I smiled or laughed each time she paused expectantly in her recital.

"What do *you* think about them?" she asked suddenly. "And televised bullfights and executions?"

I shrugged.

"Why does the government allow it?" she demanded.

For the first time I caught a glimpse of an anger behind her placidity. In bed she was a wanton. Now I saw a hint of an emotional (if not intellectual) passion that might equal the physical.

"The government allow it?" I laughed. "Lydia, you *are* naïve. The government *encourages* it!"

"But *why?*"

"For very practical reasons. Psychological studies have proved that violence and sex on TV act as a catharsis, a visual safety valve for hostility and aggression."

"I don't believe that," she said sharply.

"In any event, it's not the main reason why—"

I was silent then while the waitress removed our emptied dinner plates. She brought us a pot of espresso (mostly chicory) and, proudly, fresh apples (two). They were huge, bright, red. And mealy and tasteless. But Lydia appeared to be delighted with hers. I watched her large, strong teeth chonk into the fruit. When she swallowed, her entire soft throat convulsed. It was oddly exciting to watch.

"What is the main reason that the government encourages permissiveness on TV?" she asked finally.

"Well, in the media industry there are two main cartels: print media and electronic media. They claim to be complementary. In a few insignificant ways they are. But actually they are quite competitive, especially in obtaining advertising revenues. Now the government cannot license print media. The last time they tried it, in 1990, the result was catastrophic.

"But the government does have some ways of manipulating the electronic media. This they can do legally since all radio and television stations must be licensed by a government agency. It's easier to influence an industry whose very existence depends on official grant. And for that reason, it's vital to the government that the electronic media grow while the print media decrease in importance. So the government encourages permissiveness on TV. People who once could only scan sex scenes in books and magazines, can now view it—in three dimensions and color. Thus the electronic media attract larger audiences. Thus their advertising revenue increases. Thus they grow stronger, make more love, and the need for TV station owners to retain their licenses becomes even more imperative. Thus stronger government control of their editorial policies. That's why you see fornication and bullfights and executions on your home set. Do you follow all that?"

She seemed shocked. I thought what I had explained was obvious to everyone.

"I can't believe it," she said.

99

"Believe it. It's operative."

"But don't you—you personally—object to government control of media? Any media, in any form?"

"I'm just an em following orders," I said. "What can I do?"

We finished our coffee in silence. She opened her purse, then paused to look at me.

"Do you mind if I touch up my makeup?" she asked innocently. "I know I shouldn't do it at the table."

In some ways she was delightful. Almost as ingenuous as Millie.

"Please do." I laughed. "I might even touch up mine."

"You don't wear much."

"No, not much. A friend of mine has been after me to use eye shadow."

"Oh, no," she said quickly. "Please don't do that."

I watched her apply lip rouge.

"Beautiful color," I said. "What is it?"

"The color is called Passion Flower. Does that jerk you? The lip rouge is Amour Now."

"*That* jerks me," I said. "Amour now or later?"

She tried to smile mysteriously, but she was too open and honest to bring it off. We both laughed and left the restaurant hand in hand. It had been a profitable dinner.

We went to a nude performance of *Swan Lake* at Lincoln Center. The audience seemed to enjoy it—oohing and ahing whenever the em star performed a *grand jeté*—but I found the whole thing absurd. I think Lydia did, too. At least, she made no objection when we left before it ended. We stopped at a federal grogshop where I bought a lovable bottle of cherry liqueur which the manager assured me was made from real cherries. I also bought Lydia a national lottery ticket. She laughed happily.

"If I win I'll give you half," she vowed.

"Good. An ef in my Division won a thousand a few weeks ago."

"I want to win a million."

"I hope you do. What will you do with it—after you give me my half?"

"I'll buy a farm," she said dreamily. "Somewhere far off. Lonely and deserted. I'll buy animals—dogs and horses and cows and chickens and cats. And I'll raise my own food. I'll have a little lake, and I'll swim every morning. I'll listen to the wind and watch the stars."

I think she was serious. But of course there were no places like that anymore.

We went back to her home by taxi. The cabs had changed; they were electric now. The drivers hadn't changed; still choleric and unpleasant as ever. We also had to endure a Cab-Alert installation that flashed color slides at ten-second intervals and, by recorded messages, advised us what to do about wet armpits, bowel irregularity, and a breath that wilted flowers.

Lydia had an apartment that reflected her personality: unassertive, pleasing, calm. I had to keep reminding myself this was the ef who provided Harris with a going-away present: the fiddled Somnorific.

"Sit over there," she said casually, motioning toward the slip-covered armchair in the living room. "It's the most comfortable chair I have. Would you like this cherry stuff in Smack or on ice—or how?"

"Just straight," I said. "And just a small glass. It's sure to be sweet."

Obediently, I sat down in the armchair. She was right—it was comfortable. While she was in the kitchen, I ran my fingertips lightly over the slipcover on both sides. Leon Mansfield had been right, too; it was amateurish; I felt the bump of the mike. When she came in from the kitchen, I was leaning back, relaxed, my mouth close to the concealed bug.

"Cheers," I said, lifting the plasticup she handed me.

She pulled a hassock across the floor and sat at a lower level, near my knees.

"But you don't seem so cheerful tonight," she said. "Depressed?"

"A little."

"Your service?"

"I guess so. It's been bothering me for some time now. Recently it's become worse."

"Want to talk about it?"

"Want to, but can't."

"Security classification?"

"Yes."

"I won't repeat it."

That was a giggle. She wouldn't have to.

"Oh, Lydia, it's not that I don't trust you. I know you wouldn't

101

do or say anything to endanger me. Or your father."

That startled her, but she recovered quickly.

"I can't believe you and Daddy would do anything wrong," she said.

"Depends on your definition of wrong, doesn't it? Tell me this: Is it wrong to refuse to obey the legal order of your ruler when you feel, in your heart of hearts, that the order you are given is immoral?"

She was silent, staring at me.

"Nick, I can't make a decision like that for you."

"I know you can't. I'm not asking you to. It's all mine."

"But maybe it would help if you talked it out."

I shrugged.

"I doubt it, Lydia. I've been over and over it, again and again. I've considered every possible argument, for and against. And I just don't know what to do."

"Nick, for God's sake, what *is* it?"

I sighed. "Well . . . I might as well tell you. But don't—please, please, don't—breathe a word of this to anyone. It involves behavior control. Or, as it was once euphemistically called, 'behavior modification.' But I'm talking about behavior control by chemical means, not by psychological conditioning."

"You mean by giving an object a pill or injection?"

"I wish it was that simple. But it's not a single object I'm talking about; it's an entire population. Look, the principle is an obso one. More than seventy years ago we started putting traces of iodine in table salt. It practically eliminated goiter in this country."

I paused to see if she reacted. If she, as I suspected, might be a victim of hypothyroidism. But she showed nothing but fascinated interest.

"Then we put chlorine in our water to make it potable," I continued. "Then fluoride—all chemicals."

"But they're like—like medicine!"

"Right. No one but the ignorant could possibly object. But we established the principle of involuntary ingestion of chemicals by government decree. All right, now take this situation: We have a prison riot. The warden and several guards have been seized as hostages; the prisoners threaten to kill them. They're destroying the prison. We can go in with armored tanks and flechette guns. Sure, a lot of objects will be stopped, but the riot will be over. Now every prison in the country is supplied water from a central source, pipe or

102

tank. Wouldn't it make more sense to put tranquilizers or hypnotics in the drinking water to subdue the entire prison population without loss of life? Wouldn't you opt for that?''

"Yesss," she said. "I guess I would."

"What about Harlem, or Watts, or any other ghetto being torn apart by a race riot? Rather than an armed confrontation, wouldn't you prefer that the riots be calmed by adding say, a soporific, to their water supply? Only for as long as it took to end the riot? Then the authorities could discuss the issues involved with objects not inflamed by blood lust or an uncontrollable urge to burn, baby, burn. Wouldn't you opt for the drug?''

"I don't know," she said slowly. "Now it's getting complicated. I might approve if it meant saving lives."

"It would," I assured her. "But it's become more difficult than you imagine. Because now we have a whole arsenal of drugs that affect behavior. We can make an object as fierce as a tiger or as mild as a kitten. And not only a single object, mind you, but by adding the chemical to food or the water supply, we can manipulate populations—in prisons, schools, towns, cities, nations, the world.''

"You're talking about chemical warfare."

"Not necessarily. I'm talking about behavior control—although I admit the fine line between that and chemwar gets finer each day.''

"But you said you had a particular problem?''

"I do. About a year ago—well . . . a little less than that—an African nation was admitted to statehood in the US. We can do a lot for them—socially, economically, medically, culturally. But they have one tribe, about ten thousand objects, who are national fanatics and oppose US statehood. These objects are primitives—unbelievably cruel, without conscience, burning and looting and stopping. They can cause absolute chaos in a young state trying to pull itself up from the mud of ignorance and poverty. The other objects in the state number about four million. They want nothing but a peaceful existence, a chance to improve their standard of living and educate their children. Should the ten thousand rebels be allowed to thwart that desire? Most of the dissidents live in one very restricted area. Most of them draw their drinking water from one lake. We could calm them all tomorrow by sending planes over the lake to drop a few centiliters of a clear liquid. That would be a temporary solution. We could make it a permanent solution simply by substituting a different chemical. You understand?''

103

"Oh, yes. Oh, yes. I understand."

"But if we poisoned the lot, the international outcry would be—well, just something we don't want. So a decision has been made at the highest possible levels of our government. It will be a two-part program. First, the rebels' water supply will be treated with tranquilizers and antiaggression drugs. That will take care of the immediate problem. The long-range cure—if you can call it that—is to stop the tribe. Our prosterility drugs are not as dependable as they might be, so it was decided to take advantage of a genetic deficiency from which the rebels already suffer naturally."

"Which is?"

"Sickle-cell anemia. We've practically wiped it out in this country. Genetic manipulation led to an oral drug. In developing the inhibitor, we also learned how to synthesize a stimulator. We can stop the entire rebel tribe in one generation. Long enough to forestall any international accusation of genocide, and short enough not to endanger the social and economic development of the state. I have been ordered to work up the technology: drugs required, amounts, preferred methods of delivery, and so forth. And that, Miss Ferguson, is my problem. Now give me advice."

She sat there, hunched over on the hassock, chin cupped in palms.

"You're not going to do it, are you?" she asked quietly.

"I don't *want* to do it!" I cried. "If I don't, my career is over. But that's the least of my worries. There's always the R&R Hospice 'for psychiatric observation for reasons of public security.' They'll never let me walk away from this. Not knowing what I know."

She nodded, reached forward, took my hands in hers.

"We'll work it out," she whispered. "Somehow."

"Don't talk to your father, for God's sake," I said roughly. "That's the last thing in the world I need—the Director of Bliss learning I had mentioned this to anyone."

"No," she said. "No, I won't talk to my father."

She rose and smiled down at me. A sad, understanding, sympathetic smile. The last smile Harris had seen before he began clawing at his chest?

"Another drink?" she asked.

"No, thanks. I'm all knotted up. It won't help."

She nodded, took my empty glass, went into the kitchen, then

104

into the bedroom. I waited, wondering what she was doing. Then she came to the bedroom door and stood there for a moment, erect, arms down at her sides, palms turned forward. She was naked. She looked like an anatomy chart. I rose, turned off the lamp, moved to her.

Whatever control she possessed, and she had displayed a great deal, fell away from her in bed. The pleasant self-assurance disappeared, and something raw took its place. If she was not a practised user, she was an ardent student. I could understand Harris' infatuation. There was nothing she would not do.

The body was overwhelming, slightly tumescent, a fever to her flesh. She had an almost demoniacal strength, thrashing, bucking, flailing. And uttering animal cries. Her odor was dark, fern-rot and bog. I know it may scan ridiculous, but I was never certain she was conscious of my presence. Surrendered to a paroxysm of sensuality, she was simply lost and gone, rutting her last minute on earth and howling with delight.

Long afterward, her great breasts puddled out, nipples bleary, soft thighs spread, she looked at me with dazed eyes, coming back slowly from wherever she had been. I may have hated her then.

Smelling of her, I showered quickly and dressed. I bent over the bed to kiss her goodnight. A strong arm curled around my neck, pulled me close.

"Yes," she whispered.

In the lobby, I looked at the mailbox of 2-B, the apartment directly below hers. Dr. and Mrs. Henry L. Hammond. I knew him—or knew of him.

I circled the block slowly. Finally, on Ninetieth Street between West End Avenue and the river, I found the Kleen-Eeez Laundry van. It appeared deserted. I rapped on the side. A small circular flap, concealed in the lettering, slid aside. An eye stared at me. The flap closed. A moment later the van's rear door was opened. Leon Mansfield motioned to me.

I climbed in and closed the door behind me. The interior was dimly lighted with a low-wattage red bulb. It was fitted out with electronic equipment: tape recorders, shortwave radio transmitters and receivers, locator, tape splicer, etc. There was a canvas cot with a filthy blanket. Mansfield was seated at a makeshift desk, earphones clamped to his elongated skull. He turned one of the earphones around and waved me close.

I moved next to him, breathing through my mouth. I had had enough of other objects' odors for one day. I pressed my ear to the turned pad.

Man's voice: "We'll discuss it tomorrow."

Lydia: "Yes, Henry. As long as you got it all."

Henry: "We did indeed. Perfectly."

Lydia: "He's very troubled."

Henry: "We'll discuss it tomorrow. Get a good night's sleep."

Lydia: "Give my best to Alice. Good night."

Henry: "Good night."

Click. The tape stopped.

Leon Mansfield removed his earphones. He rewound the tape, stopped the machine, removed the reel. He fitted a fresh reel on the spindle, threaded it through. He handed me the reel he had removed and two more.

"This is what I have so far," he said tonelessly.

I was waiting to hear him comment about those bedroom sounds he had picked up, but he said nothing. I climbed out of the back door of the van, carrying the reels.

"Thank you," I said.

"A pleasure," he said.

X-9

On the morning following my dinner with Lydia Ann Ferguson, I flashed DIVSEC (Division of Security & Intelligence) and requested a complete profile on Dr. Henry L. Hammond from the National Data Bank. I was certain I'd hear from Assistant Deputy Director Burton P. Klein within the hour, demanding to know the reason for my request. I underestimated the em. He came storming into my office thirty minutes later, banging the door behind him.

"Come on in, Burton," I said genially.

My irony was wasted.

"What the hell is this about Dr. Hammond?" he shouted.

I looked at him critically.

"Calm, Burton, calm," I said. "You want me to quote correlative statistics on hypertension and mortality? Now sit down and relax. I don't like that high color in your face."

106

It worked. He threw himself into the plastivas sling at my deskside, breathing heavily, glaring at me, but gradually quieting.

He was a bear of an em, carrying an overweight torso on slender legs. He was ugly. Ungraceful. His voice was too loud, his manner boisterous, his personal habits disgusting. (He picked his nose, rolled the detached matter between thumb and forefinger, flicked it away.)

But he could no more dissimulate than he could play a toccata on a harpsichord. I took no profit from him, but I admired his openness. He was what he was: take it or leave it.

"Dr. Henry L. Hammond," I said. "Yes, I requested a profile. I'm thinking of asking him to serve on a consultant basis."

"What the hell for?"

"Burton, it's just routine," I said softly. "Hyman Lewisohn has leukemia. You know that. Lewisohn's survival is my concern. He's not responding to drugs. So I've drawn up a contingency plan if his condition continues to deteriorate. One step in that plan is parabiosis. Hammond is an expert in parabiosis. That's all there is to it."

"What's parabiosis?" he demanded.

At least he made no attempt to disguise his ignorance.

"Parabiosis is a surgical process by which two objects of the same species are linked physiologically. Hopefully for a short time. One object is healthy, one diseased. By linking their blood vessels, the healthy one takes over, or assists, the life processes of the diseased object. It has worked many times in renal failure. That pertains to kidney malfunctions. And it has worked, experimentally, with leukemic patients. That's why I want Dr. Hammond. If parabiosis becomes necessary in Lewisohn's case."

In his blunt manner, he went directly to the essence of the problem.

"Where do you get the healthy object to connect him to?" he asked.

"Volunteers." I shrugged. "Prisoners condemned to capital punishment. Others. We can work it out."

"Do you know what you're doing?" he asked finally.

I was startled. I thought at first he was questioning my professional competence. Then I saw, from his bemused manner, that it had been a rhetorical question. What the hell, he wanted to know, was going on?

I had seen that same manner in, and heard the same question from many other objects, some much more intelligent than Burton Klein. It sprang from an inability to accept change. It was a psychological condition quite similar to shock. Things were moving so fast, society evolving so rapidly, some objects simply could not cope. Mutation followed mutation so swiftly that after a while catalepsy was the only means of survival.

"Burton," I said gently, "you've been serving too hard."

"Yes, I have," he agreed. He scrubbed his face with his palms. "Things have been piling up. These terrorist attacks. I don't know where to start. And—"

"And?" I prompted when he paused.

"And other things," he muttered. "I don't know whom to trust anymore."

"Sleeping well?" I asked him.

"Somnorifics."

"How often?"

"Every night."

"That's not so good. Want to check in? Here or at a Hospice? We'll give you a workup."

"No," he said decisively. "Not now. My annual comes up in September. I can wait till then."

He got up heavily, started for the door. Then he turned.

"Listen," he said. "You talk to Angela Berri more than I do."

It wasn't a question. I didn't answer.

"You should know—"

But then he stopped, turned around again, and marched out, leaving my door open. I stared after him.

We met in my apartment about 1800. Angela Berri told us the program to accuratize the Satrat was proceeding on schedule. No problems. She and I looked to Paul Bumford.

Paul had been serving long hours; it showed. His weight was down. His naturally fair skin had an unhealthy pallor. There were dark rings under his eyes. With his vanity, I knew that must gall him. He had applied pancake makeup, but the shadows were still discernible.

"Mary Bergstrom and I have been using the King Mk. IV computer in A Lab," he reported. "I thought it best not to take the chance of alerting Phoebe Huntzinger to what we were doing."

"Good," Angela said.

"But the King is limited," Paul went on. "Especially in storage. Anyway, we broke down and coded the raw data on terrorist attacks. Nationwide. Only on the mainland. Incidents in outlying states are normal. We programmed for dates and times, types of attack, number of objects believed involved, types of installations hit, results, duration of attacks, methods of approach and escape, types of sabotage, and so forth.''

"And?" Angela demanded.

"These are preliminary printouts," Paul said. "But I think they'll hold up. It may be a nationwide conspiracy, directed from a central command. I can't say definitely. I'd guess yes. Operations appear to be organized by Geo-Political Areas. Each GPA exhibits distinct characteristics. In GPA-6, for instance, bombings predominate. In GPA-3, it's kidnappings. Times of attack and numbers of objects involved convince me the whole is organized, structurally, along GPA lines."

"Any uniformities?" I asked.

"Mostly procreation and genetic research facilities, in all GPA's. Most significant: Attacks on procreation and genetic research facilities are 82.3 percent sabotage. That indicates interior collusion. Turning a thermostat down a few degrees. Enough to destroy a culture. Poisoning rats' meal. To stop a cancer-sensitive strain it's taken thirty years to breed. In our Denver Field Office labs, a hundred aborted fetuses were uncovered over a weekend."

"Jesus," Angela breathed.

I tried to control my anger. What in God's name did they think they were doing?

"Those are my gross conclusions to date," Paul finished. "It's big. It's serious. No hint of who may be behind it. No suggestion of foreign influence. Obviously a great number of objects, including SATSEC personnel, are participating. Questions?"

"Any captures?" I asked. "Defectors? Informers?"

"None."

"Any love stolen?" Angela asked.

"Now that's interesting," Paul said. "The answer is yes. Terrorism against banks was in the usual pattern. Large sums were taken. But I think the bank hits were a diversion."

"Nice diversion," I said. "Dual purpose. Muddy the waters and finance the whole operation. Good brain there."

"Paul, you've done excellent service," Angela said.

He straightened and brightened.

"Another two days," he said. "Then we'll be finished. What's next?"

"Me," I said. "I'm next. These are the tapes supplied by Leon Mansfield. Recorded yesterday. He told me Lydia Ferguson's apartment was already being shared before he got in. The bug leads to the apartment below hers. Occupied by Dr. and Mrs. Henry L. Hammond."

Angela Berri showed no reaction when I spoke the name. I was watching for it.

"So what you hear," I went on, "has already been shared by her rulers. I knew it when I spoke. Here we go. . . ."

I started the machine. Angela and Paul leaned forward, hands clasped, heads down. During Lydia's animal cries in the bedroom, I watched them closely. Neither reacted. They listened intently, right up to Henry's last line. I switched off the machine.

Then Paul raised his head, looked at me admiringly.

"How did you ever think of that African idea?" he asked. "Using an anemic stimulator on a rebel tribe?"

"It just occurred to me. I thought it was exactly the type of activity a dissident group would be looking for. Something to discredit the US in the United Nations."

"Genius," Paul enthused. "Genius!"

Angela Berri was silent.

"Who is Dr. Henry L. Hammond?" Paul asked.

"I know him. I never met him personally, but I heard him address a meeting of the American Association for the Advancement of Science in 1993. On symbiosis. A brilliant paper. Then he disappeared, for years. This afternoon I ran a DIVSEC profile on him."

Then Angela came alive.

"DIVSEC?" she said sharply. "Did Klein question it?"

"Of course." I nodded. "But I soothed him. I told him I wanted Hammond as a consultant because I was considering symbiosis for the treatment of Lewisohn. Which I am."

She started to speak, then thought better of it.

"Hammond's profile was interesting," I went on. "He headed a team at CIT that did the research on symbiosis. More failures than successes on human objects, but definite progress. Six months after he delivered the paper at the Triple-A S, he resigned, went to Japan, and served in a Zen Buddhist monastery for two years. How does that jerk you? Then he returned, married his former secretary, and took service at CCNY teaching a very primary course in something called Human Dynamics. As far as I can discover, it's a lot of kaka.

110

Hammond and his wife live in the apartment directly below Lydia Ferguson's. Alice Hammond rules a government daycare center on Broadway and Seventy-third Street. She's a PS-7. About six months ago they applied for and were granted a procreation license. Ef. Their political involvement, to date, has been minimal. Both are registered Independents. She belongs only to several scientific societies.''

"Obsos?" Paul asked.

"No. He is twenty-seven, she is twenty-four. Both, for some unknown reason, underwent primal scream therapy about two years ago. He should have known better. Anyway, there you have Dr. and Mrs. Henry L. Hammond who, possibly, are now listening to tapes similar to those you just heard.''

They both straightened up, leaned back on the couch.

"Well . . ." Paul said finally. "Where do we go from here?"

"I know where *I* go," I announced. "This afternoon Lydia called. She just had a wonderful idea. The people downstairs, the Hammonds, have had her for dinner twice. So she feels she owes them an invitation. Will I come for dinner on Thursday to meet them?''

"Watch yourself," Angela said.

Late that night—not too late, about 2330—I was seated naked on the edge of my bed. I should have swung my legs under the thermasheet and tried to sleep. But something was puzzling me.

Paul Bumford, the last time we had been under that same sheet—not the *same* one, but an identical one—had said his happiness derived from surrender. To me, I presumed. Or at least to physical mastery. And last night I had proof of Lydia's happiness in surrendering to—well, to something. The mastery of her own flesh perhaps. There was a link there, between the two, but I couldn't analyze it.

My flasher chimed. I went over to the bedroom extension, sat down, flicked it on. The image was Angela Berri.

"Nick," she said, "why did you have to use the African idea?"

"Angela," I said, "what difference does it make?"

"What if they ask for documentation?"

"I'll tell them the truth: all oral orders, no documentation exists. It doesn't, does it?"

"Not to my knowledge," she said.

"Good. Besides, that was three years ago. It's operative, isn't it?''

Then she looked at me, eye to eye, on the screen.

"Perfectly," she said. "One of the most lovable ideas you've ever had."

"Thank you, teacher," I said.

She smiled and switched off.

I was the last to arrive at Lydia's apartment. But she wasn't upset. Just happy, apparently, to see me. I kissed her cheek, left her to serve in the kitchen, went into the living room to introduce myself.

Dr. Henry L. Hammond had changed little, physically, since I had seen him at the AAAS meeting five years ago. He was a big em, stalwart, with a natural Valkyrie hair style and a full, blondish beard. His lips were an intense cherry-red, but I did not believe it was makeup. His palm stroke was dry and hearty.

His wife, Alice, obviously pregnant, was small, mousy, and seemed composed mostly of grays: gray hair, a grayish tinge to her skin, a gray silk dress, gray plastipat shoes, a necklace and bracelet of slate chips set in pewter. She was quiet, contained, watchful. The more dangerous of the two, I judged.

Hammond and I chatted briskly. Inconsequential topics: the high cost of food, the difficulty of getting cabs when it rained, the dearth of decent housing in New York. Finally, his wife spoke:

"Where do you serve, Dr. Flair?" she asked.

I told her. She nodded, with a half-smile. Then she rose awkwardly and went into the kitchen, presumably to help Lydia with the dinner.

"Pardon me, Dr. Hammond," I said. "My memory may be playing tricks, but didn't you serve on parabiosis?"

"Oh, yes," he said casually. "But that was a long time ago."

"You're no longer in the field?"

"Oh my, no. I took a two-year sabbatical to visit the Orient. When I returned, I discovered I was simply out of it. Things had moved along so rapidly in my absence that it would have taken me years to catch up."

"I know exactly what you mean." I laughed. "Sometimes I'm afraid to take a threeday. The world progresses while I'm away."

"Progresses?" he said. "Well, it certainly changes."

"And what are you doing now?"

"Conditioning. At CCNY. Basic stuff on human motivations. But I find it very satisfying. Teaching the young, I mean."

Then we were called to dinner. We sat at a round plastisteel table

112

in a small alcove. The table was lighted with electric candles, the little bulbs shaped like flames, with flickering filaments.

Lydia had prepared a casserole in her microwave oven: prorice and proshrimp—shaped and tinted like the real thing. It also contained slices of green propep, bits of natural ham, and natural onion. It was edible.

We went through the confusion of passing plates about, spooning out the main dish, dividing a prolet salad that could have used more synthetic herbs and spices. Then, all served, we settled down to consumption.

Dr. Hammond was wearing obso clothes: flannel slacks and a rough tweed jacket. He withdrew a pair of yellowed ivory chopsticks from his inside breast pocket. He manipulated them with great dexterity, demonstrating how it was possible to pick up a single grain of rice. His wife gave me the impression of having witnessed this trick previously, too many times.

"Mrs. Hammond," I said. "I haven't—"

"Alice," she interrupted gravely.

"Alice." I smiled. "A first-name basis is profitable. Call me Nick. I haven't yet congratulated you and your husband. When is the child due?"

"The last week in August."

"Congratulations! Ef or em?"

"Ef," she said.

"Wonderful."

"We wanted an em," she said.

Lydia and Hammond were silent, bending over their plates.

"I'm sure you'll be delighted with a little ef," I said. "You'll see."

"Dr. Flair, do you—"

"Nick."

"Nick, do you approve of the government licensing pregnancies and dictating the sex of the child?"

"Approve of it?" I said cautiously. "Perhaps not approve. But I accept it. I recognize the necessity."

"What is the necessity?"

"Why . . . it's the Fertility Control Act."

"I know. But what is the necessity for *that*?"

"Well . . . it's very important, socially and economically. When sex predetermination drugs were developed, a few years before the FCA was passed, it was discovered that half a million ems more

113

than the norm were being bred annually. Parents opted for them. Lewisohn was the first to point out the dangers of that. At the time, more than fifteen years ago, they were very real dangers: increased male homosexuality due to a gross surplus of ems, psychological deprivation of efs when they were old enough to realize they were not first choice, a decline of culture consumers since efs predominate in this market, and so forth. All the FCA does is decree the most favorable social and economic ratio. Computerized estimates are made annually of how many babies are to be bred. The government still authorizes more ems than efs, I assure you. But you probably know the statistics of ef and em longevity rates. Even today, widows over sixty-five far outnumber widowers of the same age. But we're slowly bringing the numbers into balance. And, most important of course, the FCA has achieved Zero Population growth. Now, as longevity increases, we're considering going to Minus-Z Pop. To ensure every living object adequate breathing room and a decent environment.''

"You make it sound so logical," she said.

"It *is* logical."

"But isn't the FCA a restraint of individual freedom?"

"No doubt about it," I said promptly. "Like traffic laws and required radiation inoculation of children. For the common good."

"All I know," she said, "is that we wanted an em baby and are not allowed to have one."

"It's a weakness I have," I acknowledged sadly, "to speak in statistics and percentages and ratios and Z-Pop growth. But these things are part of my service. I tend to treat objects as numbers. I forget the personal traumata that may be involved in obeying a very logical and practical government decree."

"You see the forest but not the trees," Henry Hammond said.

"Right," I agreed. "But you must realize I've been conditioned to do exactly that."

"Well," he said, "at least you recognize it as conditioning."

"Yes," I said. "I do."

"Nick," Lydia said suddenly, "can a hypnotized object be made to do something against his will? Something he knows is morally wrong?"

I looked at her in surprise.

"Of course," I said. "If the hypnotist is clever enough."

"You mentioned conditioning," Alice said. "Can a conditioned object be made to do something against his will? Something he knows is morally wrong?''

It was a beautiful orchestrated performance. I wondered if they had rehearsed it.

I knew the operative answer to Alice Hammond's question, but it didn't fit my role.

"You've opened a different can of worms," I said. I tried to appear disquieted. "There's been a great deal of research on the subject, but no definitive answer. As yet.''

"How do you feel about it?" Henry Hammond asked. "What's your personal opinion?''

I paused a long moment, staring down at my empty plate.

"I'd say no," I said finally, in a low voice. "I believe, regardless of the length or intensity of conditioning, an object's operative nature will eventually surface.''

They said nothing. Their expressions didn't alter. But I felt I had scored points. It was all a lot of kaka, of course. They were talking about psychological behavior modification. If I wished, I could describe to them the effects of an existent drug that simply demolished all their airy-fairy theories. They were such innocents, playing a game the rules of which had changed while they were picking up a single grain of rice with obso chopsticks.

I insisted on helping Lydia clear the table and sterilize the dishes. The Hammonds went into the living room. I couldn't overhear their conversation. It wasn't important; I'd be hearing soon enough on Mansfield's tapes what they had discussed.

I learned sooner than that. After our chores, Lydia and I joined them in the living room. Talk was desultory. Nothing significant. Until. . . .

"By the way, Nick," Dr. Henry Hammond said, "Alice and I have a summer place, up near Cornwall. Know where it is?''

"On the river, isn't it? South of Newburgh?''

"Glorious view," Alice said.

"Built on the ruins of an Indian trading post," Henry said.

"Almost a hectare of land.''

"Clean air," Alice said.

How could I resist?

"Alice and I are going up on Friday morning to open the place for the season," Henry went on. He paused to light an enormous oompaul pipe, puffing mightily, blowing out great clouds of blue

115

smoke. He was really a ridiculous em. "We were wondering if Lydia and you would care to come up for Saturday? We're having a few interesting people in."

I had been planning to start a threeday on Friday morning, but I didn't hesitate.

"A profit," I said. "Lydia?"

"Oh, yes." She nodded. "Sounds like fun."

"Can you get a car?" Henry asked. "You could train to New-burgh, and we could pick you up there. But a car would be easier. It's a profitable drive."

"No problem," I said. "I'll requisition one from the motor pool. One of the advantages of serving our beneficial government."

We all laughed. I was in.

I returned to the compound shortly after midnight. Paul must have tipped the gate guard to flash him when I signed in; he was waiting outside my apartment door.

"I was worried. The whole thing worries me. Is it going to be all right, Nick?"

" 'The future belongs to the untroubled,' " I quoted him.

He had the grace to blush.

I let us in, locked the door behind us.

"What happened?" he asked.

"Wait a minute. Let's get Angela in on this. I'll tell you both at the same time."

"You can't. She flew down to Washington this evening. The Deputy Directors are meeting with DIROB tomorrow. Cabinet meeting on Thursday."

"Shit." I thought a moment. "She usually stays at the PS hostel, doesn't she?"

"Well, she checks in there. God knows where she sleeps."

I grinned at him.

"Try to get her, will you? I'll pour us a petrovod. I need it."

Paul was still on the flasher when I returned to the living room He finally got through to the Public Service hostel in Arlington. Yes, Angela Berri was registered there. No, she was not in her room. Yes, she had left a number where she could be reached. Paul repeated it, then switched off.

"That's DIROB's private number," I said. "He murt be having a buffet dinner for his Deputy Directors and headquarters staff before the meeting. He usually does."

"*Before* the meeting? Why not after?"

"Who knows? Maybe they've all lost their appetites by then. Try her there."

I stood behind Paul, playing with his ear while he punched out DIROB's number. He got the image of an em server in an earth-colored zipsuit. There was a lot of noise, people moving in the background. Finally Angela came on.

"Yes, Paul?" she said crisply. "Where are you?"

"Nick's apartment."

"Can it wait?"

He looked up at me. I shook my head.

"No," he told Angela.

"Call you back in five minutes," she said, and switched off.

Paul arose, and I took the chair in front of the flasher. Angela was back on in about three minutes. This time she was seated at a desk in what appeared to be a study or library.

"You look lovely," I told her.

She smiled. "Thanks. Is that what you called to tell me?"

I laughed.

"There's more. They want me to meet people. This Saturday. At a place near Cornwall. That's up the Hudson. Just south of New-burgh."

She thought a moment.

"Yes," she said finally.

"I've already agreed," I said. "But the place should be shared. Or at least scouted. And fast."

She nodded.

"Send Mansfield. Give him three hundred. You have it?"

"I can get it."

"Good."

"I don't know the exact address."

"Just give Leon the name. Let him take it from there. Tell him to call you when it's set."

"Right. Enjoying yourself?"

She made an O of her mouth, extended her tongue, wiggled the tip lasciviously.

"Wicked ef," I said.

She switched off.

"You heard all that?" I asked Paul.

"Yes. Bitch! Who's the meeting with?"

"Very vague. 'A few interesting people.' You'll hear the tapes."

"Are you in, Nick?"

"Almost certain. I played it very cozy tonight, but they think they have me in a bag. That African business I invented to tell Lydia. They've got it on tape."

"Oh-ho," he said. "Blackmail."

"Well . . . just call it pressure."

I had no way of contacting Leon Mansfield, other than making that annoying trip up to West Forty-second Street. He had given me no number to flash; he wasn't listed in the directory. I decided to wait till noon, hoping he'd call by then.

I spent the morning doing a workup on my Division's budget for the coming year. It was axiomatic in Public Service that you inflated your proposed budget by approximately 20 percent, knowing it would be cut by approximately 10-15 percent. Fiscal game-playing.

Ordinarily, I would have stuffed all the raw data into a computer, pressed the button, and let it chug out the estimate in minutes. I would still do that, eventually. But there was a factor involved that few other government budget-makers had to wrestle with.

A great number of projects my Division was serving on were classified. Some were unknown to the Chairmen of the ruling Congressional committees. A few were even unknown to Angela Berri and DIROB. I had to conceal funds for these projects by diluting them to several other known and approved programs. And, of course, I could make no records of this double-entry bookkeeping. Budget-making was not particularly difficult, but it was time-consuming.

I was still hacking away at it, about 1115, when Leon Mansfield flashed me from a public booth. This time he was on camera. He looked weary.

"Same place as last time," he said. "Half an hour."

He switched off. I cursed the em. But I had no choice. I drew a propane-powered sedan from the motor pool and drove up to the Mess Hall on Seventh Avenue. I had the 300 new dollars in my purse. Parking, as usual, was a nightmare. Finally I pulled into a restricted zone. I stuck a card, "Psychoanalyst on Call," on the windshield. Someone in my Division had them printed up as a joke. Incredibly, they sometimes worked.

Leon Mansfield was at the same table near the plate glass window. He looked seedier than ever. He had a package with him. I slid into the chair next to him.

"Couldn't we have met at your office?" I asked.

"No. I don't have an office. They tore the building down yesterday."

"I suppose you've been moving," I said.

He shrugged. "I left everything there. Nothing I wanted."

I had a sudden, sharp attack of Random Synaptic Control. Images flickered by. . . .

. . . the wreckers' ball flinging high against a blue sky.

. . . tons of steel crunching into stone carvings on which an Italian immigrant had served slowly and lovingly 100 years ago.

. . . great clouds of acrid dust, jagged holes in the walls, crumbling brick, wooden staircases knocked flat, a gigantic gilt eye staring up from the rubble.

. . . and all the odd detritus of Mansfield's office obscenely exposed, opened to the wind. Blowing away: posters, books, magazines, photos, pictures—all blown and scattered.

I took a spansule from my side pocket and popped it dry. Mansfield watched me with interest.

"On something?" he asked.

"Increases my sex drive," I said.

He lost interest.

"Got some tapes for you," he said listlessly. "Slow job."

"It's quickening," I said. "Dr. Henry L. Hammond. He's on the tapes. The apartment below Ferguson's."

"The em who's sharing?"

"Yes. He owns a summer place. Near Cornwall. That's—"

"I know where it is."

"He and his wife are going up Friday morning. I want you to get there first. Share it, if you can. If not, just scout. Take some Instaroids. I'll need to know by tomorrow. Can you handle it?"

"Sure. How much did she tell you to give me?"

I took the love out of my purse, passed it to him under the table. He riffled the bills with a grubby thumb.

"Three hundred," he said. "The dear lady. Never too little. Never enough."

"I thought it was generous," I said.

"Hmm?" He looked up at me, through me. "Generous? Oh. You misunderstood me, Mr. Nicholas Flair. Yes, it's generous for the service."

"Then what did you mean by 'Never enough'? Never enough for what?"

He shrugged and tried a ghastly smile.

119

"Dreams," he said.

His personal problems had a very low priority rating on my Anxiety List. I started to leave, then sat down again.

"Just out of curiosity," I said, "when did you stop believing my story about a cheating ef user?"

He looked at me in astonishment.

"Stop believing? I never started. You said Angela Berri sent you."

I took the package of tape reels and left. Out on the sidewalk, I glanced back. He had taken out his pocket chess set and was continuing the game that seemed never to end.

On the following afternoon I met him again at the Mess Hall. He told me what he had done at the Hammonds' summer place and handed over another envelope.

"How can I get in touch with you?" I asked. "Do you have a new office or an apartment?"

"No. I'm living in the Kleen-Eeez van."

"Living in it?" I said. "Where do you wash up?"

"Subway toilets," he said.

Great conspiracies. Nationwide plots. Vital plans astir. Important state secrets endangered. And one of the principal actors living in a laundry van and using subway toilets. It called for a 100-year Somnorific.

That evening we gathered in my apartment, standing at my white plastisteel service table, the overhead fluorescents pulled low.

"Here are the Instaroids that Mansfield took," I said, passing them around. "This is a rough map he drew of the site. The house is just south of Cornwall on Hudson, before you get to the state park. The dirt access road leads off Route 218, crosses abandoned railroad tracks here, curves toward the river. The house is on a bluff overlooking the river."

"Nice-looking place," Paul remarked.

"Hammond told me it was built on the ruins of an Indian trading post, and it looks it. The foundation is natural fieldstones set in mortar. The rest is all wood. Hand-hewn beams. The originals. Very obso. Some of the knee braces and rafters are modern. Glass windows with plastisteel storm shutters. Poor security, Mansfield reports. He got in with no trouble. That em is a whiz on locks. Downstairs: one large living-dining room, kitchen, small pantry, toilet. Upstairs: one bedroom, a study-library, a nest. Lots of obso furniture."

"Inside walls?" Angela asked.

"Painted plaster. The walls are unusually thick. But emplacing cameras would be a structural service. We don't have time."

"So?" she asked.

"Paul, let me have those shots for a minute. Here, Angela. And here. Two obso phones. One in the downstairs living room, one in the upstairs study."

"Did Mansfield share them?"

"No. He was concerned about an electronic sweep."

"Smart," Paul said.

"Oh, yes. He guesses something of what's happening. So he put a tap on the line. It's an overhead wire, on poles, coming down the access road from the highway. He says it's a direct wiretap, the best he could do in a short time. The transmitter is concealed under a plastic insulator close to one of the poles. Mansfield claims it's invisible from the ground. He'll receive in his van, parked off the highway, about a kilometer away, hidden in the trees. All right so far? Angela?"

"If they sweep the house electronically—and I think they will; I think Mansfield is right—can they detect the phone line sharing?"

"I don't know. Paul?"

"Doubtful," he said. "Unless they measure power loss. That could only be done through the phone company."

"All right," I said. "We'll go with the phone line tap. We'll get all incoming and outgoing calls. But that may be nil. We need interior conversations. Question: Should I be wired? Personally?"

"How?" Paul asked. "Something taped to your ribs? Too dangerous, in case of a search. Dental implant? Rectal implant? Ingested transmitter? All detectable."

"Aren't we crediting them with more talent than they probably possess?" Angela said.

"No," I said. "Paul's right. And it's my cock. I say no."

That ended wiring me for hi-fidelity broadcasting.

"There are other solutions," I said, "but they all require time to set up. We could use a laser to pick up window vibrations. Or an ultrasensitive telescopic mike. But all that involves heavy equipment, difficult to conceal. I don't see us getting any physical evidence. We'll have to go with my memory. I'll take a Supermem intravenous and try to stay in theta as much as I can."

"My God," Paul said, "with several people gabbling around you? Practically impossible."

"I'll try," I said. "We have no choice. Angela, another problem."

"What?"

"Look at this map. Cars coming off the highway turn onto the dirt access road and head down toward the river. Those abandoned railroad tracks are set in an obso wood crossing. But—here, scan this Instaroid—the planking has shrunk and been worn away. If you were driving, you'd naturally slow down before bumping over the tracks. Foliage on both sides. If Mansfield could conceal remote-controlled cameras, we could get photos of the visitors."

"Marvelous," Angela said.

"Great," Paul said.

"Here's the problem," I said. "I have no way of reaching Mansfield to tell him to emplace the cameras tonight. And the Hammonds are going up tomorrow morning."

"No problem," Angela said. "I'll get in touch with him tonight. As soon as I leave here. I'll tell him what we need. He'll have the cameras in before the Hammonds get there tomorrow morning."

"You have a number for Mansfield?" I asked.

"I can contact him," she said.

I didn't pursue it.

"All right," I went on. "Then we're set on the sharing for Saturday. Now sit down and listen to the tapes."

We moved to the living room and sat in a row on the couch. We listened to the dinner party at Lydia's. None of us spoke until the machine clicked off.

"Very good, Nick." Angela nodded approvingly. "You manipulated them beautifully."

"I liked your answer to the question on conditioning," Paul said. "Fancy footwork."

I rose, went over to the machine, changed reels.

"Just a little more," I said. "The Hammonds were obviously in no hurry to leave, so finally I left. This is the conversation after I departed."

I started the tape.

Lydia: "He's nice, isn't he?"

Alice: "You like him, Lydia?"

Lydia: "Yes. Very much.

Alice: "Be careful. You know what happened last time."

Lydia: "This is different."

Henry: "Well, in any event, I think he'll do. Clever. Creative mind there. But not deep, of course. I'll wager he's never answered a koan or known satori.''

Alice: ''Yes, dear. I think he's going to be very valuable to us. Lydia, you've done a fine service.''

Lydia (faintly): ''Thank you.''

Lapse of eleven seconds.

Lydia: ''I do like him, you know. I wouldn't want anything to happen to him.''

Henry: ''We all know the risks involved. He'll know them, too. Before he volunteers.''

Alice: ''I think we should go now, dear.''

There were the usual thank-yous and goodnights. Then the sound of a door closing. I switched off the machine.

''That's all,'' I said.

''You're definitely in,'' Paul said. ''No doubt about it.''

Angela looked at me. Curious expression.

''The ef profits from you,'' she said. ''Mightily.''

''That needn't concern us,'' I said. ''What stresses me is that on all the tapes we've heard, hours of them, there's been no mention of the stopping of Harris.''

''My God, you're right,'' Paul said.

''I was hoping for a confession,'' I said. ''Or at least an obvious reference.''

''Oh, but there was,'' Angela said quickly. ''On that last tape, Lydia said she liked you. Alice said, 'Be careful. You know what happened the last time.' Then, at the end, Lydia repeated that she liked you and hoped nothing would happen to you. She was making a reference to what happened to Harris.''

''Possibly,'' I acknowledged. ''It's one interpretation. Another could be entirely innocent. Alice merely referring to an unhappy affair that Lydia had in the past. Then Lydia, at the end, expressing a normal anxiety that something might happen to me if I join in on the bombings. It's just not definite. We haven't tied them to Harris' stopping with any physical evidence. Well . . . no use worrying it. Perhaps I'll get what we need this weekend. Let's hope so.''

After they left, I sat in my suspended plastifoam sling and went into my own blend of alpha and self-hypnosis. I came out of it twenty minutes later, calm and relaxed. As far as I was concerned, it was as good as Hammond's satori.

I had brought home a single file to scan. It was an abstruse report from my Genetics Team. It concerned a process known as "auto-adultery," which one of our laboratory wits had dubbed "masturbation carried to its logical conclusion." Briefly, it was a technique of taking the DNA from the egg of one human ef and using it to inject another egg from the same object and fertilize it. The child bred would be, genetically, entirely the ef's, with no em sperm involved. In the process we were developing, entry into the "mother" egg was made by laser surgery.

The technique was still experimental, of course, but the concept had been proved feasible. There was no reason why it could not be made generally available. I hesitated to imagine the social, political, and economic consequences. Even more important, I had doubts of its genetic value.

Even assuming a Grade A genetic rating of the efs selected for such procreation, wouldn't there be a deterioration of the gene pool, simply by the loss of variety supplied by the em sperm? In other words, would we be risking a kind of inbreeding, a never-ending reproduction of identical efs? (An ef's cell contains no Y chromosome.) Perhaps it was em chauvinism that conditioned me, but I felt the dangers were real.

What it all came down to, I computed, was—what kind of a society did we want? Ten years from now? Fifty? A hundred? We had not yet decided that.

It was best, I thought, to cultivate pragmatism, trying to cope with each change as it developed. The science of futurism had its limits, doomed to failure by the invention, discovery, development of mutations impossible to foresee.

One thing I was certain of: There was no way, *no* way to halt change. Or even to postpone it. Declare a moratorium on all scientific research, destroy all laboratory equipment, dismantle all the paraphernalia of science, and still you would have someone, somewhere, ef or em, pacing in a drafty attic perhaps, scrawling symbols on a blackboard, erasing, scribbling more.

We could not stop the future. We could only hope it didn't stop us.

We arrived at the dirt access road a little before 1145 Saturday morning.

"There it is," Lydia said.

She nodded toward a marker at the roadside: a large pseudofolkart cutout of a human hand, one finger pointing toward the river. The knuckles had HAMMONDS' POINT painted across them in flaky red paint.

"Cutesy," I said.

I turned slowly onto the dirt road, slowed even more as we bumped over the rusted railroad tracks. I looked about casually. If Mansfield had installed the cameras, he had performed a good service; I didn't spot them.

I had expected the "interesting people" to be there before us, waiting. But only a single car was parked outside the house. I guessed it to be about a 1980 model. Hammond had a yen for the obso.

He came out the front door, waving, as we pulled up. He was wearing a brown corduroy suit, suede bush boots, a checked flannel shirt. He was smoking his silly pipe. The country squire.

We had brought them a two-kilo package of probisks, the round container a reasonably accurate plastic imitation of an old English biscuit tin. Of course, it was labeled "Olde English Tea Biscuits." Hammond was delighted.

We went into the kitchen where Alice was preparing food. She kissed Lydia's cheek, smiled at me. Even in a cheerfully patterned "rustic" dress, she was a gray ef. Lydia stayed with her while Hammond took me on a tour of the grounds. We went first to the edge of the cliff overlooking the river. The view was magnificent. He swept his arm around in a fustian gesture.

"Imagine all this as it was originally," he commanded me. "Virgin forest as far as the eye could see. Untouched. Unspoiled by the hand of white men. And then, coming up the river in their birchbark canoes, a band of red Mohawks, with the pelts of mink and otter and beaver to trade."

I was tempted to ask, "Do you really think the Mohawks traded this far East? And did they really have mink pelts?" But I wouldn't interrupt his glorious oratory for the world.

It continued as we wandered about the house. He pointed out the thick stone walls of the foundation.

"Actually a fort," he revealed. "Not all the Indians who arrived came to trade."

Politely, I admired everything. In truth, it was a pleasant place on this mild spring afternoon. I heard birdcalls. As promised, the air was clear. The sky was cloudless azure.

"And now," he said, "the *pièce de résistance*. Follow me. . . ."

Pièce de résistance, I mused. That must be Mohawk for "unwilling squaw."

We went back into the kitchen. The efs looked up from their service.

"I want to show Nick the tunnel," he said, excited as a boy.

"Henry, you'll muck up everything," Alice snapped at him.

"Just take a minute."

With his heel, he pulled a rag rug aside. It had concealed a trapdoor with an iron ring set into a recess so the floor was perfectly flat. He looked for my expression of surprise. I obliged.

"Y'see," he explained, "in case of Indian attack, they held them off as long as possible from behind the stone walls. But if push came to shove, they nipped down through here. Now follow me. Watch your head, Nick."

He bent and, with some effort, raised the trap.

"Original hinges," he said proudly. "Hammered iron."

He took a cadmium-celled lantern from a kitchen shelf and led the way down a narrow wooden staircase. I followed cautiously. At the bottom, we stood on a packed earthen floor. He moved the light about. It was a small chamber, not too deep; we had to stoop. The walls appeared to be marl. It was cooler and damper than the upstairs rooms.

"Probably used for a fruit cellar," he said. "To store apples and such during the winter."

"And firewater," I said maliciously.

"What? Oh, yes. That, too. Now follow me closely, Nick, and watch your head."

He led the way into the small opening of a tunnel cut through the clayey earth.

The walk, or creep, took only a few minutes. We came up against a barred iron gate, fastened on the inside with an obso chain and padlock. We looked out onto the surface of the river, a few meters below us.

"Escape?" I said.

"Right!" he said triumphantly. "Out through this gate and you practically step onto the beach."

"You think they kept a boat moored?" I asked.

"Shouldn't wonder," he said portentously.

He looked at me expectantly.

"Amazing," I breathed.

He seemed satisfied.

We retraced our steps. When we came to the wooden stairway leading up to the kitchen, he paused and played his torch behind the steps. He found a small box, held it out to me. He beamed the light to illuminate the contents. I peered in.

"Arrowheads," he whispered. "Three. Genuine. Indian. Arrowheads. I found them in the dirt floor of the tunnel."

"Amazing," I repeated.

He nodded solemnly in agreement. Dolt.

We had a reasonably profitable lunch. We filled our plates from the pot of stew simmering on the obso electric range and brought them to the dining table in the big room. There was also a large bowl of greens.

"All from plants in the woods," Hammond bragged. "All natural. You've never tasted anything like this before."

That was not reassuring. During our tour I had identified at least three toxic species, including a particularly noxious toadstool. But I said nothing. Nor did I make any reference to the missing "interesting people" I had been invited to meet.

We all served in the cleanup after dinner. Then we sat in chintz-covered chairs in the living room while Hammond lectured on Oriental philology. His accent was atrocious. Finally, recalling his duties as host, he brought out a small bottle of something. He and I took drinks; the efs declined—thus proving their superior intelligence. Lydia was making a valiant effort to stay awake. Alice knitted placidly, pushing back and forth in an obso wooden rocker.

It was close to 1630 when we heard the sound of approaching cars. Hammond stopped his monologue immediately, rose, looked out the window.

"Here they are," he announced. I thought his manner suddenly tense, but perhaps not.

The four objects who came through the door, ef and three ems, had arrived in two cars. I could not see the license plates, but perhaps Mansfield's cameras had caught them.

The newcomers were dressed casually. The taffy-haired ef was wearing a jolly plaid zipsuit with an overjacket of plastifur. Two of the ems had black turtleneck sweaters. They looked like brothers. One carried a small cassette machine. I knew what *that* was. Those three were young. The other was an obso, perhaps forty. He was a short, barrel-shaped em, chunky through the shoulders. He had a great, black walrus mustache. Dyed, I suspected.

127

I recognized him immediately. Dr. Thomas J. Wiley. He was a genetic biologist who had won several prizes for his services on shortening normal gestation periods by enzymatic manipulation. I had studied with him at Harvard. But that had been almost ten years ago; I doubted if he'd remember me. He did.

"Nicholas Flair!" he said, coming toward me with outspread arms. "After all these years! How nice to see you again."

He gripped me in a surprisingly strong embrace, then withdrew to slap my arms while he examined me critically.

"Yes, yes." He nodded. "A few more lines. What, no fountain of youth from that respected Division of yours?"

"Not yet, sir," I said. "We're serving on it."

He nodded again, suddenly sober.

There was a flurry of introductions. The tall, willowy ef was Martha Wiley, the doctor's daughter. She was also serving in her father's specialty. The two ems were, as I had guessed, brothers: Tod and Vernon DeTilly. Tod was a nuclear physicist, Vernon a neuropharmacologist. It was Tod who circled me casually, glancing occasionally at an instrument on his wrist. I was happy I had not swallowed a transmitter.

Chairs were brought from the kitchen. We settled in a rough oval, only Dr. Wiley standing. He was evidently the leader.

"Well," he said genially, "here we all are. Dr. Flair, we know you for a very brilliant, very talented young man. You see? I do not say 'em.' Man. We would not waste your time. Also, we have a long drive to make, another visit, so I will speak bluntly and to the point."

I looked at him in puzzlement, then looked around at the others. They were all staring at me.

"You see, Dr. Flair," he continued, "all of us in this room are members of a secret organization that—"

I rose hastily to my feet, held up a hand.

"Please, Dr. Wiley," I said. "I think perhaps I better leave."

"No," he said. "I think perhaps you better stay."

"If it's anything that might compromise my official—"

Now he held up his hand.

"We do not have the time," he said. "Vernon, play the tape."

Obediently, the DeTilly em pressed the Start button of the cassette machine held in his lap. I heard my own voice. . . .

"About a year ago—well . . . a little less than that—an African nation was admitted to statehood in the US. We can do a lot for

128

them—socially, economically, medically, culturally. But they have one tribe, about ten thousand objects, who are national fanatics and oppose statehood. These objects are primitives. . . .''

Dr. Wiley made a gesture. DeTilly stopped the tape. I turned slowly to look at Lydia. Her face was flushed but her chin was up; she returned my stare without flinching.

"Lydia!" I said with shocked disbelief.

"Following orders." Wiley shrugged. "Playing an important role."

"Oh, yes," I said bitterly. "I presume this secret organization of yours has high ideals?"

"The highest," he said.

"But you are quite willing to use despicable means to achieve your ends—is that it?"

"Any means!" he said in a passionate voice. "Any means, including violence, murder, terror, blackmail, that will bring this obscene government of yours to its senses."

How I wished I had *that* speech on tape. We'd have popped the lot of them into R&R and drained them.

"I don't wish to debate the morality of what you're doing."

"No," he agreed unexpectedly. "The time for debate has passed. Now is the time for action."

I was waiting for him to say, "Those that are not for us are against us." But his daughter said it.

"Dr. Flair," she said solemnly, "those that are not for us are against us."

I looked around the oval of staring faces.

"Time, Dr. Flair," Wiley warned.

"I don't understand," I said. "What do you want?"

"We want you to serve with us to the limit, and beyond, of your energy, talent, and devotion to the cause."

In how many forgotten revolts and revolutions had those ringing words been spoken?

"You're asking me to risk my career to—"

"No," he interrupted. "We're asking you to risk your life. Well?"

"You can't expect me to decide now, this minute?"

"Can and do. Well?"

I collapsed back into my chair, sat a minute with lowered head, hand covering my eyes. What melodrama! Finally I straightened up, raised my head, looked at Dr. Wiley.

"At least tell me what you want me to do. So I can make an informed judgment."

"Informed judgment?" he repeated. He smiled suddenly, full lips pulling back from big white false teeth. "Yes, I remember Nicholas Bennington Flair and his informed judgments. Your fellow students called you 'The Thinking Machine.' Did you know that?"

"I heard."

He slapped his palms together briskly. "All right. So you can arrive at an informed judgment—we want, primo, all documentation of that little African assignment mentioned on the tape."

"Impossible," I said. "No documentation exists. All oral orders."

"I told you," Tod DeTilly said.

"A disappointment." Wiley shrugged. "But not fatal. Secondo, that famous severed head in your lab. Fred."

"What about him?"

"A photo or film of that head has never been released to the media. Correct?"

"Yes, that's correct. Why needlessly antagonize antivivisectionists and dog lovers?"

"Exactly. But I am certain such photos and films do exist. We want them, or copies of them."

I sat back, crossed my knees, put back my head, stared at the ceiling, apparently deep in thought.

"Dr. Wiley," I said flatly, "what proof do I have—or *any* evidence, for that matter—that you are what you claim to be, members of a secret organization?"

"I assure you we are. Nationwide, and growing daily."

"So you say. But how do I know it's not just the seven of you present in this room? Just seven hotheads. You want me to risk my life for you seven?"

They looked at each other, back and forth. Finally, Alice Hammond spoke:

"Tell him, Tom," she said flatly. "If he decides not to come in. . . ." She shrugged.

I knew what that shrug meant. The sweet ef. . . .

"You've heard of the Society of Obsoletes?" Wiley asked me.

"Those lunatics?" I cried. "Surely you don't—"

"Wait, wait—" He stopped me. "What you see in the Society of Obsos are eccentrics: antivivisectionists, ecology freaks, health food fanatics, occult religionists. That is exactly what we want you to see. That is the public image of the Society: a conglomerate of harmless loons writing letters to the media, marching in silly parades, making ineffectual demonstrations. But the Society is actually a two-tier organization. The second layer, the basic one, hidden, secret, is composed of professionals like ourselves. Scientists, mostly, but also teachers, businessmen, union leaders, journalists, academicians, politicians—all bound together in one determination: to stop the US Government from pursuing the course it is on, and to steer our society's destiny in a different direction.

"What direction?" I demanded.

"If my phrases sound obso to you, forgive me. But there are no new words or better words available. A society of personal liberty, freedom, justice, equality. A diversified society of individual choice, not decree by the Public Service. Does that satisfy you?"

"Dr. Wiley," I said earnestly. "I believe you are sincere. And the other objects in this room are sincere. But sincerity isn't enough. Can you give me evidence—any evidence at all—that what you've told me is operative?"

Again they looked at one another, heads swiveling.

"We've gone this far. . . ." Martha Wiley said.

"Dr. Flair," Tod DeTilly said, "you know about the recent wave of bombings, assassinations, kidnappings, and sabotage against scientific research facilities?"

"I've heard of them," I said cautiously.

"I'll bet you have." He laughed. "Not all of them were made public. Correct?"

"Yes."

"I will name a few that were *not* made public," he said. "The only way we could know about them is by having planned them and carried them out. Will that convince you?"

"Yes."

"In your Denver Field office, a hundred aborted fetuses destroyed. A cancer-sensitive strain of rats poisoned in Dallas. A cyclotron sabotaged in Illinois. A neurosurgeon assassinated at Berkeley. Is that sufficient—or do you want more?"

"That's sufficient," I said. "I'm convinced."

"Well then," Dr. Wiley said genially, "now that we have delivered our secrets to you, let's return to the secrets we want you to deliver. I have already mentioned the photographs or films of Fred. In addition, we have prepared a little list. Martha?"

She took a paper from her purse, unfolded it, rose to hand it to me. I scanned it swiftly. I was genuinely shocked, and let it show. I looked up at Wiley, feeling a sour smile stretch my face.

"It appears you have infiltrated my Division," I said.

"Oh, yes." He nodded. "We have objects everywhere."

Again I scanned the list. All the material they wanted—letters, reports, statistical studies, tapes, films—all concerned classified projects. Some had a higher priority than others, but none were known to outsiders—supposedly.

"Very technical material," I commented. "Quite specialized."

"I believe we will be able to compute it, Dr. Flair."

"I'm sure you will," I acknowledged. "But if this is the sort of thing you're looking for, why on earth do you want a photo of Fred? What possible good will that do you?"

"Surely you're not as obtuse as that, Dr. Flair?" he said. "Media exploitation."

"Oh-ho," I said. "You've decided to go public?"

He laughed.

"A nice way of putting it," he said. "Yes, our national leadership has decided the time is ripe to bring our activities to the attention of the public. To publish our aims. To make an appeal for public support. The reproduction of Fred's photograph and films in facsimile newspapers and on TV will show even the most indifferent citizen exactly what the government is doing, and show it in shockingly dramatic fashion. The secret material we are asking you to furnish will provide added ammunition. It will be a two-part program of public enlightenment and education: What we are against and what we are for."

I scanned again the list I held in my hand.

"I can't simply walk out of the compound carrying all this," I said. "If you have members inside, you must be aware of our security precautions."

"Oh, sure," Vernon DeTilly said, grinning cheerfully. "Your problem is getting the material out of the files—right?"

"That's not the big problem," I said. "I could manage that—at great risk. But how do I get it out of the gate? Every package is opened and searched. I am required to open my purse and empty my pockets every time I pass through, no matter how many times a day. X-rays. Metal detectors. Ultrasonic detectors. Odor analysis. The instrumentation is extremely effective."

"Microfilms?" Tod DeTilly suggested. "Or microdots?"

"In what kind of carrier?" I asked. "And by what means— swallowing? No, thanks. Not this mass of material."

"Broadcast?" Vernon DeTilly said. "To a mobile receiver parked outside the fence?"

"Impossible. We are constantly monitored electronically. They'd be on me in seconds."

"Mail?" Henry Hammond asked.

"Packages fluoroscoped," I said. "Letters opened on a random basis."

"Isn't restricted material *ever* taken out of the compound?" Lydia Ferguson asked faintly, then blushed at having ventured to speak in this august assemblage.

"Of course." I nodded. "But then you need a pass signed by your ruler. In my case, that would be Angela Berri, DEPDIRSAT. In addition, the gate guard is required to flash the ruler signing the pass to verify its authenticity."

"A problem," Dr. Wiley agreed. "It will be difficult, I know. But we have great faith in your intelligence, creativity, and talent at synthesizing an informed judgment."

"What you're saying," I told him, "is that I have no choice."

"That is correct, Nick," he said gently. "You have no choice."

"How do I contact you?"

Wiley looked at Hammond.

"I'll be in the city next week," Hammond said to me. "Alice is staying out here, but you can flash me at our apartment."

"By Monday," Dr. Thomas J. Wiley said.

"Monday?" I was incredulous. "You're only giving me two days to come up with a viable plan?"

"I told you," he said. "We have great faith in your talent."

I drove Lydia Ferguson back to New York through the gathering twilight. It was a trip made in morose silence.

"I'm sorry, Nick," she said once.

I didn't answer.

"I suppose you hate me," she said sometime later.

I didn't answer.

But then, the lights of Manhattan glowing across the river, I thawed.

"No," I told her, "I don't hate you. I know you did it from a deep belief."

"Oh, yes." She sighed. "A deep, *deep* belief."

She put her head on my shoulder, hugged my arm. We drove u
to her door that way.

She asked me to come up. If I hesitated, it was because I feare
she might want me to listen to all her rationalizations of her deep
deep belief. I had had enough histrionics for one day. But he
motives were simpler.

"Please?" she said, touching me.

When we were naked in her bed, she teased my body with ho
fingers.

"You're so profitable, Nick," she murmured. "You've used
lot of efs, haven't you?"

"No," I said, "you're the first. You routed my maidenhead.'
She laughed.

"And ems?" she asked.

"Of course."

"I've never tried it," she said.

"With ems?"

"Don't be silly." she giggled. "You know what I mean."

"I'm bisexual," I admitted. "By intellectual choice and physica
predilection. I think most objects are, admittedly or not. The sexua
preferences of obsos were conditioned by biological necessity and
hence by society. Neither prevail today. Efs can procreate withou
sperm. The preservation of the species is no more vital than it:
limitations. Now we can indulge our operative natures, which ar
androgynous."

"What does all that mean?" she asked.

"That I like to use both efs and ems."

"Oh, yes," she breathed. "Use me."

Perhaps her betrayal of me, via the tape on the African incident
excited her, empowered her. She was aggressive, bold, a leade
now, not a follower. Even while taking profit from her strong
attack, I puzzled her motives—and mine. Once again it came bacl
to mastery and surrender, but on a primitive level.

Even with my ears pressed flat between her sweated thighs,
pondered if what we felt was not operative on a social and political
perhaps even a philosophical level. It would not be the first time tha
physical spurs had a counterpart in moral and mental passions
Indeed, some obso thinkers believed it all one: a finite quantity o
"life force," dammed in the gonads, sure to break out in the cortex
It was interesting.

I resolved to move Paul Bumford's suggestion of an Ultimate Pleasure pill, the UP, from the Tomorrow File to an active project. It would require an immense amount of service: analysis by neurophysiologists of the physical nature of the orgasm, analysis by neuropsychologists of the emotive factors involved, and finally synthesis by specialists who, to my knowledge, did not yet exist: neurometaphysicians. It might be necessary to condition an entirely new breed of scientific investigators before the problem of the UP could be solved. Difficult. Arduous. But I hardly dared envision the reward. Simply the world and all.

X-10

Later—for months—I was to wonder to what extent the events of the following week were due to planning or due to chance. But that kind of deliberation is fruitless, of course. You become immobilized in a thicket of determination, free will, and-accident. A lot of kaka. Every object must make a choice between speculation and action. I had opted for action. I was willing to endure the consequences of that choice.

One curious consequence—I confess frankly—was a haunting suspicion that the satisfaction I felt in Lydia's bed that Saturday night sprang from a subconscious realization that I was using a doomed ef. But I didn't wish to compute that thought further.

Sunday:

In the morning I picked up a packet of Instaroids from Leon Mansfield at the Seventh Avenue Mess Hall. They were good, clear photos of the four visitors and the license plates of their cars. I delivered the packet to Angela Berri. By evening, she had obtained the home addresses of the four. I believe she served through Lieutenant Oliver of the New York Peace Department. It wasn't important; we never employed the input.

At our evening conference, I addressed Angela and Paul for almost an hour, describing the Saturday meeting at Hammonds' Point. I used the actual words of the participants as much as possible.

"So," I concluded, "that is what happened. We have no physical evidence of their complicity. I have the list they gave me—the

135

restricted material they want. But the list itself proves nothing. Common bond paper. Smudged fingerprints. A dicto-typeprinter we might identify, if we ever find the machine. They are intelligent, wary objects.''

"Is Dr. Wiley the leader?'' Angela asked.

"Of them? Yes. But I think his authority is limited. He spoke of 'our national leadership' in a tone that leads me to suspect he is not a member. If Paul's analysis is operative, if their activities are organized on a Geo-Political Area structure, then I'd guess Wiley is director of GPA-1. But he may be only their recruiting chief.''

"Suggestions?'' Paul said.

"When I saw that escape tunnel leading to the river bank, I thought it would be simple and obvious. Mansfield could plant incriminating material in there, from the river exit. I'd arrange a meeting with all of them. We'd alert Burton Klein and his bully boys and take the lot. We'd have them cold. But then Henry Hammond said his wife would be out there all week. We can't have Mansfield prowling around. Too much risk. We can forget the tunnel.''

"I agree.'' Angela nodded.

"I need a solution by tomorrow,'' I said. "The deadline. Here's a scenario—a little complex, but I think it will serve. I call Hammond tomorrow. I will obtain the material requested and deliver on X day at Y hour. His question: How will you get it through the gate? My answer: I will bribe the gate guard. That simple. I have fiddled the whole security setup by bribing the key object. His question: How much? My answer: Fifty thousand new dollars. Hammond will then say he has to check with his rulers—that probably means Wiley—and flash me back. All right so far?''

"With me,'' Angela nodded.

"Me, too,'' Paul said.

"All right,'' I went on. "Hammond flashes me back. Now it begins to get cute. His rulers are interested. But can I trust the guard? Meaning, can they trust me? They suspect I may want the love for myself. Or perhaps that fifty thousand will be for the guard, but it will just be the down payment on a blackmail plan that will go on and on. Hammond is a loon. I can manipulate him, implant the possibility of blackmail in our first conversation. I agree that the guard may prove to be too greedy. So I suggest that when I deliver the material, I bring the guard with me. They take still photos or tape of the guard receiving the payoff. Then they've got him hooked. He can't blackmail; he's implicated. They're home free—they think.''

''Who plays the guard?'' Angela asked.

''I will,'' Paul said.

''No good.'' I shook my head. ''They're inside, in my Division. They might have a file on you. It's got to be an object they know nothing about. A low-rank object. Angela, you've got to draw an em from Burton Klein.''

''No,'' she said definitely. ''Not yet. He'll have to be called in eventually, when we take them, but not yet.''

She rose and paced about my apartment, hugging her elbows. What an ef! Tight and tough as a tungsten coil. A brain that, by nature or conditioning, targeted instinctively. And the power she exuded! Not because of her rank. Put her on a factory assembly line and it would still be there. I wanted very much to be using her at that moment.

''Leon Mansfield,'' she said decisively. ''He'll do. We'll dress him up in a gate guard's zipsuit. What the hell is it? Brown? Tan? Nick, will Mansfield do?''

''No,'' I said. ''He's got to be in Public Service. That's the whole point of having them photograph the payoff. Evidence of attempted bribery of a Public Service employee to obtain restricted documents.''

''We can sign Mansfield on as a temporary consultant,'' she said.

''It might serve.'' I nodded. ''I think so. Obviously, they won't have a line on him. They won't be able to check out his Public Service record. If the meet is soon enough, it will go. Yes, I think we can fiddle it. All right. I set up the meet. I bring the evidence. Mansfield plays the gate guard. They take photos of him accepting the love, photos we'll use later to prove bribery. Then Klein moves in. Timing. It's all timing.''

''Yes—timing,'' Angela agreed. ''But we can strucutre all that. Paul?''

''Nothing wrong I can compute,'' he said slowly. ''Nick, do they carry weapons?''

''They didn't on Saturday,'' I said. ''I'm sure of that. Wiley said they had a trip to make, another visit. They wouldn't risk a random stop-and-search on the road. These objects are not simpletons.''

''All right,'' Angela said. ''Let's go ahead with it.''

"After I have it set up," I said. "I'll brief Mansfield. Then I'll brief Burton Klein."

"But at the very last minute," Angela warned. "His Division may be infiltrated, too."

She thought of everything.

Monday:

0945. I flashed Dr. Henry Hammond from a station outside the compound. I told him I thought I could diddle a gate guard. But the object had a Grade D genetic rating, and I wasn't sure I could trust him. If the guard cooperated, it would be from cupidity, not from a desire to overthrow the US Government. Hammond said he would have to "consult my rulers." I gave him my apartment code.

1745. Hammond flashed me back. He said his rulers approved of the plan, "in principle," but needed to know the gate guard's name and how much love he wanted. I told him the guard was Leon Mansfield, and he'd probably want 50,000 new dollars.

2330. Hammond flashed me again and said his rulers instructed me to offer Mansfield 25,000 new dollars.

Tuesday:

0930. I flashed Hammond and said the guard would take 35,000, but no less. He said he'd relay the message.

1840. Hammond flashed me at my apartment and said the 35,000 was acceptable. But could I compute any way to ensure the future silence of Mansfield other than stopping him, since his rulers avoided personal violence whenever possible. A giggle, that. I answered by saying that the most obvious solution would be to make the payoff before witnesses, in an isolated place where the transaction could be photographed. Like Hammonds' Point. He said he'd get back to me.

Wednesday:

0830. A call from Hammond to my apartment. He was off camera. He said his rulers approved of the plan. I was to bring the material requested to his summer place on Saturday, at 2030 precisely. I was to be accompanied by the bribed guard, Leon Mansfield. No one else. At that time, 35,000 new dollars would be turned over to Mansfield and the deal would be filmed. I said that was just dandy. I was almost certain they meant to stop Mansfield and reclaim their funds.

I was about to leave for my office, thinking of how to brief

AssDepDirSec Burton Klein on what would be expected of him, when my flasher chimed again. My father came on screen. He didn't look well.

"Nick," he said, "Mother's ill." His voice was unsteady.

"Bad?"

"Yes. I think so. She's in bed. I don't know. Bradford is here. He says she's just going. She won't eat."

"Can he get some fluid into her?"

"He says it'll have to be under sedation."

"She wants to die."

"Nick, make her live."

"How? We can strap her into machines. Shove tubes into her veins. Keep her heart pumping. Is that what you want?"

"No," he said. "You?"

"No," I said. "Let her go with will."

"I remember how it was at first," he said. "When we—"

He stopped suddenly. The brute wept. I waited patiently.

"Ahh," he said, "memory is a curse."

"Is it?" I said. "Put Bradford on."

"I can't," he said. "He's upstairs with her. He said about two weeks. Maybe more. Nick, I've got to go."

"Go?"

"Our plant in Connecticut. There's been a tragedy. We've lost a whole run of Poo-Poo Dolls. They're falling apart on the shelves. Something went wrong."

"Yes," I said.

"I stand to lose half a million."

"Yes," I said. "When do you want me?"

"As soon as possible."

I couldn't get a government hypersonic to Detroit. The regular flight had been suspended since six months previously, when a courier plane letting down over Lake Erie had swamped a pleasure boat with the sonic boom. Six objects had drowned. "The investigation is continuing. . . ."

"I'll get a commercial flight from Kennedy," I told my father's flickering image. "I'll be there at 1223."

"I'll hold my jet until you come in," he said. "I'll have the copter there to take you to Grosse Pointe."

We switched off. I moved precisely. I flashed my own office. One of my secretaries was in. I told him to book me on commercial

Flight 128 to Detroit, leaving at 1058. I told him to requisition a Section copter to get me to Kennedy. I flashed Paul Bumford's office. He wasn't in yet. I left a message: I was leaving on a threeday; he was to call Angela Berri for details. I flashed Angela's apartment. Her serving ef came on. She said her ruler was showering. I told her to get Angela to the flasher. Angela came on, wet, hair dripping, a big pink plastowel wrapped around her.

"What, Nick?"

"My mother is ill. I've got to take my threeday now."

"Take as long as you need."

"Can't. The meet is on for this Saturday."

"It's set?" she asked, coming alive.

"Definitely. Less than an hour ago Hammond flashed me. It's Saturday night at 2030. I'm to be at Hammonds' Point with Mansfield and the things they want. Paul will contact you. Have him pack the classified material in a bag, a box, a carton—anything. A transmitter at the bottom. Are you tracking?"

"Yes."

"Burton Klein will receive. The code is—listen carefully—the code is, 'That's everything you wanted.' Repeat."

"That's everything you wanted."

"Correct. Then Klein moves in—fast. I'll be back by noon on Saturday. I'll pick up the carton and Mansfield and drive up to Hammonds' Point. Any problems so far?"

"Nooo," she said slowly.

"Angela, you'll have to brief Klein and Mansfield. Will you do that?"

"Of course," she said briskly.

"The important point is the timing. Klein will have to be in position before I get there. Show him the Instaroids and map of the site. And Mansfield will have to be rehearsed on his role."

"I compute," she said. "Not to worry. Everything will be set by the time you get back. Nick, I'm sorry about your mother."

I was about to switch off when suddenly she held up her palm.

"Nick," she said, "will Lydia Ferguson be there? On Saturday?"

"I don't know," I said. "Is it important?"

"Yes," she said. "We want to take as many of them as possible. Especially Lydia. To tie them in with stopping Harris."

That made sense to me. I looked at my digiwatch.

140

"I'll flash Hammond," I said. "I'll arrange it."

"Good service, Nick," she said.

I took another few minutes to call Hammond. I explained I had to go out of town on personal affairs, but I would return in plenty of time for the Saturday meeting. I asked him if he'd drive Lydia Ferguson up to Hammonds' Point. I'd meet her there and drive her back to the city Saturday night.

"Of course, Nick m'boy," he said genially. "Of course."

X-11

I had time to scan two files on the flight to Detroit. The first originated in the Culture Section of the Department of Bliss. It dealt with the problem of televised executions. Ratings were down. Although not stated in the memo, it was in the state's interest—as I previously explained—to keep TV viewing audiences at optimum levels.

Capital punishment had been legislated in 1979, but only for federal crimes. Originally, these included treason, espionage, military desertion, kidnappings in which the victim was stopped, bombings or hi-jackings of interstate carriers, and assassination of government servers.

Over the years, the list of capital crimes had been enlarged to include all kidnappings, all homicides, threats and acts of terrorism against the state, use of and trafficking in restricted drugs, forgery of federal specie (including BIN cards), acts of public terrorism, defiling the US flag, willful political dissent with the intent of overthrowing the government, and "slanderous and/or libelous actions taken against public servers."

The guilty were executed by electric chair. Not only was it a popular TV special, but it was believed that TV exposure of capital punishment had a socially beneficial effect on those contemplating similar crimes.

In any event, ratings were off. The CULSEC memo asked for suggestions for more "visually stimulating" methods of execution that might regain the lost audience. The answers seemed obvious to me. Hanging, garroting, or even the revival of the guillotine would certainly prove more visually stimulating. And when these methods palled, as I supposed they eventually would, there was always drawing and quartering.

I scrawled quick notes on the border of the memo. One of my secretaries would transcribe them into acceptable officialese.

The second file, a thick one, was labeled "Hyman R. Lewisohn." It concerned the health of the em who, more than any other object, was the source of innovative ideas for the social, political, and economic progress of the US.

Lewisohn's genius had come to the attention of the government in a curious manner. Early in 1973, at a diplomatic reception in Teheran, an aide of the economic counselor to the US Embassy had been chatting with the Shah.

"That was quite an article by your Professor Lewisohn," the Shah mentioned.

"Ah yes, Excellency," the aide said, as smoothly as he could. "Remarkable."

The Shah looked at him closely, then smiled.

"Yes," he said. "Quite remarkable!"

An hour later a coded cablegram went to Washington: RUSH URGENT RECENT ARTICLE PROFESSOR LEWISOHN.

The article and the author were finally tracked down. Hyman R. Lewisohn was an obscure professor of economics at an obscure Midwestern liberal arts college. His article had been contributed ($25 honorarium) to an obscure monthly trade journal of the petroleum industry.

Working with only a primitive desktop computer, Lewisohn had proved, quite simply, that petroleum was too valuable to be burned as fuel. His theory was based on estimates of the finite quantity of petroleum in the world. He then computed the future cash value of heating oils, kerosene, gasoline, lubricants, naphtha, and similar products versus the future cash value of plastics, chemicals, drugs, dyes, fertilizers, and—a pure conception at the time—synthetic protein.

Lewisohn was offered a US Government post. He refused. The rank-rate was doubled. Again he refused. An Undersecretary of State was sent out to talk to him. It must have been a bewildering interview for the public server.

Hyman R. Lewisohn was the orphan of immigrant German Jews.

He was a victim of achondroplasia, with the enormous bulging forehead common in such cases. In addition, he had a crop of coarse red hair, paid absolutely no attention to his grooming or even to his personal cleanliness, and deliberately discouraged personal relationships by a rude and offensive manner. This included expectorating on the floor, loudly deriding the opinions of others, lewd gestures, and so forth. But he had one thing going for him: He was a genius.

Eventually, he stated his terms for public service. He was to be paid 100,000 new dollars annually. Living and working quarters were to be provided, with a relatively small, compact, versatile computer. His expenses for periodicals were to be paid, including the obso romantic novels to which he was addicted. The government agreed immediately, making the most lovable bargain since the purchase of Alaska. We had bought the power of Lewisohn's creativity.

And now that power was stopping. The file I scanned contained the most recent contingency plan from the Chief Resident at Rehabilitation & Reconditioning Hospice No. 4, near Alexandria, Virginia. It was not encouraging. The obso em was not responding to treatment. Bopne marrow transplant was recommended. I realized I had to go down there myself and scan him. His continued existence was—well, essential. That was all I could say.

When I came down the ramp at the Detroit airport, I was met by the blue-haired copter pilot. She was wearing her Chinese red zipsuit with the embroidered "flAIRToys" across one breast. The other disembarking ems looked at her voraciously.

"I'm supposed to guide you," she said archly.

"Oh? Where?"

"To the private plane area. Your father's over there, waiting at his jet. And the copter's parked there."

My father was standing at the cabin door of the sleek twin-jet. There were three objects with him. One em was Ben Baker, his production manager, carrying a plastic box. The other two were assistants, one ef, one em. Introductions were made. We all stroked palms.

"Thanks, Nick," my father said. "I knew I could depend on you."

"How's Mother?"

"No change. Ben, show him."

143

Baker took the lid off the box he was carrying, held it out to me. I bent over to look. The stench drove me back.

"Jesus Christ!" I cried. "What *is* it?"

"What is it?" my father repeated bitterly. "When it left our Connecticut factory five weeks ago it was a perfect Poo-Poo Doll. Something happened."

"Something sure as hell did," I agreed.

The mess in the box was putrescent. It stank. The plastic body of the doll had deteriorated, decayed almost to the point of liquidity. The rot had discolored the dress, stained the hair, even corrupted the little plastiglass eyes. It was a small corpus. Fetid.

"Ben," I said, "what caused it?"

"I wish I knew," he said miserably. "That's the most automated toy production line in the world. Computerized quality control. Bells go off if anything isn't just perfect. Automatic temperature and fluidity controls. Foolproof. Fail-safe. But we lost a whole run."

The ef assistant spoke up.

"Everything since that run has been perfect," she said. "We've done heavy analysis. They look fine."

"How long did the bad run last?" I asked.

"A week," Ben Baker said. "Actually a little less than six days. Before, the dolls were fine. After, the dolls were fine. But during? Murder!"

"We can't let it happen again," my father said furiously. "Never!"

On that happy note we separated. I watched my father's jet take off. Then I took the copter to Grosse Pointe. The ef pilot didn't stop chirping.

"What's your name?" I interrupted once.

"Beryl," she said. And started up again.

We landed on the front lawn. I handed my case over to a sad-faced Charles and went immediately to my mother's bedroom on the second floor. Shades and drapes were drawn. But enough late afternoon light came through to pearl the room. Mrs. McPherson was seated woodenly at my mother's bedside. I went over to the bed, picked up the feather hand, tried to find a pulse.

Head turned. Eyes opened slowly. Widened in consciousness. Then recognition.

Weakly: "Hullo, chappie."

"What's this?" I said sternly. "What's this?"

"Terminal nostalgia," she said.

I caught my breath.

"Don't fake me, chappie," she said.

"Have I ever?"

"No," she murmured. "No, no, no." In diminishing volume until I couldn't hear. "No, no, nooo. . . ."

I went over to one of the windows. I think I leaned my head against the frame. I was alert, aware of my own symptoms. Mental dislocation. Light-headedness. Something new: Physical vertigo. Weakness in the knees. A tilt. I thought I might fall. . . .

. . . annual visits to the cemetery at Mt. Clemens when I was a child. The grave of an older sister who had stopped at the age of three months from a respiratory infection. "Susan Bennington Flair, May 3, 1967—August 14, 1967." A smirking granite cherub.

. . . natural bacon frying for breakfast. A treat on Sunday morning. The kitchen filled with the scent. Dividing up the thick Sunday newspaper, a section to each. Gobbling bacon, shouting news items to each other. Rollicking.

. . . my parents dressed to go out. Mother in a strapless black velvet gown. Her bare flesh glowing. *Glowing!* Excitement and electricity. Her naked body moving inside the gown, bursting to spring free. A choker of small diamonds, no brighter than her sparkle. Goodnight, Nick! Goodnight! Goodnight!

. . . a midnight storm when the thunder. . . .

I flipped a spansule into the air, caught it in my mouth. A salted peanut. I swallowed it down. In a few moments the trembling ceased; memories faded.

I went back to my mother's bedside. I saw the dark green jar on the bedside table, picked it up, spilled a few of the pills into my palm. I recognized them.

"Did Dr. Bradford tell you about these?" I asked Mrs. McPherson.

She nodded.

"Please don't leave them at the bedside." I moved the jar across the room, to a dresser top.

I ate alone in the gloomy dining room. I sat at one end of the long oak table, surrounded by lost whispers and forgotten laughs. I had a slice of proham, a cold salad made of propots, two slices of natural

145

tomato—ruby red and mealy. I did what I could with it all, forking it down, staring at the walls, listening to echoes.

Then, in the library, I poured a large natural brandy. I took it up to Mother's bedroom.

"I'll stay awhile," I told Mrs. McPherson.

She nodded and left. I sat in a cane-backed armchair, sipping my drink, watching the bed. Occasionally my mother stirred, moved uneasily, groaned or muttered. It was not natural sleep. That dark green jar contained a potent barbiturate.

I went over to the bed, put my hand lightly on her hot forehead. She relaxed, calmed; the moans ceased. I was standing there, feeling the paper-thin skin beneath my fingers, when Mrs. McPherson returned. She was carrying a tray of dishes, covered with a large plastinap. She hadn't been gone more than fifteen minutes. She wasn't giving an inch. Mother was *hers*. I left the two of them. Together.

It was a black night, mild and moonless. A tug hooted somewhere. A jetliner droned over. Then the silence crept back. I walked slowly down toward the water, peering about for the garden table and chairs. I found them, finally. I sat there in the dark, sipping my brandy slowly, almost tonguing it.

I stirred, eventually, when bright lights flashed on in the guesthouse. I heard loud music. New jazz. It was probably Beryl, dancing about in her red zipsuit or inspecting her bare breasts critically before a mirror, peering at them through a cloud of cannabis smoke. I went back to the house and called Millie. No answer.

I poured another brandy, took it up to my suite. I showered, dressed in tooty civilian clothes, called Millie again. No answer. I finished the brandy in two gulps. There was an effect now, a welcome lack of caution, irresponsibility triumphant. I drove into Detroit, singing.

Millie wasn't at her apartment. I started a crawl of taverns we had visited together. I drank a petronac, petrovod, petrorum—whatever I saw first; it made no difference. I didn't find Millie. By midnight I was moving sideways through a blurred world, slipping by everyone, giggling.

I found her finally. I was in a tumultuous place, somewhere, raised my head from my drink, looked in the mirror. A stranger there. And over his shoulder, across the room, there was Millie, sitting with another ef and two tooty ems. I swung around on the barstool, so quickly that I spun off, staggering.

"Hey," I yelled. "Hey, Millie!"

I went banging toward them, knocking into tables, chairs, shoving objects out of the way. A burly em suddenly stood before me.

"Be good or be gone," he said pleasantly.

I got a knee into his groin and he went down, mouth open. Grinning, I clawed my way toward Millie.

"Hey, Millie!" I called joyously.

Then I was in an alley. I was on the bricks, slime under my cheek. I doubled over, drew up my knees, covered my face with my hands.

They took me with their boots. Not speaking. Just breathing hard. It hurt. How it hurt.

Just before I went out, I heard an ef screaming, "Stoppit! Stoppit! Stoppit!"

I came up slowly. Through a bloody haze I was staring at a plaster ceiling, paint chips peeling away. My chest was cold and wet.

I looked down. Millie was rubbing a plastinap of Jellicubes along my ribs. I looked around. Her apartment. And two uniformed bobs from the Detroit Peace Department, watching. One held my BIN card, one my purse.

"Oh, Nick," Millie said anxiously. "Are you tip-top?"

Beautiful question.

"Tip-top," I nodded. "What time is it?"

"Almost 0200. How do you feel?"

"I told you. Tip-top. Would you make me some coffee?"

She scurried off. I slowly swung my legs over the edge of the bed. Cautiously, I sat upright. Something was wrong on my left side. I probed gently.

"Broken?" one of the bobs asked.

I took a deep breath. No sudden, sharp anguish. Just dull pain.

"I don't think so. Contused perhaps."

"You want to press charges?" he asked.

"That wouldn't be wise," I said. "Would it?"

"No," he said. "It wouldn't."

"Did I cause any damage?" I asked.

"You kicked an em in the balls," the other bob said. "The manager."

"Can I have my purse?"

I took out my wallet, riffled the bills. I thought some love was missing. But I had spent a lot.

"You think fifty will make him feel better?" I asked.

"Fifty will cure him," one of them said.

I handed over the fifty, then added twenty more.

"Sorry for the trouble," I said.

"It happens." One of the bobs shrugged. "But an em like you—in a place like that. You want to watch it."

They both nodded virtuously. I was given back my BIN card. They departed. I was getting out of my clothes when Millie returned, bringing a plasticup of something black and steaming.

"Oh, Nick," she said sorrowfully, looking at me.

"I vomited?"

"Yes, you did."

"Not in here? " I asked, horrified.

"No. In the alley. When they were picking you up."

I took a sip of coffee. If it had any flavor, I couldn't taste it. It wasn't important. It was hot and wet. I took slow sips as I continued undressing.

"I'll wipe off your clothes," Millie said. "With a damp rag."

"Thank you." I smiled. "Later. Is my face all right?"

"Your right ear is a little scratched. From the bricks. But you can hardly notice."

I examined myself. Red blotches on shoulders, arms, ribs, hips, thighs, calves. I knew what color they'd be tomorrow, and the next day, and the next. And I could feel the pain starting in my back and buttocks. A complete service.

"Do you have any tape, Millie?"

"Tape?"

"Any kind. Mending tape? Electrician's tape?"

"Nooo, I don't think so. Nick, should I go out and get some?"

"At 0200? Thanks, dear, but no. Do you have an old thermasheet I can rip up? I'll send you a new one."

"Don't say that. You don't have to give me anything."

I tore long strips. I held one end in place, then slowly revolved. Millie wound me like a mummy. I kept telling her to keep it tight. Finally my thorax was wrapped, armpits to waist. It still hurt. But it would hold. I tucked in the loose end.

"I'm sorry, Millie," I said. "Please excuse me. I know I ruined your evening."

"Oh, Nick . . . I was so happy to see you again. Why didn't you call?"

"I tried."

It seemed a ridiculously formal conversation. A naked em, chest mummified, standing before a fully dressed ef.

"Another coffee?" she asked.

"No," I said. "Two liters of cold water."

"Do you think—" she asked tentatively.

"Let's try," I said. "But you must be very gentle."

"Ever so gentle," she cried happily. "I'll do *everything*!"

But I didn't let her. For some reason I couldn't compute, it was important to me that I give her profit. I never penetrated her child's body that night, not once, but I employed lips, tongue, fingers, eyelashes, toes, until she was screaming with delight, and I had to hush her, fearing the neighbors would call the bobs again.

It went on and on. She seemed insatiable, but I would not end until she signaled me. Finally, she pushed me away and lay back exhausted, rosy and sweated.

"Who is Lydia?" she gasped.

"Lydia?" I said. "I don't know any Lydia."

"In the alley. Just before you passed out. You said, 'Lydia.' "

"Did I?" I said. "That's interesting."

Late the next morning I watched while Dr. Bradford examined my mother. She was awake, babbling nonsense.

"Yes, yes," Bradford kept saying. "Yes, yes."

I followed him out into the hallway. He was a short, thick, comose man. About my age. Competent.

"Well, doctor?" I asked him.

"Well, doctor?" he said ironically. "You want her force-fed?"

"No. You want off the case?"

He thought seriously about that.

"I should," he acknowledged.

"Strap her in—"

"Oh, don't give me all that kaka," he exploded angrily. "I've heard it all before. I simply have to do nothing—right? As if sins of omission are less tainted than sins of commission."

"You want off," I said stonily, "you're off. It won't change things."

"Goddamned son of a bitching bastard!" he cried furiously. He actually stamped his foot.

"My sentiments exactly, doctor," I said.

"Ahh," he said. "The dear lady."

This quote from Leon Mansfield startled me.

"Would you come up to my rooms, please?" I asked him. "A professional consultation. I have some natural brandy."

"Only sensible thing I've heard today," he grumbled, and followed me up the stairs.

I poured us each a glass. Then I stripped down. He took a look at the colors.

"Pretty," he said. "Hit by a truck?"

"Two of them," I said. "Check the ribs, please."

He helped me unwrap the stripping of torn sheet. He probed me gently.

"Breathe deeply," he commanded. "Again. Again. Pain?"

"No punctures," I said. "No fractures. I think."

"Contusions," he said. "Here and here. Drive back with me. We'll take some plates."

"No," I said. "It's not that important. I'll have it done when I get back to New York. I have wide tape here. Just strap me up."

"Idiot," he growled.

"Exactly," I agreed.

He taped me up. We finished our brandies. He wanted to give me a meperidine. I insisted on a codeine. It took me another brandy to get it. By the time he departed, he was feeling no pain. And neither was I.

I wandered about the grounds. A gray, overcast day. I was gray and overcast. Codeine plus hangover. But I was computing in a dazed kind of way, jumping circuits.

I think I ate something. I know I visited my mother again. We held hands and chatted away like magpies. Mrs. McPherson didn't seem shocked, but I know Mother and I were trading absurdities. It pleased Mother. I think. It certainly pleased me.

Afterward, the pain coming on again, my whole body aching, I debated: Another codeine? No, I decided. Because the anxieties were worse than the pain. So I popped a new manipulated amitriptyline I just happened to have in my case. It worked on me like a hypnotic. Get rid of the anxieties and then you can sleep.

I slept until noon. I took a sponge bath and shaved carefully. I was tracking. A little deliberate, a little dulled, but functioning. My bruises hurt like hell. I accepted the pain gladly. I had been lucky and I knew it.

I spent most of the day with Mother. She had been off barbiturates for almost twelve hours; I thought it safe enough to allow her the natural vodka she craved. I cut it with water, but she didn't notice. Her color improved, her spirits perked, she laughed.

The copter had taken off for the airport at 1700, to pick up my father. At 1730, I took a bottle of natural brandy and glasses out to the lawn table. I waited for him there, not drinking. It was almost 1840 before I heard the copter throb. Beryl came slipping in neatly, hovered, set down gently. A skillful ef.

Ben Baker got out first, then turned to assist Father. He climbed out wearily, clumsily. Sad to view. They ducked low as the main rotor revved, then slowed to a stop. I stood, called out. They saw me and came over. Both were obviously fatigued, depressed.

"Nick," my father said.

Ben Baker nodded briefly. I gestured toward the brandy.

"Medicine," I said. "Doctor's orders."

They accepted gratefully. Father downed his in one gulp, shuddered, drew a long breath, then held out his glass for a refill. We all sat down at the metal table.

"How is she?" my father asked.

"Better," I said. "A little. I got some fluid into her."

"Eat?"

"No. You have any luck?"

Baker shook his head gloomily.

"Can't find it, Nick," he said. "Checked out everything. It couldn't have happened, but it did."

"And might happen again," Father said. "Goddamn it to hell!"

"Faulty input?" I suggested.

Baker shook his head. "No way. We're still using plastic from the same shipment. It's up to specifications."

"Maybe heavy analysis of the spoiled doll will tell the story," I said. "Wait for that."

Neither seemed cheered by the possibility.

"Ben," I said, "give me a rough idea of how the doll is made. The process. Just the highlights."

"We get the plastic in pellets," he said. "Mix for flesh color desired. We market the Poo-Poo worldwide. White, pink, tan, yellow, red, brown, black. The plastic is melted down, poured hot into alloy molds. Front molds and back molds. The Poo-Poo tubing and devices are laid in the back mold. The front is pressed on and heat-welded. Excess is sheared. The complete body is dunked for cooling and washing. Then it goes for eye insertion, facial stenciling, wig-gluing, dressing. These are semihand operations. Then inspection and packing. Shipping. That's it.''

"But the plastic is controlled?"

"Absolutely. Fluidity and temperature. Automatic.''

"What about the molds?"

"Steam-scalded after every impression. Practically sterile.''

I computed the problem a few moments. We all watched the night creep in, darkness flowing around us, coming from the lake like fog.

"Ben," I said, "where does the factory get its water?"

"What water?"

"When you wash the hot doll bodies to cool them and rinse off scrap.''

"In a tank," he said. "Constantly running, constantly flushed.''

"Where from?"

"The Connecticut River. We pump in one end and have a gravity flow out the other.''

"Is the intake filtered?"

"What are you getting at, Nick?" my father demanded.

"Ben, is the water intake filtered?"

"A gross filter. Just to take the crap out. Nick, we don't *drink* the stuff.''

"What's upstream from you?"

"Nick, I'm not following.''

"What is this?" my father asked again. Bewildered.

"What kind of factories are upstream from you?"

"Oh—let's see. . . . A foundry. Alloys. A bauxite refinery. Some small tobacco-processors. A rayon manufacturer. A few others. I don't know them all.''

"Do they exhaust into the river?"

"Not if they want to stay out of jail. You know the law.''

"But an accident? Or maybe a quick dump at night, hoping no one could trace it? Like that rayon factory, pouring carbon disulphide into the—''

"Jesus Christ!" he shouted.

He stood suddenly, spilling his brandy all over the table. He began running awkwardly toward the house, elbows flopping out at his sides.

"What?" my father cried in alarm. "Where is he running? What's happening?"

"Calm down." I soothed him. "He's going to flash your Connecticut factory to order objects to check on accidental or deliberate spills in the river from upstream plants. The ruined run of dolls was probably rinsed in polluted water. Maybe carbon disulphide sludge from the rayon factory. Why didn't you dunk the hot doll bodies in sulphuric acid and be done with it?"

"Oh, God." He groaned.

"You've got to monitor the water intake," I told him. "Constant analysis. It can be done automatically."

"Nick-ol'-as!" he shouted, leaned over, pounded my back. My bruises. I tried not to wince.

"You've got to come into the business," he said. "*Got* to!"

"Let's not go into that again."

"Nick, I'm getting old," he said piteously. "I need help."

He watched Beryl finish strapping down the copter. She glanced toward us, then waggled off toward the guesthouse.

"You need help?" I said scoffingly.

"Not with that." He giggled.

He dragged me up to the house for dinner, hugging my arm, laughing like a maniac.

"I feel twenty years younger," he declared. "I want to buy you something. Anything. What would you like?"

"Nothing," I told him. "You know I've got everything."

It was almost 2200 before I could get away from them. I pleaded a heavy schedule on the following day. I left them in the library, glassy-eyed and belching, trading coarse and not very funny jokes. I felt sorry for Beryl. Briefly.

I looked in at my mother on the way upstairs. She appeared to be sleeping. Mrs. McPherson was sitting there, ramrod straight in her chair. But her eyes were closed. They opened when I put a wool blanket softly across her.

"Thank you, sor," she whispered.

At the top, in my suite, I checked the glued thread from the jamb to the door of my secret place. It had not been disturbed. I switched on the light, locked the door behind me. I stacked the four books alongside the sprung Morris chair, poured a brandy, settled down. . . .

Egon Schiele had done many nudes, em and ef. The thighs were deliberately spread, genitalia represented in almost finicky detail. I found these portraits so harrowing, I could not view them without dread. The artist had gone beyond sexuality. I sensed something of death in beauty, beauty in death.

At this point in time, I wanted only to look into the eyes of the self-portraits. There was a demented possession there. But perhaps I considered it "demented" simply because it was foreign to me, not part of my conditioning.

When you cannot comprehend what is being said, if an object seems to be wildly pleading in a language utterly unknown to you, then your instinctive reaction might well be fear. Terror. That was close to what I felt, staring into the burning eyes of Egon Schiele. I strove to compute. There was something for me there. I wanted to learn what those eyes knew.

X-12

I called Ellen Dawes from the Detroit airport, told her what flight I was taking, asked her to have a Section copter meet me at Kennedy. She must have alerted Paul Bumford; he was waiting at the compound pad when we let down.

"Nick," he said, "what happened to your ear?"

"Stumbled and scraped it on a brick wall. Nothing serious."

"How's your mother?"

"All right, thank you. Are we set?"

"Everything ready. We've got—"

"Wait a minute. Let's go over it with Angela."

"Can't. She's gone down to Washington."

I thought a moment, then nodded.

"That's Angela," I said. "So she can be the first to tell DIROB his daughter was arrested for homicide and crimes against the state."

"More likely tell the Chief Director," Paul said. "Anyway,

154

she's made arrangements for an open line to DIVSEC from 1990 on.''

I glanced at my digiwatch.

"We've got time. Come up to my place. I need a fresh zipsuit. You can fill me in there.''

In my apartment, Paul followed me into the nest. When I stripped down, he saw the taping and bruises. His eyes widened.

"My God!'' he breathed. "Nick, what the hell happened?''

"Nothing happened. A disagreement.''

"Are you all right?''

"Of course. Minor aches and pains, that's all.''

"What's under the tape?''

"Jesus Christ, Paul,'' I shouted. "Don't stress me. Possibly a crack or two. I'll have a plate taken tomorrow. I'm functioning. I'm perfectly capable of winding up this whole thing. Now . . . what have you got?''

He pouted.

"All right.'' I sighed. I patted his cheek. "I'm sorry I yelled at you.''

He brightened.

"I don't mind, Nick. Really I don't. I know you've been pressurized.''

"Just tell me what's happening.''

"Burton Klein has been briefed. He and a squad of twenty objects left here at midnight. They're in position now, reporting every ten minutes to DIVSEC. So far everything is quiet, no unusual activity.''

"Good.''

"Before we left, Klein picked out a car for you, a white sedan. There's a beeper under the hood. Klein will track you in.''

"That was smart.''

"The car is in the motor pool now, under guard. The carton of material is in the trunk. I assembled it. Everything on the list.''

"Transmitter?''

"At the bottom. We've got omnidirectional mikes: they'll pick up everything. The Electronics Team rigged it. We checked it out here, but Klein will stop you on the road up there for a final check.''

"Were you there when Angela briefed Klein?''

"No, she briefed us separately. But I talked to Klein later. He's a

155

pig, Nick, but he knows what he's doing."

"As long as he knows the code."

"He does. He said to ask you if you wanted a gun. You can draw one from DIVSEC if you want it."

"A gun? What for? These objects aren't thugs."

"I told that to Klein. He said maybe you should carry one—just in case."

"No, thanks. I don't anticipate any violence. If Klein knows his service, no one will be injured."

I came into the living room, zipping up my fresh uniform.

"Now what about Mansfield?" I asked.

"Angela said she briefed him and furnished a gate guard's zipsuit. She said to pick him up at 1700 at 'the usual place.' That's all she'd tell me. She said you'd know where it is. Do you know, Nick?"

"Yes."

"No one tells me anything," he grumbled. "Anyway, are the times right?"

"Barring accidents. If I'm to pick up Mansfield at 1700, I better leave here in about"—I glanced at my digiwatch—"in about forty minutes."

"Can I come with you, Nick?"

I smiled at him.

"No way. But thank you, Paul."

"You will be careful?"

"Of course. Anything else?"

"No, I . . . Oh, yes, another thing: Angela has already given orders for their interrogation. After Klein takes them, they're to be separated and sent to Hospices 2, 4, and 7. She said we'd get better results if we kept them apart."

I shook my head admiringly.

"She thinks of everything," I said.

"She surely does," he said. "Bitch!"

We ran through the whole thing once more to make certain the timing and communications were as foolproof as possible. Paul said he'd wait at DIVSEC headquarters for news of how the raid went. That reminded me of something else.

"Did Angela arrange for an Uncle Sam?" I asked.

The law allowed the security section of any government department to make arrests for crimes against the state, providing the arresting officers were under the command of a server of the Bureau of Public Security (formerly the FBI) of the Department of Rewards. (The DOR had originally been called the Department of Justice, then the Department of Merit, then the Department of Virtue, and now the Department of Rewards. Everyone agreed the title was not quite right yet. The Office of Linguistic Truth was working on it.)

In any event, the law requiring a BPS server to be in command when arrests were made by security officers of other government departments was easily circumvented. A token BPS officer was requisitioned, put in nominal command, and the necessary documents executed. The borrowed BPS object, who was rarely present at the time and place of the arrests, was known in Public Service circles as an Uncle Sam.

Paul assured me Angela Berri had remembered to requisition an Uncle Sam. The required papers had been filed in Washington. Everything was legal.

I picked up Leon Mansfield at the Mess Hall on Seventh Avenue at 1700, after driving the white sedan around the block twice, despairing of finding a parking space, and finally double-parking in front of the restaurant. I could see him inside, playing his chess game. I honked the horn twice. He looked up, saw me, folded his little chessboard, put it in his pocket, and came out to me.

He was wearing a soiled raincoat, but took it off before he got in the car. His tan zipsuit, a gate guard's uniform, fitted reasonably well.

"Who's winning?" I asked him.

"What? Oh, you mean the chess game. Well, when you play yourself, you win and you lose. Am I right, Mr. Nicholas Flair?"

"Right." I nodded and swung into traffic.

He didn't say a word while I maneuvered over to the West Side Freeway.

"Did Angela Berri give you your orders?" I asked, as we headed north.

"I have my orders. The dear lady."

After that, there was no more talk. He seemed unusually reticent. I was just as happy; his cryptic comments, always hinting at something beyond the obvious, were wearisome.

157

When we were about thirty meters from the access road to Hammonds' Point, I slowed down, trying to spot the sign. An object came out onto the highway, signaled us to a halt with a swinging lantern. There was a red filter over the lens.

He was wearing a white plastisteel helmet with transparent faceguard. His body was bulky in nylon-alloy armor: cuirass, cuisses, greave. He looked like an obso baseball catcher, before soccer became the Great American Game. He came around to the driver's side.

"Dr. Flair?" he said.

He turned the torch on my face, briefly.

"Yes," he said. "I've seen you around. I'm Art Roach, X-0 of DIVSEC. Flair is here."

I looked around, thinking he was speaking to someone else. But then I saw his throat mike. The miniaturized transceiver would be in his helmet.

"Where's Klein?" I asked.

"Roger," he said. "Pull off to the side a moment. Please."

His voice was cold, cold. I pulled onto the verge, cut the motor. The silence out there had a ring to it.

Roach came back to my side.

"Yes, sir," he said. "Will do. Where is the package, Dr. Flair?"

"In the trunk."

"Can we run a communication check? Please."

Obediently, I got out of the car. I unlocked the trunk. Roach backed off a few paces and motioned me to him.

"Say something," he said. "Please."

" 'I never saw a purple cow,' " I recited. " 'I never hope to see one. . . .' "

"How was the voice level?" Roach asked. "Very good. Yes, sir. I'll tell him. Dr. Flair, Klein wants you to wait here a moment. He's coming up from the communications van. No smoking. Please."

In a few moments Klein appeared, coming out of the brush. I would have recognized that big, square torso and spindly legs anywhere, even brutalized with helmet, faceguard, armor. He was carrying a flechette gun slung over one shoulder.

"Burton," I said, gesturing toward his armament, "is all this necessary?"

"Regulations," he said. "You're transmitting loud and clear. You can go ahead."

"Are they here?"

"Yes. About an hour ago."

"All of them?"

"Martha Wiley is missing. You want to wait for her?"

I thought a moment.

"No," I said, "do you?"

"No," he said. "Let's take what we've got. Listen. . . ."

"Yes?"

"What's Mansfield doing in this? He's not PS."

"Just bait," I said. "We needed someone they couldn't check."

"I don't like it. Something smells."

"Burton."—I sighed—"we had to set up a bribery trap."

"I should have been handling this. How can a bribery charge stand if he's not a PS?"

"Angela said she'd sign him on as a temporary consultant."

"I don't like it," he repeated. "She says my Division is infiltrated. That's a lot of kaka. I trust every one of my ems."

"Burton, will you calm down? Everything is set; let's get it over with. You know the code?"

" 'That's everything you wanted.' "

"Right. Then you move in. Come in fast, Burton."

"I know my service."

"And take plenty of photos, still and tape. All the objects, the love, the restricted material—everything."

"I know my service," he repeated stubbornly.

I started back to the car, but he put a hand on my arm. I turned. He switched off his throat mike.

"Flair—"

"Yes?"

"How are you going back? After it's over?"

"I'll drive back," I said, puzzled. "With Mansfield."

"Let me come with you. Mansfield can go with my ems."

"Well . . . sure."

"Will you wait for me? It may take some time before we get them searched and on their way."

"What's this all about?"

"I just want to talk to you. Alone."

"All right, Burton. I'll wait."

"Thanks. I've got to tell someone. I don't know how to handle it. Go ahead now."

I got back in the car and started up. We bumped slowly over the railroad tracks, pulled up at the side of the house. The porch light went on. Henry Hammond came out, peered down at us. I got out of the car, lifted my hand to him.

"You're late," he said. And went back inside.

Leon Mansfield got out of the car, carrying his soiled raincoat draped over his arm. I went around to the rear trunk, opened it again, unleashed the carton. I left the trunk lid open. Mansfield followed me up the steps, into the house. Hammond switched off the porch light, closed and locked the door behind me. I looked around. Lydia Ferguson. Alice Hammond. Dr. Thomas J. Wiley. Tod and Vernon DeTilly. Henry Hammond.

I caught their excitement immediately. Eager eyes on the carton of goodies I was carrying. I moved toward the wooden dining table. Lydia cleared it hastily of a bowl of wax fruit and two pewter candlestick holders. I smiled at her, set the box carefully in the middle of the table. I jerked a thumb over my shoulder.

"Leon Mansfield," I said.

They started how-are-yous and nice-to-meet-yous, but Mansfield interrupted roughly.

"Where's my love?" he demanded.

Wiley pointed at a black plastic case on one of the chairs. It looked like an obso doctor's bag.

"Right there," he said, smiling. "But Mr. Mansfield, surely you don't expect us to hand it over until we have examined what we are buying?"

"Nothing to do with me," Mansfield said harshly. "I don't know what it is and I don't want to know. I done my job. I want my love."

"Of course, of course," Wiley said smoothly. "But just in case you may, some day, decide you want more than agreed upon, surely you'll have no objection if we photograph your receiving the love?"

Mansfield looked slowly about the circle of faces. Pupils contracted in his phlegmy eyes. That thin, pointed face became cruel. I fancied even the tip of the long, prehensile nose quivered. He convinced *me*.

"Cute," he said harshly. "Goddamned cute."

Vernon DeTilly moved slowly around until he stood between Mansfield and the door. He put his back against the door, folded his arms.

"Well, Mr. Mansfield?" Dr. Wiley asked genially. "What is it to be?"

Mansfield hesitated, apparently pondering. Tod DeTilly helped make up his mind. He went over to the black plastic case, unlatched it, upended it over the couch. The contents spilled out. Packets and packets of new bills in the brilliantly hued abstract designs adopted in 1989.

Mansfield stared at the spilled love. He actually licked his lips. The em was a natural thespian.

"Take your lousy pictures," he said hoarsely.

They had a camera prepared, threaded with a reel of color Instaroid. They turned the lamps toward Mansfield, switched on the overhead light so he was brightly illuminated. Tod DeTilly photographed him taking a bundle from the hand of Dr. Wiley, counting a sheaf, stacking the packets of bills.

"Fine, fine." Wiley chuckled. "That should do nicely, Tod. Now just one more thing: Let's take a look at the presents Dr. Flair has brought us."

We clustered around the table. The carton was unstrapped. I removed the lid, began taking out documents, tapes, reels of film, a box of slides, specimen jars, etc. As I emptied the box, I cautiously probed beneath. But the Electronics Team had done good service; the transmitter was below a false bottom. I tilted the carton to show Wiley it was empty.

But he and the others were too busy to pay attention. They were eagerly, almost frantically shuffling through the mass of material. Each item bore a red label, RESTRICTED, and below, in small type, a warning that unauthorized viewing or disclosure was a capital offense.

"Excellent," Dr. Wiley crowed. "Excellent!"

"That's everything you wanted," I said in a loud voice.

Burton Klein was right: He knew his service.

It seemed to me I had no sooner spoken than the room, the house, the entire world was bathed in a brilliant, white, almost phosphorescent light.

"You are surrounded," a thunderous voice boomed out. "You cannot escape. This is Division of Security, Department of Bliss.

161

Open the door. Come out one at a time. Hands on top of your head. You are surrounded. You cannot escape. This is Division of Security, Department of Bliss. If you come out now, one at a time, hands on top of your head, you will. . . ."

The deep, resonant voice thundered on and on, never ending. That tremendous noise and the blinding light had the effect intended: We stood shocked. Trembling. Small, helpless animals shriveled by fear.

Dr. Thomas J. Wiley recovered first. He realized at once what had happened.

"*You*, Dr. Flair?" he shouted. "Your informed judgment?"

I didn't answer.

He turned to the others, tried to smile, didn't quite make it.

"All of you," he yelled, to make himself heard above the thundering voice from outside. "Do as they say. Do not resist. There is no hope. God help us all."

He went to the front door, unlocked it, swung it open. Then he put his hands atop his head and stepped through. Almost immediately the thundering voice ceased, cut off in mid-sentence. The glaring floodlights dimmed.

I looked at Lydia Ferguson. Her head was bowed. She was blushing and would not glance at me.

The behavior of the others was predictable: Alice Hammond, proud, feeling her gravid abdomen. The DeTilley brothers, furious and frustrated, about to follow Wiley out the door. Henry Hammond utterly destroyed, riven by terror.

I looked through the open door. There was a circle of armored ems. Their pipe-barreled flechette guns were pointed at the house. I saw the burly figure of Burton Klein coming toward the steps. He pushed up his faceguard.

"Move out," he shouted. "Make it—"

Then everything came apart.

Klein had one foot on the lowest step.

I heard three sharp cracks from inside the house. Next to me. Three rapid shots.

Klein's heavy face disintegrated into red pulp.

He went down.

The surrounding ems opened fire. Boom of flechette guns. Whiz of steel darts.

Dr. Wiley was safe. Tod DeTilley was safe. Both stood, guarded, beyond the firing line.

Vernon DeTilly was on the porch, hands on top of his head. The fusillade caught him, tore him apart.

Then I was on the floor, head turned sideways. I could see Lydia Ferguson. She was on the floor, eyes closed.

Alice Hammond was down too. Spouting blood from a hundred punctures. A sieve. Henry Hammond was behind the couch. I could not see Mansfield.

I heard a high, cracked voice: "Stop firing! Stop firing! Stop firing!"

Was that me?

Silence.

I raised my head slowly. An armored monster stood braced in the doorway. A black pipe pointed at me.

"Flair," I cried. "I'm Flair!"

"Who fired?" Art Roach demanded.

"I don't know. I didn't see."

"Where's Mansfield?"

"I don't—"

But then we heard the boom of a flechette gun, muted. From down near the river. X-0 Roach turned and ran. I climbed shakily to my feet. Armored ems came crowding through the door.

It took almost two hours to get it sorted out.

Burton Klein was stopped. So was Vernon DeTilly. Alice Hammond was going. She aborted: a stopped ef fetus. But we had Wiley, Tod DeTilly, Lydia Ferguson, Henry Hammond.

We photographed everything: the living prisoners, the corpora, the scattered love, the restricted material on the table. Roach confiscated the bag of bills. I made him sign a receipt. I repacked the DIVRAD carton, locked it in the trunk of my white sedan.

Then I went to the river, sliding and slipping down the bank, grabbing at trees to keep from falling. An armored em was guarding the corpus of Leon Mansfield. He had been sliced in two. Literally. At short range, a flechette gun will do that.

"He came through that tunnel," the em said excitedly, pointing to the opening a few feet above us. "I waited for him to unlock the gate. He dropped to the beach. I told him to freeze, but he raised a pistol. So I blew him away."

"What kind of pistol?"

"Rocket. Every slug carries its own power."

"I know."

"Good penetration at short range," he said professorially. "Inaccurate at long. I guess he stopped Klein."

"I guess so." I nodded. "You were stationed here? By this tunnel exit?"

"Sure."

"Who ordered you?"

"Klein did. He said there was an underground tunnel, and they might try to escape. I figured he was right because when he placed me here, we found a boat. Tied up right over there."

"A boat?" I said. "Birchbark canoe?"

"What?" he said. "No, it was a little plastic runabout with an electric kicker. We took it away last night."

I turned to go back.

"Hey, Dr. Flair," he whispered.

I stopped. He looked about furtively.

"See what I found in the pocket of his raincoat," he said.

He showed me. Three. Genuine. Indian. Arrowheads.

"You think I should turn them in?" he asked.

"No, keep them," I said. "They're not important."

So I drove back to New York alone. No Leon Mansfield. No Burton Klein. I tried to think of nothing. I tried alpha. I tried self-hypnosis. Failure. So I gave myself over to it. Remembering. Computing. I did not, honestly, believe I could have foreseen from the input.

Paul Bumford was waiting for me when I drove through the gates of the compound. I didn't get out of the car. He came over to my window and bent down. His face was ashen.

"Burton Klein was stopped?" he said.

"Yes. And Leon Mansfield. And Alice Hammond. And Vernon DeTilly."

"My God," he breathed. "Nick, what happened?"

I tried to keep my voice as normal as I could.

"Listen carefully, Paul," I said. "I want you to go to the pad, requisition a copter, and go over to Ellis. There I want you to check passenger registers for the twenty-four hours preceding and following the stopping of Frank Lawson Harris. Only the hypersonic flights to and from San Francisco."

"Nick," he said, "what am I looking for?"

"Goddamn you!" I screamed at him. "Can't you follow orders? Get moving!"

He stumbled away, shocked, glancing back nervously over his shoulder.

I tracked precisely then. I returned the sedan to the motor pool. I got a receipt for it. I returned the restricted material to the NDO's (Night Duty Officers) of my Genetics, Chimerism, and Neurosurgery Teams. I got receipts. I returned the empty carton and concealed transmitter to the NDO of the Electronics Team. I got a receipt. I was functioning.

Then I went back to my apartment. I took a hot shower, taped ribs and all, and pulled on a plastisilk robe. Butterflies in flight on a dark-green background. I mixed a large vodka-and-Smack. I turned out all the lights, settled down in the darkness.

I was on my third drink, almost dozing, when the doorbell chimed. I rose, switched on lights. I opened the door.

Paul stood there, trembling. I pulled him inside, locked the door behind him, handed him my drink. He drained it, just swallowed it down as fast as he could, then looked about wildly, gasping.

"N-n-n," he stammered.

I got him over to the couch and seated. He bent far over, head down between his knees. That was encouraging; he was beginning to function. I went into the nest to get two phenothiazines from my cabinet. He popped the slugs dry without asking what they were.

We sat quietly for a while.

"When did you compute it?" he asked finally.

"On the trip back."

"Do you want to know what I found? Or *do* you know?"

"I can guess. I may not have the times exactly right. Angela flew to San Francisco the day before Harris was stopped. On the night he inhaled the fiddled Somnorific, she flew back. She was in New York for two or three hours. Maybe four. Then she turned around and went right back to California."

"Close enough." He groaned. "Nick, what are we going to *do*?"

"Do? We're not going to do anything."

"You mean she's going to get away with it?"

"Yes," I said. "She is."

"But her name is on the passenger register!"

"So? She came back because she forgot something. Or she had an important meeting with a pol or a supplier that night. Do you really want me to take those passenger lists to the Chief Director and claim they are proof that Angela Teresa Berri committed homicide?"

"Then she did it?"

"Of course."

"Herself?"

"Had to be. Harris would let her into his apartment. Gladly. He was on her Headquarters Staff. She had probably used him before. So she used him again—and left a present. The fiddled Somnorific."

"Then she went back for the container?"

"Oh, no. She was in California by then. Mansfield picked it up. He could get by any lock. He had a talent for it."

"But why would he do it?"

"For love. He had dreams."

"What about tonight? How did she fiddle that?"

"Double, triple, quadruple-cross. At least. She promises Mansfield a lot of love to assassinate Klein. She tells him there's an escape tunnel Klein doesn't know about. Then, in her briefing of Klein, she tells him there's an escape tunnel to the river, and he better guard it. Pretty?"

"But you were scheduled to brief Klein and Mansfield. Until your mother got worse, and you went on a threeday. What if you had been here to brief them, and told them both about the tunnel, and warned Mansfield it would be guarded?"

I shrugged.

"She would have thought of some other way to stop them."

"I can understand her stopping Mansfield. After all, he knew she had stopped Harris. But why Klein?"

"That's sad." I took a deep breath. "He wanted to drive back with me. Said, quote, 'I've got to tell someone. I don't know how to handle it.' Unquote. He probably had evidence that Angela is on the suck."

Suddenly, unexpectedly, Paul laughed. It might have been the phenothiazine.

"But why us?" he asked finally. "Why did she bring us into this whole thing?"

"Paul"—I sighed—"you still don't compute this ef. She doesn't think the way we do. We see problems. She sees opportunities. That's very *political* thinking. We must learn to think that way."

"Nick, I'm not tracking."

"Let's imagine we're Angela," I said. "Here is her input of, say, a few months ago. One: She's on the suck and learns that Burton Klein suspects it. Two: She realizes the Satrat is being fiddled. That's serious; it's her responsibility. Three—very essential this: She has a hyperactive desire for power. Political power. Up the PS ladder. Become Director of Bliss. Sooo. . . . She assigns Frank Harris to Pub-Op, Inc., to help uncover the Satrat rigging. He comes up with the name of Lydia Ferguson. Beautiful. To you and me—a problem. To Angela—an opportunity. But Harris isn't moving fast enough. Maybe he has an operative reaction to the ef. It's possible. I know. And Klein is getting closer. Now Angela has to consider a time factor. How much time has she got before Klein blows the whistle? Or someone in Washington starts wondering why the Satrat is so high while the terrorism rate is increasing?"

"My God," Paul breathed. "I'd have cracked."

"Would you?" I said. "Not our Angela. She breathes better when the oxygen is thin. She computes carefully. Probably all of three minutes. I'm not joking. She's not a thinker; she's a feeler. Primeval. She stops Harris. She brings us in to make certain she can pin a homicide conviction on Lydia Ferguson via the Individual Microbiological Profile she knows we've been working on. If Lydia is taken for homicide and crimes against the state, her father, DIROB, has to resign. *Has* to. At least. If he can avoid arrest himself on suspected complicity. It all computes for Angela. A dream. Klein is stopped. Mansfield is stopped. And along the way, Frank Harris, Alice Hammond, and Vernon DeTilly are all stopped. Angela couldn't care less."

He shook his head in wonderment.

"Nick, she scares me."

"Does she? She is of our species. She belches, farts, pisses, defecates, bleeds, stops—even as you and I."

"What do you suppose she's doing now?"

"Now? This minute? Probably gulping the Chief Director."

"Nick!"

167

"I mean it. Within a week she'll be DIROB."

"And you?"

"I'll be Deputy Director of the Satisfaction Section."

"You'll take it?"

"Of course."

"Payoff?"

"Well . . . really a token of her regard. Angela doesn't have to do it. She knows that. I couldn't prove a bit of what I've just told you. But she'll toss me a bone to keep me happy. That's the way she functions."

"What about me, Nick? Can I be your Assistant Deputy Director of Security and Intelligence?"

I looked at him pityingly.

"Paul, you still haven't computed how this ef's brain works. It's my guess she'll move up to DIROB. Her first official act will be to transfer Security and Intelligence to Washington, as part of her Headquarters Staff. She doesn't want another Burton Klein situation."

He nodded despondently.

"But if I get DEPDIRSAT, you can have Research and Development. With Mary Bergstrom as your Executive Assistant. And three secretaries. Corner office. Does that please you?"

"Sure, Nick."

I looked at him sympathetically.

"It's difficult to acknowledge you've been played for a fool, isn't it?"

"Yes," he agreed. "Very difficult."

"It is for me, too. Let's go to bed."

"Oh, yes!" he cried.

I punished him until we were both panting with pleasure. Finally I pushed him away. We lay gasping.

"ESP?" I asked.

He nodded.

I turned onto my side, scrawled one word on a pad on the bedside table. Then we set to again, flopping like spawning salmon.

Later, not having disengaged or even moved, I said drowsily, "What is it?"

"One word, or more?" he asked.

"One."

168

"Revenge!" he said.

I showed him my scribbled note: "Patience."

"Oh, God." He groaned. "How could we have been so far apart?"

"Not really," I said.

BOOK Y

Y-1

So it came to pass in the Department of Bliss. . . .

Angela Teresa Berri became DIROB. I, Nicholas Bennington Flair, became DEPDIRSAT. Paul Thomas Bumford became Ass-DepDipRad, with Mary Margaret Bergstrom his Executive Assistant.

Angela Berri's first official edict as Director of Bliss, as I had predicted, transferred the personnel, duties, and responsibilities of the Division of Security & Intelligence to her headquarters staff in Washington, D.C. It reduced my Section to three Divisions, but I was not disappointed.

I told Paul: "At least it proves I'm beginning to compute the way she does."

"It also means a lot of problems for us," Paul grumbled. "Now we are required to go to her for a security check on anyone. And as for investigating her, forget it."

"You're too easily discouraged," I said. "What any brain can do, a better brain can undo. Remember, as DEPDIRSAT I now award contracts to independent servers and suppliers of my Section."

My complacency was stopped almost immediately.

Angela Berri's second edict came in the form of a printed notice, return receipt requested. To all ranks, PS-3 and higher. . . . Henceforth, all bids involving contracts in excess of 50,000 new dollars would be processed by DIROB's headquarters staff.

"Well?" Paul said.

"Pretty," I acknowledged. "She's still one step ahead of me—and anyone else in the Department computing heavy larceny. Notice the cutoff limit—fifty thousand new dollars. That's the way this ef operates: Scatter crumbs to the peasants so they won't become too jealous of cake on the lord's plate."

"What are you going to do about it?" Paul asked.

"At the moment? Learn my new service."

That is what I did. I believe Paul Bumford served just as diligently learning the duties of his new rank. I assisted him when I could, but it wasn't often. He came up to my penthouse apartment a few times, usually to ask questions about those privy matters he had not been aware of: the restricted projects I had initiated.

In turn, I received little assistance from Angela Berri in mastering my new service. I could appreciate that; she had her own new service to rule, more intricate than mine. I saw her at monthly DOB meetings in Washington, but most of our contacts during the early summer of 1998 were on the flasher, brief and businesslike. We were both learning to swim in new waters.

After one of those DOB staff meetings, at a reception at her luxurious apartment in the Watergate Complex, she called me into the study. Art Roach was present, standing by the door while Angela and I talked. Roach was now Chief, Security & Intelligence, for the entire Department of Bliss.

My initial impression of the em had been correct; he *was* cold. A tall, rawboned figure. Close-cropped hair, so blond it was almost white; pink scalp showed through. Large, protuberant ears. Bloodless lips. Eyes as colorless as water.

He listened, blinking slowly, as Angela told me that Lydia Ann Ferguson, Dr. Thomas J. Wiley, Tod DeTilly, and Dr. Henry L. Hammond had been drained.

"Could I scan their journals?" I asked. "Or hear the tapes?"

"You have no need to know," Angela said.

I computed the reason for that: Lydia Ferguson hadn't confessed to stopping Frank Harris.

"I hope you destroyed the organization," I said.

"Not completely," Angela said. She was toying with a letter opener on her desk. A miniature Turkish scimitar. "Art and I felt it would be unwise to stop the entire apparatus. Others might start a similar association under another name. By leaving a skeleton of the Society of Obsos intact, we can infiltrate it. Keep an eye on their activities. Learn the identities of new recruits. Clamp down any time we want to. Nick, we've got to get the terrorism level down and the Satrat up.''

''I hope, at least, you've cleaned out my Section,'' I said blandly.

''Of course,'' Angela said blandly. ''Almost a hundred objects.''

''That's fine,'' I said blandly.

I repeated this conversation to Paul Bumford the following day.

''Do you think what she said was operative?'' he asked.

''Operative to the point where I asked about SATSEC. After that, a lot of kaka. I'm certain we still have members of the Society of Obsoletes in the Section. But in addition, we now have Art Roach's doubles. Save yourself, Paul.''

He nodded grimly.

Y-2

It wasn't until after the July Fourth threeday that I felt I had mastered the routine of DEPDIRSAT. I could begin to act on what I had been computing since Angela Berri made a fool of me. At that point in time, my plan was vague. My only input was the ef herself: shrewd, ambitious, greedy. The shrewdness I could not condition. The ambition I was powerless to control. I could manipulate the greed.

It began innocently enough. Everything I did had to appear innocent. I asked Phoebe Huntzinger to have dinner with me at *La Bonne Vie*. It couldn't have been more public.

The Assistant Deputy Director of the Division of Data & Statistics was an uncommonly attractive ef. Not yellow, not tan, not café au lait. Not bronze, nor dark. She was *black,* with a purplish undertone to the epidermis.

She must have carried Benin genes; the characteristics were unmistakable: aquiline nose with splayed nostrils; almond-shaped eyes, large and slanted; wide, sculpted lips curved as artfully as a bow. It was not difficult to imagine that more than a century ago she might have been a favorite of the Oba's court in southern Nigeria. Now she ruled one of the largest computer installations in the US.

Not too surprising. The Bini were famous for their prowess with numbers.

We ordered. I lighted her cannabis cigarette.

"How's the new service, Nick?"

Her voice was deep, throaty, without being thick. Good resonance.

"Getting settled in. I think I'll find it profitable."

"Good. Anything I can do to help. . . ."

"Thanks, Phoebe. I may take you up on that. I see the Satrat's down again."

"I know." She sighed. "It irritates me. The raw data we're processing now from the polling contractors is uniformly lower than their tapes of just a few months ago."

"Don't worry about it," I soothed her. "It will stabilize soon."

She raised those huge, lustrous eyes to stare at me. Her expression didn't change.

"Fiddling?" she said.

I nodded.

"It's been stopped," I said. "Just keep using the raw data."

"I knew it had to be that. Nick, it's going to make my long-range predictions inoperative for awhile."

"I know."

"It would help if I knew the time period when the fiddled tapes were supplied. Then I could excise that and reconstruct my projective curves."

"I can't tell you that, Phoebe, I honestly can't. I just don't know. Do the best you can with what you have."

We had a profitable dinner. I kept her talking about her service. She was voluble about the regenerative potentialities of computers: devices capable of breeding. I found it interesting.

"Phoebe," I said finally, "I want you to take a trip."

"A trip? Where to, Nick?"

"The Denver Field Office. You know they're doing most of our cyborg research. I see their reports, and they've been stalled for months now. They're working with soft laser beams, precisely aimed, to pick up electrical activity from the central nervous system, much in the manner of an EEG. Then the signals are amplified and analyzed by computer with a typewriter printout."

"What hardware are they using?"

"A Golem Mk. III."

"Very good. What's the problem?"

"They've been able to pick up sensations from the objects' brains and identify them: colors, scents, sounds, and so forth."

She was interested now, leaning forward across the table.

"Shape identification?" she asked.

"Yes, on a primitive level. The object is shown a circle, square, star, cross, and the computer spells it out: circle, square, star, cross. Good results. But they're stuck there. They can't pick up conceptions."

"The problem may be in the equipment or in the technique. The laser beam may not be sensitive enough. It may be poorly aimed. Their signal booster may not be strong enough. The Golem may be poorly programmed."

"That's why I'd like you to go out there, Phoebe. Check into every phase of their technology. See if you can suggest improvements. All right?"

"Of course, Nick. I could use a change of scene. But why the sudden interest in cyborgs?"

"Lewisohn's condition. He shows no improvement. I'm trying to foresee every eventuality."

The next day, about 1400, I flashed the copter pad. I asked if Phoebe Huntzinger was there, They told me she had taken off for Kennedy about an hour previously. I thanked them and switched off.

I went over to her office. Her Executive Assistant was a sluggish em with the unlikely name of Pomfret Wingate. Known as Pommy. He was the organizer and director of the Section's little-theater group. They called themselves the Masque & Mirth Society. Atrocious players.

I chatted with Pommy a few minutes. Or rather, I listened to Pommy chat, describing the Society's coming season that would include a nude performance of *King Lear*.

Finally I mentioned casually that I was serving on the budget and wanted to scan a list of contractors and suppliers the Section had dealt with for the past five years.

"Surely, Mr. Flair," he said. "But it won't include anything over fifty thousand new dollars. Those reels were sent to Washington. DIROB's orders."

"I know," I said. "I just want to scan the small fry so I can make an informed estimate of expenses for the coming year. Could you get that for me?"

"Surely, Mr. Flair," he said.

I sat at Phoebe Huntzinger's cleared desk, running reels through her viewing machine. I made heavy notes in case anyone looked in and wondered what I was doing.

I was looking for a regular supplier who specialized in one particular product, who was not located on the East Coast, and who operated with a limited physical plant and few servers. I found three possibles.

I finished in an hour, returned the reels to Pommy, thanked him profusely.

"Surely, Mr. Flair," he said. "Don't forget the nude *King Lear* on October tenth."

"Who's playing Lear?" I asked.

"I am." He giggled. "Nothing but a beard!"

"Wouldn't miss it for the world," I said.

I took the list back to my office and sat computing the three candidates. I looked them up in a thick *Directory of Contractors and Suppliers,* an indepsec publication of the Department of Bliss. One of the three was eliminated immediately. It was too large; it was publicly owned. A second I set aside because of its sole product: electronic prosthetic devices for the armless and legless. I couldn't see any logical justification for a sudden increase in its sales.

The third supplier listed was small, located in San Diego, California. It specialized in hallucinogenic drugs: mescaline, cannabis, bufotenin, lysergic acid diethylamide, etc. Its sales to SATSEC had averaged about 30,000 new dollars annually over the past five years. The directory stated it was a privately owned corporation, employed twenty-four servers, had a good credit rating, owned a somewhat obso physical plant valued at approximately 200,000 new dollars. There was no record of any government prosecution or even investigation of illegal trafficking, mislabeling, or unexplained loss of inventory. Unusual for a company producing hallucinogens.

The name was Scilla Pharmaceuticals, Inc. I wasn't sure I could afford it, assuming they were open to a tender. I spent the evening computing my personal finances.

Over the years, my mother and father had each given me 50,000 new dollars, the legal gift limit. It was tax-exempt and would reduce taxes on their estates when they stopped. And although I had never lived frugally, I had managed to save a small proportion of my rank-rate, lecture fees, love from writing assignments, etc.

I kept my cash balance in the American National Bank to a

necessary minimum. Most of my assets were in common stocks of publicly held corporations. About 50 percent was invested in Flair Toys, my father's company. I trusted his acumen. The other half was almost all in drug manufacturers. I usually knew, weeks or months in advance, when a pharmaceutical company was close to the solution of a difficult research problem, and might announce a new commercial product shortly.

In 1979, all stock exchanges in the US had been merged into one, the Consolidated Stock Exchange, CSE. For a monthly leasing fee, they provided an electronic push-button device, slightly smaller than a shoebox, that tied in with your flasher line. Simply by punching out the symbol of your stock, the current price was shown on a small screen.

That evening I ran my list of love affairs through the stock scanner (popularly known as the "suicide machine"). The total came to a little more than 150,000 new dollars. A few miscellaneous investments in insurance policies, government, and municipal bonds, etc., plus my ANB balance, brought my total to almost 200,000 new dollars. It would, I judged, be sufficient, either converted into cash or as collateral for a loan.

I flashed Paul Bumford. He came on screen in a dressing gown, holding an official record I recognized as a directory of DIVRAD objects serving in Field Offices. He was still learning.

"Paul," I said, "you've been serving too hard. Come on up for a few minutes."

"Nick, I really better—"

"It's a lovely night," I said. "But wear a sweater or jacket. We'll sit out on the terrace and have a drink."

He stared at me a moment. Then he computed.

"Ten minutes," he said.

"Fine," I said lightly. "See you then."

The last few months had mutated him. He was no longer pudgy. The girlish flush was gone from his skin. The face was thinner, harder. His whole bearing was more confident. He carried himself with an almost authoritative arrogance. Serving as administrator of so many objects had done that.

We took our vodka-and-Smacks out onto the terrace. It was a gorgeously mild night, but at that height the wind had an edge. We sat in the shadowed corner where, not too long ago, we had plotted with Angela Berri. My penthouse was swept electronically once a week. But that meant nothing. The sweeper might be reporting directly to Angela Berri. Or to Art Roach.

I went through it as briefly as I could. It wasn't even a plan. It was a plan for a plan. I blocked it out for him, suggesting what might be done, alternative approaches, what we might hope from luck and chance. I finished.

"Well?" I asked.

"Complex," he said.

"Richly complex," I agreed. "But only in the details. The overall design is elegant. Almost pretty. I gather you're not interested."

He leaned forward, hands clenched between his knees. He almost hissed. I was startled by the venom in his face.

"You think I haven't been computing this?" he demanded. Voice low and intense. "Every minute. Waking and sleeping. Ways. Means. Methods. Plots. Plans. Including inviting her out to lunch, saying, 'Oh, Angela, look at that woman in the funny hat,' and then slipping a bomb in her drink."

"I know," I said sympathetically. "But that's stupidity."

"I *know* it is," he said passionately. "I knew it when I thought it. But I thought it, Nick, I actually *thought* it. Your way is best."

"You're sure?"

"I can't better it. Dangerous. For both of us. But the possibility of success is there. Jesus, Nick, you've got to be so *careful*."

"Not only me," I said. "You, too. Then you're in?"

"Whatever you ask," he said.

I leaned forward. He leaned forward. We kissed. Then we leaned back. Both of us took a deep breath. Knowing we had crossed a line.

"What's first?" he asked.

"That lawyer in Oakland—the one who discovered who owns Angela's beachhouse. What's his name?"

"Sam Gershorn."

"Flash him tomorrow. From outside the compound. Tell him you have an obso friend who's retiring and thinking about the San Diego area. Ask Gershorn if he can recommend an attorney in the San Diego area who handles investments, especially industrial properties and real estate."

"I'll do it tomorrow."

We started to rise from our chairs, then Bumford settled back. He touched his lips with two pressed forefingers.

"What input do you have on Art Roach?" he asked.

"Not much. Subjective reactions. Not a profitable em. Potentially violent."

"Yes. I've been making a few cautious inquiries. Here and there. He used around the Section a lot. All efs. A stallion. And not nice. Rough."

"Psychopathic?"

"Probably. Sado. He put one ef into a hospice. About a year ago."

"I didn't hear anything about that."

"Angela glossed it."

"She did?" I pondered that tidbit. "Yes, that makes sense. That's how she knew Burton Klein was investigating her. Roach was her em inside DIVSEC. She bought him by covering up his assault. I told you: She doesn't see problems, she sees opportunities."

"He's a danger, Nick. As much as she is."

"I know."

"We should get a control on him."

Paul was right. I computed the problem, then forced myself to compute the opportunity. It would be difficult, with Art Roach stationed in Washington. But it could be fiddled.

"You're not going to like it, Paul," I said.

"I told you, whatever you ask."

"Your new secretary. Maya Leighton."

"What about her?"

"Bisexual?"

"Possibly. I think so. Why?"

"Is she using Mary Bergstrom?"

"I doubt it. Maybe. I don't know. Is it important?"

"Very. We can't afford to alienate Mary. Can you find out if they're users?"

"I'll try."

"Paul, *do* it. Casually, humorously, if you can. If not, a direct question."

"All right. Then?"

"I've got to use Maya."

"Nick!"

"Got to."

"I don't follow."

"To set up Art Roach."

"Ahh."

"You don't profit from the idea of my using Maya?"

"No."

"Paul, it's necessary."

"I know, I know. How will you get her together with Roach?"

"No idea. Yet. I'm just winging it. But the first step is determining if she's right for the service. What do you think? Is she ambitious?"

"Very."

"Sexually curious?"

"Yes."

"On anything? Smoking? Drinking? Popping?"

"On *everything*. But she functions. And very well."

"So?"

"Yes. You may be right, Nick. You always are. I'll set it up."

"No, *I'll* set it up. Friday night. You and Mary Bergstrom and Maya Leighton come up about 2100. We'll have a few drinks, smoke a little hemp, talk a little business. Nothing about *this*. Understand?"

"Of course."

"During the evening, I'll get Maya aside and suggest she leave with you and Mary, and then come back up here about a half-hour later. You know nothing about it."

"I compute, Nick."

"She may return or she may not. If she doesn't, we'll have to find another ef. If she does, I'll take it from there. Paul, are you certain you control Mary Bergstrom?"

"Certain."

"Are you users?"

"No."

"Then how do you control her?"

"Well. . . .Well, we talk. I listen to her. I even listen to her play the flute. She doesn't have any friends. So I—"

"Paul? What is it? Do you have an investment in this ef?"

"Nick, I swear to you, I don't know. I don't really know. That's operative. I do know she'll do whatever I say."

"That's good enough for me. Let's get moving on this."

"Thank God! At last!"

After he left I had another drink. I paced the floor. I knew what

179

was bothering me. *I* should have thought of the idea of getting a hook into Art Roach. Paul Bumford was not only becoming more confident, he was creating fresh and operative ideas. I wasn't certain that development was lovable.

I took an eight-hour Somnorific.

Y-3

On Friday morning, I sat down to a breakfast of dissolved orange-flavored concentrate (500 mg of ascorbic acid per teaspoonful), probisks, and a hot cup of coftea. As I munched and sipped, I scanned the front page of my facsimile *Times*.

The lead story, under a three-column head on the *left*-hand side (human behavior analysts had finally realized that most non-Judaic objects scanned from left to right) carried a Washington, D.C., dateline. It concerned a speech delivered by Angela Berri, Director of Bliss, to the national convention of the Actuarial Guild of America. Angela stated at the outset that the ideas she would express were based on the concepts of Hyman R. Lewisohn.

A radical revision of the Social Security laws was proposed. An object who had contributed to the SS fund all his serving life, and to which his employers had contributed, would have an equity in that fund. It would not end when he stopped. It could be bequeathed. It would be part of his estate.

Such a law, if enacted, would mean a revolutionary adjustment of Social Security deduction rates. An upward adjustment, of course. It would also mean the US Government was getting into the life insurance business. I could well believe the New York *Times* report that Angela's proposal had been greeted by the assembled actuaries with "incredulous murmurs."

That was of no importance to me. What I found of interest was Lewisohn's basic conception. For some time, I had suspected that all the ideas from his prodigious brain were not simply fragmentary answers to fragmentary problems. I imagined that extraordinary em had conceived a Plan, and every suggestion he made was part of a visualized design.

That filthy, cantankerous dwarf was putting together a new world, *his* world. I could not perceive its delineation. But I knew,

180

knew, there was a grand Lewisohn Plan. He was creating a mosaic, a piece here, a piece there, chuckling obscenely. I found it a stress to manipulate SATSEC. He read his obso novels, vilified his doctors and nurses, scorned the rot of his corpus, and jauntily encompassed us all.

The moment I arrived at my office I flashed the Chief Resident at Rehabilitation & Reconditioning Hospice No. 4. He came on screen almost immediately, with his habitual manner of expecting every call to presage disaster. Dr. Luke Warren was a perennially worried little em. His field was biomedicine, and he was good. Not just competent, but *good.*

"Luke," I said, "how are you?"

He told me—at length. I had heard the story before: Hyman R. Lewisohn was destroying his sanity.

"Insulting, is he?" I asked. Knowing the answer.

"Insulting? Nick, *that* I could take. But he's obscene. Yesterday he threw a full bedpan at the morning nurse. His language and habits are filthy. The only way I can get anyone to attend him is to bribe them with extra threedays. We had to put him in restraint to clean him up, and then he complained to the Chief Director who ordered me never to do that again. He pulls out his tubes, spits out his pills, urinates on the floor. Nick, he's a beast."

"I know, I know," I said. "Luke, you've got a megaproblem; no doubt about it. How is he responding to treatment?"

"Not good. Want to go to marrow transplant?"

"No. Not yet. It'll incapacitate him for too long. Have you ever used the BCG vaccine with irradiated tumor cells?"

"A few times. Nick, it just postpones the inevitable. I think we'd do better to go to the marrow now."

"Tell you what. Suppose I come down next week and we'll talk about it. Maybe I can persuade him to stop acting like a depraved child."

"Oh, God, would you do that? It would be a big help."

"I'll flash you on Monday and we'll set a time. Don't tell him I'm coming. But alert your team; I'll want a colloquy."

I switched off and looked at my next week's schedule. That would be an all-day consultation. Lewisohn was suffering from acute myelogenous leukemia. There were several methods of treatment; if one didn't serve, you tried another. You hoped the patient would hang on until you found something effective.

Ellen Dawes came in for the morning ration of real coffee. She was her usual smiling, pleasant, unflappable self; a good way to start a hectic day.

When Angela Berri had moved to Washington, she had taken two of her four secretaries with her. That left me two short. I brought Ellen with me. Now I was one down. Paul Bumford, with the addition of Maya Leighton, had his appropriate three. But of course, I had wall-to-wall plasticarp while his, in my former office, ended twelve inches from the baseboard. Also, I had a private nest, a small kitchen, and windows on three sides.

I had an 0930 meeting scheduled with Frances and Frank von Liszte the twin Assistant Deputy Directors of the Division of Law & Enforcement. I went over to their conference room, at their request, since they wanted to make a presentation that involved big charts, graphs, visual aids, etc. Also, they wanted the top objects of their staff to be present. As I had expected, the meeting dealt with the legal problems of inheritance generated by the Biological Revolution.

At that point in time, we had developed fourteen methods of mammalian reproduction, seven of which had been used successfully on human objects:

1. Artificial insemination
2. Artificial enovulation
3. Parthenogenesis
4. Fertilization *in vitro,* the fetus brought to "birth" in an artificial placenta
5. Auto-adultery (resulting only in ef offspring)
6. Embryonic cloning
7. Sexual intercourse

This list, of course, did not include embryonic or gonadal transplants, which posed similar legal problems.

In artificial insemination, did the child inherit from the mother's husband or from her donor? Could the husband sue for divorce on the grounds of adultery—even if he had agreed to the impregnation but changed his mind later?

In artificial enovulation, did the child inherit from the ef who bore it, from the ef who donated the fertilized egg, from the em who provided the sperm, or from the husband of the ef who bore the child?

In cloning, where as many as twenty identical offspring had been produced from a single embryo, did all progeny inherit equally?

182

I had heard all these problems discussed before, endlessly. But in that morning's conference, new input was added. The von Liszts, after a great deal of research, had come up with reasonably firm statistics on the number of objects in the US bred by methods other than using. They also displayed charts showing computerized projective curves on the number of such objects to be expected in five, ten, twenty-five, and fifty years. It was brain-boggling.

"Well," I sighed, after the presentation, "what solution do you suggest—or was this just a preview of my future migraine?"

I derived a lot of profit from Frances and Frank von Liszt. They were attractive twins with their infantile complexions, flaxen hair, light blue eyes, young profiles. I could believe the rumor that they used each other. Why not?

Now, speaking alternately, they explained what they proposed. They were getting nowhere with bar associations. The debates on recommended legislation were futile. What the von Liszts suggested was an official government "position paper" that would at least give a basis for logical and informed discussion by interested jurists.

I questioned them and their staff closely. Did a child born of electrical parthenogenesis have *any* legal father other than a dry cell? If clones were brought to "birth" at different times, either in an artificial placenta or by implant, would the one born first be the senior, inheriting from the natural father?

It was a lively discussion. I enjoyed it. I had no law degree, but I knew molecular genetics better than they. I finally approved of their plan to draw up a preliminary government position paper. I also suggested they give some thought to a discussion with academics of the government's Science Academy with a view to creating a new field of Biological Jurisprudence: objects conditioned in genetics *and* law.

I went back to my office, not optimistic that their proposed position paper would ever be allowed distribution to the civilian bar associations for which it was intended. Too controversial. And if it was distributed, would it help clarify the issues? The kaka would continue, perhaps even intensified.

Paul Bumford was waiting for me. I took him into my inner office and closed the door.

"All set for tonight?" I asked.

"Yes. We'll be up about 2100."

183

"No fancy dress. Just an informal get-together."

I was speaking to the suspected sharer as much as to him. He computed.

"Another thing, Paul," I said. "Please get out a Telex to all the Hospices asking how many parabiosis volunteers each can furnish for a leukemic victim. Don't mention Lewisohn by name. The less publicity on this the better."

"You're going to parabiosis?"

"Not immediately. Just preparing. Anything else?"

"No, that's all. Walk me to the elevator?"

"Sure."

In the crowded corridor, a zipsuited throng was noisily waiting for high-speed elevators to take them down to the building cafeteria.

"San Diego," Paul murmured. "Hawkley, Goldfarb and Bensen. Got that?"

"Yes."

"Hawkley is the only senior partner still alive. Sam Gershorn says he's one year younger than God. But he has some smart junior partners."

"Good. Can you come up early tonight? Just you. About 2030. The efs at 2100."

"Uh-huh. Important?"

"No. Just talk. For the Tomorrow File."

"Fine. I'll fix it. See you at 2030."

As DEPDIRSAT, I carried weight at the motor pool. I had first choice of the Section limousine, a huge, black, diesel-powered Mercedes-Benz. Reserved for my exclusive use was an electronically powered two-door Chevrolet. I took the small sedan and drove up to Canal Street, to one of the public flasher stations scattered around the city. I wore a light raincoat over my zipsuit.

I sat in a small booth and after about five minutes of spelling the names for Information operators, I finally got through to Hawkley, Goldfarb & Bensen in San Diego. I made certain my raincoat was zipped up to the neck; my uniform wasn't visible.

A plumpish, matronly secretary came on.

"Hawkley, Goldfarb and Bensen," she said, in a surprisingly deep, emish voice. "May I serve you?"

"Could I speak to Mr. Hawkley, please? My name is Nicholas Flair. I'm calling from New York."

"I'm sorry, sir. Mr. Hawkley isn't in today. Could you speak to someone else?"

"To Mr. Hawkley's secretary, please. I'd like to make an appointment to meet with Mr. Hawkley."

"Just a moment, please, Mr. Flair. I'll see if she's in."

She went off-screen. A full-color reproduction of one of Van Gogh's self-portraits unexpectedly took her place. And I was treated to a symphonic rendition of Bach's *Jesu, Joy of Man's Desiring*. It was a new device introduced about a year previously. When a commercial operator had to hold a call, she switched on a gadget that simultaneously showed an "ageless painting" and played "immortal music." So the caller wouldn't get bored waiting. I wondered how long it would be before there were similar gadgets showing illustrations from the Kama Sutra and playing "Gimme Head Blues."

When Van Gogh disappeared, and Bach was cut off in mid-strain, the ef who appeared was very young, very blond, very—

"Yes, Mr. Flair?" She dimpled. "I am Mr. Hawkley's private secretary. May I serve you?"

"I'm calling from New York," I repeated. "I'm coming out to San Diego next week and would like to make an appointment to meet with Mr. Hawkley to discuss possible investments in real estate and industrial properties in the San Diego area."

"And may I ask who referred you to us, Mr. Flair?"

"You may ask, but I won't answer. It's not important."

She didn't seem shocked, or even surprised by my answer. She was making no notes. I suspected our conversation was being taped.

"Would Tuesday afternoon at 1500 be satisfactory, Mr. Flair?"

"Fine. I'll be there."

"In case Mr. Hawkley is unable to keep the appointment, how may I get in touch with you, sir?"

"Unfortunately, I'll be out of town and unavailable," I said. "But I'll check with you Tuesday morning to confirm the appointment."

I stopped at a government grogshop in the neighborhood and picked up four bottles of Bordeaux. The clerk swore—"On my mother's grave"—the wine had been made from real grapes. I didn't believe him for a minute. In the early 1980's the multinational cartels had started buying up French vineyards. The prices of natural wines and brandies went so high that the only things left for most objects to drink came out of oil wells.

In my office, I had Ellen Dawes get through to Phoebe Huntzinger at our Denver Field Office. It took almost fifteen minutes to locate Phoebe in Denver's Computer Room. When she came on screen, she was wearing white paper coveralls. She looked her usual cool, imperturbable self.

"Nick," she said. "How are you? Checking up on me?"

"Of course," I said. "I thought you might have taken off for Rio. How are you, Phoebe? Any luck?"

"A little. We've tuned the laser and boosted the amplification. The signal is stronger now, sharper, but preliminary tests still don't show much more than they did before."

"Still no conceptions?"

"No. Just sensations and inconclusive tests on simple words like 'Go.' 'Come.' 'Walk.' 'Run.' Things like that. Then we tried emotive words: 'Cry.' 'Shout.' 'Frown.' 'Scream.' 'Smile.' And so forth. A little progress there."

"Fine. I think you're on the right track. Who's the Team Leader?"

"An em named Stanley. That's his last name. Peter Stanley. Know him?"

"No. Good?"

"Well. . . .He's enthusiastic'."

"That helps. Is he around now?"

"Just went out for coffee, Nick. Anything I can do?"

"Phoebe, the problem there may not be the technology. It may be in the experimental objects. When Stanley gets back, suggest he try hallucinogens on the objects prior to test. Especially lysergic acid diethylamide. If it intensifies sensation the way the freaks claim, it may get a conception through to the computer."

"Wild idea," she said.

"Worth trying. Probably nothing, but you never can tell. If he's short on hallucinogenic drugs, tell him to requisition more. I'll approve."

"I'll tell him, Nick. It's nice out here. I profit from it."

"Don't stay too long. You might not come back."

I was assigned a private serving em from the Maintenance Department to keep my penthouse in order. He was ordered to serve six hours a day, four days a week. I suspected he served about ten hours a week and watched TV the remainder of the time. It was cushy duty. Knowing the customs of the lower Public Service ranks, I supposed he had paid his ruler something for the assignment. In any event, my apartment was kept reasonably clean. I could detect no pilferage or search of my personal effects, so I was satisfied.

The em, a bearded obso, was just going off duty when I arrived home. I gave him one of the bottles of wine I had purchased and told him not to come in on Saturday until after 1200. He asked no questions; the wine was answer enough.

I undressed, slid into bed, napped until 1900. Then I rose, showered, pulled on a fresh summer-weight zipsuit. I wore no underwear. I switched on a music cassette—Vivaldi's *Four Seasons* —opened one of the bottles of Bordeaux, and sampled it. It might not have been produced from grapes, but a clever chemist had compounded it; it was light, dry, with good body and bouquet. Only the acrid aftertaste betrayed its test-tube origins. I tried a drop or two on a plastowel. The stain washed out immediately. That was encouraging. I once performed a similar test with a "genuine grape Burgundy." Not only was the stain indelible, but two hours later there was a hole in the towel.

The air conditioning had been turned on full all day; the apartment was almost painfully cold. I stepped out onto the terrace, sliding the thermopane door closed behind me. I wandered around to the west side. The setting sun looked like a human ovum.

It was a hot July evening, the atmosphere supersaturated, the air smelling distinctly of sulphur. There had been an inversion layer over much of GPA-1 for the past two days; objects doing outdoor service wore masks over nose and mouth, glared at the murky sky with red-rimmed eyes. I went back into the chilled interior thankfully. It might smell of Freon, but it was better than breathing smoke, ash, soot, hydrogen chloride, carbon monoxide, sulphur dioxide, and air that had been filtered through too many lungs before it was my turn.

Paul Bumford arrived promptly at 2030. I poured him a glass of wine. I noted he was wearing a minimum of makeup.

"Let's go out on the terrace for a moment," I said. "I hate to do this to you; it's brutal out there. But I want you to see the sunset. The one advantage of air pollution; magnificent sunrises and sunsets."

We stood at the rail, watching the sun slowly stop. I talked rapidly in a low voice. I recounted my San Diego conversation and the call to Phoebe Huntzinger.

"That Denver project is one possibility for increased use of hallucinogens," I explained. "Tonight, when the efs are here, I'm going to bring up the subject of the Ultimate Pleasure pill. We'll discuss methods of development. Follow my lead. Volunteer nothing. Let one of them suggest a hallucinogenic approach. Compute?''

"Yes. But aren't we going at this ass-backward? We don't have the factory yet.''

"We will,'' I said. "Scilla or some other. While we're serving on the factory, we've got to plan increased need for LSD, mescaline, and all the rest. Check your files of ongoing projects, and see what you can do. On Tuesday, you'll have to go to San Diego with me. A perfect cover: I'm taking you out to meet the Field Office objects and familiarize you with their service. All right?''

"Fine.''

"I'll make the arrangements. We'll take the courier flight out Tuesday morning. I'll come back Wednesday morning. You stay on a day or two, serving with the FO. I'll see Hawkley on Tuesday afternoon. I'm taking civilian clothes, but all you'll need are zip-suits.''

"Going to use your real name, Nick?''

"Have to. Sooner or later I'll have to identify myself and sign papers. We can't afford the dangers of a fiddled BIN card. Besides, the Field Office is in San Diego, and my father has a factory out there. There must be a hundred objects in that city who know me by sight. Too risky to forge a new identity. I'll chance it.''

"How will Hawkley contact you?''

"On Monday I'll go uptown and lease a mailing address, or desk space—whatever it takes. If I have to show my BIN card, I will. But if I pay in advance, I doubt if they'll want identification. See any flaws?''

He pondered a moment.

"What if Hawkley doesn't go for it?''

"Then I'll stay on another day, or until I find a sharp attorney who can handle it all and keep me hidden.''

"Nick, you're taking all the risk. I'm not doing anything.''

"Oh, but you will,'' I assured him. "You will, indeed. If the deal goes through, you may have to pay a visit to Scilla. You'll have good cover: You're checking the facilities of your suppliers. And while you were visiting the DIVRAD Field Office, you thought you'd stop by and say hello, and so forth, and so forth. But all that's futuristic. Right now, the important thing is to get control of that factory and build up its sales. Let's go back in; I'm beginning to sweat."

"You said you had something for the Tomorrow File. Can you talk about it inside?"

"Good point. No, I'll give it to you now. This morning I had a long meet with DIVLAW. They want to draw up an official position paper on how inheritance should be handled in all methods of reproduction. You're familiar with the problems?"

"Yes."

"Incredibly complex. No precedents in litigation. DIVLAW's solution is fragmentary, a hodgepodge. No solution at all. How's this for the Tomorrow File: All created objects, *all* objects, regardless of reproductive technology, become wards of the state. No orphans. No bastards. No daughters. No sons. All objects created have legal equality. The government acts *in loco parentis*. And inherits all. Well?"

"Nick? Are you serious? *No* inheritance? *No* family at all? It would take a century of conditioning."

"It could be done in less," I said. "The difficulty isn't liquidation of the family as a social unit. That's been going on for generations. The sticking point is individual motivation. If an object was prevented by law from bequeathing love to heirs, would the object lose desire to amass it?"

"You mean, how would government inheritability affect the profit motive?"

"Well . . . call it the acquisition drive. A desire to succeed in a capitalistic society. That's the problem."

"Nick, answer me one thing?"

"What's that?"

"Do you have a plan?"

"A plan?"

"A design. A coherent view of the future. The suggestions you've made recently for the Tomorrow File seem to fit a pattern. I can't visualize it. But I sense something there."

I was startled. Exactly what I had thought about Lewisohn's ideas that morning. Paul was no fool. This needed thought, review of my own suggestions, long and careful computation to determine if synthesis was possible. And if it was, would my plan and Lewisohn's be complementary or antithetical? It was interesting.

"I have no plan," I said shortly. "Let's go inside and cool off."

Mary Margaret Bergstrom was a husky ef, solid as a stump, and as shapely. Her face reflected nothing of her intelligence. Features heavy and coarse. Complexion sallow. I looked in vain for animation. The eyes were, if anything, wary. She seemed to have suffered, in the past, some awful hurt, and was determined not to risk pain again. But perhaps I was romanticizing. It was quite possible she was simply overconditioned. It was happening frequently with younger scientists: pure objectivity and complete incapacity to make value judgments.

I courted her while Paul and Maya Leighton inspected my cassette library. I lighted Mary's cannabis cigarette, kept her wine glass filled, strove desperately to find a subject, other than our service, that might rouse her. I found it by accident when I congratulated her on hitting the national lottery for one thousand new dollars.

Within minutes we were having a lively discussion on gambling —odds, horse vs. dog racing, soccer vs. jai alai, roulette vs. chemin de fer, poker vs. gin rummy, and the mathematical possibilities of winning at the daily numbers drawing. Maya and Paul joined us; talked quickened, gestures became more vigorous. I opened the second bottle of wine.

At this point in time, the US Government, in addition to sole ownership of the nation's grogshops, also sponsored lotteries and operated a nationwide chain of betting parlors. All gambling was legalized in 1983, and prostitution a year later. Casinos and bordellos were now as much a part of government activities as day-care centers and veterans' hospitals. The income from bets on sporting events alone was sufficient to reduce the personal contribution rate (formerly the income tax rate) by 5 percent.

I discovered that Mary Bergstrom was an addicted gambler. I wondered if Paul had been aware of it. If so, why hadn't he told me? Mary's knowledge of odds, spreads, points, combinations, and all the other details of wagering was encyclopedic. We listened, fascinated, while she described a system of winning at roulette she was devising with the help of a King Mk. IV computer. We resolved to make a visit, *en masse,* to the Central Park Casino as soon as Mary's system was perfected.

Then our conversation became more general. I drew them into a gossipy discussion of personalities in SATSEC, who was using whom, what marriages were planned, divorces scheduled. My news that Pomfret Wingate was to play the lead in a nude performance of *King Lear* sent the efs into almost hysterical laughter.

"Well"—Paul shrugged—"if it gives him pleasure, why deny him?"

"And speaking of pleasure," I said, rising to turn off the cassette player, "here's a puzzle for you all. What is the greatest pleasure, the ultimate pleasure, a human object can know? Paul?"

"Physical orgasm," he said promptly.

"Mary?"

"Gambling," she said. "And music."

"Maya?"

She was a queenly ef, almost as tall as I. Soon after entering my apartment, she had taken clips from her coiled red hair and let it tumble down her back, to her waist. Her official zipsuit had obviously been altered to display her body to advantage: wide shoulders and hips, narrow waist, long legs.

She had enormous hazel eyes, generous mouth, impudent smile. Her eye shadow was mauve, the false lashes extraordinarily thick. Her ears bore huge clamp rings, not on the lobes but on the pinna. A tooty fashion. Her zipper was pulled low enough to exhibit cleavage. She wore a black velvet mouche, star-shaped, on the upper, shiny bulge of the right breast.

When I spoke her name, asking her the ultimate pleasure a human object could know, she raised her leonine head slowly in a cloud of cannabis smoke and looked at me mockingly.

"The greatest pleasure?" she said. "Almost any pleasure if you surrender to it completely."

"Now that *is* interesting," I said, "because—"

"Wait a minute, Nick," she said. I think she was smiling. "We've answered. Now it's your turn. What do you think is the ultimate pleasure?"

"That's easy," I said. "Danger."

"Physical danger?" Mary asked.

"Possibly. Perhaps a better word would be peril."

I believe I lied successfully.

Then we were all talking at once. We smoked up a storm, finished the wine, started on petrovod and petronac. The conversation bubbled, ebbed, exploded anew: sex, cannabis, alcohol, drugs, art, music, gambling, danger, dancing, crime—which might be the most pleasurable?

191

"All in all," I said finally, "you pays your love and you takes your choice. Too bad we can't come up with something to intensify the pleasure of the means we select."

"Drugs can do that," Mary said. "Or so it's said. I've never tried them."

"Drugs?"

"Hallucinogens," Maya said.

"That's an idea I hadn't thought of," I said slowly. "Paul, we might consider that."

"What's this all about?" Mary Bergstrom asked.

"Paul and I were discussing the possibility of developing a pleasure pill, the Ultimate Pleasure pill, the UP. Then we realized we couldn't start until we knew what we were looking for. What *is* the Ultimate Pleasure? There are four of us here. We have at least four different answers."

The efs were interested now, leaning forward intently.

"I still think it could be done," I said. "Hallucinogens would certainly be one line of approach. Paul, this is DIVRAD's service. Why don't you and Mary and Maya try to come up with a plan, a system of attack. What are the immediate goals? Intermediate? Final? How many servers will we need? What specialties? How large a budget? Should we try it here or farm it out to a Field Office? Or is it so big and complex that we need several teams working on it in several places? Could you do that?"

"Of course," Paul said. "The first target, obviously, is a basic conception of what we're looking for. Mary?"

"It could be physiological," she said slowly. "Or emotional. Or mental."

"Or something even deeper," Maya said.

"Deeper?" I said. "Instinctive."

"Perhaps," she said. "Something like that."

Paul and Mary started discussing how they might begin to outline a plan of attack on the problem.

"Maya," I said, "come on into the kitchen and help me make some coffee."

"Real coffee?" she asked.

"Close enough," I said. "After another petronac and another Bold, you won't know the difference."

She laughed and followed me into the kitchen. I asked her to leave with the others and then return a half-hour later.

"All righty," she said blithely.

It didn't seem to make any difference to her.

After they all left I switched the air conditioners to exhaust and got rid of the cannabis smoke. I cleaned up the living room, stacking plastiglasses and ashtrays in the sink. I washed my face with cold water. Gradually the buzzing in my brain dulled to a pleasant drone. I stood erect, closed my eyes, lifted my arms sideways and attempted to touch forefingers over my head. I didn't miss by much.

I might have been reasonably sober, but Maya Leighton was still flying when she came back. She strode in, kicked off her sandals in the living room, and was in the darkened bedroom before I got the front door locked. I left one lamp on, then followed her into the bedroom. Her zipsuit lay in a crumpled heap near the bed. I picked it up, shook it out, draped it over a chairback.

"Sleepy?" I asked.

"Far from it."

Her voice was full, musical, but not as confident as she intended. A slight tremor there. I looked at her, the bed dimly visible in nightlight from the undraped windows. She stared back at me, eyes enormous and black. Glistening. The huge earrings lay on the bedside table.

"What is that on your left thigh?" I asked.

"A tattoo," she said.

"A tattoo of what?"

"A scarab," she said.

"Scarab? That's a dung beetle."

"Yes. A dung beetle. Bite it."

I bit it.

She was lying on her right leg, hip, shoulder. Head pillowed. Hair flung. A lush Circe. Her body was more than baroque. There was extravagant opulence. It came perilously close to being a caricature of an ef's body.

There was a bursting heat in her. Almost feverish. Eyes half-closed, glimmering. Mouth half-open in a pant. But she was conscious and aware. She did not surrender, as Lydia Ferguson had, to her own sensuality. But to my demands. A fine point, but significant.

I used her. Or did she use me? I knew my motive. It was, I thought, more devious than hers. But still. . . .

She seemed hypersensitive. I suspected drugs, but could taste nothing on her lips or tongue but sweet saliva.

I used her painfully, but I could not daunt her. I had to know, you see. I left bruises and the marks of teeth on that tumescent flesh. She did not object or cry out. But opened herself to me, urging on the night.

Y-4

The hypersonic wheeled out over the Atlantic, accelerating, gaining altitude so rapidly that G-force pressed us back against the semireclining seats. I viewed the telescreen as the coastline fell away. We circled again, then passed through the sonic wall with a barely perceptible shudder. The plane straightened, headed west for San Diego at a gentler climb. We pulled up our seatbacks. The white-clad stewardess began pushing her cart down the aisle. Paul Bumford returned to his facsimile *Times.*

"Nick," he said, "look at this."

I glanced down, then settled back, closed my eyes.

"I scanned it," I said. "At breakfast."

It was a short item. Only a few lines. . . .

The corpus of a young ef had been washed ashore near Falmouth, Massachusetts. It had been identified as Martha Wiley, daughter of Dr. Thomas J. Wiley, noted genetic biologist, who had been taken two months previously, charged with subversion and crimes against the state.

"Probably suicide," Paul said.

"Probably," I agreed, my eyes still closed.

Then the stewardess paused at our seats. We each took a plasticup of coftea. Paul also took a package of probisks. He dunked them in the hot brown liquid.

"You're losing a secretary," I told him. "I'm taking Maya Leighton onto my staff."

"All right. She'll work out then? With Art Roach?"

"I think so."

"How will you bring them together?"

"I'll find a way."

"How much will you tell her, Nick?"

"As little as possible. I don't think she'll pry too much. As you said—a good brain."

"I've been thinking about it," he said. "Suicide, I mean. For the Tomorrow File. Making suicide illegal."

"I agree the numbers are horrendous," I said. "Especially among the young. But what do you propose—making suicide a capital crime?"

"I know that's senseless, Nick. But what if the law decreed capital punishment for the suicide's immediate family? Wouldn't that be a deterrent?"

"No," I said. "Suicides are usually in a hyperemotional state. Or extremely neurotic or psychotic. Don't expect them to compute rationally the consequences of their act."

"Did you like her, Nick?"

"Maya? Very much. A puzzle."

"How so?"

"Total surrender. But I can't compute the reason."

"She recognizes it. She suggested it when you asked her to name the ultimate pleasure. So it must be deliberate choice."

"That's what she said. But she may be rationalizing a weakness. We all do it. You are cowardly; I am cautious. You are miserly; I am prudent. You are a spendthrift; I am generous. We all conceal— no, not conceal, but prettify our weaknesses."

"What is your weakness, Nick?"

I laughed.

"My fatal flaw? I want life to have charm."

I closed my eyes again, leaned back, relaxed. I could feel a gentle forward tilt. We had already started letting down for the Pacific.

"I still think suicide belongs in the Tomorrow File," Paul said stubbornly. "A law making it illegal. With penalties stiff enough to make would-be suicides think twice."

I opened my eyes to stare at him.

"Why do you feel so strongly about it, Paul?"

"Because it fits right in with what you've suggested—about the government inheriting healthy organs from stopped objects. And all new objects becoming wards of the state, no matter how they were bred. If those suggestions are valid, then suicide becomes a crime against the state. If you stop yourself, you're destroying government property."

"That's interesting," I said.

We came in low over Point Loma. The cabin telescreen showed a fine view of the harbor: pleasure boats, tuna fleet, Coast Guard cutters. After the jammed frenzy of the N.Y.-D.C. axis, the Southern California scene was open, yawning, whitewashed in the summer sun.

Paul and I splurged, taking one of the new steam-powered cabs to the Strake Hotel in Chula Vista. It was Paul's first trip to San Diego. I pointed out the DIVRAD Field Office as we drove by. He was impressed by the heroic bronze statue of Linus Pauling in front of the main building.

"But it's a small installation, isn't it, Nick?"

"Larger than you think. The labs are underground."

We claimed our hotel suite. I flashed Hawkley's office and confirmed my appointment at 1500. Then we cabbed back to the FO, arriving a little before 1000. They had been alerted to our coming; we were taken directly to Lab 1 where the Chief was waiting for us.

The San Diego Field Office specialized in molecular and biochemical genetics. Their list of accomplishments was impressive.

The servers were remarkably young, eager, innovative. They spawned a thousand new ideas annually. Most proved loveless, but it didn't seem to discourage them. I had noted that about DIVRAD servers: The farther they were removed from the political pressures of New York and Washington, the more freewheeling and creative they became.

The Chief of the FO was one of my favorites, Nancy Ching, a jolly yellow ef as cute and plump as an Oriental doll. On my last trip to San Diego, Nancy and I had become demented on plum wine and amphetamine, and had used each other with much giggling delight.

She greeted me with a hot, smeary kiss, grabbed our arms, and dragged us on a whirlwind tour of her labs, chattering incessantly. She spoke a rapid patois of technical jargon and tooty slang. I caught about half of it; Paul seemed to have no trouble at all. In a few moments he was talking in similar fashion. Two of a kind.

Suddenly Nancy stopped, tugged me around to face her.

"Oh, Nick," she said, "DIROB flashed you just before you arrived. You're supposed to flash back at once."

"Why on earth didn't you tell me that before?"

"Because I wanted you to myself. Let her wait—the bitch!"

I glanced at Paul. He was looking at her admiringly. I knew she had made a friend for life.

"You can flash from my office on the second floor," Nancy said. I'll give Paul the fast, thirty-cent tour, and then we'll join you up here. I've laid on a gorgeous lunch for you in the conference room."

I sat at Nancy's desk while the FO operator put me through to Washington.

Angela Berri came on screen.

"Nick," she said, "what the hell are you doing out there?"

"Good morning, Angela," I said.

"Good morning, Nick," she said. "What the hell are you doing out there?"

"Showing Paul the scenery."

"When are you coming back?" she demanded.

"I'll probably return tomorrow morning. Paul will stay on a day or so to learn what's going on."

"I want you in Washington on Friday night. A dinner with the Chief Director and his wife. At their home. It's important."

"It's awkward," I said.

"Why?"

"I have an appointment in Alexandria on Friday. To examine Lewisohn."

"Fine. Come over to my place in the evening."

"Angela, I'll have my new secretary with me."

"What for?"

"To take notes."

"Nick, when did you ever need notes?"

"Since I got a new secretary."

That thawed her. After she stopped laughing, she said, "Bring her along. We'll find something for her to do."

"Maybe Art Roach can entertain her for the evening," I said casually.

"Why not?" she said.

"Who'll be there? At the dinner?"

"Just you, me, the Chief Director and his wife. I've got something to discuss with him."

"While I keep the wife busy?"

"Of course. Wear your uniform and decorations."

"Where do we stay? At the Alexandria Hospice?"

She thought a moment.

"No," she said. "Come to my apartment. I can put you up overnight. Separate bedrooms, I presume?"

"For whom?" I asked.

She smiled and switched off.

I finally found Nancy and Paul in another corridor. They we standing before a closed door, staring through a small square transparent glass. On the inside, I knew, it would be a mirror.

". . . third month," Nancy was saying as I came up to the "All vital functions normal. A strong, healthy ef. We decided o rhesus monkey."

"Compatible DNA," Paul said.

"You plenty damn smart for a white em," Nancy said perki "Get your call through, Nick?"

"Sure," I said. "Nothing important. What have we here?"

"Take a look. Fertilization, *in vivo,* with rhesus sperm. An new interspecific drug we've been working on. Normal gestati period. The object is coming along nicely."

I stooped a little to peer through the glass. Lydia Ann Fergus was sitting on the edge of the bed. Hands folded in her lap. She w staring out through the window, beyond the white bars, at t endless blue sky.

It came on fast. . . .

. . . dissecting a frog when I was seven years old. Taking out heart and putting it carefully aside. Watching gravely while continued to pump, for minutes in diminishing rhythm.

. . . the look of surprised hurt on a child's face in Central Pa The string of his helium-filled balloon had slipped from his finge The blue balloon floated slowly upward. Then, caught by the win it whirled away.

. . . George Bernard Shaw: "Liberty means responsibility. Th is why most men dread it."

. . . in a darkened car. A street on upper Manhattan. A wa hand touching me. "Please?" she had asked. "Please?"

I fumbled in my pocket, found the dispenser, popped a spansule

"Nick?" Paul said anxiously. "You all right?"

"Yes," I said. I jerked a thumb toward the glass. "Very impr sive, Nancy. Now what do we have to do to get something to around here?"

"Right now," she said. "I warn you, Nick—all my Te Leaders will be there. We're ganging up to you."

"Don't tell me," I said. "Let me guess. You want more love

"How on earth did you know?" She giggled.

It was a delightfully noisy, confused lunch. Almost everythi served had been grown in the Field Office's hydroponic beds. The few protein substitutes were made from soy rather than petroleum. I hadn't had such a flavorful feast in months.

As we gobbled, we squabbled. The usual kaka: pure versus applied science; the impossibility of an absolute value judgment; action versus speculation; the influence of technology on the future of science; and so forth, and so forth. I had heard it all before. I let Paul attempt to answer their questions and respond to their complaints. It was time he learned to handle, to control, to manipulate these free and sometimes abrasive debates. I thought he did rather well.

Finally, I glanced at my digiwatch. Almost 1330. I pushed back from the table and stood up. The room quieted. Everyone looked to me.

"Lousy food," I said. "About what I'd expect in a dump like this."

They laughed delightedly. Strange. The young prefer insults. How old must one be to learn to accept gratitude gracefully?

"And now," I continued, "I expect to be presented with the bill. Let me guess. . . . You are against further love being spent on chimerism by transplant. You are in favor of enormous sums of love being spent on chimerism by genetic tinkering. Well, this is my decision. . . ."

They were silent, staring at me expectantly, wide-eyed. . . .

"My decision," I said, "is that Paul Bumford, your new ruler, will make the decision. Good-bye, all. Stay happy."

I marched out, to a chorus of groans, boos, laughter, catcalls. Paul came running after me into the corridor.

"Nick!" he gasped. "You're not serious?"

"I'm serious." I nodded. "It's your decision. Make it."

I changed into civilian clothes at the hotel. I took a cab to Hawkley's office, in a new skyscraper overlooking Balboa Park. The building was as cold and sterile as an operating theater. The offices of Hawkley, Goldfarb & Bensen weren't much better. They occupied the entire thirty-fourth floor, and appeared to be carved from a single block of white plastisteel. If a robot had taken my hat I wouldn't have been a bit surprised. It was not encouraging.

I gave my name to the matronly receptionist. She murmured into an intercom. I stood waiting. In a few moments a knobless panel opened in the wall; the young, blond private secretary came out to collect me.

"Mr. Flair?"

"Yes."

"Follow me, please."

"To the ends of the earth."

I had hoped for a dimple. But there was no reaction. I followed her haunches down a long, apparently endless corridor. On both sides of that nightmare alley doors led away to—to what? Offices? Closets? Cells?

There was no human sound. A slight hum of machinery. Or perhaps I was humming to myself. We went through a door to another, much shorter corridor. At the end, a door. What a door!

It was oaken, the wood looking as though it had been excavated from primeval ooze and laid out on desert sand to dry and bleach. The outside hinges were unpainted iron, fancifully wrought, fastened to the wood with clumpy studs. There was no hint of plastiseal, no sign of any futuristic fakery.

"I'll buy the door," I told the blond ef.

"He'd never sell it," she said.

She bounced her knuckles off the wood. Like rapping the Great Pyramid of Cheops. Then she swung the door outward. It moved with nary a squeak.

"Mr. Nicholas Flair," she announced.

I stepped inside, past her. She disappeared. I heard that massive door thud shut behind me.

If there had been a single feature of that remarkable room unconvincing or not essential, I would have thought it more stage set than office. But I did not see anything leased, and there was nothing I did not want to own.

It was obso, of course: pine paneling; curtained windows; maroon velvet drapes; a mahogany desk; shelves of leather-bound law books, glassed in. And brass lighting fixtures with green shades, buff ceiling, watercolors of ancient sailing ships, a table of carved walnut, a liquor cabinet made from a campaign chest: inset hardware and brass corners. Over all, a musty, antique odor; paste wax and oil, old wood and polished metal.

The obso em sitting motionless behind the enormous desk belonged there: fly frozen in amber. He appeared to be ninety, at least. He was not bald, but white hair had thinned to a halo. Keratoses of scalp, temples, backs of hands lying palms down on the black desk blotter.

Clear, almost colorless eyes. Penetrating stare. A hooked beak, fleshless. Lips that had faded into the surrounding skin. A haze of eyebrows and lashes. The corpus thin to the point of emaciation.

The voice was shockingly deep, strong, resonant. I had expected a frail whisper.

"Forgive me for not rising," he said. He moved a finger toward a thick cane hooked over a corner of the desk. "I move as little as possible."

"That's quite all right, sir," I said.

He did not, I noted, ask me to be seated.

"Sir. . . ." I said. And paused.

He gave me no encouragement. He was stone. Posture, manner unyielding. I knew at once it had been a mistake. Not fatal—but still a waste.

"I am interested in making an investment in the San Diego area," I said rapidly. Determined to speak my piece and leave with as much dignity as I could salvage.

"Investment?"

"Yes, sir. Preferably in real estate or industrial properties."

"You have something specific in mind?"

"Scilla Pharmaceuticals. They are—"

"I know them," he said shortly. "No, I'm afraid I can't help you."

That was clear enough. I turned, took two steps, had my hand on the huge brass doorknob when he spoke my name for the first time.

"Mr. Flair," he trumpeted. "Dr. Nicholas Flair. Deputy Director of something called the Satisfaction Section. Of something called the Department of Bliss. Of something called the Government of the United States of America."

I took my hand off the knob, turned back.

"That is correct," I said.

"The name Flair is not unknown in this city," he said coldly. "I like to know who is coming across the country to see me. It wasn't difficult to find out."

"I didn't think it would be," I said. "I admire your thoroughness—if that's what you want from me."

"It isn't," he said. "I couldn't care less what you think of me."

"Then our business is at an end, sir," I said.

Again I turned to go. Again his voice stopped me.

"Your father is wealthy," he said. "Has a good reputation. You seem to be in no need. You hold a responsible government job."

"So?" I said.

"Just to satisfy an old man's curiosity," he said. Eyes squinting. "Why should a young man in your position want to invest in a drug manufacturer that sells to the government you work for? Shoddy, Mr. Flair. I don't like shoddy."

I looked at him. It was obvious what he thought.

"My motive is not what you suspect," I told him.

"Oh? Then what is your motive?"

I should have walked out then, of course. But I wanted to make a chip, at least, in that icy superiority.

"My motive, sir?" I said. "Revenge."

If he had been given adrenalin IV, the result could not have been more astonishing. The sunken cheeks flushed. The cold eyes took on a sparkle. He pushed himself upright in his straight-backed chair.

"Revenge?" he said. "Revenge?"

I stared at him, astounded by the sudden change in his appearance. He had, literally, come alive. He raised a steady hand, pointed across the room at the polished liquor cabinet.

"On the lower shelf, young man," he said. "The squarish decanter and two balloons, please."

I hesitated a moment. Then I did as he asked. I brought the bottle and brandy snifters back to his desk. He waved me to a leather armchair. Then he unstoppered the decanter, poured the two glasses one-third full, pushed one of them toward me. His movements were slow but not tremulous. We lifted, nodded, sipped.

I almost gagged. It was liquid fire. He smiled happily. I thought it was a smile; there was a crinkling.

"Burgundian," he said. "From the grape dregs. An acquired taste. Like revenge. Tell me what you think I should know."

I kept it brief. I did not mention Angela Berri by name. I said only that my target was an object in a high government position who was on the suck. I outlined my plan. He listened intently, not interrupting. But his eyes never left mine.

I finished. I waited for his reaction.

"An outlandish scheme," he said finally. "Farfetched."

"Yes, sir," I agreed. "It's a great advantage. The object couldn't possibly conceive of anyone going to all that trouble."

"And expense," he said shrewdly. "It's going to take a lot of money."

"A lot of love," I said mischievously.

"Money," he repeated stubbornly.

I laughed. "Money it is," I said. "How much?"

"How could I possibly know at this time? A lot. You want complete ownership? Or will a partnership suffice?"

"Ownership, if possible. Or any arrangement that will give me access to the offices. The chief executive must be ruled by me."

"I see." He pondered a moment. "Of course, you want your name kept out?"

"Of course. I thought you might be able to set up a dummy corporation, or some kind of a holding—"

"Don't tell me my business," he said crossly. "There are many new discoveries and products of which I am not aware, I'm sure. But now you're talking about something as old as Cain and Abel. We used to call it a 'fuzz job.' "

"I don't believe I've ever heard the expression."

"To fuzz the ownership of a particular property. Hide it behind layers of owners of record. Lots of papers. That's the secret: lots and lots of legal documents. The true ownership can always be traced, of course. But only after a great deal of time and effort. By then, we will have accomplished our purpose."

"*Our* purpose?" I repeated. "You're willing to take this on?"

"Oh yes," he said. "It's human. Very human indeed. It almost convinces me that there's hope for you yet."

"Hope for *me*?"

"For you, your generation, your world. That it's not all urine specimens and computer printouts. There's some blood left."

I smiled politely and lifted my glass.

"To blood," I said.

We made what arrangements we could: his payment, maximum love to be expended, transfer of funds, communication. He suggested the code. Thirty years previously he had written a thin book: *Early Monasteries of Southern California.* It had been privately published. He still had a dozen volumes left, and gave me one. If he sent me a letter of numbers, including 19-3-14, it would mean the fourteenth word of the third paragraph on page 19. Simple and unbreakable. Providing, of course, the key wasn't known to the interceptor.

I leaned across the desk to shake his frail hand just before I departed. I knew a palm stroke would offend him.

"Mr. Hawkley," I said. "A pleasure."

"Yes, young man." He nodded. "It will be a pleasure. You must tell me all about it. When it's over."

"When it's over," I agreed. "Meanwhile, sir, our Gerontology Team has come up with—"

"No pills, no pills," he said sharply. Then, to soften his refusal, he patted the brandy decanter gently. "This is my medicine."

I left him then. No fear of failure. With my ideas and energy and his experience. . . . But the euphoria may have been due to the marc. Put *that* in a pill and my fortune was made!

Y-5

At that point in time, according to regulations, I should have turned over to Paul Bumford complete rule of the Division of Research & Development. I did not do so for the following reasons:

1. Paul, although able and talented, was inexperienced in the administration of many objects, despite his previous service as my Executive Assistant.

2. There were a number of ongoing projects in DIVRAD which I had originated or to which I contributed. I could not withdraw my personal service suddenly without loss of creative momentum.

3. The transfer of the Division of Security & Intelligence to Angela Berri's headquarters had left me with only three divisions. Two of these—Law & Enforcement and Data & Statistics—practically ran themselves; they required a minimum of administrative supervision. Hence, I could devote more time to DIVRAD.

If my future actions were questioned, if I was called to account by a Board of Inquiry, those were the three explanations I would have given for my conduct—and all were operative.

But the real reason I could not—had no desire to—relinquish the rule of the Division of Research & Development was considerably more complex.

The popular belief was that laws (policies) of the US Government were made by the Legislative branch and administered by the Executive. It was cynically believed that the Public Service (formerly Civil Service) was a necessary boondoggle of bookkeepers, accountants, statisticians, computerniks, clerks, etc.—mindless and servile paper-shufflers interested only in obtaining the highest possible rank-rate for the least possible effort.

A dangerous assumption.

Actually, it was quite possible for a bureaucrat to make policy. In fact, it was frequently a required part of his service. Congress might legislate the broad outlines of policy. But inevitably, it was a lot of kaka until bureaucrats translated law into action. How they translated it was, in effect, how US society functioned and evolved.

I had, long ago, realized that the Division of Research & Development, of the Satisfaction Section, of the Department of Bliss, wielded political clout far beyond its size and status on the government's Table of Organization. No object, ever, surrenders power voluntarily. I was not about to yield the enormous power of DIVRAD to Paul Bumford, or to anyone else.

The governing factors were these:

1. The Executive, Legislative, and Judicial branches of the US Government did not yet fully appreciate the significance and consequences of the Biological Revolution and the increasing contribution of all scientific disciplines to the political world and the manner in which life would be lived. The general public was almost totally unaware of what lay ahead—not in 100, 50, or 20 years, but tomorrow.

2. After the death of President Harold K. Morse, there was no one object in the higher echelons of government who, by conditioning or inclination, was capable of recognizing what was happening. A few Congressmen had degrees in science. Most were woefully ignorant. Even the staffs of Congressional committees whose service was to oversee DIVRAD's budget and operations did not have the necessary expertise.

Power abhors a vacuum. I rushed in. I cannot list here, for want of space, the areas in which I—*I*, personally—could make national policy through DIVRAD. And not policy of little importance, but policy that would affect the society we lived in, and society for generations to come. A single example will suffice. . . .

Annually, an item of X-million new dollars for "gerontology research" was included in DIVRAD's requested budget. Congressmen and staffs of the ruling committees assumed the love was for investigation and cure of biomedical disorders of the aged. During my tenure at DIVRAD, the requested sum was never reduced. Never. It would have been politically inexpedient. The rapidly growing number of obsos were voters. And increasingly vocal in their demands.

So, annually, I was granted X-million new dollars for gerontology research, with no restrictions as to how the sum was to be spent.

The legislators had no more knowledge of gerontology than they had of molecular genetics.

I had several options, including:

1. Prolong life itself. That is, attempt to extend the physical life span to, say, 100 or 125 years, by heavy research into the mechanism of stopping. But that might leave us with an enormous population of senile, dribbling oldsters, to be supported by the taxes of younger generations. The care of obsos was already an onerous economic burden. How long before euthanasia of all those over Y years of age was legislated?

2. Improve the middle life. That is, devote those X-million new dollars to research in arteriosclerosis, arthritis, senility, and other deteriorative disorders, to ensure a relatively healthy old age without appreciably increasing the longevity rates. But to what purpose? The obsos would still be retired nonproducers and nonconsumers.

3. Extend immaturity. Spend those gerontology research funds to prolong youth, keeping the young young for a longer period, so that one-half of an object's life might be spent in conditioning, the second half in producing, and all of it in consuming.

These were but three of the options I faced in determining how gerontology research love was to be spent. I have simplified my choices, of course. There was an almost infinite number of additional factors to be considered.

For instance, the human species is by nature conservative. That is, objects resent and are fearful of change, despite the fact that change is the only constant of biological and political history. This abhorrence of change becomes stronger as objects grow older. Obsos cannot cope with change. It bewilders them. So even naturally intelligent and well-conditioned oldsters frequently waste their energy providing obsolete answers to obsolete questions, like bad chess players. Did we really want a society of doddering conservatives?

I go into such detail to illustrate my thesis that bureaucrats *can* make vital policy. And, more than any other department of Public Service, DIVRAD made policy that affected the life and future of every object in the US and, eventually, every object on earth.

That was why I was unwilling to relinquish this awesome power. Sometimes it is necessary to cultivate madness.

My activities during the several days following my visit to San

Diego provide a more precise conception of my responsibilities and the decisions I was called upon to make.

Leo Bernstein ruled the miniteam conducting research on the severed head of Fred III. At the age of eighteen, Leo was, in my opinion, one of the top three biochemists in the world. Certainly the fattest. When he was thirteen, Leo had published a brilliant theoretical paper on the virus causing plantar warts. It had led to chemotherapy for rodent ulcers of the face and scalp, and suggested an entirely new approach to the treatment of all epidermal carcinomas.

Leo's only defect was that he knew exactly how good he was.

He waddled into my office, tossed a computer printout onto my desk, lowered himself sideways onto a chair, and with much grunting effort hoisted his bulging thighs over one of the arms.

"Make yourself at home, Leo," I said.

He couldn't be bothered with irony, small talk, or common courtesy.

"Take a look," he commanded. He gestured toward the printout. "We checked the numbers three times. It's operative."

I scanned the printout. It was stupefying. I had been away from the lab too long. Things were moving too fast.

"Where the hell's the bottom line?" I said.

"On the bottom. What's the matter, teacher?" he jeered. "Can't keep up?"

I forgave talent anything, including distended egos. I scanned the printout again. Again. Finally I computed the meaning.

It was exciting, but I wouldn't let him see my pleasure. In brief, what Leo's team had done was to stabilize the deterioration rate of Fred's brain. They hadn't yet halted the natural stopping of brain cells and loss of electrical power. But they had firmed the *rate* of decline. A small step, but an important one.

"Not bad," I acknowledged. "But a breakthrough it ain't."

"Don't jerk me." Leo grinned. "It's great and you know it."

"What are you using?"

"You'll never guess."

"That's why I'm asking."

"Ergotamine."

My astonishment drew a burst of laughter from him. But he didn't know the cause of my reaction. Ergotamine is an alkaloid of ergot, with a chemical structure similar to that of lysergic acid, a hallucinogen. Marvelous. Everything was going my way.

"Excellent," I said. "Nervy thinking. Stick with it."

"Of course," he said. "Increasing the dosage. I'll have Fred's deterioration ended in a month."

"Leo," I said, "if you're ever wrong, may I be the first to know?"

He laughed again, made a rude gesture, grabbed up his computer printout, waddled out of the office. He was an obese young em. But no fat around his brain.

Maya Leighton came into my apartment wearing a floor-length plastilap cloak in kelly green and an enormous tooty nosering of braided elephant hair. As usual, there was about her an aura of febrile expectancy. From my conditioning at the Science Academy I suddenly remembered an obso medical term: thyrotoxicosis. But perhaps I was playing doctor.

I took the cloak from her shoulders. She was wearing an em's shirt, the tails rolled up and knotted beneath her gourdish breasts. There was a wide span of naked torso. Smooth, tanned. A large umbilicus with a protruding yolk stalk, a little tongue. Beneath were rough pants, belted low on the pelvis. Wisps of pubic hair sprouted like sprigs of parsley. Between heavy bosom and wide hips, that incredibly slender waist.

"We're going to Alexandria on Friday," I said. "You and I. To the Hospice. I want to take a look at Lewisohn."

"All right," she said equably. "That will be nice. Can we drive?"

"Good idea. We'll start early. Take our time. Do you drive?"

"Oh, yes! May I? Part of the way, at least?"

"Of course. We'll stop for lunch along the way."

"A picnic lunch."

"Or at some amusing roadside restaurant."

"Maybe near a lake or river."

"We'll eat outside. With wine."

"We'll throw crusts to the swans."

We both laughed. I leaned to tongue her breasts.

As usual, Maya was eagerly complaisant, almost perversely so. Mastery excited me. I felt no sadistic tendencies, but still. . . .

We showered together, tissues raw and swollen. I mentioned, as casually as I could, that after the Alexandria visit, we would go into

Washington where I had a dinner engagement.

"But you won't be left alone," I told her. "We'll stay at DIROB's apartment."

"All right."

"Her Chief of Security will take care of you," I said. "His name is Art Roach."

"All right."

"He has a bad reputation."

"Bad?"

"He's a rough em. You understand?"

"Yes."

"Will you be careful?"

She laughed and presented her great soaped ass to me.

I had a two-hour conference with Frank and Frances von Liszt and their top attorneys of the Division of Law & Enforcement. It was a relaxed, unstructured meeting. I had convened it to discuss progress in an ongoing project to write an addendum to the Fertility Control Act. When completed, the proposed law would be submitted to Congress for debate and, I hoped, legislation.

The new law would require compulsory sterilization of habitual criminals, the feebleminded, insane, drug addicts, chronic alcoholics, and those suffering from incurable genetic disorders and/or abnormal sexuality.

I felt very strongly on the need for such a law. You must realize that the service of DIVRAD fell into two time-frames. We were seeking to prevent mental retardation and physical disorders by genetic engineering; i.e., we were trying to improve the quality of the gene pool of the future.

Simultaneously, we were seeking to cure living victims of those same disorders, and thus improve the quality of life in the present. Sometimes, happily, a discovery in one time frame also proved efficacious in the other. More frequently, our successes in genetic engineering far surpassed our victories in the treatment of existing victims. Hence the need for compulsory sterilization.

I wanted to present a proposed law as logical and complete as possible. As usual when dealing with subjects as sensitive as this—a law that limited personal liberty for the public good—the main difficulty was precise definition of terms. What was insanity? Feeblemindedness? Abnormal sexuality?

Source material covered the long conference table. With as many

209

opinions as sources. No consensus. I could see the von Liszts and their staff were bewildered and disheartened by this mass of conflicting views.

"Look," I told them. "You're getting bogged down in a quicksand. Don't consult any more authorities. Don't scan any more learned papers or listen to distinguished scientists and scholars. You have quite enough here to assimilate."

"But it's so contradictory," Frances burst out. "Nick, we just can't reconcile all these viewpoints."

"Impossible." Her brother nodded. "And not only disagreement on definitions of the physical and mental disorders warranting sterilization, but also a zillion objections to such a program on religious, ethical, and political grounds."

"Now you're getting into value judgments," I warned him. "In an area where there are no universal values. We cannot let ourselves become involved in a moral debate. It would go on forever, never be settled, and nothing would be accomplished. Somehow we have to create a situation in which we are above such a debate—or beyond it. A situation in which opposition is, if not hopeless, at least ineffectual."

"And how do we do that?" one of the attorneys demanded. "You're asking for guaranteed success."

"No," I said. "Just better odds than we have now. All right—give me a minute and then I'll throw you some raw meat."

They quieted, lighted up their Bolds, whispered softly to each other. I sat where I was, at the head of the table, looking with some distaste at the mounds of research. A lot of thoughts there. Ideas. Theories. Kaka. If I let it, science would be pushed back to the four elements, demonology, dowsing, and belief in the soul.

"All right," I said loudly. "Here's what we do."

Heads snapped up. They looked at me expectantly.

"For some time I haven't been satisfied with the Genetic Rating program. It was originally established under the Fertility Control Act to be exactly what its title indicates: classification of objects by genetic quality. The big error was to assign to human examiners the authority to determine Genetic Ratings. There are good GE's and there are bad ones. But all suffer from one defect: They are human. It was inevitable that subjective judgments would be made. The entire Genetic Rating program should have been computerized from the start.

"That will be our first step. The switch to computerization can be made by administrative decree without enabling legislation. I anticipate very little opposition. As a matter of fact, I think the move will draw general approval. You've all heard the stories of bribery of GE's, and other rumors as to how they are influenced by personal and political considerations. The main opposition will come from the GE's themselves when they learn they're being replaced by a King Mk. V. But there aren't enough GE's to cause a major flap, and they'll be assured of transfer to other services with a rank-rate equal to or more than their present love.

"Now I want you to work very closely with Data and Statistics in planning the programming for determining Genetic Ratings. Make certain that minus-ratings of sufficient weight are given for precisely those disorders for which we will eventually require sterilization."

A gasp ran around the room. They turned to look at one another. They understood now what I was planning.

"Once computerized Genetic Ratings are operational—we should be able to do it in a year, at most—the Sterilization Addendum will then be submitted to Congress. We'll have to give it an attractive title—like the Gene Pool Improvement Act, or something like that. It will be based solely on Genetic Ratings. The opposition will then find no human objects to debate. You can't argue with mechanical thinking. Having already accepted computerized Genetic Ratings, they'll find it difficult to object to the use of those ratings to improve the quality of life today and the quality of the gene pool tomorrow. I don't say they'll be completely silenced. Of course, they won't be. But we'll have broken their teeth. I think we can win this one, and the plan I have outlined is exactly how we'll do it. Any questions?"

There were no questions.

Phoebe Huntzinger returned from the Denver Field Office. She marched into my office. Her usual placidity was not evident. She was disturbed and trying to control it.

"Phoebe," I said, "how was the trip?"

"The trip? Fine. I like it out there. Would you believe they still have snow up in the mountains?"

"I believe. You like the objects?"

"At the FO? Some good brains there, Nick."

"I know. So what's the problem?"

She tried to laugh. "It shows?"

211

"It shows. A crisis at Denver?"

"Not so much a crisis as just plain, everyday, run-of-the-mill stupidity."

"Can it be glossed?"

"What? Oh, sure, Nick. It can be handled."

"All right. Then there's no crisis. Now what is it?"

"Do you know how they're running this game?"

"On this particular project? Roughly. Nine laser beams pick up the CNS electrical activity. They scan in overlapping disks, like radar beams. Right so far?"

"Right."

"Electric synapses show on screen and at the same time the bedside computer determines location, duration, and strength of the cerebral signal. That information is amplified and fed into the master computer for translation into printout. From a trigger in the brain, we get an actual word in type. Correct?"

"Correct. Pretty good for an old em like you. Is there *anything* going on in this Section you don't know?"

"Cut the kaka. What's the problem?"

"You're hoping for a conception from the experimental object. A complete declarative sentence. Nick?"

"Yes."

"Impossible."

"Why impossible?"

"What do you think is the vocabulary of the master computer? How many signals is it programmed to accept and translate into words?"

"Oh . . . I don't know. Three thousand? Five thousand?"

"Two hundred."

"You're joking?"

"I'm not. That computer can never give you a conception, Nick. It only knows two hundred words, and almost all of them are adjectives and adverbs. Few verbs. No pronouns. It's great for picking up sensations and emotions. Hot. Pink. Green. Soft. Blue. Happy. Red. But a complete conception? Forget it. Unless your idea of a declarative sentence is: 'Sad red warm hurt cold loud.' "

I got up, moved to the window, stared out into murky sky. I tried to control my anger. I knew there were two factors that negated the best efforts of the best futurists: human genius and human stupidity. You could construct the greatest mathematical model in the world, but all your agonized planning could be brought to dust by a

ukemic dwarf creating a new idea in a hospice bed or by a stupid
cientist who neglected an experimental element so basic that no
ne thought to question it.

I turned to face Phoebe Huntzinger. I tried to smile. She tried. We
oth failed.

"Not fatal," I said. "Peter Stanley?"

"The Team Leader? Yes, Nick. That's his name."

"I'll take care of him. Phoebe, does this project interest you?"

"Yes. Very much. Let me serve on it, Nick. The things I do
round here are routine. My Division runs itself. You know that."

"All right. That master computer in Denver—a Golem?"

"Mk. III."

"What's the storage potential?"

"Vocabulary? Maybe ten thousand words tops, on the basis of
put from the bedside computer."

"Flash WISSEC. They've got basic vocabulary lists from five
ords to fifty thousand. Ask for copies of one, three, five, and ten
ousand words. Program Golem to its limit. Got that?"

"Sure."

"What about the in-brain technology? Any chance of a foulup
ere?"

"I don't know, Nick. It's not my field."

I nodded. "I'll take care of it. As soon as you get your word lists,
et back to Denver and start the reprogramming. Thanks, Phoebe."

She smiled warmly at me.

"Nick, if I wasn't married, I'd suggest you and I use each other.
ne night at least."

"Why not?" I said. "Your wife won't mind. By the way,
hoebe, that Denver project never has been named. I've been
arrying it on the budget under Gerontology Research. I think we'll
ring it out of the closet now and give it a name. Make the servers
eel they're on something important. We'll call it Project Phoenix."

"Whatever you say, Nick."

Paul Bumford returned from the San Diego Field Office on
hursday morning. He flashed my office to report in. On screen, he
ppeared thin, hard, drawn.

"Tired?" I asked him.

"Busted my ass," he said. But he was not grumbling. If any-
ing, he seemed proud of his labors, confident of his mastery of his
ew power.

213

"How did you resolve the chimerism debate?" I asked him.

"I told them I would phase out the transplant program and provide more love for genetic manipulation. Nick?"

"Excellent. Good judgment."

"I passed the test? Thanks, teacher."

"Paul, break the news gently to the Chimerism Team here. Better yet, just don't mention it. Reduce their love gradually over a period of a year. Eventually, they'll get the message."

"That's what I planned to do," he said crossly. "How about a serveout and swim later today?"

"Fine. At the DIVSEC gym. Meet you about 1700."

At 1630, I left my office and walked over to the small gym and swimming pool on the compound grounds. It was not the large communal gym-pool, available to servers of all ranks, but was located in what had formerly been the headquarters building of the Division of Security & Intelligence.

When Angela moved DIVSEC to Washington, leaving behind only a guard company for compound security, their offices were assigned to objects from other divisions who required more room for their service. The small gym and swimming pool that had formerly been reserved for the exclusive use of DIVSEC had now, by my decree, become a private facility for the use of PS-4 rank and higher.

Paul was serving out in the gym when I arrived. He was using the horizontal wallbars. Arms stretched over his head, he had suspended his body a few inches above the floor. With his back pressed against the bars, he was slowly raising and lowering his legs from the hips.

I had changed to plastilast briefs in the locker room. Paul was wearing a plastilast clout. His body had always been androgynous. But now he had lost weight; he had a waist; I could see his rib cage. He was no longer pudgy. I fancied even his skin tone had changed. It was no longer blushed. And it was taut. Plump curves had disappeared. Muscles were discernible.

"You're looking good," I said.

I jumped up to grab a bar alongside him. I began to replicate his exercise, lifting my legs from the hips, slowly, then slowly lowering them.

"Nancy Ching?" I said. "What's your input?"

"Superior," he gasped. "Elegant brain. Good ruler. Her servers follow."

214

"Use her?" I asked. "After I left?"

"Yes," he said. "At her cottage, north of La Jolla Bay."

I felt something.

"Fine." I exhaled. "She's profitable."

"Election," he said, trying to breathe deeply as he exercised. "Off-year election out there. Local Congressmen."

I turned my head to look at him. His lovely body was sheened.

"Don't tell me Nancy is involved? She'll stop her career."

"No, no. She just mentioned this obso in office will probably be returned. She said he's a clunk."

"So?"

"His support is mostly from obsos. This is for the Tomorrow File. My idea. Nick, why should obsos have the vote? No one under sixteen has it. Why objects over, say, fifty or sixty? It's not right. They don't produce, and their consumption rate is nil."

"Disenfranchise the obsos? Good. Solve the political problem of their conservatism. Excellent thinking, Paul. Add it to the File. Let's go to the bikes."

They were bicyclelike mechanical contrivances bolted to the floor. You could adjust the tension on the pedals. An odometer showed meters and kilometers. Paul and I mounted onto the saddles.

"Set it at five," I told him. "One new dollar on a kilometer."

"You're on," he said.

We began to pedal madly.

"That thing in Denver," I said. "Printout from brain signals."

"Yes."

"I coded it Project Phoenix."

"Oh?"

"The computerization was mucked."

I told him what Phoebe Huntzinger had told me, how the computer vocabulary had been shorted.

"Oh, God," he groaned.

"Get rid of Peter Stanley. He's the Team Leader."

He turned his head sideways to glance at me.

"Terminate him with prejudice?" he said slowly.

"Not permanently, you idiot. Transfer him. A tsetse fly station in darkest Africa—something like that. Just get rid of him."

"All right, Nick."

"I want you to go to Denver and check out the in-brain technology. There may be a balls-up there, too."

"Nick, for God's sake, I've got a full plate."

"Then send Mary Bergstrom. She can compute what's going on."

He was silent. We were both pedaling our stationary bicycles as hard as we could. Gripping handlebars with sweaty hands. Knees plunging up and down. Leaning forward. Gasping. Striving.

"What's stressing you?" I panted.

"You," he said. "What you're doing. Goddamn it, Nick, it's *my* Division. I rule it. I'm AssDepDirRad. Can't you let me make the decisions?"

"You object to my decisions?"

"No, but let *me* make them. Your decisions are operative, but I want to make them first. You've been acting like a—like a—" He paused in fury and frustration. "Like a mogul!" he burst out, pedaling crazily.

"Mogul?" I shouted. "I haven't heard that word in years!"

"Well, that's what you are—a mogul."

We pedaled away furiously, glancing occasionally at each other's odometer. We were about equal. I strained to draw ahead.

"Power," I gasped. "I recognize the symptoms."

"Because you suffer from it yourself."

"Right! You don't seek it out. It seeks you. It's a passion, a virus. It's incurable."

"You've got it and I've got it."

"Yes. Can't we serve together?"

"Sure," he said.

"One kilometer," I said, peering at my odometer. I stopped pedaling, swung off the saddle. I stood trembling, knees water, heart thudding. Paul stopped pumping, swung slowly from his machine.

"You win," he said. "Owe you a dollar."

He walked away. Steadily. Not looking back. I glanced at his odometer. It showed slightly over one kilometer.

I took one hand off the wheel and placed it delicately on her hard, tanned thigh. She was wearing a miniskirt. Fresh zipsuits and makeup were in a small overnight case on the back seat.

"Look what I have," she said.

She unzipped her purse. I took my eyes off the road a moment to glance down. A red dildo.

"Got a jerk for Indians?" I asked her.

She laughed.

"I like the color: Come-Along Red. Nice?"

"Oh, yes," I said. "Electric?"

"Ultrasonic."

"Turn your bones to water," I warned her.

"I don't care."

"Shock therapy?"

"Well . . . it just feels good."

"The endless problem of therapeutics," I said. "Risk versus benefit."

She laughed again and hiked her little skirt higher.

"You're cute," she said.

I had been certain the day would prove a disaster. It began in rain, what Hibernians call a "soft day." Gray, wet, endless. Not gusty or sweeping; nothing as dramatic as that. Just a slow, unreeling curtain of drifting water. Polluted enough to stain cloth.

I requisitioned a hydrogen-powered sedan from the motor pool. Speed and acceleration were not the best, but it could churn out 100 kph without faltering. Just what we needed for the run south.

Except that every driver in New York was going to Alexandria, Virginia, that Friday morning. Or so it seemed. It took us an hour to get through the new Morse Tunnel to Jersey City. The freeway south was clogged, an infarcted artery: stop start, start stop.

Then suddenly, almost instantaneously, it ran free. I moved the hand accelerator switch. At the same time the curtain of rain lifted. Someone rolled it up. Just like that. The sun was there in a clearing sky. Blue. Maya Leighton sighed and pushed out her long legs. And I put my hand lightly on her bare, cool thigh. It might, I thought, it just might serve.

"Maya, where are you from?"

"GPA-5."

I guessed Iowa.

"What made you pick geriatrics?"

"I want to live forever."

She switched off the air conditioning and lowered the window on her side. I lowered mine. The fresh air seemed washed. Sun-warmed. She took off her jacket, unbuttoned her blouse to the waist, put her hand inside. She began to hum. Not a tune, a song. Just a hum, a not unpleasant drone. Her eyes were closed.

"Maya, what do you want?"

"Excitement," she said drowsily.

217

"I can give you that. Pain, too."

"That's excitement," she said faintly.

I thought she might be napping. She was a lazy animal. She required long hours of sleep.

I drove steadily, letting the astronauts zoom by. The wide road lulled. Suddenly, without willing it, I was at peace. We—she, I, the car—were floating and stationary. The new world revolved beneath our wheels.

I made the long curve onto the new elevated freeway that had been completed north to Mt. Holly. Eventually it would link with the Morse Tunnel to Manhattan. At that point in time, it was completed from Mt. Holly south to Washington, D.C. Once on it, you were captive. You could turn off for Philadelphia, Wilmington, or Baltimore. Otherwise, you had no place to go until you saw the Capitol.

"Good-bye, swans," I said.

"Good-bye, roadside paradise," she said sleepily.

"We'll pull off," I promised her. "They don't let you starve. Exactly. Do you prefer a fake English tavern or a fake German biergarten?"

"You decide," she murmured. "You say."

Her hand flopped limply sideways. Into my lap. Her fingers tightened gently. She began to play.

"Keep that up," I warned her, "and the result will pop my zipper and poke up through the steering wheel. Then some idiot will cut in front. I'll make a hard turn, and fracture my engorged penis. You, naturally, will then provide medical attention. And I will go to my very important dinner engagement this evening with my *Laternenpfahl* in splints. Is that what you want?"

"You're mad," she giggled.

"I suspect so," I sighed.

She turned sideways on the passenger seat, lying with her head in my lap, her hips turned. I took my right hand off the wheel and slid it into her unbuttoned shirt. I pinched a nipple as hard as I could between my knuckles.

"Yes," she breathed.

We stopped for lunch at one of the approved turnoff "Rest-Ur-Haunts." This one was a fake Italian ristorante. We dined under an outside arbor, enclosed by washable plastic lattice. Overhead were clumps of purple plastirub grapes and green leaves. On the tables were imitation empty Chianti bottles, fitted with plastiwax candles

218

and flame-shaped bulbs with flickering filaments. Battery-powered. The false bottles even had browned, peeling labels. It was swell.

We returned to the car trading small belches from the proveal, propep, natural spaghetti, red wine. Frank Lawson Harris, where are you now?

She surprised me; an uncommonly skilled driver. She was relaxed, almost negligent. Hands lightly on the wheel in the approved 10-2 position. Fast, but not careless. Skirt pulled up to her pudendum. Eyes on the road. Elbow on the window rest. Sensitive touch. But excited.

"Can I go faster?" she said.

"Sure."

We went faster. I responded to that, remembering Millie and me whirling around that darkened track in Detroit.

"Whee!" she said.

As usual, speed took me out. I could forget my mad Potemkin's Village scheme to hang Angela Berri by her soft heels, forget the groans of today and the moans of tomorrow. The whispers of yesterday.

"Are you wearing anything?" I asked her.

"Beneath? No."

"Will it bother you?"

"Yes," she said. "It will bother me. *Do it.*"

I twisted my body sideways. She spread her legs eagerly. I buried my face. She tasted of . . .

"Petronac-flavored," she said. "A new douche."

And so we sped into the Nation's Capital.

I took the wheel then. It cost almost two hours to get through Washington traffic, across the Potomac, down into Alexandria. But I welcomed our slow progress. It gave me time to compute the ef at my side.

There were contradictions. I knew—and Paul Bumford concurred—that she had a sharp, alert brain. But I found her, physically, a yawning animal, almost indolent, willing server to sensuality.

Her scientific discipline was geriatrics; all her conditioning had been directed toward alleviating the ills of the aged and the extension of life. Yet she had come to our attention by her suggestions for two euthanasic programs. She had told me glibly, "I want to live forever." But my original take on her had been correct: She *was* terminally oriented.

219

There had been a brief moment in my life when I had believed there was still hope for the human species if there remained but one unpredictable object. But that was youthful romanticism. After I squirmed into the snakepit of national politics, I realized that a ruler must equate the unpredictable with the unreliable. The future was too important to leave to whim.

We were rolling through the lovely Virginia countryside when I decided there was less to her than met the eye. She would not be a problem.

Hospice No. 4 offered a pleasant prospect: several hectares of plastiturf surrounding small plots of natural meadowland, trees, a well-groomed orchard. The buildings were three levels high, constructed of antiqued plastibrick with plastirub ivy attached to the south walls. A curved driveway of Glasphalt led to the portico of the Headquarters Ward. A small spur of this driveway turned off to the receiving and emergency building, marked with a large sign: WELCOME WARD.

The various buildings were in a loose cluster. They were, I knew, connected by underground passageways. Utilities, power sources, computers, and classified labs were also underground. It was a design that was, with minor modifications, standard for government hospices all over the US.

Also standard was a single building that stood apart, unconnected to the others by above- or below-ground passages. It looked exactly like the other wards. The only difference was the plastisteel wire netting over the windows. The netting was molded white. You could hardly see it in the late-afternoon sunshine.

This was the Public Security Ward. It was in this building that objects guilty of politically unacceptable behavior were rehabilitated and reconditioned. It was also where government servers guilty of activities inimical to the public interest were drained. It was also where most of our scientific research on human objects was conducted. Generally, this was limited to the testing of new pharmaceuticals. More esoteric research was the province of my Field Offices.

I do not wish to imply—that is not my thrust at all—that this building was a prison ward of dark dungeons, beatings, torture, starvation, or any other kind of repression whatsoever. Quite the contrary. It was a reasonably clean, cheerful, bright, efficiently operated facility. It was open at all times to duly authorized inspectional or investigative bodies of the US Congress, and was so

220

inspected and investigated frequently. We had nothing to hide. Everything was legal.

It must not be inferred that at this point in time the US was what the Society of Obsoletes termed a "police state." The communications media were still privately owned and allowed to express their views freely, even if those views were critical of government policy, as they sometimes were. Private property rights were still cherished and protected by law. And the public could still vote, choosing between the two political parties. In fact, during the Presidential election of 1996, 16 percent of the qualified electorate had cast ballots. So the US could hardly be called a police state. Far from it.

We were no sooner parked, getting out of the car, when a group of white-clad figures debouched through the main door of the Headquarters Ward. They awaited us on the porch. I recognized Dr. Luke Warren.

"Welcoming committee?" Maya Leighton asked.

"Yes," I said. I was about to warn her not to speak unless spoken to, to follow my lead in all things—but then I thought better of it. Let her behave as she wished. It would give me additional input on her potential.

We went up to the porch. Introductions and palm stroking began. I gathered fresh evidence of a new social habit I had first noted a few months previously.

The palm stroke had generally replaced the handshake by the mid-1980's. Human behavior analysts believed its origin was the palm slap of black "studs" and "cats," widely used in the 1960's. The violence of that gesture was modified in the palm stroke that had become an almost universal token of friendly greeting. Originally the palm was offered with the hand held vertically, thumb and fingers closed. Palms were pressed as much as stroked.

I had noticed a new modification that signaled status. The server, or inferior, was, more and more, offering his hand in a semihorizontal or sometimes flat position, palm upward. Almost in supplication. The ruler, or superior—by rank, wealth, age, or fame—would then stroke the proferred palm with his own hand turned downward. Almost a benediction.

So we went through the ceremony. All palms were turned up to me. All palms were turned down to my secretary. I was amused, and took care not to show it.

Besides Dr. Luke Warren, the Chief Resident, the only other

object of significance to this account was Dr. Seth Lucas, introduced as the junior resident who had day-to-day responsibility for Hyman Lewisohn's condition. It was the first time I had met Lucas, although I had scanned his file before approving his assignment to the case.

He was a tall, thin (almost scrawny) black with the somewhat glassy stare of a contact lens wearer. His features were quite ordinary. He was nineteen years old and was an honor graduate of the Science Academy's Accelerated Learning Course. He had majored in biochemistry and specialized in psychopharmacology. His record in Public Service had been excellent, but not brilliant. A tiny red tab in his PP (Psychological Profile) called attention to "potential racism against blacks."

Dr. Luke Warren bustled about, gnawing crazily at his upper lip, blinking like mad, continually running both hands over his bald pate, as if to press water from his nonexistent hair. He wanted to shepherd us into the colloquy immediately. It was all set up. It was all planned.

I told him that was impossible. I wished to make a personal examination of our famous patient first. Face fell, shoulders slumped. I had dealt his always frail confidence another stout kick. Too bad. In certain objects, one cultivates apprehension. They perform best when fearful or even desperate.

So, with Dr. Seth Lucas showing us the way, Maya and I went to see Lewisohn.

"Seth," I remarked to the black doctor. "Seth. The evil brother of Osiris."

We were walking down a wide, polished corridor, stepping aside occasionally to avoid bustling nurses, pushed beds, wheeled equipment.

"That's right," he said, not smiling. "Seth, the evil brother of Osiris. That's me. Except my brother's name is Sam. Sir."

I looked at him curiously, remembering suddenly.

"Didn't you publish recently?" I asked him.

Then he came alive. Smiling. He looked even younger when he smiled. Little boy playing doctor. White paper gown. Electronic stethoscope hung around his neck.

"Yes, I published," he said. "About six months ago. In the *Psychopharmacology Bulletin*. You scan it?"

"Sure," I said. "'The Influence of Cocaine on Catecholamines in the Treatment of Schizophrenia.' Right?"

222

He laughed with delight.

"Right! What did you think?"

"Elegant organization," I said. "But you're full of kaka."

He bridled.

"How so?"

"The results of that experiment of yours can't be replicated. We tried. I think your problem may have been contaminated coke. What's your clearance?"

"Red-3," he said.

"I'll get it raised to Red-2," I promised him. "Then I'll send you some restricted stuff they're doing in the Spokane Field Office. I think you'll be interested."

"Thank you," he said gratefully. "I'd like that."

We stopped outside Lewisohn's suite. I stepped into a nest across the hall to scrub my hands with germicide and dry them over the hot air outlet and ultraviolet beam. As habitual and meaningless as a devout religionist crossing himself as his bus speeds past a church.

I went back to the door of the suite where Maya and Lucas were waiting.

"How's he doing?" I asked him.

"No better, no worse. An hour ago the count was—"

"All right"—I interrupted him—"I'll get all the gruesome details at the colloquy. What's his mood?"

"Today, not so bad. It scares me."

"Scares you? Why?"

"I'd rather have him ranting and raving."

"I compute." I nodded. "Well . . . we'll see. Maya, when we go in, stand away from the bed where he can see you. If I look at you, clear my throat and raise my chin a little, you go over to the window and look out. Have your back turned to him and bend to look out. Bend far over. Got that?"

"Of course."

"When you turn back into the room, have the top button or the top two buttons of your blouse open. Then come over to stand close to the bed. Understand?"

"Yes."

Dr. Seth Lucas had been looking back and forth from Maya to me during this exchange. But he said nothing. He didn't grin.

"Let's go," I said.

It was a conventional VIP hospital suite. The electrically operated bed dominated. Emergency equipment was hidden behind a screen. A private nest with tub and shower. A parked electric wheelchair. A separate sitting room with sofa and two armchairs of orange plastifoam. A 3-D laser TV set. There were books, papers, tape rolls, and film reels everywhere. A viewing machine. A facsimile newspaper machine. Two flashers and three phones, one in red fitted with a scrambler. A small, desktop computer. Rolls of computer printout.

When we entered, Lewisohn was in bed. The top third raised. He was scanning a thick manuscript through spectacles that looked like the bottoms of obso bottles.

He didn't look up until Dr. Lucas closed the door behind us. Then Lewisohn pushed his glasses down on his mottled nose and stared at us over the rims.

"Dr. Nicholas Bennington Flair," Lewisohn said in his harsh, grating voice. "Born too late. Should have been a Borgia. One of the bad ones. A poisoned dirk at your belt, a poisoned ring on your finger. Wooing a lady with a love song on a lute. Kissing her just before you murder her so you might rule a duchy inherited by her weak brother to whom you have been supplying young boys and drugs from the East."

I looked at him, trying not to show my shock. It had been almost six months since I had last seen him. The deterioration was evident. He was stopping.

"Still reading those crappy novels of yours?" I said disgustedly. "No wonder we can't get any service out of you."

Observers usually thought our insults, our obvious hostility masked a hidden and deep affection. I wasn't so sure.

His eyes slid away from me and locked on Maya Leighton. He continued to speak to me while he stared at her.

"Think you're going to prod me with those filthy fingers of yours?" he demanded. "Be gone. I don't need you. I don't need anyone."

I glanced at Maya, cleared my throat, raised my chin a little. She moved casually to the window. Lewisohn's eyes followed her. She bent far over to peer out. Her legs were slightly spread. The miniskirt hiked up farther on her long, tanned legs.

"Who's she?" Lewisohn shouted furiously. "What's she doing here?"

"Maya Leighton. She's a doctor, too."

"Doctors!" he shouted. "I'm surrounded by doctors. I'm up to

224

my asshole in doctors. All of you get the hell out of here.''

But his voice lacked his usual ferocity. He continued to stare at Maya's bare legs. I moved closer to the bed. I looked down at him.

It is extremely difficult to generalize about the symptoms of leukemia. In many cases there are only minimal signs of physical deterioration; the gradual stopping may be concealed by rosy cheeks, a sweet breath, grossly normal vital functions. But the rot is there: milky blood, tumerous bone marrow, a serious lowering of the defense mechanism against infection.

In Lewisohn's case, however, degeneration of the corpus was plain. Tissue had shrunk. That dwarfed body seemed even smaller, more distorted. The coarse red hair had thinned to a fuzz. Features had condensed so that the protruding forehead was obscenely bulging. Pale lips. Sluggish eyes. Pinched nostrils in a thick nose. I bent over him.

''Get the fuck away,'' he said. ''Don't touch me, you Italianate bastard.''

All diagnosticians have their individual bags of tricks. In this case, diagnosis of the disease wasn't necessary; I knew what was stopping him. But I wanted to know more about his condition. I leaned far over to sniff his breath. Foul. Sour predominating. His skin also had a stale scent. I inspected his fingernails. Milk-tinged with bluish half-moons. I pinched the skin on the back of one hand. The ridge slowly, slowly flattened out. But not entirely.

He let me tinker with him because Maya had turned from the window and come back to the bedside. She had unfastened the top two buttons of her blouse. The shining cleavage between her heavy breasts was clearly visible. Lewisohn had pushed his glasses back into place. He was still staring at her. She regarded him gravely.

''Hello, Maya,'' the old man said in a low voice.

''Hello, Mr. Lewisohn,'' she said in a soft, tremulous voice. ''I can't tell you what an honor it is to meet you. I'll never forget this moment.''

She sounded as if she meant it. Perhaps she did.

''Pull up a chair,'' he said to her.

I went back to the door where Dr. Lucas had been standing silently, arms folded. I motioned him outside. We closed the door, leaving Maya inside with Lewisohn.

''Not good, is it,'' Lucas said.

''Are you usually given to understatement?'' I asked with more sharpness than I intended.

"Dr. Flair," he started, "I've been—"

"How do you get along with him?" I interrupted.

"As well as anyone. My father was a son of a bitch to live with. I'm used to it. We jive one another."

"Jive? I haven't heard that word in years. Who runs the tests? Who takes the blood?"

"I do."

"What do you want?"

He was startled.

"What?"

"What do you want, Seth?" I repeated patiently. "From your career. From life. Want to serve in a hospice?"

"Jesus, *no*! I'm just putting in my time."

"Well then?"

"Research," he said promptly. "I profit from that."

I nodded. What I was computing might work out.

"I can do that for you," I said. "What will you do for me?"

He looked at me shrewdly. If he had agreed immediately, I would have canceled him on the spot. But he was trying hard to be prudent. Still, I caught his excitement.

"What do you want me to do?" he asked cautiously.

"Not much at the moment. I want you to talk to Maya Leighton, as much as you can. Observe her. Get some input. Then I'm going to flash you tomorrow and ask if you believe you can serve with her. You'll rule."

"Sure," he said. "I'll do that."

"Fine. Where's the colloquy?"

"Conference Room B. Downstairs."

"I'll find it. You wait for Maya. The two of you come down together."

I opened Lewisohn's door. Maya was sitting at his bedside, holding his lumpy hand. Leaning forward. Loose blouse gaping. Her legs were crossed. Cool, tanned thigh. The other calf bulging sweetly.

"Get the fuck out of here!" Lewisohn roared.

"Up yours," I snarled at him. "Serve a little and earn your keep, you monster. Maya, five minutes."

She nodded. I closed the door.

"Give them five minutes," I said to Lucas. "Then knock at the door. Maya will come out."

I went down to the colloquy, synthesizing. I needed a friendly base in the Washington-Alexandria area. Hadn't someone said war is geography?

Conference Room B was crowded when I entered. A chair had been reserved for me, front row center, next to Dr. Luke Warren. I took my place. Lights dimmed.

The colloquy had been beautifully organized. Warren was on top of his service, though no one would ever convince him of that. It began with a fifteen-minute presentation. He had put the entire thing on tape.

We had the whole story in color: tissue slides, magnified computer printouts, filmed microanalysis, blowups of those deranged leukocytes dancing about madly, color comparisons of serum, charts, percentages, projective curves. I was vaguely aware of the door of the conference room opening and Maya and Seth Lucas entering. But I was concentrating on the screen. It was not encouraging.

Then the tape ran blank, lights came on, we all blinked. Warren turned to me and gestured toward the stage. A podium had been set up there, to one side. I rose, moved up the two steps, turned to search those young faces. Young! There was even a group of five thirteen-year-olds assigned to the Hospice by the Science Academy for practical training as part of their conditioning. That had been my idea and I was proud of it.

"First of all," I started, "before we get into a screaming match—"

There was a titter of laughter.

"—I'd like to congratulate Dr. Luke Warren and his associates for one of the finest scientific presentations I've ever seen. Luke—well done!"

There was an enthusiastic snapping of fingers. Warren ducked his bald head, blinked ferociously, gnawed his upper lip, blushed happily. First the kick, then the pat. That was how this object had to be manipulated.

I went on. "Now then, I have just examined the patient. I hadn't seen him for six months. His physical deterioration is obvious and ominous. Question: Is that deterioration due to the disease itself or to the irradiation treatment? Oh—before anyone eagerly volunteers—let me say that I will listen to anything you have to offer. I welcome your opinions. But the final decision must be mine." I paused. "After all, it's my ass that's in the sling."

That won them and loosened them. They roared with sympathetic laughter. The give-and-take became fast. Sometimes angry and heated. Consensus: Physical deterioration was basically due to the nature of this disorder in this particular victim. Similar deterioration, though rare, was not unheard of. But it had been compounded by the radiation treatments, which should cease immediately.

"I concur." I nodded. "We're getting nowhere. Even worse, neither is the patient."

Again, laughter. I knew, of course, that Warren had planned this colloquy to condition his young staff as well as to inform me. He had been exactly right to do so.

"Second question," I said. "What do we do now? With the understanding that it is not sufficient to keep this object's vital functions animate. I hope you all recognize that his service as this country's most creative theorist is necessary—no, it's *essential* to the future of our society. He must not only be kept alive, he must be kept capable of serving. And if that isn't enough, we must also consider the personality and character of the em himself. I am sure you are all aware of what a quiet, gentle, cooperative, profitable object he is."

Loud groans and laughter. They knew him.

"So that's our input. One: Keep him alive. Two: Keep his brain functioning. Three: Tailor our treatment so it will not adversely affect his willingness to contribute his very unique service—I mean this very seriously—to the planning of our future world. Dr. Warren, is this symposium being taped?"

"Why, yes," he answered nervously. "I thought—"

"Excellent," I said. "I'm glad it is. All right—let's have suggestions on where we go from here."

It was a wild-and-woolly session and I profited from every minute of it. I think what gave me most pleasure was that I could keep up with them. I had fears, occasionally, that my increasing service in social and political fields might leave me lost in the disciplines from which all my power stemmed—scientific expertise. Things were moving so rapidly, on so many thrusts, that to fall behind was to perish.

The first suggestion offered, predictably, was for bone marrow transplant. I explained, for the umpteenth time, that this difficult, painful treatment would incapacitate Lewisohn for long periods of time. During which his service would be lost to the US. The Chief Director would never approve.

Second suggestion: Connect him to a strainer. This was our name

228

for a machine that operated in a fashion not unlike kidney dialysis. Briefly, the strainer sieved useless, immature leukocytes from the bloodstream. It required a three-hour connection every twenty-four hours. I knew Lewisohn well enough to know he would never allow it. He didn't want to live *that* much to endure the strainer for the remainder of his days.

Several additional suggestions offered by the young Oncology Team at Rehabilitation & Reconditioning Hospice No. 4 were brilliant, none the less brilliant for the fact that I had already thought of them and included them in my contingency plan. One was the injection of laboratory-grown antibodies. We had recently made great advances in breeding specific antibodies *in vitro*. Some had proved efficacious in the treatment of multiple myeloma.

Another suggestion came from a bioimmunologist. She suggested treatment with tuberculosis vaccine and dead cells from stopped leukemic victims. Excellent.

I was wondering if anyone might suggest parabiosis. Dr. Seth Lucas did. The treatment was relatively brief, he argued. Lewisohn would have to be connected to his partner about an hour a day.

"And how do you suggest we persuade him to do that?" I asked. "To have his veins and arteries tied to a stranger at his side, for whatever period of time? You can't sedate him every day. He'll compute what's going on and fight it. One call to the Chief Director, and that's it."

"Easy," Lucas said. "We build a special suite. Partitioned. Tubes lead from Lewisohn through a blank plastiwood wall. He'll never see his partner. We tell him we're monitoring his blood. I think we can get him to lie still for that. He's fascinated by machines. We'll tell him it's an automatic blood analyzer, a computer. He'll go for it. We should have no trouble getting objects to connect him to. And it's better than a strainer; there's a possibility of a cure."

I was profited. I had selected the correct object for the scheme I had in mind.

"Not bad," I acknowledged. "We could even make up an inoperative computer printout to show him. Thank you, Dr. Lucas. And thank all of you. Dr. Warren, if you will be kind enough to furnish me the original tape of this conference, it will be of great help to me in making an informed judgment."

I paused. Then, slowly, I descended the two steps of the stage to stand on the floor of the conference room. On their level.

"A final note," I said. "A personal note. A sermon, if you will. My text is cancer, and the long, arduous search to find a cure. Many of you are aware, I am sure, that in obso days it was believed this disorder was a single disease for which a single cure might be found. It was only with the passage of years, and much service, that science became aware of the complexity of the problem. Cancer, as we now know, is many diseases with many causes, many symptoms, and demands many cures. Today we take most of those cures for granted. I ask you to remember the time required to produce them, and the services of thousands of objects, singly and in teams, that contributed to those cures. But I don't wish to rehash medical history. I only want to point out that the conquest of cancer, to date, is the most frighteningly complex task science has ever undertaken. Even today, when computers relieve us of much of the analysis and synthesis, we still don't know all the answers. This colloquy today is evidence of that! My thrust is this: On a personal level, I ask you not to be disheartened by complexity. On the contrary, I urge you to accept complexity. In fact, to seek it. You are individually capable of computing far more than you are now called upon to do. Life is no longer simple—if it ever was. Science is no longer simple. And certainly our society and the world are no longer simple. They are organs of incredible complexity. And to understand them, to manage them, we must, each of us, become infinitely complex ourselves, capable of assimilating, computing, and acting on millions of bits: facts, observations, emotions, instincts, experience, and so forth. Do not fear complexity. Do not be dismayed if human values and aims prove to be just as complex as the conquest of cancer. Open your mind to the complex. Train your mind to encompass more, more, more. Then the future will truly belong to us. Thank you."

They all stood to snap their fingers frantically. I was not certain they computed what I meant. But I did.

Following the Watergate scandals of the 1970's, heavy structural changes had been made in the US Government. In 1979, a weak—and frequently witless—President had signed an Executive Reorganization Bill. In the words of a political commentator of the time, "Today, with one stroke of his pen, the President reduced the White House to the size of a privy."

Briefly, the ERB legislated the removal of all departments and agencies from control of the Chief Executive. What had been the

Cabinet became independent Public Service Departments, ruled by PS directors. All departmental directors were ruled by a Chief Director who was appointed by the President with the advice and consent of the Congress. The Chief Director could be, but need not be, a PS server. He had tenure to the age of fifty-five unless removed from office upon conviction of wrongful acts, carefully spelled out in the enabling legislation.

In effect, the Chief Director became the manager of the US, ruling through the Public Service. The intent was for the PS merely to administer laws passed by the Legislative Branch.

In the almost twenty years the Executive Reorganization Bill had been law, two results had become increasingly apparent:

1. The President's role was reduced to that of a titular "head of state." He visited abroad and received foreign dignitaries. He awarded honors and presided over national ceremonies. He addressed the citizenry on the need for morality, law, order, patriotism, and the prompt payment of voluntary contributions (taxes). He kicked out the first ball on the opening of the soccer season. He met with delegations of Indians, Boy Scientists, and crabby veterans of World War II. He launched atomic-powered dirigibles and chatted, via TV, with our colonists on the moon. He barbecued proribs on the White House lawn and spent at least two days in each nation that elected to become a new state in the US. But his administrative powers were nonexistent. The Chief Director ran the government.

2. The purpose of the ERB had been to curtail the swollen power of the Executive Branch. That it did. But it also created a fourth branch of government, the Public Service bureaucracy. By 1998, it ruled 89 percent of *all* government servers (96 percent, including the military), and had amassed more political power than the other three branches combined. As pointed out previously, we not only administered the laws of the US, but in the manner of bureaucrats everywhere, in all times, we *created* policy.

Our present Chief Director, Michael Wingate, had held office for seven years. His particular interests were economics and foreign policy. He was said to be science-oriented, and I believed that to be operative. Although I had never met him personally, I had received a cordial handwritten note from him thanking me for my assistance on "our recent project." He was referring to my suggestion for the use of a sickle-cell anemia stimulator on the recalcitrant African tribe.

The Chief Director and his fourth wife lived in a pleasant,

unpretentious home (surrounded by a guarded, barbed wire fence) in the Georgetown area. I drove Angela Berri from her Watergate apartment in her smart, steam-powered sedan. We were both wearing zipsuits with decorations. Angela was carrying a thin, shiny briefcase linted to her wrist with a silver-alloy handcuff and chain. She didn't tell me what the case contained and I didn't ask.

The security precautions at the gate were as stringent as those at the compound in GPA-1. We were not allowed entrance until our BIN cards and voiceprints were electronically scanned, approved, and recorded. Then came visual identification by closed-circuit TV to the house. Then the gate was opened. The surrounding lawn was brilliantly illuminated by floodlights.

A serving em in a black zipsuit opened the steel-backed front door. But before he could close it, the Chief Director came rapidly toward us, smiling, hands outstretched. My initial reaction was to the em's warm charm. Then I was surprised by his shortness. In his TV and film appearances, he had seemed much taller. But that could have been manipulated, of course.

I knew something of his background. It was interesting. He was forty-two, a Natural Male, and married only Natural Females. His father had been a successful inventor, mostly of gadgets and small electric and electronic devices. But one invention, a machine for "aging" whiskies and wines almost instantaneously, had proved enormously lovable. It exposed alcoholic beverages to actinic light. It could not produce a twenty-five-year-old cognac in seconds, but it could take the raw edge off petroleum-based alcoholic drinks and make them potable. It was used in almost every distillery in the world.

Michael Wingate inherited his father's wealth at the age of twenty. He could have spent his life in indolence. But he earned a doctorate in social engineering and came to the attention of the government with his PhD thesis on the practicality of direct TV broadcasts to foreign countries via satellite. His ideas had been adopted, but objections in the United Nations became so heated that the US was forced to sign a covenant that restricted all international satellite radio and TV broadcasting to UN control.

(As I dictated the previous paragraph, I became suddenly aware that Michael Wingate's background was not too unlike my own. This was an insight that had not occurred to me before. Perhaps it explains why I was prepared to take profit from the em even before meeting him.)

232

Wingate joined Public Service, rose rapidly in rank, and was appointed Chief Director in 1991. His brilliance was almost universally recognized and his wit admired.

"Angela!" He smiled. She bent slightly to take his kiss on her cheek.

He turned to me and beamed.

"Dr. Flair!" he said. "This *is* a pleasure. I've been waiting a long time for this meeting."

That solved a question that had been puzzling me: Why had Angela called me to Washington? She was too crafty to initiate contacts between her servers and rulers. Now it was obvious: *He* had commanded my presence.

His palm stroke was slow, firm, dry. He looked like a beardless Santa Claus: white hair, rubicund complexion, pug nose, blue eyes twinkling merrily. An appearance, I knew, that served him well in the political jungle. His brain was quick, dark, devious. He preferred the plot to the plan.

"Grace will be down in a moment," he said. He chuckled suddenly, for no reason I could tell. "Let me show you about. Then we'll have a drink in the library before dinner."

He bounced ahead of us, full of energy and delight. Throwing doors wide, pointing out antiques: rugs, paintings, sculpture, porcelain—all on loan from the National Gallery. This home and all its furnishings were owned by the US and provided as the "Georgetown White House" for the use of the Chief Director.

It was larger than the exterior had indicated. Three early Federal houses had been combined, walls removed or archways and doors inserted. Rooms ran into rooms. Ceilings soared. Quaint cubbyholes abounded. Colors were light; fresh flowers were everywhere. It was all bright, cheerful, comfortable and pleasant.

But still. . . . In almost every room black zipsuits moved casually, shadows, ems and efs. None of them obviously armed. One em, in a red zipsuit, an officer, stood aside to let us pass, grave and reserved. Servants all. But members of the Chief's personal guard. Formerly the Secret Service. Now officially called the Household Staff. They were everywhere. Michael Wingate ignored them.

Finally, he led us into the library. He had, I noted, a need to touch. His hands were on my arm, shoulder, back. He stroked Angela's hair, clasped her waist, held her hand briefly. When he poured an already mixed beverage from a plastic decanter bedded in a bucket of Jellicubes, he handed us each our plastiglass, then curled our fingers about it with both hands. An interesting tic.

"Well," he said happily, holding up his glass. "Happiness and long life to all."

We smiled politely. I looked about. Like my father's library in Grosse Pointe. With one vital exception: These books had been read. I could tell: uneven rows, stained bindings, bookmarks poking up, a few lying on open shelves, bindings down, spread wide.

"Dr. Flair," the Chief Director said. He paused. "Nick? All right?"

"Of course, Chief."

"Nick, how is Lewisohn?"

I gave him a brief, concise report. The em's deterioration. The best we could hope for. The worse we might expect. What I proposed to do next. He listened intently, head cocked to one side. The bright smile on the lips, but not in the eyes.

"Nick," he said. "I'm sure you understand the importance of this em's survival?"

"Yes, sir. In a functioning condition."

"Precisely," he said. "Functioning. We need that."

"Chief," Angela said, "from what Nick says, it may require a heavy outlay. The use of—uh—volunteers. A new staff. And perhaps—"

"Anything." He waved away all the details. "Don't even pause to question it. Whatever you need. My responsibility. You have full authority. Is that clear, Nick?"

On that last question, the velvet glove split and I saw the iron fist: blue eyes deepening, lips pulled tight, the whole face suddenly harder, austere. This em would not suffer failure lightly.

"I compute." I nodded. "You have my—"

But then the library door opened suddenly. The Chief's wife stood framed. Angela and I rose to our feet. Wingate, the happy bunny once again, bounded over to take her hand and lead her into the room.

"Ah. . . ." he said. "Oh. . . ." he said. "Grace, you look lovely. Just lovely."

So she did. My first reaction, purely visceral: I must use this ef.

She was a head taller than he and, I judged, half his age.

Bare feet, spatulate, with big-toe rings set with clusters of red stones. Garnets?

Loose-flowing gown in a flowered pattern. Natural silk perhaps. Sleeves to her wrists. Draped to her ankles. High on her neck.

234

Long hands. Smooth, tapered fingers. Tanned. A tiny gold chain for a wedding band.

Dark eyes. Violet? Brown? Heavy brows. Curved brows swooping down on veined temples.

Wide mouth. Full lips. Slightly parted. Glistening. Upper teeth somewhat protuberant. Long canines.

Sharp nose. V-chin. Sinuous neck.

What little I could see of her flesh—ankles, feet, wrists, hands, neck, head—was complete, an almost discernible line about her. She was within. Contained.

Hair the color of fresh ashes. As fine and fragile.

Sculpted ears.

I would lick those first.

"Please forgive me," she said, smiling at Angela. Giving me a flick. "I tried three sets of earrings, then gave up."

Thick voice. Almost syrupy.

We all—even Angela—waited on her. Her presence demanded it. Though her manner was never less, nor more, than quiet, attentive, sympathetic, understanding. But she seemed so *sure*. A teacher. Even her laughter was detached.

It was an unmemorable dinner—surrogate food—served efficiently but with no panache by black zipsuits. A natural Israeli white wine was palatable; a red petrowine, actinized, was not. One amusing detail: Angela Berri ate her entire dinner with her right hand, the briefcase still shackled her left wrist. No one commented. I wondered, idly, if the Chief Director might have the only key. If so, he made no effort to relieve her discomfort.

He dominated the conversation during a gelatinous pâté, cold potato soup, an entree of chilled canned salmon (molded inexpertly into the shape of a fish), a salad of prolet. This synthetic lettuce was produced in endless sheets, the rollers stamping the veins and crinkles of the natural leaf. Then the sheets were cut into small squares and merchandised in plastic bags. It might well be used to stuff mattresses.

Chief Wingate, in a droll, eye-rolling manner, recounted his tribulations in dealing with a small, emerging nation of the Far East. Its representative in Washington had expressed interest in joining the US. Diplomatic tactics in this case demanded gifts, bribes, long letters swearing undying fealty to the current monarch, and, finally, supplying the Ambassador with the corpus of a popular TV star, a comedienne who weighed about 100 kilos.

"And how did you get her to cooperate, dear?" Grace Wingate asked. Dutiful wife, feeding her husband lines. "Bribery?"

"Oh, no." He chuckled. "She agreed voluntarily. Didn't even have to appeal to her patriotism. She said no one had asked her for years and years!"

Laughter fluttered around the table. Artificial lettuce.

"Is it worth the trouble, Chief?" Angela asked.

"I think so." He nodded. Serious now. "Not from any great contribution they can make, but simply from their numbers. Almost four million. Their resources aren't all that exciting, although there may be oil off the coast. But we must constantly keep in mind our need to increase our consumer pool. Nick, what do you think?"

His sudden, direct question startled me. I had a distinct impression I was being interviewed.

"A Zoo Nation," I said.

"Zoo Nation?" He looked at me quizzically. "I've never heard the term before. Yours?"

"I believe so. Yes, sir."

"How do you define a Zoo Nation?"

"An undeveloped—or underdeveloped—political entity that has nothing to offer but its history, hunger, culture, and poverty. Limited natural resources. And most of those can now be synthesized. Or adequate substitutes produced. No science and no technology."

"Surely they could be developed as a viable nation," Grace Wingate said sharply.

I turned to look at her.

"To what purpose?" I asked. "Assuming it could be done. I'm not certain it could be. Science and technology progress at a geometric rate. Attempt to raise a Zoo Nation to our status—or Russia's, or China's—and by the time that was accomplished we'd be so far ahead they could never catch up. Never. But I think they could achieve a reasonable level of prosperity as a Zoo Nation, a well-ordered Zoo Nation. Income from tourism and handicrafts. Assistance with their sanitation and public health. Perhaps some light cottage-industry. A limited amount of education. Bring the first-rate brains to the mainland for advanced conditioning. But don't expect to make a Japan from a Chad. Develop it deliberately as a Zoo Nation. Encourage its native culture. Make it a kind of human game park, protected, allowed to grow. Within limits."

"Limits?" Wingate said. "Z-Pop?"

"Or Minus-Z. Depending on arable land, rainfall, birthrate, disease, and so forth. A computer study would give you the optimum population. The vital factors are not to expect too much from or promise too much to a Zoo Nation. There is quality in nations, just as there is in objects."

"Mmm," the Chief Director said. He stared at me. Pausing as the servers removed our dinner plates and brought dessert. Thick slices of the new strain of seedless watermelon. They had removed the flavor with the seeds. But the coffee was genuine. With an oily film from poorly washed cups.

"Interesting," he continued. He slipped a saccharine pill into his coffee. "You judge national quality by the degree of scientific and technological development?"

"Of course." I smiled. "My conditioning."

"And how would you rank the US?" he asked. "Compared to, say, Russia, Pan-Europe, China?"

"Forget Pan-Europe," I said. "They have the brains but not the love. As for Russia and China, I can give you only an uninformed judgment. I am not cleared for restricted research in the physical sciences."

"What is your 'uninformed judgment'?"

"In the biomedical disciplines? Compared with Russia and China? Grossly equal. We're ahead in molecular biology. Russia is ahead in bioimmunization. China is ahead in psychopharmacology. But still, as I said, grossly equal."

"But you feel we're not doing enough?"

"Not nearly enough."

He threw back his head and laughed.

"I get that thrust from all sides," he said finally. Spluttering. Wiping wet eyes with his plastinap. "But rarely as openly or as honestly. What do you suggest we do?" Then, ironically: "I'm sure you have many ideas on the subject, Nick."

I caught an angry glance from Angela Berri. But I ignored her wrath and his irony. I didn't care. It was an opportunity. I would have been a fool to avoid it.

"Yes." I nodded. "I have many ideas on the subject. The Science Academy and the National Science Advisory Board were steps in the right direction. But not enough. There must be clear communication between the scientific community and government. A continuing dialogue. And in a participating, not merely an advisory capacity."

"I thought most scientists were deliberately—even enthusiastically—nonpolitical," Chief Wingate said mildly. "If not antipolitical."

"Obso scientists were," I acknowledged. "And are. Many younger scientists are activists. They—we—recognize that science has always been political. That is, it is based on the values of the society in which it exists. The same holds true for art, of course. And economics. No human activity exists in a vacuum. All are influenced by and, in turn, influence the social medium. Today, science is the megafactor of tomorrow. We ignore it at our peril."

"You feel very deeply about this," Grace Wingate said softly.

"Yes, I do. And it's operative. Remember, we are the first species that can control its own evolution. Compute *that* and its consequences."

"And what do you suggest?" the Chief asked. Somber now. "For today? Where do we start?"

"A separate department under your rule, sir. The Department of Creative Science. Bring together all the government's scientific activities in one efficient and effective political body. Right now, the government's scientific activities are scattered all over the place: atomic energy and solar research in the Department of Natural Resources; weaponry and chemwar research in the Department of Peace; plant biology research in the Department of Agribusiness. Et cetera. The most important, the most promising projects in basic research are restricted. So the overlapping and duplication of effort are disgraceful. I realize that sometimes this state of affairs is desirable: planned disorganization with several teams working on identical projects unknown to each other. But in this case, the disorganization is unplanned. There is no centralization, no firm management. Science demands control, political control, for optimum value to the state. Conditioned political scientists are the answer. If a purely objective scientist, working alone in his lab, was to come up with a guarantee of physical immortality, a public announcement of such a development would simply wreck our economy and our society. We make a thousand discoveries a year, none as world-shaking as that, but the consequences of every scientific advance should be evaluated economically and politically before it's made available. A Department of Creative Science could do that. Am I making sense?"

"A great deal of sense." Chief Wingate nodded. "A great deal indeed. I agree with your thrust. And I thank you for expressing your views so lucidly.''

He glanced at the digiclock on the wall, then looked to his wife. A signal apparently passed between them, although I did not catch it. Grace Wingate rose to her feet. We all followed.

"Nick," the Chief Director said, "I'd like a favor from you."

"Of course, sir."

"Angela and I have things to discuss. My wife has a meeting to attend. May I prevail upon you to accompany her and see her safely home?"

Mrs. Wingate smiled faintly.

"My profit," I said.

We separated. The Chief led Angela into the library, his arm linked in hers. She still carried that thin briefcase. Grace Wingate asked me to wait a few moments while she changed.

When she came bouncing down the stairs, I was startled by her costume. She had suddenly lost five years. At least! Long ash hair flamed down her back. A middy was closed with a loosely knotted light blue scarf. A white pleated skirt stopped just above her bare knees. She wore white plastivas sneakers. If she had tried to sell me Girl Scout cookies, I wouldn't have been a bit surprised.

She smiled at my reaction to her appearance.

"Well!" I said. "Are we going to a marshmallow roast?"

Then she laughed, took my arm, led me to the door. We waited silently while the heavy bolts were drawn, the door swung open. Two outside guards accompanied us to a waiting diesel-powered Mercedes limousine. Chauffeur and guard in the front seat, closed off from us by a shield of bulletproof glass. The windows also had the green-tinted nylon layer. As we rolled through the opened gate, a sedan with four black zipsuited occupants followed us closely to Wisconsin Avenue, M Street, and onto Pennsylvania Avenue.

"We're visiting the President," I guessed.

She laughed again. A throaty, gurgling laugh. She seemed freer, relaxed, glad to be out from behind that barred door.

"I'm going to church," she said. Hint of mischief in her voice. "I'm a religionist. Did you know that?"

"No, Mrs. Wingate, I didn't. Which religion?"

"Beist."

"Deist?"

"*Bei*st. I'm sure you've never heard of it. It's very new."

"How many members?" I asked her.

"Oh . . . perhaps a hundred."

"That's not a religion," I said. "It's a cult."

"Beist," she repeated. "We have a small chapter here, and in New York, and in San Francisco. But we make no effort to recruit. If objects hear about us and want to attend meetings, they are welcome. We ask nothing from them. We own no property. Meetings are held in members' homes or, as tonight, in offices or stores. It's all very informal. Unstructured. We hope to keep it that way."

"And what does a Beist believe?"

"A force. A Life Force. We prefer not to define it. We accept the mystery. We welcome the mystery. We say the individual is not immortal, but the human species is. We say all life is growth, with purpose. To merge finally, and become one with that Life Force."

"Vaguely mystic," I murmured.

"Is it? Perhaps. You said tonight at dinner that we are the first species capable of directing and controlling our own evolution. We accept that. We say the human species, now, today, is the highest form of life but will direct its evolution, over thousands and thousands of years, to a higher form, something finer, that will eventually become one with the divine essence of the universe, the Life Force."

She stopped suddenly, turned sideways from the waist, stared at me.

"Well?" she demanded. "What do you think?"

"You want me to be honest?"

"Of course. You must always be honest."

This last was uttered in such a sweetly innocent tone that I could not scoff.

"Mrs. Wingate," I said, "I can't—"

"You may call me Grace," she said.

"Thank you. Grace, I'm glad your new faith encompasses manipulated evolution. But when you speak of a Life Force, a divine essence, you lose me. Consider my conditioning. All scientists—well, certainly most—equate the individual corpus with a clock. Nothing divine about a clock. Dial, hands, wheels, pivots, gears, springs: a mechanical device. Reproduce it exactly—so many teeth in the gears, ratios just so—put tension on the spring or provide some other power source, and away it goes. Tick-tick-tick. Nothing mysterious there. Similarly with the human corpus. But infinitely more complex. Not only mechanical, but electrical and

240

chemical. Still, the corpus is *stuff*, no matter how complex. Bone, blood, tissue, cells, enzymes, hormones, glands, organs, skin, muscle. All *stuff*. And the time will come when we can produce it all, assemble it correctly, and then away it will go, the heart beating steadily—ca-thump, ca-thump, ca-thump. But no finger of God will poke down through the clouds and touch it. No divine essence will be injected. No Life Force will be needed. It will be purely a laboratory product, a reasonable facsimile of the real thing. We're closer to that synthesis than you might think. Where does that leave Beism?''

''But don't you see?'' she said excitedly. ''We accept all that. It's all part of the purpose. To evolve into something finer and better. When you can create a living human in the laboratory, won't you try to improve on it?''

''Probably. In fact, undoubtedly.''

''Well, there you are!'' she said triumphantly. ''You're part of it, part of the Life Force, whether you recognize it or not. And— Oh, we're here. Nick, would you like to attend? You don't have to, of course. But you're welcome, if you'd like to come in.''

''I'd like to very much.''

This particular meeting of the Beists was held in the back of a commercial laundry on Sixteenth Street, behind the White House. There were, perhaps, thirty objects present. There was one ef in the uniform of a naval commander, and I recognized the junior Senator from South Dakota. The others were a diverse lot. Most, apparently, middle class, but with a sprinkling of artisans, zipsuits from several Public Service ranks, a few adolescents, a few obsos, a tall, dignified em in Arabic robes.

The congregation stood against the walls, or sat on a miscellany of folding chairs, or perched on cold pressing tables and laundry machinery. The mood seemed light, carefree, informal, lively. There appeared to be no ceremony or ritual. Grace Wingate left me a moment to whisper to a plump young ef with stringy hair and a complexion disfigured by a bad case of *acne vulgaris*.

Grace rejoined me. I had ''reserved'' a seat for her alongside me on a long metal sorting table. If we had leaned back incautiously, we'd have fallen into empty wire bins labeled Shirts, Skirts, Sheets, Towels, Drawers, etc. Just the place to seek the divine essence.

The dumpy young ef stood up before the gathering. Gradually, the congregation quieted. The ef introduced herself as Joanne Wilensky. She welcomed newcomers. She regretted there was no literature on the Beist movement to distribute, but suggested those interested might question any members present after the formal meeting was concluded.

"We can't answer all your questions," she said. A smile that made her almost pretty. "Because we don't know all the answers. Beism is as much a seeking as a knowing. Perhaps you can help us. We hope you can. Does the secretary have anything to report?"

The junior Senator from South Dakota rose and read two short letters from the Beist chapters in New York and San Francisco. Both reported increased attendance at their most recent weekly meetings and growing membership. The secretary announced with some pride that he now estimated the total number of Beists in the US at almost 200. Fingers were snapped.

Joanne Wilensky then asked if anyone else cared to speak. An em in a bronze-colored zipsuit rose and stated he was about to be transferred to Yuma, Arizona. He requested permission to start a Beist group there. The congregation voted approval enthusiastically. The wave of the future.

The Wilensky ef paused a moment, surveying the group slowly. She was a dowdy figure, shapeless, in a wrinkled plasticot dress.

"Is she the minister, or priestess, or guru?" I whispered to Grace Wingate.

"Sort of. It all started with her. But we take turns leading the meetings. She doesn't get paid or anything. She's a presser in this laundry."

"Scientists believe—" Joanne Wilensky began in a hesitant, stammering voice—and then she proceeded to tell us what scientists believed, repeating almost word for word the comparison of a clock to a human corpus I had made to Grace Wingate in the car. I had seen Grace speak to her, but I was startled at how accurately the Beist leader was repeating my thesis.

"But the life of the clock comes from a coiled spring," she stated. "Or from an electric outlet. Or from a battery. Where does the life of a human come from? Not from on high, the scientists say. Not from the finger of God poking down through a cloud. Then from where? Why should this combination of blood, tissue, cells, and organs result in animate life? Because, say the scientists, it is the nature of the materials used, being so constituted that in proper combination life begins. That is no answer at all. *Why* should the constitution of the materials be of such a nature? *Why* should the proper combination of those materials result in a beating heart? It is the *why* we seek. It may or may not be the touch of a Divine Creator. It may or may not be the blind functioning of chance. God or accident: Is there any difference? But we believe there is a reason, a purpose. We know not what. But we ask the scientists this question: Why do they exist? Or we? Or stones, stars, fish, and the universe? Why a something and not a nothing? Nullity, complete nonexistence, would prove nonpurpose. Existence presupposes purpose.''

And so forth, and so forth. A stew of not especially new ideas. She made the mistake so many religionists make of trying to justify their faith by reason. Then they're in my court, and I can slaughter them. If I started a new religion, I would have but one law, one justification: Believe. Faith confounds reason.

I said much the same thing to Grace Wingate on the ride back to the Georgetown White House.

''Don't you believe in anything?'' she asked me.

''Of course. In the immortality of the human species and the ability of science to ensure that immortality.''

''But to what purpose?''

''My Personality Profile says that I am goal-oriented. That is true, but in the short run. I am essentially pragmatic. I am not concerned with teleology. A lot of kaka. A waste of time. There's too much to be done today. For tomorrow.''

Suddenly, unexpectedly, she put a hand on mine. She leaned toward me.

''Will you be my friend, Nick?'' she asked. A whisper.

''Of course.'' I smiled. ''Do you have to ask?''

''Do you know what was in Angela's briefcase?''

''No. I obviously have no need to know.''

She sat back, huddled into the corner of the wide seat. She stared at me thoughtfully a long moment. In the gloom she seemed suddenly older, despite the girlish middy, the ashen hair misting about her shoulders. I was conscious of the bare legs, the curve of her upper arms.

''I want to tell you,'' she said.

''I don't think you should,'' I said.

''I *want* to.''

''Please don't. It's wrong for you to talk about restricted material, and dangerous for me to listen.''

''Then I'll tell my husband you tried to worm it out of me, that you tried and tried to get me to reveal what's going on, but I refused to tell you.''

I looked at her in astonishment. Shocked by her resoluteness.

"Why would you want to do that to me?" I asked her. "I have done you no harm."

Then she was weeping. Hand over her eyes. Shoulders hunched, shaking. Hair a scrim about her face. Little sounds came out of her. My hand crept sideways, found her free hand. She gripped my fingers with surprising force.

"All right, Grace," I said gently. "What's this all about?"

"Angela," she said. "And Mike. What she's doing. With Mike. To Mike."

Mike? Chief Director Michael Wingate, manager of the US. It sounded odd. Did President Harold K. Morse's wife call him Harry? Probably. And here was Grace Wingate worrying about Mike. Knowing Angela, I thought she probably had cause for worry.

"Grace." I said her name softly. I gripped her hand tightly. "I want to be your friend. Tell me what is in Angela's briefcase."

We were on M Street, approaching Georgetown, and she spoke rapidly in her deep, throaty voice. What she told me seemed anticlimactic. But I did not at that point in time fully compute the Washington world. I was not conditioned to assigning operative political values. It was my first experience as a major mover and shaker. Later, when I learned the techniques of power politics, I realized the importance of what Grace Wingate told me that night.

This had been the sequence of events:

1. Hyman R. Lewisohn had run a definitive computer study of the US Government's assets in real property. The inventory included public lands, military bases and hardware, natural resources (estimated), power generating facilities, and such real estate as shipyards, factories, homes, universities, hotels, motels, schools, zoos, wholesale and retail businesses, etc. Most of the last-mentioned had reverted to US ownership upon the default of government loans or for nonpayment of voluntary contributions.

2. The total proved simply astonishing. The US was by far the largest landholder, the largest shipbuilder, the largest *everything* in the world. This enormous capital had been amassed not deliberately but by a slow process of accretion, almost by accident. The US Government now owned and operated, either directly or through license, hamburger stands and swimming pools, parks and playgrounds, macaroni factories and airlines, golf courses and bordellos, bridges and distilleries, shipping lines and private mints, an

orchard in Florida, and a trout stream in Oregon. Even whole towns that had grown up about military bases.

3. It was determined that all these enterprises were under the direction of or operated by several Public Service departments. Natural Resources handled public lands and parks. Commerce handled hotels, motels, factories, stores. Bliss handled nursing homes, hospitals, recreation facilities. Agribusiness handled farms, food processing plants, supermarkets. And so forth.

4. Lewisohn's plan was to maximize income by bringing all US Government profit-making properties under the management of a new Public Service department, the Department of National Assets. He argued that by centralized control, modern management techniques, stricter accounting procedures—by operating US-owned business as an efficient conglomerate might—income from government property could be increased by 38.6416 percent and result, if desired, in a 4.2674 percent tax reduction.

5. Chief Director Wingate, his staff and directors were enthusiastic about Lewisohn's proposal. But the creation of a new Public Service department would necessitate enabling legislation from Congress. Wingate wasn't so enthusiastic about stirring up the Whigs (formerly the Republican Party). And they would certainly be stirred up by the revelation of the incredible total of real property held by the US Government that would have to be made in any Congressional hearing on a bill to create the proposed department.

6. Angela Berri had suggested a way out of the difficulty. Instead of a new department, a new section in the Department of Bliss, which she ruled, would be established. New sections were purely an administrative matter and required no Congressional approval. The new section would perform all the functions of the new department proposed by Lewisohn. It was a detailed prospectus for this new section that Angela was carrying in her chained briefcase to discuss with the Chief Director.

Dear Angela! For an ef on the suck, I could understand how tempting the new section must seem. All that love rolling in from government properties all over the world. If she skimmed only one-tenth of one percent, she'd be the wealthiest ef in the world within five years. Temerity! Greed!

"I'm not sure I can do anything about this," I said slowly to Grace Wingate. "If your husband wants to avoid a Congressional confrontation, I can't see any choice but to opt for Angela's plan."

She turned away from me, staring out the window.

"She owns you, too, I suppose," she said dully. "You've probably used each other."

"Yes, we've used each other," I said. "No, she doesn't own me. Give me a little time. Maybe I can compute something. If you want me to be your friend, if you want me to help you, you must trust me. Can you do that?"

She turned to look at me. Despair in those dark eyes.

"I have no choice." she said. "Do I? I have nowhere else to —I can't let her—They—she and Mike—Nick, I want to keep my husband! But she—and she thinks I—you don't *know* what she—"

"I know, Grace," I murmured. "Believe me, I know. I'll do everything I can. I'm on your side."

She leaned forward, kissed my cheek swiftly, pulled away. We stopped before the barred gate. Guards came over to inspect us.

We found Angela Berri and Chief Wingate seated casually in a parlor-type room in the front of the house. It was furnished with three TV sets, a game table, a cellarette on wheels, and slightly worn chintz-covered armchairs and sofas. Angela no longer had her briefcase. There was nothing in the manner or appearance of either of them to indicate how their discussion had gone. Perhaps I imagined they were seated an unusual distance apart.

Wingate rose to greet us.

"Good meeting?" he asked his wife.

"Oh, yes."

"Let's have a nightcap," he said.

He glanced at me, made an almost imperceptible motion of his head. Obediently, I followed him over to the cellarette. He busied himself with the bottle of apricot-flavored petroqueur and four small, stemmed glasses.

"Did you attend?" he asked in a low voice.

"Yes, sir. I did."

"Reactions?"

"Certainly not apocalyptists. Quite the contrary. I think they're harmless."

"They are," he said. "At this point in time."

"Not politically oriented," I observed. "Unless what I saw was a front."

"No, it's operative," he said. "I had them profiled. Nick, that suggestion of yours for a new Department of Science. . . ."

"Department of Creative Science, sir."

"Yes. Spell it out in a personal letter to me. Purpose, organization, staff, estimated budget, and so forth."

"Be happy to, sir."

He handed me two filled glasses, looked swiftly at the chatting efs, turned back to stare into my eyes.

"No need to go through channels," he said quietly. "Bring the prospectus directly to me. Don't mail it. No endorsement copies. You compute?"

"Yes, sir."

We each carried two glasses back to the efs. Wingate handed one of his to Grace; I gave mine to Angela. We sat in a rough square, efs at the ends of a sofa, ems in distant armchairs. Each in a corner.

"Nick," the Chief said, rather languidly, "that suggestion of yours for a new Department of Science. . . . I wonder if you appreciate the political problems involved in getting a new Public Service department approved by Congress? The opposition would be heavy: the small but loud group that is against any extension of PS hegemony, obsos, the antiscience faction, antiabortionists, most religionists, rulers of existing government research sections in other departments, and industrial lobbyists with sweetheart contracts with those sections. A can of worms. It wouldn't be easy to get the enabling legislation passed."

"I'm sure it wouldn't, sir."

"But suppose we decided to make a fight for a new department," he said casually. "Any suggestions on tactics?"

I caught a warning glance from Angela. Wingate was, I knew, drawing me out on the possibility of creating Lewisohn's new Department of National Assets. He had no way of knowing I recognized his stalking-horse. Nor did Angela. She was concerned only that I might say something to endanger her plan. But I could safely ignore her warning; I could always plead ignorance and innocence.

"I don't believe the establishment of a new department would present insuperable difficulties, sir," I said pompously. Ingenuous I. "It seems to me one way to approach the problem would be to introduce—at the same time you introduce the new department bill—another bill so controversial, so certain to arouse strong passions and angry dispute, that with all the howling going on—media debates, demonstrations, strikes, boycotts, and so forth—why, you might stand a much better chance of slipping by your new department bill with a minimum of opposition."

247

He stared at me a moment. Expressionless. I risked a quick glance at Angela. If looks could stop, I would have been cremated in my armchair.

"A throwaway bill," Wingate mused. "Something we know will be defeated. But we put up a valiant fight. It takes off the heat. In other words, a decoy bill. I do believe you have a talent for politics. What you suggest—"

At that precise instant. Explosion. Loud. Heavy thump. Ground tremble. Inside me. Tinkle of broken glass. Softer thump. Wisconsin Avenue or all around? Shake and flutter. Looks. Frozen. Cuaght. Shatter of automatic rifle fire. Boom of flechette guns.

Wingate: "Down on the floor! All of you!"

Angela a cat. Up. Two quick steps. Soft, gymnastic roll onto one shoulder. Then. Under a table. Hands and knees. Spine arched. Head up. Lips drawn back. Snarling.

Door burst. Black zipsuits.

Ems kneeling. Glass breaking. Another thump. Mirror shattered. Myself moving in a dream. Stop-action. Down on one knee. A razor stripe across the back of my left hand. Shallow slice. Dark blood welling. No pain.

Wingate at the window.

"Goddamn it, get down! Sir!"

A red zipsuit inside. Door slammed and bolted.

"Down! Down! Down!"

Grace Wingate gliding to her husband. Grasping his shoulders. Turning him. Interposing her body between him and the jagged windows. Hugging him close. Looking into his eyes. Angela spitting. Furious. The efs magnificent.

A chatter of gunfire from black zipsuits at the windows. Smoke. Smell. Sharp crack. Whine of steel splinters. Portrait of John Quincy Adams with three eyes. Final burst. A human wail. High-pitched scream.

Silence. We wait. Trembling. Black zipsuits reload. With shaking hands. I look down. A few drops of urine. Nothing shows. But I know. Wingate goes to the cellarette. Begins to fill glasses. Steady hands.

"Oh," he breathes. "Ah," he breathes. "The worst this year."

He turns. Sees my blood, starts toward me. I wave him away, knot a handkerchief, pull it tight with my teeth. Angela crawls out. Straightens up. White.

"Stay here," Wingate says. Rushes out.

The black zipsuits are still at the windows. Not moving. I take them brandies. They drink. Not taking their eyes away from the night.

Wingate comes back with a kit. My wound is ridiculous. A slice across the knuckles. Already clotting. I dab it, tape it. The bandage stains slowly. Then stabilizes. Angela grips my arm, her grin a forgiveness. Grace Wingate kisses my cheek. Again. Soft, yielding lips. Syrupy as her voice. Her body would come apart in my hands. Just disintegrate. No. Unfold. And reveal mysteries.

"We lost an em on the gate," Wingate reported. "Three injured. They lost four stopped. Two injured. All of them. We think."

"Who?" I asked.

He shrugged.

"Oh . . . who knows. Animals."

The Chief ordered an escort to see us back to the Watergate Complex. A gray sedan preceded us. Driver and three armed guards. A gray sedan followed us. Driver and three armed guards. The red zipsuited officer in command was an ef. She insisted on ushering us safely inside the door of Angela's apartment. When the door was closed, locked, bolted, chained, I glanced through the peephole. A black zipsuit stood outside.

"Welcome to Washington," Angela said. "District of Columbia."

"But the love isn't bad," I said, and we both laughed.

When Maya Leighton and I had arrived late that afternoon, I had been impressed by the apartment. Now, after an evening in the Wingates' pleasant, comfortable, lived-in, slightly shabby home, these rooms seemed stagy. Everything glistened or glowed. Ashtrays were not only empty but polished. Artificial elegance.

When we had arrived, Angela had not yet returned from her office. A serving ef in an earth-colored zipsuit let us in, showed us the two double bedrooms, nests. We bathed separately, changed into our uniforms, waited with a drink for Angela's return.

She rushed in, stroked palms, gave Maya a sharp, searching look, then disappeared to dress for dinner with the Chief Director. While she was absent, and Maya and I sat in silence, sipping vodka-and-Smack, Art Roach rang the chime. He was wearing his red zipsuit.

What a chilly, bloodless em he was. He inspected Maya Leighton drowsily, blinking. I recognized the look. There are certain surgeons who enjoy cutting. The two departed, for an evening of fun and frivolity. I had already warned Maya. I could, I told myself, do no more.

Now. Angela and I safe inside the guarded door. We were sunk in uncomfortably soft armchairs. Enveloped. Drowning. She stared at me.

"You're a fool, Nick," she said. Finally.

"A fool? How so?"

"When the Chief asked you how he might pass a bill for a new department."

"So? I answered him as honestly as I could. Would you have me stutter, 'I don't know,' or 'I have no idea.' Then *he* would have thought me a fool. And *you* a fool for giving me my rank. Is that what you wanted?"

"Oh . . . no." She sighed. "I suppose you're right. You just didn't know."

"Know what?"

"Nothing. You have no need to know. I wonder if your secretary is home?"

I waved toward the door of the second bedroom.

"Take a look," I told her.

She rose, kicked off her shoes, padded to the bedroom door. She opened it, peered in cautiously, closed the door.

"She's here. Sleeping naked."

"Any obvious cuts, bruises, contusions, welts, or scratches?"

She looked at me curiously.

"Ah," she said, "I see you know Art Roach. No, she looks rosy and whole."

We looked at each other and laughed. We were both very vulgar objects.

"Speaking of wounds," she said. "How's yours?"

"I'll survive," I said. "How often does that happen?"

"Assault on the Chief? Third time this year. It's always pillowed. The neighbors are all in PS. No one talks."

"He was good. So was his wife. Lovely ef."

"Yes."

She looked toward the bedroom door. Seeing, I knew, the naked Maya sprawled sleeping.

"I'm charged," she said.

"That's understandable." I nodded. "Violence. Danger. Adrenalin."

"Don't you feel it?"

"Of course. Flip a coin?"

"Don't be silly. Is she het or bi?"

"Bi. I think. Don't really know, ma'am."

"Would you mind if I tried?"

"Not at all. But Roach probably just used her."

"So?" she said. "That just makes the cheese more binding."

"You're a dreadful ef." I laughed.

"I know." She smiled coldly. "Dreadful. An object inspiring dread. And don't you ever forget it, Nick."

She went into Maya's bedroom. Closed the door behind her. In a moment I heard a burst of laughter. Then murmurings. Then silence.

I stood up, stretched, looked around. I poured myself a petronac at her futuristic bar, then slumped down again in that womb-chair. I sipped the brandy and, for a moment, plotted her destruction.

I couldn't compute it through. Too many variables. I thought of Grace Wingate. What she . . . What I . . . I couldn't compute it through. Insufficient input.

I came around to Lewisohn's suggestion for a new Department of National Assets. His Grand Plan was becoming increasingly evident. I should have seen it before. Opening the United States to foreign nations. A national bank. Converting Social Security to conventional insurance. And now centralizing the management of the nation's real property. The leukemic dwarf was creating a corporate state. Eventually, a corporate world. It was that simple and elegant.

I could live with it, I decided. I moved to the other bedroom. Undressed slowly. I could live with it. Every successful corporation, conglomerate, multinational company depended on research and development for growth. Enter Nicholas Bennington Flair. Machiavelli in a silver zipsuit.

I inhaled an eight-hour Somnorific and plunged out.

Y-6

In the forty-eight hours following my return to GPA-1 from Washington, I made a number of administrative decisions that were to have far-reaching effects important in this account.

I constituted a "Group Lewisohn" that would be responsible for the continued creative functioning of our famous patient. The Group would be headquartered at Rehabilitation & Reconditioning Hospice No. 4 at Alexandria, Virginia, and would be under the nominal rule of Dr. Seth Lucas. Second in command would be Maya Leighton. I transferred her to GPA-2 and briefed her on what I expected from her. In the treatment of Lewisohn . . . and in the treatment of Art Roach.

I informed Angela Berri of the creation of Group Lewisohn (later, Maya Leighton was to refer to it, in my presence only, as "Grope Lewisohn") via a conventional, low-priority mailed memo.

I flashed Seth Lucas, told him his new assignment, and instructed him to proceed with the construction of a suite designed for the parabiotic treatment of Hyman R. Lewisohn as he, Lucas, had described it during the colloquy at Hospice No. 4.

I also remembered to have his security clearance raised to Red-2.

I had a heavy four-hour meet with Paul Bumford. We dealt with a plan for drawing and storing an Individual Microbiological Profile for every object in the US, as a means of positive and precise identification. Then our discussion turned to our project for developing UP, the Ultimate Pleasure pill. We agreed basic research fell into three gross areas: physiological, psychological, mental. Overlapping, of course. There was a fourth, worrisome research area: metaphysical in nature. But we could not define it and postponed action until more input was available.

We decided to organize three miniteams in our field offices: physiological in Houston, psychological in Spokane, mental in Honolulu. None would be aware of the final goal of their service. Simply that we wanted to determine the origins of pleasure.

Paul had an additional matter to discuss. In the most recent bulletin of the Bureau of Public Security on current crime statistics, he had noted that the arrest rate for use, sale, or possession of restricted drugs was up 0.4 percent.

"It's statistically insignificant," he admitted. "But I think it's large enough to justify action. In fact, action might be a plus if someone in Congress or the media picks up on it."

"So?" I asked him. "What do you suggest?"

"A study of possible chromosomal damage due to habitual use of hallucinogens. Having Nancy Ching set up a team out in San Diego.

With increased need for hallucinogens for research. From Scilla Pharmaceuticals, of course.''

"Paul," I said, "I'm proud of you. And when you send out your directives on the UP Project, be certain to mention the use of hallucinogens as one possible approach."

On the evening of the second day I picked up a long coded message from Simon Hawkley at my mail drop. I spent most of the night decoding it with the aid of his book on the early monasteries of California. I completed the service about 0430, and fell into bed. Exhausted.

I was awakened at 0740 by a flash from my father in Grosse Pointe. My mother had stopped in her sleep the previous night.

I gave the orders I had to give. I didn't anticipate being absent more than three days.

"Can I come with you?" Paul Bumford asked.

He had met my parents. Once. My mother had liked him. My father had not.

"All right," I said. "Thank you. I may stay on a day or two, but you come back right after the funeral. Let's take the Bullet Train. A few more hours will make no difference. We'll try for a compartment. I have a lot to tell you. In camera."

I had time to make some purchases in the enormous compound PX before we left. I wondered if Lewisohn had included the worldwide PX chain in his list of the US Government's real property. Probably. At eighty-six new dollars for a middy blouse, it had to be a lovable enterprise.

Aboard the Bullet Train to Detroit, we sprawled comfortably, uniforms unzipped, shoes kicked off. We pulled the shades; the landscape en route was not inspiring. I told Paul first about my establishing Group Lewisohn in Alexandria.

"Advance toward the guns," he remarked.

"Exactly," I said approvingly. "Paul, you're becoming very perceptive. Washington is where the action is, and we need a base there. Maya's proximity to Art Roach can do us no harm. She's been instructed to supply me with a profile on him. Everything: personal habits, sexual kinks, daily routine, prejudices, speech patterns. And so forth."

"What do you hope to learn?"

"Anything. Maybe after he uses, he talks. Some ems do. Is he left-handed? What pills does he pop? Does he use a lighter or matches? I want to know everything about him. Now take a look at this. . . ."

I took a paper from my briefcase and handed it across to him. It was my decoding of Simon Hawkley's long message.

Yes, Scilla Pharmaceuticals in San Diego would probably be amenable to a takeover, if the love was right. The current owner, Anthony Scilla, was fifty-two and had recently suffered two mild strokes. His family was urging his retirement. The company had strong union contracts with two years to run. Scilla himself had even stronger loyalties to his executive staff. Terms of sale would probably include rank security for top management.

Paul Bumford scanned this financial kaka quickly. But when he came to the bottom line, he slowed. Lips pursed. He emitted a low, hissing whistle. Then he looked up at me. I was suddenly aware he had stopped using eyeshadow. His makeup was much more subtle than it had been.

"Nick," he said, "I was going to offer to help out. To throw my little pittance into the pot if it would help buy Scilla. But my contribution would be pissing in the sea. You can't manage this, can you?"

"I couldn't last night," I admitted. "After I decoded, I was ready to reject the whole thing and try to concoct a new plan. That was last night. Then this morning I woke up, my mother has stopped, and I'm her sole heir. That's what I mean by chance and luck. Who could have computed. . . ."

"A sweet ef," he said in a low voice. "I took profit from her. Very much."

"Yes," I said. "And she profited from you. 'Terminal nostalgia,' she said. She knew. It's true. Nostalgia is desperation. When you can't cope. It'll probably take a year for probate. Mother had the faith of a French peasant or Chinese shopkeeper: Paper is no good, put everything in gold or diamonds. So it will take time to realize. But I know my father will lend against it."

"A sweet ef," he repeated faintly.

"Yes, yes," I said impatiently. A little angry, perhaps, that his grief should seem greater than mine. "But I now have the funds. Zero in on that. Let's futurize. . . . Assuming Angela takes the bait, and assuming we're able to obtain hard evidence that she's on the suck, where do we go from there?"

"Go?" Paul said. "Why, we take her."

"Take her? How? Go to Art Roach, the ruler of Security and

254

Intelligence, and demand her arrest? No way. He's her creature. He'd have us both in a Cooperation Room so fast we wouldn't know what happened until we were given the Informed Consent Statement to sign.''

"Then, if we have the evidence, don't go down. To Roach. Go up. To the Chief Director.''

"Yes.'' I nodded. "That's logical. But life isn't logical. Politics isn't logical. No, strike that. Politics is logical. But a different kind of logic. No value judgment implied, but *different*. Not the linear logic of science. Infinitely more complex. More input. More variables. Angela and the Chief Director are users.''

"Oh, Jesus.'' He groaned.

I told him about the dinner with the Wingates at the Georgetown White House. He interrupted once.

"Nick,'' he said, "I've been meaning to tell you. Wingate. Chief Director Michael Wingate. Phoebe Huntzinger's Executive Assistant is Pomfret Wingate, the em who's going to play *King Lear* in the nude. I thought he might be related to the Chief Director. Remember Franklin Ferguson and Lydia Ann? But there's nothing to it. They're not related. Chief Wingate is an NM, and Pommy is an AINM.''

"Good,'' I said. "Glad you thought to check.''

But I was disturbed. The possibility should have occurred to *me*.

I continued describing the dinner with the Wingates. Paul listened intently, bent forward, head lowered. I related everything except the final armed attack against the Chief Director. Paul had no need to know.

"What's your reaction?'' I asked when I finished.

"Involved,'' he said. "But more plus than minus, I think. We should be able to manipulate Grace Wingate. She asked for help. She might provide more to us than we can offer her.''

"Well . . . equal, certainly. One hand washes the other. But I agree with you that she's an important factor. Or will be when we go to the Chief Director with evidence of Angela's snookering.''

"Beism, you said?''

"Yes, Beism. Not Deism.''

"Sounds wild. And with a New York chapter?''

"That's what she said.''

"Nick, suppose I look them up and join the group. Wouldn't that help?''

I didn't like it. I didn't know why at that point in time, but I instinctively rejected the idea.

"I could do that, Paul."

"No, no," he said earnestly. "Too obvious. You told her your objections to Beism. You came on strong for science. She wouldn't accept a sudden conversion. Nor would her husband. It would look exactly like what it was: opportunism. But I could do it."

"To what purpose?"

He grinned at me.

"If you want a precise scenario, I can't supply one. But it might help. Nick, I want to help."

He half-rose to his feet, leaned across to me, kissed my lips. The caress surprised, pleased me.

"Long time since we've done that," I breathed. "Too long."

"Yes," he said. "All right then if I become a Beist?"

His reasoning was valid. But still. . . .

"All right," I said reluctantly. "But keep it pillowed."

"Sure. Now, Nick, about this Department of Creative Science—where did *that* come from? It's not in the Tomorrow File."

"I know it isn't. But the Chief Director asked me for ideas on how to bring scientists into government. I winged it."

"And brilliantly," he said. "Have you prepared the prospectus yet?"

"No. Who's had time?"

"Can I provide some input? Wild ideas? Include them or not, as you like."

"Of course. All contributions gratefully accepted."

I think we both dozed. When finally, slowing for the Detroit terminal, I opened my eyes, Paul Bumford was awake and staring at me.

Later, when I was to recall the events of those two days, scenes and images were remembered in short takes. Out of sequence. A badly spliced film. I thought at first it was an extended attack of Random Synaptic Control. Then I realized that, because of emotional strain, the alcohol I drank, the pills I popped, those two days were recollected as a discontinuous series of incidents. In my memory a time frame did not exist.

Paul and I were elevated to the roof of the high-rise crematorium surmounting the Detroit terminal. My father's helicopter was awaiting us. A new ef pilot: dark, thin. Petulant mouth.

256

Paul glanced at plane and pilot. Then looked sideways at me, raised his eyebrows.

"My father's toy," I said.

I had resolved to take no drugs before her funeral. It was to be a kind of penance. The only penance I was capable of. I was not capable of it.

After the burial of the urn, after my weeping father, weeping Mrs. McPherson, weeping Miss Catherine, and weeping Charles had stumbled back to the house, Paul and I stood staring at the freshly turned earth.

Through the trees, drifting, came the two young ems, neighbors who had so amused my mother. Wispy creatures from the adjoining estate. Both barefoot, wearing identical plasticot caftans decorated in an overall pattern of atomic explosions.

They were carrying armloads of natural flowers: something long-stemmed and purple. They asked if they might leave them on my mother's grave. I nodded. They put them down gently.

"She was a beautiful human being," one of them said. The one with a ring in his nose.

"Yes," I said. "Thank you."

"Who were *they*?" Paul breathed when they ran away. Startled fauns.

"Friends and neighbors," I said.

"The kind of ems who give homosexuals a bad name," Paul said. "Flits."

"You've changed," I told him. "You wouldn't have said that a year ago. In that tone."

" 'When I was a child,' " he quoted, " 'I spake as a child. When I became a man, I put away childish things.' "

"Now I'll give you one," I said. " 'Upon what meat doth this our Caesar feed, that he is grown so great?' "

Paul wrote:

In your prospectus to the Chief Director re the establishment of a Department of Creative Science, I presume you will include an introduction explicating the relationship between science and politics. Do not neglect to point out that the development of birth control pills and their wide acceptance affected the Women's Liberation movement of the 1960-

1970's: a classic example of how science and technology influence sociological change.

"What data banks does your company buy from?" I asked my father.

He looked at me curiously.

"Consolidated or Federated," he said. "Occasionally some of the smaller ones. Why?"

The government's National Data Bank was the largest, of course. It maintained a complete computerized file on every object in the US. It issued BIN cards, recorded genetic history, military service, political activity, criminal accusations and convictions, credit rating, income taxes, marital status, awards and honors. Everything. By law, information stored in the NDB could not be revealed to anyone outside the government, or inside for that matter, who could not prove a need to know.

But private data banks had proliferated. Several attempts had been made to curb their activities by licensing, as Sweden had. But in 1998, there was little regulation of their operations. Most of the commercial data banks were specialized, dealing with such things as credit rating or personal interests or purchasing habits, etc. If you wanted a list of all seventy-year-old obsos in the US with an annual income of 10,000 new dollars and an active interest in shuffleboard, there was a data bank to provide names and addresses. Or if you wanted information on a specific object, for whatever reason, enough love paid to enough data banks would buy a profile almost as complete as if you had free access to the National Data Bank.

Sometimes I wondered how long it would be before the definition of "privacy" in your dictionary began "Obsol." And how long before it began "Obs."

"I want a profile on Angela Teresa Berri," I told my father.

"Ah," he said. "DIROB. She rules you, doesn't she?"

"Yes," I said. "And I also want a profile on Art Roach. He's ruler of Security and Intelligence of the Department of Bliss. That's why I don't want you connected with it in any way. Can you scam it?"

He didn't ask why I wanted the information. My father wasn't afraid of me, but I thought possibly he was in awe of me.

"I think I can do it." He nodded. "I'll place the orders through a supplier who owes me. What do you want?"

"Everything," I said. "Down to the moles on her ass."

"She has them?" he asked.

"She has them," I said.

He laughed.

"All right," he said. "But it'll take time."

"I have patience," I told him.

My mother's corpus was cremated, according to law. By custom, flaming took place following the funeral ceremony, lay or religionist. Then the plastilead urn containing the ashes of the stopped would be placed in a deposit box in a high-rise crematorium. A simple marker attached to the door. The long corridors of deposit boxes were decorated with frequently changed bouquets of plastirub flowers.

But in this case, my mother's corpus had been flamed soon after stopping. The urn had been delivered to a local church for the service. My father intended to bury her ashes on the grounds of our Grosse Pointe estate. It was illegal, but he had bribed local authorities. I approved of his arrangements.

The service was held in an Omni-Faith church, across Mack Avenue from Sunningdale Park. It was an A-frame structure of white plastisteel panels inset with long, narrow windows of colored plastiglass in abstract patterns. Rosy light fell on the altar where the gray urn had been placed. The church was crowded. I was surprised by the number of objects. I had expected her obso friends. But there were so many young objects present. Adolescents. What their relationship to my mother had been, I did not know. But they may have been strangers, their attendance due to simple curiosity in a church service.

It was a short ceremony. The pastor said she was not gone. Though she was stopped, he said, the memory of her kindness, beauty, and good humor would endure. We would recall her many charitable deeds, he said. We would speak her name, and tell children of her. So she would remain alive. A small choir sang a rock lament.

Millie Jean Grunwald was delighted with my gifts. Gifts for her. Gifts for me.

"Oh," she kept saying. "Oh, oh, oh."

The gifts were a middy loosely tied with a light blue scarf. A white skirt that ended above her bare knees. Plastivas sneakers. And a long wig of ashen hair (nylet) that flamed about her shoulders.

How artful. Carrying her tenderly to the bed. Ministering. She a surrender, wavering. Slowly the scarf, the middy, the skirt. I held my breath. It was sacred. I guided her fingers. She opened the mystery to me.

We were so slow. Just drifting. I wasn't sure when sperm spurted. If it did. It made no difference in my dream.

"You're going to be rich," my father told me. "Not rich rich, but rich. Everything she had is yours."

"How much?" I asked.

"Oh . . . maybe half a million new dollars."

New dollars. Interesting. They were always "new." In 1979, Lewisohn had persuaded the US Government to go to an Index System. The original idea was Brazilian. Lewisohn improved on it. Everything in the US economy—prices, wages, interest rates—was linked to the Cost of Living Index. As the index rose, as it did, inexorably, so rose every other economic factor in an intricate relationship.

The setting up of this system had required ten years of intensive computerized service, calculating the monetary, financial, and economic equations. The terms of all outstanding contracts—mortgages, bonds, stocks, insurance policies, etc.—had to be renegotiated. It was a horrendously complex task.

Yet, when completed, the Index System served reasonably well. It demanded, of course, that the US dollar be devalued, or you'd need a wheelbarrow of dollars to purchase a loaf of bread. "Revaluation" was the term used, rather than "devaluation," for semantic reasons. After each revaluation, old bills were declared obsolete and without value. New dollars, in new designs, were put into circulation.

The Index System proved to have one unexpected benefit: It halted hoarding completely, either by misers or by objects seeking to hide illegal cash from the government. No longer could the criminal conglomerates store bills in safe deposit boxes. After each revaluation, old dollars could be exchanged for the new currency at government banks. Questions were asked.

"Half a million new dollars," I repeated to my father. "I imagine probate and sale of the gold and other assets will take at least a year."

"Probably." He nodded.

"Will you lend against it?" I asked him. "I may need large sums for a short time."

"Of course," he said. "As much as you want."

"I insist on paying interest," I said.

He was offended.

Paul wrote:

In the prospectus for the Department of Creative Science, it will be necessary to make certain projections, describing the role of science and technology in the world of tomorrow. Just as inevitably, objections will be made that our vision of the future is "inhuman." It is important that we stonewall this attack. One approach: Point out the subjective nature of the term "inhuman world." What is human? What is inhuman? Cro-Magnon man might very well have found Renaissance Italy inhuman. Queen Victoria, I am certain, would have thought amniocentesis inhuman. Yet today it is accepted casually as a proved and useful diagnostic technique. I am convinced the technology we suggest today will similarly be accepted casually tomorrow.

We were in the library. Drinking brandy. Paul, my father, Ben Baker, my father's production manager, me. After a while we could talk.

"Hey, Nick," Baker said. "Look at this."

He brought a box from a corner, lifted the lid under my nose. The putrescent corpus of a Poo-Poo Doll. The same stink.

"Not again?" I said. "Another bad run?"

"What are you looking at?" Paul said.

The production manager shoved it at him.

"My God!" Paul cried. "What *is* it?"

I told him about the Connecticut River spill, the polluted rinse water in my father's factory, the ruined dolls.

"But this one is deliberate," my father said. "We got those doll bodies so they decay within predictable time limits. And that's not all we've got. It's going to be big, Nick."

I looked at him. Not certain.

"What's going to be big?"

"I'll tell you," he said. "A couple of weeks after we solved— after *you* solved the problem of the spoiled run—I went over to Ben's place for an outdoor barbecue. Ben's youngest daughter— What is she, Ben? Five? Six?"

"Penny is five," Ben Baker said. "Smart as a whip."

"Right," my father said. "Well, when I got there, Penny and

261

some of her friends were having a funeral for her pet turtle which had just died. They were burying him in a cigar box. Regular funeral: ceremony, procession, a grave, a piece of cardboard for a marker. The kids were crying. It was the real thing."

"Did exactly the same thing when our canary died." Baker nodded.

"Right," my father said. "Well, Ben and I got to brainstorming a doll that stops. Get it? The Die-Dee Doll. After the kid buys it, it begins to decay. I mean the body of the doll and the face just fall apart. The eyes sink. The hair falls out. I knew it could be done. After all, I have a BS in chemistry."

"And I suggested a death rattle," Ben said. "We could do it with a fused Japanese battery and noisemaker. The kid hears the death rattle, at any hour of the day or night—we can't program it *that* accurately—and knows her doll is dead. It's all falling apart by then."

"Right," my father said. "Then the little ef has the funeral. Now get this, Nick—this is where the love comes in. The basic Die-Dee kit is just the doll itself: young, pretty, blue eyes, blond wig. Other colors for other ethnic markets, of course. But the accessories! First of all, a model doctor's kit: toy stethoscope, plastic scalpel, bandages—the works. Then, when the doll rattles and stops, a plastic snap-together coffin. Get it now? And a little shovel and a plastic marker for the grave. A blank marker, shaped like an obso tombstone, so the kid can write on it the doll's name and age and whatever else. Well? Nick? What do you think? About the Die-Dee Doll?"

I stood up slowly and poured brandy in all the glasses.

"Well," I said. "That's quite a conception. Unusual. You'll get a lot of flak on it, of course."

"We're prepared for it," Ben Baker said.

"Right," my father said. "We've already got the go-ahead from our house child psychologist. Excellent emotional catharsis, he says. Teaches the child to feel. Second of all, we've paid out some good love for a motivational research survey. Kids between the ages of four and ten, both efs and ems, are fascinated by stopping, Nick. Third of all, we went to an independent psychological testing lab. That cost ten thousand new dollars, Nick. We got some big names in child psychology. Really big. You'd be surprised. They substantiated our in-house em. The Die-Dee Doll is recommended for emotional catharsis. Aids normal adjustment to stopping."

262

"Well, Nick?" my father asked.

"I think you've got a winner," I said.

Paul Bumford caught my warning glance and kept his mouth shut.

"I told you!" my father said. He leaned forward to slap Ben Baker on the knee. "I told you Nick would go for it!"

"When do you go into production?" I asked.

"As soon as we can get approval," my father said. "The sooner the better."

He and Baker began to exchange their coarse jokes. I signaled to Paul and we withdrew. Paul was sleeping in a second-floor guestroom. I stopped in with him for a nightcap and a Bold:

"Nick," he said, as soon as the door was closed, "that idea— that Die-Dee Doll—" He choked on the name. "—That will have to come to my Division for approval."

"Of course," I said mildly. "Why do you think my father and Baker were giving us that sales pitch?"

"Well, I'm not going to approve it."

"Oh? Mind telling me why?"

"Two reasons I can think of offhand. One, the projected sale of a toy doctor's kit along with a doll inexorably fated to stop. So the young ef, or em, is conditioned to the inefficiency of medicine and science."

"A possible result," I admitted. "If the child makes the connection, comes to that conclusion."

"Has to!" he said hotly. "Secondly, the child is conditioned to an image of stopping as putrescence, ugliness, and stench. Even the word 'die' is used. That goes against our national psychological thrust that has taken generations to reinforce. We don't want a society of objects pondering on stopping. Before you know it, they'll all be sitting around naked, cross-legged, contemplating their navels. Do we want a world of mystics or a world of producers and consumers? I'm going to reject the Die-Dee Doll, Nick."

"I can overrule your rejection, you know," I said.

"Are you going to?"

"We'll talk about it when the time comes," I said.

Paul wrote:

I would not favor a conventional bureaucratic hierarchy for the proposed Department of Creative Science. Rather than a Director served by deputy directors and assistant deputy directors who are specialists in one scientific or technological discipline, I recommend the Director rule a board of "omnists" that would constitute his second line of command. These "omnists" I see as objects conditioned in several scientific and/or technological disciplines and who can appreciate the interrelationship of those disciplines. "Renaissance man" was the term used for both objects of wide interest and expertise in several arts. I suggest the term "omnist" to describe a Renaissance object of science.

I was preparing for my visit to Millie Jean Grunwald. Paul Bumford knocked on the door of my suite. When I answered, he handed over a sealed manila envelope.

"My notes on the prospectus for the Department of Creative Science," he told me.

I weighed the envelope in my hand.

"You've been serving," I said.

"Yes. I wanted to finish them here. I'm taking a late flight back tonight."

"The copter will take you to the airport," I said.

"Yes," he said. "Your father arranged it."

"Well. . . ." Strained silence. "Have a good flight. I appreciate your coming."

He nodded.

"I'll see you back in GPA-1," I said.

He looked me up and down. My tooty costume.

"Going somewhere?" he asked.

"Yes. Into Detroit."

"Ef or em?"

"Ef," I said.

"Nice?"

"*My* toy," I said.

I sat in my "secret place," staring at the paintings of Egon Schiele. Searching for answers. As always, I was dazzled by those explosions of color, the raw sensuality, the brooding despair, the probing so deep it seemed to me a scalpel rather than a paintbrush had exposed the live nerve and set it tingling.

And, as always, the answers eluded me. I was convinced they were there, but I could not decode them. Suddenly I had an infamous thought: I wanted Egon Schiele alive. Then I could take him, send him to an R&R, into a Cooperation Room where, after he had signed an Informed Consent Statement, I could drain him and learn what I sought. But the em was stopped. And I could not read the testament of his art.

Paul wrote:

Re planning for the DCS, the problem of projection is always the same: What kind of a world do we want in 20, 50, or 100 years? Agreement will be difficult, if not impossible, but planning *must* be started unless we are to leave the future to chance and accident. Our Tomorrow File is certainly a good beginning.

Nick, I know the quality of your mind, and I wish you would give some thought to the eventual establishment of social classes based on procreative techniques. From highest to lowest: Natural, Artificial Insemination, Artificial Enovulation, Placenta Machine, Embryonic Cloning, Parthenogenesis, etc. Within each class, of course, status would be determined by genetic quality.

I wasn't enthusiastic about this suggestion. My first impulse was to reject it. But I could not reject it totally. As Paul requested, I computed it.

The heavy conflict, to any object of reason, is between the tomorrow you desire and the tomorrow you expect.

Y-7

By the mid-1980's, the US Postal Service had reached such a nadir of inefficiency that in desperation Congress had amended existing law to allow the establishment of commercial postal services. Although their rates were higher, they did provide some degree of privacy and some assurance that a letter mailed from Point A to Point B would not end up in a dusty pigeonhole at Point K. Gradually, the US Post Office was reduced to the handling of parcels and a service called Instamail by which open letters were electronically scanned at Point A, broadcast to Point B, reproduced in facsimile on a standard form and, one hoped, delivered to the addressee. No privacy, of course, but useful for form letters and nonconfidential correspondence.

I had instructed Maya Leighton to send me reports on Art Roach via commercial mail, addressed to my rented box number in the Times Square section of Manhattan. On August 14, I left the compound in uniform and drove uptown. I flashed Simon Hawkley's office in San Diego and told his secretary I would be out there the following Tuesday and would contact Mr. Hawkley upon arrival.

I then stopped at my mail drop and picked up the first report from Maya. As I was coming out of the building, an obso em, handsome, well dressed, looked scornfully at my silver zipsuit and said clearly, "Jinky shit."

I think everyone in Public Service had experienced this kind of personal hassle. One reason why the wearing of official uniforms outside government compounds had been made voluntary rather than mandatory.

A few hours later, in my office, I scanned Maya Leighton's report, laughed aloud, tossed it across my desk to Paul Bumford.

Subject from GA-8. Georgia, I think. Cracker. No wonder he's so silent. Every time he opens his mouth he betrays his conditioning. Or lack of it. Brains in his penis. He's very brainy. Heavy signet ring middle finger left hand. Loose kidneys. But frequently constipated. Doctors himself. *Everything!* But mostly laxatives and nasal sprays. Pimples drive him wild. Very clean personally. Rushes to the nest after using. Can't pass a mirror without glancing at his image. With approval. Nick, a beautiful, *beautiful* ass! You wouldn't believe! A muffin! Loves steam rooms, saunas, massage. Exercises strenuously every day. But hooked on the saunas. A kind of ceremony? Not intelligent—but shrewd? Hoo-boy! Nick, I was amused at first. Now he's beginning to wear. Such a child. When he starts calling me "Mommy" I resign. He has absolutely *no* pubic hair at all. Well, of course, he has. But it is so blond, so fine, you must get up very, very close to see it. Miss me, you fork-tongued bastard?

Paul scanned the letter swiftly. Then he laughed, too.
"Sardonic ef," he said. "What do you want done with this?"
"Dictate it onto a belt," I said. "Leave out all personal refer-

ences to me. Then send it down to your Neuropsychiatry Team and order them to start building a Psychological Profile."

"It would be a lot easier if we could get into the Personnel Files and scan his original PP."

"It would," I agreed, "but we can't. He rules those files. What do you want me to do—flash him and say, 'Oh Art, by the way, could you send me a copy of your PP? I want to know what makes you jerk.' No, this is the only way to do it. I don't need it on Angela because I compute that ef. And we'll be getting background and financial input on both of them from my father's private data banks. Just tell the Neuropsychiatry Team the subject is an object applying for sensitive service and we need a preliminary profile. No problem."

"Nooo," he said slowly. "No problem."

I stared at him.

"What's *your* problem?" I asked. "Something inoperative here?"

"No, no," he said hastily. "I was just computing. For the Tomorrow File."

"Oh? What?"

"These Psychological Profiles—they're part of the Personnel File of everyone in Public Service. Right?"

"And the military. And universities. And academies. And every decent-size company, corporation, foundation, and conglomerate in the US."

"In other words, they're valuable?"

"Valuable? Invaluable! They cull out the nuts. And objects too ambitious or too creative for a particular service. What are you getting at?"

"Everyone should have a Psychological Profile. Every citizen of the US. To be included in the National Data Bank."

I shook my head.

"Illegal," I said. "A PP requires a value judgment. By law, the NDB can only be a repository for raw data."

"So change the law." He shrugged.

"For what purpose? What benefit?"

"Nick, you know what's been happening to the Satrat."

"Yes. It's soft."

"Soft? It's limp! And terrorism is increasing."

"How do you know that?"

"I hear things, Nick. Just as you do. Bombings, kidnapping,

assassinations. All over the place. Well, if we had a Psychological Profile in the National Data Bank on everyone, computerized, maybe we could weed out the violence-prone, the crime-prone, the nonproducers and the underconsumers. A PP updated every five years, or two years, or annually, would certainly flash warning signs. It could cut down on terrorism, reduce crime, give us a clearer picture of the number and identity of enemies of the state."

"Yes," I said promptly. "I think you've got something there. It's interesting. Add it to the Tomorrow File. And while you're at it, send me a tape of the entire file. I want to include some of our items in the prospectus for the Department of Creative Science. There's a meeting of DOB early next month. While I'm in Washington, I'll deliver the prospectus to the Chief Director."

"Nick," he said, not looking at me, "are you going to mention me? You know, as source of some of the ideas?"

"Not to worry," I said. "I'll spell your name right."

He grinned at me then. I could remember when it was a little boy's grin.

I took a commercial jet to San Diego. It stopped at St. Louis, Tulsa, Phoenix. But I didn't regret the time lost. I used it to dictate notes into my Pockacorder, organizing ideas on the prospectus for the Department of Creative Science. I knew I not only had to convince the Chief Director of its value, but I had to provide—in a brief document—sufficient ammunition to make it politically viable. I had to manipulate his mind from concept to reality.

I decided, in the introduction, to move swiftly from the specific to the general.

"As recently as two hundred years ago, ours was an agrarian society. An em might spend his lifetime in the same log cabin, chinked with mud, in which he had been born. He woke to a cock's crow, washed in well or stream water, donned garments woven and sewn by his wife, ate a breakfast of foods raised on his own land, turned his fields with a wooden plow pulled by a horse, sold what extra produce he could for needles and glass, read his Bible by candlelight, fell exhausted onto a rope bed covered with a straw tick. Ignorance, poverty, near-starvation, and hard, grinding, endless labor. Muscle labor.

"Today, two centuries later, the average em wakes on a plastifoam mattress when his radio alarm clicks on. He adjusts the temperature of his shower by regulating taps through which flows water brought from hundreds of miles away. He cleans his teeth with an ultrasonic strigil. He dons garments knitted of fibers made from petroleum. He drives an electric-powered vehicle. He serves in aseptic, air-conditioned surroundings. He rules machines that provide brute labor. He eats foods, nutritional foods, vitamin-enriched, of an astounding variety. He is able to learn from or be entertained by an amazing array of sight, sound, and scent appliances. He lives longer and he lives better.

"Science and technology have effected this change from the society of two hundred years ago. Revolution is a mild word for it. But since science advances exponentially, the next two hundred years will be, not revolution, but change so fundamental that those living today have less possibility of visualizing it fully than the em of 1800 conceiving today's world.

"With these advances in medicine, comfort, personal fulfillment, and increased opportunities for all objects, have come new problems: the possibility of nukewar, uncontrolled population growth, despoilment of the environment, a shortage of energy, etc., etc. It could be said that science and technology have created these problems.

"If this is operative, then science and technology can solve these problems. When the need becomes imperative, the human brain will find a solution. Otherwise, we would be apes, would we not?"

I played the tape back and listened intently. It would need greasing, but the gist was there. It was at once a challenge and a promise. It was almost a crusade. I felt it would impress Chief Director Michael Wingate because he would recognize the political potential. No one is against tomorrow.

I called Hawkley, Goldfarb & Bensen from the jetport and was told Simon Hawkley would see me at 1400. I purchased a map of San Diego at the newsstand. I sat down on a plastic bench, put my attaché case flat on my lap, spread out the map. I found the approximate location of Scilla Pharmaceuticals. I refolded the map—not on the original creases, naturally—left the terminal and rented a diesel-powered two-door Ford sedan, one of the new Shark models. The attendant gave me directions on how to get to the La Mesa area, to Alvarado Road.

I am conscious of having dictated the preceding paragraph in simple, declarative sentences. It is indicative of my actions at that point in time. After reflection and planning comes the go or no-go decision. This is the stage, I believe, at which most objects falter. Anyone can reflect. Anyone can plan. The crunch comes with the move from thought to action, a giant step that requires energy, resolve, and a willingness to accept change.

In any event, I became aware that once the go/no-go decision was taken and I had opted for action, a linear logic all its own took over. A led to B which led to C, etc., almost with no volition on my part. Pilots speak of "the point of no return," the exact second when their diminishing fuel leaves no alternative but to continue the flight, they hope to their destination. I believe I reached my point of no return on that hot afternoon of August 20, 1998, in San Diego, California.

Did I believe in omens? Yes, I believed in omens, and Scilla Pharmaceuticals was a pleasant surprise. The main building was small, two stories high, built of cinder blocks painted a celery green. The architecture was inoffensive. There was a loading platform, several smaller outbuildings, a circular drive of white gravel. The landscaping was attractive: trees, bushes, shrubs, lawn—all obviously well tenued, neat, clean. There was a chain fence around the area, a smartly uniformed guard at the gate.

I drove past slowly, staring, made a U-turn and drove past again. I was briefly tempted to stop, go inside on some pretext or other, and take a look at the interior. But I decided against it. I was satisfied with my first impression: a small, clean, moderately prosperous drug factory. It seemed to fit my needs exactly.

A few hundred yards past the gate the road was bordered by trees for a short distance. The shoulders of the road were wide; a driver could safely pull off onto the verge. Traffic, at that time of day, seemed minimal. At night, I guessed, it would be practically nonexistent. We could park in the shadow of the trees with our receivers and recorders.

I drove slowly back toward the business section, computing possibilities and variables. The difficulties were numerous, but not unconquerable. Mostly physical problems: equipment, timing, tactics. I might even bring it off by myself, but it would be awkward. I needed assistance. Which brought me back to something, or someone rather who had been troubling me. Paul Bumford.

He was, of course, my co-conspirator. Having divulged so much to him, having made him privy to my motives and plans, I should not at that point in time have even questioned his further involvement. He was already in. I could not deny it. But still. . . .

A year previously there would have been no problem. He was then my creature. But the events of the past six months—the smashing of the Society of Obsoletes' conspiracy and Paul's elevation to AssDepDirRad—had given him power. That was, as I had told him, a virus. He was as much a victim as I. But I knew it for what it was. And could, I thought, cope, recognizing the responsibilities and dangers of power. But did Paul?

I drove directly to the offices of Hawkley, Goldfarb & Bensen, and spent almost fifteen minutes searching for a parking space. Finally I did what I should have done in the first place: I parked directly in front of the building in a No Parking zone. A uniformed doorman seemed to pop up out of the Glasphalt sidewalk, but I had a five-dollar bill folded, ready to slip into his palm.

"I'll only be a few minutes," I said.

He glanced at the bill.

"Take your time," he said.

Up to the thirty-fourth floor in a high-speed elevator that smelled of an estrogen-based perfume. Then down those chilled, empty corridors. The massive plank door swung shut behind me. Thudding. I was not conscious of having stepped into the past. I had stepped into an executive's office on the star Arcturus. It was all foreign to me, including the unwrapped mummy propped behind the mahogany desk. Those exhausted eyes stared thoughtfully at me. Again, the scrawny neck stretched from a starched white collar, a shiny alpaca jacket.

"Sir," I said, "I trust I find you in good health?"

He demanded language like that.

He waved me to a chair. He already had the decanter and two balloons ready. He poured me a half-glass with a slow, steady hand.

"I live, young man," Simon Hawkley said.

We plunged right in. He had a sheaf of papers ready and flipped them over steadily, explaining what he proposed. My initial investment would be in a new corporation formed for the purpose of establishing a franchised chain of porn shops. Quite legal. The porn shops would then purchase controlling interest in a new company formed for the purpose of establishing a drive-in three-dimensional laser movie theater. Which in turn would invest its assets in a new factory to produce redi-mixed frozen salads with forty-eight different artificial seasonings. Which would. . . . A classic "fuzz job."

"To accomplish all this," Simon Hawkley said at one point, "I will need a power of attorney from you, young man. This is where a certain degree of trust on your part is essential."

271

"A degree of trust, sir?" I said. "I always thought of trust as complete and absolute, or nonexistent. You have my trust, Mr. Hawkley."

He liked that. The silver lips compressed in what I hoped was a smile.

I signed all the documents he shoved toward me. I wrote out a check for an enormous sum drawn on a Detroit bank where my father's loan against my inheritance had been deposited in my name. Hawkley immediately called in the bountifully hindquartered secretary. She took my check and BIN card and departed to open my account.

We raised glasses, sipped, looked at each other. Quite solemn.

"Now then—" I began.

"Now then," he rumbled in that surprisingly deep, resonant voice of his. "Now then, you will need a personal representative at Scilla. Under the terms of sale, the executive staff stays on. You are allowed to bring in a chief executive. I have a man for you. I vouch for him completely. Agreed?"

"Agreed."

"He is on our payroll, so your expense will be minimal. He is young, intelligent, sharp. Versed in business law. He will spend a minimum of two or three hours a day at Scilla, familiarizing himself with the operation. Auditors will go in every month. You will not be—uh—I believe 'scammed' is the new word, Mr. Flair."

"That is the word." I nodded. "But it never occurred to me that I would be scammed, sir. But there is—"

"Our man," he rumbled on, "whom you will meet shortly, will occupy the private office of the former owner, Anthony Scilla. Now, you will want the office shared. I recommend Chauncey Higgles, a British organization of excellent reputation. They have a branch office in this city, on Market Street. We use them frequently. Dependable. Discreet. The salesperson you want to deal with is Mrs. Agatha Whiggam. I have alerted her to your interest. She tells me that Higgles has in their files complete floor plans of Scilla, as they do of almost every other building, office, store, and factory in the city. I suggest you follow her instructions."

I looked at him with admiration.

"Mr. Hawkley," I said, raising my glass to him, "we're two of a kind."

"Umm," he said.

He swung slowly back and forth in his high-backed leather swivel chair. He gazed at me dreamily from those faded eyes.

"Mr. Flair," he said, "you are an adventurer."

"Yes, sir," I said. "I expect so."

"Perhaps a buccaneer?"

"Perhaps," I agreed.

Again the stretched smile. I think he saw himself in me. I know I saw myself in him. Strangely enough, I had never felt that sense of identity with any object except Angela Teresa Berri. And here we were, plotting her destruction. If the three of us ever got together, we could rule the world and all its suburbs.

The blond secretary returned with bank forms, a receipt, a book of checks, my BIN card. I signed where I had to sign, including a dozen blank checks. I kept only my BIN card; he retained the other documents.

"We'll wait for your Detroit check to clear," he said. "But unless you hear from me differently, you may proceed with your plans in two weeks."

He was speaking to me, but his eyes were following the haunches of the young ef as she marched out of the office. The massive door boomed shut behind her.

"Art is long, and time is fleeting," Simon Hawkley said.

"Yes, sir," I said. I wasn't certain what he meant. If anything.

He sighed, looked down at his liver-spotted hands.

"The man you are about to meet is Seymour Dove," he said. "He is neither a clerk nor a junior partner. But he occupies a very special position in this office. Originally, he trained for the stage. He is very handsome and has great presence. He also had enough intelligence to realize the theater—stage, movies, TV—did not offer the rewards he desired. So, at a relatively late age—his middle-twenties—he took a law degree and minored in business administration. But his previous stage experience has proved valuable, as I have reason to know. Also, he is a happy man. That helps."

"Yes, sir," I agreed. "It surely does."

He slowly slipped an obso hunter from an inside pocket, flicked it open, glanced at the face, clicked it shut, slid it back into the hidden pocket.

"Mr. Dove will be with us in two minutes."

If only I could manipulate SATSEC as efficiently.

273

Initially, Seymour Dove overwhelmed me. Dismayed me. I saw a big, beefy em, handsome and brutish, clad in harsh, bright California colors. A horseblanket-plaid jacket, fire-engine-red slacks, a lace shirt unbuttoned to his navel, capped teeth, bronzed skin, red hair so perfectly teased it had to be a wig, makeup artfully applied, plastigold sandals on bare feet, enormous sunglasses that not only blanked his eyes but covered half his face. A sight.

"Hi, dads," he said.

I turned to look at Simon Hawkley in astonishment. Was this—But he was silent, regarding me gravely. I turned back to Seymour Dove. He was pulling up a chair, unasked, beginning to speak rapidly in a flat, hard voice, totally unlike his flutey "Hi, dads."

"Here's what you want," he started. . . .

Then, as he spoke, I caught on. He wasn't wearing clothes; he was wearing a costume. He was auditioning for a role. He would wear those garments as chief executive officer of Scilla Pharmaceuticals and earn a reputation as a microweight, a playboy. But he'd watch the books. He'd report to Simon Hawkley the moment he got a nibble from Washington. He'd keep his private office sacrosanct and oversee the sharing installation.

"Is that about it, dads?" he asked, switching back to his stage voice.

I stood up, leaned across the desk to shake Hawkley's paper hand. Then I stroked palms with the seated Seymour Dove.

"My worries are over," I said.

The California whites gleamed at me.

"Depend on it," he said.

Y-8

On September 10, Paul Bumford came to my office to discuss matters of mutual interest. He had been serving tough; his thinned-down physique and almost gaunt features showed it. But he was cool, precise, informed. If he had problems—and I knew he had—he showed no signs of being unable to handle them.

Finally, after we had concluded the agenda agreed upon, he returned to me an Instox copy of the DCS prospectus I had submitted to him for comment.

"Well?" I asked.

He grinned. "Nick, it's magnificent."

"Really?"

"Really. If he rejects it, he's a fool. But he won't reject it."

"How do you know?"

"I just feel it."

I laughed. "Well . . . I trust your instincts."

"Do you? Nick, don't change a word of it. It's great. And thanks for the plug. More good news . . . Mary Bergstrom and Phoebe Huntzinger are back from the Denver FO. Everything on Project Phoenix is go. Mary made some suggestions on the scanning areas of the lasers. Phoebe says the computer is as ready as it'll ever be. Tests started yesterday."

"Fine," I said. "That's fine."

I consulted some notes on my desk pad. I was conscious of him staring at me. I looked up. Our eyes locked.

"So much going on," I said, "I thought it best to make notes."

"Of course." He nodded.

"Now then," I went on, "the DOB (we pronounced it Dob) is meeting on Tuesday of next week. Do you have time to go down to Washington with me?"

"I'll find time."

"Good. And I want Mary Bergstrom to come along. We'll drive down on Monday, directly to the Alexandria Hospice. They'll put us up for the night. I want you and Mary to meet Group Lewisohn."

"Why?"

"Oh . . . just to familiarize yourselves with their operation," I said vaguely.

"In other words, I have no need to know?"

"At the moment, no," I agreed. "But you might."

"Oh? Your contingency list for Lewisohn?"

"That's right."

"The trouble with contingency plans," he said, "is that they all have a built-in defect. The objects who devise them can't resist trying them out to see if they'll succeed."

I thought it time to show my teeth.

"Are you objecting to my efforts to keep Hyman R. Lewisohn alive?" I asked coldly.

"No, no!" he backed off hastily. "My God, Nick, you're touchy lately."

"I admit it." I sighed. Having made my point. "The moment we

275

get the Scilla business concluded, I'll be my usual sweet self again.''

"Scilla," he said. "Ah-ha! I've been saving the best news for last.''

"What about Scilla?" I asked sharply.

"I've gotten the need for hallucinogens to over a hundred thousand new dollars during the next fiscal year. Projected.''

I smiled. "Paul, that's great. Just great!''

"Yes." He nodded. "I won't be modest. It's great.''

"All right, now here's what you do: Send me a Request for Suspension of Bidding form. State that you'll need the hallucinogens in the amounts detailed for the purposes noted. State that Scilla has been our supplier in the past and you recommend them on the basis of tested purity of product, responsibility for delivery, and so forth. And the amount involved, in your opinion, is not sufficient to advertise competitive bidding among the drug cartels. Then I'll put my endorsement on it, forward it to Data and Statistics, and they'll send it on to—''

"Got it right here," he said.

He picked the document from his case, glanced at it briefly, placed it on my desk with a flourish.

I laughed. "Paul, you're way ahead of me.''

"That's right," he said.

We estimated it would take about a week for the request to clear Data & Statistics in GPA-1, and another two weeks to be processed by Angela's Purchasing Department in Washington. If she was going to take the bait, it couldn't be before late September, perhaps early October.

I was content to wait. I would be patient. Sometimes anticipation is more satisfying than realization.

I wasn't so patient with the preliminary reports Paul was receiving from his Neuropsychiatry Team: the psychological profile of Art Roach. Of all scientific jargons, sociological gobbledygook was the worst. Closely followed by psychiatric guck. I wanted objective judgments. I received such kaka as "anal positive . . . cyclothymic personality . . . severe status orientation . . . probable overcompensating inferior . . . possible paranoiac schizophrenia, etc., etc.''

In my disciplines, a gene is a gene, a cell is a cell, a virus is a virus, and a brain is never a mind. I wanted their language to be as exact.

Finally, in desperation, I posed a series of questions, through Paul. The answers that came back substantiated my splanchnic opinion of the em.

Art Roach was shrewd without being intelligent. He was deeply conscious of the circumstances of his birth—he was a bastard—and his lack of conditioning. To reinforce his self-esteem, he pampered his corpus—mirrors, massages, saunas, laxatives, and nasal sprays. He was motivated by status almost totally. His sadistic sexual behavior served to obliterate his essential belief in his own unworthiness. He was a slave striving to be a master.

To my question, "If status is threatened, is this object capable of violence?" the answer was unequivocal and mercifully short: "Yes."

The private data bank reports on Angela Berri, sent by commercial mail to my father and forwarded by commercial mail to my letter drop, were less revealing. I scanned the background material swiftly: "NF . . . born in Chicago . . . father a bartender . . . etc., etc." It wasn't important. No one had roots anymore. History was inoperative.

The quality of her brain had been, apparently, recognized at an early age. She received advanced conditioning, then was accepted by the Science Academy at the age of thirteen. I was already aware of her doctorates and of her career after she entered Public Service.

Something I hadn't known: She had been married at the age of eighteen to an em named John Findlay. He had suicided three weeks after their marriage. No details provided. None were necessary. I could guess.

I spent more time scanning reports of her personal finances and credit rating. At first glance, they revealed nothing. Her total wealth was substantial, but nothing that could not be accounted for by her annual rank-rate. She neither deposited nor withdrew sizable sums at regular intervals. Her expenditures seemed to be what might be expected of an ef with her income. The totality did not form a mathematical model of the greedy object I knew her to be. Until. . . .

I was scanning an Instox copy of her household insurance policy. I zipped the fine print. It seemed normal. I went back for a slower scanning. Ah! She was paying insurance premiums on more than 100,000 new dollars' worth of personal jewelry and furs. This in an age when some of the wealthiest efs leased their jewelry and furs.

The policy had a footnote to this assessment: "See Appraisal Affidavit No. 6-49-34G-2-B."

I searched for this document, but it was missing from the file. No matter. She could not resist adorning her corpus—with gems and costly furs that were hers alone.

So I believed the insurance policy, without yet knowing how she had managed to cover the purchases of 100,000 new dollars' worth of jewelry and furs. I was saddened, because greed seemed to me so drab. There are more admirable vices.

I decided to take the limousine to Washington, D.C. These trappings of official majesty counted for something in the Nation's Capital. In Manhattan, the new breed of pimps selected the identical vehicles: big, black, sedate, silent, powerful. Tooty cars to drop off street whores along Park Avenue.

Our chauffeur was a perky, red-wigged ef with the face of a choirboy and a corpus to match. I wondered how much love she had paid the ruler of the motor pool for this cushy assignment. Whatever, she seemed to be happy; her humming never ceased. Finally, Paul leaned forward and pressed the button that raised the bulletproof, soundproof plastiglass partition between driver and passengers. Then he settled back. Mary Bergstrom was seated solidly between us, knees together. So we drove south. Stiff. Rarely speaking. A grim trip.

At Rehabilitation & Reconditioning Hospice No. 4, we went immediately into colloquy with Group Lewisohn. In addition to Dr. Seth Lucas and Maya Leighton, the Group now included a hematologist, a neuropsychologist, two oncologists, an interne, three nurses, a dietician. We went over the most recent scannings quickly. There had been little change, physically, since my last visit. No grave deterioration, but no improvement either.

"It's not the scannings that bother me so much," Lucas said nervously. "But I think there's been a loss. The object refuses to let us test motor ability. So the loss may be psychological. But I'm convinced there's a growing lassitude there. Maya?"

"I concur," she said promptly. "He doesn't grab my tits anymore. Physical? Psychological? I can't say. Both, probably. But there's a definite slowing down. One symptom is a lengthening of verbal response. Nick, we're with him every day, so we can't determine its significance. You haven't seen him for weeks; you'll be able to compute it easier than we can."

"All right." I sighed. "I'll take a look. Is he serving at anything?"

"At something." The psychologist nodded. "Lots of books, computer printouts, confidential reports. He hasn't volunteered any information and, of course, we haven't asked. But his morale is degenerating. No doubt about it. It may be due to his current service or it may be physiological in origin."

"Thank you, doctor," I said. I meant it ironically, but he missed it.

"You're welcome," he said.

"Is it depression?" I asked him.

"Close to it."

"Is he eating?" I asked the dietician.

"Poorly. We're giving supplements by injection. When we can. He's a difficult patient."

"The understatement of the year." I looked at the blood em. "Doctor?"

"Nothing's serving," he said gloomily. "A very stubborn case."

Then we all sat in silence a few moments. I was thinking—and I presumed the others were computing along similar lines—how important the survival of this disgusting, magnificent object was to my own career. His life had become my life. I would not let him go without a struggle.

"The parabiosis suite?" I asked Lucas.

"Almost finished. Want to take a look?"

"Yes. Paul, you and Mary and Maya come along. Then we'll beard the ogre in his den. I thank all of you."

The new suite designed for the parabiotic treatment of Hyman Lewisohn had a fatal flaw. I pointed it out as calmly as I could. The purpose of the massive and lovable alteration of three hospice rooms was to shield him from the fact that his veins and arteries had been snugged with the veins and arteries of a healthy "donor" or "volunteer" or "partner" whose natural immunity might help rid Lewisohn's circulatory system of the proliferation of immature white cells.

Lewisohn, I knew—we all knew—would not willingly endure this vital linkage. He scorned personal relationships, intimate relationships. They sickened him. He gloried in his independence, in his uniqueness. To such an extent that he rejected every opportunity for friendship. I do not wish to dwell too long on the neuropsychiatric motivation of this em's behavior, except to point out that his physical ugliness, his achondroplasia, was undoubtedly the gross motivating factor. But unfortunate as that might have been, it may also have been the stimulus of his creative energy. Such things happen.

In any event, I had no wish to "cure" this psychic twitch. In fact, it was to my interest that he continue to function as before. My only concern was his continued existence and ability to serve. Nothing more.

So I pointed out to Dr. Seth Lucas that the dividing wall erected between Lewisohn's new suite and the room in which the donor would reside was much too thin. Sounds would carry. Lewisohn would become aware of some object existing on the other side of that partition through which ran the tubes and wires necessary for the exchange.

We spent almost an hour planning how the dividing wall might be improved: widening, the addition of insulation, the use of ultrasonic baffles, the placement of Lewisohn's three TV monitors to mask sounds from the donor's chamber, etc. Maya Leighton proposed that visitors' chairs and Lewisohn's computer be placed on the side of his bed away from the wall, manipulating his attention in that direction. An excellent suggestion.

Then we all trooped down one floor to examine the patient in his present quarters.

I saw at once what Maya Leighton and Seth Lucas had meant by the object's lassitude. His obscene insults were as vituperative as usual. But they came fitfully, in bursts, almost as a duty to maintain his reputation. Or his ego image. But between outbursts were periods of a condition distressingly akin to catatonia: head turned aside, eyes unfocused, jaw hanging slackly. That enormous skull seemed more distorted than ever; the corpus had shrunk. Skin on neck and shoulders hung loosely, without tone. Spittle gathered in the corners of his mouth. Maya wiped it gently away. He looked up at her dully. She took his hand. I watched. His fingers did not curl about hers.

I remember thinking, bitterly: The bastard is going.

I introduced Mary Bergstrom and Paul Bumford. He did not acknowledge their presence. Finally, he gathered enough energy to demand of me when he'd be out of this "dungheap."

280

"Soon," I promised him. "We're moving you to a new suite. Upstairs. More room. More privacy. You'll like it there."

He cursed me mechanically, then lost interest, looked about vaguely. Seth Lucas fussed at him, watching the electronic monitors. The little white spheres bounced across the black screens or traced graceful curves. Thankfully, there were only minor aberrations. *Ping-ping-ping. Ka-voom, ka-voom, ka-voom. Ahh-waa, ahh-waa, ahh-waa.* Soft sounds of existence.

I noted Paul surreptitiously examining a pile of books stacked at the bedside. There was the usual disorder of computer printouts, folders, manuscripts, envelopes with the red tags of restricted material. But I could not believe the em was capable of serving productively in his present state.

Outside, we held an impromptu, low-voiced colloquy in the corridor.

"Paul?" I asked.

"Going."

"Mary?"

"I concur."

"Yes," I agreed. "Seth"—I turned to him—"you have that list of potential donors from FO's and hospices. Start bringing them in for serological workups. Begin with twenty. We'll make our initial choices from them."

"Right."

"Get a crew on that wall immediately. Prepare to start parabiosis next Wednesday. I'll come down with a surgical staff from GPA-1 to help you with the hookup. Now . . . where can we get a vodka-and-Smack in this necropolis?"

They all laughed. Dutifully.

On our way to the Executive Lounge, I drew Paul Bumford aside for a moment.

"What were the books, Paul? Alongside Lewisohn's bed?"

"I only saw three of them: *The Methodology of Modern Revolution. A Psychohistory of Terrorism.* And *The Roots of Social Discontent.*"

"Oh?" I said. "That's interesting."

Beds had been reserved for us in Transients Quarters. I could forgo the honor; let Paul Bumford and Mary Bergstrom endure those hard cots. I knew Maya Leighton had leased a small apartment in Hamlet West. I pleaded my need in doleful tones. She had a dinner engagement that evening with Art Roach. I told her what to do: Flash him and cancel it, claiming a sudden medical emergency.

"And so it is," I assured her.

"So it is," she agreed. "It'll be wonderful losing him for a night. How much longer do I have to jerk him, Nick?"

"Three months max," I told her. "But probably only a month. Maybe a little more. Can you endure?"

"If you say so."

"Maya, your reports have been a big help."

"But he's such a yawn, Nick, *such* a yawn. There's nothing *to* him. After the novelty has worn off."

I insisted on cooking dinner for us. It took an hour's touring of local markets to find a natural steak, four small, sad natural potatoes, a natural Spanish onion. We settled for green probeans, a plastipak of synthetic scallion greens, a half-kilo of prorooms—"Taste-engineered to please the most discriminating palate." And a liter of actinized brandy.

It turned out to be an unstructured, improvised, and rather splendid evening. At least, I enjoyed it, and I tried to please Maya. Her profit, being part of mine, *most* of mine, was important to me. Also, at that point in time, I was in need of mindless bliss. She was always in need of mindless bliss. This is merely an observation, not a value judgment.

I baked the minuscule potatoes in Maya's microwave oven, chilled them swiftly in the quik-freez section of her refrigerator, then sliced them and fried them with chopped onions and scallion greens. The steak was microwaved, the probeans and prorooms cooked together, then turned into the frying pan at the last moment for a coating of oil and seasoning. The whole thing was palatable, eminently palatable.

Perhaps our enjoyment was whetted by the brandy. We attained a level of beaming inebriation and held it for hours, not becoming maudlin, slovenly, physically uncoordinated. But relaxed in an almost floppy state, grinning continually, occasionally teasing, playing like puppies. I could not recall ever feeling such a sense of physical belonging with another object.

Late in the evening, she leaped from my lap—we had been munching each other—hauled me to my feet, tugged me toward her bedroom.

"I have something to show you," she said.

"You've had toothbud transplants on the labia majora?"

"How did you guess?" she giggled.

What she had to show me was a shelved cupboard filled with all the paraphernalia of a sophisticated sexualist.

"Why, Maya," I murmured, "I didn't know you cared."

"I joined the Thrill of the Month Club about three years ago," she said. "But I've only been collecting seriously in the last year. I have some rare items here."

"Rare, indeed," I agreed.

Dildos: wood, rubber, plastic, steel; capable of being filled with hot water, metal bearings, mercury; or vibrated electrically or ultrasonically. Japanese Ben-Wa balls; German breast oscillators; French ticklers; US artifical vaginas; British Electro-Cops; inflatable sex dolls, ef and em, life-size, fitted with wigs and costumes, with heat elements and vibrators; coitus splints; molded tongues covered with nodules; clitoral stimulators; penile extensors; desensitizing cremes, lotions, and sprays to delay orgasm; vibrating fingers; dildo harnesses; vibraginas; penis rings; studded penis sleeves; open-mouthed rubber masks; double-vibrators for vagina and anus; purse-sized vibrators; erotic statuary; a "gun" with a penis barrel that "ejaculated" when the trigger was pulled; false breasts; condoms and vibrator sleeves of every conceivable abrasive design; jellies, oils, sprays. And much, much more.

"I don't know how they can sell that stuff," she said. Vestigial morality there. "Isn't there a law against it, Nick?"

Her naïveté amused me. Yes, there was "a law against it." Several. But it was deliberate government policy not to enforce those laws. The reason given for the government's inaction was the doubtful constitutionality of those laws and the subsequent difficulties in obtaining convictions.

The operative reason why the government allowed—Allowed? Encouraged!—the increasing technologizing of sex was the continuing need to achieve and maintain Zero Population Growth. Anything that contributed to Z-Pop was in the public interest. Hence this proliferation of false penises and artificial vaginas (the expensive models trimmed with mink). Similarly, the federal government had quietly passed the word to state and local law enforcement agencies to overlook laws still on the books making homosexuality and lesbianism criminal offenses. Z-Pop was more important.

"Now then," I said, rubbing my hands before this cornucopia of mechanical delights, "what shall we start with?"

Maya had a pharmacopoeia in her nest. I made full use of it the following morning. After a liter of cold water, a vitamin injection, an energizing inhalant, and two methylphenidate spansules, I began to believe my original diagnosis of ambulatory quietus had been exaggerated.

The brandy bottle was quite empty, but I found a new half-liter of petrorum in the cupboard under the milk. I mixed a large rum-and-Smack and sipped it while showering and using Maya's dipilatory face creme. I called for a cab. While waiting, I examined my features in the bedroom mirror. Except for a small bite mark low on my neck, there were no obvious signs of the previous night's debauch. And certainly no psychic scars.

Maya was still sleeping. That great, lush corpus sprawled across the rumpled sheet. Tangled hair. Slack flesh. Bruised breasts. Smeared makeup. I heard the doorbell chime—the taxi driver—and bent swiftly for a final lick.

"Who?" she said drowsily.

I laughed, and left.

We took the limo into Washington, Mary Bergstrom sitting between Paul and me, as before. During the trip I questioned both on Group Lewisohn personnel and operations. Generally, their reactions were favorable, though both felt Dr. Seth Lucas, while talented, was too young and inexperienced for the responsibility he held. I agreed, which was one reason I ruled his decisions so closely. Also, of course, if Lewisohn survived, I wanted no doubt as to whom the credit belonged. If that seems egocentric, allow me to point out that I was also quite willing to accept the consequences of failure.

We pulled up before the old HEW Building on Independence Avenue, now headquarters of the Department of Bliss. Three limousines were parked in line before us. Two were identical to our own hearselike vehicle. The third was a white Rolls-Royce.

"That belongs to DEPDIRCUL," I told Paul. "He thinks it enhances his image."

Paul snorted.

He and I got out of the car, carrying our attaché cases. I leaned down to speak to Mary.

"Sight-seeing?" I asked her.

"I'd like to," she said faintly. "This is my first visit to Washington."

"Take the car," I told her. I glanced at Paul. "Suppose we all meet right here at 1600 this afternoon for the trip back?"

"Thank you," Mary said. "I'll be here."

Paul nodded. We stood there a moment, watching the limousine pull away.

"That was kind of you," Paul said. "Lending Mary the car."

"I'm a kind em," I said. "Some kind. Paul, after the conference I want you to move around. Talk to objects you know on Headquarters Staff. Not Security and Intelligence, but others. Talk to reporters. Then go up to the Hill. Check in with the staff members. If you bump into a familiar Congressman, stroke palms and tell him what a splendid service he's doing. But the staff members are more important. Buy lunch or drinks."

"What do you want?"

"Anything on terrorism rates. Current social discontent. We know the Satrat is soft, but I don't think it's giving us an operative scan. The demographics may be off."

"You're thinking about Lewisohn's books?"

"Yes. I believe he's serving on possible solutions. And if the Chief Director assigned it, the situation must be getting near flash point."

"Nick, we better move faster on the UP pill."

It took a lurch of my brain to realize he was already computing the social, economic, and political consequences of a drug that provided Ultimate Pleasure. Particularly if the manufacture and distribution of that drug were controlled by the government.

"Right," I said. "We'll review progress on the trip back. Now let's walk into the cage."

We marched up to that ugly heap. There were a few reporters lounging about, a few photographers. No TV coverage.

"Get them, Larry," a voice shouted. A photographer stepped in front of us, aimed his camera, clicked the shutter.

The shouter, a reporter named Herb Bailey, on the Washington Bureau of a news syndicate, came strolling forward to stroke our palms.

"Nick," he said. "Paul. You two look full of piss and vinegar."

"At the moment," I said, "Paul's full of vinegar, and I'm full of piss. Got to get inside, Herb."

"Sure," he said. "But just for the record, Deputy Director, do you anticipate any earth-shaking decisions resulting from this meeting of the Department of Bliss?"

"Just for the record," I said. "No comment."

He shook his head dolefully. "The Dragon Lady runs a tight ship. What about off the record?

"Herb"—I sighed—"this is a routine monthly meeting of DOB. We have nothing heavy pending on the Hill. Zilch. Now let me ask you a question: Why the photographer catching Paul and me? We're not news."

"You will be if you get blown up inside." He grinned.

I glanced toward Paul.

"Happy Herby," I said. "The public servants' best friend."

"Herb," Paul said, "are you sticking around until the meeting ends?"

"I suppose I'll have to," the reporter said disgustedly. "Just to get the canned handout."

"Buy you a drink?" Paul asked.

"That's the best bribe I've had this week."

The Department of Bliss, at that point in time, was organized into five gross divisions:

1. Prosperity Section (PROSEC), ruled by a Deputy Director (DEPDIRPRO), was responsible for all welfare, poverty, and antihunger operations, plus what was formerly Social Security, now called Personal Happiness.

2. Wisdom Section (WISSEC), ruled by DEPDIRWIS, controlled all federally financed conditioning programs, from nursery schools to universities, including the Science Academy.

3. Vigor Section (VIGSEC), ruled by DEPDIRVIG, administered public health laws, including HAP (Health Assurance Plan) that had replaced Medicare, Medicaid, etc.

4. Culture Section (CULSEC), ruled by DEPDIRCUL, was in charge of all government programs in communicative and performing arts, including what had formerly been the Federal Communications Commission, Commission of Fine Arts, American Battle Monuments Commission, Architect of the Capitol, National Foundation on the Arts and the Humanities, etc., etc.

5. Satisfaction Section. My section, SATSEC, of which I was DEPDIRSAT.

Angela Teresa Berri, DIROB, also had a constantly expanding Headquarters Staff. Its two main groups were: (1) Security & Intelligence, ruled by Art Roach, which in addition to the duties indicated by its title, also controlled all personnel files of the Department of Bliss; (2) PUBREL, the public relations and publicity group for the entire Department.

And, of course, Angela now had a small army of Administrative Assistants, assistant AA's, legal counsels, specialists, secretaries, clerks, and Congressional liaison representatives who did the Department's lobbying on the Hill.

The monthly meeting of DOB was held in a cavernous conference hall which Angela Berri, thankfully, had had redecorated. Each Deputy Director was supplied with a comfortable swiveled armchair upholstered in real white leather. On the glass before him, exactly positioned, was a carafe of ice water, a plastiglass, two sharpened pencils, a pad of legal-size yellow paper. Behind each DEPDIR sat his Administrative Assistant, in a straight-back, upholstered chair. All proceedings were taped.

In addition to the tape engineer, Angela was served by her chief legal counsel, her AA, her executive secretary, the chief of PUBREL, and Art Roach. They like everyone else in the room, wore the zipsuits of their rank.

The structure of these meetings was quite unlike the conferences of SATSEC Angela had ruled in GPA-1. According to Public Service regulations, all departmental conferences began with the reading of what was properly called the "Menace," a statement rattled off by DIROB's Administative Assistant:

"Accordingtoregulationfortysixdashbeesubsectiononethree-dashkayoftheinternalsecurityprovisionsofthePublicServiceco-deasamendedbysubsectiononeohtwodashgeeadoptedsixMarch-nineteeneightynineallpresentareherebyinformedtheseproceed-ingsarerestrictedandanythingsaidheardscannedorobservedwi-thintheconfinesandlimitsofthismeetingaredeemedofaconfid-entialnatureandnothingshallbedivulgeddisclosedproclaimed-revealedormadeknowntoanyobjectgroupor...etc.,etc."

Penalties were not specified. They didn't have to be.

After this cheery introduction, Angela would speak, usually briefly, bringing us up to date on the progress of legislation affecting DOB. She would then relate any additional information of governmental plans and activities she thought might be of value or interest to her Deputy Directors. At this particular meeting, after running quickly through an especially dull recital of Congressional action, or inaction, Angela concluded by saying:

"You may be interested to learn that the Chief Director has decided to ask for enabling legislation establishing a new department of Public Service, to be called the Department of National Assets. The DNA will rule the management and income of all real property of the US. Any questions?''

She looked directly at me. With hostility. What an ef! I knew she blamed me—partly, at least—for her loss in this particular political cockfight. I did admire her then: the tailored gold zipsuit, pointy breasts, whippy corpus bathed in the soft beam of a spot directed onto her chair. A wig of parsley curls. Her witch's face perfectly symmetrical, almost frightening in its lack of blemish. So composed. So *sure*. Exuding power as naturally as sweat. I could look at those green-painted lips and marvel where they once had been. On me.

''Nick,'' she said tonelessly, ''you seem amused.''

''Only because of the name of the new department,'' I said smoothly. ''Department of National Assets. DNA. That's my Section's abbreviation for the molecular basis of heredity. Deoxyribonucleic acid. The double helix. Why we are what we are. It seems an apt title for a department dealing with national assets.''

There were a few smiles, a relaxation. I think the others were vaguely conscious that an unpleasant confrontation had been avoided.

''Very good, Nick,'' she said. ''Well, let's get started. Anyone?''

Problems presented and discussed during that particular meeting —with one exception—were of monumental inconsequence. My own report, though deviously contrived, could have had little significance to the others present. I said that my Division of Research & Development had noted an increasing arrest rate for drug abuse, and we had started a research program to determine possible chromosomal damage from habitual use of hallucinogens. They all looked at me blankly.

The reports of the other Deputy Directors were equally as enervating.

DEPDIRCUL read a long, numbing research study on the feasibility of including commercials in the US Government's satellite broadcasts to every nation wealthy enough to own TV receivers. The conclusion was that commercials of products distributed internationally would provide a dollar revenue approximating 83.4 percent of the total cost of providing the world with free US films, US cartoons, US news programs, artfully interspersed with short features on happy US servers on the assembly line, tuna fishing off

California, the splendid array of electric bidets available to US citizens, and the whitewashing of Mt. Rushmore.

Heavy interest in buying commercial time on US satellite TV broadcasts had already been expressed by Kodak cameras, Ford cars, IBM typewriters, Pepsi-Cola, and Jiffi condoms ("I'll be with you in a Jiffi!").

It was decided to recommend to the Chief Director that such commercial time be sold.

DEPDIRWIS, a tall, gaunt ef with a reported predilection for young, plump boys, complained of the scruff she was receiving on the government-sponsored program to provide methylphenidate tablets for hyperactive children in elementary schools. It was the same drug I had popped a few hours previously to overcome hangover depression. With the children, of course, the reaction was exactly the opposite: It sedated them.

It was agreed a new public conditioning program would be necessary to convince unreasonably anxious parents of the benefits of the drug to their children. It was so ordered.

I came alive only during the presentation by DEPDIRPRO. This fussy little em, a prototype bookkeeper, droned through a list of depressing numbers that revealed how much love the US Government was expending on indigent, nonproductive, and underconsuming obsos. Including costs of food, clothing, shelter, medical care, etc.

I was alerted because it had been Maya Leighton's memo on exactly the same subject, when she had been a member of my Gerontology Team, that had first brought her to our attention. I remembered her suggestion, now in our Tomorrow File. I was conscious of Paul Bumford shifting position behind me, and knew he remembered it, too.

DEPDIRPRO begged for possible solutions to his dilemma, saying:

"The annual drain on the US Treasury is rapidly approaching the point where it will no longer be financially tolerable. To say nothing of the essential unfairness to young, productive, consuming, tax-paying objects of our population."

"At the moment," Angela Berri said immediately and crisply, "the possibility of euthanasia is not politically expedient, and I want no discussion of the subject. But I will welcome any other suggested solutions for this serious problem."

There was almost a minute of silence. Then I raised my hand, tentatively.

"Nick?"

I told them SATSEC had been aware of this problem for some time, that it was difficult and vexing, that we had expended a great number of object-hours brainstorming the situation. And we had evolved what might be, at least, a partial solution.

I then, briefly, explained the program of Government-Assisted Peace: X dollars paid to each indigent obso who signed a life-release statement, that sum to be spent or bequeathed before painless suicide, the means of which would be provided by the government at no extra cost to the object.

I pointed out that details would have to be refined: the amount of the grant, the wording of the voluntary release statement, the time allowed between signing and stopping, and so forth. But SATSEC estimated, I lied casually, that a minimum of ten million new dollars annually, and probably more, could be saved by the plan. *Not* euthanasia, I emphasized. Purely voluntary.

Again there was silence while they all stared at the water carafes on the table, at the walls, the ceiling, anywhere but at each other. Finally Angela turned to her Public Relations chief.

"Will it play in Peoria, Sam?" she asked.

He hunched forward in his chair, a benign, rubicund em with flashing rings on three fingers.

"If you want my tip-of-the-tongue reaction," he said, "I would say yes. We got a motivation study here, of course, and we got some in-depth emotional analyses. But like I said, my instinctual gut feeling is go."

"Vic?" Angela turned to her legal counsel.

"In my opinion—" he began.

"Yes or no, Vic," she said sharply.

"I think we can manage it."

"Very well, Sam." Angela nodded at the PUBREL chief. "Move on it. Good computing, Nick. Anything else? Anyone?"

"Strange," Paul Bumford said as we moved out of DOB headquarters into that bright afternoon sunlight.

"What's strange?" I asked.

"That PROSEC business and Government-Assisted Peace. I had no idea that items in our Tomorrow File might be implemented so soon."

"That's what we're creating it for, isn't it? It's not just a Christmas list. It's a plan, a practical program that may not be feasible today but that we expect to be tomorrow."

"You're right, of course." Paul nodded. "But tomorrow has become today so quickly. It's just the speed that surprises me. Well . . . there's Herb Bailey waiting for his drink. I better start my rounds. Where are you off to?"

"Chief Director," I said shortly. "To deliver the prospectus for the Department of Creative Science."

"He's out of the country," Paul said. "Left yesterday for talks with the British on their joining the US."

"I know," I said. "I'll leave it with his wife."

"Oh-ho," Paul said.

I stared at him.

"We agreed she may prove lovable to us."

"No argument, Nick," he said hastily. "I may soon be meeting the ef myself."

"Oh?"

"I joined the New York chapter of the Beists. A national convention is planned for next month. Here, in Washington."

"Where are they going to hold it—in a phone booth?"

As anticipated, I had trouble at the gate. They took an electronic scan of my BIN card, ran a voiceprint check through their central computer, made me walk through a metal and explosives detector.

(Since 1981, by UN agreement, all explosives legally manufactured anywhere in the world contained a radioactive signature.)

After all this, I was told the Chief Director was out of the country. I expressed chagrin at my ignorance, then asked to see Mrs. Wingate. Reluctantly, they flashed the main house and I showed my phiz on screen. Grace Wingate vouched for me, I was allowed entrance, escorted to the bolted steel door by an armed guard.

She waved aside the zipsuited butler and held her hands out to me.

"Sorry about the fuss, Nick," she said. Somewhat breathlessly. "How *are* you?"

"Well, thank you. And you?"

"In shamefully good health, doctor. Hungry? A drink?"

"A drink would be nice. I just stopped by to drop off a report the Chief Director wanted delivered personally. It's restricted."

"I'll make certain he gets it personally," she assured me. "Let's go in here. . . ."

She led the way into that same slightly shabby, chintzy parlor-type room where we had all been seated when the bombs boomed and flechettes sang during my previous visit. The portrait of John Quincy Adams still had a third eye.

She looked about vaguely.

"Oh dear. No ice."

She pressed a concealed button. A black zipsuit materialized instantly from somewhere.

"Modom?"

"Some Jellicubes, please, John."

"Immediately, modom."

She waved me to the lumpy couch. She seated herself gracefully and looked at me with sympathetic interest.

"Have you been busy, Nick?" she asked.

I had the oddest impression of a little girl stumbling about in her mother's high heels, pearls down to her knees, wearing a crazy chiffon gown and oversized garden hat. With makeup awkwardly painted on in patches.

But Grace Wingate was wearing tawny pants so tight they could have been sprayed on. A knitted tank top of some sheeny material, cut wide at neck and arms. Ashen hair flung loose. Spatulate feet bare. About her neck, partially covering the cleavage between her tanned breasts, was a silvery, oversized reproduction of a snow-flake, hung from a leather thong.

"Your necklace," I said. "Beautiful."

She grinned with delight, forgetting I had not answered her question.

"I do thank you. It's a new alloy of silver, palladium, and platinum. It was given to me by the manufacturer. But of course we're not allowed to accept gifts. So Mike paid for it. The wholesale price. That's all right, don't you think, Nick?"

I laughed. "Yes, I think that's all right. Perfectly legal. It's lovely."

"Well, they're all over now, but this is the first striking of the design."

She looked down at the gleaming snowflake, stroking it. Her long fingers were close to the soft bulge of her breasts. Fingernails touched her sinuous neck.

I could not fathom her. She seemed an odd combination of the fey and the profound I could not analyze. That line that enclosed her

292

sculpted corpus appeared to complete her. But I had the sense of a force bursting to spring free. I just did not know. She was unique in my experience.

The black zipsuit returned with a tub of Jellicubes, then disappeared. I mixed vodka-and-Smacks for both of us. We hoisted plastiglasses to each other, smiled, sipped delicately. Then we sat in silence. I wanted her to make the approach. Finally. . . .

"You said. . . ." she murmured faintly. Then stopped.

"Yes, Mrs. Wingate?"

"I asked you to call me Grace. Will you not?"

"I want to," I said. Still smiling. "But it's difficult. Your husband is very important."

"I know. Oh, God, do I know. Nick, what have you—"

I pursed my lips and pressed them with a forefinger. So dramatic! A Restoration comedy. She rose and moved toward French windows. I joined her there. We looked over a rather scrubby garden. A kneeling em, head shielded with a white riot helmet, was loosening dry soil about azalea bushes.

";You must be patient," I urged her. "I promised to help, and I shall. Grace, tell me—are you certain? Of your husband and Angela Berri?"

"Oh, yes."

I had to force her, not only for my own need to know, but to make her face it and say it.

"Are they users?" I asked.

She tried to speak but couldn't. Finally she nodded dumbly. I wanted to tongue that vulval ear revealed as her fine hair swung aside.

"Do you have any letters, documents, tapes—any physical evidence?"

She looked at me scornfully.

"*Physical* evidence? I have all the *physical* evidence I need. Nick, a wife *knows*!"

"Yes, yes," I said quickly. Convinced.

She put a hand on my arm.

"Nick," she said, "you're my only hope."

In retrospect I can be objective. But at that particular moment in time, I was so overwhelmed by her proximity, her presence—scent, the matte of her skin, dark eyes, syrupy voice—that I would have said anything, done anything to prolong the interview.

293

"I asked you to have patience," I repeated. "A month, two months, possibly three. No longer."

"Then you'll—you'll—" She couldn't finish.

"Yes," I told her. "Then I'll stop Angela Berri, or myself be stopped. Is that guarantee enough?"

We stood motionless, not speaking. Did her look turn to sympathy? To pity? To acquiescence? To complaisance? I simply did not know. A pulse fluttered low on her neck. I wanted to swoop and kiss it still. Strange that even then—so early—I was aware of what was happening.

There was a sharp rap at the parlor door. The moment shattered. We turned back into the room. A black zipsuit announced scheduled visitors. I made a polite farewell, leaving my prospectus to her.

At the doorway, smiling her good-bye, one hand rose almost languidly and touched the back of my head, my neck.

"Thank you, Nick," she said.

I was lost, I thought suddenly. For some reason I did not wish to compute, the thought pleased me.

It took almost two hours, in a cab, and visits to five jewelry shops before I was able to locate and purchase an exact replica of Grace Wingate's necklace—a silvery snowflake swinging from a leather thong.

But I was only ten minutes late for my meeting with Paul Bumford and Mary Bergstrom in front of DOB headquarters. I climbed into the back of the limousine and we started off for New York immediately.

"Well?" I asked Paul.

"Worse than we supposed," he reported. "Very heavy social unrest. They're pillowing most of it—but who knows for how long? Bombings, assassinations, arson, kidnappings. A complete mosaic."

"Who?" I asked.

He shook his head. "That's what's so weird. Everyone agrees it's not organized. Just a kind of general discontent."

"But *why*?" I said loudly. Angrily. "They never had it so good."

"The pee-pul." Paul shrugged. "Who knows?"

"Show them," Mary Bergstrom muttered sullenly.

We both, Paul and I, looked at her in astonishment. But she volunteered nothing more, and we went on as if she had never spoken.

The remainder of the trip was spent reviewing input from the Field Offices at Houston, Spokane, and Honolulu, dealing with the physiological, psychological, and mental sources of pleasure. Even these preliminary reports generated grave questions. We drove through gathering darkness, debating the nature of happiness.

Y-9

I visited my Times Square mail drop every day. Nothing from Simon Hawkley. Anxiety growing. My position was perilous. I was owner of a factory selling drugs to my own department of government. I knew what the results of discovery would be.

Finally, on September 20, rainy, windswept, I found a short, coded message from Hawkley. Just three series of numbers. Decoded: FISH BITING. CALL.

I called San Diego from a corner booth. We kept our conversation as brief and cryptic as possible. A letter had arrived at Scilla Pharmaceuticals from Headquarters, Department of Bliss. It was signed by an Edward T. Collins. His title was Commercial Coordinator, Security & Intelligence. It stated that since Scilla was engaged in the production and sale to the US Government of restricted drugs, according to Public Law, Section DOB-46-H3, subsection 2X-31G, the premises, the production methods, and the distribution procedures of Scilla were required to be examined and approved periodically. At 1500, on September 29, Mr. Art Roach, Chief, Security & Intelligence, would arrive at Scilla to make such an inspection.

I told Simon Hawkley I would get back to him with instructions for Seymour Dove well before Roach's arrival.

I discussed it with Paul Bumford that night.

"You really think they're taking the bait?" he asked.

"Definitely," I told him. "Those *in situ* inspections are customarily made by a road crew, PS-4's, conditioned for that service. I never heard of an S-and-I chief inspecting a factory personally."

"You don't seem too happy," he said.

"I'm happy enough. I suppose, subconsciously, I was hoping Angela would make the approach personally. But I should have

295

known better. I should have known she'd use Roach as a bagman, keep a level between her and the overt act. Then, if push came to shove, she could terminate him with prejudice. Well, we'll have to manipulate Roach and compromise her through him. Let's get started on the scenario. The first consideration is the time frame. . . .''

There was never any doubt that Paul and I would have to be in San Diego when the trap was sprung. In fact, we'd have to be there a day or two earlier to help install and test the sharing equipment in Seymour Dove's office at Scilla, and to instruct and rehearse him in his role.

"Getting out there with a legitimate cover should be no problem,'' I said. "I have a backlog of threedays. You can go out to inspect Nancy Ching's operations in the FO. The problem is— where do we stay? The letter Scilla received states that Roach will arrive at 1500 on September twenty-ninth. But what if he takes a threeday and gets there on the twenty-seventh, or maybe just a day earlier to scout the ground? His profile says he is shrewd, clever, suspicious. We're so close now, Paul, we can't take the chance of getting out there early and discover we've checked into the hotel where he's staying. Am I being paranoid?''

"My God, no!'' Paul said. "We can't leave anything to chance. It's risky enough as it is. How about Nancy Ching's place on the beach?''

"Think she'd let us have it?''

"Of course.''

"Yesss,'' I said slowly. Computing. "I think that would serve. We'll stay out there as much as possible, going into the city only when it's absolutely necessary. That should reduce a chance meeting with Roach to the ult min. Now let's talk about what equipment we'll need. Chauncey Higgles, Limited, will supply the heavy stuff. But we'll need cameras, film, maybe some personal devices. Just in case.''

We served long hours for three evenings. We went over the Personality Profile of Art Roach, trying to determine how he might react in certain situations. We pored over the Federal Criminal Code to determine what kind of evidence we'd need to stop Art Roach and Angela Berri.

Finally, the scenario was in a form where anything added or subtracted would just be tinkering. We agreed to go ahead with what we had. I sent a letter to Simon Hawkley the following morning by commercial mail. Merely: "Arriving Sept. 27. Adventurer."

After our planning was completed, in the few days prior to September 27, I served hard, clearing my desk for the threeday I announced I was taking. I doubted any emergency would arise. But if it did, I told Ellen Dawes she could contact me through my father in Grosse Pointe, Michigan. I sent my father a letter instructing him to forward any messages for me to the San Diego Field Office.

We arrived in San Diego, on a commercial flight, a little before 1100, Pacific time, on the morning of September 27. We rented a black, two-door Dodge sedan, a Piranha, with a high-performance eight-cylinder internal combustion engine. Nancy Ching had closed her beachhouse for the season, but had readily agreed to lend it to Paul. She had promised to leave the keys in the sand under the first step of the porch.

We drove directly there, stopping just once to pick up vodka, Smack, some sandwich groceries. It took us about an hour to get the place aired out, to unpack, and settle in. Then I called Simon Hawkley to announce our arrival. I told him from then on, I would deal directly with Seymour Dove at Scilla and keep my contacts with him, Hawkley, to a minimum. He approved of my caution. I thought he might wish me good luck, but he didn't. Perhaps he didn't think I'd need it.

I then called Seymour Dove at Scilla, told him where we were, asked when he could join us. He said two hours. I told him we'd be waiting. And so we did. Wait. We spent the time discussing unexplored approaches in the development of the UP pill. I know I felt no nervousness about our current activity. If Paul felt any, at this late stage, he hid it very well.

I had alerted Paul, but still he was startled when Seymour Dove sauntered in. A vision in peacock blue, including blue sunglasses, blue sandals, blue bone earrings, blue eye shadow, and a blue, feathered hat left over from the road company of *The Three Musketeers*. He grinned at us, whites flashing against that incredibly tanned skin. Then he twirled slowly for our inspection, arms akimbo.

"Jerk you?" he said.

Paul laughed, and we all stroked palms. We made vodka-and-Smacks and prowurst sandwiches. Then we started on the details of the scenario.

We all agreed that the sharing operation should be kept as simple as possible. Seymour Dove pointed out that with the number of serves at Scilla, assigned to all levels of the main building, including the basement, it would be practically impossible to place clandestine wiring and power sources without being observed. We would have to opt for self-powered devices. The critical danger was that such devices could usually be detected by a portable meter, or even a wrist monitor. Art Roach might well be carrying or wearing either.

I believed I had the answer to this problem. In scanning the Chauncey Higgles, Ltd., catalogue, provided by Mrs. Agatha Whiggam, I had noted a new (1997) device which seemed almost to have been designed with our mission in mind.

It was a conventional, one-meter TV receiver, a console model available in three furniture styles: Contemporary, Traditional, and Mediterranean. It was not one of the new 3-D, laser-holograph sets, but still utilized a cathode tube. However, installed within the tube, photographing through the plastiglas faceplate, was a miniaturized TV camera, picking up both sight and sound. It was powered by the electric current supplying the television set.

Its greatest advantage was that the set was always "hot." That is, diminished power was constantly fed to the picture tube so that, when the viewer clicked the On button, it was not necessary to wait ten seconds for the set to warm up; the image appeared on screen almost instantaneously. Thus, if the set was checked with a meter, of course it would show a power flow, for a very innocent reason.

We agreed that such a set, designed for home or office, would be entirely appropriate in the executive suite of Scilla Pharmaceuticals. The monitor was small, compact, and would easily fit into the back seat of our rented Dodge sedan. The monitor consisted of a loudspeaker, a 20 cm viewing screen, and a TV tape attachment by which voice and visual communication could be recorded. We, in turn, in the car, could talk to Seymour Dove via his TV set.

So it was decided that Paul and I, with the monitor, would park in the copse of trees bordering the road that ran in front of the Scilla plant. The trees, fortunately, were in the opposite direction from that Roach would probably take in arriving at the factory by taxi or rented car. The chances of his spotting and recognizing us were minimal. And our parking area was well within the claimed range of the TV camera transmitter.

Then we went over Seymour Dove's role. Several times. I gave him a page of dialogue we had prepared: questions to ask Art Roach, the answers to which, we hoped, would implicate Angela

Berri. Dove was a quick study. He scanned the page swiftly, nodded, handed it back.

"All right," Paul said. "Let's try it. Pretend I'm Art Roach."

They went into the suggested dialogue:

Paul: "So you see, Mr. Dove, if you want that contract, it'll cost you."

Dove: "How much?"

Paul: "Ten percent."

Dove: "Ten? My God, there goes my profit."

Paul: "Not at all. If the contract figures out to a hundred thousand, bid a hundred and ten. You'll get it. No loss to you. You get the hundred. We get the ten. Up front."

Dove: "Up front? Jesus! How do I know I can trust you. No offense to you, but I've never seen you before. I've never even *heard* of you. You're in Security and Intelligence. All my dealings up to now have been with Satisfaction Section."

Paul: "Who did you deal with in SATSEC?"

Dove: "The last purchase order was signed by Nicholas Flair. But before that, it was Angela Berri."

Paul: "That's who you're dealing with now."

Dove: "Berri? But she's Director of Bliss."

Paul: "That's right."

Dove: "You mean she's in on this?"

Paul: "She's in all right. She's your guarantee."

Then Seymour Dove looked at me, troubled.

"Something wrong?" I asked him.

"I don't know," he said hesitantly. "Look, I don't want to damper this thing. I'll serve on it. You ems know what you're doing. You know the objects concerned. But . . ."

"But what?" Paul asked.

"I've been involved in deals like this before," Dove said, shaking his head. "Believe me, it's never that easy."

"Well," I said, "you know what we want. If Roach doesn't follow the scenario, you'll have to play it by ear."

"That I can do." He nodded.

I admired the em. He appeared to welcome the challenge. A new role at the San Fernando Playhouse. He was the star and would get great reviews. He had the unreasoning confidence of all actors.

We spent the following morning and early afternoon installing and testing the equipment. Paul and I picked up the monitor at the Chauncey Higgles, Ltd., warehouse on Sampson Street. Then we drove to our stakeout under the trees. Higgles delivered the fiddled television set to Scilla Pharmaceuticals in a van chastely marked "New World TV Service & Repair." Seymour Dove had it positioned at one end of his long office, against the wall. The hidden camera covered practically the entire room. The image we received on the small monitor screen was remarkably detailed. Not as bright as I would have liked, but adequate. Sound reception was excellent.

Paul drove me back to the beachhouse, then left to put in an appearance at the Field Office and take Nancy Ching to dinner. I went for a swim, then walked down the road to a seafood restaurant and gnawed futilely at a rubberized abalone steak afloat in an oleaginous sauce. Finally I gave up, returned to the cottage, made two more prowurst sandwiches. I washed them down with vodka-and-Smacks, while watching a televised execution. A rapist-murderer was being hanged. It was messy. But I imagined the ratings would be lovable.

We were in position by 1430 the next day. Well off the road. Practically against the tree trunks. We had brought sandwiches and cans of Smack. Not so much to assuage hunger, but as an excuse for parking in case a highway patrol car stopped to look us over.

Paul sat in the back seat, tending the monitor. I sat up front, behind the wheel. I held the mike, on a short cord. We both watched the screen. Dove's office was empty.

At 1440 an ef secretary came in and placed a folder on Seymour Dove's desk. She scratched her ass before departing. I don't believe either Paul or I smiled.

Dove entered the office about 1450. He came over to stand directly in front of the television set.

"Receiving?" he asked softly.

"Fine," I said. Just as softly. "Picture and sound good."

He stood motionless a moment.

"Would you like to see my impersonation of President Hilton?" He grinned.

"No," I said. It was the first time he had evidenced nervousness.

He went back behind his desk, sat down, began to scan papers in the folder the secretary had left.

1455.

1500.

1505.

Dove glanced once toward the TV set, seemed about to speak, then thought better of it.

At 1525, Dove's desk flasher chimed. He switched it on. We could see no image on the flasher screen. It was obviously a phone call.

"Seymour Dove," he said. His voice was steady and loud.

We couldn't hear the reply.

"Yes," Dove said. "How are you, Mr. Roach? . . . Yes, sir, we're all set and waiting for you . . . I see . . . But what about the inspection? . . . I see . . . Well, yes, of course . . . When? . . . Yes, I can make it by then . . . of course . . . The Strake? Yes, I know where it is . . . Shall I ring your room? . . . Fine. See you then."

He switched off the flasher. Sat a moment in silence. Rose heavily and came over to the TV set. He looked directly at the screen.

"It's no-go," he said. "He's not coming out to inspect. He wants me to meet him at 1700 at the Strake Hotel."

Paul and I stared at his miniature image on the TV monitor. Then we looked at each other. I wondered if my face was as pinched and drained as his.

I spoke into the mike: "We'll drive down to the plant. Can you meet us just outside the gate? Across the road."

"Sure," he said. "Will do. Sorry, Nick."

We moved down the road, pulled off into the shoulder opposite the Scilla gate. In a few moments Seymour Dove came out into the main building, walked down the graveled driveway.

"Sorry, Nick," he repeated.

"Not your fault," I said shortly. "I should have trusted your instinct. It *was* too easy."

"Where are you meeting him?" Paul asked. "His hotel room?"

"In the lobby," Dove said. "At 1700. I suppose we'll go someplace from there. Some safe place. His room, a restaurant, maybe just a ride. In *his* car. He's cute."

We were all silent. Trying to compute a way.

"Look," Seymour Dove said finally, "you told me you brought a body-pack and some other trinkets from New York. Want to wire me and hope for the best?"

"Negative," I said. "If he's this cautious, he's sure to be carrying or wearing a monitor. If he discovers you're powered . . .

well, just forget it. No, I think all you can do now is meet with him and see how much you can salvage from the scenario."

"I'm willing to testify if you want him on extortion or bribery conspiracy."

"Forget it," I told him wearily. "Just your word against his. All it would accomplish would be to start them checking into the ownership of Scilla. That I can do without. How did he sound?"

"Roach? Sharp, hard, no hesitation. He's done this before."

"Shouldn't wonder." I sighed. "All right, meet him. Can you come out to the beachhouse later and fill us in?"

"Sure, Nick. Shouldn't take more than an hour or so after 1700. Unless he chisels a free dinner. I'll get to you as soon as I leave him."

Paul and I returned the TV monitor to the Higgles warehouse. Then we drove back to La Jolla Bay in silence. The beachhouse seemed airless and deserted. The sun was beginning a long, slow slide into the sea. From the porch we could see a few naked swimmers, a picnicking family group, a couple of nude efs suntanning on plastilume sheets. There were no birds.

I had bought a liter of lovable natural brandy. We were going to drink it to celebrate our triumph. We drank it to numb our defeat. The bottle was almost half-empty when Seymour Dove stalked in. He slammed the door behind him. He went directly to the brandy bottle, poured a glassful, drank it off the way I'd drink a glass of Smack. Then he looked at us.

"That em," he said, "is one cold monkey."

We said nothing. He took off his jacket, kicked off his sandals, slumped into a plastivas sling.

"You'll never guess where he took me," he said.

"Wait, wait," I said hurriedly. "Don't tell us. Let me compute this. I'll tell you where you went."

Suddenly it was important to me that I got this correct, that I could reason where a man like Art Roach would take a prospective victim to dictate terms. I reviewed everything I knew about Roach. Input, storage, retrieval.

"I'll tell you," I said. "He took you to a steam room or sauna."

"My God," Dove said. "You're exactly right. A sauna. How did you know?"

"I know Roach," I said. Feeling better. "He dotes on saunas and steam rooms. And where can you be certain the man you're cutting isn't wired? In a sauna or steam room, of course. Where you're both bareass naked.''

"Well," Dove said, "I'm glad you turned me down on the body-pack. I don't know what he would have done if he had spotted it while we were undressing. And he was wearing a wrist monitor. I haven't met many objects who scare me, but that em is one of them. Be careful of him, gentlemen. He bites.''

"How much did he want?" Paul asked.

"A modest five percent. I followed your scenario. He did, too—up to a point. I said five percent would kill my profit. He said to add it on the top. But he wanted the five percent up front. I asked what guarantee I had that if I paid the love, I'd get the contract. That's when he departed from the script. He said the only way I could prove his sincerity—that's the word he used: 'sincerity'— was *not* to pay the love. Then I wouldn't get the contract, and I'd know positively he hadn't been scamming me. Beautiful?''

"He never mentioned Angela Berri?" I asked.

"Never. Not once. He implied he had complete rule of contract awards. He was the only object I had to deal with. No one else.''

"How does he want the payoff?" Paul asked.

"If I agree to his terms, I go to Washington on October 20 and check into any hotel. I call him at the hotel where he lives—the Winslow on N Street. I act like an old friend unexpectedly in town, looking him up. He'll give me instructions on delivery then.''

"Uh-huh." Paul nodded. "At a place of his choosing. And you're to bring the love in cash. Small, untreated bills. Nothing larger than a twenty. In nonconsecutive serial numbers.''

"However did you guess?" Dove said.

We all laughed. I don't know why, but suddenly we all had the idea we were still alive.

"Well?" Dove asked. "Should I plan to be in Washington on October 20?''

"Sure," I said. "With the love. I'll be in touch with you or Simon Hawkley before that.''

We sat a few minutes after he left. I think what most pleased both of us, although we didn't mention it, was that our basic premise had proved out: Roach *was* on the suck. And by reasonable inference, so was Angela Berri.

"Paul," I said suddenly, "let's get out of here. Let's go back. Right now.''

"Nick, we've got reservations on a morning flight."

"So? Change them. Get on the flasher. See if there's a flight tonight we can make. I've got to get moving. Even if it's only from Point B to Point C."

We made it, with minutes to spare. The jet was only one-quarter filled. In fact, there was only one other passenger in the first-class cabin. He had his left leg encased in a heavy cast. It stuck out into the aisle. We stepped over it carefully on the way to our seats.

"Sorry," he said cheerfully. "Skiing. I zigged when I should have zagged."

We smiled sympathetically.

After takeoff, we each took our three free drinks: vodka-and-Smacks. They lasted to Phoenix. There we started on what remained of the natural brandy, which we had thoughtfully brought along. We nursed it to Tulsa. Pleading dehydration, we got two more drinks from the stewardess and sipped those to St. Louis.

Meanwhile, we had been brainstorming the logistics of the payoff: Seymour Dove to Art Roach, Washington, D.C., October 20, 1998. We came up with many ingenious scenarios. A lot of kaka. The only possible solution was to have Seymour Dove swallow an internal mike and transmitter. Or implant a set in a molar or in the rectum or in the external auditory meatus. But if Art Roach wore a wrist monitor, he could detect any of those. Checkmate.

At St. Louis, our crippled fellow passenger debarked, slowly and painfully, leaning on crutches. We watched him move himself up the aisle to the open door, assisted by the stewardess.

"My God," Paul said, "he must be dragging twenty pounds of plaster in that cast."

"Probably plastiment," I said. "Half the weight, one-third more strength."

"Why not an inflatable splint? One-hundredth the weight."

"Can't use an inflatable splint," I said. "Not on a load-bearing break."

We took off from the new St. Louis jetport, heading for GPA-1. The fenced compound. Home. I closed my eyes.

"You want to sleep?" Paul asked.

"No. Go up to the galley. See if you can wheedle some more booze."

He came back in a moment, giggling.

"Well?" I said.

"Look," he said.

I opened my eyes. He had four miniatures of vodka. He handed me two.

"Stole them," he said.

"Good em," I said. "Fine service."

I twisted off the little plastic cap. Drained half in one swallow. Closed my eyes again.

"Paul," I said dreamily.

"What?"

"Ever see an inflatable splint?"

"Of course I've seen an inflatable splint. Are you drunk?"

"Just enough. A double sleeve of opaque heavy-gauge plastic. Compressed air forced between the sleeves. After inflation, it's hard as a rock. Keeps the fracture rigid. Right?"

"Nick, for God's sake, what's all this about inflatable splints?" I opened my eyes.

"Very scientific. Very objective. Given: Two objects. Problem: To share their conversation. Known factor: One object cannot be equipped for sharing. Ergo: Equip the other."

"I know, I know," Paul said. Impatient now. "But *how*?"

I told him.

"Nick. . . ." he said. Almost choking. "You're either mad or a genius."

"Can't I be both?" I asked.

Y-10

I had decided to grow a beard and mustache. No reason that I could analyze. Just whim. I wanted something vaguely Vandyke, but perhaps a bit more squarish.

I had showered and was standing naked in front of the nest mirror. I was inspecting five days' growth of beard, debating whether it was long enough to trim, when my doorbell chimed. I padded out.

"Yes?"

"Nick, it's me. Paul."

I let him in, relocked the door. He followed me back to the nest. He sat on the toilet seat lid, watched me fuss at the new growth with a little pair of fingernail scissors.

"Itch?" he asked.

"It did the first few days. What's on your mind?"

"You don't really want to know, do you? Not everything!"

I sighed, put down the scissors, pulled on a robe.

"All right, let's have a nightcap. Just one. Then you can tell me."

He followed me into the living room, sat on the sofa. On the edge. I knew his moods. He was winding himself up to something. I brought us each a petrorye on Jellicubes, and sat down opposite him.

"All right, Paul," I said, "let's have it."

"Your father's application for permission to manufacture, distribute, and sell the Die-Dee Doll came across my desk today."

"And?"

"I'm going to reject it. As being 'Inimical to the public interest.'"

"Yes. You told me you would."

"Nick, I'd like a chance to explain the reasons for rejection to your father."

"You know I'll probably overrule you on the doll?"

"Yes, I know that."

"But you still want to explain your position to my father?"

"Yes. It may sound silly to you, but I keep thinking I can get him to withdraw it."

"No way," I said. "He smells love. But you rate a try. Paul, we've both been serving hard. Suppose we take a threeday together to Michigan?"

"Sounds good," he said. Brightening. "Let's do it."

"Fine." I rubbed the new hair on my chin. "Maybe by the time I get back objects will stop asking if I forgot to shave."

He tried to smile. That night he looked—somehow sad. He had the look of an em who had come to some momentous decision he meant to carry out, though it would bring him no profit.

I came close to bringing out the bottle of petrorye and asking him to stay the night. I believed then, and I believe now, that he would have accepted gladly. I also believe that it would not have altered what happened.

We took the Bullet Train to Detroit, treating ourselves to a compartment. With two bottles of natural wine to lubricate the trip. It was October 8. There was a threat of winter in the air: wind with a

306

bite, smell of snow, a lowering sky. The feel of things coming to an end.

This time the copter pilot was an em—was my father changing his religion?—but wearing the usual Chinese red zipsuit with the usual logo embroidered across the chest. On the short flight to Grosse Pointe, he told us Father was out of town but was expected back the following day.

Miss Catherine had prepared a cold supper for us, served by Mrs. McPherson in the echoing dining room. Both Paul and I were ravenous, and ate hugely. The meat dish was some kind of processed pork substitute, a cold, lardlike loaf. Side dishes came from a nearby food factory where fruits and vegetables were grown in enormous plastic greenhouses. Humidity, temperature, artificial sunlight, carbon dioxide, soil nutrients, and water were rigidly controlled. The resulting produce was enormous in size but, though unquestionably natural, was something less than tasty. They were "working on the problem." I suspected it was the soil used: reprocessed and dried sludge from Detroit sewers.

We dawdled over ersatz coffee and my father's decanter of natural plum brandy. Our conversation was meandering and rather bawdy. Mainly, it concerned the government's puzzlement over what to do about an international airline that had recently started "The Sultan's Flight," US to Europe. The ticket cost included, according to the advertisement, "a single act of normal coitus" with one of the young hostesses aboard. Consummated in small, curtained cubicles called "Harem Huts." It all seemed to be legal.

Finally, before midnight, we straggled upstairs.

We wasted the following day—a delightful experience. Somehow it made us superior to time, to spend it in such a profligate manner. We wandered about the grounds, had a lazy lunch on the terrace, skipped stones over the water (Paul was quite good), and chased a squirrel through the woods.

When my father arrived, late in the afternoon, we were waiting for him on the porch. He came bounding up the steps, grabbed me in the usual bear hug, shouted "Nick-ol'-as!" several times, stroked palms with Paul, bundled us into the library, shouted for a tub of Jellicubes, vodka, Smack. When Mrs. McPherson brought the tray, I noticed my father was using up what remained of my mother's natural potato vodka. I couldn't expect him to pour it down the sink. I don't know why I felt a pang.

He immediately began a loud and enthusiastic account of what he had been doing: rushing from Connecticut to Indiana to North Carolina, setting up production facilities for the Die-Dee Doll. Paul's lips compressed, his face congealed, he set his drink slowly and carefully on the floor alongside his chair.

"Mr. Flair—" he started. Voice cold and steady.

"—an entirely new concept," Father burbled on. "A system of snap-together assembly that should—"

"Mr. Flair," Paul repeated. Louder now. He stood up.

"—in terms of—" my father said. And paused. Suddenly.

"I'm going to reject your application to produce the Die-Dee Doll," Paul said. Again loudly. Distinctly. "As a matter of fact, I already have. As being inimical to the public interest."

"What?" Chester K. Flair said shakily. "What are you talking about?"

"Yes, sir. The Die-Dee Doll. I've rejected your application to produce."

"Jesus Christ," my father breathed.

He sat down heavily, took a long pull of his drink, looked at us, back and forth, with hurt, bewildered eyes.

A marvelous act. Paul would never know. But I saw at once that my father had already considered the possibility of rejection and computed how to handle it.

" 'Inimical to the public interest'?" he said. Incredulously. "How can you *say* that?"

Paul repeated, in greater detail, the reasons he had already stated to me. I thought they were valid arguments. Finally—this was a new one—the concept of burial in the ground in a plastic coffin conditioned disobedience to the federal law requiring cremation.

My father listened closely, and gave every evidence of growing perplexity.

"Paul," he said, "it's just a toy. Nothing more. I'm not out to condition or recondition the kids. I must tell you—and I swear it—I really don't compute what you mean. How could a toy do what you say it does? Listen, I've got the signed statements of some of the best child psychologists in the country. Really big names. They all say the same thing: The Die-Dee Doll will do no harm. In fact, it will do good. *Good,* Paul. 'Emotional catharsis.' 'Normal adjustments to stopping.' 'Relieves irrational childish fears.' I've got the papers to *prove* it, Paul. All right, if you insist on the last part, about the burial, I'll change it. Instead of a coffin, we'll supply a little cremation oven. How about *that,* Paul? The kid can burn up the stopped Die-Dee Doll, oven and all. Will that do it?''

Paul looked at me with a kind of wonderment, shaking his head.

"I'm sorry, Mr. Flair," he said. "My rejection stands."

He turned, marched from the room, closed the door softly behind him. My father watched him leave, then stared at me.

"What's *with* that little butterfly?" he demanded. "He eats my food, drinks my booze, sleeps in my house—and then he pulls this kaka?"

"He's doing what he thinks is right," I said mildly.

My father grunted. He mixed us fresh drinks. He took his to a club chair opposite mine, slumped into it, regarded me gravely over his raised plastiglas.

"You can overrule him, can't you, Nick?" he asked quietly.

I nodded.

"You going to?"

"I haven't made up my mind yet."

"Well. . . ." He sighed. "Do what you think is best. Don't let our father-son relationship affect your service. Just judge me like any other applicant."

"I will," I said solemnly. He was hilarious.

"Now let's talk about other things," he said. "You been getting those private data bank reports on Angela Berri and Art Roach?"

"Yes," I said. "Thank you. They've been very helpful."

"Good," he said. "I had a lot of trouble setting that up. But as long as the reports are getting to you and helping you, that's all I care about. And the love? Have any trouble with the transfer from the Detroit banks?"

"None whatsoever," I said. "The love was there when I needed it."

"Glad to hear it," he said. "Anything I can do for my boy really makes me happy. Well, Nick, let me know what you decide on the Die-Dee Doll."

"Of course," I said. "As soon as possible."

Suddenly he was looming over me, grinning down at me, his great paw crushing my shoulder.

"Thanks, *son,*" he said. "Now I think I'll take a little stroll and relax."

"Who is she?" I asked.

"Who?" he asked innocently. "Oh." He laughed. "Oh . . . in the guesthouse. Well . . . she's a musician."

I held up a hand, palm out.

"Please," I said. "Don't tell me what she plays."

He was still laughing when he went out the library doorway, banging the frame on both sides with his wide shoulders as he went through.

I finished my drink. Then, from the library phone, I called Millie Jean Grunwald. Thankfully, she was at home. Better than that, she was entertaining a girlfriend. They were watching a Spanish bullfight on the telly, via satellite, and eating sandwiches of prorye spread with premixed peanut butter and grape petrojelly.

"Yum-yum," Millie said.

I asked how she and her girlfriend would enjoy the company of two young, horny ems.

"Yum-yum," Millie said.

I went up to Paul's room, walked in without knocking. He was standing at a window, staring out into the darkness. Hands thrust into his pockets.

"Come on," I said. "We're going into Detroit."

"What for?" Dulled.

"Life."

"No. You go ahead without me, Nick."

"Don't you want to meet my girlfriend?"

He turned then to look at me. I knew; he *was* curious.

"Three's a crowd," he said cautiously.

"Four, in this case. She's got a girlfriend visiting. Don't know who. I probably never met her."

"Well. . . ." He hesitated. "Listen, Nick, what did your father say after I left?"

I told him exactly what my father had said. He was aghast.

"My God," he said. "Between father and son? That kind of interaction?"

I shrugged. "That's the way we are. That's the way we all are."

"I'm glad I never knew who my father was."

"It can be an advantage," I admitted. "At times."

"Then you're going to overrule my rejection? Approve the Die-Dee Doll?"

"Do I have any choice?"

"Nooo," he said slowly. "I guess not."

310

I thought it time to bring him up to speed.

"Before you hate him, or me, too much, Paul, remember that what he did for me also benefited you. Enough of this kaka. Let's get tracking."

On the ride into Detroit, we stopped for a two-liter jug of red petrowine. I think we were both in the mood for something harsh and primitive.

Paul was shocked, perhaps a bit frightened by the dark, bricked street down near the river. The suppurative smell of things. Echoing footfalls. Feeble pools of light from obso streetlamps. The apartment over the porn shop. A display of dusty phalli.

"Nick," he said. Looking up at the cracked windows. "Do you come here often?"

"Every time I'm in Detroit."

"And you've never had your throat slit?"

"Every time I'm in Detroit."

He laughed. "Now I understand your bruised ribs. You were lucky."

We rang, were admitted, climbed the creaking stairway. The efs awaited us at the top of the stairs, arms about each other's waist. Millie, with all her bountiful blessings, looked like the mother. The girlfriend's name was Sophie. No last name volunteered or requested.

During the late 1980's and early 1990's, for almost a decade, a series of great droughts and famines had bloomed like a firestorm across Southeast Asia, India, Africa, South America. It was said that 500,000,000 objects stopped. That may have been operative. No one would know. The "developed nations" (what does that mean?) did what they could with token shipments of proteins, fats, vitamins, etc. It was all useless. The world listened to the chuckles of Malthus.

The famines were, at first, given heavy media coverage. Until it became a bore. We stared at staggering animals, stopping objects, cracked earth, withered foliage. Heard the cries of the victims, animals and objects. So similar. What impressed me most was the expression on the faces of the very young. Outrage.

Sophie had much that same look. And curiously, she had the physical appearance of a famine victim: joints poking out against parchment skin, thinness to the point of emaciation, faintness of speech, eyes abnormally large. I guessed that, like Millie, she was one of a flawed clone group. Paul didn't flinch.

311

We drank quite a lot of the red petrowine. We danced. I recall that at one point, Paul and I engaged in a kind of adagio routine with Sophie, throwing her back and forth between us. She was a loose rack of bones. She adored the rough play, urging us on with piggish squeals. Millie couldn't stop laughing.

What else? Paul crawled across the floor on hands and knees, Sophie perched on his back. Her sleazy shift was pulled up to her waist. The naked pelvis was a shadowed hollow. Bones jutted whitely. Wiry hair bristled. Millie and I applauded this performance wildly. We were then sitting up in bed. About Millie's neck, suspended from a leather thong, the silvery snowflake hung between sweated breasts. My gift to her.

Then we four were naked. A tangle on the crumpled sheet. Paul and I drank wine from them. This amused us all. But the alcohol stung when they took us into full mouths. We bit their flesh. To screams. The taste of the two efs was quite different: Millie soft, sweet, pulpy; Sophie tart, hard, astringent. Paul and I knocked foreheads as our tongues met in some viscous trap. We discovered Millie was able to suck her own nipples. Sophie locked her heels behind her head and pouted that bearded mouth to all. We knew the world would end the next instant.

During that fevered night I lurched out into the hallway, found the nest. And there was Paul, standing on the closed toilet, his head and shoulders out the opened window. He appeared to be inspecting the rear wall of the adjoining buildings.

"Paul, what are you doing?"

He came inside slowly, climbed down.

"I had to get some air," he said. "I thought I was going to faint."

"Sorry," I said.

"About what?"

"Sophie."

He stared at me.

"Nick," he said, "believe this. It's operative. The best orgasm I've ever had in my life."

"Oh?" I said. "Why?"

"Why? Why? I'm not sure."

"Try."

"Complete mastery. I owned her."

"That's interesting," I said.

312

Physical pleasure demands deliberation. Passion is for beasts. The second half of that *Walpurgisnacht* was cool, muted, considered. Occasionally painful. We all moved slowly in a grunted dream. Some things we could not do. But tried.

By dawn we were emptied. I slept on the floor. When I awoke aching, I found the other three on the bed, spoon-fashion, hands grasping swollen flesh in sleep.

I moved them about. Slowly, gently. They did not awake, but muttered, groaned. It was more pained stupor than sleep. I arranged the efs on their backs, knees raised and spread. Paul turned, twisted, his flaccid genitals plastered to his thigh.

It was Egon Schiele, of course. I had recognized it the moment I saw their rawness. Now, exposed, I dimly glimpsed a truth and began to understand. It went beyond sexuality. To a primitive something. A dark mystery I could not deny. It drew me, this wonder long sought. It was almost a revelation.

Paul and I got home safely. I bathed and went to bed. I presumed he did the same. I know I didn't see him until late that afternoon. I was forcing myself to eat some food, on the terrace, and trying to stop a bursting thirst with a tall vodka-and-Smack. Paul took his place opposite me, nodding. He was quite pale. I suppose I was, too.

Later, carrying a second vodka-and-Smack, we wandered out onto the grounds. We wore flannel bags, heavy sweaters. There was, thankfully, a nip in the wind. It dried sweat, brought a welcome chill. I did not mention the previous night. Nor did Paul. I think we were both too awed by what we had done.

"About the UP pill," I said. "Are you up to speed?"

"Yes."

"Reactions?"

"On the physical factor, I can see a reasonable hope. Houston says it will definitely be addictive, psychologically if not physiologically. I see it as a combined narcotic and euphoric. I think the chemistry can be solved."

"I concur. But you don't sound too enthusiastic."

"I'm not. Nick, if all we want is the world's greatest physical jerk, we might as well go to an opium-based derivative, or an amphetamine, and have everyone in the country on the nod or grinning their way through life in a semipermanent state of goofiness. That's not what we want, is it?"

313

"You know better than that."

"Honolulu was equivocal. They didn't say yes, and they didn't say no. Except for Ruben's report."

"Oh-ho. You caught that. Know the em?"

"Never heard of him before."

"I served with him on a memory project. Very quiet. Shy. A chess genius. With a fantastic ability to go straight to the jugular of a problem. You notice that while everyone else in Honolulu was trying to analyze the mental factor in happiness, only Ruben realized it may consist of no mentality at all. What was it he said? 'The total absence of conscious ratiocination may prove to be the dominant mental factor in states of euphoria.' That's pure Ruben. It's even the way he talks."

"He also said, in his report, 'Mental happiness may result from complete absence of responsibility.' Interesting."

"Yes. Well, Spokane was unequivocal. They said flat-out that, psychologically, happiness is such a subjective state that there is no common denominator. Do you believe that?"

"I don't want to, Nick. If it's true, we can forget about the UP pill."

"Well, I don't believe it. Paul, we'll never get a pill with one hundred percent effectiveness. What pill has? Even aspirin is ineffective on some subjects. If we can jerk even seventy-five percent, I'll be satisfied."

"You have a very low satiety level."

I laughed. We continued our stroll. Wandering through the trees. Crunching dried leaves underfoot. I began to believe I might live.

"What is Lewisohn up to?" Paul asked abruptly.

"I was wondering when you'd get curious. As nearly as I can tell, his plan is mainly economic. I don't believe he's done any computing on the social organization it will demand. He probably assumes social form will follow economic function."

"What's the economic plan?"

"A corporate state," I said. "That's as close as I can come. Evolving into a corporate world. All means of production owned by the government. Planning takes over the role of the marketplace."

"The individual buys stocks or bonds in the government?"

"Possibly. Perhaps the total of voluntary contributions determines an object's share. I don't believe Lewisohn has yet considered the problems, the social problems."

"It would have to be authoritarian. The government."

"Of course. But no more than, say, General Motors or IBM. A benevolent despotism. Written into law. You better make notes on this in the Tomorrow File."

"Yes. I will. It implies a class society, doesn't it?"

"If Lewisohn has computed it at all, he probably envisions economic classes: rulers, managers, servers. Not too different from what we have now."

"With free vertical movement between classes?"

"I would imagine so. Paul, why are you so interested in Lewisohn's plan?"

"Because right now he's serving on social unrest. But I see nothing in his proposed world, as you describe it, that would eliminate the unrest."

"The UP pill might."

"Perhaps. But we agreed we don't want something to keep servers perpetually dopey. They've got to produce. How about the UP pill as a reward?"

"For producing? Now you're just substituting a drug for love. That solves nothing."

"Yes. Yes, Nick, you're right. Let me compute this a little more."

On the following day, in our compartment aboard the Bullet Train to GPA-1, Paul returned to the subject.

"If the purpose of the UP pill is to curb social unrest," he said, "then it cannot be considered by itself, a new drug, *in vacuo*. It must be developed in the context of the social situation."

"In other words, you're saying we should work backward from the purpose? Determining the social goal, then developing the UP pill that achieves it?"

"In a way. Nick, we've got to create a *political* drug."

"A political drug," I murmured.

"Exactly. The UP pill must be effective, physiologically. But it cannot succeed as we want it to unless it is encapsulated in a social organization that reinforces it. One has no greater value than the other. But both sustain each other, mutually dependent."

"Are you saying then that purely *physical* joy—Ultimate Pleasure, if you will—is sufficient if the social organization is so computed as to provide the mental and psychological factors of operative happiness?"

"Yesss," Paul said slowly. "That's about it."

"Yes," I said. "I think so, too. Let's serve along those lines."

315

We came out into the low ceilings and rancid, littered corridors of the Pennsylvania Station in New York. At one point in time a huge railroad depot had stood here. Modeled after the Baths of Caracalla. With enormous, delicate, soaring spaces that dwarfed objects and at the same time, strangely, enobled them. But that cathedral was before my time. I never knew it.

Y-11

On October 15, I was to take the 1300 air shuttle to Washington, D.C. But I had several official duties to get through that morning. Paul Bumford accompanied me on my rounds. Whenever we had the chance, whenever we were alone, we went over once again the details of the scenario for the next five days.

Our first visit was to C Lab where Paul's Memory Team leader was staging a demonstration for us. They had been serving on the physical transfer of memory from one object to another of the same species. They had developed a derivative of purified RNA, from the donor object, hyped with a chlorinated uracil. Since, at that point in time, we had an evidentiary indication that memory was both a chemical and an electrical process, the Memory Team was experimenting with a very low-frequency current, in the range of human theta waves, to boost the effect of the injected chemicals.

In this case, the donor was a young em chimpanzee. He had been trained to pull a lever that released a food pellet. Positive behavioral conditioning. He was then sacrificed. Lovely word. RNA was extracted from his brain, purified by a newly developed cryogenic process, and combined with the uracil compound.

This mixture was then injected into the internal carotid of an untrained em chimp of the same breeding group—a "brother" of the donor. At the same time the untrained chimp was fitted with a metal helmet, self-powered, that generated the theta waves.

We all crowded around the one-way glass window looking into the chimp's room. In a moment, a lab server carried him in. The chimp's arms were clamped about the ef's neck. She gently disengaged him, set him in the middle of the floor, left the room. The chimp stared about curiously. He looked like a little, hairy astronaut.

316

"Haven't been starving him, have you, Ed?" I asked the Team Leader.

"Sure," he said cheerfully. "We need all the help we can get."

"As long as you haven't trained him," Paul said.

"I swear," the Team Leader murmured.

We watched the chimp in silence. He rose to all fours, put his head back, yawned. He scratched his ass. Exactly like the Scilla secretary Paul and I had watched on the TV monitor in San Diego.

Then the chimp looked around, bounced up and down once or twice as if to loosen his muscles. He ambled over to the food dispensing panel.

"He's going for it," someone breathed.

Almost without pausing, the animal reached up, yanked the lever, released it, lifted the metal cover of the chute, removed the food pellet, popped it into his mouth and began to chew, grimacing.

"Son of a bitch," someone said. Wonderingly.

Strangely, there was no elation. I think we just looked at each other, stunned. I know I was trying to compute the significance of what I had just seen. What it meant. What it could lead to. Physical transfer of memory. The power!

"Congratulations, Ed," I said finally. Shaking his hand. "Try it again. And again. And again. Publish nothing. It looks good."

He took me aside for a moment.

"How's the RSC, Nick?" he asked.

"Fine," I lied. "No problems."

"Good. When are you due for a hippocampal irrigation?"

"February."

"See me before then. We've been serving on something new."

"Will do. Congratulations again, Ed. Very impressive."

If we had one triumph that morning, we also had one disappointment. We stopped by Phoebe Huntzinger's office in the computer complex. I knew she had been monitoring Project Phoenix in Denver. She had come to feel it was her baby. Baby wasn't growing.

"Nothing," Phoebe growled. The moment we walked in. "Nothing plus nothing gives you nothing."

Her heavy brogues were propped up on a desk littered with books, pamphlets, journals, papers. Paul and I pulled up chairs facing her.

"Mary Bergstrom checked out the brain technology," Paul said. Defensively. "She says it's operative."

Phoebe nodded glumly. She was fretted by this problem.

"Nick," she said slowly, "if it was a nice day out, and I passed you in the hall or outside, what would you say to me?"

I looked at her.

"All right, I'll play your game," I said finally. "I'd probably say, 'Hello, Phoebe. Nice day.' "

"Precisely," she said. Bringing her feet down from the desk, hitching her chair toward us. "You'd say, 'Nice day.' But you'd say it like, 'Niceday.' In effect, you wouldn't use two words, an adjective and a noun. You'd use one word, 'Niceday,' as a kind of label for the kind of day it was. Compute? You'd not only say, 'Niceday,' but you'd think, 'Niceday.' A combination of two words, a union that describes verbally *and in your mind* the kind of day it is. You don't think 'nice' and then think 'day' and then put the two together. You get input from the sky, the sun, the air, and then your brain leaps immediately to the label, 'Niceday.' "

"So?" Paul said. He was interested now. Leaning forward to stare at her.

"See this kaka?" she said. She pushed at the stacks of books on her desk. "Linguistics. How we are conditioned to think in words. But more than one object suggests we don't think in words at all. Not individual words. A lot of our thinking is in phrases, even sentences, that constitute labels. Niceday, howareyou, hardrain, hotsun, cutekid. Compute? Nick, send me out to Denver. I want to reprogram that damned Golem to pick up a couple of thousand basic, primitive verbal labels in the English language. I can make up my own list from all this—" Again she shoved at the research on her desk. "And it may help us pick up coherent thoughts. It certainly can't do any harm. All we've done so far is print out a few individual words."

"Phoebe," I said, "sounds to me like you'll be making Golem sensitive to clichés."

"All right, all right," she said. "Clichés. Call them that if you want. That's what ninety percent of human speech consists of, isn't it?"

"Cynic," I said. "Well, you may be right. Clichés may be the basis of rational speech. We've got to start somewhere. Paul? Reactions?"

"Phoebe," he said, "how will the computer print it out? In a series of words without space breaks?"

"No, no," she said. "It's a simple circuitry trick. The thought will be picked up by the input bank as connected phrases or sentences. The printout from retrieval will be properly spaced and punctuated.''

Paul looked at me.

"Nick, let's try it," he said. "Nothing to lose."

"Right," I said. "Phoebe, have a good time in Denver. Orrather, have a goodtime."

October 15, 1998.

1630: I arrived at Rehabilitation & Reconditioning Hospice No. 4, Alexandria, Virginia, via taxi from the airport. I immediately sought out Chief Resident Luke Warren and informed him I would be his guest for the next five days. During which I intended to monitor the reactions of Hyman R. Lewisohn to the new parabiotic treatment. Lewisohn had already been connected to the first "volunteer," a young em from Texas. He was a former border guard of the Immigration Service who had been found guilty of actions detrimental to the public interest in that he accepted bribes to allow unlawful immigration across the border. From the US into Mexico.

I also told Dr. Warren I would need accommodations in Transient Quarters and the use of a radiotelephone-equipped car during my stay. He made the arrangements immediately, apologizing for the only radiophone car available, a diesel-powered, four-wheel-drive Rover.

1645: I called Paul Bumford in New York, reported my arrival, gave him the number of the mobile phone in the car assigned to me. I then called Angela Berri's office at DOB Headquarters to report my whereabouts. I had intended to speak only to an assistant or secretary, but Angela herself came on the flasher screen.

"What's up, Nick?" she asked.

"I am," I said.

She tried to smile. It wasn't only my feeble joke; she seemed worn, features honed down to tight skin on sharp bones. I thought her manner subdued, if not depressed. Her service as DIROB could account for that; I had learned that routine administration can be more wearying than the most demanding creative assignment.

I told her I'd be in Alexandria for the next five days, personally ministering to Lewisohn. She accepted the news casually.

"How about dinner or a drink?" she asked. "Whenever you get a chance."

"A profit," I said. "May I flash you at any hour of the day or night?"

Then she became the "old" Angela, did something with her mouth and tongue, and switched off, smiling wickedly.

1710: I drove to the first public phone booth I could find and called Seymour Dove in San Diego. I gave him two phone numbers: the R&R Hospice and my radiophone-equipped Rover. He told me he expected to check into the Morse Hotel in Washington, D.C., by noon on October 20. With the 5,000 new dollars, as demanded by Art Roach.

1730: I returned to the Hospice. Dr. Seth Lucas was off-duty, but Maya Leighton was there. In her private office. Feet up on her desk. Tanned legs spread. Leaning far back in a tilted chair. No panties. The tattooed scarab showed. She was leafing through a unisex fashion magazine (*TOOTY: For Those Who Dare!*). She saw me at the door. Her chair slammed down. She came out of it as if propelled.

"Look at the beaver!" she marveled. Stroking my face with both palms. "Look at the dickety twitcher! A devil! Nick, now you look exactly like the Devil!"

She groped my testicles and pursed for a kiss.

1750: I looked in on Lewisohn, leaving Maya to prepare for her evening with Art Roach. She said he always left before midnight, to drive back to his hotel suite in Washington. I told her I'd call to make certain the coast was clear before I came over.

Lewisohn was sleeping, and so was his donor. I checked the instrumentation, then went back to the Group Lewisohn office to scan the most recent reports. Lewisohn's blood count had stabilized and was holding. The donor's leukocyte count was up. That was to be expected.

Reading the record of this radical treatment, I wished, briefly, that Dr. Henry L. Hammond was alive and available for consultation. But after his arrest in the fiascoed Society of Obsoletes' plot, he had been drained and his corpus assigned to the National Survival Bank. That facility ruled the storage tunnels in the Tetons where the US Government kept its hoard of frozen sperm, fertilized and unfertilized eggs, blood, organs, and complete corpora. In case of a nukewar. They were continually in need of fresh deposits.

2030: I stopped time at a porn movie. Single ems were encouraged to hire young, lubricious efs ("hostesses") for companionship in small, foul-smelling balcony cubicles (one lumpy sofa), or sim-

320

ply to sit alongside during the performance and supplement the action on the screen with whispered promises or threats, whichever you preferred.

2315: I parked down the block from Maya's apartment, concealed in shadow. The street was as I remembered it. Her apartment was on the ground floor of a two-story town house. It had both a front and a rear entrance. Important to our plan.

2350: The windows of her apartment suddenly blazed with light. I scrunched down further in the seat of my Rover.

0020: Art Roach strode quickly from her front door. Turned to wave. He got into his four-door, black Buick, an official "command car," and drove off. Still I waited.

0100: I found a phone booth, called Maya. She said that as far as she could determine, he had forgotten nothing. If he followed his usual pattern, he wouldn't return that night.

"Hurry," she said.

0125: She was in a surly mood. She admitted it.

"It's that pile of kaka who just walked out of here," she said wrathfully. "He thinks he owns me. Nick, for God's sake, how much longer?"

"Five days," I said.

She came alive. Rushing at me, flinging herself atop me. She was wearing only an em's undershirt, something thin and clinging, with shoulder straps and deeply cut armholes. One breast plunged out.

"But you have to do a favor for me," I said. "One final favor. Then we're home free."

"Anything," she murmured. She was rubbing her cheek against my new beard. "I'll do anything."

I explained slowly what would be required of her. She listened intently. Her questions were to the point: "But what if he—" "But what if we—" I had the answers ready. I gave her the fail-safe alternatives to all his possible reactions to the scenario.

She agreed immediately. But I don't believe her motives were those I anticipated. There was her dislike of Roach, of course. But something more. I sensed it. A tasting of power. A feeling of mastery. It was something new for her. She found it sweet.

We went over the script, in detail, two more times. She provided additional valuable input: Roach was right-handed; he smoked continually, at least two and sometimes three packs a day; he wouldn't touch cannabis; he didn't use a lighter; he was continually running out of paper matches. When he lighted a cigarette, he

321

cupped both hands around the match and cigarette, like a sailor in a gale. Excellent.

I told her that her role would begin on the evening of October 18. She would invite Art Roach to a dinner in her apartment. A dinner she would prepare for him.

"Anything unusual in that?" I asked. "Anything to make him suspicious?"

"Of course not. We've had dinner here a dozen times. He likes to eat with his shoes off."

I took a white envelope from my inside pocket and handed it to her. It contained 500 new dollars. Various denominations. She opened it. Thumb riffled the bills. Widening eyes turned up to me.

"It's not for this Roach thing," I said hurriedly. "It's from me to you. For putting up with my nonsense. I didn't have time to get you a gift. Buy yourself a pretty."

She was one of those objects sexually excited by the sight of love. I could tell. She felt the bills. Flipped through the stack again and again. Did everything but smell it. Excitement growing. The power of love.

October 16.

1040: I called Paul again at GPA-1 and asked him to call me from an outside phone. When he returned my call, I told him what additional equipment we'd need. He said there would be no problems; his Electronics Team carried most of the devices in stock and could easily assemble what they didn't have. The Neuropharmacology Team could provide the remainder. Paul had merely to tell the team leaders their cooperation was needed on an urgent classified project. They would ask no questions.

1110: I spent almost two hours with Group Lewisohn, giving the patient a workup. I could only bully, but Maya Leighton could wheedle. Between us, we got what we wanted. All gross indicators were encouraging. Even his color and skin tone had improved as his rejuvenated blood was returned to him through plastirub tubing.

His disposition, of course, was as repellent as ever. Only Maya's pattings and strokings allowed us to complete our tests. We were filing out when he suddenly shouted, "You bastard!"

Naturally, we all turned around, startled. His ugly mouth stretched in what I assumed to be a grin.

"You all know what you are, don't you?" He chuckled. "Flair is the particular bastard I want at the moment. The rest of you get the fuck gone."

The door closed behind them. I came back to his bedside.

"I should let you stop," I told him. "You're more trouble than you're worth."

He could accept that kind of language. It confirmed his misanthropy. It comforted him.

"Look at the beard," he said. "The lean and hungry look. Ah there, Cassius. Or Iago." He stared at me. "No," he said. "A cut-rate Machiavelli." The idea seemed to amuse him. Then: "Where do those tubes go?" he demanded.

They led from his arm through the thick, soundproof wall separating him from the former Texas border guard.

"Continuous blood analysis," I said glibly. "Constant monitoring on a linked computer. We put it behind a wall so the noise wouldn't disturb you. Want to see the latest printout? It looks good."

"Fuck you," he grumbled. "No, I don't want to see the latest printout. You'd fake it, you monster."

He was right. I would.

"Now what the hell is this?" he shouted.

He took a manuscript from a stack alongside his bed and threw it at me. I caught it in midair. Glanced at it. An Instox copy of my prospectus for a new Department of Creative Science.

"Oh?" I said. "The Chief Director sent you a copy?"

"Oh?" he said. Burlesquing my innocent tone. "The Chief Director sent you a copy? Just what are you plotting, you devious whoreson?"

"Plotting?" I said. Righteous indignation. "I'm not plotting anything. I suggested the idea to the Chief. He was interested and wanted to see it expanded. That's all there is to it."

He stared at me.

"It's all a mouse in a cage to you, isn't it?" he said finally.

"Now look," I said. Anger in my voice. Feigned? I don't know. "If you're going to give me the canned lecture on science versus humanism, forget it. I've heard it from better brains than yours. I've heard it in a hundred lecture halls, conditioning sessions, symposia, and colloquies. You know what it all adds up to? Kaka. Rich, refined, intellectual kaka. Let other objects debate, endlessly, morality and value judgments. I won't spend a microsecond wringing my hands and pleading, 'What does it all mean?' To act is all. I'm just not teleologically oriented. I'm only interested in the tomorrow I can compute and plan. The future that can be manipulated."

"You think scientists can do a better job than politicians?"

"We couldn't do worse, could we?"

"Yes," he said.

Which, from him, was almost praise.

"Who's this Paul Bumford you mentioned?" he said.

"You met him. A small, slight em. He was with me the last time I was here."

"Oh. That one. The one memorizing the titles of the books I was reading."

That shook me.

"He's got some fresh ideas," he went on. "And you're giving him credit."

"Of course," I said. "They were his ideas."

Again I saw that caricature of a cynical grin. Lips drawn back, yellowed teeth showing it in an ugly rictus.

"Round and round it goes," he said. "And where it stops, nobody knows."

"I don't know what the hell you're mumbling about," I told him, "and I don't think you do either."

He turned his face to the wall through which his blood was disappearing, to reappear young, cleansed, whole. I took his silence for dismissal and left. The old fart had bounced me.

1400: We took Maya's tooty little sports car. We spent all afternoon finding the right location. It had to be on a secondary road between her apartment and a tavern, an all-night drive-in movie, a cabaret, a grogshop—something like that. The road, preferably, would be bordered with trees. The spot selected should be within quick walking distance of a public phone. In a booth, store, gas station—anyplace. Any phone available around midnight.

We didn't find the perfect spot, of course. But the one we selected would serve. Light traffic in the afternoon, probably less at night. Direct route from Maya's apartment to a roadhouse called the King's Pawn. Maya said she and Art Roach had been there before. They served food and featured a transvestite pianist after 2100. There was a roadside phone booth a five-minute walk from the place we selected. Most of the road ran through a wood.

2200: I drove my Rover back to the selected location to inspect it at the anticipated time of action. It looked better. It was quite dark. Traffic was minimal. Trees menaced on both sides. The road itself was a paved two-laner. The shoulders on both sides sloped down steeply. Nice.

October 17.

1020: It is hardly an original observation: The basic motivation of all living things is self-interest. This is, to be sure, a generalization. As operative and inoperative as all generalizations. But still, the hard rock of self is there. In *Homo sapiens*, it may be—usually is—slicked over with various camouflage: patriotism, mercy, devotion, sacrifice, altruism, duty, and so forth. Sometimes you can hardly see the rock.

In manipulating Dr. Seth Lucas, my only problem was in determining where the young black's self-interest lay. As expected, it proved to be a melange.

"Seth," I started, "I haven't had a chance before this to tell you what a fine service you've been pulling with Group Lewisohn."

I believe positive behavioral conditioning is more useful than negative.

"Thank you, Dr. Flair," he said. Straightening. Consciously mature. "It's been great experience for me. I've learned a lot."

"Nick," I said. "Any problems?"

"Nothing I haven't been able to handle. Nick. Lewisohn himself is my heaviest migraine. But I knew that before you organized Group Lewisohn."

"All the indicators show go," I said. "We'll just have to wait and see. Meanwhile, Seth, I have a heavy migraine myself. I'm hoping you can help me."

"Of course," he said. "Anything I can do. Nick."

We were in his tiny office, seated at his desk. We were both sipping a plasticup of brown liquid the Hospice cafeteria called coffee. I rose from my chair, walked lightly to the corridor door. I yanked it open suddenly, peered out cautiously. I locked it shut from the inside.

"What the hell?" the kid said. "Nick?"

"Seth," I said, "I'm going to ask you to do something for me. I know the request will sound strange to you. All I ask is for you to hear me out. I'll explain what will be required of you. Then you can say go or no-go. The decision is entirely yours. Whichever way you decide, it shouldn't have any effect on your rule of Group Lewisohn. Will you listen?"

"Well . . . sure. Nick."

Speaking slowly, earnestly, I explained to him that a certain object (unnamed), a server of DOB, had been accused of activities dangerous to public security. I had been ordered to cooperate in proving or disproving those accusations. I would need his, Dr. Seth Lucas', professional assistance.

"This object," I said, "this em, will be brought into the Welcome Ward at approximately 2400 tomorrow night. You will be informed of the exact time of his arrival. Then you will send for me. I will be sleeping in Transient Quarters. This object has a security clearance equal to mine, higher than yours. Are you aware that such an object can only be treated by a medical doctor or psychiatrist with an equal or higher clearance? It's regulations."

"Oh sure," he said hastily. "Nick."

I doubted he had ever heard of that regulation. But it was operative.

"So I must be in attendance before this object is treated in the Welcome Ward," I said solemnly. "From that moment on, he will be my responsibility."

"Will he be injured?"

"Not at that point in time. But he will be unconscious."

I then explained what would be required of him. His features grew increasingly bleak as I related details. He was spooked. It was understandable. Nothing in his conditioning had prepared him for activities of this nature.

"Of course," I said offhandedly, "if you would feel safer if you had a direct order, signed by me, to account for your actions, I'll be happy to oblige."

"No no no," he said hurriedly. "That won't be necessary. I just don't see—"

I leaned forward, grasped his arm, lowered my voice.

"Seth," I whispered, "I'd like to tell you more. I really would. But there are certain things you have no need to know. And believe me, it's better that way. Just let me make one thing perfectly clear: If you do this, you'll be performing a valuable service for the Department of Bliss. And for your country. I can't make you any promises, but I'm sure you'll find, a few weeks from now, that your Department and your country are not unappreciative."

I thought then I had touched all bases. And so I had. He was bewildered, shaken, frightened. But he was in.

1640: Paul Bumford and Mary Bergstrom arrived. They had come down from the GPA-1 compound in my limousine. No chauffeur; Mary did the driving. The heavy equipment was locked in the trunk. Paul was carrying the drugs and small devices in a plastic shopping bag advertising "Maxine's Smoked Salmon and

Imported Delicacies.'' I remembered Leon Mansfield sleeping in a laundry van and using subway toilets. It's the bizarreness of existence that continually bemuses me.

They settled in at Transient Quarters and made their presence known around the Hospice. Paul seemed charged, brittle, almost fatalistic. He didn't smile or laugh very often. But recently he had become increasingly serious. If not solemn.

Mary Bergstrom I never could compute. I had no input on *her* self-interest. Paul said he controlled her, and had proved it. But to me, she was essentially an unknown quantity. I thought her cold, introverted, frustrated. Unattractive and rather dull. None of this, of course, affected her usefulness.

1900: I treated us all—Maya, Mary, Paul, myself—to dinner at a restaurant recommended by Dr. Luke Warren.

It was a crowded room; we didn't discuss business. But afterward, we drove to the scene of the crime. We parked; Paul, Maya, and I got out and took a look. We couldn't see any difficulties. Paul approved. We were there almost five minutes, and not a single car passed on the road.

We drove back to the Hospice. Maya transferred to her sports car. We followed her back to her apartment. She pulled into the driveway that curved around to the back entrance. We parked right behind her. Paul and I got out and joined her. He handed over the drugs. They were in three small plastic containers. Color-coded caps: red, white, and blue. Red held the anaphrodisiac, white the instant narcotic, blue the thirty-minute narcotic.

Then I showed her the matches. Apparently an ordinary packet of paper matches. An ad on the cover for an IUD with the legend: ''Close cover before striking.''

''The moment he lights up,'' I told Maya, ''turn your head away. Have your window down. Get your head outside and breathe fresh air deeply. Got that?''

''Sure,'' she said. ''How long does it take?''

I looked at Paul.

''Probably within thirty seconds,'' he said. ''A minute at the most. Make certain he doesn't fall forward and hit his head on the dash. We don't want him to injure himself.''

He meant it seriously. Maya and I laughed.

I tore two matches from the folder. Holding them at arm's length, I struck them. They flared. I turned my head away. They both burned halfway down, then went out when the saturation was consumed. I dropped them onto the gravel driveway.

Then I placed the match folder on the shelf over the dash.

"You'll drive?" I asked Maya.

She nodded.

I positioned the matches directly in front of the passenger's seat. I bent the cover open.

"Don't use them by mistake," I cautioned her. "We want you wide awake."

We went back to the Transient Quarters barracks. I thought sleep would come easily; I had done everything that could be done. But at 0200 I shoved a six-hour Somnorific up my nose.

October 18.

1000: Dr. Seth Lucas reserved two rooms in the Welcome Ward, as I had instructed. Into one, he moved a portable laserscope and the other equipment we'd need. He locked the door. I had told him if he got any flak, refer it to me.

Sure enough, Dr. Luke Warren found me in the offices of Group Lewisohn. He asked why it was necessary to reserve two of his precious rooms. He was unexpectedly determined. I think he was astonished by his own temerity.

"Departmental business," I told him. It had worked once; I tried it again: "If you want a signed order, I'll give you one."

"Butbutbut. . . ." he stammered.

"You have no need to know," I said coldly.

1930: I phoned Maya Leighton's apartment from the Hospice.

She answered: "Hello?"

"Is Jack there?" I asked.

"Sorry," she said, "you've got the wrong number." And hung up.

Signal. Our pigeon was in the coop.

Paul and I departed in my Rover. Mary Bergstrom took the plastic shopping bag up to the locked room.

2030: We were parked down the block from Maya's apartment. All our lights were out. I had a feeling of inexorableness and could wait patiently. Paul was in a voluble mood. He may have popped an energizer. I let him talk.

2140: The lights behind the shades of Maya Leighton's apartment went out. Paul and I straightened in our seats, peering.

"She's got him," I said softly. "Clever ef."

2145: Maya's tooty little sports car backed swiftly out of the driveway, swung around in the street, paused, headed off. We followed, well back. Paul had the infrared binoculars out, pressed to his eyes.

2150: "Normal," he reported. "She's driving. Normal. Normal."

"All *right*, Paul," I said. "Just tell me if anything happens."

2205: "There!" Paul cried. "Flare of match on his side. He's lighting up! He's using the matches! He's using the matches!"

"We'll soon know," I said.

2210: The red sports car slowed appreciably. We pulled up until we were trailing by twenty meters. A bare arm came out of the driver's window. A hand flapped at us languidly.

"Marvelous, marvelous ef!" I laughed. "He's out."

"Oh, yes!" Paul giggled. Almost hysterically. "Oh, yes! Oh, yes!"

2235: She pulled off the deserted road, into the shadow. Her car was tilted downward, hanging up on the steep shoulder. We parked right behind her. Paul and I got out, hurried up to her car. I was on the driver's side.

"Go?" I asked her.

She was lighting a cigarette. With her own lighter.

"Cake," she said. "You manipulated him beautifully. Clunked almost instantly. Dropped cigarettes and matches in his lap. I've got them. He started to fall forward, but I pulled him back."

Paul had the door open on the passenger's side. Feeling for a pulse in Roach's neck. Lifting his eyelids.

"Pulse slow," he reported in a low voice. "He's under deep."

I went around and helped haul Art Roach from the car. We finally got him unfolded, lying on the shoulder of the road.

Maya Leighton got out and joined us. She left the driver's door open. She took a final puff of her cannabis, dropped it to the ground, rubbed it to shreds under her foot. She looked at her car.

"Good-bye, sweetie," she said.

"I'll pay all expenses," I assured her. "It'll be as good as new."

The three of us got behind the car and pushed it over the shoulder of the road. It crunched down into the trees. The right front fender crumpled. The car tilted crazily.

We hauled Art Roach down there, dragging him on pavement, gravel, short scrub. To mess him up. We arranged him artistically. On his back, arms flung wide, one ankle hooked over the sill on the passenger's side. The door had sprung and he had been thrown out of the car. What else?

We climbed back onto the shoulder of the road.

"Let's have the drugs, Maya," Paul said. He was tracking now.

She gave him the fiddled matches. Roach's cigarettes were tossed down atop his corpus. Paul inspected the three plastic containers before he slipped them into his purse. There was one anaphrodisiac capsule missing. Maya had slipped that into Roach's first drink. To cool his ardency. Make him more willing to leave the apartment. If he had refused to leave, the instant narcotic would have smashed him in the apartment. Then Paul and I would have wrestled him out of there into Maya's car, and the plan would have proceeded on schedule. If he had agreed to visit the King's Pawn, but hadn't used the narcotized matches en route, Maya still had the thirty-minute narcotic pills to fiddle his last drink at the roadhouse. He'd have clunked on the trip back. Fail-safe.

Maya Leighton looked at me, squared her shoulders, lifted her chin.

"All right, Nick," she said crisply. "Let's have it."

Without pausing to reflect, not wanting to reflect, I slammed her in the jaw with the heel of my hand. She went flying back down into the gully, one hand out to break her fall.

She sat up on the ground, shaking her head groggily. She looked at her palm. It was scraped raw, beginning to ooze blood. She wiped it on her blouse. Ripped two buttons open. Took clips from her hair, let it fall free. She climbed to her feet. Came up the bank to us. Rubbed a bloodied palm across her face.

"You'll pay for all this, you bastard." She grinned at me.

"Any time," I told her. "A profit."

I made certain she had small coins in her purse. Then she started walking down the road to the public phone. Paul and I got into the Rover, drove back to the Hospice, undressed, slid into our cots in Transient Quarters. I may have been whistling.

2350: A nurse came down between the two rows of cots. She was carrying a flashlight. A puddle of white light jerked along at her feet. I closed my eyes.

She leaned over me, shook my shoulder.

"Dr. Flair," she whispered. "Dr. Flair, wake up."

"Wha'? What?" I sat up suddenly. "What is it?"

"Dr. Lucas asks you to come to Emergency. At once, doctor."

"What's wrong? Is it Lewisohn?"

"No, not Lewisohn. The ambulance just brought in two accident

330

cases. Maya Leighton and an em. Dr. Lucas says it's urgent, doctor.''

I began to dress. I waited until she had left the barracks. Then I tapped Paul and Mary Bergstrom. Their cots were side by side.

"They're here," I said. "Let's go."

The interne ruling Emergency was completely confused. The night dispatcher had sent an ambulance in answer to Maya's phone call. By the time it returned with Maya, bruised but conscious, and Art Roach, unconscious, Dr. Seth Lucas was on the scene. After Maya had identified Roach as Chief of Security & Intelligence, DOB, Lucas had refused to touch the case and warned the befuddled interne not to interfere. At that moment he sent for me.

"You did exactly right, doctor," I told him. In a loud voice. Everyone listening. "This em can only be treated by me. Regulations. Let's get them upstairs. Paul, you and Mary assist. Dr. Lucas, please give us a hand. We'll take them on the wheeled stretchers."

"I can walk," Maya protested.

"Just lie still," I told her sternly. "You may have internal injuries."

We wheeled the two stretchers rapidly into the elevator. On the second floor, we paused in the corridor outside one of the reserved rooms. The unlocked room.

"Mary, Seth," I said, "you two take Maya in, get her cleaned up. A big bandage around that hand. Hospital gown."

"No way," Maya said. Climbing off her stretcher. "I'm mobile. And I'm not going to miss the fun."

It didn't seem the right moment to assert my authority over her. If I had any.

"All right," I said. "Let's get on with Roach."

The five of us got in each other's way getting him off the stretcher onto the hospital bed. Finally, I made the two efs and Paul stand clear. Seth Lucas and I stripped Roach down. Maya's first report had been accurate: The em was blessed.

"It looks like a baby's arm with an apple in its fist," I said. The standard encomium. "Paul, let's have the syringe first."

He took his plastic shopping bag from the closet, extracted a hypogun. There was a sealed vial in the case. Actually a cartridge to fit the gun.

"I'll do it," Paul said.

If he wanted to demonstrate his complicity, fine.

"In the neck," I told him.

He loaded the gun expertly, cocked it by pulling back the spring operated plunger. He placed the muzzle on the side of Roach's neck, pulled the trigger. There was an audible "Pflug!" sound. The indicator on the gun showed empty. Paul replaced it in the shopping bag.

We had decided on a purazine compound in a liquid that could be subcutaneously injected. We administered two cc's. It would produce a temporary memory block for approximately eight hours prior to the time of injection. The memory erasure with this particular compound was not permanent. Within a week or two, Roach would remember everything. By then, we hoped, it would make no difference.

He was lying naked, supine on the hospital bed. I pulled him across to the left side. I straightened his left arm. Now everyone was serving. Roach's digiwatch was removed from his left wrist, placed on the bedside table.

"The signet ring?" Mary asked.

"No, no," I said hurriedly. "Leave it on. Identification that it's really his arm. He'll recognize it."

The portable laserscope was brought close. The bed had to be raised electrically so that Roach's arm could be slipped easily into the image tunnel. Then the laserscope was moved to one side. Dr. Seth Lucas wheeled over a sturdy stainless steel table covered with a towel on a square of plastirub padding. On the table were two natural-rubber blocks and a surgical mallet.

Roach's forearm was laid across the rubber supports. Just below his elbow and just above his wrist. The arm was supported about five cm above the table surface.

"Seth," I said casually, "give it a whack."

I had intended to break Art Roach's arm myself. But after Paul had proved his loyalty by administering the memory inhibitor, I computed it might be wise if Dr. Seth Lucas also performed an overt act.

Lucas picked up the surgical mallet. Suddenly his face was glistening with sweat. He looked at me. Appealing.

"Try for the radius," I said. "A simple break. Not a compound fracture."

Almost blindly, he hit Roach's arm. Too close to the wrist, and

332

such a light tap I doubted if it would bruise the skin.

"Give me that," Mary Bergstrom growled. She grabbed the mallet roughly from Seth's nerveless hand.

We moved in closer. Mary pursed her lips, studying the white, almost hairless arm. She pulped the flesh feeling for bone position and thickness. Then, with a look of utter concentration, she raised the mallet and smacked it down.

We all heard it. I was convinced Roach's arm had been shattered into a million pieces. But no, it appeared whole. No jagged splinters of bone protruded.

"Laserscope," I ordered.

Paul and Lucas (breathing heavily) held Roach's arm immobile while the table was rolled away and the laserscope moved close. The arm was slid into the tunnel, the set switched on. We crowded around the viewing screen. There it was: a definite hairline break in the radius, midway between elbow and wrist.

"Beautiful, Mary," I said. "Just what we wanted."

"Thank you," she murmured. "Another tap? A light one, just to enlarge it?"

"No, no," I said hastily. "This will do fine. Paul, take the plates, from various angles. Make certain the signet ring shows."

We took a holder of 3-D holographic laserpix. Dr. Seth Lucas departed with the film to have it processed by the night crew in the lab. We wheeled the tables out of the way. Paul and I moved Roach back into the center of his bed while Mary pressed the two sections of his cracked arm tightly together.

Paul took the inflatable arm splint out of his bag of tricks and handed it to me. I slid my hand inside, felt about cautiously.

"The Electronics Team did a good service," Paul said.

He was right. The self-powered transmitter was no larger than a postage stamp, and almost as flat. What bulk it had came from the plastifoam padding in which it was encased. So it wouldn't press into the arm and impede circulation.

We gently pulled the limp plastic sleeve over Roach's cracked arm. It reached from just below his elbow to the limits of the metacarpals, the large knuckles. His fingers, and that signet ring, hung free.

We attached the bottle of compressed air provided by Dr. Seth Lucas. We began to inflate the splint. Slowly. Smoothing out the wrinkles. Pulling it taut. I kept an eye on the splint valve. When the

333

dial showed the recommended pressure for the splint, I gave it an additional two psi, cut it off, detached dial, tube, valve nipple. The splint was rigid, hard as plaster.

"Let's check it out," I said. "Paul, you go. We'll keep talking."

I gave him the key to my Rover. We had put the receiver on the back seat, covered with the topcoat I had brought down from GPA-1.

Paul left. Maya Leighton said, faintly, "I think I better sit down."

Mary and I whirled to look at her. She was suddenly quite pale, forehead moist. Mary got to her first, helped her into a chair, felt for her pulse. I rummaged through Paul's shopping bag, found the half-liter of natural brandy I had asked him to provide. I poured a double dollop into a Hospice plastiglass, held it to Maya's lips.

"A little at a time," I told her. "Gently, gently. You deserve it all. You were magnificent."

"I was, wasn't I?" She smiled wanly. "Did you have to break his arm?"

"Yes." I nodded seriously. "We did. We could have put the splint on a whole arm and told him it was broken. But what if he insisted on proof? Show him someone else's plates? What if he wanted to see it himself on the laserscope, or asked for another doctor, another set of plates? Or went to another Hospice? Also, we couldn't put a bugged splint on Seymour Dove's arm. Roach is very cautious, very careful. He'd have been immediately wary of taking a bribe from an em with his arm in a splint. Roach would have suspected an implanted bug. But it won't occur to him that *he* might be shared. This way, he won't take the other em to a sauna or steam room. And because the splint covers his left wrist, where he usually wears his digiwatch, he'll have to wear the watch on his right wrist. That reduces the possibility of his wearing a wrist monitor and discovering he's a walking broadcasting station."

"You thought of everything," Maya marveled. Sipping her brandy.

"We tried to anticipate every eventuality." I nodded. "But tonight was just preparation. We're not home free. Now we—"

The door was unlocked. Paul strode in. Grinning from ear to ear.

"Clear as a bell," he laughed. "We're home free."

"Mary," I said, "will you take care of Maya? Get her cleaned

334

up, into a hospital gown. Bandage that hand. Maybe a romantic head bandage, a turban, would be nice."

Maya looked at me.

"What I've got aching you can't bandage," she said.

That brandy had served quickly.

October 19.

1010: I was in the offices of Group Lewisohn. Had been since 0800. A Hospice nurse was sitting with Art Roach. Her orders were to call me the moment he showed signs of regaining consciousness. When the call came, I grabbed up the file of laserpix and went directly to his room. He was sitting up in bed, looking as ridiculous, helpless, and furious as any object wearing a short paper gown slit up the back. He gawked when I came in.

"What are *you* doing here?" he demanded. Instantly suspicious.

"Nurse," I said quietly, "would you leave the room, please."

After the door closed behind her, I went up to his bedside. I lifted his right wrist. Pressed the inner surface professionally. Not bothering to count.

"How are you feeling?" I asked sympathetically.

"Lousy," he said. He repeated: "What are *you* doing here?"

"I've been here for five days. Treating Hyman Lewisohn. Angela knows where I am. When you were brought in, they called me. Because of your security clearance." I added virtuously: "Regulations."

"I know the regulations," he said angrily.

Suddenly he realized what I had said.

"Brought in?" he said. "Brought in from where? When?"

"Don't you remember?"

He groaned, rubbed his free hand across his forehead.

"I don't remember a damned thing since—since—what day is this?"

"October 19."

"Then it was yesterday. The eighteenth. I was sitting in my office at Headquarters. About 1600. I was signing requisitions. That's the last thing I remember."

"Oh-oh," I said. "That doesn't sound so good. Let me take a look."

Fear came into his eyes. We had been counting on his hypochondria.

"What is it?" he gasped. "What's happened to me?"

I didn't answer. I pressed him back onto the pillow. I shoved up his eyelids, beamed a pencilite into his pupils. Then I felt his skull, fingertips probing through his fine, brush-cut hair.

"Hurt here?" I asked. "Here? Here? Here?"

"No. No. NO! Goddamn it, doc, what's wrong?"

I don't like to be called doc.

"Loss of memory might indicate possible concussion," I said coldly. "But I see no gross indicators. Eyes clear. No cranial contusions. But that amnesia bothers me. Maybe we should take some tests."

"What kind of tests?" he cried desperately.

"Very simple," I said cruelly. "We go into the brain with a needle—local anesthetic; you won't feel a thing—and draw off some fluid for analysis."

"My brain feels fine," he said. Shaken. "Just fine."

"Sure it does," I said softly. "The brain has no capacity to feel pain inflicted on itself. You think everything's normal, and then—"

I snapped my fingers.

"My God," he breathed.

"Well," I said briskly, "we'll discuss that later. Now . . . how's the arm?"

"This?" he said. He raised the inflated splint in front of him and looked at it with wonderment. "What the hell *is* it?"

I shook my head. Discouraged.

"You really don't remember, do you? You broke your arm. We put it in an inflatable splint. Want to see the plates?"

I held the laserpix to the light. I pointed out the hairline fracture. He saw his own signet ring.

"Will it heal okay?" he asked anxiously.

"It should," I said. Doctorial hedging. "You'll have to carry it in a sling for about two weeks. I don't anticipate any complications. Any other aches or pains?"

"My neck," he groaned. Rubbing it. "Here, on this side. It hurts."

Where Paul had shot him with the hypogun. I inspected it carefully.

"Just a minor bruise," I told him. "If that's all you've got, you're lucky. After that accident."

"Accident?" he cried. Horrified. "What accident?"

"Oh, that's right. Amnesia. Well, do you remember having a date with Maya Leighton?"

"Yes. Yes, I remember that. I was supposed to go to her place for dinner last night."

"Very good," I nodded approvingly. "Now do you remember being there?"

"No. I don't remember that at all."

"Oh. Too bad. Well, according to Maya, you arrived on time, had dinner, and then, about 2140, you both decided to go out. Some cabaret or tavern. The King's Pawn, I think it was. Does that ring any bells?"

"I don't remember going there last night. But I know the place. We've been there before."

"Well, you and Maya were on your way there. Maya was driving. It's a two-lane road. A semitrailer was coming in the opposite direction. Some nut swung out to pass just as the truck went past you. Maya swerved to avoid a head-on. Her car went off the road, down into a gully, banged into the trees. Thankfully, she wasn't driving too fast. The doors were sprung, you were both thrown out. No one stopped to assist. Maya came to, and, when she couldn't bring you around, staggered down the road to call for help."

I could almost hear his synapses clicking.

"Who did she call?" he asked.

"The Hospice. Here. She knows the regulations. She wouldn't call the local cops. So they sent out an ambulance from the Welcome Ward to bring you and Maya in."

"What happened to the car?"

"Maya's sports car? Banged up considerably. Ruined front fender. Probably need new doors. It's in a garage over in Hamlet West."

"How's Maya?"

Sweet em. I thought he'd never ask.

"Maya's doing fine. She's got a bad hand and scalp lacerations, but we can't find anything worse."

"Listen, doc, can you gloss this? I mean, I don't want to get Maya in any trouble."

It was his own muffin ass that was troubling him.

"Well. . . ." I considered thoughtfully. Frowning. Chewing my lips. "I can probably gloss it at this end. Lose the file, and so forth. As a personal favor to you. . . ."

"Oh sure, doc. I'd really appreciate it."

"Look," I said, "suppose we do this. Suppose you stay here

337

until noon tomorrow. You'll be able to gloss that at your office, won't you?''

"Well . . . maybe," he said doubtfully.

"I'll take another look at you tomorrow morning. If everything shows go, you can check out. By noon. October twentieth. Then you can consult the Medical Section at Headquarters if you need further treatment. How does that sound?"

"Sounds fine," he said. Almost laughing. "Sounds real good."

Why shouldn't it? He could make the meet with Seymour Dove.

"There's your digiwatch," I told him. "Your zipsuit, underwear, shoes, and so forth are in that closet. I have your identification, BIN card, wallet, and keys in a downstairs safe."

"Keys?" he said. "Was I driving?"

"You drove over from Washington. Your car is parked in front of Maya's apartment. I'll have it brought over here. Anything else?"

"Can I visit Maya?"

"You better stay flat on your back as much as possible if you want to get out of here tomorrow. But I'll send her in for a short visit. She's just next door."

"Good, good," he gurgled. "Maybe she can fill me in on what happened."

And maybe the anaphrodisiac was wearing off.

1845: Paul had connected two tape decks to the receiver in the back of the Rover. One was temporarily switched off, the other was operative and voice-actuated. We ran through the tape that evening.

Most of it was kaka: Roach snarling at nurses, Roach trying to lure Maya Leighton into his hospital bed for a session of rub-the-bacon. "No way," Maya said firmly. Apparently pointing to her turban bandage. "Can't you see I've got a headache?"

Roach made two phone calls. We couldn't share the entire conversations, of course—just his part. One call apparently went to his office. He explained he was personally investigating a "serious security problem" at R&R Hospice No. 4, and expected to return to Headquarters the following day.

The second call apparently went to his residence hotel. He told them he would be absent for a day, but was expecting an important phone call from a Mr. Seymour Dove. He gave the hotel his phone number at the Hospice and instructed them to tell Mr. Dove to contact him there.

I immediately called the Morse Hotel and left a message for Mr. Seymour Dove. He was to call *me* as soon as he registered.

And so the checkers went flying about the board.

October 20.

1135: I was in the Group Lewisohn offices. Paul was monitoring Roach's gimpy arm in the Rover, moved to a deserted end of the Hospice parking area.

Seymour Dove called me from the Morse. I explained the situation, told him to call Roach's hotel and then call Roach at the Hospice as he would be instructed. I asked him to give me ten minutes before making the call to Roach.

1150: I was out in the Rover with Paul when we heard Roach's phone ring. His conversation went like this:

"Harya. . . .Yeah. . . .What hotel? . . . Real good. You got it? . . .Fine. . . .No problem. . . .Be in the lobby at, oh, say 1400. I'll meet you there. . . .Yeah, 1400. . . .Right. . . .See you then."

After he hung up, I called Dove's hotel room on the Rover radiophone. I told him to meet Roach at 1400, play the role he was expected to play, and try to follow the original San Diego script as closely as he could.

"We'll be shared?" he asked.

"Yes," I said. But I didn't tell him how.

1210: I went up to Roach's room. He was already dressed, slipping his digiwatch onto his right wrist.

"Harya, doc," he said genially.

He had the splinted arm in a sling, a wide strap of plastiweb around his right shoulder.

"How does the arm feel?"

"Real good," he said. Rapping the splint with his knuckles. "No hurt at all."

I went through the stethoscope charade. Lifted his lids to peer into his eyes. Took his pulse.

"Well . . . all right," I said doubtfully. "But check with your Medical Section as soon as you get back."

"Oh, sure. Where's my bumf?"

"Right here." I handed him all his identification. He began stuffing it into his pockets. "Your car's out in front," I told him. "Take care of yourself."

He was still checking to make certain no one had raped his wallet when I walked out. I went directly to the Rover. Paul had all the equipment ready. We were away and heading toward Washington before Roach came out of the Welcome Ward.

1410: We were parked across from the Morse Hotel. We saw Art

Roach come down the street, striding purposefully. Actually, we heard him before we saw him. His arm was picking up street noise: honk of horns, screech of brakes, a siren, bits of passers-by conversation. Paul got his Instaroid movie camera fixed and focused before Roach turned in to the hotel.

We picked up a lot of lobby gabble. Interference from somewhere. Then, suddenly, voices clear enough to understand. Both tape decks were running now:

Roach: "Car accident. A kid ran out and I had to go off the road to avoid hitting him."

Dove: "My God!"

Roach: "Nothing serious. Come on outside."

In a moment, they came through the powered revolving door, Roach first. Seymour Dove was carrying an attaché case. Paul got busy with his camera, adjusting the telephoto lens. They crossed the street to the park, looking both ways.

"Good shot," Paul murmured. "Got them together."

He continued to photograph the two men. They walked through the park slowly. No conversation. Roach looked about, spotted an empty bench that apparently appealed to him. He led Dove over to it. Seymour set the attaché case down between his feet.

"Very good," I said approvingly. "Can't share a random park bench, can you, Art?"

I pulled the Rover away from the curb, circled until I found a parking space across the park, almost facing them. Paul got film on the two of them, huddling together. Then switched off the camera.

Roach: "—out in time. But it worked out real good. Mind opening your coat?"

Dove: "My coat? What for?"

Roach: "Just standard operating procedure."

We saw Seymour Dove unbutton his violet velvet topcoat. We saw Roach pat all the pockets, feel the seams.

Roach: "Now your jacket."

Dove: "What is this?"

Roach: "Just take a second. The jacket. . . ."

We saw him give Dove a quick frisk, patting pockets, waistline, trouser legs. He even bent over to feel Dove's moccasins.

Dove: "I'm not shared, if that's what you're afraid of."

Roach: "Afraid? Not me. But if you're bugged, *you* better be afraid. Did you bring it?"

Dove: "Yes. Five thousand new dollars."

Roach: "Small bills? Unmarked? Out of sequence?"

Dove: "Just the way you told me. It's in twenties."

Roach: "In the case?"

Dove: "Yes. Want to take a look?"

Roach: "Why not? Is it locked?"

Dove: "Yes."

Roach: "Just bend over casually and unlock it. Then hand it to me. Slowly."

"Get this," I said to Paul hurriedly. "It's the actual payoff."

Paul switched on the camera again. I watched Dove lift the attaché case. Roach took it from him, placed it on his lap. He opened the lid halfway, peering inside. He inserted his right hand, began pawing.

Dove: "It's all there. Five thousand new dollars."

Roach: "I know you wouldn't scam me. I'm just making sure there's nothing else in here."

Dove: "A bug? Would I do that? Listen, I'm taking an awful chance doing this."

Roach: "What do you think *I'm* taking?"

Dove: "But how do I know I'm not throwing it away? If you don't come through, Scilla Pharmaceuticals is stopped. We've made heavy investments in raw materials and new machinery. We need that contract."

Roach: "Don't worry. You'll get your contract."

Dove: "I wish I had a guarantee."

Roach: "This five thousand is your guarantee."

"What a good little boy he is," I whispered to Paul. "This time he's following the scenario."

Roach: "Can I have the case?"

Dove: "Sure. Take it. Here's the key."

Roach: "I'll return it to you."

Dove: "No need. It's yours."

Roach: "Thank you very much. Real good doing business with you." We watched the two ems stand, stroke palms. They separated, Roach carrying the case in his free hand. He walked across the park, angling away from us. Dove headed back to his hotel. We watched Roach.

"He won't go to Headquarters." Paul frowned.

"Doubt it," I agreed. "Not with the loot. He wouldn't go directly to Angela's apartment at the Watergate, would he?"

341

"I don't know," Paul said. Worrying it. "I don't think so. She wouldn't allow it."

"No. She wouldn't. Maybe he'll go directly to a bank, put it in a safe deposit box. But I don't think so. He'll want to count it. Examine it. That means his place. The Winslow on N Street. We'll lose him in this traffic if we try to follow. Want to take a gamble?"

"Sure. The Winslow it is."

We left the park, headed for N Street.

"We've got him, haven't we, Nick?" Paul said happily.

"Screwed, blewed, and tattooed," I agreed. "He's down the pipe. One down, one to go."

We were parked across the street, near the corner, when Roach drove up to the Winslow Hotel in his official black Buick. He got out, carrying the attaché case. We heard him say, "Be down in twenty minutes, Al," to the doorman. Then he went inside.

"Now what?" Paul said.

Suddenly, at his question, I felt a curious lassitude. Having come so far, I wanted to rest. Hadn't I done enough? Hadn't enough been accomplished? I had to flog my resolve, telling myself it would all be wasted if I didn't finish. But I was weary.

"Got any uppers?" I asked Paul. "Amphetamine? Anything?"

"The Pharm Team gave me a new methylphenidate. Experimental. No results yet. Want to chance it?"

"Sure," I said. "I have nothing to lose but my balls."

He fished around in his shopping bag. He came up with a plastic container of spansules as big as suppositories.

"For whales," I said. "Where's the size for humans?"

"This is them." Paul laughed.

I sighed. "Give me one. Maybe there's a water fountain in the lobby."

We had a big, horsey briefcase among our gear. We packed it with everything I thought I'd need.

"Are you still getting him?" I asked.

Paul moved his head closer to the receiver speaker. He turned up the volume, cautiously moved the tuning knob. What we heard could have been Roach moving around in his hotel room. It could have been anything. Then we heard a toilet flush.

"That's him," I said. "On my way. Get it all. If you hear anything bad, or if I don't come out within an hour, take the other tape to the Chief Director."

I started to duck out of the car. Paul pulled me back, kissed me on the lips. I was surprised. And pleased.

"Take care, Nick," he whispered.

He had said the same thing to me on the helipad of the compound when I was starting off to meet Angela Berri in her California beachhouse. Was that aeons ago? Or yesterday?

There was no water fountain in the hotel lobby. But there was a unisex nest in the cocktail lounge. I went in there, used a cupped palmful of water to bolt down the giant energizing spansule. I could almost feel it thud into my stomach.

Do something, I urged it.

I was turning to leave when an ef came out of one of the toilet booths, adjusting her skirt. She looked at me.

"I suck cocks," she said.

"Who doesn't?" I said.

It was a stuffy obso hotel, with a color photograph of the Washington Monument over the registration desk. Not the kind of place that encourages wandering about the corridors. I called Roach on the single house phone. It rang seven times before he answered.

"Yes?"

"Art Roach?"

"Yes. Who's this?"

"Flair. Dr. Nicholas Bennington Flair. I'm downstairs. I've got to see you."

"What the hell for?"

"About your condition. The results of tests we took. It's very important I see you at once."

He panicked. "Oh, my God! What is it, doc?"

"I must see you immediately. What room?"

He was standing outside his door. He practically pulled me inside.

"What is it, doc?" he demanded. "What about the tests? What's wrong with me?"

I sat down near a glass cocktail table. I set the briefcase at my feet, opened it, took out the threaded tape deck. He watched me. First in astonishment. Then warily. His attaché case was not in sight.

"Nothing wrong with you," I said. "Cracked arm. That's all. But you're strong as a horse. And not much smarter. Sit down. Something I want you to hear."

343

I stared at him. Slowly, almost tentatively, he slid into a chair at a diagonal to mine. Not across the table. Clear of the table.

I switched it on. We listened to his entire conversation with Seymour Dove. When it came to an end, I switched off the tape.

"There's another tape," I told him hastily. "Exactly like this one. Elsewhere. And films of the entire meet."

"And I suppose the bills are marked?" he said bitterly.

"What else?" I shrugged.

That was inoperative, but he couldn't be sure.

We sat in silence for at least a minute. Then he stood. I stood.

"Motherfucker!" he shouted.

It was more an expletive than an accusation.

Then he came at me. Good arm reaching for me.

I was not unmuscular, and I had a kind of desperate courage. Not quite hysterical. But even in that state it would never occur to me to strike an opponent with my fist if a more effective weapon was at hand.

I bent to slip his lunge, picked up a heavy plastilead ashtray with rounded edges. As he was starting his turn, I clipped him just to the left and low on the occipital area.

He went down, going "Houff!" Then he was still.

I replaced the undamaged ashtray on the table. I bent over him, felt for pulse and respiration, peeled back his eyelids. He was already blinking, snorting, curling up into the fetal position. I patted him over and found a weapon, a short-barreled rocket pistol.

Then I went back to my chair, sat down, lighted a Bold. My hands were trembling slightly. I abhor violence. I sat silently, staring at him.

"I'm all right, Paul," I said loudly. "Everything's fine."

After a while, Art Roach roused. He looked at me from the floor.

"You're fast," he said admiringly.

"Thank you," I said.

He glanced at his pistol on the table in front of me. No way. He climbed to his feet, staggered over to his armchair, sat down heavily. He lowered his head between his knees.

"Dumb-ass," he said dully. "I'm a dumb-ass."

I didn't say anything.

"You come here with enough to take me," he said in a grumbling voice. Shaking his head. "But you don't just take me, like you could. So you want to talk deal. Right?"

"Right," I said.

"Stupe," he said mournfully. "I've been a stupe all my life. What do you want?"

"Her," I said.

"Oh, Jesus." He groaned. "Do I gotta?"

"Yes," I said. "You gotta."

I didn't have to spell out for him what would happen if he didn't "gotta." He knew. But he was a pro and wanted to know how it had been fiddled. I told him: the phony accident, the memory block, the broken arm, the shared splint. It had been *his* arm, but he wasn't angry.

"That was *beautiful*," he breathed.

"Yes," I said. "Now let's get to it. I know she's on the suck. Where does she hide the love?"

It was an interesting story. He had been shrewd enough to keep records, figuring they'd be a bargaining factor if Angela ever decided his activities were contrary to the public interest. From that, I guessed he had his own private little scams going which she tolerated as long as he didn't become too greedy.

I had thought her method of concealing her booty would be original and complex. It proved depressingly simple. There was, it seemed, a well-organized band of thieves serving at the National Data Bank. They were all assigned to the Stopped Section where, according to law, the BIN cards of all stopped objects were returned, flamed, and their names and registration numbers erased from the master computer tape.

BINS of stopped objects flowed into the NDB at a rate of approximately 10,000 per serving day. It was not difficult for the crooks to extract from this flow certain BIN cards expressly ordered by a growing list of customers. The going price had risen to 1,500 new dollars per card.

Angela Berri had a standing order for cards of stopped efs whose age and physical description approximated hers. The stopped efs were victims of accidents, disease, murder, suicide, etc. When Angela purchased such a card—the unlawful possession of which, incidentally, made her liable for execution, under certain circumstances—she merely attached her own photo, sent Roach to a large city to open a bank account under the stopped ef's name and number.

Once a year, under her orders, he closed out each account and moved it to another bank, under new identification. This was to thwart annoying investigation by the Voluntary Contribution Commission of the Department of Profitability. They hadn't even come close to her.

Roach had a complete record of her current deposits, which he handed over to me. I also received a lengthy list of government contracts on which she had received kickbacks. And a neatly written journal of her other peculations: unlicensed dealing in grains and other foodstuffs; part ownership of a small refinery producing methanol ostensibly for sale as a solvent, though a goodly percentage of the output was diverted to a distiller producing champage; and—Angela! Shame!—ownership of a very posh, very secret Washington, D.C., bordello called, by its habitués, "The Sexual Congress." This last was, of course, completely illicit, since the US Government had a monopoly on bagnios.

That would seem to be enough, I told Art Roach, packing up my goodies. I would do everything I could to pillow his involvement in these disgraceful shenanigans. He might be called on to testify, but I doubted if that would be necessary. He might even be able to retain his rank-rate and continue to serve as Chief, Security & Intelligence, DOB.

He brightened at that.

"You'll be taking over her spot I suppose," he said. "Real good."

I looked at him in amazement.

"Whatever gave you that idea?" I said.

"Why else would you be doing this?" he asked.

I could have explained to him that Angela Teresa Berri had grievously wounded my amour propre, and in that area I was as sensitive as a Sicilian. But he would not have understood. Besides, there might be something operative to what he suggested. Not a vulgar ambition to have the title Director of Bliss. But an almost unconscious thrust for power.

I didn't answer him, but turned to go. He spoke before I reached the door.

"I told her to watch out for you," he said.

"Oh?" I said. "Why?"

"Listen," he said, "it takes one to know one."

I wasn't certain I knew what he meant by that, and didn't want to know. I took the elevator down, my spirits rising as the cage descended.

I could move mountains. Do anything. I told myself it was me, *my* talent, *my* will. But way down deep in that prune I called my heart, I knew it was partly, mostly, that experimental energizer. That wonderful whale-sized spansule. I was on air. Not walking on air. Just on air. Floating.

I leaned down to talk to Paul through the opened car window.

"That new methylphenidate . . ." I said.

"Yes?" Paul said.

"Make notes. Too euphoric. Loss of visual perception. Slight mental displacement. Some verbal slurring. No obvious impairment of muscular coordination. Improved audition. Ego inflation. Got that?"

"Yes," Paul said. "I'll remember. Want to stretch out on the back seat awhile, Nick?"

"No," I said, "I do not want to stretch out on the back seat. Did you get all the Roach stuff?"

"I did," Paul said happily. "A complete tape. That's it, isn't it, Nick?"

"That's it," I said. Climbing into the car. "That, indeed, is it."

I picked up the mobile phone, punched the numbers of the Chief Director's residence.

"Who you calling?" Paul asked.

"Grace Wingate."

"What the hell for?"

"Wheels within wheels," I said mysteriously. I tried to wink. Both eyes closed at the same time.

Mrs. Wingate wasn't at home. They refused to tell me where I might reach her.

"That reporter," I said to Paul. "Herb Bailey. What outfit does he work for?"

"Federal Syndicate."

"Right," I said. "Make another note on the new energizer. Negative memory effect."

I finally got through to Herb Bailey and asked him if he could discover the whereabouts of the Chief Director's wife.

"I probably could," he said. "Why should I?"

"Because I will then give you the scoop of a lifetime, Scoop," I said.

"Are you drunk?" he demanded.

"Of course I'm not drunk. Do me a favor, Herb. And I have got something for you."

"Fat chance," he grumbled. But he left the line open, was gone a few minutes, finally returned. "The Society Desk says she's scheduled to visit a school for retarded clones this afternoon. It's in Chevy Chase. The New Hope School."

"Thanks, Herb," I said. "I appreciate it."

"What's the something you've got for me? You running away with the Chief Director's wife? She's a prime cut."

"No," I said shortly. Displeased. "It's something else. If I give it to you, can I join the Anonymous Sources club?"

"Sure."

"Keep an eye on the Department of Bliss for the next few days," I told him. "Big shakeup due."

"No kidding?" he said. Interested now. "How big?"

"Enormous," I said, and hung up.

"Was that wise?" Paul asked.

"The Washington game." I shrugged. "Besides, I'm tired of being wise. I think I'll be foolish awhile. You better drive. In my manic mood, I'll be worse than you. I want to go to the New Hope School for Retarded Clones in Chevy Chase."

"She's there?"

"Yes. Visiting. Not enrolled."

"Should I wait for you?"

"No. You go back to the Hospice. Make a copy of that film in case of accidental erasure. And better make Instox copies of the records Roach gave me. In the briefcase. You never can tell. . . ."

"Now you're tracking," Paul said. "Where are you going after you see Grace Wingate?"

"Things to do," I said. "Worlds to conquer. I may not be back to the Hospice until tomorrow."

"When are you going to see the Chief Director?"

"Also tomorrow," I said. "It's all in the Tomorrow File."

As we drove off we heard, via Roach's broken arm, a toilet flush.

By the time Paul had located and delivered me to the New Hope School for Retarded Clones, in Chevy Chase, the giddy effects of the methylphenidate had evaporated, leaving dregs of vague anxieties and dim terrors. A year was ending. A century would soon end. I shivered inside my silverized zipsuit. I should have worn my topcoat; the wind was a knife.

There were three limousines parked at the curb. Black zipsuits stood near the cars. They inspected me coldly. Apparently I didn't look like a potential assassin; they allowed me to walk up the brick path and enter the school. The exterior was white enameled tiles. It looked like a subway station turned inside out.

I asked for the Chief Director's wife. I was told she was completing her tour and would be out soon. I waited patiently, staring at children's crayon drawings taped to the walls, wondering how old the "children" were.

She came out eventually, surrounded by a retinue of Administrative Assistants, social secretaries, guards, a few reporters, photographers.

I stood, took a step forward. She prepared to exit, glanced up. Startled. Then the fading smile grew again. She came over to me, hand outstretched. We stroked palms. I had the impression of rigidity beneath cool softness.

"Nick!" she said. With pleasure. I thought. "What are *you* doing here?"

"I must speak to you a few minutes," I murmured. "Alone. Before you get in your car. It's important. Anywhere we can go?"

Lips tightened, paled. She was wearing a smooth helmet of white felt. It covered her ears. Her hair was tucked up, out of sight. The wide-collared natural wool coat, simple as a smock, left the long stem of her neck exposed.

"There's an outdoor playground," she said. Tentatively. "Around to the side. I think it's empty now. All the—ah, children are inside. We could go there. But only for a few minutes. We have another stop to make. At an orphanage. They're expecting us."

"The playground sounds fine," I said. "It won't take long."

She went back to speak to her assistants. They looked at me doubtfully. But eventually they all filed out ahead of us. Then she led the way around a curved walk to a small, fenced playground.

We sat apart on a slatted bench. I glanced about. Already there was a black zipsuit at each of the playground's three gates. They were all regarding us gravely. For the first time I realized the full import, and danger, of what I was doing: a public tête-à-tête with the wife of the most powerful man in the US Government.

"Have things changed between you and your husband?"

"No," she said shortly. "If anything, they're worse. We had an argument last night. Screaming. I cried. I'm so ashamed. And ashamed of bothering you with my problems."

She tried to smile.

"It's still . . . *her*?"

"Yes. Nick, I don't know what she's done to him. He can't break loose. I think he wants to. Really. But she seems to have him under some kind of—of a spell. I know how foolish that must sound."

349

"No, no. Not foolish at all."

I spoke mechanically. I was computing. I had assumed Chief Director Michael Wingate was merely a victim of Angela's sexual expertise. But her ownership of an illicit bordello opened another can of worms. It would not be difficult for Angela to share the private rooms of the Sexual Congress. What a leverage that evidence might give her! Over the Chief Director, Congressmen, journalists, lobbyists, Public Service executives, judges—the whole political bestiary of Washington, D.C. She had murdered; blackmail was within her ken.

"How did it end?" I asked. "The argument?"

"It didn't end. It will go on and on. Until our marriage ends. I know."

"No," I said positively. "That's not going to happen. Take a gamble?"

Lids raised. Dark, somber eyes stared into mine.

"A gamble?" she said. Smiled suddenly. "What odds?"

"Long," I admitted. "But it's my gamble as well as yours. I'm taking it."

She stared at me a long moment. Once again her features ran that curious gamut of emotions; perplexity to sympathy to pity to . . . what?

"All right," she said. Stiffening her back. "What is it?"

"Here is what you must do . . ." I started. Coaching her. Nicholas Bennington Stanislavski Flair.

She must go to her husband that very evening. She must present him with an ultimatum. No, not an ultimatum exactly, but a declaration of her intent. Either he would agree never to see Angela Berri again, or she, Grace Wingate, would simply leave him. Pack up and walk out. I told her exactly how to conduct herself during the meeting: state her resolve, make no threats about adverse public relations, speak quietly in a firm, dignified tone, wear something sexy. But subtle. Keep the interview as short as possible. Speak her piece, tell him the decision was his to make, she loved him and wanted to continue as his wife. And he must decide within twenty-four hours. That was most important. Within twenty-four hours.

"Can you do all that?" I asked her.

"Yes," she said.

Two hours later I was seated in the cocktail lounge of the Morse Hotel. I had asked for Seymour Dove at the desk. But he had already checked out, was on his way back to San Diego. So I was drinking a vodka-and-Smack by myself. My first opportunity to spend leisure alone for many, many months. I was enjoying it.

I dined somewhere. A crowded, horrendously expensive French restaurant. It required ten new dollars slipped to the maître d' to bypass the crowd waiting to claim their reservations. The food was undeniably natural—but what was the use? The best chefs in the world couldn't compensate for its lack of flavor. Within a generation or two, the sense of taste would be as debased as the sense of smell was at that point in time. Sighing, I dug into my "baked potato." What they had done, of course, was to salvage a blackened shell, discarded by a previous diner, fill it with cheaper mashed potatoes, and shove it under a microwave broiler for a minute to give it a realistic crust.

I had two natural brandies at the restaurant bar on my way out. A black ef, wearing an obso nun's robe, scuttled through the door and succeeded in handing out small pieces of paper to several bar patrons before the maître d' and two waiters hustled her out of there. My paper read: REPANT FOR THE TIME IS AT HAND. Even the holy couldn't spell. I strolled out in an expansive mood. This was my world. Let others waste their days weeping.

I spent hours walking Washington that night. From Lafayette Park to the White House. Down Pennsylvania Avenue to the Capitol. Around to the Library of Congress. Back to the National Gallery of Art. All the way down the Mall to the Lincoln Memorial.

It was easy to feel indulgent about Washington, D.C. Despite the presence of foreign embassies, of couriers arriving and speeding off to every corner of the earth, despite its architecture—some of it incredibly gross, some incredibly elegant—Washington remained insular. A marbelized village. A company town. Its one product was government; its one raw material was power. Departments and offices and agencies and facilities had been distributed all over the US. But no one doubted where the thrones were.

Eventually, I went to a phone booth. I called Angela Berri. It was almost a reflex, an automatic response, an emotional knee-jerk. My soul had received a light tap below the patella.

Her greeting sounded fretful, weary. But after some idle chitchat, she seemed to thaw; her voice warmed.

I suggested an immediate picnic on the White House lawn.

She suggested a naked *pas de deux* on the Capitol steps.

It went on like that for a while, each suggestion topping the last in outrageous public lewdness. Finally I asked her to join me somewhere for a drink. She said she was too exhausted to consider stirring from her apartment. But she wanted very much to see me. I was to come to her Watergate apartment at once.

Which was what it was all about in the first place.

Exhausted, she may have been. Without makeup or uniform. But I saw no diminution of her unique primitive force. If anything, her languor only heightened, by contrast, the flash deep in her eyes, the electricity of her sudden gestures. She was wearing a black silk robe. Carelessly. A plain robe. It gaped at neckline and thigh. A full sleeve fell back to reveal a bare arm. That pampered body was cut into white sections. An effect at once abstract and stirring.

She gave me a straight petrovod on Jellicubes. She was not drinking, but she was smoking—something. I could not identify the odor. Not cannabis. She saw me sniffing.

"Perfumed hash." She smiled. "Want to try?"

"No," I said. "Thanks."

She smoked slowly. A small, jeweled pipe. I sipped my drink slowly. She crossed her knees. The robe fell back. One bare foot bobbed.

"I'm weary, Nick," she said suddenly. "I've begun to flip in and out. Occasionally. Is that bad?"

"Anxieties?" I asked.

"No. Not really. Nothing I can't handle. Just a—it's difficult to describe."

"Flipping in and out?" I asked.

"Reality," she said. "You play a role long enough, hard enough, and the role takes over. You're all role."

"Disorientation," I said. "Want something for it?"

"Yes," she said. Rising. Holding out her hand. "I want something for it. Come along."

None of Maya's hardware for her. Not that night. Just her depilated body and a curious need for tenderness. For warm affection. For close, protective snuggling. The ruler ruled. The master mastered.

The problem was. . . .The problem was. . . .Well, the problem was this: Was her mood operative or plotted? Was her soft languor real or structured? Was her surrender valid or scenarioed? I didn't know. For certain. And not knowing, I would have been a fool to assume anything but falsity.

That's the way we were. That's the way we all were.

No sexual sophistication that night. No tricks, gimmicks, gigs.

Just a slow, lazy petting to arousal. At one point we lay slightly apart, not touching. I could not compute the rapture.

I would have preferred her to ravage me. Absolution? That lacking, I could only serve her. I was a knight, and gathered her close. A young body came bonelessly into my arms.

Usually we laughed with delight. That night we were silent. Obediently she lay upon her back, spread silken thighs. Curled snake arms about my neck. Linked snake legs about my back. But silently, in a shy, docile manner. I penetrated her as gently as I could, as deeply. It was her mood.

There was some illumination from the nest light. I arched my back to see her face. Eyes closed. Lips slightly parted. Gleam of wet teeth.

"Don't go away from me," she murmured.

I bent to scrape my new mustache and beard across her breasts. She responded to that; I could feel her return. From wherever she had been. She had no right to try to escape. We are all here. Fingernails rived my shoulders. Legs tightened.

She was velvet on steel: the languor suffused with steamed blood she could not deny. But no further murmurings, whispers, cries, moans. In silence, deliberately, we used each other, sensing when our rhythm was one.

I don't know how long we lasted. A lifetime, I suppose. Eventually, of course, we could no longer control our deliberation. Our rhythm controlled us; conscious will eroded. My fingers slid to join my penis. I had one wild, frightening impulse to tear her apart. But that was gone almost as quickly as I recognized it.

Our summit was calm, satisfying. Certainly for me. And, I believed, for her. We flowed together in a kind of dance. Her extended arms and legs now feebly stroking the air. My pelvis squirming in rut. Open mouths were slicked together; tongues beat a slow tattoo. Good-bye. Good-bye.

Y-12

Early the next morning I took a cab back to the Hospice in Alexandria. I found Paul, Mary, Maya, and Seth Lucas having breakfast together in the cafeteria. I drew a plasticup of black coffee and joined them, pulling up a chair.

"How's Lewisohn, Seth?" I asked.

"Well . . . all right."

"What does that mean—'Well . . . all right?' "

"Count's up. Just a bit. Not appreciably. Not significantly."

"How often do you take it?"

"Every eight hours."

"Take it every four. Keep me informed. Mary and Paul and I will be leaving this morning."

"Everything all right, Nick?" Paul asked.

"Everything's fine," I assured him. And then. "Coming up roses. Load the limousine. We'll be starting back this afternoon."

I showered, shaved, trimmed beard and moustache, donned a fresh zipsuit. With decorations. I waited until Dr. Seth Warren was about to start his rounds, then requested the use of his office. I told him I would soon be gone. He happily granted my request. I knew I made him nervous. But then life made him nervous.

I had decided to start with Chief Director Michael Wingate's Administrative Assistant, a capable ef named Penelope Mapes. The headquarters of the Chief Director were located in the obso Executive Office Building. Since the Presidency had been reduced to what was essentially a ceremonial role, the White House was completely adequate for the Chief Executive's activities.

I sat behind Dr. Warren's cluttered desk and flashed the Executive Office Building. When an operator came on screen, I identified myself and asked to speak to Administrative Assistant Mapes.

"Just a moment, please, sir," the operator said.

I saw her punch buttons furiously. But Penelope Mapes didn't come on screen. Instead, I got an em I recognized, although I had never met him personally. His name was Theodore Seidensticker III. His title—unlikely anywhere except in Washington, D.C.— was Executive Assistant in Charge of Administration to the Administrative Assistant.

I identified myself as he inspected my silver zipsuit and decorations. I asked to speak to Penelope Mapes.

"Sorry, Dr. Flair," he said stiffly. "The Administrative Assistant is not available."

"Not available." That meant she was in conference, in the nest, ill, nursing a hangover, stopped, or under the desk of Theodore Seidensticker III enjoying a little *fellatio alla veneziana*. That last remark suggests my mood of the moment.

I then asked to speak directly to Chief Director Michael Wingate. Seidensticker looked at me pityingly. He said that was quite impossible. The Chief Director was in conference and had a full calendar for the remainder of the day. Checkmate. We sat and stared at each other.

The Executive Assistant in Charge of Administration to the Administrative Assistant was a tall, bony, sniffy character with a cold, Brahminical look. Even his posture was designed to demonstrate his uprightness. He was reputed to be the Lord High Executioner of Wingate's court. I decided, that moment, he was just the em for me.

I explained, as briefly as I could, that I had a matter of the greatest urgency to lay before the Chief Director. A matter of the greatest sensitivity. Allegations had been brought to my attention indicating conduct inimical to the public interest by an object high—very high—in the Chief Director's administration.

He didn't consider, hesitate a moment, or ask any questions. It was evidently a situation with which he was not unfamiliar.

"I will see you at 1200 precisely, Dr. Flair," he said tonelessly. "Please bring whatever documentation you have in your possession."

We left the Hospice amidst fond farewells. I stroked the palms of Warren and Lucas. I kissed Maya's cheek. I promised to return as soon as possible. A prospect that sent Warren into a paroxysm of blinking, pate-stroking, lip-gnawing.

Mary parked the limousine at the curb outside the Executive Office Building. I told Paul I expected to be an hour, no longer. He agreed to wait right there, in case I was finished earlier. I marched into the building, carrying my loaded briefcase. Ted the Stick was faithful to his word; he saw me at precisely 1200. *Precisely*.

I had prepared my story. I told him that a month previously I had been visited by the chief executive of Scilla Pharmaceuticals of San Diego. A drug manufacturer with whom SATSEC had had lovable dealings in the past. He had claimed he was the victim of extortion by Art Roach, Chief, Security & Intelligence, Department of Bliss. If he paid off Roach, he was guaranteed a government contract. I had advised Scilla to play along. A meeting was arranged, the Scilla president was shared, and this was the result.

I then played the Art Roach-Seymour Dove tape for Theodore Seidensticker III. Watching his face as we listened. No change of expression on those horsey features.

I had then, I went on, confronted Art Roach with the evidence of his criminal behavior. He had been immediately contrite, even tearful, but claimed he had attempted the shakedown under direct orders of Angela Teresa Berri, Director of Bliss. Since she ruled him, he followed her orders, knowing what he was doing was contrary to the public interest, but fearing to disobey her. His career was at stake. To prove his horror and disgust of her illicit activities, he had compiled a record of her infamy. This he had delivered to me voluntarily, trusting in the mercy of those who would judge his own participation in her nefarious schemes.

I then placed the remaining evidence before Seidensticker: the list of fiddled contracts, grain deals, the methanol refinery ripoff, ownership of the Sexual Congress. He donned steel-rimmed spectacles to scan the documents slowly and carefully. Perhaps I imagined it, but I thought his thin lips pressed thinner still when he learned of Angela's proprietorship of the bordello. Could Ted the Stick be a regular customer? (Every Thursday evening. 1800 to 1900. Precisely.)

Finally he pushed the material away with the tips of bloodless fingers. Ugh. Dirty stuff. He took off his glasses, massaged the bony bridge of his nose.

"If possible, sir," I said, "I would like to ask for compassion for Art Roach. He is not an intelligent em. I believe his story, that he acted as he did under orders."

I owed Roach nothing. But he had certain specialized talents that might be of use to me in the future. It was worth one tentative effort to save him.

"Roach isn't important," Seidensticker said. Voice of doom. "Angela Berri is."

"Can it be glossed, sir?" I asked anxiously. "Allow her to resign for reasons of personal health?"

He pursed those knife lips, considered the matter gravely. A gourmet inspecting a menu.

"It might be possible to gloss," he acknowledged, "if it was not for that distressing business involving the National Data Bank. That gang must be cleaned out, and all their customers taken. With so many objects involved, it will be almost impossible to put a pillow on the affair. No, I'm afraid Angela Berri must pay the penalty prescribed by law."

He didn't smack his lips. Exactly.

He leaned toward the flasher, punched a number. Three digits. I couldn't see the screen from where I was seated, but it was obvious to whom he was speaking.

"Sorry to interrupt the Chief Director, sir," he said in a lackey's voice. "But something of the utmost urgency has come up. I have Dr. Nicholas Flair with me, and—"

"Who?"

"Flair. Dr. Nicholas Flair. Deputy Director of Satisfaction Section, Department of Bliss. He has brought a matter to my attention that I believe demands the Chief Director's immediate decision, sir."

Michael Wingate's office was impressive. And quite unlike his home. It occupied half of the top floor of the EOB. Cold, futuristic decor and furnishings. It was divided roughly into thirds. A serving area: plastisteel desk, swivel chairs, maps and charts on the walls, flashers, phones, Telex printers, etc. A sitting area with a chromium cocktail table, inflated chairs and sofa, radio and television sets. A dining area: a glass table large enough to seat eight, pantry, a well-equipped bar, a stereo set with a screen for film cassettes.

Seidensticker knocked on the outer door and waited for the "Come in!" before he entered. I followed a few paces back. The Chief Director was in the "parlor" area, seated on the inflated couch alongside a short, plump, obso hausfrau. I recognized her at once from newsphotos and TV appearances: Sady Nagle, Deputy Chief Director for Domestic Affairs. (When her appointment was up for confirmation, a Congressional critic grumbled, "My God, she's so ugly she couldn't have had a domestic affair in her whole life.")

The Chief Director rose to greet us. He nodded at Ted the Stick, then turned to me with a strained smile. The pleasant, twinkling Santa Claus was gone. He seemed to me an em under considerable strain. I could guess the reason for his tension. The twenty-four hours his wife had given him were ticking away.

"Nick," he said. "Good to see you again."

"My profit, sir," I said.

He introduced me to Sady Nagle. She was across the room. I bowed in her direction. She smiled sweetly, bobbed a great mass of iron-gray hair. She was so ugly she was charming.

"Nick, entertain Sady for a few minutes, will you? Mix a drink if you like or ring for the steward.''

He and Seidensticker went back to the office area. The Chief Director sat down heavily behind his desk. The Executive Assistant was carrying my briefcase. He stood at Wingate's elbow and began to lay out the evidence: tapes, film, lists, journals, notebooks. He leaned far over Wingate, whispering, whispering. . . .

''May I get you a drink, Miss Nagle?'' I asked.

''Sady,'' she said. In an unexpectedly hoarse, emish voice. ''Tea would be nice. For that you push the little button over there by the pantry door. Then Tommy comes in. He knows how I like my tea. In a real glass. And whatever you want.''

I did as she instructed. I pressed the little button, a red steward appeared immediately, listened to my request, nodded, disappeared.

''Come sit here,'' Sady Nagle called to me. Patting the couch beside her. ''You're really a doctor?''

''Really.''

''So tell me, Nick . . .'' she went on. ''I can call you Nick?''

''Of course.''

''Tell me, Nick, what kind of a doctor are you? Head? Foot? Stomach? Heart? A professor maybe?''

''All kinds,'' I told her.

''Good.'' She smiled approvingly. ''So tell me, doctor, what do you recommend for an endless headache?''

''Two aspirins every four hours,'' I said. ''Endlessly.''

She laughed until her face was pink.

Her tea was brought, and my iced Smack. We had a most enjoyable conversation. I had never met an object who could *listen* as well as she. She asked personal questions about my birthplace, my parents, why I wasn't married. But never did I feel she was prying; I felt she *cared*.

She was said to be a political genius, the one object in the US perfectly attuned to the wants, needs, ambitions, and dreams of the political heirarchy and the public. And to their sins and weaknesses. I could believe it. It seemed difficult to withhold a confidence from her, and impossible to deceive her. I think her gift, in addition to that ugly, grandmotherly appearance, was that she could never represent a threat. She was sympathetic, disarming, and so worldly-wise and understanding that if I had suddenly blurted out, ''Sady, I have just betrayed an ef I admire,'' she might pat my arm and say, ''You shouldn't have done that, sonny.'' And I would then be less

358

horrified by my deed than by the realization that I had diminished her good opinion of me.

"Nickola," she whispered. Leaning close. "What you and the Stick brought up . . . it's serious?"

I nodded.

"I knew," she said sadly. "I could tell. The poor boy is so upset today. His stomach? I asked him. But he said no, it's not his stomach. Not his feet. It's his wife, no?"

"Partly," I said. I could keep nothing from her.

"That poor girl," she said sorrowfully. "So lovely. I tell you, Nickola, what we women have to put up with you wouldn't believe."

I was rescued by the Chief Director. In a cracked, almost angry voice, he called, "Nick, would you come over here a moment, please."

When I got to the desk, he was standing at a window, staring out.

"Does Angela know anything of this?" Wingate asked. Tonelessly. "Is she aware that *you* know?"

"No, sir," I said. "Not to my knowledge."

We stood there silently another minute. At least. Then the Chief Director turned to us slowly. I hoped I might never again see an object's face so tortured. He was a stranger, twisted out of shape. Blank eyes looked at me without seeing. Then slid over to his hatchet.

"Take her," he said harshly.

An hour later I was curled up on the back seat of my limousine. The radio was on, turned low. The current jerk-and-jag star, Jock Rot, was singing, "If you don't like my artichoke, please don't shake my bush." I went to sleep to that.

I slept all the way to Manhattan Landing. It was a good sleep, deep and dreamless. At the guardhouse of the compound I picked up an urgent message from Ellen Dawes, asking I flash her the moment I returned.

We left Mary to return the equipment to the night duty officers and the limousine to the motor pool. Paul and I went up to my office.

Paul kicked off his shoes, sprawled wearily on my couch. I stood behind my desk, flipping quickly through the red messages.

"Satisfaction Rate is down point five," I said.

Paul groaned.

I tossed the messages aside. Sat down in my swivel chair, put my feet up on the desk. Paul and I drank in silence. I don't know why we didn't feel more elation. We had done what we set out to do.

"Will you get DIROB?" Paul asked. Languidly.

"No," I said. "I don't think so. Directorships are in the political realm. I don't have enough clout."

"Surely you'll get *something* out of it?"

"I got what I wanted," I said. "Didn't you?"

He didn't answer.

I finally called Ellen Dawes. She said Phoebe Huntzinger had been trying to contact me all day. Phoebe had said it was very, very important, and I was to flash her at any hour of the day or night, whenever I returned.

"Thanks, Ellen," I said. "I'll flash her right now. Sorry to bother you."

I switched off long enough to break the connection, then switched on again and punched the number of the Denver Field Office.

"What is it?" Paul asked.

"Phoebe Huntzinger in Denver," I said. "Probably about Project Phoenix. Says it's important."

Paul got up, came around to stand behind me, watching the flasher screen. The Denver Field Office operator came on. I asked for Phoebe Huntzinger.

"Yes, *sir*, Dr. Flair!" She grinned. "At once, Dr. Flair, sir!"

"Now what the hell?" I muttered.

The flasher flicked to a scene of bedlam. A mob in the background. Shouts, calls, laughter, screams. Total confusion. A naked ef dancing about.

"Jesus Christ!" Paul said. "Have they gone mad?"

Then Phoebe was on screen. Grinning and more than slightly drunk. Holding a plastiglass of something.

"Nick!" she screamed. "Nick, you old fart!"

She was bumped, shoved. Objects kept poking their heads over her shoulders to get on camera.

"Phoebe," I yelled, "what the hell is this? What's happening?"

Someone shoved a piece of computer printout at her. She held it close to the flasher camera eye. Our screen filled with print. Paul and I leaned forward to see.

XXXXXX I XXXXXX

XXXX I FEEL XXXXX

XXX I FEEL GOD XXX

XXXXXXXXXXXXXXXX

We scanned it. Looked at each other. Realization growing.

"Phoebe!" I screamed. "Phoebe!"

The printout was jerked away. She was grinning at me again.

"We did it, daddy!" she yelled. "We really did! The first declarative sentence! A conception! Brain to computer printout! Untouched by human hands!"

" 'I feel god'?" I repeated. "What is—"

"No, no!" she screamed. "It's a little booboo in the circuitry. 'God' wasn't fed into the memory bank. It should be 'good.' 'I feel good.' We can correct it. No problem. A little slippage. 'I feel good.' We did it, Nick!"

"Put it up there again," I yelled at her.

She held up the computer printout.

XXX I FEEL GOD XXX

Paul was laughing now. I was too. Everything we had bottled up for days, weeks, months came bubbling out. All our disappointments, fears, tensions, anxieties, terrors. All released. We hugged each other, roaring, screaming, tossing papers into the air, dancing wildly, stamping our feet.

XXX I FEEL GOD XXX

We had done it. Done it! Picked up an object's thought and printed it. Negated will. Tapped the brain. We were all one now. All one!

XXX I FEEL GOD XXX

BOOK Z

Z-1

Chief Director Michael Wingate sent me an Instox copy of Angela Teresa Berri's voluntary statement. It was delivered by courier and stamped "FYEO-S&D" on every page. For Your Eyes Only—Scan and Destroy.

Clipped to the sheaf of manuscript was a small, handwritten note: "Thanx. M. W." So apparently he was appreciative of my service.

I saved the mss. for late-night scanning, in the privacy of my apartment. I had succeeded in purchasing a case of natural beer, allegedly of Dutch origin, from a black-market pusher. The entire case was chilling on the bottom shelf of my fridge. Scanning Angela's *mea culpa* seemed as good an occasion as any to sample my treasure.

The medical report attached to Angela's statement described an ef of basically good health, in a somewhat debilitated state. At some point in the past, she had been hysterectomized and had undergone plastic surgery for the implantation of polyurethane sacs of silicone gel to increase the rotundity of her buttocks. I had not been aware of either operation.

The psychological diagnosis listed strong competitive drive, oral orientation, possible narcissism, positive self-esteem, and other labels of a similarly general nature. The final notation—"severe depressive anxiety"—was, I would say, normal under the conditions in which she had found herself following her arrest. But the citation of severe depressive anxiety served another purpose. As I well knew. It justified treatment by cocaine or some other alkaloid to relieve the symptoms. The report ended as I knew it would: "Subject signed Informed Consent Statement voluntarily." Of course.

In 1998, the judicial system of the US operated approximately as it had for 200 years. An object charged with a serious criminal offense was tried by a jury of his peers in a public court. However, in 1991, the Public Security Control Act created an additional court within the federal judiciary. It was designed to deal solely with crimes against public security or prejudicial to the public interest. Trials under the PSCA were held *in camera*. Rather than a jury, the verdict was decided by a board of appointed judges whose security clearance was sufficiently high to enable them to hear and consider evidence of a sensitive nature. Appeal could be made through higher channels in a manner similar to that specified in the Code of Military Justice. But in the great majority of public security cases, especially those involving objects in Public Service, full confessions with a signed and witnessed Informed Consent Statement reduced most trials to an automatic plea of guilty before a single judge.

That was what happened to Angela Teresa Berri. Her sentence, as prescribed by law: "To be determined in such a manner as to maximize the convicted object's future usefulness and benefit to the State." The trial judge, after accepting and recording the guilty plea, invariably released the corpus of the convicted object to the US Government's Chief Prosecutor. That officer, in turn, usually transferred the corpus to the Public Service Department in which the object had been a member. The convicted object was then assigned to "service of the greatest public benefaction."

I opened another bottle of that delightfully biting beer and began scanning Angela's statement. It had been transcribed from dictated tapes. There was a great deal in it that was discontinuous, some that was irrational, and some merely gibberish. Considering the conditions under which the statement had been given, that was understandable.

I turned first to that portion of Angela's confession dealing with the conspiracy of the Society of Obsoletes, previously described in this record. I was concerned as to Angela's account of my activities and involvement in that affair. But nothing she said implied any serious improprieties on my part. In fact, she gave me generous credit in helping thwart the plot of Dr. Thomas J. Wiley, *et al.*

I then started at the beginning and scanned straight through. Finishing the manuscript and my fourth bottle of beer just before 0200. It was interesting. Not only had she murdered Frank Lawson Harris, but she had manipulated the suicide of her husband when she was eighteen.

Her ownership of the Washington, D. C., bordello, the Sexual Congress, was a fairly recent business venture. It had not been used for overt blackmail attempts, although she was aware of the membership. She had a few other minor scams going of which Art Roach was unaware.

There was no mention of her relationship with Chief Director Michael Wingate. But of course I might have been supplied an edited copy of her statement.

The final page of the manuscript was a copy of a document assigning the corpus of Angela Teresa Berri to Hospice No. 17 for "service of the greatest public benefaction." This Hospice was a small facility, near Little Rock, Arkansas, that was, and had been for many years, engaged in a single project: the chemical synthesis of human blood. I scanned their reports regularly. The most recent had announced the survival of a human subject for twenty-two hours following complete transfusion of a newly formularized fluid.

Incidentally, the assignment to Hospice No. 17 was signed by the new Director of the Department of Bliss. He was Chapman, the fussy little bookkeeper type who had formerly been DEPDIRPRO. I told Paul I was not disappointed. But I may have been.

Four days after the Congressional elections, Paul and I received invitations to a dinner party to be held at the Chief Director's residence in Georgetown, to honor B. Anthony Chapman, the new Director of the Department of Bliss. Such an invitation was a polite command. In the lower left-hand corner of the card was printed "Decorations, *s'il vous plaît*." From which I inferred this was to be a gathering of official guests only: all Public Service. If civilians had been invited, the instruction on expected dress would have included "Red tie, *s'il vous plaît*."

Paul and I discussed our travel arrangements. We agreed that guests would probably include the Chief Director's personal staff, directors of all Public Service departments, section deputy directors of Bliss, and some division assistant deputy directors. We would be fools to arrive at this august assemblage in a battered, dusty cab after having taken the air shuttle to Washington. We opted for a drive down in my limousine. Chauffeured, of course.

En route, we reviewed our options on the Ultimate Pleasure pill. We agreed it was no longer a go/no-go decision; the problem now was how to formulate the directive to the Houston Field Office, what parameters to set for the new drug they were to develop.

"By its very nature it would have to be addictive," I pointed out. "In any social context. To be of any value. Psychologically addictive, if not physiologically."

"Physiologically addictive," Paul said definitely. "*Must* be. You know the numbers on cannabis, amphetamines, barbiturates. We're looking for a universal drug. That demands physiological addiction."

"Well . . ." I said slowly. "I suppose you're right. Psychological addiction is too chancy. But we want a formula with a constant effect. Something that doesn't produce tolerance. Easily self-administered. That means ingestion or inhalation."

"You're ruling out the needle?"

"Aren't *you?*" I said. Surprised.

"No. Nick, I think you're missing an important factor here: administration of the UP as ritual or ceremony. Popping a pill or sniffing an inhaler can't do it. But the needle can. Penetrating the corpus. A sacred rite. It needn't be intravenous; a subcutaneous injection would serve as well. Better. But there should be a period of preparation required, sanctified or holy equipment, a *process* of administering the drug as involved and satisfying as taking communion. Nick, we've got to PR this thing. Part of the jerk must come from the act itself."

"Any suggestions?"

"Yes," he said determinedly. "I ultimize the UP as something like those disposable one-shot morphine Syrettes they put in first-aid kits. Needle attached. Sterile. No danger of serum hepatitis. The UP shot attractively packaged, difficult to unwrap. This must take time. The used container must be turned in before a new one is awarded. To help prevent OD's."

"Awarded?" I picked up on that. "Is that how you see it, Paul? As an award?"

"Has to be," he said firmly. "For any service that benefits the state. To mildify terrorism. To reward increased production or consumption. To ensure military discipline. Whatever might be in the public interest. Production and distribution rigidly controlled. Public execution for illegal manufacture, sale or possession. It might even be used as a reward for limiting procreation. Another factor in the Z-Pop campaign."

I looked at him with something like wonder.

"You've really been computing this," I said.

"Yes." He nodded. "I have. I see it as cocaine-based. If we can't get Bolivia or Peru into the US, we can cultivate the shrub in factory-farms. In addition to the coke, we'll want an addictive factor. That's where it gets dicey. Almost any addictive factor will add a tolerance problem. But I think we can strike a risk-benefit balance. And an aphrodisiac. Perhaps an orgasmic trigger. It's going to be one hell of a cocktail. Can I get Houston moving on a crash basis?"

"Crash away," I said. "Top priority, top security. Weekly reports. Send me an Instox of your directive."

"Will do," he said happily. "Now we're moving. Nick, I—" He stopped suddenly. I turned to stare at him.

"Well?" I asked.

"It's something for the Tomorrow File."

"Oh? What is it?"

"I don't think you're going to like it."

"Come on, Paul, don't play cozy with me."

"Well, it's not actually my idea. It's Mary Bergstrom's idea. With an assist from Maya Leighton."

"Mary? Maya? What the hell *is* it?"

"Well, when we were all down in Alexandria, the night you disappeared after you braced Art Roach, I took the two efs and Seth Lucas out to dinner. Talk got around to Z-Pop. I explained how difficult it was to achieve when longevity rates were increasing every year."

"Paul, I hope this doesn't concern euthanasia for obsoletes. You know it's politically inexpedient."

"No, no. Not euthanasia. I explained the arithmetic of population growth to them, how a reduced fertility rate is nullified if life span continues to increase. So then we started talking about longevity. Mary said longevity was primarily characterological. Inherited trait. Then Maya said, if it was genetic in origin, why couldn't it be engineered? Nick, we all started talking at once. Maya said, to her knowledge, no one has ever done any heavy research on the chromosome pairs that carry the long-life genes. Mary said she saw no reason why they couldn't be identified and manipulated. She futurized a predetermined life span. Adjustable to the needs of society. Nick? Reactions?''

"Yesss," I said slowly. "For the Tomorrow File."

"And it's definitely *not* euthanasia," Paul said triumphantly.

There were as many black zipsuits as guests milling about the barred gate to the Georgetown White House. There was no relaxation of security precautions. Invited guests and wives, husbands, children, relations, users, friends—all, one by one, filed through the metal detector, showed BIN cards and invitations, were identified by voiceprint or vouched for on closed-circuit TV.

Then up the driveway to the steel-paneled door. Inching along the reception line. Chief Director Michael Wingate. Grace Wingate. Director of Bliss B. Anthony Chapman. Mrs. Chapman. A fluttery ef with the face of a parrot. Rapid palm strokes. Smiles. Move along. Murmured phrases.

Then into the gathering crush. All doors thrown wide. Black zipsuits bearing trays. Paul shoved his way through; I followed in his wake. Pausing to stroke palms. Smile.

"Paul, I need a drink."

"Here. In here."

He elbowed. Pushing. He would have his way. He drew me to a bar. His eyes were shining. There he was. Being entertained in the home of the Chief Director of the US Government. Mama would have been so *proud*. I looked at him closely. Who *was* he?

"Nick, what's wrong?"

"Nothing's wrong."

"You look so strange."

"My genial, party look."

"There's Sady Nagle! There. Over there."

"Would you like to meet her?"

"Of course. They say . . ."

Noise increased. In volume and intensity. And heat. The crush. I lost Paul. I found myself with an empty glass. Edging back toward a bar. Then I was dancing with Theodore Seidensticker III, sliding in the opposite direction. We did a mad tango, revolving to get around each other.

"Ah there," he said. He did something with his face. I think he intended it to be a friendly smile. It frightened me.

"What happened to Roach?" I asked him.

"Who? Oh. Very cooperative. Demoted. Fined."

"Thank you," I said piously.

We scraped past. I had a terrible urge to goose him. I envisioned him suddenly plunging forward. Outraged and shaken. The full glasses he was carrying splashing on an ef wearing a tooty evening gown with portholes through which bare breasts bulged strabismically.

The doors of the dining room were thrown wide. The buffet awaited. Disposable food. Come and get it!

Objects were so deliberately casual. What a jerk! The slow saunter. Not really caring. Hunger was vulgar. Then the nonchalant inspection. Then the heaped plate. Where *was* she? I searched the crowd.

"Are you Nick Flair?"

"I am. Penelope Mapes?"

"Yes. The Chief Director's AA. I've been wanting to meet you."

A short, plump ef, downy as a bird. Enormously efficient at her service. It was said. But at this moment flushed, breathless. Her palm stuck.

"He speaks so highly of you."

"He's very kind."

She pushed or was pushed tightly against me. I thought her pneumatic. If her pudendum was depressed, her buttocks would expand. Compress her bicep, and the fingers would swell. Penetrate her with a respectful rod and, hissing faintly, the corpus would deflate in your arms. An empty envelope of skin smelling faintly of lavender.

I didn't like this party. Where *was* she?

"He speaks so highly of you," Penelope Mapes repeated throatily. Eyes glazed. Staring at my beard.

"Would you like a ringlet?" I asked. "To tuck beneath your pillow?"

"Oh, *you!*" she said.

Paul rescued me by squeezing nearby. I reached out, dragged him close, pushed the two together, introduced. Paul was delighted. The Chief Director's Administrative Assistant!

"Oh, *you!*" she was saying as I slid away.

The thought of heaping a plastiplate with that gelatinous food was more than I could endure. I had another vodka-and-Smack.

I stroked many palms. Supinely with departmental directors. Vertically with deputy directors. Pronely with assistant deputy directors. Joe Wellington, the Chief Director's PR Chief, insisted on shaking hands. As his left hand gripped my right arm just above the elbow. Numbing.

"Nick baby!" he said.

"Joe baby!" I said.

A billow of cannabis smoke parted and there she was. Centered in a semicircle. More a golden chemise than a sheath. Quite short. Bare arms. Bare legs. Golden sandals. Ashen hair bound up in a high swirl. The completed nakedness apparent. Lips parted. The teeth. Glistening. Head slightly lowered to listen to the em beside her.

She was wasting herself on him. On them. On everyone but me. Dark, somber eyes rose and caught my stare. Lips bowed in a quick smile. She looked slowly away. That brief lock of glances cut into. . . .

"Nick!" the Chief Director shouted. "So glad you could make it!"

He was Santa Claus again. Perhaps that had been Angela's fatal flaw. She had one role that devoured her. This em flipped a dozen masks off and on. Quik-change.

"Marvelous party, sir," I said.

"Is it?" he said. Chuckling. "Not when you're giving it! Got enough to eat and drink?"

"Plenty," I assured him.

"Good, good. Paul Bumford here?"

"Yes, sir."

"Find him, will you? Both of you upstairs in about fifteen minutes. Second door on your right."

"Yes, sir."

"Hello, hello, hello!" he caroled. Bouncing away. Stroking every palm in sight. Touching. Patting. Feeling. Pressing. Physical contacts for everyone. I turned to search for her, but the cannabis curtain was down.

"What's this about?" Paul asked.

"I have no idea," I said.

We trudged up the stairs. Second door on the right. A black zipsuit inspected us coldly.

"Do we knock?" I said. "Or walk right in?"

"Both," Paul said. He rapped sharply, paused a second, opened the door. We entered. I closed the door respectfully behind us.

It was, I supposed, an upstairs sitting room. Small. Cluttered with odds and ends of obso furniture. Many chairs. Many. Two couches. Stained prints on the walls.

Chief Director Michael Wingate. Deputy Chief Director for Domestic Affairs Sady Nagle. Administrative Assistant Penelope Mapes. Assistant to the Administrative Assistant in Charge of Administration Theodore Seidensticker III. Chief of Public Relations Joseph Wellington. All of them suddenly sober, suddenly solemn.

"Sit anywhere," Wingate commanded. Short, abrupt gesture. Santa Claus had departed. Genghis Khan had returned.

Paul and I listened in silence to what he had to say.

He told us the prospectus for the new Department of Creative Science—which he understood was the result of our joint efforts—had been distributed for comment. To certain selected objects in Public Service, Congress, the judiciary. Also, to objects in the highest echelons of academe, science and law, labor and industry, organized religion, and consumer/environmental Gruppen.

"Although I myself was high on the DCS—" Wingate said. Somewhat wryly. "—it was necessary to test the political viability of the product. Too many causes lost—even just causes—engender an impression of ineffectuality. Not only in others, but in oneself."

I began to appreciate this em's talents and experience.

He continued, looking mostly at me, but shifting his glance occasionally to Paul. His assistants sat mute, regarding us both without expression.

Wingate said initial reaction to the concept of a Department of Creative Science had been almost universally favorable. But the great majority of advocates—even those most enthusiastically supportive of the role of science and technology—were troubled and/or dismayed by what they considered to be our alarmist predictions of the future. What he wanted to learn, Wingate said, was had we included those predictions of extreme change in an effort to bolster our case? If we had, he felt we were guilty of oversell. Or did we sincerely believe tomorrow would produce the problems we had envisioned, necessitating the solutions we had suggested?

"Sir," I said, "new problems demand new answers."

"Sonny," Sady Nagle said. In the kindliest of tones. "Even if those terrible things you predict should happen—and I'm not saying you're all wrong; some of them I can see starting today—you suggest such radical solutions you scare us. Because what you suggest, sonny, is impossible. Just impossible."

370

"Why impossible?" Paul demanded.

"First of all, sonny," she said, turning to him, "some of your ideas are illegal. Just that—illegal. Other ideas, which may be legal, are a spit in the face of what remains in this little country of morality, religion, tradition, and social order."

"I don't think you understand," Paul said hotly. "I don't think any of you really understand. You just don't grasp what we're trying to tell you. And that is what President Morse said ten years ago: This society is obsolete. It's creaking along, parts falling off, levers jamming, fuses blowing, the whole outmoded mechanism coming to a shuddering halt."

It was too late to switch him off or try to mollify what he was saying. He was on his feet now. Pacing. His voice louder. They were all listening intently. Following him with their eyes as he strode about the room.

"Illegal?" he demanded. "Then change the laws. Tradition? As ephemeral as slavery and dueling. Morality? Someone said it's all a matter of time and geography. Religion? Valuable, but only as a function of the state. Social order? It is what the government says it is. Yes, the solutions we propose are radical. Or may appear radical. Because the problems are new. Have never been faced before. Zero population growth. Energy crunch. World-wide terrorism. Ecological decay. Genetic engineering. Nuclear blackmail. All relatively new problems. That not only demand new solutions, as Nick said, but demand a new way of computing. Of seeing the interdependence of all human activities. A lot of things that have been cherished for a long, long time will have to go. *Must* go! There are no absolutes. Free elections? Free speech? The Bill of Rights? Freedom of worship? Personal privacy? They've all been restricted during times of crisis. And they are all relatively young concepts. Some of them less than two hundred years old. They worked well for that timespan. But we can no longer afford them. We must compute new concepts, a new Bill of Rights, to see us through the approaching crisis. And it is coming. As certainly as I know the reality of our presence here, in this room, I know it is coming. And the only way to even begin to cope is to put away the slogans of yesterday, the shibboleths of today's political system and social organization. I put it to you this way: Is there one of you who would not voluntarily relinquish your individual freedom if, by relinquishing that freedom, you helped guarantee the survival of the human species? That is not just a 'what if' question. It is an exact statement

371

of the choice we may some day soon be facing. Yes, Nick and I suggested a radical program. Because only strange new ideas can ensure the survival of our society. Of our species. That is what we're really talking about—survival. The Department of Creative Science will be the first step toward bringing science and technology into a policymaking role in the US Government. Reject it, and you reject the future.''

He ended suddenly. I could hear the sounds of the party downstairs: laughter, cries, music, the stomp of dancers. But in that frowsy room, silence banged off the walls. No one moved.

Finally, Chief Director Michael Wingate drew a great breath. He looked about slowly. Not seeking reactions, but reassuring himself as to place and time. Then his eyes came to Paul and stayed there.

"What I shall say," he stated in a low, firm voice, "does not imply concurrence with everything Paul said. Nor should my total agreement with his views be inferred. However, I have decided to go ahead with exploring the most feasible scenario for establishing a new Department of Creative Science. I ask you all to submit your ideas to me as soon as possible. I thank you for your close attention. I suggest we now return to the party, singly or in twos. So as not to attract attention or comment. Thank you.''

Paul and I were the last to leave. He was still shaking. I thought it best not to say anything at the moment. We rejoined the throng downstairs. We were separated.

I wandered through the thinning crowd. Objects were waving, calling, departing. I smiled my way into that chintzy sitting room. John Quincy Adams' third eye had been repaired.

Then fingers touched my wrist.

"Nick," Grace Wingate said. Somewhat breathlessly. "I haven't had a chance to thank you.''

I looked down upon that soft hand laid upon my arm. She drew me gently into an alcove. We were both smiling determinedly: hostess and guest in a polite and inconsequential dialogue.

"I don't know how you did it," she said, "and I don't want to know. But she's gone, Nick. She's gone!''

I nodded.

"I don't know how I can ever repay you," she said.

"You look lovely, Grace," I told her.

Too ingenuous to accept praise casually. Her hand rose automatically to her gathered hair. Fingers poked at floating tendrils. I thought she flushed with pleasure, suddenly conscious of her body. She glanced down at the glittering overskin.

"Nick, is it—is it too—"

"No," I assured her gravely. "It isn't too."

If she was suddenly conscious of her body, I was suddenly conscious of my . . .

"Do you ever walk out?" I asked. The fool's smile still pulling my face apart.

"Walk out?"

"Casually. Shopping. A museum. A matinee."

Then she understood.

"I don't," she said. "I can't," she said. "I won't," she said.

"Lovely party!" someone cried. Drifting past. Grace lifted a hand. Head turning. Tilted.

I couldn't breathe. That line of completion enclosed her like a sharp halo. She was an ancient child. As fresh and knowing. The open, tender parts of her, pristine, might exude a scent of new worlds. I had dangerous visions of mad profits. Reason fled.

"I couldn't," she murmured.

Blackmail was not beyond me. At that moment. Nothing was.

"After what I—" I said. And paused.

"The Beists," she said. Finally. "Paul is a member. Can you come to Washington? He can bring you. I'll be there. Nick?"

Suddenly we were up to our assholes in idiots. Chattering and laughing. All I could do was stretch my smile to pain and nod at her over the heads of surrounding guests. She had tossed me a crust. I would have taken a crumb. I watched the hostess move, laugh, throw back her glistering snake head. I entered into that vulval ear and rested.

Paul and I started back for GPA-1 at 0215. We traveled through the new day. Languid with exhaustion.

"Listen," Paul murmured, "do you think they took me seriously?"

"I don't know if they did," I said. "I did."

"Did I frighten them?"

"Probably."

"Good. But it served. Didn't it, Nick? We got what we wanted."

"Yes," I said.

373

Z-2

At that point in time, mid-November, it seemed to me the whirligig increased speed. I, who had opted for action, became aware of the lure of rapid movement for its own sake. Without reason or destination. I felt a curious unease. The world on a fulcrum. Teetering.

During that period I suffered a severe attack of Random Synaptic Control that lasted almost five minutes and left me riven.

Even more disquieting was Hyman R. Lewisohn's lack of affirmative response to parabiotic therapy. Unless his vital readouts showed a sudden and unexpected upcurve, my prognosis was negative. The physioanalytic computer concurred. I returned, once again, to my contingency plan.

We had exhausted conventional protocols long ago. Arabinosylcytosine. 6-Thioquanine. Daunorubicin. L-Asparaginase. Vincristine IV. Prednisone. 6-Mercaptopurine. Methotrexate. Cyclophosphamide. Ara-C. Hydroxyurea. We had tried them all in dozens of combinations and protocols suggested by the pharmacoanalytic computer.

In addition to therapy for the acute myelogenous leukemia, Lewisohn had been and was being treated for leukemic infiltration of the nervous system. This called for intrathecal (injection into the spinal fluid) of methotrexate and aminopterine, as well as oral pyrimethamine. We had ended radiation therapy.

We had shifted to more experimental compounds of limited value. With no better results. Although, for a brief period, the object responded to 1-2 chlorethyl-3, cyclohexyl-1-nitosourea.

We had tried unblocking antibodies with a compound based on the original Moloney regressor sera. We had then turned to immunization with tumor antigens, utilizing living tumor cells pretreated with Vibrio cholerae neuraminidase. Nothing served.

The penultimate therapy, in which we were then engaged, parabiosis, was an attempt to transfer immunity with lymphocytes from immunized donors. The donors had underachieved the norm. In fact, the second had unaccountably developed leukemic symptoms from Lewisohn's infected blood.

I have presented this brief precis of Lewisohn's therapy to justify what lay ahead for him: the final step in my contingency plan. I had become convinced it would prove absolutely necessary. There was no choice.

Shortly after the hookup with the third donor, I went down to Alexandria to scan the most recent computer printouts. I saw no indications of improvement; the em was going. All the staff of Group Lewisohn concurred. I took their signed statements to this effect.

I was sitting in Lewisohn's room, close to his bedside. A roll of printout on my lap. But I wasn't scanning it. I was staring at him, computing what had to be done. The place. The time. How many objects would be needed. The chances of success. It never occurred to me, of course, to tell him what I planned. I could imagine his reaction. The horror.

He was somnolent. Heavily drugged. He had not stirred when I entered the room. I sat patiently, wondering if Paul had been correct. He had said all contingency plans have a built-in defect: the author wants to ultimize them, to see if they'll serve. That dictum was just operative enough to disturb me.

Lewisohn's eyes opened. Finally. He was staring directly at me.

"Jack the Ripper," he rasped. He made a weak gesture. "Where do those tubes go? The ones to the wall?"

"I told you a dozen times. We're monitoring your blood. Instant analysis. It looks good."

"Thank you, Doctor Pangloss," he said wearily. And looked away.

I nodded toward the stack of books at his bedside.

"What are you serving on?" I asked him.

"Go to hell," he said. "Besides, it isn't important."

"What *is* important?"

"The weakness," he said. "I can't think. It's draining me. Give me a pill."

"What for?"

"I'm sick and tired of being sick and tired. One pill. An injection."

"No way," I said. "We're not through with you yet."

"What good am I to you? My brain is mush."

"It'll come back," I told him.

"When?"

"Soon. Soon."

"My brain is dying."

"No," I said. "The corpus. Not the brain."

He turned his head slowly. Looked at me. I feared I had said too much.

"You devious devil," he whispered. "What are you plotting?"

"I'm planning to make you well," I said. "To end your pain and your weakness. Is that so bad?"

He began to curse me then. Forgetting his suspicions. Which was what I wanted.

During November and early December, Paul Bumford and I spent an increasing number of hours in Washington, D. C.

Out of all the confused and contentious meetings and conferences and colloquies of those weeks, the scenario for the Department of Creative Science was slowly structured. We could not have come to the necessary compromises without the knowing counsel of Joseph Tyrone Wellington. Of all objects! The Chief Director's Public Relations Chief.

I had always thought the em a microweight. With his petrobon complexion. Wirewool muttonchops. "Nick baby!" A breath of cold cigars. Shallow, blue eyes. Lips remarkably rosy, brown-rimmed. A smile on the face of the tiger.

But the Chief Director did not surround himself with fools. Soon after Wingate's go decision, Joe Wellington took me aside and cautioned me not to take public relations lightly. "The trick," he said, "is to cross-fertilize substance and image so the resultant hybrid has the strengths of both and the weaknesses of neither. Example: God as substance, Jesus Christ as image. Think of the crucifixion as a PR scenario, and you'll compute what I mean."

With his aid, the following proposals were drafted for the Chief Director's consideration:

1. I would remain as Deputy Director of Satisfaction Section, Department of Bliss. But I would be appointed to Director (Temp.), enabling me to wear a crimson tab on the right shoulder epaulette of my silver zipsuit. The purpose of this promotion was to signal Congress and the public the importance the Chief Director attached to proposed legislation establishing a Department of Creative Science.

I would continue to reside in the compound at GPA-1, but make frequent trips to Washington, D. C.—two or three times a week—to rule the DCS operation there and to consult with the Chief Director and his staff. This arrangement would also ensure my continued rule of Project Phoenix, the Fred III research, the UP project, personal care of Lewisohn, and several other restricted projects.

2. Paul Bumford would be promoted to Deputy Director (Temp.), with the crimson tab on his bronze zipsuit. A small office would be established in the Capital, ruled by Paul, and he would take up permanent residence in Washington.

Paul's main responsibility would be personal relations with Congress and members of committee staffs. Via Sady Nagle. My main responsibility would be public relations with rulers and organizations of all scientific disciplines. Joe Wellington would manipulate lecture tours, convention addresses, symposia, TV appearances, planted magazine articles, perhaps a ghost-written book, etc.

3. At the same time we pushed the concept of a Department of Creative Science, we would also urge the establishment of a Joint Committee on Creative Science by both houses of Congress. To oversee the budget, plans, and activities of the new Public Service department. Something for everyone.

The Chief Director approved of the main thrust of our program *in toto,* making only a few minor adjustments. For instance, we had suggested Paul's Washington office be established in the headquarters of the Department of Bliss. Wingate rejected this, pointing out that it would give the impression of DCS being ruled by or an offshoot of DOB. He wanted DCS to parturiate as completely new and independent. He was right.

Paul's service as AssDepDirRad was taken over by Edward Nolan, formerly leader of the Memory Team. Mary Bergstrom was moved to Washington to serve as AA in the DCS office. Paul and I, jointly, leased a furnished home in the Chevy Chase section. The new Metro link extended out there. Since a Metro link was also operating to Alexandria, transportation to Hospice No. 4 would be simplified.

The house Paul and I shared in Chevy Chase was pleasantly decrepit. It was an obso structure, brick with wood trim, badly in need of pointing and painting. The furnishings seemed to have been accumulated rather than selected: they were of all periods, in various stages of disrepair. But the house was adequately heated, undeniably comfortable, and had more rooms than we would possibly need. Shortly after we took possession, Paul asked me if Mary Bergstrom could take over one of the bedroom-nest suites since she was not happy in the studio apartment she had found on Franklin Street. I saw no reason to object. Mary moved in.

We had a carefully programmed housewarming, of course. Catered. A pro forma invitation was sent to the Chief Director and Mrs. Wingate. They sent their regrets. A previous engagement. But everyone else we invited put in an appearance. Even the Chairman of the Senate Government Operations Committee and two influential members of the House Government Operations Committee.

More important, we had an excellent turnout of media reps, Congressional administrative assistants, and general counsels and staff members of both GO Committees. Their cooperation was essential if we were to win preliminary approval of the DCS and move enabling legislation onto the floors of both Houses for debate and vote.

Sady Nagle served as hostess, and Joe Wellington had brought over his entire staff to make certain things moved smoothly. It was a large, friendly, noisy party; we hadn't skimped on alcohol, cannabis, or food. Everyone recognized it as a lobbying ploy, but the AA's and committee staff members were flattered by the attention we paid them and the importance we obviously attached to their goodwill.

I limited my drinking and played the genial host strenuously. As did Paul Bumford. We had previously agreed I was to manipulate the media reps while Paul concentrated on the pols. The arrangement served well.

"Good party," Herb Bailey assured me. "As parties go in this town. At least the booze isn't watered."

"What do you think, Herb?" I asked him. "Have we got a chance?"

"Don't be so impatient," he told me. "You'll learn that there's time, and then there's Congressional time. No one's in a hurry in this town. Or they might get all the nation's business cleaned up in a month or two, and have to go back home to their constituents. Who the hell wants to do that? By the way, I never thanked you for the lead on the DOB shakeup. Thanks. Got anything else for me?"

"Yes," I said. Solemnly. "Something very big indeed."

"Oh? What is it?"

"I'll keep an eye on what you write about the DCS before I decide whether to give it to you."

"Jesus Christ," he said disgustedly. "You're learning fast."

"I learned that at my father's knee."

"Which reminds me," he said. "My little girl has been pushing me to buy her one of your father's new Die-Dee Dolls."

He didn't have to say more.

"Don't spend the love," I told him. "I'll have one sent out to you from the factory. You should get it in time for Christmas."

"Thanks, Nick," he said gratefully. "I appreciate that."

I knew he would. One of the Government Operations Committee Representatives left early for another party. He took Maya Leighton along with him. I knew *he'd* appreciate *that*. Politics is objects. But so, it may surprise you, is science. In many respects. Winning a research grant, manipulating the race to be "first," earning credit for a discovery, or scamming your team leader—all are not too unlike getting a piece of legislation through the US Congress. The stakes may be higher in Washington, that's all.

After the final guests straggled away, Sady Nagle and Joe Wellington joined Paul and me for a final coffee and postmortem. We agreed the housewarming had been a success. An effective kickoff for the DCS campaign.

"I wish the Chief Director had been here," Paul fretted. "It would have made it more important."

Nagle and Wellington laughed.

"Sonny," Sady said, "believe me, he's got more important things to worry about. He's given you a chance. What more do you want?"

"He's testing the water," Wellington explained. "If he sees the DCS is going, he'll link himself more closely. If it doesn't look good, he'll pull clear. He has his personal image to consider. You heard what he said: He can't afford too many failures."

"This isn't going to fail," Paul said coldly. "I guarantee that."

After Sady and Joe departed—kisses all around; Washington had adopted many of the conventions of show biz—Paul and I lingered over a bottle of natural brandy we had *not* served our guests.

"What's bothering you?" I asked him.

He looked at me thoughtfully.

"I must never forget how perceptive you are of my moods," he said.

"That's right, Paul," I said lazily. "You must never forget that. So what's bothering you?"

"Sady Nagle is an obso. You know that."

"And?"

"She's never had any memory conditioning."

"Paul, she's Deputy Chief Director for Domestic Affairs. The Chief's political expert. She's supposed to know more about what keeps the country ticking over than anyone else."

"You know how she keeps her records?"

"How?"

"On file cards. Would you believe it? A card for every Congressman, for every governor, for every magnamayor and minimayor in the country. One for every big pol and little pol. Superlawyers and superbankers. Judges and wardheelers. Business execs, labor barons, college presidents, and professors with clout. Prime TV and newspaper factors. In other words, the Establishment. Movers and shakers. She's got them all. Thousands and thousands of file cards. With name, address, phone number, date of birth, brief physical description, political affiliation, voting record, marital status, conditioning, personal likes and dislikes, if any. And so forth. Then she's got a cross-file on dates. She sends out birthday cards, anniversary cards, condolence cards. To the pols and to their parents, spouses, children, grandchildren. It's incredible!"

"Seems to serve." I shrugged. "She's on top of the political scene. The Chief Director depends on her."

"But that card file's so *obso*," Paul said angrily. "Nick, do you know how Judidat functions?"

"Judidat? Is that the legal outfit?"

"It's a legal service. Available to attorneys. At a lovable fee, of course. Suppose an object is indicted for homicide. Or any other crime. The defense attorney retains Judidat. They come into the community where the alleged crime was committed. They do a public opinion poll in depth. Heavy motivational analysis. Everything goes into a computer, and they get a complete personality profile of objects whose sympathy is with the accused. Say the PP show white, em, under thirty, limited conditioning, strong parental influence, conservative politics, deep religous leanings, undersexed, whatever. All right, now the defense attorney knows what to look for in the voir dire. He tries to get a jury as close as possible to the Judidat profile. Then, after the jury is selected, Judidat moves in closer to construct life histories and psychological profiles of the individual jurors. Into the computer again. Out comes an analysis that dictates the thrust of the defense attorney's arguments, what questions to ask, what areas to avoid, what triggers to pull. How, in fact, to manipulate the jury. Judidat's attainment rate runs around ninety-plus."

"Paul, what *is* this?"

He was smiling at me. A sly smile. Almost ferrety.

"Nick, I want to bring one of Phoebe Huntzinger's whiz kids down from GPA-1 to study Sady Nagle's silly file card operation. And then to design software to get the whole thing on tape. Set up a political Judidat process so we can run Congress through a computer and get the most effective arguments for the DCS, what areas to avoid, what triggers to pull. We'll start with Congress, but eventually we'll include everyone in Sady's file. The entire Establishment! The whole power structure! Think what that could mean to us—and the Chief Director too, of course. Instant analysis of the viability of proposed legislation. Accurate percentile predictions of success. What buttons to push for maximum response."

"You think Sady will lend her file cards to your computernik?"

"No way. Not voluntarily. She sleeps on them. But you and I know there are ways. . . ."

"Forget it," I said loudly. "Too much risk. Alienate Sady and we're stopped. Just forget it. It's for the Tomorrow File."

"The Tomorrow File?" he said furiously. "This is for today. Right *now*. We can't wait. Nick, we can get the whole thing set up on a computer in GPA-1. Top security. Crash priority. We can have it serving in time to give us the answers on this DCS project."

"No." I shook my head. "Absolutely not. It would obsolete Sady Nagle completely and probably get Wingate questioning our motives and solutions again. We narcotized him the first time around. Something like this would revive all his suspicions. Put it in the Tomorrow File."

"For God's sake, Nick!" he shouted. "We've got to start moving the Tomorrow File to actuality. You said so yourself. You said it's not just a Christmas list; it's a plan of action!"

"But you're moving too fast. You'll clever us both right into Cooperation Rooms. Being drained. Forget it!"

He didn't accept it easily. An ugly pout twisted his mouth. He jumped to his feet. Slammed palms together. The sharp crack of something breaking irretrievably. Then he put his hands on his hips, stalked angrily about the room. He didn't look at me. Finally he stood with his back to me. I heard him take several deep breaths.

"All right," he said. Controlled voice. "All right. We'll do it your way. I'll put it in the Tomorrow File."

"Good. That's best, Paul. Really it is."

"Are you going to tell the Chief Director about the UP project?" he asked suddenly.

He caught me by surprise. I couldn't compute his sudden jink.

"Why . . . no. I hadn't planned to. We having nothing to show him, Paul. Not yet. It's just a concept."

"But it's a political drug."

"Sure, if it authenticates. But what's the point of telling him now?"

"Just a thought," he said casually. "I'm going to bed."

A week before Christmas, 1998, I drove down to Washington from GPA-1 in my official sedan. I was carrying gifts for Paul, Mary Bergstrom, Maya Leighton, and Seth Lucas. And a liter of natural bourbon for Joe Wellington, a jeweled owl's head brooch for Sady Nagle, a natural silk scarf for Penelope Mapes. I also had a gift for Grace Wingate: giant hoop earrings of hammered silver. But still undecided if I might risk the giving.

I had not endured the aggravating traffic jams on the New York-Washington freeway merely to celebrate the birth of Christ in the Nation's Capital. A meeting of the D. C. Beists was scheduled for the evening of my arrival. Hopefully, it would provide an opportunity for my first meeting with Grace Wingate since the Chief Director's reception for DIROB.

Paul had transferred his membership from the New York chapter of the Beists to the Washington organization. He suggested, in view of our new ranks and close identification with the Department of Creative Science legislation, it might be discreet to wear civilian clothes to the meeting. I concurred. I slipped the tissue-wrapped silver earrings into the pocket of my tweed jacket and carried a vodka-and-Smack into Paul's bedroom while he finished dressing.

I sprawled on his chaise lounge and watched him fuss with butterfly bowties in front of a wardrobe mirror.

"Polka dot or paisley?" he asked.

"Paisley," I said. "More festive. Is this going to be a Christmas party?"

"Something like that," he said. "We're all supposed to bring something. I had a cake delivered. We have a place of our own now. Did I tell you that?"

"No. You didn't."

"Oh, yes. A meeting hall over a delicatessen. You can get

heartburn on the elevator. With a uninest and a small room for administration. I'm secretary-treasurer.''

''Congratulations.''

''Thank you. More than two hundred members, and growing. I think I can make something of it.''

''Why?''

''It's a giggle.''

''Paul.''

He turned to stare at me. How he had changed in the past few months! Now he looked like a young Napoleon: broad brow, brooding eyes, sweet lips, a darkling cast to his expression. Withal, a cold, firm resolve in those effeminate features.

''I know you think it a giggle,'' he said.

''But *you* don't?'' I asked.

After our blast over computerizing Sady Nagle's card file, I thought our relationship had regained its former tenor: open, candid, easy.

''Oh, I suppose it's a laugh now,'' he said. ''Like all religions. But I see something in it.''

''And what is that?''

''Primus: Beism is not only *not* antiscience, but whatever codified beliefs it expresses advocate increased scientific research and social change. Secundus: A new society might do worse than encourage a state religion. As a kind of emotional spine. A new patriotism.''

''Oh-ho,'' I said. ''Pope Paul.''

''The first.'' He grinned.

The new Beist meeting hall was simply a large, square, dusty room with a stage at one end, elevated two steps above the floor. It was almost filled when we arrived. The number of Beists surprised me. I had a fleeting impression of having left pregnant rats in a cage and returning a few nights later to find the cage crowded and swarming.

Paul left me to claim one of the cane-backed chairs on the rostrum. Reserved for the governing board. The last time I had attended a Beist meeting, the movement seemed unstructured, with no desire for rulers. I wondered what role Paul had played in this nascent power pattern.

I glanced about casually. I could not see Grace Wingate.

The meeting was called to order with the banging of a gavel. We all found places on those hellishly uncomfortable chairs. Joanne Wilensky, as dreary and acned as before, welcomed members and newcomers. She called on a chapter officer to make a membership report.

This ef, wearing the zipsuit of a PS-3, read a short statement. There were now Beist chapters in fourteen towns and cities. Total national membership was estimated at close to three thousand. I was astounded. It seemed to me very rapid growth for such a rinkydink cult.

Then Secretary-Treasurer Paul Bumford was called on to make his report. It was a remarkable performance. Without notes, he delivered a concise, number-filled account of his office. He spoke for almost ten minutes. Without hesitation or stumble. His memory conditioning was obviously successful.

Even more surprising to me was what he said. The Washington, D. C., chapter of the Beists now had a bank balance exceeding ten thousand new dollars. Paul said that since the only existent office equipment was an obso typewriter (donated), he strongly urged that the sum of three thousand new dollars be approved for the purchase of a new electric typewriter, a mimeograph machine, stationery, and the requisite office supplies. His suggestion was put in the form of a motion and overwhelmingly adopted.

The evening's speaker was then introduced. He was Arthur Raddo. A young em with lank blond hair falling untidily over his forehead. Enormous eyes with a fervid stare. Flat lips he licked constantly. Wearing a wrinkled, soiled zipsuit of a PS-5. His physical appearance gave the impression of limp ineffectuality. But his voice was unexpectedly loud, passionate. Still, I was certain he was a frail.

He said that up to that point in time, the Beists had been content with rather vague canons and implied scripture. What was needed, Raddo proclaimed, was a start on structuring the Beists' beliefs, to put them into written form, in a sort of Bible to which all members might voluntarily submit and adhere.

In addition, he said, such written prescriptions would serve as a basis for proselyting. For the time had passed when Beism could be content with the casual addition of the bored and curious and lonely to its membership rolls. The time had come to move actively to build numbers, require discipline, exercise power.

If Beists were sincere about the evolution of the human species into a single superrace, he said, then they must devise a program to purify the blood. That was the phrase he used: "purify the blood." But he never defined it, and I could only assume he actually meant to improve the gene pool. Although he never concretized how this was to be done. "Purify the blood!" he kept shouting. "Purify the blood!"

"We cannot stand still and talk and hope," he concluded. "We must sacrifice ourselves if the future is truly to belong to us. To the single, divine human race."

There was a moment of silence. Then an enthusiastic snapping of fingers. In spite of his nuttiness (surely there was pathology there), it had been a well-organized speech. Point led to point. A was easy to accept. If you accepted A, you had to accept B. And, of course, B led to C. I could hardly believe this insipid object was capable of such artfulness.

The meeting was brought to a close by the Wilensky ef's announcement that a contributed "holiday feast" was available to all members and guests in the administration room. There was a swift surge of hungry Beists.

Paul chatted a moment with other officers on the platform, then came down. We moved toward each other.

"Well?" he said. Smiling. "What did you think?"

"About what?"

"The speaker, for starters."

"A wowser," I said. "Where does he serve?"

"I'm not certain. Bureau of Printing and Engraving, I think. He comes on a little heavy, I admit. But every religion has its fanatics."

"How long have you had a board of directors?" I asked curiously.

"Oh . . . a few months," Paul said vaguely. "The membership was getting too large. We needed some kind of formal structure. Environment determines social organization, you know. Then you get a positive feedback."

"What the hell are you talking about?" I demanded.

"Oh, look," he said. "There's Grace Wingate. She's waving at us."

So she was. I moved slowly through the throng. Never taking my eyes from her. She watched me approach. Smiling. Paul had disappeared. So had everyone. And everything. She was wearing a bottle-green silk sheath. A black suede coat about her shoulders. Sleeves hanging empty. Her hair was down. She was beautiful. I could not compute why.

"Nick!" she said. "Merry Christmas!"

"Merry Christmas to you. Are you as well as you look?"

"Better." She laughed. "You can drop my hand now." And laughed again. "What a rogue you are!" Determinedly light.

"Was," I said. "Have been. Not now."

The smile faded slowly.

"Would you like something?" I asked. "Food? I can get it."

"No, nothing, thank you. We were at an embassy party and were late getting away. So sorry we couldn't get to your housewarming but . . . you know."

In another moment we'd be agreeing what a severe winter it threatened to be and wasn't it a shame that the entire crew of Sealab 46 had been lost when the hull unaccountably cracked.

"I really must run," she said nervously.

"Can we sit a moment?" I asked.

"A moment," she said. Finally.

And all during this our eyes had not unclinched. Had not wavered. Somewhere around us was movement, laughter.

"I have a Christmas present for you," I said. Suddenly deciding. "Will you accept it?"

Appreciable hesitation. Then: "Yes," she said.

I handed over the tissue-wrapped package. Her eyes lowered as she unwrapped it softly, timorously, just far enough to see what it contained. "Ahhh," she breathed. Then looked up at me again.

"Beautiful. Nick, they're beautiful. I thank you."

"Yes," I said.

"But I have nothing for you."

I stopped myself. I could have told her.

"Grace, am I to see you only at Beist meetings? Must I join? Is there no other way?"

It troubled her. But I had to know. If she wanted it no-go, now was the time to signal me.

"I am never alone," she said. In such a low voice I could hardly hear.

"Never?"

"Not outside. But. . . ."

"But?"

She shook her head. Ashen hair flaming.

"This is very wrong," she said.

"Not wrong," I said. "Just difficult. Couldn't you come to New York? For shopping or the theater?"

"I could," she said. "But with a secretary. And guards. Always guards."

I was deliriously happy. Because, I thought, my only problem was logistics.

"Grace," I said, "come to New York. Plan a week or two in advance. Tell your husband. Tell him that at your reception I invited you for lunch the next time you were in New York, and you're going to take me up on it. Send me a note when you'll arrive. Does that sound all right to you?"

"Yes."

"Will you do it?"

"Yes. What about the secretary and guards?"

"I don't know. At the moment. I'll think of something."

I hoped my erection was not obvious. I wondered why our flat words seemed to me the most erotic conversation I had ever had. Our eyes locked again, promising. . . .

"Do you sleep naked?" I asked her.

She caught her breath. Went quite pale. Those somber eyes seemed to grow in size and intensity. Dark beacons. I thought her lips trembled. A knuckle went to her teeth.

"Nick," she said. "Please. Don't."

"Do you?" I persisted.

"Yes," she whispered. At last.

"Think of me?" I asked.

She nodded dumbly.

"Here we are," Paul Bumford caroled brightly. "Best cake in the house. If I have to say so myself."

He was balancing three plastiplates with slices of chocolate layer cake, three plastiforks. He sat down with us, and Grace Wingate remarked how lovely the lighted Christmas trees looked along the mall.

We had finished the cake, were standing, beginning our farewells when a black zipsuit came pushing through the crowd of Beists. They fell silent as he passed. Drawing back. Watching him. No expression.

"Ma'am," he said to Grace Wingate.

"What is it, Tim?"

"We just got a call on the car phone. Do you know if Director

Nicholas Flair and Deputy Director Paul Bumford are here?"

"I'm Flair," I said. "This is Deputy Director Bumford. What is it?"

"Sir," he said, "the Chief Director would like both of you to join him at his Georgetown residence as soon as possible."

Paul and I glanced at each other.

"Mrs. Wingate," I said. Bowing slightly. "It's been a profitable evening. Merry Christmas and Happy New Year."

"Oh, yes," Paul said. "From me, too."

"Thank you both," she said. Wooden smile. "Perhaps I'll see you at home."

Penelope Mapes met us at the outside door. Led us through the hallway maze to the library.

"I called your place in Chevy Chase," she said. "Mary Bergstrom told me where you were. Are you both Beists?"

"Paul is," I said. "I'm just an innocent bystander."

The plump squab giggled dutifully.

"Penny, what's this all about?" Paul asked.

"Penny." That was interesting.

"I'll let the CD give you the gruesome details," she said. Knocked, and swung open the library door. Chief Director Michael Wingate rose from behind the desk.

"Nick!" he said. "Paul! So glad you could make it."

He introduced us to the other two ems in the room. But I knew one of them well. And recognized the other. We all stroked palms.

Dr. Winston Heath was Chief of the National Epidemiology Center in Frankfort, Kentucky. I had known him for years: a cold, unemotional technician. Capable but limited. No imagination. He was the palest live object I had ever seen. Blanched.

The other em was R. Sam Bigelow, Chief, BPS—the Bureau of Public Security (formerly the Federal Bureau of Investigation). In all the photos of him that appeared in newspapers, magazines, books, and in his frequent TV interviews, he looked like a frog. In person, he looked like a frog. A suspicious frog. He glowered at Paul and me. Not looked, but glowered. I felt immediately guilty.

We found chairs. Penelope Mapes faded into the background. That ef had made effacement a fine art. I wondered if Chief Director Wingate demanded her presence for the same reason gynecologists insist their nurses be present during an internal: to forestall cries of rape.

"This conversation is restricted," the Chief Director mentioned casually. "I need not quote applicable law. I'm certain you're aware of the penalties. The situation is this:"

Then, speaking rapidly but distinctly, Wingate related the pertinent factors. Two weeks previously, there had been a heavy outbreak of botulism in GPA-11 (Idaho, Wyoming, Montana, and both Dakotas). Since then, slightly more than 1,200 cases had been reported. Of those afflicted, approximately three-fourths had stopped. During the same time period, seven botulism cases had been reported from East Coast areas, sixteen from the West Coast, and scattered cases elsewhere.

"Dr. Heath," the Chief Director said, "will you take it from here?"

"Average number of botulism cases annually per total population for the past ten years," Heath said in a dead, lecturer's voice, "is 2.17. For the entire US. Naturally, our first thought was massive food poisoning. A bad shipment of canned *something* into the stricken area. Although that would not account for the cases on the East and West Coasts and the few scattered all over the US. But we computed that it was possible that tourists, traveling through GPA-11, had taken some of the spoiled foodstuff home with them. We immediately sent an investigative team into GPA-11, of course. They found absolutely *no* evidence of food poisoning. In fact, victims came, for the most part, from families who consumed identical meals. But only one object of several was poisoned. It could not have been the water supply since, as you know, the *Clostridium botulinum* is anaerobic. And besides, the water supply was ruled out because only a relatively few of the total population were affected. Most botulism results from inefficient home-canning. No evidence of that. As you are probably aware, commercial canning processes have been so completely automated, with such a multiplicity of quality controls, that the risk factor in commercial food processing is practically nil. That's it. Any questions?"

"Stop rate, doctor?" I asked.

"It's 76.1967, doctor."

"Age of victims, doctor?" Paul asked.

"Between nine and eighty-three, doctor. Very few of the very young. At the age of fifteen, the curve begins to rise. Slowly. It accelerates at maturity. Reaches a peak at fifty-plus, then declines slowly. One odd incident: the stopping of a four-month-old ef from botulism. The single infant case recorded."

"Any common denominators, doctor?" I asked. "Industrial pollution? Occupation? Clothing? Sports? Drinks—soft or alcoholic? Any drug intake common to all?"

"Negative, negative, negative, doctor," Dr. Heath said bleakly. "We've checked it all out."

"You're certain it's botulism, doctor?" Paul asked.

R. Sam Bigelow looked at him coldly.

"We're certain," he said. "Heath told you what it is. We checked it out in the Bureau labs. That's what it is."

The Chief Director turned to me.

"It's not over, Nick," he said. "Case incidence is beginning to decline slowly, but projective curves show more than a thousand objects eventually stopped."

"What was the diagnosis of the local physicians, doctor?" I asked Heath. Worrying it.

"Botulism, doctor." He nodded. "Some of them recognized it immediately and were able to reverse it. Some missed it completely. It *is* rare these days, Nick; you know that."

"We've been able to pillow it," Chief Director Wingate said. "The media have been very cooperative. No one wants panic."

"You said victim age peaks at fifty, doctor," I said to Heath. "Do you see any significance in that? Lowered resistance?"

"Can't see it, doctor." He shook his head. "There were many juveniles. Afflicted objects over the age of eighteen constituted 71.83 of the total. It appears to be an adult disorder, but not exclusively so."

We were all silent then. Staring blankly at each other. I computed what I had heard. The detail that impressed me most was that Dr. Winston Heath, Chief of the National Epidemiology Center, still believed that *Clostridium botulinum* was anaerobic.

It was not his fault, of course. The doctrine of "need to know," applied to scientific research, is stupid—and frequently fatal. As witness that stop rate of 76.1967 percent.

I glanced at R. Sam Bigelow's toadish scowl, then addressed the Chief Director.

"Sir," I said, "are Paul and I to assume, by the presence of the Chief of the Bureau of Public Security in a colloquy involving a public health problem, that there is reason to believe the epidemic may be—"

"Now look here, you—" Bigelow growled at me. Frog eyes popping.

But Wingate waved him down.

"No, no," he said. "A very cogent question. Nick, about two years ago a black revolutionary group tried to contaminate Denver's water supply. Last year, a group called SON. . . . Ever hear of them?"

"Yes, sir," I said. "Society of Nothing. Around San Francisco. Mostly senseless assassinations. They were in all the media."

"Right." He nodded. "We took them just before they were about to feed cyanide gas into the air conditioning system of a federal think-tank in Oakland. We have absolutely no evidence of any terrorist participation in this botulism outbreak. We have received no letters or threats. We've checked our undercover agents carefully. No hint of any activity. No one in the media has received letters or threats. It may be just a medical fluke. Something no one will ever be able to explain. But I've got to cover all bases before I bring the matter to the attention of the Joint Committee on Internal Peace. That's why Chief Bigelow is here. That's why you're here. I need all the help I can get. I keep thinking that if it happened once, in GPA-11, it can happen again. Anywhere. Surely you can understand my concern."

"Of course, sir."

"Any ideas?"

"None at the moment, sir. Paul?"

"None." He shook his head. "Can we have some time on this, sir?"

"Of course." Wingate tried to smile. "You two are the very lively brains pushing a Department of Creative Science. I'm hoping you—and science—can make a significant contribution toward solving this problem. You understand?"

We understood; the velvet glove was peeling off the iron fist.

Everyone rose; the meeting broke up. Penelope Mapes came out of the shadows to open the door for us. But before we disbanded, I had the opportunity to draw Dr. Winston Heath aside.

"Doctor," I said, "it's been a pleasure seeing you again. How is the family?"

"Fine, doctor," he said. Brightening as much as a skeleton with skin can brighten.

"And that boy of yours? Scheduled for the moon colony, wasn't he?"

"That memory of yours," he said. Shaking his head. "Yes, he's up there now. We get a teleletter every week. He wouldn't be anywhere else. Enjoying every minute."

"Paleogeology, isn't it?"

"Yes, that's his discipline."

"Fine. Fascinating stuff. Doctor, about this botulism business— I don't for a moment doubt your analysis, or the diagnoses of the attending physicians, or the backup opinion of the BPS labs, but tell me—was this done on the basis of the clinical picture?"

"Of course, doctor." He looked at me strangely.

"Of course, of course," I soothed him. "Entirely understandable. Do you think you could send me some bits and pieces at GPA-1? Maybe a little blood? Just to confirm your findings. Substantiate your judgment. You know the kind of hardware we have. Excellent stuff. Some experimental. It would help us. Give the labniks a problem—right? A challenge. Who knows?"

He was thoroughly confused. As I meant him to be. All he could assimilate was that supportive testimony on his analysis could do him and the National Epidemiology Center no harm.

"Of course, doctor," he said. "Happy to cooperate. Most of what we have is frozen. But we do have some pickled stomach, I believe, and a few other things. And some very interesting slides. I'll send you what I can."

"Fine, doctor," I said. Clapping him on the shoulder. "Just fine. All contributions gratefully accepted."

We both laughed.

"Since the matter is of such high priority and top security," I said. Leaning closer. Lowering my voice. "—Perhaps you better send it by personal courier."

"Of course, of course."

"Doctor," I said heartily. Slapping his palm. "It's a pleasure serving with you on this."

He couldn't blush with happiness. But he became less pale.

"And, doctor," I murmured, "I'm looking forward to serving much closer with you in the future."

I may have winked. I meant, of course, that the National Epidemiology Center would become part of the Department of Creative Science, and I would be ruling him. But the whole bit was lost on him. A very dull em.

"My God," Paul said. "Wouldn't it be marvelous if we could compute this botulism thing? What a leg up for the DCS!"

"Yes," I said.

We were driving back to Chevy Chase from the Georgetown White House. Paul was in an ebullient mood.

"It would solidify us with the Chief Director," he said. Almost laughed. "He'd get behind us all the way."

"Yes," I said.

"How the hell are they getting botulism, Nick? Got any ideas?"

"Ideas?" I said. "Not a one."

"That question you asked the CD about Bigelow being there— you think it's a programmed operation? Terrorist?"

"Could be."

"But *how?*"

"Don't know, Paul."

"But the motive? No letters, no threats. Even if it was an outfit like the Society of Nothing, they'd make phone calls to the media, and so forth. You know how high the ego factor is with terrorists. Why would anyone do it without taking credit?"

"What?" I said. "Oh," I said. And grimaced. "I don't know, Paul. Maybe just to destabilize the government. As basic as that."

Paul was silent. I thought he was shaken. Then he made one of those increasingly frequent jinks that vaguely disturbed me.

"Nick, we need a security officer," he said.

"What?"

"At the DCS office. We're adding objects. Expanding. And dealing with a lot of classified bumf. We need a security officer. For starters. And eventually, a security staff."

"So? Get one."

"How about Art Roach?"

"*Roach?* Why him?"

"Nick, he's down to a black zipsuit. He'd be grateful for the chance. And we own him, Nick. I've still got his tape with Seymour Dove. He'll behave. And he knows his service. Doesn't he, Nick?"

"I suppose so. All right. Maybe we owe him something. Bring him over from DOB. Serve through Penelope Mapes; she'll arrange it."

"Right, Nick. Now we're beginning to move. Don't you feel that, Nick? That things are coming our way?"

"Yes," I said.

I took a hot shower. As hot as I could endure.

I slipped naked into bed. Knowing I would be long awake. I wanted to be.

When I had been shopping for a Christmas present for Grace

Wingate, I had seen—in a unisex boutique in Manhattan's Olympic Tower—a tooty blouse of a gauzy, see-through fabric. Artfully imprinted on the front, in color, were female breasts. When the blouse was worn, you could not be certain what you saw was real. That was the jerk.

Lying immobile, awake in bed, my jerk was in not knowing if the ef was real, existed or created. My own illusion. *Why?* Her neck was too long. Chin too pointed. Nose too thin. That flame of ashen hair. Undoubtedly tinted. Undoubtedly. The voice too fruity. And was there not an absence of fine intelligence? She did pick up on things. But not immediately. Certainly not Angela Berri's sharp wit. And certainly not Millie Jean Grunwald's young, tender innocence. And certainly not Maya Leighton's skilled and enthusiastic sensuality. But still . . . Still. . . .

What? *What?* Why was I willing to risk all, everything, for a convoluted ear?

Z-3

I served tough on institutionalizing the speeches I was to deliver to establishment groups all over the mainland US. And, if time allowed, in overseas suburbs.

I was jotting additional notes in my office in the GPA-1 compound when Ellen Dawes buzzed to tell me a courier had arrived with a delivery for me. Personally signed receipt requested. It was a steel box from the National Epidemiology Center, sealed with metal straps and plastiwax marks.

I signed for it, shoved it under my desk. I flashed Bob Spivey, leader of the Neuropharmacology Team. This wasn't his discipline—it wasn't anyone's, actually; we had no special chem-an team—but Spivey ruled an em named Claude Burlinghouse. The Sherlock Holmes of chemical analysis.

When Spivey came on screen, I explained what I wanted.

"Extreme priority and security," I told him.

"You want Claude, I suppose?" he asked.

"Who else? Robert, this stuff is mucho toxic."

"The fishbowl?"

"I'd say so, yes. How soon?"

"What have you got?"

"Bits and pieces of a corpus long stopped. Botulism indicated."

"Oh-ho," he said.

"Yes," I said. "But not necessarily inert."

"Three days?" he asked.

"One," I said.

"Settle for two?" he asked.

Laughing, we agreed on two. He said he'd send a messenger to pick up the specimens.

Then fat Leo Bernstein banged my door open. Without knocking. As usual. I watched Leo lower his bulk slowly into a chair, drape his bulging thighs over one of the arms.

"How long since you've seen your piccolo?" I asked him. Cruelly. "Without a mirror?"

"Who wants to see my piccolo?" He shrugged. "Not me. Nick. I'm out of a job."

I stared at him a long moment. I knew the brain that hummed away in that lardy carcass. But if he didn't chisel off some of the blubber, that brain would be smothered to a stop in another ten years. I didn't want that.

"What do you mean out of a job?" I asked him.

"Fred is stabilized. No weight loss. The EEG is firmed. That hound's brain is immortal. Until someone pulls the plug. Doesn't that make you feel glad all over?"

"Congratulations, Leo."

I knew how many long hours he had served on the project. There wasn't another biochemist in the US—in the world!—who could have done it. The fat slob was a genius.

"Want to see the bumf?" he asked.

"No. I'll take your word for it."

"So I'm out of a job."

"Don't say 'job,' " I told him. "Say 'service.' "

"Say shit!" he said. Disgustedly. "Anyway, I'm finished. Got nothing to do."

"Oh?" I said. "Well, there is. . . . No, forget it."

He looked up.

"What?"

"No, nothing. Sorry I mentioned it. Just forget it, Leo."

"Goddamn it, what *is* it?"

"Leo, I'll flat with you. It's a top priority service. Hot security. Right up your plump kazoo. But I don't think you're the em for it."

"Why the hell not?" he demanded angrily.

"Leo, I told you," I said patiently. "It's top priority. I need the answers yesterday. That means I need an object with energy. Active. Someone who can get around. Look at you; you're a blob. Too bad. You'd have gotten a lot of profit from it."

"Nick, what the hell *is* it?"

I shook my head.

"Can't tell you. Ult sec. You have no need to know. But you talk about the head of Fred III being immortal. The object who comes up with the answers to this tickler *will* be immortal. And no one will ever pull the plug on *that*."

He groaned. I had him then. And knew it.

"Look, Leo," I told him. "I'll put you on this if you'll do something for me."

"What?" he said. "Anything!" he said.

"Lose three pounds a week. Promise, and I'll assign you. Then I'll weigh you. Down in the gym. We'll check every week. The first week you lose less than three pounds, you're off the project. How about it?"

"Sure, sure," he said. "I'll drop three pounds a week. Really I will, Nick. Easy."

"At first," I said. "Not after a month or so. But you stick to the three-pounds-a-week loss until I get you deflated. I'll tell you when to stop. Agreed?"

"Agreed," he said. "Sure, agreed! What is it, Nick? What's the project?"

"Just what you've done on Fred III," I said. "But for a human object."

We stared at each other. But really only I was staring at him. His eyes were on me, but his stare was inward. He was immediately computing, calculating, analyzing, figuring, determining the parameters of the problem, how to define it, how to encompass it.

"I'll need more staff," he said.

"As many as you want."

"Big budget for Tinkertoys."

"You'll get all the equipment needed."

"I can go so far *in vitro*," he said. "But sooner or later I'll need human volunteers."

"You'll get them," I said. "And I get three pounds a week."

"Goyische Shylock," he said.

I gave Bob Spivey and his Neuropharmacology Team—particularly Claude Burlinghouse—the two days he had requested for heavy analysis of the specimens forwarded from the National Epidemiology Center. I was certain, almost, what they would finalize. But I needed confirmation.

The fishbowl was in K Lab. Similar installations were frequently shown on TV and movie screens. A sealed, glass-enclosed room. No one within. Objects stood outside, manipulating specimens with long, jointed, remote-controlled grabbers. Stuff was brought into the fishbowl via a sterile lock. Chemanalysis computers were inside. Readouts or printouts were outside.

It was a slow, careful process. Especially when dealing with toxic and/or radioactive matter. The human factor was still important. In the handling, choice of technology, selection of equipment, presentation of evidence. Experts ruled our world. And not only attorneys and CPA's.

Standing outside the fishbowl with Bob Spivey and others on his team—all of us in white paper gowns and caps, like so many eager butchers—I watched with fascination while Claude Burlinghouse manipulated his stainless steel arms, hands, and fingers inside the glass. With deliberate, beautiful delicacy, he slid a mounted, microshaved specimen into the slot of a chemanalysis computer. A steel hand reached up slowly. A shiny forefinger pushed a button.

Burlinghouse turned to us.

"That's it," he said. "The last. Lousy specimens."

It took less than a minute for the final analysis. It was but one of a dozen that had been completed during the previous two days. An ef operator, sitting at the console of the master pharmaceutical file computer, added the information to what she had already stored. She faced both a cathode readout screen and an electric printout typewriter. She could have her choice or could combine the two. For instance, if she punched the readout button and then typed on the input board: $CH_3COOC_6H_4COOH$, the screen would immediately read ASPIRIN. Impressed?

But of course the master file computer was capable of infinitely more complex tasks than that. In its memory bank it had stored more than a million recipes consisting of elements and compounds. Fed input by the physiocoanalytic and chemanalysis computers, it would ponder a millisecond or two, then tell you what the stuff was you had submitted. Or, if it was an original mixture, unstored, the computer would laconically remark, on screen or typed, UNKNOWN.

I knew what was coming—and it did. The operator pushed buttons, and almost immediately the screen showed: RESTRICTED. 416HBL-CW3.

Bob Spivey, Claude Burlinghouse, the others—all looked at me. Disappointed.

I stared at the screen. Then said, "Erase. Everything."

Horrified, she looked to Spivey for confirmation. He nodded. Obediently she pushed a button to wipe the screen. Then she got busy blanking the input from the satellite analytic computers.

"Thanks, Robert," I said to Spivey. Stroking his palm. "Flame the specimens. Thank you, Claude." Stroking his palm. "Just what I wanted. Good service."

I strode away. Leaving them all floating. But they had no need to know.

Next stop: the office of Ass DepDir Rad. Edward Nolan, the em who had taken over from Paul Bumford when Paul moved to Washington. Ed was absent on a threeday. But I got no hassle from his Executive Assistant: She readily allowed me access to his safe. The combination had not been changed since it had been my safe, or since it had been Paul's safe. So much for security. And the drug code book was still on the upper shelf, left-hand corner. I was certain I remembered, but I felt it wise to check. I flipped pages, scanned, and there it was: 416HBL-CW3. Just as I recalled it.

It had started almost fifty years previously with the US Army's Office of Research & Development, as it was then called. *Clostridium botulinum* was but one of hundreds of protozoa, fungi, and bacteria they tinkered with in developing positive approaches to chemwar: poisons, pollutants, nerve gases, incapacitators, hypnotics, etc. At that point in time, it was believed *C. botulinum* toxin was the most virulent. Since then, of course, improved products had been developed.

We now skip to 1988. Interest in *Clostrium botulinum* had waned. There were simpler and more efficient means available.

But in 1988, a US intelligence sleeper in the Soviet Union reported a laboratory in Vitebsk had suddenly organized a restricted research project on botulism. The report was confirmed by other sources, and the flap was on.

Several US scientific agencies were put on a crash basis to

develop: (1) Botulism as a viable chemwar agent; and (2) A defense against botulism used as a viable chemwar agent. One of the agencies assigned to this service was the Division of Research & Development, SATSEC, DOB. Which was how I became intimately acquainted with *Clostridium botulinum*. I was eighteen at the time.

Approximately six months after the Phase II alert, it was learned that the Vitebsk lab was doing exactly what had been reported: It was researching the causes and prevention of botulism. Because there had been an outbreak of food poisoning in the Pinsk area, caused by spoiled canned blintzes. The Vitebsk research led to improved commercial food processing in the Soviet Union.

But before our Phase II alert was rescinded, civilian scientists under contract to the US Army had succeeded in developing a fully aerobic strain of *Clostridium botulinum,* easily cultivated *in vitro.* Suspended in glycerol, it could be sprayed on standing crops or dumped into water supplies. Quite lethal. To my knowledge it was only used once, in a field test. An obscure Marxist revolutionary in Guatemala had been manipulated into accepting a good Havana cigar. The tip of the cigar had been painted with the new compound. He lighted up, puffed, rolled the cigar around his lips. "Too sweet," he remarked. His last words.

That was 416HBL-CW3—the aerobic strain of *Clostridium botulinum.* It was in the specimens forwarded from the National Epidemiology Center. It was what was stopping all those objects in GPA-11. I had no doubt that the epidemic was programmed. But how, and by whom, and for what reason, I hadn't the slightest idea.

I intended to fly to Washington the following day to bring my discovery to the attention of the Chief Director. But late that same afternoon I received a note, via commercial mail, from Grace Wingate. Pleasant but cool. She and her aide would be in New York the following day on a shopping trip. She was writing to take advantage of my kind invitation to lunch. If that was possible, I could make arrangements through her aide. Number given.

416HBL-CW3 could wait. There was no rush, since there was no antidote. I immediately flashed the social secretary. A very imposing dragoon of an ef came on screen.

"Louise Rawlins Tucker speaking," she said crisply. "Ah, may I be of service?"

I identified myself.

"Ah yes, Dr. Flair," she said. Consulting a list on her desk.

"We have you down for luncheon tomorrow in New York. Will that be satisfactory?"

"Yes, of course," I said. "What time will—"

"Ah, we have you down for 1300," she said. "We prefer the Café Massenet, since the premises are familiar to our security staff. Ah, will that be convenient?"

"Yes. Very."

"Ah, splendid. The party will consist of Mrs. Wingate and myself. And security staff, of course. But they will not be dining with us. The headwaiter, Henri, will have a secluded table for us in your name."

"Thank you. And I—"

"Ah, please be prompt, Dr. Flair," she said. "We do have a very tight schedule. Looking forward to meeting you in person."

I was about to return the compliment, but she clicked off. Ah.

It didn't give me much time. But I had computed how Grace Wingate and I might be alone together. Briefly. And not in my apartment, a motel room, or a lavish suite in one of the *maisons d'assignation* that had become the Park Avenue equivalent of hot-pillow joints. It was too early in our relationship to plan such a maneuver. And with her aide and security guards in attendance. . . .

I flashed a rental agency that specialized in elegant antique and classic cars. I knew exactly the vehicle I wanted; my father had had one in his collection: a 1972 Jaguar XKE. The agency had two available, one black and one fire-engine-red. I chose the red. In January, 1999, it would be impossible to be inconspicuous in a car like that, regardless of the color. I slid my BIN card into the flasher slot. While they were verifying my credit rating, I made arrangements for the car to be delivered to the compound gate at 1200 the following day.

It was, I knew, not a car that accommodated more than two comfortably.

The next morning I flashed Ellen Dawes and told her I would not be in the office until late that afternoon. If any insuperable crisis arose, I could be contacted at the Café Massenet after 1300.

"Nothing less than the end of the world," I told her. "On second thought, not even for that."

"I understand," she laughed.

"And I left you the coffee ration in the top file drawer. Under *C*. For coffee."

She giggled delightedly.

I had decided on civilian clothes. A suit of Oxford gray flannel with a Norfolk jacket. Shirt of white natural linen with a Lord Byron collar. Plastisilk scarf of sky blue. Black plastipat moccasins with tooty tassels. I wore a plaid cloak thrown casually over my shoulders. I smelled of elegance.

When I checked out at the compound gate at 1210, there was a gang of security guards around my red Jaguar, admiring the lines and listening to the chauffeur's lecture on the car's performance potential.

"What a cock-bucket!" one of them marveled.

"You going cruising for cush, Dr. Flair?" one of them asked.

"No," I said, "I'm taking my dear old grandmother for a spin in the country."

I don't think they believed me. I signed for the car, handed the chauffeur a pat, slid behind the wheel. If I smelled of elegance, the car smelled of love. Natural glove-leather upholstery; natural burled-walnut dash. If burial had been legal, I would have opted for that car as my casket.

I pulled up in front of the Café Massenet. Directly in front. I had an instantaneous audience: passersby pausing to goggle at the car's sensuous lines. When I alighted, carrying my plaid cloak, I attracted almost as much attention.

"Big porn star," someone said knowingly.

The doorman awaited me under the canopy. I had his pat ready.

"I'm Dr. Flair," I said. "With Mrs. Wingate's party."

"Of course, Dr. Flair."

"I'd like to leave the car right there."

He glanced down at the folded bill before slipping it inside his white glove.

"Of *course,* Dr. Flair!"

"I'm Dr. Flair," I said to the headwaiter. "With Mrs. Wingate's party."

"But of course, Dr. Flair! An honor, doctor!"

He snapped his fingers. Someone took my coat.

"I am Henri," he murmured. "Allow me."

He removed a minuscule bit of lint from my shoulder.

"This way, if you please, doctor," he said. "Mrs. Wingate's special table."

Heads turned to watch our passage. The trappings of power. The only objects who scoff are the powerless.

It was unquestionably the best table in the room. Secluded, but with a fine view of everything. I was the first to arrive. As I had planned. I bent my knee. A chair was gently nudged under me. The pale pink napery was so stiff it was difficult to bend.

"While the doctor is waiting?" Henri suggested diffidently. "A something?"

"A something would be nice." I nodded. "Perhaps champagne as an aperitif?"

"Oh, excellent," he chortled. "May I suggest a '91 Piper? It was a very good year."

"The Piper will be fine," I said.

"And just in time!" he cried. "For here are the ladies!"

If my entrance had occasioned glances, theirs attracted stares. The preceding black zipsuit marched past me, hand in pocket, into the restaurant's kitchen. And stayed there. Presumably guarding a back entrance. A second sentinel, an ef, took up a position behind and to one side of our table. Impassive. The third remained near the entrance. I relished every minute of it. The panoply!

"Mrs. Wingate," I said. Having risen. "How nice to see you again. And you must be Louise Rawlins Tucker. A profit."

When we were all seated:

Grace: "Nick! Did you see that antique car parked out front? What a beauty! It's all red, and so lovely!"

I (negligently): "The Jaguar? Oh, yes. It's mine."

I knew, instinctively, that Louise Rawlins Tucker, personal aide and social secretary to the Chief Director's wife, would be important to our scenario. During lunch I paid court. Not neglecting Grace Wingate, but trying to make the duenna feel she was guest and partner more than server and chaperone.

It was not difficult. Though her physical appearance was offputting—she was more yeoman than dragoon—she had an easy manner and a pretty wit. More significantly, she had an obviously deep affection for her young charge. That made us co-conspirators, did it not?

The luncheon ritual went swimmingly. Louise was wearing a dove gray flannel suit, not too unlike my own in cut. That was good for a laugh. Grace was wearing—I could not have been conscious of it since I did not remember it.

Once, while I was speaking, she reached up, listening, looking into my eyes, and twirled a vagrant strand about her finger. Slowly twisting and stroking. Ems have gone to war for less.

402

About Louise Rawlins Tucker:

She was an obso, quite large, with enough lumps and blotches to remind me of leonine faces. But she was obviously not a victim of *Mycobacterium leprae;* simply an unfortunate, unprepossessing ef. With a wry, self-deprecating charm that included amusement at her own officiousness.

I wondered—part-wondered—if she sensed my interest in Grace Wingate and might not be a closet romantic. Because, under my gentle prying, she revealed that she had devoted most of her adult life to the care of her widowed father. A professor of Romantic Literature at Georgetown University.

"Isn't all literature romantic?" I asked.

"Ah," she said.

Then, upon her father's stopping, she had created a whole new life for herself.

"I don't know what I'd do without Louise," Grace Wingate said fondly. Putting her soft, tanned hand on the other ef's claw. "Just perish, I suppose."

"Ah, I'd do anything for you, angel," Louise Rawlins Tucker vowed. Fiercely. *"Anything."*

I had the oddest notion that she was speaking to me. A promise. And a warning.

When we went outside, preceded and followed by black zipsuits, there was an admiring audience circling the red Jaguar. The doorman looked on benignly.

"Nick," Grace Wingate said, "is it really yours?"

"For the day," I said. "A ride?"

"Oh! What a profit!"

She looked to Louise Rawlins Tucker.

"Grace, you can't," her aide said. "We're running so late."

"A half-hour," I pleaded. "Around town. Through Central Park. You and the guards can trail us."

"Louise?" Grace said. "Please? May I?"

"Ah," the yeoman said. Looking at me. "Well. . . . Twenty minutes. No more. We'll be right behind you."

So they were: two black limousines following my every turn. I didn't care. I was alone with Grace. I laughed. She laughed.

"You *are* a scamp!" she said. "Do you ever run out of ideas?"

"Never," I said. "But this is a one-shot. We can't do it again."

"No," she said. Regretfully. "I suppose not. Oh, Nick, it's *such* a car."

It was. It handled like a muscled ef. I turned smoothly into Central Park, heading north, making the grand circuit. Children were sledding. Booting a soccer ball through the snow. Chasing. There were dogs. Objects were sauntering. Couples. Users, I supposed.

"Grace," I said.

"What?" she said.

"Nothing," I said. "Just Grace."

She put her hand lightly on my arm. A few months previously she had told me of her love for her husband. How she would do anything to preserve her marriage. And now she was. . . . But I didn't think less of her for that. It made her infinitely more precious. Idealism was for scoundrels. I wasn't that. Quite. Nor was she.

"Grace," I said again.

"Yes?"

"What are you wearing?"

"Didn't you notice? Brute! I wore it just for you."

"All I could see was you."

She could not snuggle; the limousine was close behind. But her arm moved sideways. Hand probed. I moved up casually in my bucket seat so she could clasp my waist.

I took a deep breath.

"I love you," I said.

It didn't hurt.

"Yes," she said.

"Will you say it?" I asked her.

"No," she said. Quite low. "Not yet."

"But you shall?"

"I think so. Please, Nick. Time."

"Oh, yes." I nodded. "As much as you want. And then I shall have your ears."

"My ears?" She was astounded.

I told her how I worshiped her ears. She was amused. And touched. I thought.

"I'll cut them off and mail them to you," she said. "Dear, sweet Nick." She touched my beard. Quickly.

"What are we to do?" I asked.

She thought a long moment. But I knew she had already computed it.

"Do you like Louise?" she asked.

"Yes. Very much."

"She lives alone in this big house in Chevy Chase. Not too far from where you and Paul live. Since her father stopped, she has become very social. Her parties are famous. Very tooty. Mike is away a lot. Out of the mainland. It would be all right if I went to Louise's parties. Mike would approve."

"Would Louise? I mean, would she invite me?"

"Yes. If I asked."

"You trust her?"

"With my life."

"Exactly," I said. "It may come to that."

"I'm willing. Are you?"

"There's a sharp curve up ahead," I said. "To the left. I'm going to speed up suddenly. We'll be around the turn before the limousines catch up. They won't see us. I can bend to you. You can bend to me. Briefly."

"Yes," she said.

So we did. We kissed. Oh.

The next day I took the air shuttle to Washington. I had flashed ahead to set up a facial with the Chief Director. Penelope Mapes came on screen.

"I've got to see him," I said.

"No, Nick," she said. "He's got a full plate."

"It's about GPA-11," I said.

"Oh," she said. "Take a beat."

She went off screen. Then came on a moment later.

"Should Bigelow be there?" she asked.

"Yes."

"Take two beats," she said. And disappeared again. Finally she came back on.

"Got you in," she said. "At 2030 tonight. Here, at the EOB."

The shuttle got me to Washington an hour before my meet. I took the Metro to the Lafayette Square stop. I was carrying no luggage. I intended to stay overnight, but I had clothes and toilet gear in the Chevy Chase place. As I did in Grosse Pointe. It would, I thought, be nice, some day, to settle. Put down roots. Obso thinking. To settle was to stop.

I was still early for my meeting with the CD. I walked in, unannounced, to the office of the gestating Department of Creative Science. After all, it was *my* office. In the basement of the EOB. A

405

suite of three rooms, in the disarray of enlargement. No one about. Machines shrouded. But in the inner office, Paul's sanctum, lights and the sound of voices. I pushed open the door. Paul, Mary, Maya Leighton, Seth Lucas, Art Roach.

"Ah-ha," I said. "Gotcha."

"Hey, Nick." Paul said. Genially. Uncoiling from his swivel chair behind the desk.

"Dr. Flair," Roach said. Solemnly. "I haven't had a chance to thank yawl for what you did."

"Sure," I said. "We stroke you, you stroke us. Keeping an eye on the stamps and petty cash around here?"

Then they were all silent. Suddenly.

"Art just took over," Paul said. "A few days ago. Doing good service. Some creative ideas. What gives, Nick?"

I thought the mass was stressed. But when you lived in a paranoiac world, you learned to breathe suspicion.

"Got a meet with the CD, Paul," I said. "Can you make it?"

"About the DCS?" he asked anxiously.

"No. Something else."

"Nick, I have a meeting of the Beists' finance committee."

"Go," I said. "By all means." I turned to Seth Lucas. "How's your patient, Seth?"

"Just stopped by to say hello," he said.

"Lewisohn did?"

"No, no," he said hurriedly. "No change in Lewisohn. Maya and I came over for a seminar."

"Oh?" I said. "What seminar?"

"Not a seminar," Paul said testily. "How many times do I have to tell you, Seth? It's not a seminar, it's a hearing. House Committee on Science and Astronautics, Nick. I wanted to condition Seth and Maya to the drill. They may be called upon to testify."

"They may indeed." I nodded.

"See you later, Nick?" Maya smiled at me. "After your meeting?"

It was pulling in all directions. Stretched and disturbing.

"I may be a while," I said.

"Seth is going back to the Hospice," she said. "I'm staying over with Mary out in Chevy Chase."

"Fine," I said. "Maybe I'll see you there. Paul, can I talk to you for a minute?"

It had been a curious exchange. No structure. I could not compute it. It was my fault, I supposed, for barging in suddenly.

Paul followed me out into the corridor.

"That business in GPA-11," I said. Low voice. "It's a manipulated strain of *Clostridium botulinum*. Aerobic."

He looked at me. Startled.

"My God," he breathed. "How did you get onto that?"

"Heavy analysis of specimens from the National Epidemiology Center. The strain was developed during chemwar research in 1988."

"Never heard of it."

"You wouldn't. Not the original research. Before your time. But it was listed in the restricted drug code book. I'd have thought you'd remember. Didn't you scan it when you were AssDepDirRad?"

"Well, sure," he said. "But Nick, there must be a hundred stews in that book."

A serpent began to stir.

"Close to it," I said.

"Well, there you are," he said. "How is it administered?"

"No idea," I said. "I'm telling Wingate right now. Then it's Bigelow's migraine."

"Oh? He'll be there?"

"Of course."

"Well, don't take any kaka from him, Nick. I happen to know his status is fragile."

"My son, the pol," I said.

Chief Director Michael Wingate and Chief of the Bureau of Public Security R. Sam Bigelow were seated in the dining area of the CD's office when Penelope Mapes ushered me in. The remains of a meal littered the table. Both ems appeared frayed.

"Well, Nick?" the Chief Director demanded. "What have you got for us?"

"Sir," I said, "I had heavy analysis done on specimens sent from the National Epidemiology Center. That outbreak in GPA-11 is caused by a manipulated strain of the botulism bacterium. It's aerobic. Meaning it can exist in the presence of oxygen."

"I don't believe it," R. Sam Bigelow said angrily. Frog face going in and out.

"It's not important what you believe," I said. I was, I admit, relieving my growing hostility on him. "It's operative."

"Now see here, you—" he began.

Wingate raised a hand. Bigelow's mouth snapped shut. The CD stared at him.

"Why didn't Heath know about this?" he said coldly. "More to the point, Sam, why didn't *you* know about it?"

"Listen, Chief," Bigelow said hotly, "you can't expect the Bureau's labs to know about every poison developed by the Department of Bliss."

"It wasn't developed by the Department of Bliss," I said. "This particular poison was developed by the Department of Peace. In a Phase II alert, ten years ago."

"Shit," Bigelow said disgustedly. "All right. Write it down. We'll check it out."

I looked around for something to write on. Penelope Mapes was at my elbow instantly with pencil and scratchpad. I jotted the name of the bacterium and the code number and slid it across the table to Bigelow.

"Any cure, Nick?" the Chief Director asked.

"An antidote? No, sir. Not to my knowledge. The alert was canceled before we went that far."

"Shit," Bigelow repeated. And glowered at me as if I had personally stopped every one of those victims in GPA-11.

"Then the outbreak is programmed," Wingate said. No idiot he.

"Yes, sir." I nodded. "No doubt about it."

"Any idea how they're doing it?" the Chief Director asked.

"No, sir. Not really. You might have the field investigator check out fiddled cigarettes and cigars. But it's a very long shot, considering the age-victim numbers. It's something else. Got to be."

"Don't worry, we'll find it," Bigelow grumbled.

"I'm sure you will," I said equably. The toadish em bored me. Suddenly the whole fracture bored me. Not half so significant as a soft kiss, in a closed car, on a swift turn, in Central Park.

"Grace told me you entertained her at lunch in New York. Michael Wingate said. Walking me to the door. "That was kind of you, Nick."

"My profit, sir."

"Yes. And thank you for your service on this business. We'll take it from here."

It was late, but I was able to draw wheels from the EOB motor pool. I drove to Chevy Chase slowly. Much had happened in the past hour that I wanted to compute. But all I could reckon was my own obsession.

I estimated her weight at about fifty kilos. All stuff. Wind it up and set it ticking. No different. It was operative that she was comely, but so were millions of other efs and ems. Why she? No great beauty. No great wit. She was simply who she was.

I drove in a glaze. What bemused me was my chilly somberness in computing all this. And my total disregard of the possible consequences. Dreaming of her, even doom seemed a profit.

Z-4

From an address to a cadre of fourteen-year-old neurophysiologists under accelerated conditioning at Duke University, Durham, North Carolina, February fourth, 1999:

"There was a time when a conditioned obso, expert in his discipline, might spend a lifetime studying Sumerian script. I suggest to you that this was less discipline than self-indulgence! (Laughter)

"I will not insult your intelligence by calling you the 'wave of the future.' I will say only that today, and tomorrow, your brains are needed. There is vital service to be done, a world to remake, and it is to enlist your aid in remaking that world that I am here tonight.

"When you leave this hall, you will be given Instox copies of HR-316, a bill to establish a Department of Creative Science in the Public Service, as submitted by the Chief Director to the House of Representatives for debate and approval. We hope!

"I would like to call your attention to Division III, Section 8 of that bill. It deals with staff organization of the proposed Department. You will find frequent mention of the term 'omnists.' I would like to take a few moments, if I may, to analyze for you what our computing was on this subject, and why we created the term 'omnist' to describe the scientist of tomorrow.''

From an address to the National Association of Drug Manufacturers at their convention in Miami, Florida, February fifth, 1999:

"All right, having now outlined the new bill, let me ask and answer the question: 'How will the Department of Creative Science affect your organization and the future of drug biz in the US and in the world?'

"Let me make one thing perfectly clear: We haven't yet moved the bill out of the House Committee considering it, and already, amongst those serving to do exactly that, aspirin consumption is up three hundred percent! (Laughter)

"Seriously, I believe the DCS will prove the greatest boon to the drug industry since the synthesizing of steroids. Not because there is any one division, section, paragraph, or even a single word in the bill that applies particularly to the drug structure. But because the fundamental belief of the new Department of Creative Science will be in the holistic nature of science. The goal of all science is the improvement of the species. It's as simple as that. And it is there, precisely, that you and your industry will be expected to play a crucial role.

"I suggest to you that the time has passed to consider drugs within a limited, therapeutic frame of reference. Up to this point in time, you have been engaged essentially in producing a negative pharmacology: antiheadache, antiarteriosclerosis, antipimple, antidepression, and so forth.

"We, who are devoting our energies, talents, and brains to the DCS, believe the time has now arrived to develop a positive pharmacology. We are irrevocably committed to serving closely with you in researching a whole new spectrum of physical strength and mental health stimulators, to enable the human race to cope with the future and to fulfill its potential as the most creative species the universe has ever seen." (Applause)

From extempore remarks to a symposium of hostile media students at the University of Missouri, February 8, 1999:

"What on earth makes you think you are the anointed? To sit in judgment on the actions of objects in high places? To scorn their talents, misrepresent their motives, ridicule their sacrifices?

"You are falling into exactly the same trap that demolished the reputation of professional economists in the 1970's. They saw their occupation as a discipline apart, existing *in vacuo,* with its own laws, precepts, equations, logic, and goals. Then they awoke one day to discover it was all mush. They had neglected to consider the political factor, the social element, and all their fine computing

410

amounted to a heap of kaka because their imput was faulty.

"I suggest that you ponder that example. Do you really believe you can write your news stories, shoot your documentaries, film your interviews, compose your editorials, from some slightly yellowed and stained ivory tower where reality is not allowed to intrude? Such an attitude is worse than foolish; it is dangerous. You are of this world. Your service is of this world. You deny the future at your peril."

From final remarks to a meeting of graduate neurobiologists at the National Science Academy, February 11, 1999:

"The important thing is not to waste time searching for answers to questions for which there are no answers."

I delivered 12 speeches in eighteen days, and took part in 6 symposia, 8 colloquies, and submitted to 16 radio and television interviews. I visited nursery schools, academies, colleges, universities, laboratories, factories, power installations. I stroked innumerable palms, smiled until I feared my face would crack, and was photographed in close conversation with a former President. His breath was foul.

Joseph Tyrone Wellington provided a PR staff of four. An advance em moved one day ahead of us, confirming arrangements, making contacts, setting up local media. Traveling with me were: (1) A technical em who checked out public address systems, seating arrangements, local radio and TV coverage, etc.; (2) A security em in civilian clothes who was responsible for antiterrorist planning and travel arrangements; and (3) An extremely tall, attenuated ef named Samantha Slater. "Just for laughs," Joe Wellington had whispered. Winking.

In fact, Samantha was remarkably competent and held the entire safari together. She got us where we had to be on time, paid motel bills, carried an inexhaustible pharmacopoeia, and, from the first day, when we surrendered to the hysteria, she and I used each other with profit. Frequently. Everywhere. Once, standing up in a phone booth. Once, blue with cold, on a hotel terrace. Her corpus was incredible. Like using a worm.

We finally got to Detroit where I addressed a formal dinner meeting (red tie) of richnik industrialists. I told them that, if they didn't know it already, research and development were their only

411

guarantee of continued growth. And the proposed Department of Creative Science stood foursquare for research and development. Applause was generous.

So generous that I told them that as industrial managers, they must also learn that innovative ideas in political and social orbits could be just as lovable. This time the applause was polite.

We had structured a break upon reaching Detroit. The rest of the party went on to Buffalo where I would rejoin them in two days. I cabbed out to Grosse Pointe and fell into bed. Coming down slowly from my energizer high. I awoke fourteen hours later, wishing Samantha Slater was there. She could twist her . . .

My father was away for the day on a business trip. Mrs. McPherson, Miss Catherine, and Charles seemed delighted to have my company. The weather was miserable. Extraordinarily cold. So I stayed indoors all day and the four of us played cartel bridge, the new form of contract that had been devised in 1996. We had an occasional pitcher of hot flip.

"Another small glass, Mrs. McPherson?" I'd ask.

"Oh, sor!" she'd say. "Well . . . just to keep the freeze away."

Miss Catherine helped her to bed. Charles snoozed where he was, in a library chair. They were good obsos, all of them, and had absolutely no connection with what was to follow.

I called Millie Jean Grunwald early in the evening. She sounded happy to hear from me. But Millie was always happy. I made arrangements to pick her up at 2030. Despite the weather, Millie wanted to go. I was in a similar mood.

I drove slowly through a thick night. Wet snow. Wipers licking at the windshield. I thought again of Samantha's talents. Millie was waiting for me in the doorway of her building. The porn shop, at street level, was dark, empty.

After she bounced breathlessly into the car, kissing me, and her door was closed, I gestured toward the deserted store.

"What happened?" I asked. "Out of business?"

"Uh-huh." She nodded. Then giggled. "One day they were there, the next day they were all cleared out. Nick, you should see the roaches and mice that have been coming upstairs to me since the shop closed."

Millie had a sleazy plastivet cloak across her shoulders. She pulled it open proudly to display her tooty costume: a blouse of strips of fabric gathered at neck, wrists, and waist. But gaping to reveal her naked torso. Nipples nuzzled through. And purple tights imprinted with a great orchidaceous growth, sprouting from her crotch with stems, leaves, flowers down her legs and around her ass. Boots of silver plastikid.

"Loverly," I said. "Really, it is. But the snowflake around your neck. Too much, Millie."

"But you gave it to me, Nick."

"I know. But it detracts from the overall effect."

Obediently she took it off. I slid it into my purse.

"Much better," I assured her. "Millie, you're beautiful."

"Oh, yes," she sighed. Slumping contentedly. Head falling sideways onto my shoulder. "I feel beautiful when I'm all dressed up."

She knew exactly where she wanted to go: the Lords Sporting Club. I had never heard of the club, but guessed what it might be.

The Lords Sporting Club was set off Gratiot Avenue in a whitewashed, one-story, cinder-block building. I judged it had been a former garage or supermarket. A single dim neon sign said simply: LORDS. With a red outline of a fighting cock beneath.

Parking space was ample. But lovable. So was the admittance. Behind a dock, just inside the door, a large primate in a crimson mess jacket inspected us coldly.

"Member, are you?" he asked. His voice had the peculiar harsh raspiness I usually associated with laryngeal nodules.

"Unfortunately no," I said. "May I join?"

"Twenty for a card for one," he said. "Entitles you to bring a guest. Ten each for tonight's show."

I looked at Millie. Her eyes were shining.

"All right," I said. "Credit on my BIN?"

"Love," he said.

I counted out the forty. He held each bill under ultraviolet light before he accepted it. Then he took a blank membership card from a stack.

"Name?" he asked.

"Smith," I said. "James Smith."

He wrote it in swiftly. Shoved the card across to me.

"A lot of your relatives inside," he said. Not smiling.

"All named John?" I asked.

"How did you guess?" he said.

"Take care of that throat," I said.

The interior was one large room. A crowded bar at one end. A uninest at the other. The backless bleachers were ranked about a pit of hard-packed earth. A fence of chicken wire separated the pit from the downfront rows. The room was hot, fogged with cannabis smoke, raucous with the cries of vendors and markers. But it was not completely filled; we found aisle seats about halfway up to the ceiling. Stifling.

"Isn't this exciting?" Millie said delightedly.

It was a five-match exhibition. The first event, a cockfight, was just concluding when we took our seats. One of the birds was staggering, dusty, torn. The other stalked relentlessly. The outcome seemed obvious. I looked about.

A very tooty audience. I saw one em with a metallic codpiece, artfully jointed like the arm of a medieval suit of jousting armor. There were several efs bare to the waist. Poor Millie, with her gaping strips, seemed almost overdressed. One ef, an unzipped cape hanging from her shoulders, appeared to be wearing a skinsuit in a pattern copied after Mondrian. A second look revealed she was naked, the squares and lines painted on her flesh. The em across the aisle from me wore a giant gold-plated phallus on a chain about his neck. It would not have been remarkable except that it was decorated with a small, violet ribbon bow.

There was a sudden roar. I looked back to the pit. The victor had sunk a spike into the eye and brain of the vanquished. There was a rapid flurry of feathers, a spreading stain. Handlers came forward to remove their birds. Attendants sprinkled fresh earth and swept the pit clean.

There was a harsh crackling from the loudspeaker. Then a voice boomed clear: "Second event of the evening coming up. Champion My Own Ripper versus Champion Devil's Delight."

If you wish to name your dog Champion this or that, there is no law against it. The scurviest mongrel in Christendom might be called Champion La Belle Dame Sans Merci, and no one would sue. The two dogs led into the pit were "Champions" of that order. I thought there might be a few vagrant bull-terrier genes in both, but the rest was up for grabs. One was a dirty white, the other a dirty buff. But both showed encouraging ferocity. Straining against their choke leashes, snarling, yellowed teeth naked. Eyes wild. Slavering. Doping there.

"Eight for five on the white," a frantic voice screamed in my ear. "Three to two on the tan."

I turned my head.

"Ten on the white," I said.

414

"You've got it," he shouted. Marking it down.

More noise now. Almost every seat filled. Objects leaning forward. Tense.

"Gentlemen," the steward said solemnly. "Pit your dogs."

It was a good fight. Even before it started, Millie's fingers were clamped on my knees. Pressure increased as the bout progressed. I was scarcely conscious of it. Staring at the action in the pit. Trying to follow the whirl of straining bodies. Jaws snapping for the killing bite.

Both dogs were quickly blooded. White with his left hindquarters ripped. Buff with a shoulder matted with gore and pit dirt. A feral roar ripped the room. Atavistic. "Kill 'im, kill 'im, kill 'im!"

It ended suddenly. White finally found buff's throat. He would not let go despite buff's wild writhings and tumblings. Then the bite of throat ripped free. Buff stood a moment on quivering legs. The heart still pumped. Hot blood sprayed over the first few rows.

"Ahhhh," everyone breathed.

The marker paid me off without comment or expression.

The third event was ridiculous. Two efs, one white, one black, clad in tiny *cache-sexe* with aluminum cups over their breasts, belabored each other with padded gloves. The audience grew restive during this farce. Then I saw the reason for the chicken-wire fence about the pit. It wasn't to protect the customers from violence, but to protect the performers. All the missiles fell harmlessly into the first few rows. Occasioning a few private squabbles that were more enjoyable than the languid action in the pit.

But the fourth event restored the crowd's fever. Two bare-knuckled ems, wearing only aluminum cups over their genitals. Both were heavily muscled, not young, and both showed scarcely healed scars and purpled bruises from similar, fairly recent bouts.

"Twenty on baldy," I said to the marker.

"You've got it," he shouted. Marking it down.

The encounter was strangely stirring. I could observe it, analyze it, reject it. But I was moved, physically and emotionally, in a way I could not compute. Part of it, I told myself, was empathic: identification with the crowd's mood. And with Millie's. She was quaked. Her fingernails dug deeply into the side of my thigh.

The bout lasted for a single fifteen-minute round. There was one judge, but only to warn on fouls. Decision-making was vested in the audience. They made clear from the start that the shaggy-haired gladiator was their favorite. If the fight went the full fifteen minutes, and came to a roared vote, my "twenty on baldy" was down the pipe.

It went down sooner than that. Shaggy opened a barely healed cut over his opponent's right eye. Blood streaked baldy's face, mixed with dust from the pit floor to cast a clown's mask.

Baldy was willing, if inexpert. As long as he could, he kept thudding his huge fists into shaggy's torso. You could see the reddened marks on chest, ribs, solar plexus. And, when baldy saw a target, on back and kidneys. The only results were clearly audible *whumps,* but they slowed shaggy not a whit. Methodically, precisely, he cut baldy's face to ribbons. Completely closing one eye. Goring the other. Ripping the lips loose. Breaking teeth.

Baldy's torn left ear was hanging crazily. Both eyes were blinded. Forehead, cheeks, and chin looked like filleted beef. He swayed on his feet. Arms fell slowly to his sides. He slouched. Clotted eyes peering up at the noise booming down. His knees sagged.

Shaggy had no need for skill then. No fancy footwork or artful dodging. He stood planted, estimated the distance, drew back stone knuckles, crashed them into baldy's nose. Great gouts of blood spouted. The defeated em toppled face down as if someone had axed him.

They dragged him off, sprinkled fresh earth, swept the pit smooth.

"Enjoying it?" I asked Millie.

"Nick," she said. Holy tones. "It was the most marvelous thing I've ever seen. I came."

"Good on you," I said. "Let's have a drink before the next bout. I'm thirsty."

We had miniatures of vodka-and-Smack, warm, purchased from a vendor at horrendous cost. Then, since the final attraction seemed delayed, we each had two more.

I shall never know whether the last bout on the evening's card was genuine, fixed, or—as I suspected—a sophisticated theatrical turn in which the participants were not opponents, but partners in a choreographed athletic ballet.

They entered the pit naked. The raucous audience fell silent, since both were quite beautiful. Catcalls, at the moment, would have been infratooty.

The young ef, introduced as Janet, was tall, slender, with purplish hair down to her waist. Small breasts, but well formed. Elongated nipples, faint aureole. Pubic hair shaven. Protuberant *mons veneris*. Flat abdomen. Excellent musculature. A cold, composed face.

The young em, introduced as Eric, was about the ef's height. Almost as slender, with a well-defined rib cage. Enlarged gastrocnemii indicated a dancer or runner. He was circumcised. Length of the penis was not unusual, but the thickness was. Hirsute scrotum. Well-developed pectorals and deltoids. His blond hair would have reached his shoulders, but was pulled back and gathered with what appeared to be a pipe cleaner.

The only things worn, by both fighters, were brown natural-leather gloves. Skin-tight.

At the gong, they moved cautiously toward each other. Lightly. Delicately. Bodies were turned slightly sideways. Hands and arms were held extended, waist-high. I wondered if, instead of a boxing match, this was to be judo, jujitsu, karate, kung fu, or any of the other Oriental martial arts.

It apparently was to be a combination of all, for the first blow essayed was a lightning-fast kick Janet aimed at Eric's groin. His reactions were swift: He drew back just enough to slip the flashing heel, then chopped the edge of his right hand across Janet's breast. I could hear her hiss.

I could hear it because that vociferous mob was, unexpectedly, suddenly silent. Perhaps there was a susurration, a low moan, a whispered, ''Ahhhh.'' But no shouts, cries, cheers, jeers. Even the vendors and markers were quiet.

If it was a choreographed dance, it was an uncommonly brutal one. She kicked continually, almost turning her back to him as her foot slashed sideways. Aimed always at his testicles. He depended mostly on his hands and elbows, going for her unprotected breasts. Striking with scraping blows, using the edge of his gloved hand.

I could hardly believe it had all been programmed. Both gladiators were shiny with sweat, welted from blows taken, quivering from blows launched and missed. Eric was bleeding from thigh rip. One of Janet's breasts was suddenly livid.

Then, after about five minutes of careful maneuverings, great leaps, rapid flurries, and just as artful withdrawals, they appeared to be carried away by the primitivity of their conflict. This, too, may have been programmed. But speed increased, movements became wilder. More and more frequently we heard the smack of tightly gloved fists on young flesh, crack of heel or edge of foot against bone and tendon. Gasps and sobs for breath. I fancied I could smell them. Their young sweat. Hot blood. Even their charged fury.

They couldn't have been pulling those punches and kicks; I swear they could not. Flesh became lumped and rare. Slick with blood, mottled with pit dust. And when the gong sounded, ending the bout, they refused to stop. But now they were grappling close, straining against each other. It appeared he was trying to throw her to a fall, one heel hooked behind her right knee, pinioning her wrists as she strove to smash a gloved fist into his gonads, and she was biting his ear while his head swung wildly, butting her, and their slippery loins were pressed, smacked, again and again, and then, finally, a great roar went up from the crowd and, in cadence, we all shouted, "Draw! Draw! Draw! Draw!" Like the caw of waterbirds over the lake, and it was all so stupid, and Millie was actually weeping, and I had an erection that would never end. Ever. And we, Millie and I, the crowd, stumbled slowly away, and I passed the primate in the crimson mess jacket, still behind his dock, and he stared at me bleakly and rasped, "Enjoy yourself? Mr. Smith?"

I ignored him and bought Millie a souvenir from a vendor. A small stuffed pit dog. Its coat dyed with realistic bloodstains.

I have said that passion dooms profitable using, and it does. Millie and I were tuned to a tight, tinny pitch, but nothing we did that night opened the gates we wanted thrown free. I know it was so with me; I believe it was so with her. If that last fight had been a designed ballet, then I blamed art. For always offering the receding carrot. Beauty. Mystery. Ecstasy. I wanted only the now. The flat and tasteless now.

I was worse than her; I could not stop talking that night. To her sprawled, unhearing, somnolent corpus. All my problems. All my troubles. Stress pouring from me in a hemorrhage. That sweated bed became a confessional, and I meandered on about *Clostridium botulinum* and Grace Wingate and what I planned to do to Hyman R. Lewisohn. She did not hear me. But even if she had, she would not have understood. She was a poor, retarded clone with punched breasts and punished thighs, and what could she compute of the Department of Creative Science?

At some point in time, during that verbal diarrhea, I came around to Egon Schiele, whose art, I then realized, I had been sedulously avoiding for so long. There was something there, I said aloud, something there, something in his paintings and drawings frighteningly akin to what I had just seen: Janet and Eric seeking to chop each other to deadening pain.

It was all beyond me. I glimpsed rather than saw. Until I grew weary with disemboweling myself to a gently snoring Millie. I switched off the lamp. Listened awhile to the soft scuttling of mice displaced from the vacated porn shop below. And, finally, fell asleep.

Then back to Grosse Pointe the following morning. Curiously refurbished from the previous night's folly. As if I had been flayed and then fitted with a smartly tailored suit of Juskin. Guaranteed blemish-free.

The house seemed crowded. My father had returned, bringing with him his production, marketing, and PR staffs. Ben Baker was the only object I knew. I was introduced to the others: names and faces of no significance to this account.

I sat in on the afternoon session, listening to the set speeches and the colloquy that followed. It soon became evident to me that the Die-Dee Doll was an intoxicating success. I learned that production shortfalls had limited love input during the Christmas selling season, but a new assembly plant had been brought onto line, and sales were overachieving in the postchris period.

"Ethnic markets are incredible," the sales chief enthused. "Much better than projected. Take Africa. We're airlifting the DD-4, 5, and 6 models: light tan, dark brown, black. The DD-6 in tribal dress is moving exceptionally fast. We're getting reports from our field ems that in some places, back in the bush, natives are worshiping the dolls!"

I gathered that, all over the world, little efs, and some little ems, were anxiously watching their Die-Dee Dolls, waiting for the rattle that presaged the end. In Scotland, Die-Dee Dolls in kilt and plaid. In Hong-Kong, in miniature cheongsam. In Japan, in kimono and obi. In California, in bikini (topless). In Greenland, in plastifurs. And so forth. All over the globe the final rattles sounded on the wind, and children rushed to inter the remains.

Then the meet was over; guests began departing by car and by copter. Finally, my father and I, alone, moved into the library. Giving Mrs. McPherson and Charles a chance to clean up the littered dining room.

"Nick-ol'-as!" my father shouted. Clapping me on the shoulder. "Good to see you, boy. You look peakish. Serving hard?"

"Very hard." I nodded.

"Little medicine for the doctor," he chuckled. Pouring us snifters of brandy. "I'm hearing and scanning a lot about you these days."

I said nothing.

"How's it coming?" he asked. "This Department of Creative Science? Think you'll slip it by?"

"We're hoping."

"It sounds good to me," he said stoutly. "I've spoken to a few objects about it. Heavy objects. They're sympathetic. But they'd feel better if they knew who'll be Director. I tell them you. Right?"

"Probably."

"Counting on it?" he asked shrewdly.

"Sure. But no guarantee."

"I wish you were in Washington. That's where the action is."

"They've got me on the road, doing the PR. That's important, too."

"No doubt about it," he assured me. "Very important. But Washington. . . . Paul Bumford's handling things there?"

"Yes. He's running the temporary DCS office."

"Uh-huh. Well, you know the obso stories about the traveling salesmen? How much cush they get away from home? But no one mentions how much the old lady gets at home, while hubby's away. You follow?"

"Oh, sure." I nodded. "I follow. But I trust Paul."

"Uh-huh. But D. C. does strange things to young fellers. It's like their first drunk. Their first lay. A taste of what it's all about. I've been computing. . . . Suppose this: Suppose, unofficially, I organize a committee. 'Businessmen for the DCS.' Something like that. Get some big names. Lean a little on the Washington crowd. Would that help?"

"One hell of a lot. Thank you, Father."

"And while we're leaning, we can pass a few nudges that our cooperation depends on your becoming Director. How does that jerk you?"

"I like it, I like it!" I said. As enthusiastically as I could. "I'd really appreciate that."

"Good as done," he said. Finishing his brandy in a gulp. "Well. . . . I've got a few little things to do."

I must have looked amused.

"I don't want to talk about this one, Nick," he said.

"All right."

"No jokes. Please."

"All right," I repeated patiently. "No jokes."

"This one may be serious," he said solemnly. "I'm really jerked."

"Glad to hear it."

"Would you be sore, Nick? If—"

"If you married again? Of course not. It's your life."

"Well, I haven't decided," he said. "If I do, you'll be the first to know."

"If you do," I said, "I think I better be the second to know."

"Nick-ol'-as!" he said fondly.

On to Buffalo. A speech there, and at Rochester. A private conversation with the Governor in Albany. A symposium at MIT and a colloquy at Harvard. Then back to Manhattan Landing while the others continued on to Washington.

"So nice." Samantha Slater smiled. Slowly stroking my palm. "I'm looking forward to our next tour."

"My pleasure," I said.

"Oh, no," she said. "Mine."

During the twenty-six days I had been absent, I had kept in contact with Ellen Dawes in GPA-1 and Paul Bumford in Washington, D. C., via a Portaphone, a portable radiotelephone in an attaché case. With a scrambler attachment. Paul had nothing urgent. The methodology of the programmed nutbreak of botulism in GPA-11 was still unsolved. HR-316 was coming up for amendment votes in the House Government Operations Committee. The DCS office in the EOB basement had been expanded. Art Roach had added two black zipsuits to his staff. And, oh, yes—there was a hand-addressed letter to me from Louise Rawlins Tucker. I asked Paul to open it and read it to me. Louise thanked me for the enjoyable lunch and invited me to a dinner party the second week in March, date and time to be confirmed later. I told Paul I'd take care of it when I returned.

"Louise Rawlins Tucker," he said. "She's Grace Wingate's AA, isn't she?"

"Social secretary," I said.

Ellen Dawes' news wasn't as welcome. Nothing catastrophic had occurred in my absence, but the Satisfaction Rate continued to decline, and Lewisohn's vital signals continued to deteriorate. And there was a courier-delivered letter from the Bureau of Public Security. It was marked "FIA"—For Immediate Action. That, in BPS nomenclature, was akin to California canners marking a jar "Gigantic olives."

"Hold it for me," I told Ellen. "It it was really hot, the courier would have waited for a reply. Miss me?"

"Oh, yes," she said. "We're running out of coffee."

Dear, sweet Ellen. I needed her, occasionally, to snub me back to operative values.

I was glad to get back to GPA-1. To shower with a large cake of perfumed soap. To mix a big vodka-and-Smack with a slice of natural lime from three I had found in Florida. Generally to unwind. I pulled on a tattered, soft-as-silk zipsuit and old moccasins. I riffled through the personal mail that had accumulated in my absence. Bills, mostly. Some invitations to speak, write, submit to interviews, attend symposia. One of the latter, on megapopulation, was to be held in Reykjavik. Seemed an odd place for it. Why not Calcutta?

Later in the evening, about 2130, I pulled on a hooded oilskin and dashed across the snowy compound to my office. My desk was piled high. I zipped through it swiftly.

Hospice No. 17 in Little Rock reported that a "volunteer," who had been given a total transfusion of newly formulated synthetic blood, had lasted eighty-six hours. Possibly Angela Teresa Berri. But eighty-six hours wasn't bad; they were getting there.

Phoebe Huntzinger had submitted a lengthy status update. Progress was continuing on Project Phoenix. Coherent conceptions were being drained from volunteers' brains with increasing frequency and heightened sensitivity. Her use of the word "drained" excited a realization of how valuable the new technique might prove in interrogative procedures.

Leo Bernstein's report consisted of three words: "No significant progress." But I knew Leo; nothing was significant to him except the solution. I was certain he was achieving.

I finally came to the For Immediate Action message from the Bureau of Public Security. It was obviously a form letter, composed and produced by computer, with the signature of R. Sam Bigelow printed in water-soluble ink that smudged if you rubbed it. The real thing.

The letter stated the BPS was conducting a "routine inventory" on samples of the restricted toxic substance 416HBL-CW3. In 1988, a number of samples of this substance had been delivered to various research facilities, one of which was the Department of Research & Development, SATSEC, DOB. Records indicate, shipment of and signed receipt for 5 cc of the aforementioned substance. I was to inform BPS if the 5 cc were still in possession of DivRad. If not, I was to explain when and for what purpose any or all of it had been used. Reply requested instanter.

The letter angered me. I was not angry with R. Sam Bigelow; he was just performing his service, trying to trace all known quantities of the aerobic *Clostridium botulinum* in glycerol. I was angry with myself. After the analysis in K Lab, when I had looked up 416HBL-CW3 in our restricted drug code book, I had scanned the large green star after the definition. But the proper synaptic closure had not been made. I had not interpreted that green star. It signified that a restricted drug so marked was in our pharmacology library.

Then I recalled my few moments of talk with Paul Bumford in the basement of the EOB, when I had told him that 416HBL-CW3 was the causative agent in the botulism outbreak in GPA-11. I remembered that brief conversation had disturbed me. Was it because that, subconsciously, my mental lapse was nagging? That I knew I had missed something, but could not dredge it to the surface? I had had to postpone my annual hippocampal irrigation. Perhaps that had been a mistake if my memory was beginning to stammer.

No matter. All I had to do now was to verify that existence of 5 cc of 416HBL-CW3 in our pharmacology library and so inform R. Sam Bigelow. I could not recall anyone in DivRad ever requesting and using any of the damned stuff. We had no need to paint cigars or spray our neighbors' tomatoes.

Once again, oilskin clad, I dashed across the compound. Because of the snow, the automatic car-trains were not running. I slotted my BIN card, was further identified by voiceprint check, and was allowed entrace into B Lab. Down in the third sublevel I followed a maze of underground tunnels to the drug storage area. The empty white corridors went on and on. When, good little mouse that I was, I arrived at my goal, I would receive a food pellet.

There was a night staff in the outer office of the pharmacology library: two objects playing three-dimensional chess, one kibitzing. They looked up when I came in and started to rise. I waved them down.

"I can find it," I said. "Go on with your game."

They settled back.

"Still snowing out, Director?" the kibitzer asked.

"Still." I nodded. "You may be here for days. Nothing to eat but aphrodisiacs."

They grinned at me and went back to their game. I went to the file computer, switched it on, punched the readout button, and typed 416HBL-CW3 on the keyboard. Almost immediately the screen showed: RESTRICTED SECTIONXXXROOM GXXXBIN 3XXXSTACK 4XXXPOSITION RXXX END IT.

I wiped the screen, turned off the machine, went through an inner door to the storage area. The restricted section was at the end of another long, deserted corridor. Shining plastiasb tiles underfoot, white walls and ceiling, fluorescent lighting. Subway to nowhere.

The glass doors to the restricted section were locked. As they should have been. I pushed the buzzer. Nothing happened. No one came. I knew what the problem was. Vinnie Altman, the obso night guard of the restricted drug library. And *his* problem was petroport. But he was inoffensive, serving out his final years to retirement. It was easy to overlook his mild alcoholism and taste in scanning matter.

I leaned on the buzzer again. Finally I saw him. Blinking, shambling toward the door. Carrying a magazine. He peered at me through the glass. Then his whiskey face creased deeper. He turned off the alarm, opened the two locks, slid the door aside.

"Hey there, doc," he said. "Long time no see."

I didn't mind when *he* called me doc. I stepped inside. He closed the door. The locks and alarm connected again automatically. I took the picture magazine from his hand. Danish porn for export. It was called *Gash*. So it was. All of it.

"All I can do is look," he said.

"Look but don't lick," I said. "The ink may give you a bellyache."

"That ain't where my ache is," he said. "Please sign the register, doc."

I signed the register, a big ledger, with date, time of entrance, name. While Vinnie Altman leaned over my shoulder. Watching. He exuded petroport fumes.

"I know what I'm looking for," I told him. "Go back to your education."

He shuffled over to a corner desk. The half-liter of petroport was probably in a drawer. He rationed himself. One half-liter per night. No more. Just enough to make him forget the long, empty corridors.

This area of the pharmacology library was larger than you might have expected. Mostly due to the shielding needed for the radioactive drugs. But those were in special vaults equipped with automatic dumbwaiters. The other brews, everything from cobra venom to a synthetic nicotine we had developed for treatment of vascular hemorrhage, were stored on open shelves.

It was easy to find Room G. I switched on the overhead light. I searched around and found Bin 3. In it, last on the right, was Stack 4. I ran my finger along the position labels: L, M, N, O, P, Q, and there was R. I raised my hand to lift it down. And stopped. It was a small glass flask. Airtight stopper. A line had been etched around the bottle. The marking 5 cc was clearly visible. But the level of the liquid in the flask was appreciably below the etched line.

I didn't touch the bottle. Just stood there with my hand outstretched. Evaporation was impossible. Not that quantity. What else? I could not believe there had been a research project using 416HBL-CW3 which I could not recall. But then I hadn't remembered that green star in the restricted drug code book.

I switched off the light. Closed the door softly. Walked slowly back to the outer office. Vinnie Altman was tilted back in his swivel chair. Feet up. *Gash* clasped on his lap. His head was back. Eyes closed. Mouth open. He was snoring.

"Going to check the withdrawal file," I said gently.

He didn't stir. I tiptoed quietly over to the metal cabinet.

Each restricted drug had a file card. It showed, on one side, the initial deposit stored, at what date, and any additions made, at what date. The other side showed withdrawals. An object withdrawing a restricted drug had to write date, quantity, signature.

I slid open the 400 drawer slowly, easily. I looked to Vinnie Altman. He hadn't moved. The buzz was constant. I flipped through the cards. I found 416HBL-CW3. I lifted it out carefully. By one corner. Holding the file open with my other hand. With the tips of my fingers.

The card showed an initial deposit of 5 cc of 416HBL-CW3 on November 3, 1988. There had been no additions since the original quantity was stored.

I turned the card over.

There had been one withdrawal.

On November 18, 1998.
Two cc.
I looked for the signature.
It was there.
Nicholas Bennington Flair.
In my own flamboyant scrawl.

Z-5

Two days later I was on my way to Denver. For a personal inspection of Project Phoenix. Lewisohn's condition was deteriorating so inexorably that I knew I had to expedite my scenario for his survival. While he still had sufficient strength to endure it.

Aboard the jet, sipping my fourth vodka-and-Smack of the day, puffing my third cannabis, I reviewed my actions in re the fiddled 416HBL-CW3 file card. I was satisfied that I had done all that a crafty object might do.

My first reaction, of course, upon viewing my own signature, had been akin to, say, witnessing an act of levitation. "I see it but I don't believe it." Then I thought possibly I *had* taken the *Clostridium botulinum* and had signed the file card under the influence of hypnosis. Either by a clever operator or by drug. In the precarious world of politics, at that point in time, you learned to breathe the volcano's fumes.

But the date, November 18, 1998, precluded the hypnosis theory. On that particular day, I had been in Washington, D. C., conferring with Joe Wellington. I was certain. Later, my memory was verified by a notation in my appointment schedule.

Then, still staring at the file card, still shaken, I had the wit to check the register. That big ledger in which every visitor to the restricted drug library had to note date, time of entrance and exit, signature. Sure enough, "Nicholas Bennington Flair" had entered the library at 2320 on November 18, 1998, and exited at 2345.

But I was gratified to see that the signature on the register was identical with the signature on the 416HBL-CW3 file card. I don't mean the two signatures were similar; they were *identical*. To every hook, dash, curlicue. Vinnie Altman still snoozing, still gently snoring, I brought the file card over to the ledger to compare the two.

No object ever duplicates a signature exactly. Ever. But, of course, those were not signatures. Closer examination proved that. The pressure of pen throughout had been uniform: no faintness or heaviness of line. Ergo: not writing at all, but printing or inscribing with a mechanical or automatic device. The methodology then became apparent.

Like most executives, my form letters were printed and signed by an office computer. When the quantity desired was limited, and mass distribution unnecessary, identical letters were Instox duplicated from a signed master. When many letters of varied subject matter but of routine nature were prepared, they would be typed from my dictated tapes by Ellen Dawes' assistants, scanned by her for accuracy, and "signed" with a small, portable imprinter. This was a mechanical device not unlike a postal cancellation meter. It contained an ink supply. A lever depressed a plastisteel cut that was an exact (photographic) reproduction of my signature. The cut was an em equivalent of an engraving. The "signature" looked authentic. But being mechanically reproduced, pressure was uniform throughout.

The problem of my "genuine" signature appearing on file card and ledger having been solved, to my satisfaction, I next turned to how it had been snookered. My signature meter was usually kept in my office safe. To be requested by Ellen Dawes when there were a number of letters to be "signed." Then returned to me. But not always. When I was absent from the office on those Washington trips, or the PR expedition, the meter was turned over to Ellen. She should have kept it locked up. Knowing her, I didn't suppose she did. But even locked in my safe it would not have been secure. What was?

Having relatively easy access to my signature meter, how would a terrorist group planning to steal a quantity of *Clostridium botulinum* have proceeded? Putting myself in their place, with their arcane but obviously powerful motivation, I plotted a possible scenario. During the twenty-four hours following my discovery of the missing 416HBL-CW3, I put the plan to a field test. With certain refinements.

My preparations may sound complex; they were actually not. I sent Ellen Dawes to the stationery stockroom for paper, envelopes, pads, pencils, rubber bands, paperclips, and a quantity of several forms. Including 100 blank restricted drug file cards. I only needed one. Which I filled out for 416HBL-CW3. I showed an authentic initial entry of 5 cc on November 3, 1988, and no additional deposits. The withdrawal side I left blank. I "aged" the card by scraping it several times across the surface of my office plasticarp. When I had finished, it looked ten years old. Reasonably.

I then paid a casual visit to A Lab, wandered about until my presence was ignored, and filched a 5 cc flask of glycerol. I then left the compound, briefly, to purchase a half-liter bottle of petroport at a federal grogshop. I brought the bottle to the Pharmacology Team Lab and told them I needed it doped with an instant hypnotic and a memory eraser. A restricted project. No questions were asked. The seal was carefully lifted, screw top removed, contents contaminated, the bottle restored to its original appearance.

Then, just to prove to myself the fiddling could have been carried out by a single object, I donned a greatcoat over my zipsuit and filled the pockets with my signature meter, the newly prepared restricted drug file card, the small flask of glycerol, the half-liter of fixed petroport. No problem of storage.

"Vinnie," I said. After he had turned off the alarm, unlocked and opened the door. "This is just a social visit. Someone gave me this jug of happiness. Thought you might like it."

I handed over the dozied liquor.

"Why, doc," he said. Coming out of his fog for a moment. "Mighty nice of you. Have one with me?"

"You go ahead," I said. "A little too sweet for me."

We went back to his desk where a copy of another Danish magazine, *Clit*, was spread wide. As it should have been. I waited while Vinnie poured himself a plastiglass of my petroport.

"Over the hills and far away," he said. Raising the glass and draining half of it.

Thankfully, he was seated when it hit him. I took the glass from his hand before the remainder spilled. His head had fallen sideways. He was snoring busily.

I went back to Room G, Bin 3, Stack 4, Position R. My original idea had been to bring in an identical glass flask filled to the etched line with 5 cc of pure glycerol. But close investigation by the Bureau of Public Security would have revealed the substitution. Also, I would have had to remove the original flask, taking it with me in my pocket when I left. The notion of striding on icy pavements carrying a glass bottle of enough toxic bacteria to stop the entire population of the US was not an endearing prospect.

So I merely removed the stopper of the original bottle and poured in enough pure glycerol to bring the level up to the etched line. I did this as porcupines fornicate—very, very carefully. I doubted if even heavy analysis of the contents would reveal the dilution.

I replaced the original bottle in its original position. After wiping the glass free of prints. Turned off the lights. Returned to the outer office. Carrying the remainder of the pure glycerol. Vinnie Altman was still snoozing comfortably, the eraser busily at work in his brain destroying the memory of the previous hours.

I then removed the fiddled 416HBL-CW3 card from the file and substituted the new card I had prepared. It looked right at home. But before I did that, I satisfied myself that my signature meter could have leen used to imprint my name on file card and register. It could have. Easily. But I didn't record a notice of my current visit, of course. No need.

I remembered to pour the dregs of Vinnie Altman's drink back into the bottle and then take with me the remainder of the contaminated petroport. I switched off the alarm, opened both locks, exited, slid the door softly shut behind me. Alarm and locks connected automatically. Beautiful. I had done what I could to pillow the attack upon me.

In the jet, beginning the descent to the Denver airport, I reflected again, briefly, on the problem of who had been responsible. For the programmed outbreak of botulism in GPA-11 and for the attempt to fix the blame on me. Some terrorist group, I supposed. Perhaps frantic leftovers from the Society of Obsoletes' conspiracy who had not yet been terminated. But it was fruitless to wonder.

It was much more profitable to fantasize on Louise Rawlins Tucker's dinner party to be held the following Sunday. I had confirmed date and time by flasher. She had said casually, open-eyed, "I think you'll know most of the objects, Nick. They're fun. Grace Wingate promised to come."

The Denver Field Office had been alerted to my arrival. There was an official limousine awaiting me at the gate. I did not find those trappings offensive. At the complex itself, Phoebe Huntzinger met me at the door. We went immediately to a colloquy with the new Project Phoenix Team Leader, a yellow em named Thomas Lee, and his young staff.

I listened for more than an hour. Their progress startled me.

Although I should have been habituated to rapid research. As explicated in my prospectus to the Chief Director on the Department of Creative Science, I had stated that the accelerating rate of scientific discovery was mainly due to four factors:

1. The increasing use of computer technology, especially for automatic chemo- and physioanalysis.

2. The increasing early conditioning of the young. By oxygenation of the fetus and a hyperprotein diet for selected infants, the US was producing what a French astrophysicist had called (sorrowfully, I thought) a "generation of genii."

3. The easy availability of human objects for research. This element alone contributed immeasurably to public health and happiness.

4. The exponential factor involved: discoveries leading to discoveries, a geometric progression of scientific knowledge. Our conditioning techniques and development of brain-expanding and memory drugs were hard-pressed to embrace the complexity of today's science. It had become a race, as the obso writer H. G. Wells said, between education and catastrophe.

So I tried not to appear too startled by the progress of the Project Phoenix Team. I listened to their triumphs and their defeats. Nodded. Made a few pertinent suggestions. Then we adjourned to their operating theater to observe an object currently under usage. I did not inquire about the volunteer's antecedents. It would have been infratooty.

She was a young ef. About fourteen, judging from her pubescent breasts and scrabbly pubic hair. She was tightly strapped, naked, into a mechanism roughly resembling a barber's chair. Taped with electronic sensors; IV feeding that included a mild hallucinogen. Atop her head, descending to her eyebrows, was an enormous stainless steel helmet from which radiated the spokes of the soft laser transmitters and receivers, on swivel attachments.

The operating theater was a jumble of hardware. Many primary readout screens: one for each laser scan. Computers to monitor the object's vital signals. A transmitter to the Golem computer in a sublevel. Readout and printout machines for computer retrieval. And, touchingly, a pink bedpan.

We watched, quiet, while technicians made minute adjustments of the last rods.

"Sending," someone said. Watching an EEG transmitter screen. Machines went into action. The sounds were a symphony. *Ka-*

430

tah, ka-tah, ka-tah. Chingchingchingching. Beep-o, beep-o, beep-o. And underneath all, a deep, disturbing hum. We looked to the Golem computer readout screen.

XXXI WANT TO GET OUT OF HEREXXX

XXXMUST YOU DO THIS TO MEXXX

XXXPLEASE LET ME STOPXXX

I turned to the operator.

"Could I have a printout on that, please?"

"Yes, sir."

She pushed buttons. Held the screen image while the printer chattered briefly, 350 wpm. She tore off the screed, handed it to me. I scanned it, passed it to Phoebe Huntzinger.

Phoebe scanned it.

"What do you find significant in that?" I asked her.

She scanned it again.

"Nothing special, Nick."

"All one-syllable words," I said.

"Nick, I told you Golem is limited. We're using a ten-thousand word vocabulary storage, plus phrase linkups. We're pushing the limit now."

"Phoebe, I'm not blaming you," I said. Smiling. Touching her arm. "You've done wonders. Just gives me ideas, that's all. Thanks for the show. Let's eat."

But that brief demo at the Denver FO led to consequential imperatives. (Loverly words—no? Obsos would have said, "Far-reaching consequences." But language changes. As it should. Otherwise we would still be chanting, "Whan that Aprille with his shoures sote. . . .").

When I returned to GPA-1, I began to move objects about. I sent Leo Bernstein to Hospice No. 17 in Little Rock, Arkansas, for brief familiarization conditioning on their service on the formularization of synthetic blood. I pulled Seth Lucas out of Hospice No. 4, temporarily, and sent him to the Denver Field Office to serve with Tom Lee, the Team Leader on Project Phoenix. And I brought Phoebe Huntzinger back from Denver to Manhattan Landing.

"Big service," I told her. "Clear as much storage in your computers as you can. Program two-hundred-thousand word English vocabulary, plus a thousand-item vocabulary of foreign words and phrases. Particularly those applicable to economics and government. Got that?"

"Sure, boss. Going to tell me what this is all about?"

"No. Then after you have your pachinkos programmed, set up a direct wire link with Denver. For send and return. So we can scan the input down here and interpret."

"All *right*, Nick. You don't have to draw a diagram."

"This Tom Lee—what's your take?" I asked.

"A brain," she said. "He's eighteen. Makes you feel obso—right?"

"In this juvenocracy, everyone makes me feel obso. Get hopping, Phoebe."

I sent a restricted, detailed letter of instruction to the eighteen-year-old Team Leader Thomas Lee. I ordered him to prepare a contingency logistics plan to transfer Project Phoenix from the Denver FO to Hospice No. 4.

I sent a formal letter to R. Sam Bigelow at the Bureau of Public Security. I stated that in answer to his such-and-such, dated such-and-such, my personal visual inspection had confirmed that 5 cc of the substance 416HBL-CW3 was still in the possession of SAT-SEC, and records indicated no withdrawals for any purpose whatsoever.

Then I flashed Penelope Mapes, requesting an interview with the Chief Director. Times synchronized to my satisfaction. He would be leaving for a week's tour of exmainland States on a Saturday, just one day prior to Louise Rawlins Tucker's dinner party. Fine. Penelope Mapes promised me fifteen minutes with him on the afternoon of his departure. Megafine. I remembered the comment of a lab ef who had been involved in a successful research project.

"How you doing?" I asked her.

"Just great," she had said. "Everything's coming up penicillin."

I arrived in Washington on March 15. Many happy returns, Julius Caesar. I stayed at the Chevy Chase place and spent two full days with Joe Wellington and staff, including Samantha Slater, planning the logistics of a PR excursion through the Midwest. Touting the glories of a Department of Creative Science to Establishment Gruppen. It was, I sometimes felt, a contentless ceremony. Except, of course, the ceremony itself was meaningful.

I also spent a full day at temporary headquarters of the DCS in the basement of the Executive Office Building. The babe was healthy and growing. An enlarged suite of six offices, still in the process of expansion. More noise, more objects, more franticness. There is nothing quite like political growth. It is at once fascinating, exciting, disturbing. Something like the proliferation of *Neisseria gonorrhoeae* on a petri dish.

Paul Bumford and I—Mary Bergstrom sitting nearby, a silent fury—went over the political scenario. The original bill, HR-316, submitted to the House of Representatives by a Congressman from Alabama (a "sweetheart" of the Chief Director) had, of course, been overcast. A process similar to artificially inflating a requested budget by 20 percent. Knowing you'll be cut back to your desired goal. In this case, proposed amendments in the House Government Operations Committee were nibbling away at the original bill. But nothing that hadn't been anticipated and programmed. To quell wild beasts, you toss them raw chuck. When they are surfeited, the broiled sirloin is slipped by. So it was. So it always has been.

"By the way," I said to Paul. "Something for the Tomorrow File. A federal TV cable system. The only channel. All sets licensed."

"Got it," he said. "Excellent. Especially for agitprop."

My meet with Chief Director Michael Wingate was scheduled for 1430. I was ushered into his crowded EOB office. I had an opportunity then to observe the manager of the US in action. Surrounded, crushed by advisers, aides, secretaries, guards, applicants, patrons and clients, servers and masters. Penelope Mapes was there, of course, and Theodore Seidensticker III, Joe Wellington, Sady Nagle, and a varied assortment of concerned objects from Senators to hypersonic pilots and navigators plotting the CD's flight to our overseas provinces.

Then Michael Wingate exhibited to me another side of his multifaceted character: the efficient executive. Cool under pressure. Welcoming stress. The em of almost instant decisions; a barely preceptible pause before the "Yes" or the "No." And withal, remarkably genial, pleasant. Brooking no serious opposition, you understand. Not even from Senators. But the negative always glossed by the physical gesture: palm stroke, pat, embrace, caress, playful punch. It was a marvelous performance. To watch.

"Nick!" he said. Genuine pleasure. "So glad to see you!"

I believed it. That was his gift. A charm so intense it conquered all.

"About GPA-11?" he asked.

"No, no."

"You've discovered how they're doing it?"

Then I divined part of his secret: He never listened—totally.

433

"No, Chief," I said. "I'm sorry to report I have not discovered how they're doing it."

"Bad business," he said sternly. Shaking his head. "Bad business."

In our following conversation, interrupted a dozen times, I finally was able to make clear to him why I had requested the audience. Hyman R. Lewisohn was stopping. Using conventional therapy, there was no hope for the em's survival. But I wanted to attempt radical surgery. I didn't explicate further. But before that eventuality, I wanted the Chief Director to convene an ad hoc committee of the nation's foremost civilian physicians, hematologists, oncologists, etc., to make an independent analysis of Lewisohn's present condition. And to make a prognosis. They would have open and complete access to my personal files and to the records of Group Lewisohn.

Chief Director Michael Wingate looked at me closely.

"Why do you want an outside opinion?" he asked.

"For my sake, sir," I said. No expression. "And for yours."

His glance sharpened. You could see the knife edge thinning. And glittering.

"All right," he said. "Yes," he said. "I'll order it immediately."

He motioned to an aide and began dictating a tape-recorded memo that would result in the convening of a committee of civilian scientists to investigate the present physical status of Hyman R. Lewisohn. And to prognosticate his fate. I tiptoed away while he was dictating. He waved to me as I departed. He was already surrounded by the mob. Seeking his favors. His most precious was, I hoped, waiting for me.

The home of Louise Rawlins Tucker was on Oxford Street, about two kilometers from the place Paul and I leased in Chevy Chase. The house was well-sited; it had a university air: obso red brick, aged ivy, extravagant grounds, an air of staid respectability. Its most salient feature, for my profit, was a walled garden. Now sere, with patches of blued snow still lurking in the shadows. Flagstoned walks. Bare trees and withered brush.

"I don't like evergreens," Louise Fawlins Tucker said firmly. "Ah, what is?"

There was a charming arbor. It would, I hoped, be painted in the spring. Before the wild grape sprouted. There were two semicircles

434

of benches: wood-slatted seats about a shallow depression that might have been, once, a pond. Fish? Lilies? Anything.

The dinner party was for twelve. Precisely seven ems and five efs.

"Ah, it is best to have two wandering ems," Louise Rawlins Tucker said firmly.

I had sent, at great expense, natural gladiolus. Enough to fill several vases and metal pots throughout the downstairs area. The splotches of soft color enlivened the dim, somewhat depressing interior. Louise Rawlins Tucker inspected my gift with great favor and thanked me.

"Regardless of what objects hint," she said, firmly, "you can't be all bad."

"And what do objects hint?" I asked.

"Ah," she said.

We dined, a sedate but pleasant party, from a buffet of adequate but unimaginative dishes. The proshrimp were undercooked, the prolet salad distressingly flaccid. But there was an excellent bowl of natural pasta with a prosauce hyped with what I guessed to be prorooms and natural Italian garlic sausage. Quite good. I had a second helping.

"You'll get fat," Grace Wingate said to me.

"More of me for you," I murmured.

"Awful em," she whispered. But she smiled.

Other than that brief exchange, we had engaged in no other talk except polite greetings after her late arrival. She spoke to the others; I spoke to the others. Slowly, gradually, I found myself cast in the role of a "wandering em." I was content, trying to compute the status of the guests.

They all seemed to be acquainted which, naturally, made me feel the outsider. Although I met nothing but gracious thaw and smiling pleasantry. All obsos except for Grace and myself. Two of the ems and one of the efs were Georgetown professors. A Vermont Senator and his wrinkled daughter. An ef from the higher echelons of CULSEC, DOB. Another ef, crippled, a poet who, she told me, composed by a complex word-chess-move code. I couldn't compute it. She showed me a sample poem she just happened to have with her. I couldn't compute it.

But I should not carp; they were all profitable objects. Or at least inoffensive. In their tweeds and quilted skirts. Bangles and hunting

435

stocks. Neuter objects. Precisely the background for Grace Wingate and me. For our scenario. Might as well suspect that assemblage of leprosy as of passion hidden in their midst.

The after-dinner drink, as you might have predicted, was medium-dry sherry. The glasses were elegant crystal, just large enough for an eye douche. I waited until Grace Wingate was temporarily alone. Then carried my minature sherry over to her.

"Warm in here," I said. Brilliantly.

"Yes," she said. Distantly. "Isn't it."

"There's a garden," I said. "I peeped through the draperies. How does one get out there?"

"A side door from the kitchen," she said. Faintly. "A walk leads around."

"Five minutes?" I asked.

She nodded.

"Bring your cloak," I said. "It's cold."

Carrying that ridiculous sherry, I stalked determinedly through a back hall, past two serving objects in the kitchen. They didn't even look up when I unchained the side door and stepped out. I was wearing a winter-weight zipsuit. But still the cold shocked, tingled skin. I walked about, apparently inspecting withered shrubs and frozen lawn. Breathing deeply. Plumes of white. Then I sat cautiously on one of the scabbed benches under the bare arbor.

She was with me in a few minutes. Wearing a hooded cloak that framed her face. A cloud of russet wool, and those paled features. She sat alongside me. Billowing down onto the bench.

"Not for long," she said breathlessly.

"Long enough," I said.

I maneuvered between her and the house. Anyone watching— why would anyone do that? Want to do that?—would see only my back. Perhaps the top of her head.

I set the little sherry glass aside. I took her hands. She withdrew her arms into the loose sleeves of her cloak so that our clasped hands were enveloped.

"You're freezing," she said.

"No, no," I said. "Not now. First of all, I know you trust Louise. The others?"

"They couldn't care less," she said.

"Yes, I suppose so. Grace, I can cope with my own danger. But not yours. If there's any—"

"You think I care?" she asked scornfully.

I stared at her. It was an instant when, I thought then and I thought later, we came whole to each other. Why else should I suddenly be sickened by my life's turbidity? The time's? I wanted lightness, clarity, simplicity, elegance, airy laughter and spidery beauty. I wanted Grace.

"Your husband doesn't listen," I told her. "Not really."

Her eyes widened.

"How did you know? No, not really. He doesn't. Nick, I have so much to give."

I may have looked at her in amazement. I would have laughed at that dumb line from a lesser ef. But if absence makes the heart grow fonder, it also makes it more flatulent. I was prepared to believe her; she *did* have so much to give.

I took by trying to absorb her. Not only somber eyes, patrician nose, soft lips, glistening teeth, sharp chin, stalk neck, but *her*. We spoke in low voices, short sentences. Exploring. We were emotional archaeologists. Not digging with shovels. Crass that, and counterproductive. But with dentist's pick, jeweler's loupe, camel's-hair brush. Gently uncovering and examining. Learning each other. Sentences getting longer. Voices murmuring off into sighs. Warmed hands clasping tighter.

"I've wanted," she said, "all my life to become devoted. Completely. To someone. Or something. I love Michael. But he's not the all I wanted. I see that now. I thought Beism might offer what I need. I don't think so. I need a—a target. Nick, are you a target?"

"I think so."

"*My* target?"

"I want to be. But it's your determination to make, isn't it?"

"All mine?"

"Well . . . no. But I must change my nature."

"That's a great deal to ask," she said gravely.

"Yes." Nodding. "But I want to. Grace, I really *want* to. That's something, isn't it?"

We both sighed. Happy with our anguish.

"What is it?" I asked her. Nicholas Bennington Socrates Flair. "What is love?"

She shook her head.

"Devotion," she said. After a moment. "That's what it is for me. It may be something else to you. Pleasure. Duty. Whatever."

"Devotion?" I mused. "To what?"

437

"Oh," she said. Looking about. "To anyone. Or anything. Worthy."

"Am I worthy?" I asked her.

"I don't know. Yet."

"Are you worthy? Of my devotion?"

"Oh, God, yes," she said. "I *know*."

"We may die," I said. Using a word that was not officially approved.

"I don't care," she said. Looking again into my eyes. "Do you?"

Suddenly I didn't.

"No," I said. Gripping her sweated hands inside the covering cuffs. "It's meaning, isn't it?"

"Oh, yes," she breathed. "Oh, yes. Oh, yes. Meaning. That's what I want, Nick. Meaning."

"Love," I said.

"Love," she said.

We circled down from our panting high to discuss ways and means. The house of Louise Rawlins Tucker would be our "safe place." Grace assured me she could arrange for access during afternoons. Servers absent. So we plotted. With the sad acknowledgment of how small plans must bring grand ardors low.

I suppose, later, we stroked palms politely, and nodded on parting. Then we were inside, her cloak was over her arm. I saw the simple chemise of slithery silk. Imagined the living flesh glowing within. Humid scents and clever crannies. I hoped she dreamed the same of me. And thought she might.

About ten days later, I was in Bismarck, North Dakota, addressing the annual convention of the Association of US Historians. I was not about to tell historians that history was inoperative. That it no longer offered precedents. Some of my remarks:

"As historians, you must know that most civilizations have perished. Or are perishing. Birth, growth, stop. It is the fate of most objects and most societies. Some in a wink, some longer. Some by interior rot, some by external aggression.

"But, as you also must know, some political, religious, and social corpora have continued to exist. For aeons. Not in their original form, true. Not with their original structure, laws, directions, methods, goals. But by evolving. Adjusting to new input. It is the one lesson, the one great lesson, history can teach us. *Change*.

Either change conquers us, or we embrace change, learn to profit from change.

"I am here tonight to discuss with you a change in the Public Service branch of the US Government, the proposed establishment of a Department of Creative Science. I want to suggest how I feel this new Department will change the history of the US and, eventually, change the history of the world. To help us all adjust to new input, and to help us all survive. Because that, essentially, is what we're talking about—survival."

And so forth. And so forth.

I was back in the motel. In my room. Lying naked in bed with Samantha Slater. Both of us breathing like long-distance runners. Having had our first offs. One of her amazingly long, slender, hairless legs was clamped between my thighs. Her flesh could have been squeezed from a tube. I hugged it. Just the one leg. It was enough.

My Portaphone attaché case buzzed.

"Kaka," I said.

I disentangled, got out of bed, stumbled over to the desk. The case continued buzzing while I fumbled about, pulling the curtains, turning on a lamp.

"You're all red," Samantha said.

"I wonder why?" I said. I got the case open, switched it on.

"Flair," I said.

"Nick? Paul here. Go to scrambler."

"Wait a minute." I pressed the button, turned the code indicator. "What is it, Paul?"

"Nick!" Excited. "I think I may know how they're doing it. I mean the botulism. In GPA-11."

"How?"

"Are you alone? Can we talk?"

"Reasonably."

"Look, tonight I was in the office. Helping to get out the mail. We've had a postal metering machine on order for weeks, but it hasn't come yet."

"So?"

"So we've been using stamps. Licking a stamp and putting it on every envelope. So a few days ago Senator Blamey went into Bethesda for a hernia operation. I guess you scanned it."

"No. I didn't. Paul, it's hardly an item that might excite my interest."

"Well, look," he said. Almost stuttering in his frenzy to get it out. "Blamey is important to us. He's Chairman of the Senate Government Operations Committee, you know. Well, I thought—"

"Paul, will you get *to* it?"

"Well, I thought it would be a nice gesture to send him a personal get-well-quick note. From all of us at DCS. You compute?"

"Yes, Paul," I said wearily. "I compute. So?"

"So I wrote out the letter, handwritten, and addressed an envelope. Mary Bergstrom folded the letter, put it in the envelope and sealed it. Then she licked a stamp and stuck it on the envelope."

"Paul, what *is* this?"

"That's when it hit me! Nick, don't you see? I haven't looked into it, but surely there's a possibility. What if the botulism guck is in the glue on the stamps? Wouldn't that account for the number of victims in GPA-11? The age range? The scattered outbreaks elsewhere? Tourists traveling through GPA-11 and buying stamps they used when they got back home? Nick, for God's sake, all the victims are getting the dose from licking US postage stamps!"

"Jesus Christ," I said.

"What do you think, Nick? Nick? Are you there, Nick?"

"I'm here," I said into the transmitter. "What about the infant who stopped? It wouldn't be mailing a letter."

"The four-month-old?" he said. Still speaking rapidly. Still stammering with excitement. "*One* infant, Nick. Well, what if the mother or father wrote a letter, sealed it in an envelope, then licked a poisoned stamp. And *then* picked up the kid and kissed it on the mouth! That's possible, isn't it?"

I was silent.

"What is it?" Samantha Slater asked lazily from the bed.

"Nick?" Paul said. "Are you still there, Nick?"

"I'm still here," I said crossly.

"Well . . . what do you think?"

"A possibility."

"What should I do, Nick? Wait till you come back?"

I computed a moment.

"No," I said. "Don't wait. If it's contaminated stamps, there's still a lot of them around. Get to the CD as soon as possible. Tell him what you suspect. Tell him to bring R. Sam Bigelow's bloodhounds in on it. They'll run a search and analysis. Confirm or reject. But do it immediately.

"Right," Paul said. "Understood. Thanks. Nick. I really think this is it."

"Could be," I said.

"I'm off," he said.

"Good on you," I said. But he had already disconnected.

"What was that all about?" Samantha Slater asked as I crawled slowly back into bed.

"About licking," I said.

"How nice," she said.

R

Z-6

"Paul Bumford is an ultrabrain," Chief Director Michael Wingate said gravely.

"Yes, sir," I said.

"A very lovable em," he said.

I nodded. I was not, I admit, too delighted with these tributes.

"Paul suggested to me how it was being done," the CD went on. "The poisoned stamps. Bigelow's crew went in and verified it. Fortunately, they were twenty-cent stamps, used mostly on postcards. If they had been the twenty-five cent denomination for first-class postage, we estimate the stop ratio would have had a ten-factor increase. We picked up the unsold stocks of contaminated stamps at post offices and put out a general alert."

"Public?" I asked.

"Had to be," he said grimly. "No other way. But the flak didn't last long, and we were able to limit media coverage mostly to GPA-11. Nick, one of the many things this service has taught me is the public's short attention-span. Fifty years ago a botulism outbreak like this would have been an horrendous scandal. Screaming headlines for weeks. But the Great Stamp Recall lasted in the news for two, three days. Just another catastrophe. We've all learned to live with disaster. It's part of our environment. Drought, famine, crime, earthquake, terrorism, revolution, war, radioactive fallout. If you've seen one child burn to death on TV, you've seen them all. So what's new? Too much. Too many words. Too many images. The attention span shortens. It has to. We once thought alcoholism and drug addiction were psychic surrogates for suicide. Then we realized alcoholism and drug addiction are self-defense mechanisms: the object protecting itself from depression, psychosis, or worse. Right, doctor?''

"Right," I said.

"So our attention span shortens," he went on. Broodingly. "As it has to. Must. If we are to survive."

I had never heard him talk at such length. Or so intimately. He seemed to me weary. Physically weary. Kept pinching the bridge of his nose and squinching his eyes. Those jolly Santa Claus features were slack, gray with fatigue. But I would not presume to prescribe for him. I was not his personal physician. It had nothing to do with the fact that I hoped to guzzle his wife.

"The stamps, sir," I said to him gently.

"What? Oh, yes. The stamps. . . ." He came back from somewhere. "Well, it's been determined they were printed here in Washington. The glue on the back is purchased from a commercial supplier in fifty-gallon drums. It's trucked to Washington, held in storage until needed on the press. The operation is called 'gumming.' It's done after printing but before perforation. The adhesive could have been fiddled at any step along the way. Bigelow's objects have been placed in services where they can watch what's going on. And, of course, the warehouse and printing areas are being shared. I think it was a one-shot thing. Demented. I base that opinion on the absence of any obvious motive. No letters. No threats. No demands."

"I still feel it may have been an attempt to destabilize the government, sir. Or perhaps in the nature of a laboratory experiment. A trial run to test the technique."

"Maybe. Naturally we're doing everything we can to make certain it doesn't happen again."

We were seated in his top-floor EOB office. Just the two of us. It was night. The curtains blotted out the lights of Washington, the glare bathing the White House. The only illumination came from a chrome lamp on his cluttered desk. It made a round pool of light. But farther out, from the corners of the room, the darkness pressed in.

"Well . . ." he said. Pushing himself erect in his swivel chair. "Anyway, Paul Bumford did a fine service. I'll keep an eye on that young em."

"Yes, sir."

"But all this is by the way. The reason I called you in tonight is the report on Lewisohn. From that committee of civilian doctors you asked me to convene. They're in remarkable agreement—for doctors. Prognosis negative. Just like that.''

"What is their survival estimate, Chief?"

"Three to nine months. In that area."

"Any suggestions for treatment?"

"Nothing you didn't think of. They were very complimentary about the number and variety of protocols you have tried. Very ingenious, they said. Now then. . . . You mentioned something about radical surgery as a last resort. What exactly is it?"

"Chief," I said cautiously, "just how important is Hyman R. Lewisohn? How far will you go to keep his brain functioning?"

He rose heavily from behind the desk. Stretched his arms wide, arched his back. I heard the snap of vertebrae. Then he shrugged his shoulders, rolling his head about on his neck. A tired, stiffened em, trying to loosen up. He began pacing back and forth across the office. I moved around so I could watch him. He went into the darkness, then came back into the pool of light. Darkness and light alternating. While he talked. . . .

"Lewisohn," he said. "I'll tell you about Lewisohn. It's not enough to call him our best theorist. He's more than that. All his conceptions have a hard, pragmatic core. He's a genius without being a visionary. Let me give you a for instance. Years ago—it was during President Morse's second term—Lewisohn was asked to run a research project on the possibility of global war. You *ask* Lewisohn, you don't order him. Instead, Lewisohn turned in a monumental study of the history, causes, methods, and results of conflict between nations. The entire methodology of international competition. It's still a classified document—highest classification—but I can tell you it's remarkable. Lewisohn dealt with conventional warfare, nukewar, genwar, econwar, chemwar, popwar, and a dozen other possible collisions between governments. He then analyzed the resources of the US for each type of struggle. His conclusion, which has been the unofficial policy of the US ever since it was formulated, was that the security and prosperity of the US would best be served by agriwar. Agricultural warfare. An aggression in which food becomes the primary weapon. Lewisohn computed that a heavy increase in our total acreage under cultivation, plus crash programs to develop new cereal strains and new sources of protein, would provide the 'armory' we needed. You probably know the results of those classified research programs.

Lewisohn argued that by becoming the world's larder, we would, in a sense, be providing ourselves with a certain measure of insurance against nuclear attack. What foreign government would want to risk contaminating our land with radioactive fallout and endangering our agricultural productivity? But Lewisohn pointed out that, because of the population explosion, the US would never be able to feed the entire world. Therefore he recommended a system he called 'political triage.' PT for short. Basically, PT is based on the realization that food was then in short supply and would be for the foreseeable future. Therefore food must be used strategically and tactically as an offensive weapon. Since we could not feed the entire world, we could best serve our own interests by our choice of who buys our wheat, who gets our corn, who is shipped enough soybeans and fertilizer to allow them to continue to exist as viable nations. And at what level of subsistance. Some nations inimical to us would have to go down the pipe. Others we could maintain at a starvation level, a malnutrition level, or, if we wished, a comfortable level approximating our own calorie-consumption rate. Hence the term 'political triage.' It was a breathtaking concept that Lewisohn devised. And, all in all, I would say it served us well since it was implemented. At least we've avoided nukewar. All due to Hyman R. Lewisohn. This government will go to any lengths, *any*, to keep his brain functioning. We need him. It's that simple. Does that answer your question?''

''Yes, sir.''

''Now you answer mine. What is it you want to try on Lewisohn?''

I told him.

He heard me out. Still pacing into shadow, and into light. When I had finished, he came back behind his desk.

''What chance of success?'' he asked. Harsh, cracked voice.

''I'd guess between thirty and fifty percent, sir,'' I told him.

He nodded, shoved back, continued to stare at me. Horror there?

''I suppose you want my authorization?''

''Yes, sir.'' I nodded. ''I'll need it. In writing.''

He made a sound. A grunt? Snort?

''All right,'' he said. ''Go ahead. Supreme security.''

I had asked Paul to wait for me in the DCS office. Then we'd drive out to Chevy Chase in one of the official cars that had been assigned to his department. Strange. How I thought of it as ''his department." Well, he ruled the daily administration, so I supposed the preconception was normative. It was probably everyone's.

He and Mary Bergstrom were alone in the inner office. They looked up questioningly when I walked in.

"All set?" Paul asked. "We're hungry."

"In a minute," I said.

I sat down across the desk from him. I noticed he had extended his swivel chair to its full height and had equipped it with elevated casters. It put him at a higher level than the object sitting across the desk from him. I was amused. A typical gig of Potomocracy. He had learned fast.

"Got a Bold?" I asked him.

He slid a package across the desk.

"Hitting the cannabis hard lately, aren't you?" he asked.

"Am I?" I said. "I wasn't aware of it."

"How did the meeting go with the Chief?"

"Fine. It was about Lewisohn. We're going ahead."

"Going ahead? With what? The em is stopping."

There was no way I could keep it secret from him. I had no desire to. I needed a capable AA in the Washington area. He'd have to be told, and Mary Bergstrom, and all of Group Lewisohn.

"This is top security," I said. "You both know the regulations."

Then I outlined the scenario. About halfway through, Paul rose to his feet. He leaned across the desk to me. Knuckles down. I thought at first that, like the Chief Director, he was horrified by the plan. Then I saw it enraged him. I ignored his fury.

"Group Lewisohn will serve as nucleus for staff," I went on. "I'll rule all personnel. Phoebe Huntzinger will rule the computer setup in GPA-1. I'll bring Tom Lee and Project Phoenix down from Denver to Hospice No. 4. When they're positioned, we'll switch the direct-wire link. Alexandria to New York and return. We'll pick up a time lag there, but of no consequence. Leo Bernstein will also move his project to Hospice No. 4. I'll start recruiting the surgical team immediately. Paul, I want you and Mary to handle the logistics down here. Try to get the one with Operating Theater D. It's the largest building. We'll need living quarters and feeding facilities for the entire staff inside the building. And recreation—movies, TV, music, games, and so forth. Everyone will be locked up. No one in, no one out. Until it's done. You'll have to structure the security screen. Art Roach can tell you what you'll need in the way of personnel and equipment. But don't tell him what—"

"You idiot!" Paul screamed. Face livid. Entire corpus trembling with anger. "You microbrained idiot! Do you realize what you're doing?"

"I'm hoping to save Lewisohn," I said. As calmly as I could. "That's my prime responsibility."

"Save Lewisohn?" he shouted. "Kaka! Nothing can save that em. He's stopping! You understand? He's practically stopped now. Thirty percent, you said. That's the chance of success. And for that you're endangering the whole Department of Creative Science?"

"It has nothing to do with DCS," I said.

"It has everything to do with DCS," Paul yelled. Slamming a palm on the desktop. "*Everything!* You don't know politics. You just don't know. You think when we fail on this stupid Lewisohn caper that Congress is going to be sympathetic to our plans? 'The operation was a success, but the patient stopped.' Oh, they'll profit from that! All the butchers out to gut our bill. You think you can keep Lewisohn's stopping a secret? In this town? No way! And you and I will take the blame. So why trust us with something as important as the DCS?"

"You're overreacting," I told him.

"I tell you, I *know*. You don't know, but I do. I deal with these objects every day while you're running around the country having tea with professors. This town will forgive anything but failure. When Lewisohn stops, you and I stop with him, as far as our political careers go. And maybe the DCS stops too. Right in its tracks. But even if the bill is passed, with the sperm drained out of it, they won't touch you and me with plastirub gloves. The two bright young lads who stopped Lewisohn. What in God's name were you thinking of?"

"There's a chance the operation will succeed," I said.

"A chance!" he scoffed. Still trembling. Face twisted with his wrath and frustration. "Thirty percent. Some chance! Don't you think the whole DCS is chancy? I can tell you it goddamned well is. But if that gamble isn't enough, you've got to pile chance on chance, endangering something I've served on every minute for the past six months."

"*You've* served?" I shouted. Rising to my feet. Leaning across the desk so that our faces were inches apart. "*You've* served? And what have I been doing—fluffing my duff? Whose idea was it? Mine! Who wrote the prospectus? I did! Whose record and reputation convinced the Chief Director to go along with the DCS? Mine!

All mine! You're just a server here, and don't you ever forget it. I've watched you swell and preen and gloat over the miracles you've accomplished. Kaka! Ripe, rich kaka! You've got the brain of a server, the talents of a server, the ability of a server. That's all you are, that's all you'll ever be."

Then we were both screaming at once. Spraying spittle in each other's faces. I was vaguely conscious of Mary Bergstrom still sitting woodenly, expression stony. I knew where her sympathies lay. But I didn't care. I didn't need Paul *or* her. If necessary, I could do it all myself.

Finally I pounded a fist on the desk.

"All right!" I shouted. "All right! All right! Enough of this. Enough!"

We both quieted then. And drew back. Breathing hard. We were not physically violent types, either of us. But I could taste the bile in my mouth. Smell a sudden change in the odor of my own perspiration. I think possibly if the confrontation had continued for another few minutes, we'd have been at each other's throats.

"All right now," I said finally. Trying very hard to keep my voice steady. "I'll make it simple for you. I'm *ordering* you to assist on Operation Lewisohn. *Ordering*. Do you compute that? If you choose not to cooperate, please tell me now. I will then report your decision to the Chief Director. All clear?"

He turned his back to me. Stood facing the wall. Staring at a framed photograph of the Capitol. The silence went on and on. I lighted another cannabis with shaking hands. And waited.

Finally Paul turned to face me. Unexpectedly he was smiling. A tepid smile, but operative.

"Sure," he said genially. "I'll cooperate, Nick. We both will—won't we, Mary?"

I looked at her. She nodded. Without speaking.

"Good," I said. "I'll flash Luke Warren in the morning and tell him you'll be out there tomorrow and to give you everything you need. Get moving on this."

"Will do," he said lightly. "Should we go home now?"

"No. I think I'll take the shuttle back to New York. I want to get started on a personnel roster. You can drop me at the airport."

"Anything you say, Nick," Paul said. The smile warmer now. "You're the ruler."

About three hours later I was standing on the terrace of my GPA-1 penthouse. Staring down at the lighted, deserted compound.

I had showered. Mixed a large vodka-and-Smack. Pulled on a robe. Unbelted. Before starting the preliminary Table of Organization for Operation Lewisohn, I had stepped outside. Just for a moment.

It was an unusually balmy night for early April. Sky clotted with thick clouds. Wind mild, with a hint of fairer days to come.

Spring is surely the saddest season. One thinks: "My God, *again*?"

I found I was not replaying the scene with Paul. Nor even computing the Lewisohn scenario. I was dreaming only of Grace Wingate. Wishing she was standing, loosely robed, alongside me. Barefoot, as I was. We would stand in silence, for a while. Then we would. . . .

It had scarcely begun, and yet I knew the end. I think now the most precious passions have within them the seeds of stopping. Hope is, after all, an immature emotion. The astringency of end brings to even the sweetest affair a balance of flavor. Comfortable on the palate. So that one tastes with a sad, knowledgeable nod, and murmurs, "Good."

Poetry by Nicholas Bennington Herrick Flair: "Gather ye rosebuds while ye may; the thorns come soon enough."

As I began preliminary structuring of the Operation Lewisohn scenario, I saw the problem devolved into four elements: personnel, equipment, setting, timing. All these factors were crucial to the success of the experiment, but the selection of the most skillful servers available was, I felt, of prime cruciality. I would need:

1. Surgery team
2. Computer team
3. Project Phoenix team
4. Leo Bernstein's team

In addition to these four major groups (I made a note: "Gowns to be color-coded"), I would also require such supernumeraries as a Chief Nurse and assistants, Equipment Chief and assistants, a Chief Anesthesiologist and his associates, and a Production Team who would serve as medical stage directors, getting everyone in place on cue, timing the operation to the second, and coordinating the entrances and exits of the other players to avoid a mob scene in Operating Theater D. There was also, of course, Hyman R. Lewisohn himself.

Having determined the parameters of the personnel requirements, I began drawing up "optimum skill profiles" of the objects needed. These would go to Data & Statistics to be coded, then fed into our OA (Object Ability) computer. We would then, hopefully, get a selection of names of objects in Public Service who could perform the services required. I would make the final choices myself. It was, perhaps, regrettable that I was limited to Public Service by the "supreme security" nature of the assignment. There were many talented civilian scientists, some close friends, who from a vapid idealism had refused to sign the Oath of Allegiance. Thus limiting their careers. The US Government had the love.

All this took time. It was slightly more than a week before requisitions went out all over the world, calling in surgeons, anesthesiologists, medical equipment specialists, computerniks, and surgical managers with experience in directing long and complex operations. I estimated the entire Lewisohn scenario, from first knife slice to final hookup test, would take a minimum of fourteen hours.

Meanwhile, I had satisfied myself that Paul Bumford and Mary Bergstrom were serving as promised. An entire building at Hospice No. 4 was taken over for Operation Lewisohn. To the anguish of Dr. Luke Warren. A fence was constructed, a security screen implemented. Arriving staff members found themselves temporary prisoners within a restricted area. They slept in the "Lewisohn Building," ate there, found recreation there, and communicated with the outside world only through a censor control board.

I estimated later that the total cost of Operation Lewisohn ran well in excess of one million new dollars. The subject of this governmental largesse was continued on parabiotic therapy with a special IV diet designed to maximize his physical stamina, if only temporarily, to help him withstand the trauma of what awaited him. I avoided all personal contact with him during this period.

Neither Paul nor I allowed Operation Lewisohn to impede our efforts to move enabling legislation for the Department of Creative Science through the House of Representatives. Hearings before a subcommittee of the House Government Operations Committee were scheduled to begin during the third week in April. A favorable vote there would almost ensure passage by the full committee. HR-316 would then pass to the House Rules Committee for scheduling of floor debate.

There were many strings to pull, many egos to lave. At that point in time, our primary concern was the structuring of a roster of sympathetic witnesses to testify in favor of the bill at the hearings of the subcommittee of the House Government Operations Committee. We had carefully orchestrated a group of civilian scientists, academics, enema doctors, sociologists, hygienists, energeologists, science historians, gerontologists, and nuts-and-bolts businessmen. The last were enlisted with the assistance of my father's committee: Businessmen for the DCS. He had delivered.

Two days before the hearings were to commence, I went down to Washington. I stayed at the Chevy Chase place. I flashed Louise Rawlins Tucker, and told her my whereabouts and plans. She returned my call an hour later and said I'd be welcome to join her for lunch the following day. At her home. At 1300. Her manner was grave.

I walked from our Chevy Chase place. A solitary pedestrian on a gray, weepy day. A black raincoat buttoned over civilian clothes: Norfolk jacket, turtleneck sweater, flannel slacks. I tried to walk briskly, purposefully. A neighbor on an errand. Some neighbor. Some errand.

"Out for a stroll, Dr. Flair?"

"Oh, yes. On my way to seduce the Chief Director's wife, thank you."

If I had stopped to ponder the consequences. . . . But I did not stop to ponder. Could not. I think, perhaps for the first time in my life, I "was not in full possession of his faculties." Journalese for nuts. But that's not operative. Quite. I was aware of what I was doing but could not forbear. A unique experience for me. A not unpleasant one.

If Louise Rawlins Tucker or a server had answered my ring, I might have burst into tears. But neither did. After the third ring, the door opened. It was she. She! Grace Wingate let me in. Closed the door swiftly behind me. We smiled at each other. Shakily. I think we both said, "Well!" at the same time.

She busied herself taking my coat. Turning away to hang it in a hallway closet. She was wearing a strapped tanktop in pink. Shoulders and arms bare. Pinkish-purple slacks chained low on her hips. Sandals. My hammered silver earrings. When she came back to me, I touched them. We both laughed. Brief blast. Put arms about each other's waist, walked slowly back into the house. Then it was all right. Easy.

450

There were cucumber sandwiches, I think. And cocoa. It wasn't important. We sat apart and talked. Rapidly, frantically, breathlessly. There was so much to get through. So much to learn.

Her father had been in the Foreign Office. Retired now. That was how she had met Michael Wingate—at a Department of International Cooperation reception. Her mother collected cut glass in a hobnail design. Her one brother, older, married, two children, was with the Permanent Trade Mission in Peking. She had broken her leg at the age of thirteen. Skiing. Her tonsils were out. She was ashamed of her teeth, fearing they were too large, protuberant. She had studied dance. She adored broiled natural shrimp. Green and blue were her best colors, she thought. She worshiped my beard.

I did my best to reply in kind. Telling her about myself. Even imagining things to make myself more attractive in her eyes. To mogrify my image. A desperate stratagem, I admit. But you cannot love another unless you love yourself. She watched me steadily. Gaze never flickering. Finally, sandwiches merely nibbled, cocoa merely sipped, I moved over to sit alongside her on the couch.

We clasped hands and talked, talked. . . . Circling each other. Tentatively. Then spiraling closer. Each new revelation breeding another.

She told me her husband was a brilliant em, and kind, thoughtful. But he had a hundred guises, was all things to all objects. Withal, a secret em. Because there was a wall around the core of him. She could not penetrate to what he was, really, essentially. He wouldn't let her. And, above all, she wanted to be close to someone. So close that she could lose herself. Surrender.

I warned her. I said that my moral sense was atrophied. That I had used many objects, ef and em, for my own profit. That I connived without conscience. Betrayed. That I was ego-oriented and goal-directed. Sometimes without ruth. But for all that, I had not murdered. Personally. She might think that last merely a matter of degree. But degree was all—was it not? Absolutism was the mark of a crabbed and dingy brain. And although I had—

It was then she leaned forward and pressed soft, warm lips on mine. To silence me.

"I don't care," she whispered. "About all that. You can hurt me. Nick. If you want to."

I shook my head. "I don't want to hurt you. I want to know you."

We stared into each other's eyes. And learned more than all our words. Those dark, somber eyes. Widening to bring me in. I drifted hair back from her ears. She sat erect. Trembling slightly. I felt her ears with my fingers. Probing.

"That . . ." she said.

"Oh, yes," I said. "I know."

We felt each other. Still seated, we touched. Explored. Hair. Features. Neck and limbs. Torso. Our hands fluttering. Her bare shoulders. My arms. Her waist. My chest. Legs. Yes, and ankles. All. I caressed her toes, bared by her sandals.

During that almost somnambulistic ritual, we realized—I know I did; I think she did—that we would not use each other that day. The recognition lightened us, freed us.

She was, Grace Wingate was, to me, all sweetness and light. A large corpus but fragile, elegant. In texture and movement. Complete with the buoyancy of youth. And beyond sexuality, there was, in those somber eyes, dark glance, the unknowable that sucked me in, drew me in. I wanted to dive.

"I love you," I said.

"Why do you love me?"

I told her all. Corpus. Somber eyes. Soft lips. Vulval ears. Flame of ashen hair. Touch of her skin. The naked body moving within what she wore. Toes I longed to suck. The pouting navel I imagined. The ache to become one with her. Need to . . . what? Merge? Melt into each other. Penis and vagina welded. A two-backed beast. Ultimate linkage. Then, Siamese twins. Heart and all visceral organs joined. One beat. One throb. One thought.

It did excite her. The conception. A mirror of her secret hope. She began to say why she loved me. Just as graphic. Obscure eyes flaming now. As she came alive. Words she had thought but had never spoken. Stuttering from her moist tongue. Her fantasies and mine. Combined.

She told what she would do to me. For me. Bravely. In such tones that I had to know she was willing to transform dreams of reality.

That brief afternoon was as dear as a dream recalled. Later, I remembered, we sat in the walled garden. Our secret place. Both of us cloaked against a raw drizzle. Clasping hands. We the only source of heat and joy in the universe. Radiating. Then we did not speak; we could already be silent together. With profit.

It was strange that parting—as we had to, eventually. It was a small defeat. A small stop. We both had the sense that such a necessary, practical thing as parting, that afternoon, somehow reduced our passion. Stupid, I know. But there it was.

"We must make it up," she said gravely. "So strong together that parting can mean little. Nothing. No effect."

"Even better," I said. "To make us stronger. You compute? Strong enough to be apart and loving more."

"We'll age well." She laughed. Kissing my palm. Before I slipped out the door. "Like good wine."

"Or music," I said.

"Music." She nodded.

Back to this world. The hearings opened on HR-316, A Bill to Establish a Department of Creative Science within the Public Service of the US Government, and went exceeding well. Joe Wellington had arranged for complete media coverage. Including live TV broadcasts on the federal (formerly educational) network. The parade of favorable witnesses was impressive. Their credentials were undeniable, their statements (as instructed) were short and pithy.

Questioning by subcommittee members was brief and superficial. The Congressmen were not venal. (In this regard.) Simply uninformed. We were dealing here with scientific matters of great complexity. Even the subcommittee's staff, though they might be science-conditioned, could grasp only part of what we proposed. Let alone foresee the consequences. So that opening statements and questioning dealt mainly with such matters as medical research on geriatric disorders, new methods of utilizing solar energy, the efficacy of inoculation against venereal diseases, genetic manipulation to prevent crime, and so forth.

But all this was froth. No one questioned, thankfully, the philosophy of the bill. No one asked what influence the proposed Department might wield on the political and social infrastructures. No one wondered how the future might be tilted by giving to science and technology an authoritative, policymaking role in the US Government. I believed that role would be benign. But no one asked.

I think, by the fourth day, we had all relaxed. Knowing it was going well. HR-316 was on its way to becoming the law of the land. Paul and I, having set new events in motion, turned back to pendulating projects.

"This UP thing," he said. "Houston has been expediting it. As per orders. They're up to Mk. 7. They claim results."

"Tested?"

"On prisoners. Three stoppages on Mk. 4. But that was traced to contaminated containers. They've got a prototype package for the new brew. Want to try?"

He knew my insistence on testing new drugs personally. Either by myself or members of my staff.

"The Mk. 7?" I said. "Sure. Fly in a sample. I'll try it at Chevy Chase tomorrow night. Have Seth Lucas bring over a diagnostic kit. And tape recorders. I've always wanted to know the Ultimate Pleasure."

"It's got an orgasmic trigger," he said.

"Thanks for warning me," I said. "Tell everyone to stand back."

By 2100 the following evening, we were prepared. In my bedroom at the Chevy Chase place. In attendance were Paul, Mary Bergstrom, Maya Leighton, Dr. Seth Lucas. Three tape recorders and Lucas' diagnostic kit. This was a small, portable juke, developed by DIVRAD's Electronic Team. Circuitry based on space technology. Taped sensors provided input on pulse, respiration, skin temperature, blood pressure, EEG, etc., all signaled on separate screens and recorded on paper tape automatically. With time indications along the edge.

I lay naked, the taped wires leading from my corpus to the gizmo. Lucas fussed over that. Paul and Mary handled stopwatches and recorders. A fascinated Maya Leighton held a towel.

"Your Thrill of the Month," I told her.

"Better," she assured me.

Seth checked out his pinball.

"All circuits go," he reported.

"All right, Nick," Paul said. Nervously, I thought. "I'm going to hand you the pack. The moment you take it, we start the clock. You scan the printed directions, follow them, open the pack, self-administer."

"Yes, doctor," I said. "Let's have it."

He took the UP Mk. 7 from a brown paper bag. It was a clear plastic kit. Very small. No larger than, perhaps, a plastisealed tube of glue or a dozen nails.

"Give us verbal response as long as you can," Paul said. "Don't worry about coherence. Just babble."

"Right," I said.

"This is exciting," Maya said.

Paul handed me the package.

"Start time," he said loudly. "Two one three eight point four six. *Now*!"

I scanned the instructions slowly: "This UP injection is the sole property of the US Government. It has not been licensed for manufacture, distribution, or sale by any other agency, business, group, or individual. Unauthorized manufacture, distribution, and/or sale is in direct violation of Public Law DIVRAD OL962341-B2, and subject to penalties inherent therein. To receive an additional UP injection, this package and its contents (needle and emptied tube) must be returned to your local distribution center."

"Simplify instructions," I said. "Means nothing to wetbrains."

I continued scanning:

"To use the UP injection, follow these steps carefully:

"One: Open plastic case by tearing slowly along perforated line A-B."

Obediently, I attempted to tear along perforated line A-B. It didn't serve. I broke a fingernail.

"It doesn't tear," I said.

"Correct," Paul said. "It's not perforated. The dotted line is just printed on. The whole idea is to consume time and make the object frantic. Keep trying."

I finally ripped the cardboard backing off and got the clear plastic cover loose. Paul and Mary glanced at their stopwatches, made notes of my progress.

"Two: Unscrew plastic cap from needle of Syrette."

"We need another word," I said. "Objects won't know what 'Syrette' means. And the damned top won't unscrew."

I finally pulled it off. There were no threads; it was merely pressure-applied.

"Another time-waster?" I asked Paul.

"Ritual," he said. "Go on."

"Three: Push exposed needle with a sharp, quick motion into any area of the corpus below the neck."

"No good," I said. "That might include anus, genitals, nipples, navel, et cetera. Instructions should be more explicit. Perhaps limiting target area to arms, legs, buttocks, and so forth. I'll take it in the thigh."

Their tape decks were recording my comments. Seth Lucas was

watching his screens and dials. His tape, too, was running.

"Slightly heightened signals," he reported. "Nothing abnormal."

"Here we go," I said.

I jabbed the needle into my right thigh.

"Four: Squeeze from the bottom of the tube. Using thumb and forefinger of the right hand (if right-handed) or thumb and forefinger of the left hand (if left-handed), make certain the full and complete contents of the Syrette are emptied through the needle."

"Who wrote these instructions?" I asked. "Gertrude Stein?"

I compressed the tube as directed. From the bottom to the top. It was an opaque container; I didn't know if it was a clear liquid or a milky creme.

"Five: Withdraw needle from skin and put Syrette carefully aside. Remember, you cannot be awarded another UP injection unless you return the used and emptied syringe to your local distribution center."

I pulled the needle from my thigh. Rolled over carefully so as not to disturb my taped sensors, and placed the emptied Syrette carefully on the bedside table.

I had expected it to start with a gentle euphoria. Either a numbness or a tingling. But it was a jolt.

"A hit," I heard myself say. "It's got to beeee...."

"Pulse and respiration rising," I heard Seth Lucas report. "Skin temperature up. And he—"

That was the last I heard from anyone. Then I could hear only myself: "Got to stretch it. That intro. Now. Sweat and vibrations. Memory going. Sphincter contracting. Auditory nil. Numbness beginning now. Fingers. Toes."

Then I could no longer hear myself.

There were the hackneyed hallucinogenic visual reactions moving swiftly through clouds that gradually brightened to swirls of color. Great blobs of brilliant hues everywhere. (No music; no sound at all.) Then the colors clearing, drawing back: the reverse of a drop of oil on water. Enormous well-being then. Peace, and a divine carelessness. Ultimate don't-give-a-damnness.

I see a chair. Or couch. The center of the image is clear. The edges are blurred, with striations of light. A vignette. An ef is seated. An obso ef, but not unhandsome. A heavy, scarred, and pitted face. Almost emish, but attractive. Strong. She is wearing an em's blue serving shirt. Not buttoned, but loosely tied about her heavy breasts. She is leaning back. Bare stomach and torso are soft. There are precisely three rolls of avoirdupois. I note them clearly. She is wearing faded denim shorts. Ragged. Torn off from pants. Belted with a brass buckle in a lion's-head design. Her knees are up, and spread. Bare feet on the edge of the chair. Or couch. The skimpy shorts are pulled tight across her pudendum. It is divided into two plump halves. Bulging.

I come into the picture. From the blurred edge. Coming into focus. We speak. But there is no sound. I touch her bare knee.

"You can do what you like," she says. "Hurt me if you want to."

"I don't want to hurt you," I say. "I want to know you."

I spread her knees wider, standing now between them. I scrape the insides of her naked thighs gently with my fingernails. She closes her eyes.

I kneel. I rub my mustache and beard along her legs. Then begin to kiss. Lick. I pause to look up. Her eyes are open. Somber.

"Untie your shirt," I tell her.

She obeys. Pulls the knotted shirttails free, opens them wide. Her skin is coarse, bruised. Her liberated breasts swell down. They are heavy eggplants. Purplish. Glossy. Aureoles are hardly distinguishable; nipples are retracted. I lean forward awkwardly. I blow gently on one nipple. It begins to grow. When it has extruded sufficiently, I touch it softly with my wet tongue. Her entire body leaps convulsively on the chair. Couch. I pulp the elongating nipple between my lips. The other begins to extrude. Her breasts harden. She slumps sideways. I ease her down. Put a pillow beneath her head. Her hair is quite long. Black without luster. Streaked with gray.

I take her hand, make her cup a breast. Then I kiss her lips. Lightly. Our tongues serving. As we flicker, I push her hand and breast upward. Pull her head forward, down. Her breast is full enough so that we can both kiss and suck. Simultaneously. Tongues circling the erectile nipple, meeting, circling. The taste is sharp, almost acrid.

Now her breasts are slick. Slipping from my grasp. I draw back from her. Gesture toward her shorts. Then they are gone. The opened shirt gone from her shoulders. She is naked. I am still wearing my silver zipsuit. Red tab on right epaulette.

I begin. Moving her hands and fingers to show her how she must hold herself for me. Her knees are up. Then her feet. High in the sky. A cloud beneath her hips. Warm moisture collects on my mustache and beard. She adores the beard. Worships it. I nuzzle deeper, straining my tongue. She groans.

I slide her fingers lower. Demonstrate how I want her buttocks prized apart. My fingers are coated with petrogrease. I slide into the brown rosebud.

"Am I hurting you?" I ask anxiously.

"Deeper," she says.

My forefinger probes slyly. She begins a slow paroxysm. My other hand fumbles at her navel. Exploring slickly.

Her movements become stormy. Unruly. I manipulate her. First here. There. Together. It crescends. The bruises on her coarse flesh become livid. Bright violet and yellow splotches. Then, with a great pelvis heave, she summits. I hang on, continuing my service.

I turned my eyes upward to see her expression. I saw Paul Bumford. Leaning over me.

"Nick?" he said. Anxiously, I thought. "You all right?"

"Time?" I asked.

He glanced at his stopwatch.

"From the moment you took the package," he said, "about seventy-three minutes."

I looked about the room. Seth Lucas was checking the dials and long strip of paper tape. Mary Bergstrom was regarding me curiously. Maya Leighton was grinning, the clotted towel wadded up in her hands.

"Total time disorientation," I reported.

"Get this:" I said. "Euphoric physical weakness. Visual disacuity. Total auditory loss. From the looks of that towel Maya is playing with, I gather I summited. But no memory of it. No psychic guilt. No hangover. No regrets. Quite an experience. *Quite* an experience. How much time elapsed after I stopped talking?"

They all looked at me queerly.

"You never stopped talking," Paul said. "Not for a second."

I groaned. "You mean you've got it all on tape? Even the eggplants?"

"Even the eggplants," Maya giggled. "And the bruises."

"That was interesting," Paul said. "Nick, do you agree that—"

"Please." I held up a hand. "Let's have no cut-rate psychoanalysis of my personal hangups. We're just trying to evaluate a new drug. Do you think my verbal outpouring was a result of the UP?"

"Nooo," Paul said slowly. Judiciously. "That particular reaction hasn't been reported in any other test. I think it was just your conditioning. A desire to give us—if you'll excuse the expression—a blow-by-blow account. Let's go through some physical and mental coordination workups now. Seth, how does he look?"

"Parameters back to normal," Lucas reported. "Pulse, respiration, and skin temperature just slightly higher, but nothing significant."

"You summited, baby," Maya Leighton said decisively. Enviously? "You really ultimized."

A few hours later I was in my bedroom, robed, serving at my desk. Knock at the door; I called out, and Paul entered, carrying his vodka-and-Smack, and bringing me one.

"For this relief, much thanks," I said. "Hamlet." I took a big gulp. "I'm trying to rough a report on the UP while it's all fresh. You might send it on to Houston."

"Of course. Your posttests proved affirmative. Any late reactions?"

"Warm lassitude. Pleasant. Slight physical weakness. No mental or psychological effects I can detect. Paul, if possible I'd like them to work on that initial jolt. See.if they can mildify it. A slower lead-in would be more effective. Another thing that disturbs me: Shouldn't I have been physically conscious of the orgasm?"

Paul computed a moment. Frowning.

"No," he said finally. "Not necessarily. The fantasized experience apparently was psychologically satisfying. To such an extent that you summited. While still under the UP, you felt no sense of loss, did you?"

"No."

"And when you came out of it, you felt satiety. Correct?"

"Correct."

"Then your objection now is based on your conditioning to conventional orgasm. Did the UP satisfy you?"

"Yes. Definitely, yes."

"Well, then it achieved the goal. In your case, apparently, the psychological, or psychic, ruled the physical. The effect of the UP won't be identical on all objects. Some will be aware of physical orgasm. To some objects it might be great art, music, poetry, cruelty, suffering—anything. It's formulated to be generic."

"Yes. Still, I'd hardly call an involuntary emission the Ultimate Pleasure."

"Not even in the context of your fantasy?"

"Well . . . that's a thought. It was quite a go. Strange."

"Nick, could I—no, no! Don't hold up your hand. I'm not going to analyze your dream. At least not try to individualize it. But to universalize. . . . The problem, we agreed, is not the UP injection itself, but the surrounding social and political environments."

"So?"

"Would it be reasonable to interpret your fantasy as one of submission? Total surrender?"

I computed a moment.

"I think it could be interpreted that way."

Paul nodded. Thoughtful.

"You haven't had a chance to scan the Houston interviews. But the same factor turns up in a surprising percentage of experimental object tapes."

"What factor?" I asked.

"The slave factor," he said. Looking at me steadily.

I blinked at him. I had an unpleasant feeling that he had gone beyond me. That he was off somewhere. In realms I could not appreciate.

"Let's get this straight," I said to him. "Are you suggesting the slave factor may be primary to Ultimate Pleasure?"

"Yes," Paul said. Definitely. "All indicators point that way."

"And?"

"If it proves out, it should give us a valid guide to the essential nature of the political society that might enforce and enhance that pleasure."

I stared at him a long moment. He *was* ahead of me. Computing in spheres that had never concerned me.

"You *have* made a giant step," I said.

"Yes." He nodded. "I have. Look, Nick," he said earnestly, "we agreed a political drug could only function with optimum effect in a society that complements it. Neither of us brainstormed the structure of that society. If, after additional testing, the slave factor in the UP proves to be valid, wouldn't you say it constitutes a steer to the nature of the society required?"

I shook my head.

"Maybe that UP injection does have residual and negative mental effects. Paul, there's something inoperative in your computing. It just doesn't scan. I don't know where you're off. I can't isolate it. I just feel you're wrong. In any event, assuming what you say *is* operative, what do you propose now?"

460

He hunched forward on his chair. Very serious. Very sincere.

"Nick," he said, "this Operation Lewisohn gives us a marvelous opportunity for a field test. About half the staff have already come aboard at Hospice No. 4. The remainder should be reporting in a week or so. What if I call in a miniteam of psychoneurologists from Houston as observers. We divide the staff of Operation Lewisohn into thirds. Mixed disciplines. One-third a control group. One-third on placebos. One-third on the UP. Placebos and UP injections awarded for good service and extended hours. And so forth. Let the psychoneurologists run a computer study. Analyzing hours served, efficiency, morale, physical condition, and so forth. When Operation Lewisohn is over—whether it succeeds or fails— we should have a concretized idea of the value of the UP in a realistic productive situation."

"Good idea," I said. "Let's do it."

A year ago, even six months ago, it would have been my idea.

I checked on the progress of Operation Lewisohn at Hospice No. 4, finalized plans with Joe Wellington for a PR gig through the Midwest, sent three dozen natural roses to Louise Rawlins Tucker, and then returned to GPA-1. There I spent a day serving with Phoebe Huntzinger and her computerniks. They were programming our largest hardware, a King Mk. V, with a 200,000-word English vocabulary, plus additional foreign words and phrases.

"More, Phoebe," I said.

"More?"

"Pick up a dictionary of profanity and obscenity. Add it to your storage. Shouldn't be more than a thousand bits."

"Profanity and obscenity," she repeated. "I wish I knew what this was all about."

"It's better you don't," I told her. "Rush your wire link with Denver. The moment it's through and tested, let me know."

"And then?"

"Then you pull it," I laughed. "And switch to Alexandria, Virginia. When I tell you."

"Whee!" she yelled. Tossing papers into the air. "Insanity incorporated."

It wasn't. Really. It was carefully structured. With a timetable and flow chart. I had called in a project systems em with top security, and he had served on the logistics. We had allowed wiggle room, but as of that date in late April, we were right on schedule. As to equipment and objects. We had prepared fall-back positions and fail-safe alternatives. I was satisfied we were contravening Murphy's Law.

The twenty-eighth of April. About 2315. I was in my apartment at Manhattan Landing. Packing to begin the Midwest PR tour in the morning. Computing how many Somnorifics I might need, when the flasher chimed. Paul came on. Visage grave and pulled.

"Paul?" I said. "What is it?"

"It's an open line," he said tensely. "I'll cheat on what I say. Keep your questions glossed. Got that?"

"Yes. What is it?"

"The business in GPA-11. The stamps. Sam's stakeout. Follow that?"

"Stakeout? In D. C.?" I asked.

"Yes. I got all this from Art Roach. He got it from pals in BPS. Not complete. Anyway, about an hour ago, another attempt."

"Ohhh," I breathed.

"Caught him. One em. Contaminating the adhesive. Follow?"

"Yes."

"Tried to put a tranquilizer dart into him. Sam's servers. But before it worked, he gulped. Suicided. Got that?"

"I think so. Instant?"

"No. But he's stopping. No way. You understand? A mouthful."

"That should do it," I said.

"You know him," Paul said.

"*What?*"

"Not know him. But saw him. I knew him. Met him. Talked to him. Raddo. Arthur Raddo. That pale, blond fanatic. At the Beist Christmas meeting."

"Oh-oh," I said. "The wowser."

"Yes. Served at Bureau of Printing and Engraving."

"Anyone else?"

"No word. As of now. Just him."

"Motive?"

"Not known. Sam is checking."

"I can imagine. No doubt?"

"None. He had a little bottle of the stuff. Five cc. It broke when he fell. A TDT had to move in."

I was silent.

"Nick, it's not good. The Beist connection."

"Maybe no connection at all."

"That's what I'm hoping. Or that the CD will pillow it. Because of you-know-who."

"Yes."

"I think he was just a loner."

"Hope you're right. But why?"

"No idea."

"Anything else?"

"No," he said.

"Thanks for flashing. Let me know what happens."

"Will do. Have a good trip."

"Thanks."

We switched off.

Arthur Raddo. The young em with lank blond hair falling untidily over his forehead. Enormous eyes with a fervid stare. Flat lips he licked constantly. Wearing a wrinkled, soiled zipsuit of a PS-5. His physical appearance gave the impression of limp ineffectuality. But his voice was unexpectedly loud, passionate. Still, I was certain he was a frail.

That was the em who had poisoned thousands of objects in GPA-11.

But that wasn't important. At the moment. What was crucial, to me, in Paul's staccato report, was the 5 cc flask Raddo had been carrying. The bottle that smashed when he suicided. That required calling in a Toxin Decontamination Team. A 5 cc flask of *Clostridium botulinum* in glycerol.

I immediately went into the same drill. Pulled on a raincoat. Slogged through a rainy night to B Lab. Down to the third sublevel. Into the pharmacology library. I went through a charade of looking up acetylsalicylic acid in the file computer. Because I remembered 416HBL-CW3 was stored in the restricted section in Room G, Bin 3, Stack 4, Position R.

I finally buzzed a dozing Vinnie Altman awake. He let me in and I signed the register while he breathed petroport fumes in my face. He wanted to talk. I didn't.

I went directly to the room, the bin, the stack, the position. Extracted tooth. A gap. The 5 cc flask was gone.

I stood there. Staring at that emptiness. Smelling the piercing, pinching odor of manipulation. I had been. That forgery. The 2 cc taken, the bottle left. What else would I do but replace the missing

463

liquid? Remove the original file card. Sign a letter to R. Sam Bigelow stating that *my* visual inspection had verified the original deposit of 416HBL-CW3.

And when the BPS snoops, alerted by the smashed 5 cc flask in the hand of the stopping Arthur Raddo, decided to check personally on all amounts of *Clostridium botulinum* issued to research Gruppen in 1988, how would I explain its absence from my pharmacology library? And my official letter stating it was intact and untouched?

Strangely, my first reaction was admiration. I remembered what Art Roach had said after I had explained how we had broken his arm in order to share him.

"That was *beautiful*," he had breathed.

So was this. Beautiful.

Then I felt sick.

Z-7

From an address to an international convention of neurobiologists held in Chicago, Illinois, on May 3, 1999:

"There is no precedent in history for what is happening. Those who look to the Mechanical Revolution of the Nineteenth Century or the Technological Revolution of the Twentieth Century for aid in coping with our problems will look in vain.

"For the Biological Revolution of the Twenty-first Century is unique in human experience. It deals not with materials, equipment, and tools—not with *things*—but with objects, members of the species *Homo sapiens*. It is revealing to us not only how to change objects already in existence, but how to alter our own evolution. To change both for the better, I hasten to add, so we might more easily deal with and plan for the radically transformed society that tomorrow will inexorably bring.

"As neurobiologists, you know there is nothing absolute in human nature. Nothing that cannot be manipulated for the greater health of the individual and the greater good of society. What are these alterations in the corpus we must seek if we are to insure the physical and mental health of citizens of the Twenty-first Century? Suppose we start with the brain, and consider what neurobiological

464

manipulations may be of benefit to the gene pool of the future. . . ."

And so forth. And so forth. Kaka.

Worst of all, I didn't even have the consoling presence of Samantha Slater's wormish corpus in my hotel room. At the last moment, Joe Wellington had revised the travel scenario.

"Sorry, Nick," he said, "but I need Samantha here in D.C.-ville. HR-316 is coming up for a vote next week; it's no time to scatter the troops."

It was downputting, but I couldn't stamp my foot and pout. After all, it *was* for the DCS. As I boarded the jet for Chicago, a slender em in a checkered cap bumped into me. As I entered the hotel lobby in Chicago, a plump em in a checkered cap jostled me.

A less mentally healthy object might have suffered an onslaught of paranoia. First Joe Wellington's squelch of my amour propre. Then what might have been a tail by a confederation of checkered-capped enemies. All this on top of the disappearance of the 5 cc flask from my pharmacology library.

That was no irrational suspicion. The bottle was gone, and I was responsible for it. I had glossed it as best I could by filling that accusing gap in Position R, Stack 4, Bin 3, Room G, with an identical 5 cc flask of pure glycerol. But it was literally a stopgap measure. Temporarily, until R. Sam Bigelow's noses came to check volume and analyze contents. Before that happened, I would be able to discover who was manipulating me, and for what purpose. I hoped.

After Chicago, the PR safari moved on to Minneapolis, Omaha, Denver. In the last city, I spent a day at the DIVRAD Field Office with Tom Lee, reviewing his logistic plan for moving Project Phoenix to Hospice No. 4 in Alexandria, Virginia. He had projected well. I made a few minor alterations—more to assert my authority than from any real need for change; a server's plans are *never* totally operative—and then gave him the go for the move.

On to Oklahoma City, New Orleans, Memphis. Speeches, colloquies, interviews, symposia. My only pleasure was in writing and mailing a letter, every day, to Louise Rawlins Tucker. Addressed to her. Intended for the eyes of Grace Wingate. I wrote, I suppose, many foolish things. But they gave me much joy. I had never before known the happiness of stripping oneself naked in words. Surprisingly therapeutic.

And eventually, back in Washington, D.C., May 26, 1999. On

the day I returned, the subcommittee of the House Government Operations Committee passed HR-316 with but one dissenting vote. I was in time for a sedate orgy at the home of Penelope Mapes to celebrate our initial victory. I had hoped Chief Director Michael Wingate, and wife, might be present. They were not. But Louise Rawlins Tucker was.

"How is she?" I asked.

"She's lonely," she said.

"She got my letters?"

"Of course."

I looked at her with admiration. She was taking a dreadful chance. She turned back to me then. Smile fading. Eyes hardening. Not an ef I'd care to cross.

"I told you," she said. I could scarcely hear. "Hurt her, and I'll—"

"I know, I know," I said hurriedly. "I believe you. I have no wish to hurt her. I told you that. And I told her. If something goes wrong, the CD will save her. But you must save yourself."

"And you?"

"I'll worry about it when the time comes. If it does."

"It'll be too late then," she said. Suddenly, embarrassingly, her eyes filled with tears.

I stared at that dragoon of an ef. The big, blotchy face. Like seeing a rhino cry. I couldn't compute it.

"When may I see her?" I asked softly.

"Tomorrow. Noon. My home."

"I thank you," I said. And moved away.

I left the party while Paul and Mary Bergstrom were still there. Carefully computed. I went back to our Chevy Chase home. Directly to Paul's bedroom. His desk was unlocked. After five minutes' search, I found the membership list of the Washington, D. C., chapter of the Beists. I was startled by their rapid growth: more than five thousand names. I scanned Arthur Raddo's address until I was certain I had it. A scurvy neighborhood on Sixth Street.

I located, with difficulty, two lovable liters of natural California pinot noir. I carried them both to the safe house. One for us; one to be left behind for that stern obso ef who was risking too much for our joy.

The door was opened to my third ring. For the briefest of

microseconds I was panicked by the sight of a stranger. But no, it was Grace Wingate. Wearing the same middy, blue scarf, pleated skirt, white plastivas sneakers she had worn to the Beist meeting the first night we met. What had delayed recognition was a heavy wig of russet hair. Drawn back, braided into a single plait that hung down her back. Thick and long as an em's arm.

She laughed delightedly at my astonishment. Whirled to exhibit. The pigtail flung out and struck me lightly across the face. I caught it. Held it to my lips. Thick hair. Strong. Scented.

"What on earth?" I said.

"It's real human hair," she said eagerly. "Not synthetic. From France, I think. Or Bulgaria. Some place like that. Do you like it, Nick?"

I pulled that live hawser in, hand over hand, until her back was against me. Tightly. I moved the woven plait so that it curved over her shoulder, hung down her front. I reached around to clasp it there.

"Wanton!" I whispered in her ear.

She glanced back at me. Mischievous.

"Yes, I am," she said. "With you."

It was a creamy noon. Breeze hinting of summer heat. Altocumulus high in a pellucid sky. On such a day, why should I glance about casually at the windows of strangers, overlooking our garden, our secret place, and wonder where hypersensitive parabolic microphones might be emplaced?

We sat on a curving bench in the arbor. The poor, peeling lattice that seemed fated to know July as bare and forlorn as it had endured December. The entire garden had that feel: gentle decay and soft sadness. All colors muted. All scents fragile. Even a cricket's chirp faint and hesitant.

After some initial chatter, she seemed to sense my reverie, and was quiet. Then she leaned close, back half-turned so that I might caress her glossy plait.

"You do like," she murmured. "Nick? Don't you?"

"Oh, yes. Very much."

"More than my own hair?"

"Not more than," I said. "But as much as."

She giggled softly. "I can never catch you out."

"I've had a lot of experience," I said.

I left off stroking that rope of vibrant hair. How could hair, as

467

nerveless as a fingernail, so pulse with life and seem responsive to a touch? I slid a hand beneath her loose middy. Up. Stroked, with timorous fingers, her naked back.

"Oh," she said.

I sat without moving. Regarding with wonder my wandering hand. It was not I, but my scampish fingers that searched, smoothed, probed. It was not I, I swear. That vagrant hand had its own mind, and would have its way. I felt it palm her cool, quivering flesh. Arch to scrape nails from arm to torso. Then, sneaky hand, it shifted furtively to circle her. Pull her closer. Until sly fingertips could touch her bare breasts. And stealthily search out a nipple soft and yielding as a bud. My wayward hand stopped there.

After a few minutes—my hand and I motionless—she turned to glance at me.

"Nick?" she said.

I was silent.

She moved away to face me. The lifeless hand fell limp from beneath her blouse.

"You look so strange," she said.

"Do I?" I said. "I feel strange. Something strange is happening to me."

I stood up. Shakily. Leaving my wine glass on the slatted bench. I wandered about that shoddy garden. Kicking gently at doomed plants. They would never make it. Never. I went back to sit beside her, take her two hands in mine.

"Do you believe I love you?" I said. "Love you more than any object or thing in this world? Do you believe that?"

"Yes," she said. Gravely. "I do believe that."

"You scanned my letters. You must know how I feel about you. The fantasies."

"They were beautiful," she said softly.

"I could only hint. Imply. I didn't want to compromise you, or Louise, by writing a complete scenario. You compute?"

"Oh, yes."

"It seemed to me that if we could use each other, I might very well stop with profit. I imagined how it could happen. Many times. In great detail. Scents. Tastes. The touch of you. A wildness."

"Don't you think I've thought the same? Many times? Mad dreams."

"I know, I know. And yet . . . and yet, a while ago, when I

touched your sweet breast, I knew suddenly it would be a defeat. For me. For you. For our love.''

"A defeat? Nick, I—I'm not sure I understand.''

"You think I do?'' I burst out. Almost angrily. "It doesn't scan. I know it doesn't. I know you bought that lovely wig for me. I was so excited when I felt it. And when I touched your body, I thought: It will be *now*. This afternoon. We will do it now. I can't tell you what that was. Rapture.''

"And then?''

"A cold fist clamping around my heart. That using each other would defeat us. Our love. What is it, Grace? Tell me. Do you know? I love you more, now, at this moment, than ever before. But why should I feel this? That using will ruin us. What we are to each other.''

"You feel it will—will *soil* us?''

"I don't know.'' I groaned. "I just don't know. I've used hundreds. Efs and ems. You know that. I told you that. I've done things you might think perverse. I never felt defiled. Or that I was corrupting my user. I never felt guilt. Never! But then—but then. . . .''

"But then?'' she prompted.

"But then I've never loved before. I thought it was an obso vulgarity. Now, loving, I think I want it to be new. All new. Oh, I must sound a choice idiot! I'm sorry, Grace. I wish I could analyze exactly what I felt and could explain it to you. All I know is that it's important to me. The most important thing in my life. Can you tell me? Please! Tell me what it is.''

She put her arms about me. I put mine about her. Mouths close without kissing. The moment stretched without breaking.

If she had demanded we use each other immediately, I would have obeyed. And been potent, I knew. Exhibited my expertise, taken profit and given it. But I was right: It would have been a defeat. I think she sensed it, too. For we had never been closer than on that magic afternoon, in that secret garden. Realizing that everything that had gone before was preliminary. Now we were exploring a frightening realm. Where intimacy was so profound that it was mixed with fear of the unknown.

From that day on, my life became trichotomous. All the tangled skeins twisted into three strands. The strands braided into one rope. Like Grace's glossy plait. There were a few stray tendrils: the campaign for the Department of Creative Science, and so forth. But my main concerns devolved into: My relations with Grace Wingate and the shattering self-analysis that demanded; the rowen of the botulism outbreak in GPA-11 and the missing flask of 416HBL-CW3 from the GPA-1 pharmlab; and Operation Lewisohn, the most complex administrative project I had ever ruled. A hundred talented servers to be directed and managed in such a manner as to ensure that minimal 30 percent success possibility I had predicted to the CD.

When the entire staff had gathered in the Lewisohn Building in Hospice No. 4, I convened the first general assembly in Operating Theater D. Staff sat on the tiers of polished benches that rose high above the actual operating area. They were behind glass walls that were attached to the ceiling. I stood in the arena. Speaking to them via a PA system.

As per orders, they were all wearing the color-coded paper gowns and caps of their groups. Green for surgeons and anesthesiologists. Blue for Leo Bernstein and his servers. Brown for the Project Phoenix Team. Gray for Phoebe Huntzinger's computerniks. White for nurses. Red for the Production Team. Purple for Operation Directors. These colors had not been picked by whim; they had been selected with the aid of the psychoneurology miniteam from Houston. They had advised that red and purple represented high authority to most objects. A centuries-old conditioned reflex. The miniteam itself, present to administer Ultimate Pleasure injections and placebos to the Operation Lewisohn staff, and to analyze the results, wore zipsuits.

"Colleagues," I began, "I welcome you all, and thank you for being here. The fact that you had no choice in the matter doesn't change that sentiment one whit."

Their laughter came to me faintly from behind the glass walls.

"Before continuing my remarks," I went on, "I would like to introduce our Chief of Security, Art Roach, who has a few pertinent remarks of his own. Art. . . ."

He was still wearing a black zipsuit, although we had already forwarded a recommendation for his promotion to red. When he took over the microphone, I was surprised to note that he was almost exactly my height and weight. I had always thought of him as a taller, heavier em. But that was before he became my server.

I had feared his necessary comments would be an embarrassing ramble in a fried-fritter accent. But again he surprised me. Pleasantly. His address was short and to the point. He reminded them all of the Oaths of Allegiance they had signed, and of the penalties resulting from betrayal of that Oath. Quoting copiously from official regulations, without notes, he told them that they were, in effect, to be held incommunicado for the duration of Operation Lewisohn. Communication with the outside world could be made, if absolutely necessary, only through a Censor Control Board. Every effort had been taken to make their off-hours as pleasant as possible. Any suggestions for additional recreation facilities would be welcome.

He did it all very well. Just a few "yawls." There was a polite snapping of fingers when he concluded. I took over the mike again.

"All right," I said. "Let's get to it—what you're doing here. Some of you brought from halfway around the world. At great government expense, incidentally. I want to start by talking about the brain. The human brain. . . .

"A piece of gray cheese. It's not so large. You can easily hold it in one hand. An elephant's brain weighs four times as much. But in proportion to corpus weight, it's smaller. Otherwise, elephants would be sitting where you're sitting now. (Laughter) But I don't wish to discuss the physical properties of the human brain. You know all that. You better know it, or we're doomed! I want to discuss with you today the human brain as a national asset. Or, if you will, a national resource.

"In the present state of the world today, I suggest to you now that a nation's essential strength is not in its minerals, its agriculture, its wealth, or its armaments. But in the quality of the brains of its citizens. Compute that a moment. A nation is no stronger than the brains of its citizens. And the ideas those brains create.

"In the US, we have learned, and are still learning, how to improve the quality and functioning of this essential natural resource. Isolation of the 'smart genes' and genetic manipulation. Megaprotein feeding of the mother. Oxygenation of the fetus. Scientific conditioning of the child. Positive drug therapy for memory. And so forth.

"But the growth of a nation's brain pool is not only a matter of genetics, diet, drugs, conditioning. Other factors are involved. In a sense, great brains breed great brains. History is replete with examples of times—relatively short periods—when 'schools' of great brains flourished in politics, art, literature, science, music, and so forth. There seems to be an interaction. Great brains inspire great brains. Or perhaps, more exactly, great ideas inspire great ideas. So there is an exponential factor serving here. A nation's brain pool improves at a geometric rate.

"Are you still with me? Or are you now saying to yourself, 'Enough of this historical and political kaka. What are we doing here?' Fair enough. What you are doing here is to preserve, for the US Government, the continued functioning of one of the greatest brains this nation, or any nation on earth, has ever possessed. This is what we're going to do. And this is how we're going to do it...."

I had them then. As I continued speaking, they shifted forward in their seats. Fascinated. Leaning to me. These were very brainy objects themselves; it didn't take long for them to realize they were involved in a radical and risky scientific project. But a characteristic of the human brain I had not mentioned—the absolute need to solve a mystery, to conquer the unknown—had taken hold. At the end, I casually remarked that anyone who objected to the purpose of Operation Lewisohn would be excused, without prejudice. Not one object opted for out. I hadn't anticipated there would be.

Those early rehearsals were ridiculous. Pure chaos. Even such a simple process as washing-up and sterilization became incredibly complex when a total of almost 100 objects were involved. When the preliminaries were solved, and we moved to positions, cues, and timing on the actual operation—more confusion. Paul Bumford generated an excellent idea. He suggested we paint circles on the floor. Color-coded to match the gowns of the various teams. The circles showed clearly where members of each team were to stand. Numbers within the circles designated various individuals.

With such stratagems; we gradually began to execute a coherent scenario. Four hours each day were spent merely planning physical movements and walking through our paces. Remaining hours were spent in team lectures, colloquies, and symposia in which actual techniques were discussed, demonstrated, attempted. Like well-trained gunners, each object had to know (and be proficient at) not only his own service, but the service of every fellow team-member. In case of emergency.

It all began to coalesce. I saw definite progress.

As ruler of Operation Lewisohn, I had, of course, the perquisite of free, unquestioned entrance to and egress from the Lewisohn Building at Hospice No. 4. But with the stress of early organization and the pressure of preliminary rehearsals, it was June 5, 1999, before I had an opportunity to slip away. To requisition a black sedan from the motor pool. Start out early in the evening to locate the residence of the late Arthur Raddo. My investigation had to begin somewhere.

As I had anticipated, Raddo's address on Sixth Street was in a neighborhood that had once, long ago, been fashionable. Even elegant. It had seeded. There was a government bordello or betting parlor on almost every corner. Between were licensed shops offering porn, Graeco-Roman massage, high colonics, sporting events, and a type of specialized entertainment called "Sadie Moscowitz." This was a vernacular corruption of sadomasochism. Much as, years previously, marijuana had been debased to "Mary Warner."

I parked outside the area, on a shadowed sidestreet, and walked slowly toward Raddo's address. I was wearing civilian clothes. It was still early in the evening; the streets were crowded. Tourists, mostly, I guessed. With a heavy representation of pimps, jostlers of all sexes (including children), steersmen for illegal bagnios, black-market pushers, illicit drug sellers, etc. All, victims and predators, thronging quik-thaw petrofood stands, taverns, handjob joints, cabarets, grogshops. A strange, roiling neighborhood for the home of a devout Beist. But perhaps Arthur Raddo hadn't had the love to move elsewhere.

His building was slightly more presentable than the others. Slightly. An obso red-brick high-rise. Some of the windows on the lower floors were broken. Blocked with squares of cardboard or tin. The usual litter and graffiti. The unattended lobby smelled equally of urine and carbolic.

There was a "Raddo, A." listed on the lobby directory. Apartment 2-H. I opted for the dimly lighted staircase rather than chance an elevator. The outside door of 2-H had once been handsome wood. Now the jamb and area around the lock had been slashed and hacked. I heard voices from within: the never-ending litany of a broadcast. I pressed the bell. Not only was there no answer, but I didn't even hear the bell ring. I knocked sharply. Again. Again.

Finally: "Who is it?" a voice called out. An ef's voice. Surprisingly light and cheerful. Almost a carol.

"Mrs. Raddo?" I said loudly. Wondering: A mother? A widow?

"Yes?" the carol came again. "Who is it?"

"I'd like to talk to you about Arthur," I said. Lips close to the door.

There was a pause. Then the clicking of at least three locks and bolts. The sound of a heavy metal bar being withdrawn. Squeaking.

The door was opened to the length of a short, heavy chain. A bright blue eye peered at me.

"I'd like to talk to you about Arthur," I repeated. Hurriedly. "Just a moment. My name is Flair."

"I'm not supposed to talk to anyone about Arthur," the clear voice said. "They told me."

"I'm a reporter," I said. "I'm serving on a feature. A very sympathetic feature about Arthur. I need some information."

"Will it be on the TV?" she asked.

"Of course," I said. More confident now. "But I need to know what he was really like. The truth."

"The truth about Arthur?" she breathed.

"Yes," I said. "Exactly."

The door closed, the chain was slipped. Then the door was opened. She let me in.

"I'm Mrs. John Raddo," she chirped. "Arthur's mother."

An obso ef. About sixty to sixty-five, I judged. Blued-white hair teased into tight curls. A wig? Short, plump, almost merry in appearance.

She closed the door behind me, then served on the locks and bolts. I watched. Fascinated. Finally, the heavy steel bar in place, she tried the door. Beautiful. She led the way down a dim hallway to a semilighted room.

"You're interrupting my favorite program," she said. Not angrily. Archly. "You must promise not to speak until it's over."

"I promise," I said.

We took two sprung armchairs facing the TV set. She immediately picked up what appeared to be a square of knitted wool (A sweater back? The start of a scarf?) and began manipulating large bone-needles rapidly. The blue yarn flew from a bag on the floor. Even as I watched, entranced, her nimble fingers finished a row and started back.

"I just love it." She sighed. "It's a rerun, but just as good as the first time."

I looked then at the TV set. Surprisingly, it was the same model I owned: holographic laser, 3-D. Very lovable.

I recognized the program she was watching: *The Twenty-six Best Positions*. Original programs from October to March, reruns from April to September.

Permissiveness on television had come much later than in books, magazines, movies, and on the stage. TV executives had moved autiously, carefully, following a scenario pioneered by book publishers. First, in the late 1970's, they presented self-help programs n achieving emotional maturity. Followed, in the early 1980's, by ncreasingly frank discussions of the importance of sexual fulfillment in a happy marriage. These were mostly talk shows: seminars nd symposia of physicians, psychologists, sexologists, and so orth.

By the late 1980's and early 1990's, television was presenting hows that were totally sex-oriented. There was one network series, *Iave No Fear,* that appeared in the 1991-1995 period, very high atings, that effectively glossed anxieties objects might still have bout the dangers of masturbation, fellatio, and the use of dildos and imilar gadgets of technologized sex.

Public objection to these televised lectures on sexual techniques roved to be less than anticipated. For years, ice-brained conservaves had been fulminating against sex education in the schools. ''A hild should be taught about sex in the home.'' Television execuves did exactly that. In the home, the living room, bedroom, den, atio, library, kitchen. And at your friendly neighborhood tavern.

The Twenty-six Best Positions was by far the most popular rogram. Rated in the top ten shows for the past three years. On rimetime, in 3-D, and living color. With instant replay. The articipating objects changed every year to provide variety.

I watched a close-up of a young blond ef licking the glans of a oung blond em.

''Aren't they *cute?*'' Mrs. Raddo chortled. Knitting busily. *Videotape Magazine* says they want to get married, but the ponsor won't let them. Afraid it might hurt their ratings.''

I waited patiently as the famed psychologist who hosted the rogram provided a running commentary for the action on the creen. Finally, the half-hour program ended with a trailer for the ollowing week's hour-long special on anal intercourse.

Mrs. Raddo leaned forward to switch off the set.

''Thank you for waiting,'' she said. Sighing again. ''I so enjoy e *Twenty-six.* Watch it every week. Wouldn't miss it. Not even e reruns. I've seen *Mutual Masturbation* four times. What did you ay your name was?''

''Flair, Mrs. Raddo,'' I said. ''I just have a few questions. First f all, I'd like to present my condolences.''

''Condolences?'' she said.

''On Arthur's stopping.''

"Oh," she said. Then nodded. As sadly as that merry phiz could. "Arthur was a good boy."

"I'm sure he was," I said. "What I—"

"When will it be on?" she asked. "The TV show? About Arthur?"

"Probably next fall," I said.

"The new season." She nodded wisely. "Primetime?"

"I expect so."

"You'll want a taped interview with me, of course?"

"Of course," I said promptly. "That's why I'm here. Just for background to give the host some leads on questions to ask."

"Yes, yes." She nodded briskly. "That's how it's done. I know all about it. You'll make a tape, then edit it down for the timeslot."

"Exactly," I said.

She nodded again. Happily. Busy fingers twirling the long needles. The patch of knitted wool grew before my eyes. Longer and longer.

"Mrs. Raddo," I said, "did Arthur have any friends?"

"Of course he had friends," she said firmly. "Lots and lots of friends. Arthur was a very popular boy."

"Could you give me any of their names and addresses?" I asked. "We'd like to interview them, too."

"Oh, I never met them," she said gaily. Blue eyes twinkling. "Arthur never brought any of them here. 'Mother,' he used to say, 'this is *your* home.' "

"Well, he must have met them somewhere," I said. "Did he go to any special place you know of? A restaurant, perhaps? A tavern? A cabaret?"

"Oh, Arthur wouldn't go to any place like *that*," she said. Needles flashing. "Never drank. Never smoked. Never took drugs or any of the nasty things young people do these days. Arthur was a good boy."

"I'm sure he was," I said. Desperately. "But he must have gone out occasionally. Some place in the neighborhood?"

"Well . . ." she said. Needles suddenly still. Head cocked to one side. "Let me think. . . . He did. Yes, he did go out. Something Greek. He would go to something Greek."

"A Greek restaurant?"

"Oh, no. I don't think so. More like a private club. Where he could meet his friends in a nice atmosphere."

"But with a Greek name?"

"Yes, I think so. He mentioned it once, and I asked him what it meant, and he said it was a Greek god."

"A Greek god? Bacchus? Zeus? Apollo? Poseidon? Adonis? Pluto?"

"Adonis," she said triumphantly. "Yes, that's it. Adonis."

"You're sure?"

"Oh my, yes. Adonis. I remember very well now. That was the private club Arthur went to. He met his friends there."

"Frequently? Once a week? Or twice? More?"

"Oh. . . ." She considered. The needles twirling again. "I'd say at least once a week. I remember it now because he usually went when *The Twenty-six Best Positions* came on. Like tonight. 'Mother,' he'd say, 'it's *your* program.' "

"Thank you very much, Mrs. Raddo," I said. Rising. "You've been very helpful."

"And when will the crew be around?" she asked.

"The crew?"

"The camera crew to tape the interview with me."

"Soon, Mrs. Raddo. Quite soon. You'll be hearing from us."

"Isn't that nice!" she said happily.

I was halfway down that dim hallway when she called me back. Knitting needles and wool clutched on her lap.

"Yes, Mrs. Raddo?" I said.

"There was one friend," she said slowly. "I never met him, of course. Personally, I mean. But in the last few months he called Arthur several times and they spoke on the phone. I don't have a flasher. Though I'd dearly love one. But do you know how much—"

"Mrs. Raddo," I said, "did Arthur mention his name? His friend's name? While he was speaking to him on the phone?"

"Well, not his last name," she said. "I never heard Arthur mention his last name, and I never asked. But he did use his friend's first name."

"And what was that?" I said.

"Nick," she said.

I heard the rumble of muffled drums.

Z-8

During the month of June, rehearsals for Operation Lewisohn progressed, and increased in complexity. The subject was kept animate on parabiotic therapy and massive injections of steroidal stimulants. This protocol resulted, I knew, in a false set of vital signs. His color might be rosy, blood pressure stabilized, respiration normal. But he was, for the purposes of the US Government, a vegetable. Incapable of serving. A temporary condition. I hoped.

Our basic scenario underwent constant, almost daily revision. For instance, in the cold outline of the original script, the Surgery Team, having finished their task, would move out and Leo Bernstein's Team would move in. Impossible. We had to phase out the surgeons, one by one, as we phased in the hematologists. This called for neat cooperation, microsecond precision.

We were still spending four hours a day on walkthroughs and timing. The confusion had lessened; there was no more pushing, shoving, stumbling.

When the entire staff of Operation Lewisohn were not engaged in the endless drills or sleeping exhaustedly in the unisex barracks, they were practicing their disciplines. I was especially interested in and concerned with the activities of the Surgery Team. Assigned an operation that had never before been performed.

The ST was under the rule of Chief Surgeon Dr. George Berk. A tall, slender ex-soccer star from HMS. He ran a tight ship. When he said ''Go,'' his servers went. When he said ''No-go,'' they froze. He had the macho to enforce his edicts. I didn't like to recall how young he was. Made me realize I was one year away from being an obso. Even his mustache was more luxuriant than mine.

To assist Dr. Berk and his staff, I had purchased two beautifully designed and engineered humanoids from a medical equipment manufacturer in Dachau, West Germany. They were custom-made, patterned on Hyman R. Lewisohn's exact measurements (taken while he was heavily sedated). Even to the proportions of his ears and the length of his penis.

The dummies were covered with Grade D Juskin, which closely approximated Lewisohn's coarse epidermis. Within was a plastitubular circulatory system through which a bloodlike fluid was pumped by an atomic-powered "heart." The mannequin also "breathed": the chest rose and fell. When skin was cut, the humanoid "bled." Interior organs were of various plastics: solid, sponge, glass, rubber, etc. The models had been designed to cry out when "pain" was inflicted (a cut, punch, pressure) unless a specially formularized anesthetic was first administered. This was simply a gas that temporarily neutralized the "voice-making" machinery.

The mannequins were marvels of engineering. The two replicas of Hyman R. Lewisohn had cost the US Government 100,000 new dollars each. But parts not destroyed in surgical practice could be returned to the West German factory for credit against future purchases.

The manufactured Hyman R. Lewisohns proved of invaluable assistance to the Surgery Team. They were able to plan their own surgical schedule, estimate volume of blood loss, practice on an inanimate object that reacted much as would their eventual subject.

It was, I admit, an eerie experience when I first saw the two Lewisohn replicas. Lying naked, side by side, on a wide operating table in the Surgical Team lab. We had sent over photos, hair and nail clippings, under ultrasecret precautions, and the results were astounding. There was the dwarf corpus, bulging brow, thin fringe of reddish hair, brutal features, thick lips. Had the reproductions snarled obscenities at me, I wouldn't have been a bit surprised.

If the Lewisohn copies shook me, they shattered Maya Leighton. She was not horrified by them. "Fascinated" is the operative word.

Maya had been serving as my Executive Assistant during those early stages of Operation Lewisohn. Like Paul Bumford and Mary Bergstrom, her attitude had gradually changed from cold cooperation to hopeful enthusiasm. In Maya's case, the sight of those two "breathing" reproductions of Hyman R. Lewisohn ended whatever final doubts she might have in the value of the project.

"What is it?" I asked her. Wanting to know why the sight of those two mechanical objects had so affected her.

She shook her head. "Exciting," she said. Almost in awe. I still didn't know. Then.

The Surgical Team busied themselves with the mannequins. Meanwhile, Leo Bernstein's Team had been serving with live "volunteers." I had set an arbitrary limit of three stoppages. But after what he learned from the research project at Hospice No. 17 in

Little Rock, Arkansas—the development of synthetic blood—Leo's practice on human subjects resulted in only one stoppage. And that, he suspected, was due to an allergic reaction. He stated confidently that he was ready to go. Knowing Leo, I believed that was operative.

So it all slowly came together. The equipment of Project Phoenix in Denver was airlifted down, set up in Operating Theater D. The direct-wire link with Phoebe Huntzinger's huge computers in GPA was established and tested. We ran endless game-plans, gradually pushing our own electronic equipment to the ult. Problems arose. Were solved. Defects were discovered. Replaced. Backup equipment was readied (standby generators, a secondary commercial wire link, etc.). The machines were taken as far as we could stress them. That left the objects. The pressures were enormous.

Perhaps Grace Wingate kept me rational. Or, at least, kept me from becoming monomaniac. I know I came from my clandestine meetings with her purged and refreshed. For instance. . . .

A soft, rainy afternoon in early June. Too wet for our secret garden. We stayed in Louise Rawlins Tucker's great empty house. Curled up in each other's arms on a sagging sofa. Watching the rain fall. Listening to the old house creak. I had brought her a set of antique Greek worry beads. Amber. Strung on a silken cord. We were handling the polished spheres between us. Fondling them. They were warmed by our touch.

She said—what did she say?—oh, yes, she said that our decision not to use each other would lead to a love that would be "new . . . all new." Then I laughed softly. I told her she was quoting me, my first speech on the subject, word for word. Then she reminded me that, a few moments previously, I had been speaking about devotion, and had quoted her, almost word for word. Then we both laughed. Hugging each other tighter.

Because you see, we were adapting to each other. More than that, assimilating each other. Words, emotions, thoughts, attitudes, philosophies. We really were becoming one.

Later, she said, "Nick, do you believe in telepathy?"

I had sudden, total recall of Paul and me. A long time ago. In bed together. Exchanging slips of paper. ESP. Had we communicated?

"Telepathy?" I said. "Ambivalent, I guess. Why do you ask?"

"A book I read," she said. "Years and years ago. I think it was in my mother's library. I remembered it last night. For some reason."

"A book?" I said. "What kind of a book?"

"A novel. An obso romantic novel. I must have been quite young when I read it. Twelve? Fourteen? Around then."

"It must have impressed you," I said. "What was it about?"

"I don't recall all the details, dear. But it was about an ef and an em in love. Deeply in love. One of them stops. I think it was her. It might have been him. It makes no difference. The partner who had stopped returned from beyond the grave. They used each other. The live one and the stopped one. The novel said that their love was so strong, so mighty, that it conquered stopping. Nick, do you believe that is possible?"

I looked at her. Conscious my face was twisting.

"You're crying," she said. In wonderment.

"No, no," I said. "Well. Perhaps. A little. I'd like to believe it, Grace. It's very moving."

"But do you believe it?"

"I don't know. Just don't know. Do you? Believe it?"

"Yes," she said firmly. "I believe it. And that is exactly what I shall do. Or, if you go first, what you must do. Promise, Nick?"

"I promise," I said. Did I groan? "And if we both stop? Together?"

"We'll find a way," she said confidently.

We stared at each other. So close our eyelashes were brushing. At that proximity, all focus is lost. Pupils become worlds. One falls, swimming. A sweet dizziness. It was, I thought, a kind of parabiosis. Two linked by a vital look. But a two-way flow. A merging.

The exhilaration! An ecstasy to so surrender. It was passing the point of no return, not caring. The freedom! Spirit ballooning. Everything "new . . . all new," and we might come home to a fresh world.

Any wonder that I left her, each time, "purged and refreshed"? Nothing significant but her. Our love. I cannot say why.

We left Louise's home separately, of course. I departed first. Rode the Metro link into Washington. I went directly to the Executive Office Building where I had a two-hour confabulation with Joe Wellington and his top staffers. Including the serpentine Samantha Slater.

Subject was my third and final PR gig that would take me through the Far West. Conventions, universities, think tanks, laboratories, computer installations, etc. We assumed HR-316 would be approved by the full House Government Operations Committee. The shove was to bring it to floor vote before the summer recess.

After the meeting, I walked slowly toward the Hill. Delaying my return to Hospice No. 4 as long as possible. The Mall was torn up, bordered with construction trailers and heavy equipment.

It was to be the Capital's celebration of the advent of the Twenty-first Century. A series of houses was being erected in a long line from the General Grant statue to the Washington Monument. They were intended to demonstrate the progress of American homes from 1700 to 2000. One home for every fifty years. Beginning with a log cabin and ending with a plastic modular structure. The theme: "You never lived so good!"

I was surprised by the rapid progress of construction. But most of the obso homes were authentic, borrowed from museums, historical societies, national monuments, etc. Disassembled, trucked to the Mall site, and put back together again. The 1850 home, an antebellum Mississippi slave shanty, was already complete. It stood in a small field of plastirub cotton plants. Looking unbearably forlorn. I watched activities on the Mall for almost an hour. Servers were fitting stained glass windows into the walls of the 1900 home: a Victorian bordello from Chicago.

Then I went back to Operation Lewisohn.

We had tried to anticipate every possible contingency. Including such dire emergencies as fire, explosion (terrorist bombing), power failure, and so forth. But, as frequently happens in planning of such complexity, we had overlooked an obvious and imperative need. It was Paul Bumford who brought the matter to the attention of the Executive Staff.

"Look," he said, "assuming the operation is a total success, a direct-wire link is established with the computer installation at GPA-1, the Project Phoenix scanners are serving perfectly, and Leo Bernstein is delivering everything he's promised. Then what?"

"What?" someone said.

"Then what?" Paul repeated. "We haven't planned a permanent installation," he explained patiently. "Where do we move Lewisohn? Where does he *live?* What measures should be taken for his privacy and protection?"

They all looked to me. Waiting. I admit it was my failure. I should have foreseen the problem and solved it. I computed then as rapidly as I could. But all the solutions I plotted had obvious drawbacks.

"I'd prefer he not be moved," I said slowly. "Too much risk. The ideal siting would be underground, but. . . ."

"Let's do this," Paul said briskly. "Leave him *in situ* at the conclusion of the operation. Theater D offers a lot of advantages. Plenty of walk-around space. Facilities for sterile observation. And so forth. After a reasonable survival period, we call in architects. There are several possibilities. The entire Operating Theater could gradually be lowered underground if the proper preparations were made."

"Cost a mint," someone said.

"Use the cost," Paul said. "Another possibility: Convert the entire Lewisohn Building into a gigantic bunker. Reinforce the roof and walls. Put a bombproof shell over the entire building. Cost less than an underground installation, and probably just as effective."

"Good computing, Paul." I nodded. "Call in some high-security architects and get cracking on plans."

I was not gruntled by his imaginative analysis and solution of the problem. I should have anticipated him.

The remainder of that day was spent observing the Surgical Team in a stopwatched rehearsal on one of the Hyman R. Lewisohn humanoids. Maya Leighton was with me.

They were coming up to performance level. As the mock operation progressed, the team built up to full strength. Then gradually decreased in number as, during the actual operation, they would be phased out by Leo Bernstein's Team of hematologists.

I watched two complete runthroughs. When they started the third, I decided I had seen enough. On the following day they would begin practicing actual surgical procedures, cutting into the first Hyman R. Lewisohn dummy. Still intact on the operating table. Chest rising and falling rhythmically. Shining glass eyes staring at the ceiling.

"I can't stand the thought of that cafeteria food tonight," I said to Maya Leighton. "Or the unisex barracks. Too much snoring. Too many groans."

"My place," she said promptly. "I've got two natural ham steaks in the freezer. And some other stuff. We'll pop it all into the microwave."

"Stay the night?" I said.

She looked at me. Surprised.

"Of course," she said. "You think I'm asking you just for my hams?"

483

Then we both collapsed. Almost hysterical laughter.

"Let's stop at a grogshop first," I said. "What would you like?"
She told me.

"To drink," I said.

"Oh . . . anything," she said. "Have you ever tried avocado brandy?"

"I never have," I said grumpily, "and don't intend to. Let's go. Leave the transcribing of those tapes till tomorrow."

"Yes, ruler," she said.

"Oh-ho," I said. "It's going to be one of those nights, is it?"

"I hope so," she said.

Four, perhaps five hours later, we were in the bedroom of her apartment. Not completely rational. We had drunk things. Popped things. Inhaled things. Injected things.

Maya had purchased a curious garment for herself. It must have been quite lovable. Natural rubber in a grayish-beige shade. Almost flesh-colored. Almost. It was not unlike a skin diver's wet suit. But it had gloves, feet, a hood that covered her face and hair.

Her eyes glittered through two small holes. There was an elevated, ventilated V over her nose. Mouth completely covered. All of her pressed tightly in this elastic envelope. I had helped her pull it on. Even with the aid of zippers and a powdered interior it took almost thirty minutes for her to become enshrouded. The most harrowing feature of this monstrous garment was, I thought, the carmined lips painted across her rubbered mouth.

She lay on her back, quite still. Arms at her sides. Legs slightly spread. I watched her coated breasts rise and fall regularly. The heart pumped. Fluid coursed through her vascular system. Beneath the two skins.

To me, the sight of her was at once shocking and exciting. It recalled the paintings of Egon Schiele: sexuality and dread. I couldn't begin to compute it. Darkness so profound that . . . A primitivity there. Something so crude and elemental that it stirred a forgotten bog.

Those flickering eyes. Tight rubber convexing to nipples and belly, concaving to navel and vulva. The sticky sheen of the second skin. Artfully placed seams. I bent over to stare into the eyeholes. A peer into the past. Aeons ago. The ooze. She did not assist when I put my hands upon her. Nor did she resist.

I won't attempt to analyze the psychopathology of what we did. It is not one of my disciplines.

A few days after that (blank) night—I use (blank) here to indicate a deficiency in the English language. I want a word that means you'd like to forget it but you can't. "Haunting" is close, but not exact—I found a note in my Lewisohn Building office asking me to buzz Paul when I had some open time. I buzzed him.

"Paul? Nick. I'm open. What is it?"

"Nick, could you come down here? I have something to show you—some computer printouts. Too clumsy to lug up to your office."

So I went to his office. The computer printouts weren't all that extensive. But I went to his office. I mention this because. . . .

"You don't have to scan all this kaka," he said. "Just take a look at the bottom line."

It was a preliminary report, not authenticated, from the miniteam of Houston neuropsychologists who had been running the Ultimate Pleasure testing of the Operation Lewisohn staff. Preliminary it may have been, but the results were astonishing. On an arbitrary 1 to 10 scale, efficiency of the control group showed 6.9; of the placebo group 7.7; of the actual UP group 9.6.

"It's serving," Paul said. Trying hard to keep the enthusiasm out of his voice. Trying to be the cold clinician. "The UP group is definitely hooked. Their production norms are incredible. Performance excellent. And wait till you scan the personal interviews. They'll serve until they drop for another UP injection."

"What about the slave factor?" I said.

"Confirmed. It exists in 84.8 percentile points of the total UP group. According to computer analysis of fantasy factors."

"So?" I said. "What's your recommendation?"

"First of all, I want to finalize the study here. I don't anticipate ultimate numbers will vary significantly from what we already have. But Operation Lewisohn is a special case. I want a full-scale field test. Nick, do you think your father will cooperate? Let us run a project in his factories, on the assembly lines?"

I computed a moment. "I'm sure he will," I said. "Especially if it results in increased productivity."

Paul laughed. "That's what I figured. We'll pick three generally similar factories. Plants engaged only in assembly. One factory is the control; servers get nothing. Servers in the second plant get placebo injections. In the third they get the real thing. I assume your father keeps object-hour productions records?"

"Of course. Has to. For the unions."

"Right. Well, those will give us statistical norms. Then after, say, six months of the test, we should have a clear idea of the effect of the UP on industrial production."

"And then?" I asked.

He paused a moment. The pouts had disappeared. The softness, the boyish indecision. A ramrod now, but not strutting. He had stressed himself, and found he could hack it. From that came the self-esteem he had needed. He had been in my shadow, a coattailer. Now he was . . . what? I didn't know. I literally did not know. A stranger.

More, he was moving into areas I could not compute. I was older than he: a prime factor. But age alone could not account for our growing estrangement. There was a fundamental disparity. I felt it, and I trust my corpus. What he undoubtedly saw in me as a weakness, I saw in him as a lack. I tried (sometimes failing) not to begrudge his enormous talents. I think, in all honesty, I must admit this: At that point in time, he began to frighten me.

"And then?" I repeated. After he had been silent for almost a minute.

He took a deep breath.

"Well," he said, "it's obvious, isn't it? We must do some heavy brainstorming on the theoretical structure of a society that can maximize the value of the UP. After the gross outlines are postulated, we can get on with effectualizing it. Translating theory into practice. Just for starters, we should increase our research efforts in the area of biobehavioral controls. We've got to minimize the terrorism rate."

"Scratch that last for the moment," I said. "Let's discuss the nature of this society that will maximize the value of the UP. How do you see it?"

He looked at me. Then shrugged.

"It's apparent, isn't it?" he asked. "We agreed the UP would be a political drug. Serving at max efficiency in a society that complemented it. That, to me, can mean only a heavily structured authoritarian government. Designed to take full advantage of the UP's slave factor.

He was going too fast.

"You're projecting the government as master?" I asked him.

"Yes."

"And the citizen as slave?"

"Yes. All indicators point to that relationship as the foundation of Ultimate Pleasure. Nick, it scans. No responsibilities. No decisions to make. No fears of the unknown. A planned existence. Absolutely free.''

"You're equating slavery for freedom?"

He computed a moment. Then nodded.

"You can put it that way. If it pleases you. Yes. As a matter of fact, it's operative. Conventional freedom, like morality, is a luxury. But the world cannot afford it. It's like economic competition. We both know how *un*economic that is. How unlovable. Today, and certainly tomorrow, only absolute authority can produce absolute freedom.''

"Absolute authority?" I said. "You mean absolute tyranny?"

He seemed to be doing a great deal of shrugging.

"All right," Paul said. "Call it tyranny if you wish. Absolute tyranny produces absolute slavery which provides absolute freedom which produces absolute happiness. Does that startle you? It shouldn't. Your Ultimate Pleasure resulted from a sexual fantasy of complete submission.''

"Granted," I said. "But I think you're making a fatal error. It's been nagging at me since we last discussed this. I think it's this: We agreed that the UP would be maximized in a society that complemented it. A society that offered a political atmosphere in which the UP could be utilized for the greatest good of the individual. But you're starting with a political drug of known effect and tailoring a society to fit the individual's needs.''

"Why not?" Paul said. "Society exists to fulfill the individual's needs.''

"Ah-ha," I said. "That's where you're off. Society exists to fulfill *society's* needs. Otherwise, rape would be legal and opium would be sold in slot machines. The desires of the individual are in constant conflict with the needs of society. That's what law is all about.''

"You're saying society must always be in conflict with the needs of its citizens?"

"Not their needs, Paul, their *desires.* Their fantasies. Their brutal dreams. In the perfect world, there would be no conflict. But objects being what they are, society must guard the preservation of the species against individual aggression. Look. . . . Society sets certain standards of human behavior. In our codified laws. Simply to keep the jungle from creeping in. Society cannot be constituted to pander to the lowest levels of human behavior. It must set criteria of behavior—sometimes impossible criteria, I admit—to which objects can aspire."

"That's rank romanticism," Paul said.

"Is it?" I said. "Your projected society is better? A tyranny that exploits the grossest instincts of the species? I thought you were a Beist. Believing in the human species and its eventual evolution in something divine."

"I'm a Beist for reasons of temporary strategy," Paul said. "You know that. I'm no wowser. I told you the world of tomorrow has a better chance of success with an emotional and/or religious factor. Slogans. Ritual. Flags. Prayers. Songs. The whole PR schmeer. But there is nothing in my projection of an authoritarian political society that negates what the Beists stand for."

"I think we better discuss this again," I said. "After Operation Lewisohn is concluded. I think we have a lot to talk about."

"Yes," Paul said. Quirky smile. "I think we do."

On July 2, 1999, I set out again, in civilian clothes, to the neighborhood of the late Arthur Raddo. There was no Adonis Club, restaurant, or tavern listed in the D. C. directory. So, once again, I parked on a sidestreet and ambled onto the stage. Same scene. Same actors therein. I wondered if the curtain ever came down. Certainly the sets were never shifted, the cast never changed.

I listened patiently to all the jostlers who approached me. Drugs, natural foods, Sadie Moscowitz, ef prostitutes, ems, infants. Whatever my heart desired. I let them finish their pitch, then I made mine. Where was Adonis?

It didn't take long. Less than an hour. Then an obso transvestie supplied the input. Adonis was a private cellar club. Members only. I bought the address for ten new dollars.

There was nothing outside to mark it. No sign. No lights. I stumbled down a short flight of brick steps from the street. Kicked gently at a steel door. A small panel, eye-level, slid open. I could see nothing. Darkness inside.

"Yes?" a pleasant voice inquired.

"I'd like to come in," I said.

"Sorry, sir," the pleasant voice said. "This is a private club. Are you a member?"

"No," I said, "but I'd like to join."

"Sorry, sir," the pleasant voice said. "New members must be recommended by a present member. Are you a friend of a present member?"

"I'm a friend of Arthur Raddo," I said. "I *was* a friend of Arthur Raddo."

"Just a minute, please, sir," the pleasant voice said.

The panel slid shut. I waited outside that black steel door for not one, but several long minutes. I was about to kick again when the door swung open. Not wide. Just enough to let me slip through. Then it was cracked shut and bolted behind me.

Complete darkness. A soft hand on my elbow guided me. Across a plasticarp. I came up against a piece of plastisteel furniture. A desk. I fumbled, touching. A flashlight came on. Pointed down at an open ledger.

"Sign here, please, sir," the pleasant voice said. "Twenty new dollars. Cash. No BIN card. All drinks and food purchased in cash. You are allowed to bring a single guest each visit."

"You want my name?" I said foolishly.

"We want *a* name, sir."

I signed "Mickey Mouse." It didn't even raise a chuckle. A beautifully manicured hand came out of the darkness to take my love.

"This way, Mr. Mouse," the pleasant voice said.

The inner room, the cabaret, was not so Stygian. But dark enough. I could make out, dimly, a stage, tables, booths, a bar. I thought the objects in the room were both ems and efs. The costumes fooled me for a moment. All ems.

"Table or bar, sir?" the pleasant voice asked.

"Bar, please," a said.

I was gently guided. When I could touch the bar, a swiveling barstool, the warm hand left my arm. I didn't turn to inspect him. I couldn't have made him out. What illumination there was in the room came from the weak floods focused on the stage.

"Sir?" a pleasant voice said. In front of me. I peered.

"Dr. Bartender, I presume?" I said.

"Yes, sir."

"Natural brandy, please."

"Yes, sir. Water on the side?"

"Please."

The pupil is a remarkable organ. After ten minutes I could discern the small snifter of brandy before me on the bar. I could even see, dimly, the bartender who had served me. A luscious lad. There were a few other singles seated at the bar. But most of the members at tables or in booths were couples or parties of four. Very quiet.

Very restrained. No raucousness. Possibly the most genteel frail joint I had ever visited.

The lights pointed at the stage went off. The room was in total darkness. Then the lights came on again. Bright. Blinding. A loudspeaker clicked on.

"Ladies and gentlemen, the management of *your* Adonis Club is proud to present, by popular demand, a return engagement of that exciting star performer—*Tex!*"

Curtains parted. To the recorded strains of Brahms' "The Rose Breaks Into Bloom," a tall, muscular em clumped onto the minuscule stage. He was wearing the black leather costume of a motorcyclist. Complete with tinted bubble helmet that concealed hair and features. The tight jacket, pants, heavy boots seemed to have a hundred zippers, a thousand metal studs. The zippers were languorously slid open, in approximate time to the music. As the audience sucked its breath. Nothing better being available at that point in time.

Brahms seemed to repeat three times. Eventually, the strip-biker was down to tight bikini panties and that opaque helmet. Striding the dusty stage on bare feet. The corpus was that of a weight lifter: enormously developed deltoids, biceps, quadriceps. Attractive Roman fold about the pelvis. As I should have anticipated, the buttocks were extraordinary. Peachy. When he finally removed the panties and stood naked (except for that concealing helmet), his family jewels proved to be rhinestones. No matter; the audience approved. There was a frantic snapping of fingers. He took six curtains calls. On the final call, he removed his helmet. That was a mistake.

I turned back to my empty brandy glass and signaled for a refill.

"Have one with me?" I asked the bartender.

"Sorry, sir," he said. "We're not allowed to drink with members of the club."

"Have one with me?" I repeated.

"Thank you, sir," he said.

He mixed something swiftly behind the bar. Raised the glass briefly to me, in thanks, drank, then lowered the glass out of sight. In that darkness, even I, closest to him, could hardly see what he was doing.

"Arthur Raddo," I said. "Did you know him?"

"Who?" he said.

I reached across the bar to clasp his hand. And transfer a ten.

"Arthur Raddo," I said. Wriggling my hand free. "Did you know him? Artie? Ever see him?"

"Artie," he said. "Wasn't that a shame?"

"Yes," I said. "A shame. A tragedy."

He liked the word.

"A tragedy," he repeated. "Yes, it was a tragedy."

"He came in here often?"

"Oh . . . not often. Once, twice a week. Like that."

"With anyone?"

"Not at the bar. No. He came to the bar by himself. Up to a few months ago."

"And then?"

"He came with a friend. They sat at a table. I wouldn't know about that."

I sighed. I was running out of tens. So I gave him two fives.

"Ask, will you?" I urged. "Any waiter who might have served him. Artie's friend's name, and what he looked like. The friend, I mean. What the friend looked like. Can you do that for me?"

"Well . . ." he said doubtfully. "I'll try."

"Do," I said.

"You're so sweet," he said.

I sipped my brandy while he was gone. Trying to make out my own features in the artificially antiqued mirror behind the bar. My face was wrinkled with wavering tendrils of gilt. Guilt? Who was I? I couldn't make me out.

"Yes," a voice said. And there he was again. Looming close to me out of the gloom. "Artie came in several times with a friend. Not *with* a friend. He met him here."

"Name?" I asked.

"Artie called him Nick."

"Uh-huh," I said. "Did you ask what he looked like? This friend of Artie's?"

"About your height," the bartender said. "About your weight and build. With hair about your shade."

"And with a mustache," I said. "And a Vandyke beard. Just like mine."

"Exactly," he said. "How did you know?"

"Thank you very much," I said.

"I adore you," he said.

I went reeling out of there. Remembering an experience I had at MIT when I was being conditioned on computer technology. There had been a power lapse—not a failure but a lapse—and the computer I was serving on had run wild. It had spewed out incredible nonsense until we brought it back to norm. While it was out of control, the readout screen had scanned: "Bicycle boys never into tile sky shall." That was precisely my mood at that point in time: "Bicycle boys never into tile sky shall."

But it was to be compounded. I departed that dungeon and wandered back to my car. Not computing at all. Not at all. Toward me, on the crowded sidewalk, came lurching a very tall em. Apparently drunk. Picking his nose thoughtfully.

And wearing a checkered cap.

Z-9

Opening remarks delivered at a conversazione of scientists of various disciplines, University of California at Berkeley, July 16, 1999.

"It can hardly come as a surprise to most of you here tonight that, for the past fifteen years, the foreign policy of the US Government has been based on our agricultural production. Particularly of cereal grains. This agriwar, in which admittedly we have used food as an aggressive weapon, has reduced the danger of nukewar to an irremin. For which I think we all, regardless of our political tilt, can be thankful.

"Wait—wait just a minute! I do not want this colloquy to degrade into a debate on morality. Since when has morality been a scientific discipline? I'll say only that, having spent most of my adult life in Public Service, I know it is a fatal error to confuse personal morality with political morality. The two, I assure you, have nothing in common.

"But the thesis I wish to propose to you tonight—and which I hope will be the subject of frank and lively discussion—is that the period in which the superiority of the US in agriwar was the base of our foreign policy and national security is drawing to a close. The production of protein from petroleum, the improved strains of natural grains, the development of protein from plankton, the exciting discoveries in the area of weather control, the increasing use of soybeans in the production of synthetic foods, factory farms, hydroponic gardens: all these, plus the worldwide gains in achieving Z-Pop, have reduced the importance of food as a weapon of foreign policy.

"What I suggest to you now is that is is time to consider a new basis for our national strength. The Twenty-first will, in my opinion, be the Century of Sciwar.. And unless we immediately establish the proposed Department of Creative Science, bringing scientists of all disciplines into policymaking roles in the US Government, we are doomed to become a second-rate power."

That was the last meeting of my final Public Relations tour on behalf of the DCS. I flew directly from San Francisco to Detroit on an official courier plane. Hypersonic operations had once again been approved for the Detroit area.

I was exhausted. Throat raspy. Unable to compute clearly all the problems that beset me. I suffered three attacks of RSC in California. Of increasing severity. During the last, I remembered a stuffed giraffe I had played with as an infant. I couldn't have been much more than one year old at the time. It was, by far, my most ancient memory. If I went back any farther, I'd recall swimming lazily in my mother's womb.

I arrived at our Grosse Pointe place in time to have lunch with my father. Just before he departed for a week's tour of his overseas factories.

"Nick-ol'-as!" he shouted. I submitted to the expected bear hug.

He brought me up to tick. The Die-Dee Doll was a tremendous success. Worldwide markets. Eighteen ethnic models. Forty-seven national costumes. Love pouring in. Demand increasing. The problem was production. Not in raw material shortfalls, but in assembly. And just when he was convinced the problem was insoluble, along comes that little butterfly Paul Bumford with a request that he cooperate in a field test of a new drug that might double his production norms.

"Nick, did you know about that?" my father demanded.

I told him yes, I knew all about that.

And did I think it would really serve? Would it raise his unit assembly rate?

"I think it will," I said.

"That's good enough for me," he burbled. "I'll flash Paul a go. That's one bright em. I misjudged him. I admit it. What is this stuff, Nick?"

"An injection," I said. "Self-administered."

"What does it do? Make 'em serve faster?"

"No," I said. "No recorded effect on muscular coordination, physical speed, or anything like that. It's a reward for increased production. That's all I can tell you."

"A reward?" he said. "Better than overtime love?"

"Much better," I assured him. "And much cheaper."

"That's for me." He laughed. "But we'll have to make it voluntary. You know that, don't you, Nick? The unions will insist on it."

"Of course."

"Paul knows it?"

"I'm sure he does. We'll get Informed Consent Statements from everyone injected."

"You think they'll go for it? The servers?"

"When the word gets around, they'll be lining up for shots."

"Wonderful!" he yelled.

"Yes," I said. "Wonderful."

I stood on the porch. Waving as my father's helicopter lifted off the front lawn. He hadn't married the musician. I didn't think he would. But his new black ef copter pilot seemed to be about two meters tall. With a corpus as pliant as whalebone. Green hair down to her arse. My father's vitality depressed me.

I slept ten hours. Breakfasted voraciously on orange petrojuice, proham, powdered eggs, propots, two slices of soybread, and three cups of coftea. I spent four hours playing cartel bridge with Mrs. McPherson, Miss Catherine, and Charles. Then went back to bed for another eight hours. I awoke convinced that I would find solutions for all my problems and never again see another checkered cap. I called Millie Jean Grunwald.

It was then almost 2400. I woke her up, I knew, but I had never known her to speak to me in anger, or even pique. She seemed delighted when she recognized my voice. I think she was. She told me to hurry; she had so much to tell me.

I hadn't brought her a gift. But I went up to what had been my mother's bedroom, and on the top shelf of a closet, wrapped in pink tissue paper, I found an obso French doll. One of those long-legged, long-armed, fancily dressed, floppy figures young efs once left sprawled on their counterpanes.

Into Detroit, in the antique Ford Capri. To Millie's darkened street. The deserted porn shop. But her lights were on. She awaited me.

As I had hoped, the French doll delighted her. Millie would never be allowed to breed, not with her genetic rating, and perhaps she knew it. Or sensed it. She adopted the doll as her very own immediately. Insisted on taking it into bed with us. Perched high on a pillow, its painted lips smiled down on our naked corpora. Eyes opened wide in enthralled astonishment.

Millie had gained at least ten kilos since I had last seen her. Too much Qik-Freez Hot-Qizine at her factory's cafeteria. She had scarcely any waist left. The breasts were fuller, and buttocks, thighs, calves. Even upper arms and feet. I didn't care. All of her was soft. That young, globular ass was particularly comforting. Her flesh had a fresh, infant's scent. She tasted of warm milk.

I had intended only to hold her. Listening to her long, involved accounts of what had happened to her supervisor's husband, how her girlfriend's boyfriend had betrayed her, and what a local florist had suggested to her (Millie): a free natural philodendron for a fast blowjob in the stockroom.

But there was so much of her. Her almost matronly breasts hardened under my negligent urging. Long nipples stared at me expectantly. Plump thighs parted. Knees raised and widened. The lower mouth yawned. In all conscience, could I reject her when she was already humid? And panting? And I was already humid? And panting?

I maneuvered her to hands and knees. Then pressed her head and shoulders gently downward. Until her face was turned sideways onto a pillow. Live hair flung out. Great hips and buttocks raised to me. Sleek and round. She reached up to pull the French doll down to her. Cuddled it. Kissed its pouting lips. Stroked its long, tight sausage curls. Crooned into its little ear.

She was conscious of me on a physical level. The slow writhing of her pelvis demonstrated that. But as her corpus quickened, den became lubricious, ass heatened and tautened in my grip, she never left off crooning to the doll. Whispering into its tiny ear as I, insensate, thrust. Both of us slaves. Both of us masters. I didn't know.

I do know that when I felt the onset of orgasm, could no longer restrain, I withdrew and directed jets of hot semen onto her soft buttocks and dimpled back. Watching the birdlime drip and run.

Wondering why I was doing what I was doing to this child. And she smiled, smiled, nodded, nodded, and whispered secrets into the ear of my mother's doll.

Hours later—one or several; I wasn't aware—she shook me awake. Frantic. She had switched on the bedlamp.

"Nick," she said, "wake up. Please wake up, Nick."

"What is it?" I said.

"Listen," she said.

I listened. A squeaking. Clicking. Sudden scamper.

"Mice in the walls," I told her. "Coming up from the basement. Try to forget them. Go back to sleep."

"I saw one last week," she said. "It ran across the floor and went down a hole where the pipe is. There in the corner."

"A little one or a big one?" I asked.

"A big one, Nick. *Huge!*"

"How big?"

She held her forefingers about 10 cm apart.

"A little one," I said. "*Mus,* not *Rattus.* They won't hurt you."

"They'll bite me."

"No, Millie. Not mice. They won't."

"They'll run over me and, you know, get between my legs. And bite."

I sighed.

"All right, Millie," I said. "I'll fix it so they can't get up here."

I got out of bed, naked, and went into her tiny kitchen. I found some rags under the rusted sink. Brought them back to the big room.

"I'll stuff them around the pipe," I told her. "Tomorrow you must buy some plastisteel wool, pull the rags out, and stuff the wool all around the pipe. They can't gnaw through that. Do you understand, dear?"

"Plastisteel wool," she repeated.

"Right. You stuff it around the pipe where I'm going to put the rags in for tonight."

"Around the pipe," she repeated.

"Right," I said. "Then complain to the super or the owner. Tell them to set traps or scatter poison. Tell them you'll complain to the Health Board."

"The Health Board," she repeated faintly.

I knew she'd never remember. But I'd do what I could. I got down on hands and knees, began to jam rags into a wide circular

496

crack between a vertical steampipe and the old, wooden floor. There should have been a metal flange about the pipe; there was none.

I was stuffing the rags into the crevice when I glanced at the wooden baseboard. The pipe was in a corner; walls and baseboard came to a V behind the pipe. The baseboard had been nailed in place, then painted over. But two nailheads protruded. Not more than 1 cm each. I bent forward to examine them. I had seen similar electronic devices before: nailhead microphones. Topping spikes inserted in drilled holes in the wood.

I knelt there for several minutes. Staring at them. I remembered the night with Millie when I talked, talked, talked. About things she could have no interest in. About things I should not have talked about. To anyone with less than a Red 2 security clearance. Poor Millie. She would never have *any* security clearance. Not even Red 10.

Millie's apartment had been shared. I had told her things she could not—no way!—comprehend. But Maya Leighton's apartment? Was that also shared? Had I told her things? Our last evening together, when she had worn that dreadful rubber suit, had I spoken of the botulism outbreak in GPA-11? That I might have told her didn't depress me half as much as the fact that I could not remember if I had told her or not. And the safe house? My secret garden with Grace Wingate? Was that also shared? Was *I* being shared with new drugs, new technologies I had not been told about because I had no need to know? I was not without fear. What object is?

I grasped one of the protruding nailheads tightly and began to move it back and forth. I loosened the attached spike in the drilled hole. Finally I was able to withdraw it. Slowly. Carefully. There was a wire soldered to the end. It led into the wall.

That suddenly vacated porn shop below began to make sense.

"Come back to bed, Nick," Millie called.

"In a minute, darling," I said. "Millie, is there a back entrance to this building? A back staircase?"

"Nooo," she said. Frowning. "Not exactly. There's a fire escape. It's all dirty."

"How do you get to that?"

"Out in the hall. That window right next to the door to the nest. You have to climb out the window to get onto the fire escape. But it's all dirty."

"Do you have a flashlight?" I asked her.

"Flashlight?" she said. Worried. Trying to understand, to remember.

"I'll look," I told her. "You go to sleep. I'll be back in a few minutes."

I pulled on zipsuit and socmocs. I went back into her kitchen. Finally, in the back of a drawer filled with a miscellany of cheap household gadgets, I found a small, square plastic lantern.

Out to the hallway, down to the window next to the nest door. I unlocked it, but couldn't raise it. It appeared to be painted shut. I leaned against the frame on all four sides. Then strained upward on the sash. The window didn't move. Back to Millie's kitchen, carving knife, back to window, point of knife inserted between sash and frame, run all the way around.

Finally, window open a few cm, I could get my fingertips into the crack and heave upward. Once the paint seal was broken, the window ran free. I got out onto the fire escape. Millie had been right; it was all dirty.

I rested a moment on the encrusted, slatted iron landing. But it was a warm, muggy night; I was never going to get any cooler. I stepped down cautiously onto the counterweighted stairway. As I proceeded, it swung slowly lower. Gripping the filthy handrail, I went down step by careful step. Finally the base touched the ground. I scampered down.

I was about to step off the fire escape ladder onto the paved rear courtyard when, suddenly, mercifully, it occurred to me that the moment I stepped off, the counterweighted section of ladder would rise again. I would be marooned in that fetid courtyard forever. Archaeologists would find my dried bones in a million years and contrive elegant theories to account for my presence there.

I looked about frantically. Still standing on the bottom step of that cantilevered staircase. No weight within easy reach. Nothing but a barred window. Bars on the outside. There was no alternative. Still standing on the swinging escape ladder, my weight keeping it down, I skinned out of my zipsuit. Twisted it into a tough rope. Tied arms about one of the window bars, legs about a vertical handrail support on the rusty ladder. Naked, except for socmocs, I stepped onto the paved courtyard. Still gripping the handrail of the counterweighted ladder. Relieved of my weight, the end began to rise. I let it swing up slowly. Then the knotted zipsuit snugged taut. The end of the ladder was only about a meter above the ground. I could pull it down easily.

Third problem: an unbarred but locked rear door to the deserted porn shop. But there were six small panes of glass. I broke the one nearest the lock with the heel of a socmoc. Reached in cautiously through shards still in the sash. Turned a swivel latch. The door opened creakingly. I was in.

Used the weak flashlight then. Down a musty corridor. Into what had apparently been the main salesroom. Shading the light carefully with my fingers so that it could not illuminate the dusty front window, possibly alert a prowling bobcar. I moved it about slowly. Slowly. Inspecting. Fascinated dread. I thought again of Maya Leighton lying motionless in her earth-colored rubber suit. Painted lips. Glittering eyes. And—and all. . . .

Detritus of a lost civilization. Broken phalli. Ripped vaginas. Melted dildos. Vibrators long stilled. Torn photos. Dried condoms. Cracked leather masks. Rotted artificial tongues. False breasts puddled. All the technologized sex run down and stopped.

A sexual necropolis. Dust everywhere. And mouse droppings.

Finally, in a small inner room—office? stockroom?—I found the wires leading down from Millie's apartment. The bare ends dangled over a wooden table relatively free of dust. The recorders had been placed there, of course. The operators had sat there, on that rickety three-legged stool. They had been emplaced for some time; the floor was littered with empty and stained plastic coftea containers, sandwich wrappings, dried bread crusts, fruit rinds, old newspapers. I shuffled through the last. They scanned a time period of almost five months. Long enough.

I went back the way I had come. Closed the door. Locked it. Pulled the escape ladder down. Unknotted and retrieved my zipsuit. Mounted to Millie's floor. Climbed in through the window. Closed it and locked it. Took a tepid shower in Millie's nest, with a thin sliver of petrosoap that raised no lather at all. Dried on a ragged square of thin petrocot. Then went back to the big room. Switched off the bedlamp. Climbed into bed.

"Everything all right?" Millie asked sleepily.

I turned her gently onto her stomach. I squirmed down until my face was at her tail, burrowing. I parted, probed, then pressed her buttocks tight to my fevered face.

"Everything's fine," I said to her anus.

Millie had to serve the next day, and awoke early. I was vaguely aware of her moving about. Dressing slowly. Doing something in the kitchen. Talking nonsense to the French doll that she carried about with her for a while. Then propped carefully in the corner of the couch. I wanted, desperately, just another hour or two of sleep. But I awoke, wide, when I heard her unlock the door.

"Millie," I called.

She turned back.

"Nick," she said, "I'm sorry I woke you. Go back to sleep. Stay as long as you like. Just click the door when you leave."

I got out of bed. Padded across the room to her. Took her tightly into my arms.

"You are a dear, sweet ef," I told her. "And I don't know what I'd do without you."

She flushed with profit. Hugged me tightly.

"We *do* have fun, don't we?" she said.

"We do indeed," I agreed. "Remember me, Millie?"

"Remember you?" she said. Puzzled. "Of course I remember you. You're Nick."

"I mean tomorrow." I laughed. "Will you remember me tomorrow?"

I knew she wouldn't, but I kissed her on the lips and thanked her again. She was happy because I was happy.

"I'll remember you tomorrow," she assured me. "Tomorrow's Friday. Right?"

"Right," I said. And watched her go.

I did sleep another two hours and got back to Grosse Pointe before 1100. Mrs. McPherson told me Paul Bumford had flashed twice from Washington, D. C., and I was to contact him the moment I returned. I went into the library and used the flasher there. After two wrong numbers, I got through to Paul in the DCS office at the EOB. He came on screen.

"Nick," he said, "where have you been?"

"Sleeping," I said.

"Millie," he said. "Well, listen Nick, are we still set for July twenty-sixth? For Operation Lewisohn?"

"As far as I'm concerned. I'm leaving in a few hours. Be down there tonight."

"I had this idea. . . ."

"So?" I asked. "What idea?"

"We should make an official record. On videotape. Can I effect a

500

communications team? To get it all. For history. I'll borrow objects and equipment from Joe Wellington's PR staff.''

I computed a moment.

''The basic idea is go,'' I told him, ''but Joe is not to be involved. He has no need to know. Besides, this is a very specialized type of production. Contact Ed Nolan at GPA-1 and requisition the objects who photographed that intravaginal documentary. Remember it? With the microminiaturized IBM TV camera?''

''Of course I remember it. Fine. I'll get them down here instanter.''

''No interference with performing objects. Maybe they can set up platforms out of the way. And some effective commentator. Ron Nexler. That's his name. He did the voice-over on the chimera short. Remember that?''

''Nick, will you stop saying, 'Remember that?' I don't forget; you know that.''

''If you say so. Bring the objects and equipment in. We'll have them set up, then have more walkthroughs to make certain they won't interfere with the actual surgery.''

''Got it. With Ron Nexler giving a running commentary?''

''Yes. He's scientifically conditioned. No brain, but very glib. He's just right for the service.''

''I'll get on it. It should be solidified by the time you get back tonight. I thought you'd want a permanent record, Nick.''

''Yes,'' I said. ''I do. Thanks, Paul. By the way, my father is going to flash you a go signal on the UP field test.''

''Great,'' he enthused. ''I'll start putting it together. Everything's percolating. Right, Nick?''

''Right,'' I said.

There was time before my father's copter would pick me up for the trip to the airport. I went to my third-floor aerie. The glued thread, door to jamb, was undisturbed. I sat down with the works of Egon Schiele. I lighted a cannabis. Alone.

As I turned those familiar pages once again, staring at that strong, baleful sexuality, I slowly became aware that I was never going to solve the mystery of Egon Schiele. What was the meaning behind those stopped eyes? What significance in the helpless, tormented nudes? The dread in the sight of exposed, pitilessly detailed genitalia? I could penetrate so far, but no farther. Then my descent was blocked. I was left with a horrified fascination I could not analyze.

Curiously, my failure to comprehend the work of Egon Schiele did not depress me. In fact, it led me to a realization I found oddly comforting:

There are questions to which there are no answers. There are problems for which there are no solutions.

Six hours later I was in the Lewisohn Building, Hospice No. 4, Alexandria, Virginia. Operation Lewisohn was scheduled to start at 0800, July 26, 1999. The staff spent the remaining hours in rehearsals, practice, drills. The Operation Directors devoted their time to running game-plans through Phoebe Huntzinger's computers in GPA-1. Testing our scenario for possible flaws. We programmed for every possible combination of disasters: power failures, linkage breakdowns, sudden stopping of the subject, terrorist attack, and so forth.

Difficulties were encountered, and overcome. For instance, the computer warned of incapacitation of key personnel. So we established an intraproject medical group, to minister to disabled staff members. We took extraordinary precautions to guard against food poisoning on the evening of July 25. We had already structured a fail-safe Table of Organization: Each object was numbered in relation to the importance of the assigned task. Thus, if Chief Surgeon Dr. George Berk, Green One, was unable to perform, his place would be taken by Green Two. And so on; everyone moving up a rank. Standby objects were present to fill in the lowest echelons.

At midnight, July 25, all operating staff were ordered to use a six-hour Somnorific. At the same time, the Command Staff was administered low-power, time-controlled energizers. The final countdown began. The last checkout of equipment, power supply, electronic linkages, and so forth. Phoebe Huntzinger's computers were gradually brought on line. Operating Theater D illuminated. Emergency supplies opened. Instrument sterilizers wheeled into position. Laser scanners put on warm-up. Amplifiers tested. Read-out screens and printout machines switched to On.

The results of these preparations were all reported on monitor screens to Command Central. Paul and I had agreed that I was to remain there, ruling the entire project, while he roamed the assembly rooms, corridors, labs, washup lavatories, operating area, and so forth. Reporting progress and stoppages directly to me, and only me, via a Portapager on an exclusive wavelength.

Next to me in Command Central, on my right, Maya Leighton sat at a wide desk. With Mary Bergstrom as backup. They each had a throat mike and a copy of the final schedule. We had positioned loudspeakers throughout the building.

I watched the enormous wall digiclock rotate the seconds. At 0729:45, I looked to Maya. She was watching me. I raised my hand. At 0729:59, I pointed a forefinger directly at her. She began to read quietly from the schedule. Her amplified voice boomed from the speakers:

"0730. Transportation Group to stations. Green Team and White Team to standby."

The objects assigned to the task of bringing Hyman R. Lewisohn into Operating Theater D moved to their designed positions: his hospital suite, hallway, elevator, etc. The Green Team (surgeons and anesthesiologists) and White Team (nurses and aides) moved to their assembly areas. I could watch these activities, and all the actions that would take place that day, on a bank of TV monitor screens.

These belonged to the Communications Team. The commentator, Ron Nexler, sat at a control board on my left. The videotape editor sat next to him, making a rough mix as the images came in. Neither em took his eyes from the monitor screens. As Operation Lewisohn got under way, I saw the mobile videotape camera operator, powerpack on his back, move from one area to another. Taping the preliminaries. He, in turn, was videotaped by the fixed cameras.

Ron Nexler spoke softly into a desk mike:

"Good morning, ladies and gentlemen. This is Ron Nexler speaking to you from the Lewisohn Building in Hospice No. 4, Alexandria, Virginia. In a very few moments we will witness an incredible surgical operation that has never been attempted before in the long history of the human race. This is a historic moment, an exciting moment, and we hope to show you every step in this astounding scientific achievement that may very well revolutionize the future of the world."

"0740. Green Team and White Team to washup. Transportation Group to alert. Countdown will begin by minutes from 0755 to 0759. By seconds during the final minute."

Quiet in Command Central. I watched the clock. Listened to Maya's voice, coming over the loudspeaker, and to Nexler's voice, being taped. Paul patted my shoulder, then left to begin his rounds. I scanned the monitor screens. Normal.

"0754. Coming up to mark. Transportation Group to final readiness. Green Team and White Team to alert. Countdown to start begins . . . *now!* 0755.

"0756.

"0757.

"0758.

"0759, and 60, 59, 58, 57, 56, 55, 54. . . ."

As the numbers dwindled, I could see objects all over the building glancing nervously at wall digiclocks and taking deep breaths.

". . . six, five, four, three, two, one. *Start!*"

"Ladies and gentlemen, this tremendously involved and complex surgical procedure has started. I will attempt to provide a minute-by-minute account of what is taking place. But please bear with me if the image you see does not correspond to my commentary. This is a solemn and extremely intricate project, and we in the communications field must, quite rightly, take second place to all the wonderful objects contributing their time and their talents to make this great endeavor a resounding success.

"Now you see the door of Hyman R. Lewisohn's hospital room being opened. The Transportation Group is moving in to begin their assignment. The subject has already been sedated sufficiently so he can be disconnected from all his tubes and needles. Nothing but an incoherent, muttered protest from him. Jake, could you move in closer and get that moan again, please? Now they've got him on a high, wheeled stretcher and have started him out of that room where he has spent so many lonely, pain-racked hours. Moving him toward the elevator bank. A door is being held open. . . ."

"0803. Green Team and White Team to positions. Subject on the way to Operating Theater D."

"Now, folks, the endless drills and rehearsals are paying off. Notice there is no stumbling, no bumping, no confusion. Every object knows the task required and the exact physical position and movements assigned. All serving together like the selfless angels of mercy they are."

"0805. Green Team and White Team to alert. Blue Team to assembly."

"Ladies and gentlemen, what impresses me most at this crucial moment is the absolute silence of the servers as the subject is wheeled through the wide doors of Operating Theater D. Now you can see, through the magic of a portable videotape camera, the preliminaries as Lewisohn's corpus is transferred to the operating

504

table and draped. Now the anesthesiologists begin their important service. Notice they glance occasionally to the vital signs monitors against the walls. But mostly they are listening, listening intently, to the beeps, thumps, and whistles of amplified aural signals. All these indicators are reproduced here in Command Central. I have just spoken to Dr. Nicholas Bennington Flair, the brilliant ruler of this incredible scientific project, and he informs me that Lewisohn's cardiac rate, although erratic, is presently within acceptable parameters, pulse is strong, and other vital signs are encouraging.''

I saw, on a TV monitor, the Chief Anesthesiologist nod to the Chief Surgeon. Just after Maya Leighton announced: "0821. Blue Team to standby," the Chief Surgeon spoke briefly into his throat mike.

"I'm going in," he said.

"Ladies and gentlemen, the actual operation has begun."

I thought then, and I think now, it was the longest day of my life. It was not only the slight click of the wall digiclock as the minutes ticked over in Command Central. Nor Maya Leighton enunciating her orders precisely: "Blue Team to alert. Green Team begin withdrawal in precisely five minutes. Brown Team to standby." Nor Ron Nexler's never-ending, "Ladies and gentlemen, the next miracle you are about to see. . . ." And so forth.

It was the slow, deliberate pace of what we did that day that stretched minutes to hours. I knew it could not be hurried. Should not be. But I longed for it all to be over. Done with. Finished. Won or lost. One way or the other.

It did not go perfectly. What human plan does? But we were able to cope with emergencies, improvise when required, substitute, invent. Considering the radical nature of the operation, I cannot see how our basic scenario could have been improved.

The surgeons were finished by 1600. Meanwhile we had been phasing in Leo Bernstein's Blue Team. Who, in turn, were phased out as the Project Phoenix servers, Brown Team, wheeled up their equipment and began positioning the laser scanners.

As servers came off duty, I noted they did not disappear to the cafeteria or barracks. I knew they were as worn and weary as I. Yet, almost to an object, they went immediately to the observation benches behind the glass walls in Operating Theater D. Where they could witness the climax of the project. Hunched over. Leaning forward. Elbows on knees. Chins on fists. Staring. Staring.

I had left my swivel chair only twice that day. To go to the nest.

But I was on post when the first faint signal was picked up from Lewisohn's brain by the Brown Team, at 2139 on the evening of July 26, 1999. About five minutes later, they detected a signal they felt was precise enough to amplify and attempt to translate in the GPA-1 computer vocabulary. The signal was transmitted over our direct-wire link. We waited. The printout machine chattered briefly: WHAT?

It wasn't much, I admit. But if Lewisohn's brain had stopped at that instant, I would still have deemed Operation Lewisohn a success. As the word spread of what we had done, I heard a great, muffled roar go up from everyone, everywhere, throughout the Lewisohn Building. Maya Leighton kissed me. Even Mary Bergstrom kissed me. There was a continual snapping of fingers, stroking of palms. Paul came rushing back to Command Central. I realized then his total commitment to, and belief in Operation Lewisohn. For behind came laughing servers with bottles of petropagne, natural brandy, petrovod, chilled Smack. Many nice liters of many nice things. A celebration Paul had provided. We celebrated.

Meanwhile, Brown Team were still fussing with their laser scanners. Making minute power adjustments in the amplifiers. By the time I got down to Operating Theater D, they were transmitting a stream of utile signals to GPA-1. Returns were mostly gibberish, but that was understandable; Lewisohn's brain hadn't yet been totally flushed of sedatives and anesthesia. Leo Bernstein was personally monitoring the blood serum pump and adjusting the data processing monitor that gave a continuous scan and printout of brain weight, electrical power output, oxygen level, and so forth.

The head of Hyman R. Lewisohn had been severed from his corpus. It had been placed beneath a giant bell jar. Five times the size of the glass dome enclosing the head of Fred III, the Labrador retriever. Lewisohn's head existed in a sterile environment. Laser rods, instruments, the loudspeaker wire, etc., all penetrated the protective covering, but were attached with contamination-proof seals.

The head had been cut off below the larynx, slightly beneath the voice box. But Lewisohn could not speak, since there were no lungs to provide airflow across the vocal cords. Hence the need for the scanning equipment of Project Phoenix. The head would be maintained in an animate status in a manner similar to that used to keep Fred III alive, with an oxygenated blood pump. Brain weight and

506

electrical output were monitored constantly. Lewisohn could see, and he could hear. Hence the small loudspeaker inside his bell jar.

When I first approached Lewisohn's head, the eyes were closed. The skin tone appeared waxen to me. But Leo Bernstein didn't seem unduly concerned, so I refrained from questioning him. He and two members of his staff were still adjusting flow rates and formulae. The Project Phoenix servers were just as busy. Making microadjustments on the laser rods. Watching their screens to provide maximum overlap of the scanned areas. Tuning their amplifiers on phoned advice from Phoebe Huntzinger in New York. I spoke with her briefly.

"Congratulations, Nick," she said. "You did it."

"*We* did it," I said. "Thank you."

"It was your idea," she said. "What's next?"

"I'll think of something," I said. And we both laughed.

I watched Lewisohn's head. Keratotic scalp showing through the scraggly fringe of reddish hair. Distorted skull. Bulge of domed brow. Gross features magnified by his pallor. Rubbery lips, drooling slightly. Certainly not as attractive as Fred III.

Finally, the eyes opened. Slowly. Lids rose like a weighted curtain. I moved closer to the bell jar. Picked up the small hand mike. Waited.

Eyes appeared dulled. Lifeless. But even as I watched, I saw a definite improvement. Consciousness flowing in. Animation growing stronger.

"Folks," Ron Nexler's low voice said, "Hyman R. Lewisohn's head appears to be recovering from the shock of this historymaking operation. His eyes are opening wide, and, yes, they're turning now to inspect. . . ."

I turned sharply. Nexler was at my side. Staring with fascination at Lewisohn's head. But not too fascinated to remain silent; he was dictating into a portable tape deck. Over his shoulder, the mobile videotape camera operator was recording the awakening of Hyman R. Lewisohn. For history. For one insane instant I wanted to beat them both to stopping with their own equipment. But the fury passed. They were doing their service. As I was doing mine. I turned back to Lewisohn's head.

The eyes were fully open now. Sclerae and cornea clear. Brighter. Pupils slightly dilated. The eyeballs turned slowly in complete circuits. Left. Up. Right. Down. They made two complete inspections. Surveying the inside of the glass bell jar. Distorted images of all of us outside, peering in. I knew the brain must be computing. As I anticipated, the eyes turned downward once again. To inspect the base of the bell jar. No corpus. If Lewisohn had still possessed a heart, it might have stopped at that instant. Instead, the printout computer began to chatter softly. I stepped over to it, but scanned the readout screen rather than wait for the permanent record. The translated electrical signals were not in coherent form. Understandable.

WHAT? GLASS DOME. DREAM? ALIVE. MOVEMENT THERE. OBJECTS. WHAT'S HE DOING? ABOVE. ALL SIDES. BELOW? NOTHING. NOTHING? A BASE. RODS STICKING IN. WHAT? A LITTLE SQUARE BOX. WHERE? ALIVE. YES. PAIN? NO. NO PAIN. WHO? HOT! CHRIST, IT'S SO HOT!

"Leo!" I called.

But he had been scanning the printout as it flipped from the machine. He saw it almost as soon as I did. He jerked a downthumb at one of his servers.

"Take him off five degrees and hold," he ordered.

Temperature and humidity inside Lewisohn's home were adjusted gradually downward. The computers started clacking again with scarcely a pause. It is difficult, if not impossible, to stop thinking completely. Try it sometime. The closest you can come is to think, "I will not think."

Computer readout showed that Lewisohn still did not comprehend what had happened to him. I judged it time to tell him. Primus: I wanted to anger him, keep him "talking." I guessed increased brain activity at that point in time would help rid the neurons and supporting nutritive structures of the effects of preoperative drugs and anesthetics.

Secondus: There was much we had to learn of the functioning of a detached human brain, and we had to learn it fast. For instance, did the brain have to sleep, without the need to recover from physical exhaustion? The Fred III research project had indicated that sleep is as much a function of mental recovery as of physical. But in humans? We simply didn't know.

The microphone leading to the loudspeaker within Lewisohn's bell jar was small, hand-held, with a volume control calibrated from 1 to 5. I set it at 1, and moved close to the glass. Maneuvering cautiously to avoid disturbing the projecting laser rods.

"Lewisohn," I said. In a normal, conversational tone.

It had no effect on him. His eyes did not blink. I adjusted volume control to 2.

"Lewisohn," I said again.

Eye reaction this time. Flickering briefly in the direction of the loudspeaker within the bell jar. He probably heard it as a whisper. I moved the volume control up to 3.

"Lewisohn," I repeated.

He heard that all right. Rapid blinking. Eyes focused on loudspeaker. I moved my head as close to the glass as I could.

"Lewisohn," I said, "move your eyes slowly, slowly to your left. As far as you can without feeling pain. You should be able to make me out. This is Nicholas Bennington Flair. How do you feel, Lewisohn?"

Why didn't I stand directly in front of the bell jar where he could see me without turning his eyes? Because in front of the bell jar, as close as we could get it to minimize distortion, we had set up a small viewing screen. On which Lewisohn would be able to scan books, newspapers, reports, computer printouts, etc.—all to be taped at his command. For his exclusive viewing.

"How do you feel, Lewisohn?" I repeated.

The computer printout began its soft chatter. I switched off my microphone. I looked about. Paul Bumford was standing nearby, talking with Tom Lee, Team Leader of Project Phoenix.

"Paul," I called.

He came over immediately. I drew him close. Spoke in a low voice.

"Paul, interrogation of Lewisohn will be difficult if the interrogator has to run back and forth from microphone to computer to scan Lewisohn's response. A longer cord on the mike is no answer. Then you wouldn't be able to monitor his facial reactions. Get on the flasher to Phoebe. Ask her how long it will take to program the entire stored vocabulary into vocal responses. It can be done; the hardware's available. Her computers will trigger spoken words on tape. The words should be recorded by some em with vocal qualities similar to Lewisohn's natural voice. There must be tapes of him speaking *somewhere* they can use as models."

"Right." Paul nodded. "I'll get on it at once."

"I don't want the Chief Director in here until he can actually have a 'conversation' with Lewisohn's head. Talk to him and apparently hear Lewisohn 'talking' back. Much more impressive."

"I concur," Paul said. "Marvelous idea."

"Meanwhile, assign a server to tear off printout from the machine as it comes in and hustle it over to me. Two servers would be better."

I went back to the bell jar. To my original position. I switched on the microphone.

"Lewisohn," I said. "Here I am. Nicholas Bennington Flair. Can you see me?"

The computer chattered. In a few seconds a strip of printout was held up in front of me. I scanned it: I CAN SEE YOU. WHAT HAVE YOU DONE TO ME?

I took a deep breath. Then I told him. Exactly. Everything. I came down hard on how new and revolutionary it was. How he would have stopped without it. How civilian physicians had examined him and his medical history and had agreed that he was doomed. But now his brain was, as far as we knew, as close to being immortal as any animate thing could be. "Immortal." I thought that was the key word and kept hitting it. "You will be immortal." "Your brain will never stop." "The world's first immortal object." Etc., etc. I described the precautions that had been taken and would be taken to ensure his safety: A fail-safe power supply for the machines that kept his brain alive. Gradually improved blood supply as we learned more about his needs. More physical comfort inside his bell jar. A bombproof and sabotage-proof shelter. Whatever he wanted to scan. Even his dumb romantic novels. All converted to tape and projected on the viewing screen before his eyes. No more pain. Above all, no more pain. And he could continue to serve. To serve the US Government which, in gratitude, would keep his brain animate and active. Forever.

Even before I finished speaking, the return from the GPA-1 computer came in. Was torn off in a jagged strip, rushed over to me, held before my eyes.

I had expected a stream of invective. Obscenities. Endless, gabbled curses. Blasting me for what I had conceived and what I had done. I expected that condemnation, and I wanted it. It would be a signal of Lewisohn's "normality." But I also wanted the judgment for myself. For reasons I could not compute.

But it was a brief message: MAYA. I WANT MAYA. TO TALK TO. TO SEE. MAYA.

I looked at the torn scrap.

"What?" I said into the microphone.

The response came through.

MAYA, it scanned. I WANT TO SEE MAYA LEIGHTON. BRING HER CLOSE. I WANT TO SEE HER. TALK TO HER. OR I WON'T SERVE.

I stared at that pumpkin head. Glaring eyes. Outraged. Like the starving children of Pakistan.

"Yes," I said. "All right, Lewisohn. I'll get Maya for you."

Z-10

On August 4, 1999, I was in my penthouse apartment. At the compound, Manhattan Landing, GPA-1. Trying to serve my way through four weeks' accumulation of bills, bank statements, dividend checks, scientific journals, personal correspondence, kaka.

My flasher chimed at about 2130. It was Seymour Dove. Calling from San Diego.

"Seymour!" I said. Pleased. "Good to see you again. How have you been?"

He wasted no time on pleasantries. His face, on screen, was expressionless.

"Nick," he said, "do you remember the address of the beach-house where I met you?"

"Sure. It was—"

"Don't say it," he broke in quickly. "How many digits in the number?"

I instantly became as serious as he.

"Three digits," I said.

"Correct," he said. "Keep them in mind, then duplicate the three. Now you've got a six-digit number. Right?"

"Right," I said.

"Add this number to those six: five one two seven six three one. Got that?"

"Five one two seven six three one. Correct?"

"You have the sum of the first six digits plus the seven-digit number I gave you?"

"I have it," I told him.

"Can you call me at that number, in precisely one hour?" he asked. "Call, don't flash. It's important."

511

"Will do," I said. I started to say "Thank you," but he had already switched off.

Precisely an hour later I was calling him from a public phone booth outside the compound.

"Seymour," I said, "what's this all about?"

"First of all," he said, "Simon Hawkley stopped two nights ago. In his sleep. I sent you a letter, but you probably don't have it yet."

Silence.

"I'm sorry to hear that," I said. Finally. "A gentleman. I was hoping to see him again. And tell him . . . But things . . ."

"But that isn't why I called," Seymour Dove went on. "I still have a friend at Scilla—the secretary—and about an hour or so ago she told me a government nose has been around. Investigating the sale of Scilla. Who the present owners bought the property from and when."

"Uh-huh," I said. "Did she say what agency?"

"Bureau of Public Security."

"Uh-huh. One nose?"

"Yes. An em."

"He wasn't wearing a checkered cap by any chance, was he?"

"Wearing a checkered cap?"

"Yes. Did she mention it?"

"Wait a minute. I'll ask her. She's in the bedroom."

I waited patiently. Finally he came back on.

"No," he said. "She says he wasn't wearing any hat at all. Why did you—"

"Thanks very much, Seymour," I said. "I appreciate your calling. It was kind of you."

"You'll be all right, Nick?" he asked anxiously. "Even if they trace it?"

"No problem," I said. "Thanks again, Seymour. Sorry to hear about Hawkley. Did he leave anyone? Wife? Children?"

"No," he said. "He was alone."

I was about to say "Aren't we all?" but then realized how fatuous that was. So I merely said good-bye and broke the connection. I didn't think Dove was in any danger. He was a born survivor. Was I?

Investigation of the Scilla plot. . . . That could prove fatal. If they traced ownership to me during a period when Scilla had been selling hallucinogens to my Section. How had the BPS been alerted to Scilla?

512

I had hypothecated a scenario to account for the missing 5 cc flask of 416HBL-CW3. For the fact that a known terrorist, Arthur Raddo, had a friend named "Nick" who looked like me. (Anyone could introduce himself to Raddo as "Nick," and anyone of my approximate height and weight, disguised with dark wig, mustache and Vandyke beard would resemble me in the dimness of the Adonis Club.) My hypothetical scenario even accounted for the sharing of Millie Jean Grunwald's apartment in Detroit.

Assume a terrorist group, perhaps survivors of the Society of Obsoletes' conspiracy, were authors of the plot against me. Perhaps in revenge for my role in the stopping of Hammond, Wiley, DeTilly, and the others. Assume such a dissident organization might very well have members in SATSEC. Living and serving in the GPA-1 compound. It would not be too difficult for a laboratory server to manipulate the theft of the *Clostridium botulinum*. And to forge my name on the withdrawal card.

The subsequent removal of the entire flask had been masterfully planned and executed. And timed. Since it occurred after I had answered R. Sam Bigelow's inquiry. Stating I had verified the existence of the bottle by personal inspection.

The motive for effectualizing the botulism outbreak in GPA-11 was more complex. Their prime desire, I assumed, was to implicate me in a horrendous crime. But I suspected there might have been other reasons: The whole operation could have been in the nature of a "laboratory experiment," an exercise in terrorism to hone planning techniques, and test the determination, skill, and loyalty of members.

It might also have been a deliberate attempt to destroy the Beist movement by incriminating one of its members. It was quite possible that the late Arthur Raddo was duped. A selected pigeon. Perhaps his control was an em he knew as "Nick." A bearded em he met only in the dimness of Adonis and from whom he took his orders and received the flask of 416HBL-CW3.

There were many unknowns, many possibilities. The terrorist organization scenario was not a neat, elegant solution. But I felt it explained most of the bizarre occurrences that had been bedeviling me. It might even account for the continued presence of those checkered-capped snoops, if the organization was large enough.

But now, after computing what Seymour Dove had told me, I realized a new factor had appeared in the equation: the interest of the Bureau of Public Security. Perhaps they had been alerted by their analysis of pure glycerol in the replaced 5 cc flask in my pharmlab. But I doubted that; I would have been informed of any BPS investigation in GPA-1. Or would I? Perhaps the BPS told my servers I had no need to know. Perhaps the discovery that the bottle supposed to contain 416HBL-CW3 now contained no *Clostridium botulinum* was enough to set R. Sam Bigelow's noses on my track. Hence the investigation of Scilla. Perhaps the ems in checkered caps were BPS snoops. It wouldn't be the first time they had used the technique of open and obvious surveillance to panic a suspect and start him running.

I debated if it might not be wise to go to R. Sam Bigelow, or even Chief Director Michael Wingate, and tell either, or both, that I was being manipulated. I decided it would not be wise. Because either, or both, might be doing the manipulating. Why would they desire my destruction? Because the CD had learned of my secret meetings with his wife. Possibly. . . . Maybe. . . . Perhaps. . . .

I stayed in GPA-1 for almost a week. Serving on my official duties as DEPDIRSAT and cleaning up my personal obligations. It wasn't until late in the week that I realized I was settling my affairs. As an object might do contemplating a lengthy trip. Or. . . .

When I left the compound, I flew to Washington, D. C., took the Metro to the Chevy Chase place, and left my luggage there. Showered, changed zipsuits, and went back to the Metro for the long ride to Alexandria. There I could requisition wheels from the Hospice No. 4 motor pool.

Construction had already started on converting the Lewisohn Building into an ultrasecure bombproof shelter. The heavy, windowless walls were up to the second floor. I had to show my BIN card and official ID three times, and be identified twice by voiceprint check, before I was allowed into Operating Theater D. There was a ten-object staff in attendance, twenty-four hours a day. They had been ordered to stay out of Lewisohn's sight as much as possible.

Lewisohn's head, in its domed greenhouse, sat in lonely splendor in the middle of the softly lighted theater. As I approached, I saw he was scanning a computer printout projected on the small screen in front of his bell jar. I stood as close as I could and waited patiently until he noticed me.

"Nicholas Bennington Flair!" came booming through a loudspeaker atop the computer readout screen linked to GPA-1.

The voice startled me. I knew they had completed the taping of

514

the computer vocabulary. But I had never heard the voice before. It was remarkably like Lewisohn's natural voice: harsh and yet precise, loud and angry, with an occasional phlegmy splutter.

I looked more closely at Lewisohn's head. He was still staring at the viewing screen. But his eyes were not moving; he was not scanning. I picked up the transmitting microphone.

"Yes," I said. "This is Flair."

"Satisfied?" the canned voice asked.

"Yes," I said, "I'm satisfied. The operation was a success, and the patient survived. And is serving, I see. Are you satisfied?"

Stupid question. He didn't answer. For which I was thankful.

"What are you serving on?" I asked him.

"You wouldn't understand," he thought.

"Try me," I said.

Then the lids slowly rose. Reptilian eyes focused, stared at me.

"You have no need to know," the mechanical voice crackled.

The words shivered me. It was a common enough phrase. Probably justified in this instance. But I had become abnormally sensitive to such slights. Did everyone know something I didn't know?

"Are you getting everything you want—uh—need—uh—ask for?" I said. Difficult, talking to a head.

"Yes."

"Does Maya visit you?"

"Yes."

"Every day?"

"Yes. I want to be alone with her. I want a screen around us. So those grinning apes can't watch."

"I'll arrange it."

There were many others questions I wanted to ask. Can a disembodied head still love? What form of political society did he envision for his corporate world? Did he believe, as Paul Bumford obviously did, that instinctive sexuality was an operative base on which to predicate the political nature of *Homo sapiens*? Had he done any computing of the existence of a primitive slave factor in the psychology of our species? And much, much more.

But the sight of Lewisohn's head did not encourage conversation. Particularly of an intimate nature.

"All right," I said. "I'll leave you now."

"I don't want to see you again," he thought. "Ever. If you continue to come here, I will stop serving. I will tell the Chief Director that."

"Very well," I said. Understanding. But saddened. "I won't come again. Good-bye, Lewisohn."

Then the obscenities started. Loud, rancid virulence, spewing from the loudspeaker. The serving staff looked up, startled. I turned away. Followed by that screamed filth. Created in his brain. Transformed into electrical signals. Scanned by laser. Amplified electronically. Transmitted to the GPA-1 computers. Translated, triggering taped vocal responses. Returned to Operating Theater D. Verbal excrement flung at my back as I walked out of there.

I plunged into the DCS campaign. Serving in Paul's office in the basement of the EOB. At that point in time, late August, 1999, our staff had incubated to more than fifty objects. Following what seemed to be an inexorable law of megagrowth in all bureaucratic agencies. Most of our servers were assigned to Congressional liaison, and it was to this area that Paul and I devoted most of our time.

The signal from the Chief Director, based on Sady Nagle's estimate, was that passage in the House was assured. We switched our push to the Senate. Profiting from experience, we concentrated on the staffs of individual Senators and of the subcommittee and full committee that would first consider the new Department.

Attempting to convince individual Senators was counterproductive. Difficult though it may be to believe, in August, 1999, only eighteen members of the entire US Congress had a scientific background. The great majority were lawyers, businessmen, ex-soccer stars, and former television performers. They simply did not have the conditioning to comprehend our proposals. Some staff members had, at least, a rudimentary understanding of our numbers, computer studies, plans, and projections. It was their utilization we sought.

As I endured an apparently endless succession of lunches, conferences, cocktail parties, private colloquies, and dinners, I realized the enormity of what President Harold K. Morse had accomplished. He had established an executive advisory board of scientists during his administration. He had enlarged the Science Academy and helped bring it to a level of conditioning efficiency surpassing West Point, Annapolis, the Air/Space Academy, and the Academy of International Cooperation. I became aware that our Department of Creative Science was merely one more step—but perhaps a quantum jump—Morse might have effectualized a decade earlier. If he had not stopped.

I spoke to Grace Wingate about this. Recalling my meeting with President Morse in 1990. Shortly before he suicided.

"I thought he was assassinated," she said.

"No," I said, "I don't think so. The only object who could possibly benefit from his assassination would have been his VP. And he didn't have the brain—or the ambition—to manipulate it."

"How did you meet Morse?"

"He called me in. I had published a very minor, almost poetic paper on the nature of genius."

"The nature of genius? Nick, isn't that outside your disciplines?"

"It is now. It wasn't then; I was young."

".What did you say about genius?"

"I took as my text: 'Full many a flower is born to blush unseen,/and waste its sweetness on the desert air.' Thomas Gray. Not so, I said. I argued that genius unknown is genius nonexistent. Like a tree falling unheard in an isolated forest. It produces no sound. No receiver. Genius, I said, must be appreciated to exist."

"Do you really believe that?"

"I was certain at the time I wrote it. I'm not so certain now. Anyway, that paper was how I came to meet President Morse. It was published in an obscure Southern Literary journal. But he scanned it. I believe he scanned *everything*. He called me to the White House, and I had a marvelous hour with him. What a brain!"

"What did he talk about?"

"Everything! He dazzled me. He seemed to know all I knew, and a lot more besides. A very inquiring brain. A curious brain. Always asking, always prying."

"About what?"

"Well, for instance, he recalled an obso gerontological theory: that every object, at birth, has a built-in clock. The clock is wound for a finite number of heartbeats, respirations, and so forth. When the clock runs down, the object stops. And nothing can be done to keep the clock ticking. That theory has been demolished now, but it was potent at the time. President Morse wondered, almost casually, if the same theory could be extended to human emotions. Suffering. Enthusiasm. Pain. Hope. And so forth. If we were born with a finite quantity of each. And when they were expended, they were gone. Depleted. Never to be renewed."

"Nick, he *did* suicide?"

"I have no doubt of it. Grace, I've never told anyone this—it's

517

still ultrasecret—but after Morse stopped, I was assigned as a member of an ad hoc committee of physicians to investigate. Our report was unanimous. It's filed away somewhere. He had always been a light drinker, but we found operative evidence of heavy alcoholic intake followed by massive barbiturate ingestion. There was little doubt about it. It was deliberate. He suicided.''

''But why?''

''You want my theory? That's all I can give you—a theory. His wife. A dreadful ef. But he needed her. I think—this is just my own hypothecation—I think that he finally used up all his need. It was depleted. And he found that, without it, he didn't want to live. No reason to live. Does that make sense?''

''Is your need for me depleted?''

I groaned and took her into my arms.

We were in our safe house, our secret garden. A late August day so fulsome it was almost blowsy.

''Nick, you seem . . .''

''Seem?''

''So—so reflective?''

''Do I? Talking of President Morse, I suppose. Remembering.''

''You have such a marvelous memory.''

''A curse. Sometimes.''

''You mean it's nice to forget?''

''The brain's natural therapy. Only occasionally it doesn't serve. Things buried must be dredged to the surface. And faced. Examined.''

''Nick, do you know everything?''

''Everything,'' I assured her solemnly.

We laughed. Hugged. Then I drew back, looked at her for the first time.

I had kissed, or touched, almost every part of her. Except for those hidden places I wanted to keep inviolate. Sacred. The smooth brow I could assimilate. And vulval ears. Pale flame of hair, soft lips, sharp nose, somber eyes, pointed chin. Her whippy corpus. So important. But not important. *Her*. The giving. Hers and mine.

Neither of us restrained, and we made mad vows of what we might cheerfully do at the other's bidding. Suffer. Suicide. It was a game. With the grave significance of all games. I needed her so much. And she needed me. I *knew*.

We sat together that afternoon until the sky deepened. Mostly in silence. Occasionally exchanging trivia.

"What's your favorite color?"

"Have you ever eaten natural rabbit?"

"Can you swim?"

"Do you like the scent of gardenia?"

"Do you ever pray?"

"Who was the first object you used?"

Still exploring. Still learning. Still going deeper. To profound places of such intimacy that, I think, we were both shocked. But could not end. Having come that far, we could not see a limit. We must go farther. Deeper yet. And so we did.

Strange, the way we disrated to obso speech:

"I love you. Do you love me?"

"I love you."

And didn't think it strange.

Finally, inevitably, we had to separate. I gave her the gift I had brought. A tiny jeweled scarab. A dung beetle. With a little clamp clasp. It bewitched her. She pressed it to her lips.

"Can you wear it?" I asked. Anxiously.

"Always," she said. "Hidden."

We both laughed with joy.

And that's how we parted.

I stayed in Washington, D. C. for several days. A period preceding and following Service Day. I spent most of my time in the DCS office in the EOB, although I visited Hospice No. 4 several times prior to September 8. I made no effort to see Lewisohn's head, as I had promised him. But I monitored his progress via daily status reports from the medical staff assigned to him. And I viewed films that had been made of him, without his knowledge, by a microminiaturized camera concealed in the viewing screen in front of his bell jar.

On the evening of September 8, 1999, I returned late to the Chevy Chase place. Having spent the day in Alexandria completing my final report on Operation Lewisohn. Paul Bumford and Mary Bergstrom were home, watching a live TV broadcast from the US Government's permanent moon colony. Potable water had recently been discovered, at a depth of approximately 10 kilometers.

I waved to them, went into the kitchen to mix a vodka-and-Smack. I took it up to my room. No plans except to relax. Perhaps scan some scientific journals that had accumulated. Listen to some music. I was in a cautiously euphoric mood. I had heard nothing more about the Scilla investigation. I had not seen another checkered cap. The Arthur Raddo business already seemed ancient history. It would, I told myself, all go away. Still, I thought it might be wise to find a new safe place to meet Grace Wingate. In affairs of this sort, as in crime and espionage, habitual patterns prove fatal.

Shortly before midnight, Paul knocked on my door. Carrying his own brandy and one for me.

"Busy?" he asked.

"Come on in," I said. "How are things on the moon?"

"Those lunatics." He laughed. "Because of the discovery of water, they're talking about an enormous increase in the size of our colony. Eventually applying for admission into the US as a state."

"Oh?" I said. "That's interesting. And what have you been up to?"

He slouched into a club chair facing me. Put his brandy glass to his lips. Stared at me.

"Well?" I asked.

"On the Ultimate Pleasure project," he said. "I received a preliminary report today. From Ben Baker, your father's production manager. Only on the factory in which servers are getting the actual UP injection. For the past week, production was up 69.8 percent."

"Sounds good," I said.

"Good?" Paul said. "Incredible! When you consider that only 38.6 percent of the servers signed the Informed Consent Statement. But that 38.6 percent accounted for the total production surplus. Your father should be delighted."

"He will be," I said. "Nothing from the control or placebo factories?"

"Nothing yet. Should be in this week. Nick, have you given any more thought to what we discussed?"

"Brainstorming a society to maximize the UP?"

"Yes."

"I've computed it. Some. I still feel you're overvaluing the UP. It doesn't make sense to me to predicate a political infrastructure on sexuality."

"You think that's what I'm doing, Nick?" This with a tinselly smile.

"Aren't you?"

"Far from it. But even if what you allege is operative, moral philosophies have been based on sexuality; why not political philosophies?''

"I'm not tracking."

"Nick, I'm not overvaluing the UP. Per se. I'm utilizing its most salient characteristic: the slave factor. If preliminary numbers hold up, it's present in approximately 85 percent of all UP fantasies.''

"And so?"

"I think the slave factor is more than a symptom of sexopathy. I believe there is also emotional surrender, political surrender. Even, in obso terminology, spiritual surrender. In other words, 85 percent of all objects obtain their Ultimate Pleasure from total devotion, or submission, to objects, ideas, or ideals outside themselves. It's this principle of abasement I want to utilize in predicating a new political structure for our society. It maximizes a very basic, very instinctive human drive the UP has uncovered.''

"And what about the unaffected 15 percent?"

"Ah." He nodded wisely. "You *are* tracking. Nick, those 15 percent of objects impervious to the slave factor are the big, unanswered question. A lot of heavy research to be done there. I think the answers will be found by psychobiologists. Can I activate a team?''

His sudden question caught me off balance. He was going so fast, pushing so hard, that I was dazzled. I needed time to compute. I waffled. . . .

"What do you think such a project would find?" I said.

"You want me to guess? That's all I can do at this point in time—guess. Nick, I believe research psychobiologists will find a common denominator in those 15 percent of objects unaffected by the slave factor. In addition, I think they'll find a definite correlation with genetic rating. All, or most of those 15 percent, will be found in the top and top-plus GR's.''

"And what will that mean?" I asked. Knowing his answer.

"Nick, don't you see? It demands a class society based on genetic ratings. The managers would be immune to the UP, but able to utilize it objectively for the good of society. Can I activate that research project?''

"No," I said. "I won't approve it. If I learn you've started it without my permission, I'll stop it and have you up on charges.''

His face turned to stone.

"Why?" he said. Barely audible.

"Because you're starting with a preconception. Paul, you and I

521

both know that any research project can prove anything you want it to prove. If strongly ruled. Contradata is simply disregarded. Even the structure of the project itself—organization, selection of personnel—weights the results. You already know what you want your project to find. If I let you go ahead, they'll find it. You know it and I know it.''

"You mean I'd falsify results?" Squalid smile.

"Let's just say you'd misrepresent conclusions."

"So you don't trust me?"

"On this particular matter—no."

He stood up. Trying very hard to keep himself under control. But his voice, when he spoke, was pitched higher than normal. Not hysteria, but a furious anger that threatened to break into screams and shouts.

"Nick . . ." he said. Drew a deep breath. "I'm trying to trailblaze, and you're stonewalling me. I've noticed, more and more, you've been influenced by obso moral considerations. You've been corrupted by humanism. It's decaying your judgment and perverting your decisions. You were the em who preached total objectivity. Presenting a façade of humanitarianism was to be part of the scenario. That was operative, and I believed it. I still believe it. But now you have defected. What is it, Nick? Don't you have the courage to follow your convictions to their logical ends? Well, I do. And I'm not alone; I can tell you that.

"Something you haven't realized. . . . All your brave words about the Tomorrow File not being a Christmas list, and how we had to effectualize it as soon as possible—a lot of kaka, Nick! That's exactly what it is for you: a Christmas list, a never-never inventory of brilliant ideas. Created so you can postpone actions you know are inevitable but don't have the courage or energy or desire to fructify.

"The Tomorrow File *is* tomorrow, Nick—and you know it! Right now we're on the edge, the verge, the fulcrum. The balance is shifting. The change will be enormous. Overwhelming! And the Tomorrow File is the scenario, the Department of Creative Science the organism. I thought we'd do it together. Everything we projected. But you've become an obso, Nick. In your computing. You're no longer able to keep up. You can't accept change. You've been passed. Events have gone beyond you. And ideas. You're no longer able to translate scientific principles into political doctrine. I don't know why; I don't know what's happened to you. I could guess, but I won't. All I know is that your retrogression is sad.

Personally, to me, sad. But you can't stop us, Nick. That's not a threat; it's a resolution.''

He marched out of there. I inhaled an eight-hour Somnorific and found darkness.

I came out of it about 0830 on the morning of September 9, 1999. I lay awhile in bed. Sheet pulled down to my waist. Hands behind my head. Staring at pale sunshine washed through the curtained windows. Was Grace Wingate lying alone as I was then? Perhaps I had been wrong. . . . We had been wrong. . . . I wasn't sure. . . .

Light knock on the door. Then it was opened immediately. Paul, carrying a tray. Orange petrojuice, toasted soybread, a pot of coftea, cups, saucers, cutlery, petrobutter, natural grape jelly, paper napkins.

"Peace offering." He smiled. Radiant smile.

"Greeks bearing gifts." I laughed. "Bring it over here."

He sat on the edge of my bed. We breakfasted there. Sharing the same knife, same tub of butter, same jelly.

"Listen, Nick," he said. "About last—"

"Don't talk with your mouth full."

He swallowed obediently.

"About last night," he said. "I'm sorry. But it's important to me."

"I compute," I said. "Paul, if we can't talk to each other as operatively as that, we've got nothing."

"Right," he said. "Well, I'll forget about that research project."

"No," I said, "don't forget about it. Paul, I'm not trying to demolish your theories. It's just your timing I object to. Let's get the Department of Creative Science finalized. Once that's in existence, the stratosphere's the limit. But at this point in time, we've got to walk tippytoe. Gloss all our activities on the UP. If it ever gets out, we're stopped. You compute that, don't you?"

"Oh sure, Nick."

"But that doesn't mean your ideas might not be operative. But for the future. Put it in the Tomorrow File."

"I already have." He grinned mischievously.

We both laughed. He took the tray from my bed, set it aside. Then he skinned out of his robe, slipped under the sheet. Close to me.

"What's this?" I said.

"One guess," he whispered.

"Wait," I said. "Wait just a minute."

I slid out of bed, got a liquid graphite pen and a pad of paper from my desk. Brought them back to the bed.

"ESP," I said. "Let's try it again. A two-word phrase."

"Right," he said.

We both scribbled. Then turned into each other's arms.

His corpus had become firmer. Harder. But still beneath that incredibly tender, limpid skin. Through which I could feel the rushing course of blood, heartpump, the rising heart of sexual excitement.

He put his soft lips to my nipples, loins, thighs. A sweet butcher. Carving me up. His breath was young. All of him scented. We traced each other. Flung the sheet aside. Rolling.

His eyes fluttered, closed. I eased him onto his back. Knees rose and parted. Conditioned reflex. The pleasure I felt was not heightened by penetrating an em. But heightened by guilt at surrendering to the demands of my own corpus. Brain denied. Animal all.

We fumbled some.

"Out of practice," I gasped.

He grunted.

But we finally linked, moaning. His hips pillowed. My back arched. Both of us in heat. Lightly sweated. We held back. As long as we could. Ultimizing the swoon.

We summited in a fury. Nails. Crying out. As elemental as a storm. Something despairing there. I pronged as deeply as I could. Wanting to split him. Rend. And he wanting to surrender. Rend. Sur*rend*er. From *renda*, to tear? Or from *rendre*, to give back, yield? What difference? Who was slave and who master? Both of us slick and coughing with our passion.

We pumped in deescalatory rhythm. Then rested until the slime dried and stuck us fast. Disengaged cautiously. Pulled away.

"Oh," Paul breathed. "Oh, how beautiful."

"Yes," I said.

We lay in silence for minutes. Both upon our backs. Staring at the brightening sunshine streaming through the window. Watching the mad motes dance.

"What did you write?" I asked him.

He showed me his paper: "Ultimate Pleasure."

I showed him mine: "Checkered cap."

He looked at me.

"Checkered cap?" he said. "Nick, what does *that* mean?"

"Just a thought," I said. "A vagrant notion."

"Well"—he sighed—"it didn't serve. We're far apart."

We lay in silence another five minutes. Resting. Sharing a single cannabis cigarette. Watching how the white smoke bloomed and billowed up into the strengthening sunlight. Finally:

"What are your plans for today?" he asked lazily.

"Back to GPA-1," I said. "But before I leave, I want to visit that Twenty-first Century exhibit at the Mall. After I see that, I thought I'd walk over to Union Station and take the Aeroglide home."

"Oh, yes," he said. "That's fun. It really does feel like you're riding on air."

"You've taken it?" I said, surprised. "When?"

"While you were on the PR tours," he said. "I had to go to New York, and the airports were socked in."

"Why did you have to go to the compound?"

"Talk to Phoebe Huntzinger," he said. "About the direct-wire link for Operation Lewisohn. And once to check out Leo Bernstein's scenario for moving his equipment down."

"Oh, yes," I said. "Of course. Sure."

"Well. . . ." He yawned. "I better get back to the political world. Have a good time at the Mall exhibition."

He got out of bed. Pulled on his robe and belted it. Smiling at me. A beautiful em! Then he leaned down. Kissed my lips. Patted my cheek with his fingertips.

"Take care," he said lightly.

I spent a slow morning showering, shaving, dressing, packing. It was almost noon when I took the Metro to the Mall. Carrying a thin attaché case of reports, papers, journals. Kaka to scan on the train trip north.

Finishing touches were being applied to the Twenty-first Century Celebration Festival along the Mall. Servers were testing the lighting of an enormous sign that would flash YOU NEVER LIVED SO GOOD! every three seconds until the turn of the century. Ropes were up, keeping out the general public until the following week. But that week was a preview for US Government servers; my BIN card and official ID got me past the guards with no trouble.

I started at the log cabin, circa 1700, from Plymouth, Massachusetts, and wandered slowly through American homes of 1750,

1800, 1850, 1900, 1950, up to the present. I had come prepared to scoff at this patent public relations stunt. But I found myself fascinated. Touched. Unaccountably troubled.

The obso homes had been built or assembled with careful attention to authentic detail. They might be placed in artifical settings of plastiturf and plastirub shrubs and trees. But the structures themselves were the originals or accurate reproductions. Using primary materials. The houses were complete to bed linens, pictures on the walls, tables set for a meal, rugs, bric-a-brac, etc. They were even "inhabited." By actors dressed in appropriate costumes. Silently moving through their obso roles: serving, dancing, gathering about an ancient harmonium to mouth the words of long-stopped songs.

What impressed me so? First, the *texture* of these obso homes. Rough-cut wood. Nubby plaster. Carving. Crude painting. Hooked rugs. Odd shapes. Rooms that were not boxes. I was made doubly aware of the charm of obso texture when I entered the "Home of the Present." All smooth, glossy, bland, perfect. Obso homes were palaces of error: ill-fitting beams, three steps up or down from room to room, a bow window where a flat square would have served as functionally well.

And the whimsy! All shapes of stained glass inserts. Enormous brass door-knockers. China bulldogs on the hearth. Dried flowers under bell jars. Framed tintypes on a mahogany piano. A cast-iron wood-burning stove as artfully decorated and embellished as an altar. The *humanness* of it all!

I came out of the Twenty-first Century Celebration Festival chastened by a vague feeling that I had been bred too late. I would have flourished in those obso days. Perhaps lecturing on anatomy at Johns Hopkins to an audience as bearded as I. Returning to a gaslit home of gleaming wood and glittering crystal. Logs snapping in the fireplace. Wife and children. No amusements but our own company. Conversation. Laughter. Singing.

So I exited the "Home of the Present," still thinking of the past. The way they lived. As I passed through the guarded gate, a tall, heavyset em stepped into my path. Our eyes locked. He nodded once, briefly, turned and walked quickly away. He was wearing a checkered cap.

I looked about. There were three black official sedans parked in file along Fourteenth Street, in front of me. Another on Washington Drive to my right. Another on Adams Drive, to my left. Black zipsuits standing outside each car. Watching me.

I walked slowly toward Fourteenth. A group of three, led by a short, chubby ef in a red zipsuit moved to intercept. I stopped. The officer came close. The three black zipsuits moved quietly around me.

"Dr. Nicholas Bennington Flair, sir?" she said.

"May I see your identification, please?" I said.

"Certainly, sir," she said.

She showed BIN card and official ID. A lieutenant of the Bureau of Public Security.

"Very well," I said. "I am Nicholas Bennington Flair."

I proffered my BIN card and ID. She scanned them quickly. Returned them to me.

"Thank you, sir," she said. "Dr. Flair, I have orders to take you."

Silence. We stared at each other.

"On whose authority?" I asked her.

"Warrant from the Chief Prosecutor, sir," she said.

"May I see it, please?"

"Of course, sir."

She pulled her zipsuit down far enough to extract a folded paper. A warrant for my taking. "On suspicion of activities contrary to public interest." Nothing unusual about it. But I scanned it slowly.

"Thank you, lieutenant," I said. Returning the warrant to her.

"I must now read you a statement of your rights, sir," she said.

"That won't be necessary," I said. "I know my rights."

"Please, sir," she said. "I'm required to recite it. I *must* recite it."

"Very well," I said. "Recite it."

She withdrew a crumpled card from her opened zipper and began scanning it aloud. I had the right to remain silent. I had the right to legal counsel of my choice. I could call at US Government expense. If I could not afford legal counsel, the US Government would provide such counsel without charge.

"Do you fully understand what I have told you, sir?" she inquired anxiously.

"I fully understand it," I assured her.

"Thank you, sir," she said gratefully. "Would you sign this release, please? It states only that I have explained your legal rights to you, and that you fully understand them."

She pulled a third paper from her bodice. A walking file cabinet. I scanned the release swiftly. She had a pen ready.

527

"What can I write on?" I said.

She turned her back to me and bent over slightly. On her broad, soft back, I scrawled my signature on the release. She returned all documents to her body and zipped up.

"Thank you, sir," she said.

"Thank *you*," I said. "Now what?"

"This way, please, sir."

They walked me to one of the black sedans. Before I got in, my attaché case was taken from me and I was patted down. Quickly. Expertly. Then I was seated in the rear between two black zipsuits. The lieutenant got in front, next to the driver.

It didn't take me long to realize where we were going. Across the Arlington Memorial Bridge. Past the A&N Country Club. Down into Alexandria.

"Hospice No. 4," I said aloud.

No one answered. No one spoke.

To the building set off by itself. The Public Security Ward. With white plastisteel mesh over the windows. Surrounded by plastiturf. They hustled me into the main entrance hall. Lined with stainless steel tiles. The room marked Admittance was divided by a wire grille. Several objects, ems and efs, in white hospital garb, were serving on the other side. They looked up when we entered. A small yellow em came over to the opening in the grille and stood behind a counter.

"Who made the take?" he asked.

"I did," the red zipsuited lieutenant said. "Object's name: Nicholas Bennington Flair." She slapped down the warrant. "On authority of the Chief Prosecutor."

The yellow em behind the grille turned to a data processing machine and began to type. Talking as he served.

"Flair, Nicholas Bennington. Warrant BPS-91641-99G. BIN card and ID, please."

I fished them out again, handed them over. He slid them into an electronic verifier, then typed out the numbers on his report.

"Personal property?" he asked.

One of the black zipsuits handed over my attaché case. It was unlocked. The yellow pawed through it swiftly.

"One attaché case of papers, reports, magazines. Empty your pockets, please."

I dumped everything onto the counter. He began to sort it.

"One ring of keys. One pigskin wallet containing forty-six

dollars in bills, three credit cards, and assorted membership cards. One handkerchief, white. Thirty-eight cents in change. One digiwatch, silver finish, marked 'Loxa.' One black comb, pocket size. One container of white spansules. Correct?''

"Correct," I said.

"Dentures or prosthetic devices?" he asked.

"None," I said.

"Object is assigned number 4 dash 618 dash 99," he said.

"Sign the receipt, please," the ef lieutenant asked the yellow.

They exchanged and countersigned papers. She waited until he had typed up an inventory of my personal possessions in quadruplicate. I signed all copies. She signed all copies. He signed all copies.

The BPS servers waited patiently until two objects appeared in the corridor. Coming toward us. Heels clicking. Their images were distorted by the stainless steel walls and polished floor. Two big ems. White hospital garb.

"Right," the red zipsuit said. When they had taken their places on each side of me. "That does it."

"Thank you, lieutenant," I said.

"Thank *you*, sir," she said.

I was taken to a room in the back of the ward, on the ground floor. White desk, chair, metal detector, electronic monitors. The obso ef behind the desk, wearing a nurse's uniform, looked up when I entered with my guards.

"Flair," one of them said. "Nicholas Bennington: 4 dash 618 dash 99."

"Undress, please," she said to me. "Everything. Including shoes." I stripped naked. All my clothing was folded neatly, put into a white metal box labled with my number. A receipt was typed out in quadruplicate. We all signed all copies.

I was given a cursory medical examination. Blood pressure, heart, temperature.

"Step through the frame, please," she said.

I stepped through. Nothing buzzed. She moved an electronic wand around my head, back, legs, arms. She looked into my ears with a lighted probe. Examined my armpits. Tapped my teeth lightly with a little hammer. Felt my scalp and beard, fingers prying under the hair.

"Bend over and spread your buttocks, please," she said.

I did so. She explored my rectum with a rubbered finger.

"Shower," she said.

They took me through a clear glass door into an adjoining room. I stepped into a tiled shower stall. No projections inside. No curtain. One of the guards turned a knob. A hot germicidal spray.

"Scrub your hair," one of the guards shouted. "On your head, chest, armpits, nuts, and ass."

I did as directed.

The water was finally turned off. They motioned me out onto a plastirub mat before a panel of infrared lamps. By the time I was reasonably dry, beginning to sweat, they had ready a pair of paper slippers and a one-piece paper suit. Styled like a zipsuit but closed with strips of paper tape.

They took me out into the corridor again. I shuffled along, trying to keep the heelless slippers on my feet. Trying not to trip on the long cuffs of the paper suit. They stopped me before a bank of elevators.

One of them pressed a button and leaned forward to speak into a small microphone inset in the tile wall.

"Pearson and Fleming," he said loudly. "Coming up. We have one: 4 dash 618 dash 99."

Then both guards turned and stared at a small closed-circuit TV camera mounted near the ceiling.

A loudspeaker clicked on.

"You are cleared to Three. Room 317."

An elevator door opened. We stepped inside. Another TV camera. The door closed. We went up. Door opened. We stepped out to face a white-clad guard sitting in the corridor behind a desk surmounted by a battery of TV monitor screens.

"Pearson and Fleming," one of the guards reported: "4 dash 618 dash 99 to Room 317."

The seated guard looked at his teleprinter.

"All correct," he said.

We moved to the left until we came up to a gate of steel bars. And another TV camera. We stood there a moment. Then the barred door slid sideways. Into the wall. We walked down the corridor. I heard the gate thud shut behind us.

We walked to where another guard waited outside a closed door. He held a clamp pad of teletype duplicates.

"Four dash 618 dash 99," one of my guards told him.

The em outside the door looked at me.

"Name?" he said. "Last name first, followed by first and middle names."

"Flair, Nicholas Bennington," I said.

"All correct," he told my guards. Then made a small checkmark on his pad.

He withdrew a ring of magnetic keys from his pocket. He unlocked the door. Room 317. They all stood aside. I entered. The door was closed and locked behind me. It looked like painted wood, with a small panel of clear glass. But when they clanged it shut, I knew it was steel.

I took a few steps into the sunlit room and looked about.

"Good afternoon, Dr. Flair," a metallic voice said. "How are you feeling?"

Z-11

I wish to go on record as stating that during the approximately six weeks I spent in Room 317, Public Security Ward, Hospice No. 4, Alexandria, Virginia, I was not physically abused or maltreated. I was provided with a fresh paper suit and paper slippers every week. The food brought to my room was plentiful, though bland. For some bureaucratic reason, I was not allowed salt, pepper, or any other seasonings. Although I requested them.

My sleep was never deliberately disturbed, and I was furnished with most of the scanning material I asked for. I was not allowed newspapers, news magazines, radio, television, a watch or clock, or a calendar. Nor was I allowed Somnorifics or any other drugs. However, during the fourth week, I contracted a very mild viral infection, and the nurse who had conducted my initial examination arrived to administer an injection. She would not tell me what it was, but it served excellently; I recovered fully within three days.

That was the only medication I received during my stay. Of course, it was possible that my food was drugged. Or even the water flowing from the tap in the small nest attached to Room 317. But several times a week I conducted a self-examination. Taking my pulse and testing muscular and visual coordination. I never found even a hint of covert drug administration. It was operative that shortly before, during, and for a brief period following my interrogations in the Cooperation Room, pulse rate increased. But this was undoubtedly due to a stimulated adrenalin flow, and was to be expected under the circumstances.

I exercised, faithfully, in Room 317. An hour after awakening and an hour before sleep. I practiced Yoga, isometrics, and my own version of T'ai Chi Ch'uan. In place of Somnorifics, I used self-hypnosis, alpha, and transcendental meditation. I would say that, during the six weeks of my stay, my physical health was excellent.

The objects with whom I came in contact were remarkably few. The morning guard who brought me breakfast, took me to and from the first interrogative session of the day, and who brought me lunch, was a hulking but pleasant em who said his name was Horwitz. The afternoon guard who took me to and from the second interrogative session of the day, and brought my evening meal, was a squat, muscled ef who said her name was Kineally. I called her "Princess." She liked that.

And of course, I was on nodding acquaintance with several corridor guards, head guards who watched the TV monitors outside the elevator bank, and the gate guards. I never learned any of their names. Some were polite, some were not. But there was no physical brutality. Never. At least not to me. And none that I personally witnessed. On several nights I was awakened by screams coming from nearby rooms. But they may have been the results of nightmares. It was possible.

I masturbated twice a week, on Tuesday mornings and Friday nights. Usually I slept soundly and woke refreshed. The scanning material that was provided kept my brain active and inquiring. When I wanted surcease from purely cerebral computing, I imagined what the objects looked like who spoke to me. The two Voices.

Voice No. 1 spoke to me only in Room 317. The loudspeaker was concealed behind a ceiling air-conditioning vent. This Voice was concerned with my physical well-being and daily routine. Had I slept well? Did I require anything special in the way of relaxation? A paper chess set perhaps? Were my bowel movements regular? And so forth. I was able to respond to these questions merely by speaking into the air. A sensitive microphone, probably concealed in the same vent, picked up every tone, whisper, belch, fart. As far as I could determine, Voice No. 1 was on duty 24 hours a day.

I recall once, awakening at what I judged to be about 0300, I said, into the air, "Are you there?"

Voice No. 1 came back: "I am here."

It was the Voice of Room 317. I never heard it anywhere else. I had little doubt that Voice No. 1 had me under constant surveillance. Through mirrors inset into the walls of the bedroom and nest. Even my masturbation was shared, although Voice No. 1 never alluded to it. The two-way mirrors were the only decorations in the small area. The furnishings were one bed, one chair, one desk. The toilet in the nest was seatless. The sink had recessed fixtures. As did the shower stall. I was supplied liquid soap, in small amounts, in a plastic container. The single tumbler was soft plastic. Impossible to slit wrists or throat with that. Toilet paper was supplied to me each week in thin pads. Along with paper sheets, pillowcases, and a paper towel. I controlled the air conditioning and heating in the room via a thermostat, and the illumination via a rheostat. Although the overhead light could never be completely extinguished.

"You've got the VIP Suite," the Princess told me. "You should see some of the others."

"I can imagine," I said.

"No," she said. "You can't."

Voice No. 1 intrigued me. Androgynous. At times it was definitely emish: heavy throatiness and deep overtones. Other times it was efish, almost flutey. It could be both in the same sentence. Running back and forth, soprano to baritone. The effect was not displeasing, but I could not believe it was a natural voice. I computed it might be the voice of someone I knew, a voice I might identify, and so it was being electronically distorted.

During my second week in Room 317, I asked Voice No. 1, "Are you ef or em?"

The answer came back: "Yes." Followed by a brief laugh of such a variety of tones that I became absolutely convinced Voice No. 1 was being filtered and amplified. For what reason other than that stated above, I could not guess.

Voice No. 2, that of the Interrogator, was definitely an em's voice. I heard it only in the Cooperation Room. It was beautiful. Deep, resonant, with a booming, organlike quality. A diapason there. Never less than harmonious. With a unique, echoing quality. It was only later that I began to detect a fruity, actorish dissonance.

I was taken to the Cooperation Room twice a day. At times I computed as being approximately 1000 and 1400. During the first two weeks, sessions were quite brief. A half-hour or so, I reckoned. Later, I spent two full hours in the morning and two in the afternoon. This regimen was, obviously, structured.

One fact I have neglected to mention: I never saw any objects but the guards. Although I was certain the other rooms on the third floor were occupied. On my short trips down the corridor to the Cooperation Room, I heard sounds of movement behind locked doors. Once I heard singing. Once I heard an ef's voice reciting Shakespeare: "Tomorrow, and tomorrow, and tomorrow. . . ." And frequently I smelled things in the corridor. Smells of objects. Sweat. Feces. Other things. So I knew I was not alone on the third floor, although it seemed so.

The Cooperation Room to which I was taken for my daily interrogations (seven days a week) was located in my wing of the Public Security Ward; it was not necessary to pass through any of the barred gates in the corridor to get there. It was a long, narrow room, soundproofed with white plastibest panels. There was a small mirrored panel set into each of the walls. For surveillance and filming, I presumed. The Interrogator's voice came from an overhead ventilation duct, as in Room 317, and I answered by speaking into the air. In a normal tone of voice.

During my interrogative sessions, the room contained only an enameled steel table, about card-table size, and a single plastilume chair. Both of these were immovable. Bolted to the floor. The chair so close to the table that I had to bend my knees and sidle into the seat. I noted several other ringbolts, steel loops, and small steel boxes set into the polished floor. Around the room, at baseboard level, were many electrical outlets and small connections that looked like electronic jacks. None of these were used during my sessions. Illumination came from rose-tinted fluorescent fixtures on the ceiling. Not an especially pleasant light, but not too annoying.

I had an impression that, for each session, the Cooperation Room had been hastily prepared for my interrogation shortly before my arrival. Frequently the floor showed damp patches: evidence of recent mopping or flushing. Once I noted a reddish-brown stain on the floor directly under my table, missed by the cleaning server. Invariably, when I entered the room, I smelled artificial pine. The air had obviously been sprayed heavily with a scented deodorant.

On our first exchange, I learned the Interrogator was humorless.

"For the record, doctor," Voice No. 2 boomed from the overhead loudspeaker, "please state your name, rank, and address."

"Name:" I said, "Flair, Nicholas Bennington. Rank: Director (Temporary) of the Satisfaction Section, Department of Bliss.

Address: Room 317, Public Security Ward, Hospice No. 4, Alexandria, Virginia."

"No, no," he said. Somewhat testily. "I mean your permanent address. Where you lived before you were taken."

I spoke it into the air. I felt I had scored a point. He had said, "Your *permanent* address," hadn't he? That obviously meant my stay in the Public Security Ward would be of short duration. Confidence came flooding back. I relaxed.

I had already spent some time computing how best I might reply to prolonged questioning. Reply operatively to everything that was a matter of record. Protect, insofar as possible, friends, associates, and assistants. Pillow when I was able to, or gloss. Where I was certain no evidence existed, then deny, deny, deny. Stonewall. But in such a manner that I could not later be accused of deliberate deception. "I don't remember," would serve. As would, "I don't recall," "I have no recollection of that," "I cannot state from personal experience," and similar phrases.

But during the first two weeks of brief interrogative sessions, I had little need to waffle. Questioning was direct and straightforward. It was also shallow, and seemed to be antilogical. For instance: "Are you acquainted with an ef, residing in Detroit, Michigan, named Millie Jean Grunwald?"

"Yes, I am," I said.

I naturally expected the next question, or questions, would explore the nature of my relationship with Millie. Instead, the next question was: "Did you know the late Simon Hawkley, an attorney of San Diego, California?"

And so it went. Short, blunt questions. Apparently designed only to put on record the fact of my acquaintance with or knowledge of a long list of objects.

Some of the names, admittedly, surprised me. Burton P. Klein. Alice Hammond. Leon Mansfield. Joanne Wilensky. Vernon DeTilly. I remembered them all. But was somewhat shaken that the Interrogator knew them.

I volunteered nothing. Absolutely nothing. But occasionally I tried to explain my relationship to the named object. Invariably, the Interrogator would interrupt, and in his orotund voice, say, "Yes, yes, we'll get to that later."

It took us three days to serve our way through a long list of names that apparently included every object I had had contact with since

535

January, 1998. Several names I did not recognize. The Interrogator made no effort to prod my memory. He merely accepted my negative answer and went on to another name. Were the strangers a control group, to test my veracity?

One question I found disquieting.

"Are you acquainted with Mrs. Grace Wingate, wife of the Chief Director?" the Interrogator asked.

"Yes," I said. "I am acquainted with Mrs. Wingate."

He went on to another name. Louise Rawlins Tucker.

Finally, having apparently exhausted the list of objects with whom I was known, or suspected, of having had contact with during the preceding eighteen months, the Interrogator started over again. This time he probed my relationship with the objects named. How we had met, how often we met, were we users, did we have any financial dealings, etc., etc. But again, he forbore from prying too deeply. Limiting his questions to surface relationships. It was at this point in time that Voice No. 2 took on a sonorous, almost a pompous quality. Like a prosecutor designing his inquiries as much to influence a jury as to elicit information from the defendant.

Each evening, back in Room 317, I computed the day's interrogation. I determined what I handled well, and what badly. I tried to hypothecate future areas of inquiry. Most of all, toward the end of those initial two weeks, I attempted to analyze the Interrogator's methodology. That he was following a heavily structured scenario, I had no doubt.

My first reaction to my taking had been, I suppose, like that of many objects in similar circumstances: It was all a horrible mistake. A file had been displaced, or a computer had been faultily programmed. An object could be executed on the testimony of one crossed circuit.

But those first two weeks of interrogation convinced me that it was, indeed, *I* who had been deliberately taken. On orders. I could not compute it. Less than a month previously I had received a letter from the Chief Director almost fulsome in its praise of my service on Operation Lewisohn. "One of the nation's finest young creative scientists." That is how Chief Director Michael Wingate referred to me in that letter. And now I was languishing in a Public Security Ward, charged with activities contrary to the public interest. It was incomputable.

Beginning with the third week of questioning, the Interrogator dropped his politesse. No more "Please" or "Would you. . . ." or

"Doctor" or "If you please. . . ." Inquiries became shorter, more brusque. I thought the tempo of interrogation also quickened. I scarcely had time to complete my reply before the next question was hurtling down at me. This effect, too, I presumed, was programmed. But I had little time, or inclination, to analyze technique. I was too concerned with my own defense.

"You stated you know Millie Jean Grunwald."

"Yes, that's correct."

"How long have you known her?"

"Three—no, four years."

"How did you meet her?"

"At a cockfight."

"In Detroit?"

"Yes."

"Where was this cockfight held?"

"I don't recall the address. A basement club. Somewhere down near the river."

"You were introduced to Millie Jean Grunwald at this club?"

"No. I had won a bet, and asked her and her girlfriend to have a drink with me."

"What was the girlfriend's name?"

"I don't remember. If I ever heard it. Which I—"

"What are your relations with Millie Jean Grunwald?"

"We are friends."

"Friends? Flair, how many doctorates do you have?"

"Several."

"Millie Jean Grunwald is a retardate clone. You are aware of that?"

"Yes."

"But you are friends?"

"Yes."

"Do you use her?"

"We use each other."

"Frequently?"

"Whenever I'm in Detroit. Perhaps three or four times a year."

"Do you give her gifts?"

"Yes."

"Love?"

"No."

"Have you ever discussed restricted matters with her?"

"She wouldn't understand, I assure you."

"You haven't answered my question. Did you ever discuss restricted material with Millie Jean Grunwald?"

"I don't remember."

"You don't remember? Flair, you have made that claim several times. Yet you are reputed to have the best memory in the scientific community."

"I was forced to skip my hippocampal irrigation this year, and I'm overdue on theta brushup conditioning."

"I see."

"Interrogator, you have made *that* claim several times. 'I see.' "

"You object to it?"

"It reminds me of an object who says, 'Let me make one thing perfectly clear.' Then I know I'm to be the victim of obfuscation."

"I see."

As sessions lengthened, I endured similar bursts of short, blunt questions about almost every object on the Interrogator's list. I had no opportunity to extend or explain my answers. Attempted explications were cut short. Subjects were shifted with bewildering speed and increasing frequency. Several times I found myself still speaking of the last object when a new name had been introduced. The Interrogator then snapped a command to pay closer attention to his questions.

Some objects, being stopped, I made no effort to defend. Simon Hawkley was one. Angela Teresa Berri was another. No one could touch them now.

"You and Berri were users?"

"Yes."

"Frequently?"

"Several times."

"Her apartment, yours, or elsewhere?"

"Her apartment, mine, and elsewhere."

"You have stated that you suspected her of activities contrary to the public interest."

"That's correct."

"Why didn't you communicate your suspicions to her rulers?"

"To whom? I had no knowledge of how extensive her conspiracy might be. Perhaps her rulers were involved."

"Did you think the Chief Director might be involved in her peculations?"

"Of course not."

"Then why didn't you go to him?"

"I—well, it didn't occur to me. I didn't know him personally at that point in time."

"Our records indicate that Angela Teresa Berri introduced you to the Chief Director. Is that correct?"

"Yes."

"So she was still animate when you met him. Personally. Why didn't you tell him of your suspicions then?"

"Because they were only suspicions. I had no hard evidence."

"But you have stated that you knew she had assassinated Frank Lawson Harris and had manipulated the stopping of Burton P. Klein and others."

"That's correct. I *knew* it, but had no evidence to prove it."

"Now about the Scilla business in San Diego. . . ."

By the end of the fourth week, I was no longer amused by the Interrogator's increasingly bombastic voice and denunciatory tone. I was too concerned with avoiding contradictions in my testimony and attempting to convince the Interrogator that although some of my activities might have been technically illegal, my actions benefited the US Government: A conspiracy of terrorists had been exposed and a corrupt government official was stopped. I made no love from this.

"Not even from your final sale of Scilla?"

"A very minor amount, I assure you. Hardly a tenth of my income for the year. If making love was my motivation, I would have retained ownership."

"Perhaps you became frightened."

"That's absurd."

"Is it? Let's go back to the Society of Obsoletes' conspiracy. . . . How well did you know Dr. Thomas J. Wiley?"

"I told you, I studied with him for a brief period of time."

"Did you like him?"

"Yes."

"Admire his brain?"

"Well . . . yes. Not his ideas, but his brain."

"What contact did you have with him between the time you studied with him and the time you met him at Dr. Henry Hammond's summer home?"

"No contact."

"None?"

"That's correct."

"We have in our possession a program of a symposium held at

the University of Chicago on July 14 to 17, 1997. The guest list shows that both you and Dr. Thomas J. Wiley attended."

"That's possible. There were more than a hundred objects at that symposium. I didn't know he was there and didn't speak to him personally."

"Were you and the late Lydia Ann Ferguson users?"

"The *late* Lydia Ann Ferguson?"

"Yes. She's stopped. Were you users?"

"Yes."

"Frequently?"

"No. A few times."

"Did you admire her?"

"Yes."

"Her brain, no doubt?"

"No. She was a silly ef. But I admired her."

"Listen to this tape. . . ."

Through the overhead loudspeaker came my own voice. Explaining to Lydia Ann Ferguson that I had been ordered to expedite a project that would cancel a dissident tribe of a friendly African nation. That tape should have been erased a long time ago. I tried not to reveal my shock.

"Is that your voice speaking, Flair?"

"Yes."

"The project you are discussing with an object unauthorized to receive such information was, actually, a project you conceived and finalized some time previously. Is that correct?"

"Yes."

"An ultrasecret project?"

"Top secret."

"Very well, top secret. Why did you reveal it to this unauthorized object at that point in time? She had no security clearance."

"In the first place, that conversation was couched in such general terms, she could not possibly make the connection with an actual project. In the second place—as I have stated several times before—my role was that of an undercover agent, with orders to infiltrate the conspiracy."

"Whose orders?"

"Those of Angela Teresa Berri."

"Berri is stopped."

"I know that. But you'll find in her confession a full explanation of the part I played. She praises what I did."

"We are aware of that. But nowhere in that confession does she state that she ordered you to disclose classified material to an unauthorized object."

"Ask Paul Bumford. He knew about it."

'We shall ask him. Now listen to this tape. . . ."

Again it was my voice. This time explaining to Wiley, Hammond, the DeTilly brothers, et al., how I would manage to remove classified material from the compound at GPA-1.

I waited until the tape finished. Then exploded. . . .

"I've told you and told you," I shouted angrily into the air. "I was serving as an undercover agent. It was the only way we could catch them in the act and provide enough evidence to convict."

"In the Scilla matter, concerning the crimes of Angela Teresa Berri, you stated you did not take your suspicions to a higher authority because you didn't know how far her conspiracy extended."

"And because all I had were suspicions. No hard evidence."

"But that doesn't hold true for the Society of Obsoletes' conspiracy, does it? You had more than suspicions in that case. You had hard evidence. A group of terrorists had attempted to suborn you. You had their conversation on tape. With your direct testimony, that would have been sufficient to convict. So why didn't you take the whole matter to the Bureau of Public Security?"

"Angela Teresa Berri," I said. "I did it the way she ordered me to do it."

"Angela Teresa Berri is stopped," he said hollowly, "and cannot testify to that."

"I know," I groaned, "I know."

What irked me, continually, was that what I had done was not all that awful. Illegal yes, but not awful. It had been done, was being done, and would be done by hundreds—thousands of objects in academe, multinational corporations, governments, and so forth. It had been, was being, and would be pillowed or glossed. The world would not falter for it. Good frequently resulted. Why was I being singled out for persecution and punishment? Where was the protection of my rank?

And all those "activities contrary to the public interest" I was alleged to have committed—why, they were peccadilloes, chaff, compared to my activities beneficial to the public interest. Operation Lewisohn. The overt and covert research projects I had conceived. The public health programs I had initiated. They could change the world! Lessen human pain. Reduce the anguish of future generations. Did my life's service count for nothing?

"Now about the Die-Dee Doll. . . ."

"What has that to do with me?"

"It is manufactured by your father?"

"That is correct."

"It is extremely lovable?"

"So I understand."

"Records indicate that the initial application for a license to manufacture, distribute, and sell the Die-Dee Doll was rejected by your Executive Assistant, Paul Bumford. Is that correct?"

"At that point in time, he wasn't my Executive Assistant. He was AssDepDirRad."

"But he rejected your father's application?"

"Yes."

"On what grounds?"

"The word 'Die' in the name. The inclusion of a coffin and tombstone in the doll kit. Other reasons."

"Legal reasons?"

"Yes."

"But you overruled Bumford's decision?"

"Yes."

"Why?"

"The Die-Dee Doll is a toy. A plaything. It isn't all that important."

"It isn't? At the time you overruled Bumford's decision to disapprove the Die-Dee Doll license, was this before or after your father loaned you the love to purchase Scilla Pharmaceuticals?"

"What?"

"Did your father loan you the love to purchase Scilla Pharmaceuticals before or after you had overruled Bumford's decision to deny him a license to market the Die-Dee Doll?"

"I don't remember."

The curious thing was that I *didn't* remember. I literally could not recall. It bothered me.

"Listen to this tape. . . ."

My voice again. Babbling to Millie Jean Grunwald. Spilling out my worries and misgivings about a number of classified projects. We had just seen Janet and Eric battle at the Lords Sporting Club. We had returned to Millie's apartment. Unsatisfactory sex. Then I had talked, talked, talked. To a sleeping Millie. And to the recording machine below in the deserted porn shop.

"Yes," I said dully. Although I had not been asked. "That's my voice."

"Why did you tell this unauthorized object of these matters?"

"Perhaps I was drugged."

"Drugged?"

"It's possible. At the Lords Sporting Club. In the drinks I bought. Interrogator, there are drugs to make an object speak, contrary to his will."

"Who would drug you?"

"I don't know. Someone," I said foolishly.

"How well did you know the late Arthur Raddo?"

"I've told you, I didn't know him at all. Never met him."

"But you were aware of his existence?"

"He gave a speech. At a Beist meeting I attended. I told you that, too."

"This was the Christmas, 1998, meeting of the Washington, D. C., chapter of the Beists?"

"Yes."

"Mrs. Grace Wingate was there?"

"Well. . . . Yes, I believe so. She came in later."

"Did you speak to her during the evening?"

"Yes."

"Alone?"

"Yes. No. I don't remember. I spoke to a number of objects that evening."

"But not to Arthur Raddo?"

"No. Definitely not."

"Raddo's mother, in a sworn statement, asserts he had several telephone calls from a friend he called 'Nick.' "

"So? A lot of ems are named Nick."

"Employees of the Adonis Club, in sworn statements, have testified that the late Arthur Raddo was frequently seen on the premises with an em he called 'Nick.' An em who answers your description."

"A clever manipulation," I said. "A control em in a terrorist organization is known to Raddo as 'Nick.' The control is approximately my height and weight. He is disguised in wig, false mustache and Vandyke beard. In the dimness of the Adonis Club, he could easily pass as me."

" 'In the dimness of the Adonis Club'?" he repeated. "How did you know the Adonis Club is dim? Have you been there?"

"Once."

"For what purpose?"

"After I heard that Raddo had suicided. While in possession of a bottle of—"

"Yes? A bottle of?"

"Nothing. It's not important."

"I think we will end this session at this point. We will resume at our afternoon session."

Back in Room 317. Voice No. 1 caroled, "Your fresh paper sheets will be up shortly."

"You go to hell," I screamed into the air.

"Dr. Flair!" Voice No. 1 said. Shocked.

"About the five cc flask found in the hand of the suicided Arthur Raddo," the Interrogator said that afternoon.

"Yes?" I said. "What about it?"

"You stated it was the reason you went to the Adonis Club."

"Well, goddamn it, it was!"

"Soothe yourself," Voice No. 2 said unctuously. "Soothe yourself. Take it easy. Take all the time you need. Just tell me exactly what happened."

It all came pouring out of me. Spluttered. It was a plot. A skillfully structured scenario. Of long duration. I had been manipulated. I told the Interrogator of finding the partially empty flask of *Clostridium botulinum*. My own name forged to the withdrawal card.

"Why didn't you go to the Bureau of Public Security immediately?"

"I thought I could discover the instigator. I didn't know how high the conspiracy extended."

Then, I said, when I heard of the 5 cc flask found with the suicided Arthur Raddo, I rechecked the GPA-1 pharmacology library. The entire bottle was missing. So I had replaced it. With a flask of pure glycerol. I needed time. Time to compute. Time to attempt to determine the connection between Arthur Raddo and the ongoing conspiracy to destroy me.

"So your letter to R. Sam Bigelow, stating you had verified the existence of the original deposit of 416HBL-CW3 by personal inspection—your own phrase: 'by personal inspection'—that statement was, in fact, false and misleading?"

"No, no," I protested. "Not at all. Not false and misleading. Simply inoperative."

"And you say you concealed this vital information from higher authority because of your desire to uncover the plot to destroy you?"

"Yes."

"And who did you imagine was the creator of this plot?"

"I hypothesize a terrorist organization. Perhaps the remnants of the Society of Obsoletes' conspiracy."

"That Society was canceled. All the members were taken."

"Not all of them," I said triumphantly. "Angela Berri allowed some of them to exist, to continue their activities. It's a common enough ploy. So she could keep them under surveillance. So they might lead her to other members, more important members, of whom she was not aware."

"A very ingenious explanation. Do you have any proof that this was, indeed, the intention of Angela Teresa Berri?"

"No proof, no. But it's obvious, isn't it? And they singled me out for revenge for the part I had played in erasing Wiley, Hammond, Lydia Ann Ferguson, and the others. It all synthesizes. It all computes."

Silence. I knew I wasn't convincing him. Worse, I wasn't convincing myself.

"Look, Interrogator," I said. As calmly as I could. "What possible reason could I have for becoming involved in the structuring of that botulism outbreak in GPA-11? Remember, I was the object who went to the Chief Director and the Bureau of Public Security Chief and told them about aerobic botulinum. Doesn't that prove I wasn't involved in it?"

"Not necessarily," he boomed.

"Well, what possible motive could I have for such illogical actions?"

"You have the reputation of being an ambitious em."

"So? A lot of objects are ambitious. It's characterological of intelligence."

"It wouldn't be the first time an ambitious object had artfully planned and executed a crime, using a cat's-paw as the actual perpetrator, and then assisted in the solution of that crime. To earn praise for his talent. To earn commendation from his rulers. Advancement in rank."

"That's nonsense!" I shouted.

545

During the final week of interrogation, I cannot say my mood was serene. I was deeply troubled; I cannot deny it. I knew quite well what was at stake. Me. But I did not panic, except for a few brief occasions when the Interrogator's engorged voice was not to be endured. I approached the interrogation sessions with trepidation. Not because of the questions I might be asked. But in anticipation of being subjected, once again, to those overcooked tones that flowed from the ceiling loudspeaker and seemed to fill the room.

What preserved my sanity, at that point in time, was my self-esteem. I do not know why a strong, healthy ego is generally held in such ill repute. In the circumstances in which I found myself, my vanity was my salvation.

I know many neuropsychiatrists believe that character is the psychosis we show to the world. And that the slyly contrived conception each of us has of himself is the psyche's defense mechanism against despair and madness. All this may be operative. But it is, I think, beside the point.

All I know is that I functioned in such a manner as not to degrade my vision of myself. I might tolerate the pity, or scorn, or loathing of others. I could never endure my own pity, scorn, loathing.

"And was it also part of this 'secret conspiracy' that you allegedly commanded your servers to inflict grievous bodily harm upon the corpus of a security officer of the US Government? To wit, deliberately break the arm of one Art Roach?"

"Are you humoring me, Interrogator?"

"Answer the question."

"As I've told you many times, the Art Roach scenario had nothing to do with the plot against me. Breaking his arm was the simplest way to procure evidence of the corrupt dealings of Angela Teresa Berri. It succeeded brilliantly. As soon as the evidence was obtained, I took it directly to Theodore Seidensticker III, of the Chief Director's staff."

"You told him about breaking Roach's arm?"

"I did not. He had no need to know."

"I see."

"Are you drugging me, Interrogator?"

"Drugging you? How would we drug you?"

"In my food. My tap water."

"Have you detected any drug?"

"No, but it may be something new. With no gross symptoms. A drug to make me talk."

"Surely you'd know about a drug like that, wouldn't you?"

"No," I said. "Not if I had no need to know."

I may have cackled then.

I think, in my continual computation of my dilemma, the factor I found most difficult to integrate into the overall equation was the role of Chief Director Michael Wingate. I could not believe he was unaware of my predicament. My absence would certainly have been noted by Paul Bumford and by other friends and associates. The CD could hardly be in ignorance of my whereabouts. A brief phone call or message could have freed me. "To be released for the benefit of the public." But the command never arrived. I could not account for it. Until the final interrogative session. . . .

We had been reviewing, once again, the actions I had taken to effectualize the purchase of Scilla Pharmaceuticals in San Diego. And the precise amount of love I received on the final sale, above and beyond the original purchase price and my expenses.

Then, at the end of the session, a totally new subject was introduced. I was immediately cautious.

"Did you ever meet the late President Harold K. Morse?"

"Yes."

"How many times?"

"On one occasion."

"And that was?"

"He called me to the White House for a short conversation after he had scanned a paper I had published."

"What was the subject of your published paper?"

"On the nature of genius."

"You never saw him again?"

"Not until he stopped."

"Ah, yes. You were, were you not, a member of a committee of physicians appointed to investigate the stopping of President Morse?"

"That is correct."

"And this committee, of which you were a member, then filed a report. Which was immediately classified top secret."

"Ultrasecret."

"Very well, ultrasecret. That document has never been declassified. It is still ultrasecret."

"So?"

"I will now ask you a question concerning that classified document. Consider carefully before answering. The question is this:

Have you ever divulged the existence, contents, meaning, or conclusion of that document to any object unauthorized to receive such information?"

My reply was prompt.

"No," I said. "Never."

"This interrogation is now concluded," the Interrogator boomed. Fruity voice burbling. "Remove the object."

I waited until I was back in Room 317 before I let myself compute the significance of the final question I had been asked. I lay supine upon the paper sheet, hands behind my head. I stared upward at the ceiling vent.

"Did you have an interesting session, Dr. Flair?" Voice No. 1 asked softly.

"Yes, thank you. Very interesting. I think if you don't mind, I'll skip dinner tonight."

"Oh, I'm sorry, Dr. Flair, we can't do that. The food must be brought to your room. If you choose not to eat, that's your decision, of course. But we must make it available. Regulations, you know."

"All right. Bring it up."

"Thank you, Dr. Flair."

"Thank *you*."

The reason Chief Director Michael Wingate had not intervened in the proceedings against me now seemed evident: He was aware of my relations with his wife. The final question revealed that.

I had told only one object on earth of my service on the committee to investigate the stopping of President Harold K. Morse. That object was Grace Wingate. At our last meeting. If the Interrogator had brought up the subject, it could only mean that he had evidence of my imprudence.

The fact that he had saved the subject for the final question in the concluding interrogative session, and then had delved no deeper following my denial, convinced me that the question had been intended to serve as a signal. The Chief Director was notifying me that he was aware of my interactions with Grace, and he was abandoning me. Turning his back. Walking away. Leaving me to my destiny.

There was no other explanation for that brief question. "*I know*," the Chief Director had said, in effect, "and now you know that I know."

I experienced, I admit, an initial terror. But other objects had stopped, and so should I, and so shall you. I consoled myself with that, as best I might, and resolved to act in such a manner as not to tarnish my conception of who and what I was. If self-esteem had betrayed me into seeking revenge on Angela Berri, and led to my downfall, then self-esteem would, at least, enable me to stop with as much courage and dignity possible under the dismal circumstances.

My evening meal was brought and placed on the table.

"Proveal," the guard reported. "Propots and some kind of white slimy stuff for dessert. Looks good."

"Thank you, Princess," I said.

The steel door clanged shut behind her. I didn't even rise to inspect the plastic tray with its plastic plates of plastic food. I lay on my back, watching the light fade. The darkness move in. Then I computed a problem that had to be faced.

If the Chief Director knew of my love for his wife, knew I had told her of my service on the Morse Committee, then our meetings in the safe place, in our secret garden, had been shared. Or she had betrayed me. One or the other.

It was possible, of course, that she had been forced to speak. But I didn't think it likely that Michael Wingate would do that to his wife. No, she had either spoken voluntarily, or our love had been shared, recorded, made a matter of dossiers and investigative projects. Even in that empty, deserted garden, sharing would not have been especially difficult.

She would not betray me. Could not. I knew her too well to believe that. Still. . . . The worm gnawed.

I reviewed again those intimate conversations that had been such an awesome revelation. That had introduced me to the glory of opening myself, totally, to another object, and of entering into her. The two of us one as we explored an unknown world. It was an experience of which I had never known I was capable. Had never known existed. As if I might leap from a high place and discover I could fly. As breathless and shocking and deliriously pleasurable as that.

It was quite dark outside, the illumination in my room at its lowest setting, when I came to a conclusion that almost syncoped me with its simplicity. Its purity. Whether our meetings had been shared or Grace had betrayed me was actually of no consequence. Nothing that had been done—for whatever reason—could take from me the exaltation of our love. I did not regret it. That was the operative factor: I did not regret it.

I would never know if she had betrayed me. Never. Even if our love had lasted a millennium. If we had a hundred, a thousand, a million intimate meetings. Even if we had used each other. I would never have learned her sufficiently to know if she was or was not capable of treachery.

For she was, essentially, finally, unknowable. I recognized that now. Unknowable. She was, and I am, and you are.

What will we do when the mystery is gone?

A-1

The office of the Director of the Department of Creative Science was a long box of a room. Conference area at one end. Desk, chairs, communication equipment at the other. One of the two ems in the room, wearing the gold zipsuit of a PS-1, sat in a swivel chair behind the desk. The other em, red zipsuited, stood facing him.

On the wall, behind the Director's desk, a plastic overlay graph was framed and illuminated with its own little lamp. In grease pencil markings of three colors, it was clearly shown that the Satrat and production of the Ultimate Pleasure injection were ascending curves, following almost identical percentage increases. As these two lines rose, a contrary curve, descending, marked the plunging terrorism rate.

The Director switched a tape deck to Fast Rewind. The two ems waited patiently until the empty reel filled up and the machine clicked off. Then the Director removed the full reel and placed it carefully in a cardboard carton alongside his desk. The legend on the carton: "Good-Cheer Skinless & Boneless Portuguese Sardines." It contained a vast number of tape reels.

"That should do it," the Director said. "You're certain this is the original?"

"I'm certain," the officer said.

"No copy has been made?"

"No copy," the officer said. "I know better than that."

"I hope you do," the Director laughed. "I'll prepare the transcription personally for the Chief Director. What about the Informed Consent Statement?"

"Signed, sealed, and delivered," the officer said. "Original to the Chief Prosecutor. Copies to BPS and to our files."

"Good. How did you get him to sign it? Drugs? Hypnosis? Shock therapy?"

"Yawl won't believe this," Art Roach said, "but we didn't have to use anything. He really did sign it voluntarily. He was happy to sign it."

"Oh?" Paul Bumford said. "That's interesting."

END